THE WEATHER IN THE STREETS

ROSAMOND LEHMANN

WITH A NEW INTRODUCTION BY JANET WATTS

FROST IN MAY

ANTONIA WHITE

WITH AN INTRODUCTION BY ELIZABETH BOWEN

ALL PASSION SPENT

VITA SACKVILLE-WEST

WITH AN INTRODUCTION BY VICTORIA GLENDINNING

The Weather in the Streets
Published by VIRAGO PRESS Limited 1981
First published in Great Britain by William Collins Ltd. 1936

Frost in May
Published by VIRAGO PRESS Limited 1978
First published in Great Britain by Desmond Harmsworth 1933

All Passion Spent
Published by VIRAGO PRESS Limited 1983
First published in Great Britain by The Hogarth Press 1931

This edition first published in Great Britain by VIRAGO PRESS Limited 1994
20 Vauxhall Bridge Road, London SW1V 2SA

A CIP catalogue record for this book is available from the British Library

Printed and bound in Great Britain by
Mackays of Chatham PLC, Chatham, Kent

THE WEATHER
IN THE STREETS

ROSAMOND LEHMANN

was born in Buckinghamshire in 1901, the second of the four children of R. C. Lehmann. One sister was Beatrix Lehmann, the actress, her brother is the writer John Lehmann. She was educated privately and was a scholar at Girton College, Cambridge. She wrote her first novel, *Dusty Answer*, in her early twenties whilst married to Leslie Runciman. In 1928 she married the Honourable Wogan Philipps, the artist, with whom she had one son and one daughter. In 1930 her second novel, *A Note in Music*, appeared. *Invitation to the Waltz* followed in 1932 and its sequel *The Weather in the Streets* in 1936. Both of these novels were dramatised as a BBC TV film in 1983. During the war she contributed short stories to *New Writing* which was edited by her brother: these were published as *The Gipsy's Baby* in 1946. *The Ballad and the Source* was published in 1944 followed in 1953 by *The Echoing Grove* which was to be her last novel for many years. Rosamond Lehmann then wrote an autobiography, *The Swan in the Evening: Fragments of an Inner Life* (1967) and in 1976 she published another novel, *A Sea-Grape Tree*.

Rosamond Lehmann is one of the most distinguished British novelists of this century. An International Vice-President of International PEN, Vice-President of the College of Psychic Studies, Fellow of the Royal Society of Literature, and a member of the Council of the Society of Authors, she was made a Commander of the British Empire in 1982. Rosamond Lehmann has five grandchildren and lives in London and in Suffolk, near Aldeburgh. Virago publishes *Invitation to the Waltz*, *The Weather in the Streets*, *A Note in Music*, *The Gipsy's Baby*, *The Ballad and the Source* and *A Sea-Grape Tree*.

THE WEATHER IN THE STREETS

FROST IN MAY

ALL PASSION SPENT

INTRODUCTION

The poet – and the novelist – may prove to be a prophet. Genius, said William Blake from his own embattled position, is always ahead of its time. Rosamond Lehmann, who would be the last person to link that statement with her own work, nevertheless admits that *The Weather in the Streets*, her fourth novel, was 'not exactly contemporary. I think that many people felt that this was not true to their experience when it was published. A generation later, people were beginning to say: "This is speaking to me now."'

Rosamond Lehmann's best-selling first novel, *Dusty Answer* (1927), and its two successors, *A Note in Music* (1930) and *Invitation to the Waltz* (1932), had established her as a writer of an exceptional emotional intelligence, and by 1936 her fans were avid to welcome a new novel from her. In *The Weather in the Streets* Miss Lehmann gave them a love story, though for many of them it was not what they had expected or hoped. The love in this novel is that of a woman past her first youth for a married man, and its story is not an altogether pretty one.

Readers had met these people before. In *Invitation to the Waltz* they had watched Kate and Olivia Curtis, the daughters of a middle-class English country household, await and attend the coming-out dance of an aristocratic local neighbour. Olivia, valiant but uneasy in an ill-cut flame-coloured frock, smiles, suffers, and – wonderfully – survives a first dance that comes perilously close to humiliation and disappointment. Her evening is made magically all right by a meeting with Rollo Spencer, the debutante's glorious elder brother, and a few minutes' chat with him on the moonlit terrace.

The readers who had been enchanted by Olivia Curtis at seventeen now rediscovered her ten years older: thinner, sadder, and not apparently much wiser, with a failed marriage behind her, and ahead such miseries as they might have preferred not to witness. She and Rollo Spencer meet again in a train. Her marriage is over; his is unsatisfactory. They quickly fall in love and into an affair. Olivia looks to this relationship for the salvation of her life: but it brings her unhappiness, an unwanted pregnancy and a double loss.

A number of people were not pleased. Rosamond Lehmann's American publishers, anticipating the dismay of their readership in ladies' luncheon clubs, had implored her to remove the abortion sequence. The novel's publication – complete, on Miss Lehmann's insistence – won many good reviews, but (as she recalls) 'I also had very sour notices from male critics, saying "She obviously doesn't like men, and she doesn't understand them." Though the funny thing was that it was the male critics who were apt to say what an absolute cad Rollo was. Most of the women who wrote to me – and my readers have mostly been women – said: "Oh, Miss Lehmann, this is my story! – how did you know?"'

This sense of identification has perhaps been Rosamond Lehmann's greatest attraction for her women readers. In her books they have found themselves: their own confusions and pleasures, sorrows, passions and episodes of farce. 'It looks now as if I was writing specifically about the predicament of women, though I was not conscious of it at the time. I just wrote what seemed the truth in my experience, out of something inside me – an enormous complex of experiences and emotions, my own and other people's, that I had to give expression to.'

She has always firmly resisted the 'spotters' who have plagued her writing life with attempts to attribute the characters in her novels to real people in her own life. 'I suppose because much of what I wrote dealt with romantic and sexual love seen from a subjective angle, the detective squads were rampant; also the self-identifiers; also those with a so-called knowledge of my private life more beady-eyed than accurate,' she has written.

Rollo Spencer always particularly engaged their curiosity. 'I remember Cyril Connolly for one nagging at me: "Was it so-and-so? Well, who was it, then?" I said, "It's somebody you've never known, and never will know. He has got an original, but it's not what anybody's ever thought or guessed.' It was a man who loved her, with whom she never had an affair, who 'belonged to a very uncontemporary world that has gone now. He became, for me, almost an archetype; and he haunted most of my subsequent work.'

Rosamond Lehmann admits that people and experiences from her own life have certainly gone into her books: but in the books they have acquired a new and different reality. In writing this novel and *Invitation to the Waltz* she 'saw the image' of one of her sisters in creating a character; but she insists that she did not write about that sister's experiences. The fictitious reality takes off, floats away from the original image in a new life belonging to the book alone.

Rosamond Lehmann cannot be sure whether, when she was writing *Invitation to the Waltz* half a century ago, she already had in her mind the story's sequel. 'But when I came to the meeting between Olivia and Rollo on the terrace, I think I thought: I see! *this* is what all this is about! It's unrealised now, it's broken off – but this is what I've got to deal with later.'

What comes later for Rollo and Olivia, in *The Weather in the Streets*, is love. Rollo is rich, fashionable, secure in his social and business worlds, and unhappily married to the beautiful girl with whom he was already in love in *Invitation to the Waltz*. Olivia is alone, impoverished, part of a semi-bohemian London circle.

Neither in their separate worlds, nor in the larger world of their time, can the love between Rollo and Olivia have a public life. It can have no recognition, no expression, no allowed morality, no home: no existence outside their minds and hearts. Its reality is on the other side of everything else in their lives – their families, friends, work, interests. Olivia looks out from her love, their companionship, his warm car, and sees the other world – the real world. 'Beyond the glass casing I was in, was the weather, were the winter streets in rain, wind, fog . . .' Which is stronger? 'Go, go, go, said the bird', wrote T. S. Eliot: 'human kind / Cannot bear very much reality.'

This is a novel of tenderness, but also one of courageous investigation, in which Rosamond Lehmann explores the deep recesses of people's private lives. She follows Rollo home; she accompanies his mother on her pilgrimage to Olivia's doorstep. She trails Olivia on her lonely London circuits, takes her through the abortionist's consulting rooms, and afterwards back to her bed. She probes the cracks in the carapace that encloses the chaos in Marigold Spencer's soul. She exposes the thick thread woven by money and class and social position in the frail fabric of Rollo's loyalties and loves, without which a bond may fray away to nothing. She goes into the spaces of this love affair, and transmits to us the desolation of Olivia's weeks alone, or in the colder climate of her friendships, that cast a long shadow over her hours of delight in Rollo's company. Olivia is no more a grumbler in this novel than she was in *Invitation to the Waltz*, and sometimes we seem to experience her pain, in this affair, more sharply than she does herself.

'Even trimmed up with Rollo's flowers, that room never cracked a whole-hearted smile,' she reflects, in her straightforward way, about one of her London perches.

The thing is really, I don't like living alone. The wind gets up; or else I start wondering what the people were like who lived in the room before me; dead now, and soon I'll be dead and what's it all about? . . . I sit in a chair and do nothing, or lean against the mantelpiece . . . I was alone in that room more than I thought I'd be . . .

Olivia is not a masochist and Rollo is not a cad. Yet there is pain here. Yet there is pleasantness. Their affair balances as precariously as life itself between alternatives at once almost opposite and yet almost the same. Love shimmers between friendship and passion, resentment and affection, nostalgia, exuberance and regret. A benighted weekend swings between despair and the ridiculousness that rekindles laughter and warmth. A dramatic confrontation is undercut by prenatal nausea. The agony of a miscarriage is framed in the ambiguous comfort of an accidental reunion.

The love between Olivia and Rollo warms their conversations as much as their bed; and in recording these, too, Rosamond Lehmann affords her reader a remarkable double awareness. At once we feel what the lovers are both feeling – the tension and attraction and enjoyment between them - while we are touched by the writer's unwavering perception of their separateness: the differences in their thoughts, hearts, lives.

I'd have liked to go to the smart places where people eat, and to theatres and dance places. He didn't want to. Of course it wouldn't do, he knows all those well-connected faces, they're his world . . . He only wanted to be alone somewhere and make love. 'Where can we go?' he'd say. 'Can we go back to your room?'. . . . I told him he had only one idea in his head . . . I said to tease what I wanted was a soulmate. 'You don't, do you?' he'd say, rueful, coaxing. 'And anyway,' he'd say, 'I do love talking to you. You know I do. You're such a clever young creature . . . We have lovely talks, don't we?'

We did, of course, really, lovely talks . . .

There is a conversation one night in Austria, shaded by some chestnut trees. It is the high point, the centre of the lovers' close-

ness. Next day it is gone: not only bypassed with the fragmenta-
tion of their companionship, the splitting of their routes, but
extinguished in the deeper death of their separate perceptions.
Their memories of the same shared experience are different.
Rollo's moment of commitment is to disappear into his mental
repository of good times.

In the last moments of this novel, Rollo and Olivia talk for an
allotted hour in his house. The conversation merges with all the
others they have shared. Suddenly it seems only a step away
from their chat on the moonlit terrace, or in the restaurant of the
train where they met again; and only a step away to the next
stage of their lives, whatever that is to be. They have loved each
other, and left each other; perhaps everything that could
happen between them has happened. Yet their talk, trembling
between triviality and importance, is still full of the immediacy
and uncertainty, the million possible differences, of a present
that is about to become a future.

'Do you think she went on seeing him?' said Rosamond
Lehmann, when we talked about this book. 'Yes, I suppose she
did. I expect it all went on and on, I'm sorry to say. It never
became a tragedy, exactly . . . it couldn't become one. And yet
it was.'

Was it? Perhaps. Rollo Spencer confirms, in that last conversation, that separateness that is at the root of the pain of love.
Yet his coaxing murmur doesn't belong to tragedy. It makes you
smile. It makes you love him. It helps Rollo's reader – if not
Rollo himself – bear a little more unbearable reality.

Janet Watts, London, 1981

PART ONE

1

TURNING OVER IN BED, SHE WAS AWARE OF A SUMMONS: Rouse yourself. Float up, up from the submerging element . . . But it's still night, surely. . . . She opened one eye. Everything was in darkness; a dun glimmer mourned in the crack between the curtains. Fog stung faintly in nose, eyelids. So that was it: the fog had come down again: it might be morning. But I haven't been called yet. What was it woke me? Listen: yes: the telephone, ringing downstairs in Etty's sitting-room; ringing goodness knows how long, nobody to answer it. Oh, damn, oh, hell. . . . Mrs. Banks! Mrs. Banks arrive! Click, key in the door; brown mac, black felt, rabbit stole, be on your peg at once behind the door. Answer it, answer it, let me not have to get up. . . . Etty, you maddening futile lazy cow, get up, go on, answer it at once. . . . Pole-axed with early morning sleep of course, unconscious among her eiderdowns and pillows.

Olivia huddled on her dressing-gown and tumbled down the narrow steep stairs. Etty's crammed dolls'-house sitting-room, unfamiliar in this twilight, dense with the fog's penetration, with yesterday's cigarettes; strangled with cherry-coloured curtains, with parrot-green and silver cushions, with Etty's little chairs, tables, stools, glass and shagreen and cloisonné boxes, bowls, ornaments, shrilled a peevish reproach over and over again from the darkest corner: withdrew into a sinister listening and waiting as she slumped down at the littered miniature writing-table, lifted the receiver and croaked: "Yes?"

Kate perhaps, fresh-faced, alert in the country, starting the children off for school, about to say briskly, "Did I get you

5

out of bed?—Sorry, but I've got to go out. . . ." Kate knows I never could wake up, she condemns me and is pitiless. One day I'll be disagreeable, not apologetic.

"Yes?"

"Is that Olivia?"

"Oh . . . Mother. . . ." Mother's voice, cheerful, tired, soothing—her emergency voice. "Yes?"

"Good-morning, dear. I've been trying to get an answer. . . . I thought perhaps the line was out of order. . . .?"

"No, the line's all right. Sorry, I've only just—— What time is it?"

"Past eight." Mild, unreproachful: your mother.

"Oh, Lord! There's an awful fog here, it's quite dark. Mrs. Banks must have got held up."

"Dear me, how nasty. I do hope she hasn't been careless at a crossing. There's not a sign of fog here. It's dull, just a wee bit misty, but it looks like a nice day later. . . . Listen, dear. . . ." Her voice, which had begun to trail, renewed its special quality of soothing vigour, proclaiming, before the fatal tidings: All is well. "Dad's in bed."

"Dad? What's the matter?"

"Well, it's his chest. Poor Dad, isn't it a shame?"

"Bronchitis?"

"Well, dear, pneumonia. He's being so good and patient. Dr. Martin says he's got quite a good chance—if his heart holds out, you know, dear,—so there's no need to worry too much just at present. He's making such a splendid fight."

"Is he in pain?"

"Well, his cough's tiresome, but he doesn't complain. He gets some rest off and on. Dr. Martin's so kind—he comes three or four times a day. You know what trouble he takes. I'm sure no doctor in England could take more trouble. And I've got such a nice cheerful sensible little nurse—just for night duty. Of course, I do the day."

"When did it start?"

"When did it start, did you say, dear? Oh, just a few days

ago. He would go out in that bitter east wind, and he caught cold, and then his temperature went up so very suddenly."

"I'll come at once. Is Kate there?"

"Yes. Kate's here."

"Oh, she is!" Summoned sooner than me: more of a comfort. "I'll catch the next train."

"That'll be very nice, dear. But don't go dashing off without your breakfast. There's no need. Give Etty my love."

"I will. Have you had any sleep?"

"Oh, plenty. I can always do without sleep." Scornful, obstinate, rather annoyed in the familiar way. . . . Others may have human weaknesses—not I. . . .

"I'll catch the nine-ten and take the bus out."

"Very well, dear, we'll expect you. But do take care in this fog. Don't breathe it in through your mouth more than you can help, and if you take a taxi, do tell the man to *crawl*."

"Nine minutes," said an impersonal voice.

"Remember your breakfast. Good-bye, dear."

She's hung up hastily, she's on her way upstairs without a moment's hesitation. Nine minutes have been lost. Forward, forward. Too much can sneak past, can be unsupervised in nine minutes.

Between stages of dressing and washing she packed a hasty suitcase. Pack the red dress, wear the dark brown tweed, Kate's cast-off, well-cut, with my nice jumper, lime-green, becoming, pack the other old brown jumper—That's about all. Dress carefully—hair, lipstick, powder—look your best. Don't go haggard, dishevelled, hot-foot to the bedside—don't arrive like a bad omen. No need to worry too much just at present. *Not too much just at present:* ominous words. *He's fighting*—means *he's holding his own?*—means, always—*he's defeated*. . . . Is it his death-bed? Must I dye the red, the green, must I go into Tulverton, looking pale, and buy some mourning, must I buy black gloves? Wouldn't he manage to say, if he was still just ahead of the thing that was trying to overtake him, still able

to preserve his own mixture, his particular one, sealed away
from the universal ending, the lapse into the general death of
people—wouldn't he be sure to say: If I catch you having a
funeral. . . . Surely he must have said it some time or other.
If not, if he hadn't bothered, if he hadn't had time, if Aunt
Edith were to come flowing with all her veils and chains and
overthrow him, if the Widow lurking in Mother were to
triumph, or the cheerfulness of the nurse dishearten him
beyond the remedy of malice and cynical resilience—then
black and elderly women would prevail, black armlet for
James, black-edged notepaper, and weeds and wreaths and Aunt
Edith's smelling-salts; and there'd be nothing left of the
important thing he knew, that he hadn't attempted to impart
except as a kind of spiritual wink of an eyelid, barely perceptible,
caught once or twice and returned without a word: something,
some sense he had of life and death; the lifelong private
integrity of his disillusionment.

She ran down to the next floor, telephoned for a taxi, then
opened the door of Etty's bedroom, adjoining the sitting-room.
Silence and obscurity greeted her; and a smell compounded of
powder, scent, toilet creams and chocolate truffles.

"Etty. . . .!"

At the second call, Etty turned on her pillows and groaned
"*darling* . . ." in mingled protest and greeting.

"Etty, I don't want to wake you up, but I've got to go home.
Mother's just telephoned. Dad's very ill. I'm just off."

"Oh, *darling*. . . ." She switched on her lamp, lay back
again with a heavy sigh. "*What* did you say?" She sat up
suddenly in her pink shingle cap, pale, extinct, ludicrously
diminished without her make-up and the frame of her hair.

"He's got pneumonia."

"*Oh, no!* The poor sweet. Oh, darling, have you got to
go? How *devastating*. Oh, and I do so adore him—give him
my love—*and* Aunt Ethel. Wait a minute now, darling, let me
think, let me *think*. Half-past eight—oh dear! Where's Mrs.
Banks? Not here, I suppose. Wait a minute, darling, and I'll

help you." She whisked off the bedclothes; her brittle white legs and bony little knees slipped shrinkingly over the edge of the mattress.

"There's nothing to help about. I'm all ready. I've packed and all. Get back into bed at once."

She stood up feebly for a moment in a wisp of flowered chiffon, then subsided deprecatingly on the edge of the bed.

"Oh, darling, you must have some tea or something. Let me *think*—Yes, some tea. I'll put the kettle on."

"I don't want any. I'll have breakfast on the train. It'll be something to do."

"Will you really, darling? It *might* be best. Now *mind* you do. It's *no* good not eating on these occasions, one's simply *useless* to everybody. Oh, *is* there a fog again? How *vile*. It's simply—It's almost *more* than can be borne."

She huddled back into bed and shivered.

"Just one thing. Later on, about ten, if you'd ring up Anna at the studio and explain I can't come."

"I will, darling, of *course*. I *won't* forget. Isn't there *anything* else I can do?"

"No, go to sleep again, Etty."

"Oh, darling, I feel *too* concerned." She lay back, looking stricken. "So *miserable* for you."

"It may be all right, you know. He's stronger than people think. He's quite tough."

"Oh, he *is*, isn't he? I've always thought he's *very* strong really, invalids so often are. I do *think* he'll be all right. *Promise* to ring me up, darling. Let me see, I'm dining *out* to-night, oh dear, what a nuisance . . . but I'll be in between six and seven for *certain*. I *tell* you what, I'll ring *you* up."

"All right, do, Ett. Good-bye, duck."

"Can you *manage* your suitcase? Oh! . . . good-bye, my sweet."

Pressing all her cardinal-red fingertips to her mouth, she kissed then extended them wistfully, passionately. Above them her frail temples and cheekbones, her hollowed eyes stared with their morning look of pathos and exhaustion. Like an egg she looked, without her hair, so pale, smooth, oval, the features painted on with a stare and a droop.

"Lie down again and go to sleep."

She will too.

Olivia slammed the canary-yellow door of the dolls'-house after her, swallowed a smarting draught of fog, said "Paddington" towards a waiting bulk, a peak immobile, an inexpressive disc of muffled crimson stuck with a dew-rough sprout of hoary, savage whisker—and plunged into the taxi.

Out of the station, through gradually thinning fog-banks, away from London. Lentil, saffron, fawn were left behind. A grubby jaeger shroud lay over the first suburbs; but then the woollen day clarified, and hoardings, factory buildings, the canal with its barges, the white-boled orchards, the cattle and willows and flat green fields loomed secretively, enclosed within a transparency like drenched indigo muslin. The sky's amorphous material began to quilt, then to split, to shred away; here and there a ghost of blue breathed in the vaporous upper rifts, and the air stood flushed with a luminous essence, a soft indirect suffusion from the yet undeclared sun. It would be fine. My favourite weather.

An image of the garden rose in her mind—soaked lawn, strewn leaves, yellowing elm-tops, last white roses on the pergola, last old draggled chrysanthemums in the border; all blurred with damp, with a subdued incandescence, still, mournful and contented. And him pacing the path with his plaid scarf on, his eye equivocal beneath the antique raffish slant of a Tyrolese hat, his lips mild, pressed together, patient and ironic between the asthma grooves. He can't die. . . . She rummaged in her bag for mirror, powder, handkerchief, and attended minutely to her face. A speck or two of fog-black, and my eyes look a trifle weak, but not too bad. Various nondescript wearers of bowler hats sat behind newspapers all down the breakfast car: travelling to Tulverton on business probably; or through, on to the north. . . . Here came something in a different style—a tall prosperous-looking male figure in a tweed overcoat, carrying a dog under his arm, stooping broad shoulders in at the entrance. With a beam and a flourish the fat steward conducted him to the seat opposite Olivia. He hesitated, then took off his coat, folded it, put the dog on it, patted it, sat down beside it, picked up the card, ordered sausages, scrambled eggs, coffee, toast and marmalade, and opened *The Times*.

Rollo Spencer.

A deep wave of colour swept over her face: the usual uncontrollable reaction at sight of a face from the old days. At once her mind started to scurry and scramble, looking for footholds, for crannies to hide in: because my position is ambiguous, because I'm anonymous. . . . On Tulverton platform, in the Little Compton bus, walking down to the post office, the eye of flint, the snuffing nostrils, the false mouths narrowly shaping words of greeting, saying underneath their tongues: "Now, what's your situation? Eh? Where's your husband?"—whispering with relish behind their hands: "Poor Mrs. Curtis: it's hard she didn't get that younger daughter settled. Bad blood somewhere: I always said . . ."

I won't go outside the garden, I'll wear a disguise, I'll have a shell like James's tortoise. . . .

Carry it off now, carry it off—What do I care? Snap my fingers at the whole bloody lot. Who's Rollo Spencer? He won't recognise me. I'll smile and say: "You don't recognise me. . . ." Dad's on his death-bed maybe. . . . I shan't say that.

The dog stirred about on the coat, and Rollo said something to it, then glanced across and smiled the faint general smile with which people in railway carriages accompany such demonstrations. The smile sharpened suddenly into a kind of wary prelude to recognition; and then he said in quite a pleased, friendly way:

"Good-morning."

"Good-morning."

"Revolting in London, wasn't it? It's a relief to get out."

"Yes. It's going to be heavenly in the country."

Soon, an attendant brought steaming pots, dishes, plates, set them before him. He helped himself with leisurely liberality.

"Terrific breakfasts railway companies do give one. I always overeat distressingly in trains. There's something in the words scrambled eggs, rolls, sausages, when you see them written down. . . . One look at the card and my self-control snaps. I *must* have everything."

"I know. I feel the same about ice-cream lists . . . mixed fruit sundae . . . cupid's kiss . . . banana split . . . oh! . . . banana split!"

He laughed.

"I see what you mean, but you know, the sound of it doesn't absolutely fire me—not like the word sausage. I'm afraid I'm more earthy than you. I'm afraid you're not with me really?" He eyed her solitary cup of coffee. "I hope I'm not turning you up. . . ."

"Not a bit. I'm just not a breakfaster." And only got one and sixpence left in my purse.

"Hi, Lucy. . . ." The last mouthful went into the dog's pink and white, delicately hesitating jaws.

"What a pronounced female."

"What, this one?" He looked dubiously down. "Well, I don't know. Are you, Lucy?"

The dog quivered madly and blinked towards him. She had a coat like a toy dog and her eyes were weak with pink rims. Her nose also was patched with pink, and she wore a pinched smirking expression, slightly dotty, virginal, and extremely self-conscious.

"She's horribly sentimental," he said.

"I see it's one of those cases . . ."

"How d'you mean?"

"She thinks you and she were made for one another."

"Oh! . . ." He considered. "I believe she does. It's awful, isn't it? She's shockingly touchy."

"Can you wonder? Look at the position she has to keep up. Being a gentleman's lady friend——"

He burst out laughing; and she was struck afresh by what she remembered about him years ago: the physical ease and richness flowing out through voice and gestures, a bountiful-ness of nature that drew one, irrespective of what he had to offer.

"I used to see you—quite a long time ago—didn't I?" he said shyly. "At home or somewhere?"

"Yes. I used to come to tea with Marigold. *Ages* ago. I didn't think you'd remember me."

"Well, I do. At least I wasn't absolutely sure for the first moment. . . . I've got an awful memory for names. . . ." He paused; but she said nothing. I won't tell him my name. "And you've changed," he added.

"Have I?"

They smiled at each other.

"Got thin," he suggested, a little shyly.

"Oh, well! . . . Last time we met properly I was a great big bouncing flapper. I hadn't fined down, as the saying goes."

"Well, you've done that all right now." He looked her over with a warm blue eye, and she saw an image of herself in his mind—fined down almost to the bone, thin through the hips and shoulders, with thin well-shaped cream-coloured hands, with a face of pronounced planes, slightly crooked, and a pale smoothly-hollowed cheek, and a long full mouth going to points, made vermilion. No hat, hair dark brown, silky, curling up at the ends. Safely dressed in these tweeds. Not uninterest-ing: even perhaps . . .? "All those charming plump girls I used to know," he said, "they've all dwindled shockingly."

"Has Marigold dwindled?"

"Mm—not exactly. You couldn't quite say that. But she's sort of different. . . ."

"How?"

He reflected, swallowing the last of his toast and marmalade.

"Oh, I don't know. . . . Got a bit older and all that, you know."

"More beautiful?"

"Well, if you can call it—— Haven't you seen her lately then?"

"Not for years. In fact, not since her wedding."

She glanced at him. "I think that was the last time I saw you too. . . ."

"I remember."

"Do you? We didn't speak."

"No, we didn't."

She looked away. A bubble of tension seemed to develop and explode between them. He watched me from the other side of the room. I thought once or twice we looked at each other, but he was too busy, caught up in his own world, to come near: sleek, handsome-looking in his wedding-clothes, being an usher, being the son of the house, laughing with a glass of champagne in his hand, surrounded by friends, by relations. . . . And Nicola was there too, in an enormous white hat. I was still in the chrysalis; engaged unimpressively, without a *Times* announcement, to Ivor, and my clothes were wrong: a subsidiary guest, doing crowd work on the outskirts, feeling inferior, up from the country.

"I follow her career in the *Tatler*," she said. She smiled, thinking how often the face, the figure, almost freakishly individual, had popped up on the page in Etty's sitting-room, sharply arresting the attention among all the other inheritors of renown: the co-lovelies, co-dancers, racers, charity performers, popular producers of posh children: Lady Britton at Newmarket, at Ascot, at the point to point, at the newest night-club, the smartest cocktail bar, the first night of ballet, opera; stepping ashore at Cowes, basking on the Lido, sitting behind the butts, wheeling her very own pram in the Park, entertaining a week-end party at her country home; Lady

Britton with her dogs, her pet monkey, her Siamese cat, her husband. . . .

"Yes," he said, as if with a shrug, half-amused, half-cynical, "she does seem to be something of a public figure."

One never saw him or Nicola in the gossip columns. Some people seem to lose their news value with marriage, some to acquire it. Nicola, that once sensation, appeared to have faded out. What is the clue to this?

"She's a restless creature," he said. He drank some coffee and looked uncertainly out of the window.

"Is she happy?"

"Happy? Oh, well . . ." He raised his eyebrows, and made a faint grimace, as if the question were pointless or beyond him altogether. "She seems all right. She was always determined to enjoy life, wasn't she?"

"Yes, she was."

"So I suppose she does. Or doesn't it follow? . . ." He laughed slightly. "But to tell you the truth I haven't looked into it very closely. Brothers don't generally know much about their sisters, do they?"

"I suppose you don't feel romantic about her," she said, smiling. "I always did. In fact, the way we felt about the whole lot of you! . . . You were fairly drenched in glamour. Especially you."

"Me? Good God!" He burst into such a shout of laughter that the other occupants of the car peered round their partitions to look at him. "You're pulling my leg."

"No, I assure you. You floated in a rosy veil. Marigold was always feeding us up with accounts of you, and everything you did sounded *so* superior and exciting. You didn't seem real at all—just a beautiful dream. Of course it was a very long time ago. One gets over these things." She smiled, meeting the look in his eye—the kindled interest, the light expectation of flirtation. I can do this, I can be this amusing person till Tulverton; because after that we shan't meet again. The shutter will snap down between our worlds once more. . . . He's wondering about me. . . . A person with thoughts you don't dream of, going into the country I shan't tell you why. . . .

"Well," he said, sitting back. "I've done a number of things off and on over which I prefer to draw a veil—but I swear I've never floated about in a rosy one."

"How do you know what you've done? It's all in the mind of the beholder—*We* don't know what we look like. We're not just ourselves—we're just a tiny nut of self, and the rest a complicated mass of unknown quantities—according to who's looking at us. A person might be wearing somebody else's hated aunt's Sunday black taffeta, or look like a pink blancmange that once made somebody else sick—without knowing it. . . . Or—oh, endless possibilities."

"I see," he said seriously, looking first at her, then down at himself. "It hadn't occurred to me. Even a pair of brown plus fours. . . . Could they be so unstable?"

"Oh, yes. How do you know how they might look to Lucy, for instance? . . . Once I had a simple ordinary frock, not very nice, with rows of pearl buttons on it—and someone I knew turned pale when he saw it and rushed trembling away. I had to change. But I can't just have been wearing a frock with pearl buttons, can I?"

"Good God! Did he explain?"

"No. He didn't know why. He thought it was the buttons, but he wasn't sure. He went to a psycho-analyst but he never discovered."

"What a frightfully sensitive chap he must have been!"

"Yes, he was."

"Are all your friends interesting like that?" He leaned forward over the table, his eyes teasing her in a way she remembered. "I do wish I knew the people you knew. My life's terribly humdrum."

"Is it? That's hard to believe. What is your life?"

"Oh—just a City man. I left the army, you know. Three years ago."

She suggested rather nervously:

"And—you're married?"

"Yes, married into the bargain. Three years."

"I saw about it in the papers."

"Married man, City man. What could be more hum-drum?"

"Well, it depends——"

"I dare say. . . ."

She glanced at him. He was looking out of the window. The warm, trivial, provocative play of his interest over her had been suddenly withdrawn. A hint of moodiness about him, a flatness in his voice struck an echo; and in a flash she remembered the sculpturing moonlight, their voices dropping out on to the dark, answering each other in a dream. "I've seen you dancing with somebody very beautiful." His flat reply: "Oh, yes, isn't she?" "I dare say she's as stupid as an owl," he said moodily. These things of course he wouldn't remember, but I do. They had retained their meaningless meaning; were frozen unalterably in their own element, like flowers in ice. She came down the stairs in a white dress and held up her hand to signal to him; whereupon he left me and they met far away from me, the other side of the hall. Even then there had seemed a confusion in the images—a feeling of seeing more than was there to see: the shadow of the shape of things to come. Or was that nonsense? But he had married Nicola Maude: just as I knew then he would.

His face was turned towards her again now, in rather a tentative way, as if he might be going to ask: "You're married too, aren't you?" or some such question; which to prevent she said quickly:

"Don't you like being in the City?"

He answered in the conventional tone of mild disparagement:

"Oh—it's not so bad. It's boring sometimes, but other times it's not such a bad game. Anyway, it's the only way that presented itself of turning a necessary penny. And now that my outstanding abilities have raised me to the position of

partner I give myself an occasional day off—which helps to
relieve the tedium. To-day, for instance."

"I suppose you're going to Meldon?"

"Yes, going to murder a few pheasants. I meant to go down
last night, but it was too thick. The woods ought to be looking
good. . . . You going home, too?"

"Yes. . . . Yes, I'm going home. Just for a few days."

"D'you often come down?"

"No—not very often really. No, I don't." She stopped,
feeling stubborn, choked by the usual struggle of conflicting
impulses: to explain, to say nothing; to trust, to be suspicious;
lightly to satisfy natural curiosity; to defy it with furious
scorn and silence; to let nobody come too near me. . . .

There was a flat, weighted silence. He offered her a cigarette
out of his smart gold case, struck a match for her. She watched
his hand as he lit his own. The fingers were long and nervous;
a ring with a blue engraved stone on the left-hand little finger;
a well-shaped hand, not a very strong one. She said:

"Last time we met you told me to read *Tristram Shandy*."

"And did you?"

"Yes, of course." She smiled. "I started the very next day."
It was clear as yesterday in memory: Kate gone to the Hunt
Ball with the Heriots, me reading in bed, holding little brown
calf Volume I. with a thrill of emotion, thinking: "I'm not
bereft, I've something too": not *Tristram Shandy*, but a link
with the grown-up world, the world of romance—of Rollo.
"I was awfully disappointed and puzzled. I'm afraid I gave it
up. But last year I tried again—and I enjoyed it a lot."

"Good!" he said. He seemed pleased and amused. "My
favourite idea of heaven is still a place where there's a new
volume every three months."

"I suppose you know it's one of the things men try to
make one feel inferior about? They say only a man can
appreciate it properly. Like old brandy."

"Do they?" His eyebrow lifted, he had an expression of
humorous flirtatious deprecation. "Well, naturally I'd sub-

scribe to that. I mean I couldn't be left out of a thing like
that, could I? All the same, one mustn't be bigoted. I'd be
prepared to say that every rule has an exception: and you
may be it."

"Thank you so much."

"Not at all. I must have been perspicacious enough to
detect it years ago." After a pause he added, "What a good
memory you've got."

She sighed.

"For the old times—yes, I seem to remember everything.
When one's young a little goes such a very long way. It's like
being on a rather empty road with a few signposts simply
shouting at you and a few figures looming out at you larger
than life. At least, it was like that for me. One has so little
and one expects so much."

He did not reply.

"Were you like that?" she said.

He said slowly:

"More or less, I suppose. I was awfully enthusiastic and
foolish, you know, and enjoyed everything like mad . . . But
I don't know . . . I've always been an idle sort of bloke . . .
drifting along with the stream, knocking up against things.
I don't actually remember my youth frightfully clearly . . .
Just one or two things. . . .

"The way I made bricks out of straw! . . . It's staggering
to look back on."

He glanced at her, glanced away again, said finally:

"I think you must have been rather a peculiar young
creature. I thought so at the time."

"What time?"

"The time we talked. . . . Didn't we?" He hesitated, diffident.
"At a dance we had . . . when I found you on the terrace. . . .
Didn't I?"

"Oh—do you remember that?"

"I seem to. To the best of my recollection you were a
thought depressed; and we talked about life."

"Oh dear! Yes, we did. I always did if I got half a chance. But how extraordinary!"

"What?"

"You remembering."

"You don't, then?"

"Yes. Oh, yes. Awfully well."

"Well, then, why shouldn't I?"

Meeting his eyes, she laughed and shook her head. She could think of nothing to say. He stubbed out his cigarette and gave Lucy a pat.

"But what I notice," she went on, feeling slightly perturbed, disorientated, as if she must re-establish a more impersonal basis, "is that things that have happened more recently aren't nearly so vivid. It's all a blur. Houses I've lived in—people I've been with. . . . There seems a kind of shutter down over a lot of things—although they should be more real. No images come. . . ." The difficulty of remembering Ivor with precision; or that cottage we had. . . .

"It's age creeping on," he said. "That's what it is. I suffer from the same thing myself. Though I shouldn't have expected *you* to, yet awhile."

That's the way he treated me last time. . . . She noticed a faint touch of grey at the edge of his thick chestnut hair, above the ears, a suspicion of reddening in his ruddy complexion. He must be thirty-five at least, and in the end he would look like his father. She said:

"I suppose it *is* age. Impressions pile up faster than you can sort them, and everything dims down and levels out. Not to speak of there being a good many things one wants to forget . . . so one does."

"Yes, there's that." He nodded; and after a moment said seriously: "Do you mind the idea of getting old?"

"Terribly. Do you?"

"Terribly, I'm afraid. Teeth dropping out, wrinkles, fat and slow and pompous. No more feeling enthusiastic and expectant. No more—anything."

"Yes." No more making love, did he mean? "And feeling you've missed something important when it's too late."

He nodded ruefully.

"It's the principle of the thing I object to. Being stalked down and counted out without a single word to say in the matter."

"I know. In a trap, from the very start. Born in it, in fact."

He said with a faint smile:

"I don't suppose we're quite the first people to resent it, do you?"

"No. And sometimes I think it may not be as bad as all that—that the worst is now, in the apprehension of it . . . and actually we'll just slip into it without a struggle, and accept it quite peacefully. . . ." After all, Dad had done this, and most people who grew old. . . . "We shan't long for our time over again."

"Don't you think so?" He stared out of the window.

"I think it. I don't feel it. But very occasionally I get a hint—that one day I might be going to feel it. I suddenly see the *idea* of it . . . like getting a glimpse of a place a long, long way off. You only see it for a second now and then in one particular weather; but you're walking towards it and you know it's where you're going to get in the end."

"That's a better way to look at it." He still stared out of the window. "I dare say you're right too. It *should* be like that. I expect it will . . . at least, if we've had a fair run for our money." He turned to look at her intently, and said with sudden emphasis: "And that's up to us, isn't it?"

"Yes."

"One's apt to put the blame on—other people, circumstances: which is ridiculous."

"And unsatisfactory."

"You've found that too, have you?"

Something about the way he said it startled her vaguely: as if he were insisting on an answer—a true one. What was in his mind? Wasn't he getting a run for his money? What did he want? He didn't look the kind of person to be gnawed by dreams and desires beyond his compass. . . . So prosperously handsome, so easy-mannered, so obviously pleasing to women. . . .

"I'm afraid I'm not very grown-up," he said suddenly.

"Nor am I."

"I should have said you were."

"Oh, *no!*" There was a pause; and she added nervously: "I've noticed people with children don't generally mind so much . . . about age, I mean. They seem to feel less anxious about time."

"Do they? I suppose they do," he said. "I expect it's a good thing to have children."

"You haven't got any?"

"No," he said. "Have you?"

"No."

They made it a joke, and laughed. . . . All the same, it was surprising he hadn't produced an heir. Couldn't, wouldn't Nicola? . . . or what?

"Then," she said, "there are the pleasures of the intellect. They're said to be lasting. We must cultivate our intellects."

"Too late," he said. "One ought to make at least a beginning in youth, and I omitted to do so. The fact is, I don't care much about the intellect. I'm afraid the scope of my pleasures is rather limited."

"Really?"

"Confined in fact entirely to those of the senses."

"Oh, I see. . . ." She answered his odd comically inquiring look with a lift of the eyebrows. "Well, I suppose they're all right. Only they're apt to pall."

"Oh, *are* they?"

"I was thinking of cake." She sighed. "It used to be my passion—especially chocolate, or any kind of large spicy bun. Now, it's beginning to mean less . . . much less."

He leaned back, laughing; the tension dissolved again.

"Hallo," he said, "the gasworks. We're nearly there. I've never known this journey go so quickly."

The steward advanced, pencil poised over pad.

"Two, sir?" He smiled, obsequiously arch.

"Yes," said Rollo.

"No," she said quickly.

"Please...."

He scrawled out the double bill and shortly moved on, gratified by his tip. She laid a shilling in front of Rollo.

"Thank you," she said.

"Aren't I allowed to stand you one cup of coffee?"

"Yes, certainly, with pleasure—any time you invite me. But please take this now—for luck."

"I dislike feminist demonstrations," he said.

"So do I." She picked up the shilling and put it in his palm.

He looked at it and said finally:

"Right!" He flipped it in the air, caught it and slipped it into his breast pocket.

"And I'll hold you to that," he said.

"What?"

"That cup of coffee."

The train was slowing into Tulverton. The familiar roofs and chimneys, the clock tower slid by, etherealised in the first soft gold breaking of sunlight. In another few minutes they were alighting on the platform. There stood Benson the chauffeur, brass-buttoned, capped, dignified, greeting him with respectful fatherliness, looking exactly as he used to look twenty years ago fetching Marigold from dancing-class: a kindly man of character. Jovially Rollo hailed him. A porter was already dealing nimbly with the baggage. In the aura of cap-touching recognition and prompt service surrounding him, he appeared as with a spotlight on him, larger than life-size; the other occupants of the platform a drab background to him. Jocelyn would find in the scene a fine text for a sermon of snorting moral indignation; Colin would observe with his best sardonic lip on, and afterwards act it; Anna would detach herself and stroll off to look at the automatic machines. . . . But I with my capacity for meeting everybody half-way stand meekly within his orbit and feel gratified by his attentions.

"Good-bye, Rollo."

He turned towards her quickly, as if the use of his Christian name had moved him.

"You're being met?" He took the hand she held out.

"No. Bus. I must fly."

"You'll do nothing of the sort. I'll drop you in the car, of course. Where is it—Little Compton? It's practically on my way. Here, porter, another bag."

Disregarding a feeble protest, he seized and handed over her inferior suitcase, swept her along in his wake and installed her beside him in the family Sunbeam, beneath an overpowering fur rug.

Away they glided, out of Tulverton through the narrow high street, past the market square, past the war memorial, between the more outlying rows of little red and yellow brick boxes, past the Baptist Chapel, past the gasometers, beyond the last lamps, over the bridge and skirting the duck pond—relic of a rustic Tulverton, long vanished—out along the damp, flat, field-and-allotment bordered, blue-flashing road that led to the old village.

"This feels very grand," she said. "I do wish I had a car."

"D'you live in London?"

"Yes, I do."

"A car's almost more trouble than it's worth in London. I find mine sits eating its head off in the garage most of the time."

And of course that's the reason why I don't bother to get one.

"Every time I come along this road there's a fresh outbreak of bungalows," she said. "*Look* at that one! ' *Idono* ' . . . If only I had the energy to set fire to every one of them in the middle of the night . . . except that they'd go and put up something worse. There's one somewhere called '*Oodathortit.*'"

He laughed.

"Don't you mind about them?"

He looked at her in some surprise.

"I suppose I do rather . . . when I look at them. Nasty little brutes."

"You ought to mind about them."

"Ah, but I never do anything I ought."

"England gets squalider and squalider. So disgraced, so ignoble, so smug and pretentious . . . and nobody minds enough to stop it."

"Nobody can if it wants to."

She felt his mild obstinacy hardening against her, deliberate, refusing to be lectured, quite good-humoured, half-teasing. He went on:

"It's all very interesting and degraded, I agree. But what's one to do?"

"Can't people be educated——?"

"But they have been!" he said triumphantly. "This is the glorious result: Art homes."

Oh, well, sit back in one's luxurious car then under one's great expensive, tickling fur rug and ignore it all—give one's mind to important things instead: like shooting pheasants. . . . She was dumb.

She stared out of the window and the flitting bungalows stared back at her, brazen, cocksure.

"I'd—just like to blow the whole thing up."

"Oh, anarchy! But that's not very constructive, is it?" He's laughing at me. . . . "You ought to have a remedy." Getting his own back. . . . "Personally I subscribe to the Society for the Preservation of Rural England, I think it's called, so you see I do more than you. . . . It's a magnificent object and I'm all for it. . . . I don't grudge a penny of it." He lit a cigarette. "And furthermore," he said, "I'm all for the League of Nations. But if people want war they'll have war."

"I see you're what's called a realist," she said, looking out of the window, playing with the hand-rest. People like him . . . well-padded, cynical. . . . Phrases from Colin and the rest clotted and obstructed her head, like lumps of used cotton-wool. . . .

He laughed quietly.

Some inner shock at the sound made her look round at him. What's it all about? . . . His eye was fixed upon her, alight, hard, with a sort of unconscious wariness and determination. . . . He's enjoying himself. . . . He's . . . he wants. . . . Her head whirled, snatching at questions, dissolving, her eyes stayed riveted on his. . . . What is it? . . . Fighting, subduing me. . . . What'll happen? He might hit me, kiss me. . . . She dropped her eyes suddenly. It was all over in two seconds. After a pause, she heard him say pleasantly:

"I'm afraid you must find a desert island."

"I don't want to."

I don't want to argue any more, or assert different views. *Please.* Forget about it; let everything be soothing, harmonious again. I don't know anything and I don't want to think now, to disagree with you. . . .

"What's the matter?" he said suddenly.

"Nothing." She wrenched out a narrow smile and presented it to him. "Can I have a cigarette?"

"Rather. So sorry. Dozens." His voice was kind, perturbed.

I shall cry. . . . Oh, God! God!

"The thing is really——" She applied herself elaborately to the match he held out.

"Mm?" He went on holding the match with care and patience.

"Why I'm coming home is—because my father is very ill——"

He was shocked. His hand went impulsively out towards her on the rug.

He's sorry now he had that argument, thinks no wonder I was a bit touchy, tiresome. . . .

"I say, I'm most terribly sorry. Why didn't you tell me?
How awful for you. . . ." Such sincere sympathy, such a warm
solicitous voice. . . . "I do hope you'll find it isn't so bad."

"Yes. Thank you. I expect he'll be all right. I mean—I
feel he may be. . . ." I've betrayed him to Rollo . . . to excuse
myself, to re-establish myself in Rollo's favour.

"I expect he will be, honestly I do. Daddy was most frightfully ill last winter—heart and kidneys and God knows what
—all the works. They said he'd never be able to shoot or fish
again, and have to live in an arm-chair if he ever left his bed
again—and now you should see him. He's as right as rain—
practically."

"Is he? I'm so glad." She could meet his eyes once more
and smile. The shameful, half-hysterical emotion subsided.
He's not to be sorry for me. "Do give him my love if he
remembers me." Disarming of him so unselfconsciously to
call Sir John Daddy.

"Rather. I will."

"Give everybody my love—specially your mother."

"I will indeed. I believe Marigold's coming down this
week-end."

"Oh, Marigold. . . . How lovely it would be to see her
again——"

"Well, why not? It isn't impossible, is it?"

She hesitated a minute.

"No, it's no good. . . . It's so long ago and——"

Beyond Benson's immobile cap, neck and shoulders appeared
the village green, a cluster of cottages, the farm. There wasn't
much more time. She said with an effort:

"You see your mother is a sort of symbol to me. . . . I can't
quite explain. . . . When I was a child I wanted her approbation.
She's stayed at the back of my mind—as a sort of standard for
suitable behaviour. . . . Often,—when I was in the middle of
an upheaval—a few years ago, she used to appear before me
like a reproachful vision." She laughed. "Don't look so
startled. It's quite irrational. But even now, when I've more

or less—after enormous efforts—given up minding what people think of me, it would be distressing to feel I'd—I'd disappointed her. . . . Even though—perhaps—her idea of what's a—a good kind of conduct—might be—probably is—quite different—in some cases—from mine nowadays. . . . Do you see?"

"Yes," he said, after a pause. "I see. All the same I think you underestimate Mummy's wisdom. She's a strange woman. She lives by the most rigid standards herself—and has almost complete tolerance for everybody else. It's only that she doesn't let on. . . ."

"Yes. Yes, I can believe that's true. She's one of the people who've chosen a behaviour long ago and stick to it." Like the Queen's toques—unfashionable, monotonous: but reliable, distinguished, right.

"Besides," he said, "if she likes a person she doesn't change. I've never know her to. And I believe you were always a favourite of hers."

"Was I?"

Once again, a start of surprise went through her, not at the fact, if fact it were, but at his calm statement of it. A hundred questions stirred. I was—am still—spoken of? Rollo listened?—asked questions about me?

The turn of the drive was in sight. Benson was slowing down and changing gear.

"Tell him to stop at the gate," she said hurriedly. "Not drive in."

"Are you sure?"

"Yes, truly. You see, the noise . . . it might disturb. . . ."

"I see. Of course." He tapped on the window.

But it wasn't so much that. . . .

"Well, give him your bag. Let him carry it up."

"Gracious no, I wouldn't dream of it." She jumped out and seized it. "It's very light." Not a shadow of this meeting must colour my arrival. "Please——" She gave him her hand. "Good-bye, Rollo. Thank you for kindness."

He kept her hand in his, leaning forward. Benson stood discreetly behind the door, holding it back.

"I do hope so frightfully he's all right."

"Yes. Yes, thank you."

"I do wish there was something I could do."

"Oh, no . . . it's quite all right. It's sweet of you, but please don't think at all about it. . . ."

"Might I ring up? Would it be a bore?"

"It wouldn't be a bore, only *please* don't. . . . Yes, do—if you like, I mean . . . if you think of it."

"Then I will. I'd awfully like to know. We all would."

"It's very nice of you."

He let go of her hand, looking suddenly a trifle embarrassed.

"Who would I ask for?—I mean—if I wanted to get hold of you? I'm so bad at names, I never remember."

"Oh!"—she hesitated, her colour rose. "Olivia Curtis—I'm still that. . . . I mean—I *have* been something else—I've gone back to that—Good-bye."

She took her case and hurried up the drive without looking back, hearing behind her, through a perturbed flurry, the soft mounting roar of the car as it swept him on and away.

II

KATE was at the front door to meet her.

"Hallo."

"Hallo. Whose car was that stopped at the gate?"

"The Spencers'." Olivia went in past her and put her bag down in the hall.

"The Spencers'?"

"Mm. . . . I met Rollo in the train coming down and he gave me a lift."

"Oh. . . . I saw it from the window. I suppose he's come down for the shooting."

"I suppose so. Where's Mother?"

"With him." She looked Olivia sharply over in the familiar way, thinking: she's altered the coat. Not bad.

"No change, I suppose?" She said it in the casual way Kate would require of her, her heart beginning to beat thickly, in dread and anticipation.

"Not that I know of."

"How long've you been here?"

"Since Tuesday."

Four days. And not a word to me. Did they think I'd be hysterical, or a disturbing influence or what?

There hung his old hat, his cap, on their pegs, his woolly scarf and brown fleece-lined gloves folded on the table beneath them: poignant objects. They seemed to have taken on a life of their own; to be dumb, dark, monstrously urgent questions: as dogs are whose masters have gone away.

From the top of the stairs a muted voice called down:

"Is that Olivia?"

Down floated Mrs. Curtis, smiling, to kiss her.

"Mum——" Tears sprang, her throat tightened. But her mother said with cheerful calmness:

"It's nice to see you, dear. I didn't expect you for another half-hour. Especially with such a fog in London. I made sure your train would be late. What time did you get in?"

"Quite punctually, I think. But I'm early because I ran into Rollo Spencer on Tulverton platform, and he gave me a lift out."

"Did he? Mr. Spencer? How very kind of him. It's quite out of his way, too."

"I know. He insisted."

"A good three miles. Did he drive in?"

"No, he dropped me at the gate."

"I thought I heard a car. I suppose he was on his way to Meldon?"

"Yes. For a shoot."

"Ah, yes." She wafted Rollo towards his home, his recreations, with a gracious nod. Apprehension sank away again.

The lurking threats of change, of disaster, retreated before Mother's impregnable normality. Rather pale, rather drawn and dark about the eyes, but neat, but fresh, erect, composed as ever, preoccupied with the supervision—in retrospect—of the arrival, checking up on detail with nearly all her customary minuteness and relish. . . . Mother was being wonderful.

"Did you get plenty of breakfast?"

"Yes. I had some coffee on the train."

"Nothing to eat?"

"I didn't want anything. You know I hardly ever have breakfast."

"I know you're a silly girl. No wonder you're so scraggy." She looked her daughter over with dissatisfaction.

"Oh! Must we go through this old hoop again?" Olivia flung herself down on the oak settle, and studied her shoes.

"How is Etty?" Mrs. Curtis passed on smoothly.

"Fast asleep, I expect. She was snuggling down nicely again when I left."

"Does Etty ever do anything but sleep?"

"Never—in the mornings."

"Hmm——"

The special indulgent Etty voice was no longer used. Etty had not married—not even unfortunately She both went to bed and stayed in bed too late. The whole thing was discreditable, suspicious. No longer was it tenderly remarked that Etty was such a frail little creature. She was as strong as anybody else: the trouble was that she'd been spoilt, she'd never had any backbone.

"If Etty would see to it that that woman of hers, Mrs. Binns, isn't it? who appears so very deaf over the telephone, came at a reasonable hour and cooked you both a good nourishing breakfast, if she's competent to do so, which I doubt. . . . How can you expect to do a proper morning's work on an empty stomach?"

"I don't do a proper morning's work—but it's no good putting the blame on my stomach. However full it was it wouldn't persuade people to let Anna photograph 'em, or pay their bills when she had——"

"You don't know——"

Olivia giggled, drumming her heels. Mrs. Curtis gave her a searching glance. No, not satisfactory, not sensible. . . . Not enough to eat, pretending to be warm enough in ridiculous underclothes. . . . Probably a mistake, this being Etty's p.g., though at the time it had seemed such an excellent plan: Etty just orphaned, with her little house and legacy, Olivia difficult, refusing to come back and live at home. . . . But if Olivia was out, did Etty know where? with whom? . . . when she'd be in? Never. Fatuously cooing into the receiver. . . . No attempt whatsoever at even the most tactful supervision. Idiotic . . . or deep? Slippery anyway.

"I must go back," she said briskly. "Dr. Martin will be here any minute—and Nurse must go off."

"Can I see him?" said Olivia.

"Oh, not just now, dear. He's having a little sleep. Later on you can just put your head in and peep at him. When he wakes up I'll tell him you're here. That'll cheer him up. Kate, dear, I was wondering if you wouldn't perhaps like to go for a little stroll with Nurse——?"

"Oh, were you wondering that?"

"I just thought it would be nice for her, instead of her going alone. You could take her the pretty walk. I tried to tell her yesterday how to go, but I don't think she quite took in it."

"I don't expect she wanted to. I'm sure she loathes pretty walks. She's all right. I've been quite enough of a pal for one day. I've already promised to cut out an evening dress for her. Turquoise blue satin. Scrumptious!"

"Oh, well—Fancy! I wonder what she wants it for. You wouldn't think she had many occasions to wear turquoise blue satin."

"I expect a grateful patient presented it—to match her eyes. He's going to take her out to dinner in it."

"Who is? Is he?" Mrs. Curtis was confused.

"A bottle of bubbly and a topping show," said Olivia. "Oo! I wish I was her. Is she a peach, Kate?"

"No. More of a jolly fine girl."

"Oh, well . . ." said Mrs. Curtis. "I must say it seems to me a bit cool to ask you to cut it out for her."

"It's all right, Mum, I offered. I'd rather cut out every stitch she wears for the next five years than go for a walk with her."

"Oh, well——" Really, this exaggeration and so forth . . . "Just as you like, dear. There's a fire in the schoolroom. And, Olivia, if you run through and just ask Ada she'll make you some bovril. She and Violet have been so good with the trays and everything. They're so anxious to help——"

Mrs. Curtis reflected an instant, then set off energetically up the stairs again.

"I don't want any bovril," said Olivia, low.

"Want must be your master," said Kate. "Can't you stop kicking against the pricks for *one* morning? Ada's to make it and Violet's to bring it up and we're to drink it and we'll all be doing our bit. I'll go and order it. Meet you in the schoolroom."

"Put a swig of something in mine. Port or sherry or something."

But the door had swung to.

Olivia went upstairs—ascending, ascending into the current of power. . . . In her mother's wake it seemed to flow; to concentrate at the silent threshold of his door. . . . He mustn't cough, I can't—won't hear it. But there was no sound, no odour of sickness, and the door seemed guarded. A strong resistant life was in that blank white panelled shutter, a watchful eye in the wink of the brass door-knob: Nothing shall pass here, said she from within. By the power of domestic habit, by the compulsion of household routine, death shall be elbowed out: there shall be no room for it. By the virtue of family reunion, by the protective assertion of common habits of speech, of movement and expression; by the serene impartiality of my outwardly distributed attention, by the colossal force of my inward single concentration—death shall be prevailed against. Meals shall be punctual, sheets aired, fires lit, bovril prepared and drunk, all at my bidding; and therefore nothing shall alter, not one unit of the structure shall collapse. My reserves are barely tapped yet: they shall be sufficient. By the exercise of my will. . . .

Briskly, the door of the bathroom was flung open, and out rustled a white figure, plump and crisp, across her path. Nurse. Ah, there it was, the lurking symbol, the menacing reassurance. . . . It was here, large as life, blocking the light, the efficient white flag of danger.

"Good-morning." Through the open bathroom door she saw bottles, white enamel vessels, and, on the floor, the shape of an oxygen cylinder, sinister. . . . Yes, it was here, all around. . . .

"Good-morning." The nurse held out a cool dry hand. "Are you the other daughter I've heard about?"

"Yes, I am." Eager, ingratiating, feeling sick all of a sudden. . . . Compact, short shape, broad face in its frame of white, clear full blue eye appraising her, fresh cheek, good teeth, lips strongly modelled, pale: a nurse's face, lesbian face. She devoured all in one glance. We are delivered into your hands.

"It's nice you could come. Your mother will be ever so glad to have you." Cool voice, with an edge of sub-nasal gentility.

"How is he?"

"Oh, he's quite comfortable. He's having a little snooze just now. I expect you'll be wanting to peep at him later."

"Oh, yes . . . please . . . if I might." Placate her, be obedient.

"I expect you could."

"Is he—I suppose he's—is he awfully ill, d'you think?"

"Well—pneumonia's always a nasty thing, isn't it? And at his age."

"Yes, of course . . ."

"Still, we must hope for the best. He's a good patient, I must say. Not like some. Of course he's been used to illness, hasn't he?—Makes a difference."

"Yes."

"Isn't it a glorious day? I was just going out for a little stroll round."

"Were you? Good. It's too lovely out now. I expect you're longing for some fresh air. You must be so tired being up all night. . . ."

"Oh, not too bad. Just a bit stale, you know."

"I'll see you later, then."

"Yes, that's right. Bye-bye."

Used to illness. Pneumonia's a nasty thing. We must hope for the best.

In the schoolroom, Kate was already bending over the table with pins in her mouth, the cutting-out scissors in her hand, and portions of blue material and paper pattern spread around her. She murmured through the pins, without looking up:

"I'll just slash about and she can do the rest. I'm damned if I'll fit turquoise satin over her fat bottom."

"Fat bottoms to you, Mrs. Emery—Don't trouble yourself, I beg. There'll be many only too pleased . . ."

Kate spun round with a jerk.

"God! I thought for a moment. . . . How d'you know how she speaks?"

"I've just been chatting in the passage."

"You nearly made me swallow ten pins." She bent once more over the table, and added: "Idiot."

Olivia flung herself down in the basket chair by the fire and lit a gasper.

"Still smoking like a chimney?" said Kate, through pins, beginning to cut.

"Rather, more than ever."

"How many do you get through a day?"

"Donno. It varies. Sometimes I do knock off for a day or two—if my morning cough gets too disgusting. Or if I'm short of cash."

"You simply choke up your inside with those foul fumes. No wonder you haven't any appetite. I believe that's what it is."

Cigarettes for supper, and a cup of coffee. Surprising how adequately they took the edge off one's hunger . . . how often, by oneself, when one couldn't be bothered to cook anything, or wanted to afford a movie instead. . . . Wouldn't Kate scold if she knew. . . .

"I suppose so. That, and the booze."

Above the scissors, Kate stole her a surreptitious glance. Nowadays it was apt to be a tricky business questioning Olivia. She was as touchy as could be. For the most part her immediate reaction was a sort of defiant irony, extremely boring. Anything would set her off, flaunting the no-lady pose, cracking low jokes—really awful ones— and God knows I'm no prude about language, not after eight years of Rob: but it does *not* suit females. Or else she'd simply hoot with laughter. Once, twice, dreadfully disconcertingly, she had burst into hysterical tears.

"We sex-starved women have cravings you comfortable wives and mothers don't dream of," remarked Olivia, blowing smoke-rings.

"And vice versa," said Kate tartly. She guided the crisp scissors in one unbroken line from edge to edge of the stuff.

After a pause, Olivia said:

"*She* seems to be bearing up all right."

"Who, Mother?"

"Mm. Full war paint."

Kate reflected. The words, the tone, conforming as they did to a filial convention of ribaldry for normal private occasions, wouldn't do just now—not in this crisis. Olivia showed a lack of sensibility. She said with seriousness, though without reproach:

"She hasn't had any sleep this week—not more than an hour or two. She's in and out of his room all night. She's simply amazing. I don't know how she does it. I haven't seen her fussed once."

"I suppose neither of you thought me worth informing till this morning?"

"Mother didn't want to take you away from your work if it could be helped. It was you she was thinking of."

"Oh, how very kind of her." She takes Mother's side nowadays.

"Of course we wanted you to come. . . ."

"I suppose it didn't occur to either of you I might have liked to see him before . . . I might have liked . . ." She stopped and bit hard into a thumb nail. "He and I've always got on all right. . . ."

"I know. . . . Of course. . . ." Kate was reasonable, irritated, distressed all at once. "Only you've said so often . . . You've often said it was difficult for you to get away, you were alone in the office or something."

Making that the excuse for not coming home, or cutting a visit short. . . . Oh, well. . . . That's enough of that.

"Is James coming?"

"No. Not at present, anyway. Mother didn't know what to do, but I advised not unsettling him if we could help it. She hasn't even told him. You know what he is. . . . Any excuse to be off. . . ."

What was James? He was a problem. The only male Curtis of this generation was rebellious, not inclined to conform, to settle. After the most brilliant conceit-inducing start at school, he had progressively disappointed; had failed to win the university scholarship which would have enabled him to defer the question of career for a time. Dispatched after this grave set-back to a mill-owning acquaintance of Mr. Curtis in Bristol to learn the business he had left without farewells at the end of six weeks; arriving at the front door at 1 a.m. after three days on the road, blistered, feverish, sullen. Natur-

ally that was the end of the Bristol experiment. Naturally his
wounded employer washed his hands. As for James, he explained nothing; and, though briefly bitter, not to say insolent,
about mills, voiced no preferences. At home he was disagreeable and spotty, refused all invitations to tennis parties and
dances, avoided everybody's eye, burst forth for day-long
solitary walks. In the evenings he sat in his bedroom, playing
Delius on his portable Decca and reading poetry: perhaps
writing it—nobody knew for certain: but he was known to
possess a thick furtive black copy-book. It was only a phase,
of course: boys did go like that. But it had seemed best, while
waiting for him to come on again, to send him to a French
family for a while. French was always useful; and then there
was a dark implication of the advantage of removing him
from the neighbourhood of Uncle Oswald, for whose society
he now showed an odd mingled distaste and fascination. And
then the discreet mixture of foreign emancipation and home
influence provided by Monsieur et Madame Latour of Fontainebleau might be just what was needed to soothe and settle him.
Certainly madame's elaborately eulogistic, maternally sympathetic, exquisitely penned letters about him appeared to
justify such a hope. As for James's own letters, though scanty
and reticent, they arrived regularly, contained no disquieting
P.SS. and altogether appeared the products of a normal English
youth accepting life as it was ordered for him.

But now and then Olivia remembered him that week-end
after his tramp from Bristol: sitting in the bathroom with
his trousers rolled up, soaking his swollen feet in a large bowl
of hot water and lysol; submitting to female ministrations,
silent, inhaling eucalyptus, drinking hot lemon, his masculinity
cast down, made ludicrous; his expression that of a performing
dog in a circus. He had made his gesture of independence, and
in the act of making it, he had let it crumble and be ridiculous.
Whatever savage amorphous plan for freedom had illumined
him at the start and driven him forth, he had, after all, come
home. He could do no other, he saw with incredulous rage.

He had proved nothing but his own futility, his servitude. He
would do no more. He would go into the mill. He would rot.
They had been tactful after the first shock; after the first
questions, they had attempted to conceal their profound
dismay. Nobody had brought him to book. He had been left
alone with his stubbornness and his hatred and his streaming
cold. To whom went the letters that he locked himself up to
write and took secretly to post? When the replies came, always
in the same small cramped hand, back deep, deep beneath its
surface his poor face had shrunk all day, so naked, so concealed,
fixed in a rigid frenzy, an agony of self-protection. He had
been alone. No friend had come with love and understanding
to cast forth his dumb spirit.

In the night, in London, unwillingly Olivia had thought
about him, banished him, seen him again; struck suddenly by
a crazy notion: that he now had no eyes. He had closed them,
sunk them; there were cobwebs over them. As a child he'd
had large eyes, intensely blue, of a notable shape and wild
brilliance. . . . Could I have helped him? . . . hit somehow on
the right word? . . .

Going once to his bedroom, on an impulse, the others all
out. . . . But he was not there. And oh, the room, so burdened
with him, stricken, sensual, poignant with his penned-up
mysterious youth, his harsh male unhappiness; the tidiness of
concealment everywhere, the locked drawers of the writing-
desk, the densely scribbled blotter, the poems of Eliot, Yeats,
Hopkins, Owen, the Elizabethan dramatists by his bed; the
Van Gogh landscape pinned up on the wall opposite, to comfort
him. . . . I didn't help. . . .

If Dad dies, they'll push him straight into the mill. . . .

"Kate, what do they think really? I mean, will he get
better . . . or not?"

"I don't know. I think he may."

"And we may know quite soon . . . to-day . . . ?"

"Próbably." Kate went on pinning a piece of pattern to a
length of material. "In pneumonia, good nursing counts for

a lot, and he's certainly having the best of that. But of course it mostly depends now how his heart holds out."

"Have you seen him?"

"Oh, yes. These last two afternoons I've made Mother go out for half an hour, and sat with him."

"How does he seem? Is he dreadfully—uncomfortable?"

"Well, he's restless—and his cough hurts—but not too bad."

"Does he—does he talk to you?"

"Not much. Just occasionally. He wanders a bit."

"Does he. . . .?" She bit her thumb hard again. What does he talk about?—giving himself away . . . I don't want her to tell me.

"I've nursed pneumonia before. Rob had it, don't you remember? . . . the year after we were married,—when Priscilla was six weeks old?"

"I'd forgotten."

"And I fed her just the same all the time."

Kate laid down her scissors for the first time, smiled faintly, reminiscently.

Over her unconscious face spread the expression of her life, calm, yet half-rueful, just amused, just triumphant. Kate, that young, fresh, most virginal of virgins, was a shrewd matron, capable, experienced. What look is my life giving me? Any look? . . .

"I've never nursed any one. Once Ivor had a poisoned thumb, but I didn't nurse him. He was in such a stew he summoned his mother." She giggled. "So I went off to the seaside alone for the week-end. I stayed in a pub. It was late October, it was perfect. I didn't let them know where I was, and when I came back—my hat!—— How delicate he'd always been, and how he'd been a whole day alone in the house, and he might have had to have his arm off, and she knew someone who'd started with a boil on his nose and finally lost all his legs and arms and died raving. 'Ivor won't die,' I said. 'I'll try neglect, starvation, anything to oblige. I know you'd love

to lay his death at my door. But Ivor's not the dying sort,
though he does look so pale and wistful. He's tough—jolly
tough. Like you.'"

Kate looked at her.

"You didn't really say anything of the sort, did you?" How
hard her voice was,—unkind. . . . Poor Olivia. But after all
. . . her husband; she would marry him. . . . She must have
given him a time, despising him like that.

"No, I didn't really," said Olivia, after a silence. "I spend
a lot of time devising these posthumous cracks."

"I hope they give you satisfaction," said Kate, and added,
pinning busily: "D'you ever see him?"

"I saw him in Giulio's about a month ago. He was with
a very powerful-looking middle-aged woman with a black
Bohemian fringe and a cigarette holder and a deep motherly
bosom. I think he must have been telling her about his unhappy married life. She gave me such a look."

"You didn't speak to him, did you?"

"Oh, yes. He said he was just off to France to write a novel.
I expect she's got a villa there and she'll give him nourishing
food till he's finished it. I said, 'I suppose it's about me,' but
he said no, the girl in his book was short, with red hair and
green eyes."

"Wasn't he embarrassed?"

"He didn't seem to be. . . . I don't know." Olivia was silent.
"I wonder if that was a joke of his about the red hair. . . . I
wouldn't put it past him. Damn! It never struck me. Perhaps
he's one up."

"He deserves to be, I must say."

"What do you mean?"

"Well, how could you?"

"How could I what?"

"Go up to him like that—in a public place——"

"Why not?" She flushed darkly. "We're nothing to each
other. Besides, it's much more civilised, isn't it? We haven't
got a death-feud just because we're separated. Though I know

you and Mother think we ought to have. . . . Makes it more *respectable*, I suppose."

Kate said nothing; and Olivia continued with bitter anger: "In a public place! . . . What a foul expression. You're as bad as Mother: ' Not in front of the servants.'"

Kate was a concentrated arc above the table and seemed not to have heard.

"Besides he knows Giulio's is one of my places. He knows I often go there with Anna or someone. I dare say he did it on purpose to make me feel beastly—bringing that antique cart-horse to glare at me,—just to see what I'd do."

"Keep your hair on, do. I'm not sticking up for him. I never could stand the man, as you know. . . . There, that's done, thank God." Kate flung down her scissors and stooped to pick up shreds and fragments from the floor; adding quietly, with her head under the table: "Only I just couldn't have done it myself, that's all. No offence meant."

Olivia sank back in her arm-chair and turned her face away. After a bit she said:

"Well, nor could I have—till I did it. So there. I can't explain . . . but that's just the worst of it." . . . Kate with her conventional, her sheltered successful life, tied to her husband by children and habit and affection and respect. . . . She couldn't possibly understand. . . . "He developed my nastiness from a mere seed into a great jungle. He made me so mean and bloody. . . . Well, I just am a bloody character, I suppose. And I always thought I was so nice."

"You're all right." What an idiotic way to talk. "Here, drink your bovril, I forgot it. It's getting cold." She brought the tray over from the window-seat, put it on the floor between them and sat down in the other basket-chair. They picked up their cups and began sipping.

"Only," said Kate, "as it was all so hopeless obviously from the start, I don't know why you don't want to snap out of it altogether. . . ."

"Why ' obviously '?" She fastened on the word—superior,

smug-sounding—stiffened inwardly. It hadn't been so obvious as all that, not by a long chalk. With his long-lashed greenish eyes, almond-shaped, his soft thick green-dark hair, the sweetness of his profile with its full lips and rounded chin, his pale-skinned, still-adolescent physical charm, his undergraduate's blend of verbal liveliness, shyness, sensitiveness, conceit: with all that, he'd been a natural person anyway to fall in love with.

"Well, no idea of doing any work or having a home or anything."

"He was too young."

And he was to have devoted his life to poetry. No good saying that to Kate. Those early poems, too clever, obscure, but with an individual something—they had promised, everybody said so. But the weakness in them was the weakness of his nature, basic and irremediable. They, like him, could never branch and toughen; but narrow, but dwindle and deteriorate, after the first graceful flowery outbreaking. I didn't help him. Nobody could, of course. . . . At least. . . . I think not. . . . She said with a sigh:

"We neither of us had the least idea about anything. How to behave or what things cost or how to set about anything. No practical technique whatever." His two hundred a year, my hundred had seemed any amount of money, for a start.

"I know. You never had. You always thought me earthy for saving up my pocket money." An old grievance soured Kate's voice.

"We're not all born with our wits about us like you, my love. But I bet I could give even you some tips nowadays about how to live on nothing at all. One learns if one must. But in those days I thought the Lord provided for people like us."

"One of you was to make daisy-chains, while the other coaxed the shy wild things to come around you."

"Exactly."

He was romance, culture, æsthetics, Oxford, all I wanted then. Oxford had been a potent draught, grabbed at and gulped down without question. To live the remainder of one's life in that condition,—towery, branchy, cuckoo-echoing, bell-swarmed—had seemed the worthy summit of human happiness.

"We just shouldn't have married, that's all."

"No, of course not."

"Of course not, of course not. . . . It's all very well to be so frightfully shrewd and sensible about other people's arrangements. You know as well as I do it's mostly luck. And one's first choice is more or less a matter of—of picking blindfold—practically at random, isn't it?"

"Sometimes."

"'Sometimes'! Don't you be so jolly superior. Rob wasn't your first fancy, was he? Supposing you'd married—the person who was . . . ?"

"Well, I didn't," said Kate sharply; and she coloured, after all these years, and put on the look that accused one of tactless insensibility. It *was* rather a shame to bring it up. No doubt it was true too that Kate would have made a go of it, whoever she'd married. . . . That was her nature; that was just the difference.

"What we should have done was to live together for a bit. Then we'd have had a chance of discovering . . ." How short-lived desire could be; how there could be nothing, nothing left, overnight almost; only reluctance, heaviness, resentment, only the occasional, corrupted revival of excitement, and tears and nerves, and the unforgivable words, and the remorse. . . . "But you wouldn't have approved of that either, would you?"

"I shouldn't have cared what you'd done," said Kate with a yawn. "It was none of my business. The point is, *you* wouldn't have approved of it. It's no good pretending you were so frightfully unconventional and free-lovish—in those days anyway."

Olivia was silent. It was true enough. And the trouble is I'm the same now really: wanting to make something important enough to be for ever.

"Oh, no," she said finally. "I was all for regularity. I

must say for poor Ivor he had some qualms—but I hypnotised him We were in love so we must be married. I never thought of anything else. I suppose one never gets away from a good upbringing."

"One never gets away from being an idiot," said Kate. "*Not* speaking personally."

"I must say, it's funny considering how sure you all were it would turn out badly how squawky you all were when I left him. You ought to have been delighted."

"Nobody was squawky. It's entirely your diseased imagination. Naturally Mother was anxious. Wondering what the hell you'd do next. . . ."

"Why couldn't she trust me?" Wondering was there another man? . . . Wondering what will people say? . . .

"And no money," added Kate, treating the question as rhetorical.

"Well, I didn't ask any of you for any." Olivia lit another cigarette with unsteady fingers. The blood started to beat in her face. Damn them all.

"No, you didn't," agreed Kate mildly. "I can't think how you managed." Never thought she would.

"I've managed because I swore I would." Olivia smoked with frenzy. "But it's been no picnic, I can tell you."

"I bet it hasn't." Kate was reasonableness itself.

"I have a hard life——" Her voice quavered.

"I expect it's been much more satisfactory, being on your own. I should have done the same."

Olivia laughed suddenly.

"It isn't hard really. I don't know what I'm talking about. It's all comparative. It's taught me a bit anyway—about the way some people have to live, I mean. . . ."

"What's-her-name does pay you, doesn't she?—Anna?"

"Oh, yes. As much as she can afford—more, really. *And* commission. But that's not very frequent. Nobody seems to want to be photographed. Nobody I know can afford it."

"I must try and bring the children," murmured Kate.

"She's not very good with children."

"I shouldn't think she was," said Kate, with transparent meaning. "Besides, you know, she *is* expensive."

"She's far better than any one else." That's as may be, said Kate's silence. "However, you've done your bit, coming yourself."

"Oh, well, Rob wanted me done."

"She thought you were wonderful."

"She couldn't have." A flicker of scornful pleasure crossed Kate's face. "I know I was looking awful that day. I always do after that early train journey. And her beastly lights made my eyes water. Not that it mattered much one way or the other. The results weren't so bad, I must say."

"Anna's not used to fresh young matrons from the country. She was quite overcome."

"Oh! . . . Fresh young matrons my foot! I know my looks aren't what they were, so you needn't go on."

"Nonsense!" Nonsense it was. She glanced at her. Something was gone, but Kate was a striking-looking woman. "Anyway, compared with me you're still in your teens."

Kate said nothing. It was so untrue, yet so true on the surface, it didn't bear arguing about. Those infinitesimal lines beneath her eyes, the line one side of her crooked mouth, her thinness, really almost a frail look, blast her. . . . If only she'd feed up and preserve her energy with more underclothes. . . . She looks like . . . I don't know what: nothing to do with real age: like an old child. . . . Bother—Bother. . . .

After a while Olivia said:

"How are the children, Kate?"

"Flourishing. Jane had a touch of earache last week but it went off. She didn't have a temperature, so I wasn't too worried. I must ring up George at lunch-time. Oh, Lord! I've got a million things to do next week. It couldn't have happened more awkwardly. Can't be helped."

"Perhaps he'll . . . Perhaps you'll be able to get away."

"Perhaps."

"I could stay on another few days if necessary."

"We'll see." Kate got up and stretched. "When are you coming to stay?"

"I don't know, Kate. I'd like to."

"You always say that, but you never come. The children are always asking. You're popular, for some reason. Polly doesn't even know you."

"Sweet Polly—the flower of the flock, I thought, at three weeks."

Kate said with a funny look, as if she were saying something a tiny bit embarrassing, on the sloppy side:

"We think she's a little like you. She's got your eyes."

"Really? How flattering of you and Rob! . . . Family likenesses do seem such a compliment. . . . I don't quite know why. I suppose it's because they make you feel powerful."

"Hmm. . . . Rob ought to feel powerful enough after Priscilla, Jane *and* Christopher. All the dead spit. However, I suppose I ought to rejoice." Kate rubbed her eyes. "I did think Christopher might be different. You're always told the boy favours the female. . . ." She added with bitterness: "And Mother going on every time as if I'd done it on purpose. Raking their faces for the Curtis chin and the West nose. . . ."

"Anna was mad to know if the children looked like you. She got quite moral and indignant when I said no."

"Did she?" Kate's lip curled a little; but there was a glint of satisfaction in her eye.

"Not but what Rob is a fine well-set-up specimen. In fact I think he's jolly attractive."

"Thanks."

"The thing is really we're too special to be repeated. . . . Hadn't I better adopt Polly? Three's quite enough for you to go on with. When I see the prams in the Park, I simply ache to have one to push, and lift up the steps and leave in the hall."

Kate went suddenly serious. Standing on the clipped wool hearthrug, she pulled her skirt up to let the fire get at the backs of her legs, and said finally:

"Why don't you divorce him?"

Olivia laughed.

"I follow the train of thought."

"Well, why not?"

"Too much trouble."

"You don't want to go back to him by any chance, do you?"

"God, no!"

"One day you'll want to be free and he could make it awkward for you if he wanted to."

"Why should he want to?"

"Well, you never know. You say yourself how spiteful he is. You're bound to want to marry again one day."

"Oh—I don't know. Shouldn't think so. Don't know any marrying men."

"And what about *him* wanting to be free? He might start some funny business on the sly—to get evidence."

"Oh, Lord! You think of everything, don't you?" Olivia blew out a great sigh and closed her eyes.

"You can think me as nasty-minded as you like—but he might. He might land you in a mess."

"He might—but he'd be hard put to it. My life is blameless and chaste—worse luck!"

She began to feel horribly depressed.

"You don't seem to want to give yourself a chance." Kate was implacable. "It's all very well now to knock about London on your own like you do. But you don't want to do it for ever, do you?"

"Perhaps not." Perhaps not indeed.

"Even frightfully nice——" Kate stumbled: unusual for her: went on a trifle lamely: "I mean even the most broad-minded men are a bit—well, on their guard about a woman who's legally married to some submerged person in the offing. They don't want to get mixed up——"

"Don't they? Don't they really?" Olivia opened her eyes wide.

"No, they don't," said Kate sharply. "Look here, why don't you let Rob go and have a talk to him? I'm sure he would. The longer you leave it the more difficult it'll be. Rob would be able to sort of put it to him and suggest he should give you evidence without putting his back up. Rob's awfully good with people."

"I'm sure he is." Tactful. . . . Look here, old chap, we're men of the world. . . . Cool but amiable, standing no nonsense. . . .

Olivia burst suddenly into a loud vulgar chuckle.

"Now what's the joke?"

"I was only thinking of Ivor taking a tart to Brighton for the week-end. Oh dear, it would be funny . . . the conversation. . . ."

"You're hopeless," said Kate coldly.

Out of patience, she gathered up an armful of blue satin and tissue paper and left the room.

In disgrace, thought Olivia, left alone. She went and knelt on the old hard cocoa-coloured couch by the window, and leaning on the sill looked out. Away spread the blue damp garden—just as I imagined—lit with a ghost of iridescent mist. The leaves of the walnut were down, and Higgs was sweeping them up, all lemon-yellow, into a barrow. Soon I must go down and say charmingly: "Hallo, Higgs? How are you all?" At the end of the garden rose the elm-tops with a gold shout, plump still, full sailing, but thinning, black-branch-threaded. A flock of starlings pecked on the lawn, on the path. Up they flew all of a sudden and scattered; and she heard a car change gear, hoot, and turn out of the drive: Dr. Martin.

The telephone rang, faint to her ears: someone inquiring. Kate would answer. It couldn't be Rollo: not yet. Not ever, of course. Rollo would think about ringing up, sometime to-morrow maybe; and then he wouldn't do it. Because nice men don't like to get mixed up. . . . Rollo was undoubtedly in the category of nice men, broad-minded. They are on their guard. . . .

What a queer meeting, what a queer conversation . . . getting on so well, such a long way. . . . Or didn't we really? . . . What was it happened in the car? What did it mean? I was to be punished, subjugated. . . . He must dominate. What were we near? I couldn't have been mistaken. . . . Very near, very far. . . . He could be brutal. I want to, I must, shall I never see him again? . . .

Oh. . . . This mood, this time, will pass. This heavy weight shall be lifted. Whatever happens we shall all go jogging on again somehow. The dust will settle once again upon these fly-blown images. . . . Are these all my mind shall contain? Shall no piercing shock of resurrection dislodge their tentacles, crumble them for ever? Can it be that what I expect will never be?

The smutty window, the brown street blighted with noise and rain; the stained walls; the smell of geyser, of cheese going stale in the cupboard, of my hands smelling of the washing-up bowl, nails always dirty, breaking; the figures on the stairs, coming and going drably, murmured to reluctantly, shunned at the door of the communal, dread, shameful W.C. on the middle landing. . . . The despised form in the bed, nose buried, asleep at eleven o'clock in the morning, the sheets are dirty, he is my husband, this is my life, my shoes are shabby. I shall never have a child in the country. . . .

Rollo, it wasn't all my fault, I did try. If we'd both been different, if . . .

Rollo, this isn't me, cynical, flippant: you remember me: don't judge me by what I say. They befog me with their explanations and solutions, they lay my cards on the table for me, they disapprove, they sympathise.

If I could escape to a new country, I'd soon strip off these sticky layers, grow my own shape again.

The ordinary, the unnatural day wore on. The telephone

rang, was answered; rang again. Footsteps went up and down the stairs, along the passages, creaking, subdued. Meals were swallowed punctually; tags of conversation picked up, dropped, resumed again. Soon after lunch, Dr. Martin's car returned; and when the early, fog-breathing motionless dusk crept over, there it was still, looming black, extinct, monstrous in a corner of the drive. Kate and Olivia sat over the drawing-room fire, Kate knitting with rapid fingers, Olivia darning a stocking with slow ones: a couple of dummies performing automatic gestures. As darkness fell, they gave up talking; their ears were strained for sounds from above; their bowels stirred, breathing seemed arrested. They existed only in suspense. All else, all energy and emotion, had been drained out of them to concentrate in the silent space on the other side of the ceiling; and they were powerless as ghosts.

Kate got up and lit the lamp, Olivia poked the fire. They looked out. With the increase of light in the room the darkness without had grown suddenly complete, uncompromising. It's night. Mother's been away too long, I want her to come. . . . Draw the curtains. No. The waiting car won't let us. . . .

They sat down again. All at once they heard voices, the front door opening and closing. The black oppressive bulk in the drive became a normal car, throbbed, blazed, drew away with its old familiar long-drawn rising moan and settle on the change-up.

Prepare now.

The door opened, soft, precise: the white cap was there, stuck wide, angular, vivid in the doorway.

"Hallo! All in the gloaming down here, aren't you?" Her voice was brisk and level. "Don't you believe in having light on the scene then?" . . . She gave a little laugh. "His temperature's down. He's sound asleep—breathing ever so much better. Thought I'd just pop in and tell you. Why don't you draw those curtains? Make it more cheerful, wouldn't it? Bye-bye for the present."

"What about his pulse?" said Kate. But she was gone.

"Nice of her," said Olivia.

"She's a good sort."

"Isn't it *good* . . . ?"—Choking. "I suppose we'd better just wait." . . . Carefully steadied.

They drew the curtains and stood over the fire, exchanging a brief sentence now and then. Half an hour went by. The door opened again. There wasn't one particular moment when she appeared, but there she towered, alarming, triumphant, with an unfamiliar white incandescent face.

They faced her, speechless.

"Here I am, dears." She came forward to them, smiling in secret power and triumph. "He's through it. He's sleeping—such a peaceful sleep—like a child. His pulse is steady."

"That's good," said Kate, through pale lips; and she began to breathe deeply as if she had been running.

"Of course, he's not out of the wood yet. . . ."

"No," Olivia nodded, vehement, rigid. . . .

But he will be: you've brought it off, you extraordinary woman, you know you have.

"But Dr. Martin thinks he stands a good chance now . . . with every care, of course."

"Yes."

"Nurse is with him, now. She insisted I should come down for a short time. She's been such a treasure. This room strikes me as chilly. Not a very cheerful fire. What it needs is a log. Olivia, ring the bell, dear. Have you had tea?"

"No, we haven't."

"I think we could all do with a cup of tea."

III

OPENING his eyes, he saw brass bed-rails, blue curtains, drawn, shrouding the window; darkness, suffused with muffled faint illumination. Night then. . . . Who's here? Who lit the lamp? His lids fell down again, pressed upon by an infinite but gentle weight.

A clicking, a rustle,—alive, secretive, wary: that was coal shifting, settling in the grate. All was well. This sound, this darkened room were from the beginning. The bed, the muffled light, the blue curtains; tick, flap, hush-sh-sh, the fire in the grate, in the winking bed-knobs; wide, shrunk, wide, shrunk in the fluttering ceiling. All this I know. . . .

Someone in the room, just stirring. This also was awaited. . . . Call out, perhaps. . . .

Who's moving? Where's this room? In the far-sunk depths of him, time started a gradual, a reluctant beat. When is it? Who is this, lying in a bed? His own identity began waveringly to crystallise, close over him. Apprehensive now, he opened his eyes again, saw a figure move across and vanish from his line of vision. He moved his lips and a faint sound came from between them.

There was a soft, rapid forward movement; someone by the bed. A face. . . . Well, well, well! . . . The girl Olivia. His lids fell again.

"Awake, Dad?" A tiny voice.

After a long while he sighed out:

"Very weak." A quiver fled over his face.

"I know, Dad. It's a shame. Never mind. You'll soon be better."

Sounded odd: tearful?

"You think so, do you?" That was the line. "What you doing here anyway?"

"Just sitting here for a bit—in case you wanted anything. Do you?"

He waited. . . . Want? Want? Foolish, exhausting . . .

"Little drink?" she whispered.

"No."

"Mother's downstairs, writing letters. Shall I fetch her?"

"No. No." He waited. "The other one. . . ."

"Nurse?"

"Nurse." She saw amusement break far down below his face. "Very strong woman."

"Is she? I bet she is."

"Whisks me up and down, rolls me over . . ."

"I know. . . ."

"Like a blinking baby. . . ."

Weak laughter caught them both, shook them helplessly. Tears crawled down his cheeks. When the spasm had worked itself out, he sighed heavily, groaning almost, and lay like a log. She brought a chair and sat down close beside his bed, and wiped the tears off with a handkerchief. His wasted face with its six days' growth of grizzled beard, its mouth slack, mournful, cracked with fever, was hideous, strange, distasteful to her. It was a sick old man's face—not his. But he has his forehead still. Untouched, magnanimous, it rode above the wreck, as if informed with a separate, a victorious life of intellectual strength and serenity: saying: Behold! we shall all be saved. . . .

Is he alive? Has he died? Ought I to go for someone? If he's dead, I'll be blamed. . . I let him talk too much. . . . But he said suddenly:

"Olivia."

"Yes, Dad?"

"I thought you were dead."

"Did you, Dad? I'm not. At least I don't think so."

"So it seems. Tant mieux." He sighed. "Very bad dreams. Shocking."

"It was the fever."

"No doubt. How long . . .?"

"About a week."

"Indeed."

"I turned up yesterday."

"I see. Family summoned." He smiled infinitesimally. "All here?"

"Not James."

He looked distressed all of a sudden and said, more sharply: "Oswald?"

"He's not here . . . but he shall come whenever you like. Don't worry about him, Dad."

"Poor old fellow." Another tear crept down.

"Mother didn't want to upset him. . . ."

"Why upset? He's a sensible chap. She doesn't want him here. Never did."

"He's coming, Dad, I promise you. Don't worry. I'll arrange it. Everything's all right."

Very slowly his hand came up from beneath the blankets, crawled in her direction. *Oh! Don't.* . . . She took it in hers and said, aching:

"You two shall stuff around and stump each other with *locus classicuses* and read boring books to your hearts' content. Don't worry. Don't worry about anything. Just get better quick."

He gave her hand the ghost of a pressure. The girl was a nice creature, she meant well. Oh, but so lugubrious . . . to struggle up and find yourself at the end after all. A laughable disappointment. . . . Give up, go down again? . . . No. . . . Too late. . . .

He drifted off to sleep again, his hand in hers. It felt brittle, dry, like a claw. . . . Oh, is it going to be worth it for him, after all? How in this spent declining frame could the vitality well up again to replenish him; restore this claw, this mask, to human warmth? . . . Sparing ourselves the funeral, the black, the money difficulties, only to offer him, after laborious days and nights, a rug, an invalid chair: imitations of living, humiliations; only a fettered waiting on life and death. . . .

His wife came in softly and stood by the bed. Barely perceptibly, her face altered, stiffened.

"He's asleep. He woke up and talked quite a lot, quite like himself, and then he dropped off again . . . a moment ago. . . ."

"Well . . . go and get ready for supper. I'll stay with him now."

I stole a march. I cheated. She should have had his first words, not I . . . I've betrayed her. . . .

Guiltily, under her mother's shuttered eyes, she disengaged their hands.

IV

"AREN'T you going to drink your soup, Olivia? It's one of Ada's nicest."

"No, thank you, Mum."

"Oh, come now, do try it. It's all vegetables—so good for you. I found the recipe in the *Star*."

"I don't like soup much, you know, Mum. . . ."

"What a pity. Ada'll be so disappointed. She made it specially."

"Look at me," said Kate. "I'm drinking mine up."

"Yes." Approval and exasperation struggled in Mrs. Curtis's voice. "You're a sensible girl, thank goodness."

"You can't expect to have more than one satisfactory child, Mum," said Olivia. "Not in these days."

There was a soup-drinking silence. Olivia's cup sat before her in smug reproach with its cap and button on.

"And as a child," said Mrs. Curtis, "you were always the one to have a big appetite. Kate was the fussy one."

"And now I gorge," said Kate languidly.

"You don't gorge, dear. . . ."

"It's motherhood," said Kate.

"Dad never could bear a scraggy woman."

"I know, darling, you've said so before," sighed Olivia. "That's why he picked us a Ma like you."

"Well, it's not right, and what's more it's not becoming, I don't care what people say. Your grandmother always said: 'If you go against Nature you'll pay for it.'"

"*I* don't go against Nature," said Kate. "I'm nicely covered."

"You aren't fat, dear, not a scrap. You're just nice."

"Yes, that's what I said—just nice. Though, as a matter of fact, Rob really prefers them on the skinny side."

"Nonsense. Rob has far too much sense."

Mrs. Curtis's manner conveyed an arch benevolent unperturbed reproach: for Kate, cured of that early tendency to tart defiance, of that dreadfully nervy phase she'd had after Paris—disagreeable remarks, sarcastic generalisations, tears for no reason at all—Kate had long since turned out entirely sensible and satisfactory. Kate, bless her, had slipped with no trouble into a suitable marriage within easy motoring distance. As the wife of a young doctor with a good country practice, a solid man, a man with a growing reputation; as the mother of four fine healthy children she had established herself beyond question in all eyes. No doubt she was critical still, still impatient of advice; but all the same, sitting over the fire nowadays, each with her knitting, they were very cosy, very happy together. Talk flowed on, as warm, as refreshing as a good cup of coffee. The barrier between generations was dissolved. It was almost like being young: almost—though May was gone and that blank ached irremediably, a cruel amputation—almost like having a sister again. A comfort, yes, a comfort, now that Olivia . . . now that James . . . phases, we hope; phases, of course . . . above all, now that Charles. . . . Saved, but a ruin. . . . I know it. . . . Hush. . . . Pass on.

"Did I tell either of you, Dolly Martin's getting married?"

"It can't be true!"

"Who to?"

"Well, it seems it's a young missionary out in China. She

met him some years ago—when they were both doing work in the East End—and they've been corresponding for some time, so Dr. Martin tells me. She sails next month."

"Well, well, well! Good old Pudding-face! Who'd have thought romance was nesting behind those horn-rims all these years?"

"No wonder she always looked so conceited. It just shows where there's a will there's a way, and one never need be sorry for any one."

"She's such a capable energetic girl," sighed Mrs. Curtis. "She'll be such a help to him. But it does seem a long way to go."

"Let's hope the suns of China won't reduce her. She's a luscious morsel for a missionary."

"And a very primitive place, I understand, right in the interior."

"She'll be captured by bandits," said Olivia, "for a cert. She's got just the looks they always pick on. A few more years shall roll and Dolly'll be held for ransom in a bandit lair. I see her photo in the papers now."

"These missions do wonderful work," said Mrs. Curtis with a touch of severity: for why should everything be made a mock of? "It's a hard life and a dangerous one."

"Serve 'em jolly well right for interfering," said Olivia harshly.

"People must do something, I suppose," Kate yawned.

"His name is Potts," said Mrs. Curtis, passing on with determination to the particular. "Cyril Potts,—or was it Cecil? Not a very romantic name," she conceded, smiling; for of course they thought it funny—"But Dr. Martin says he's got such a particularly nice open face. Olivia, you might send her a line, I thought. She was always more your friend."

"I might."

"I've been wondering what I could give her that would really be useful."

"A cake-basket."

"A cruet-stand . . . or two cruet-stands."

"I thought perhaps a little cheque really, then you girls could give her a little something personal. From the two of you. You needn't spend much."

"No, we needn't," said Kate. "It's the thought that counts."

"Poor Dr. Martin, I'm afraid he'll miss her dreadfully. But Phyl's coming home to keep house for him. You know she's been sharing a cottage in Wiltshire with a friend, a Miss Trotter, and breeding—now what is it?—Angoras, I think."

"Poor old Phyl," said Olivia. "It's a shame she should have to give up her career. Hard on Miss Trotter, too. You don't find a pal like Phyl on every blackberry bush."

"Yes, Dr. Martin was a little unhappy about it, but she would. She never hesitated. Those girls have always been so devoted to their father."

"And she may be able to do something with rabbits here."

Oh, give it up! . . . Plain, cheerful Martins, companions of childhood, coping efficiently with their lives, sensible women. . . . Dolly would never wake up one morning in China and tell herself: My marriage has failed and my life is empty, futile. Not she. Dolly scored heavily.

"What a divine salad," said Olivia. "What's in it—Prunes? Can I have some more, Mum, please?"

A ray of simple pleasure shot across her mother's face.

"Do, dear. I hoped you'd like it. I told Ada to put a little cream in the dressing."

And cream was nourishing. And it was all part of the plan, thought out specially to tempt, to please. And she looks so worn. I hate myself.

"Has any one taken Mrs. Skinner's cottage yet?"

And after that I'll ask for details of Miss Robinson's complete breakdown. . . . And after that. . . .

Across the table they began to ply a peaceful shuttle between the three of them, renewing, re-enforcing, patching over rents and frayed places with old serviceable thread. They were tough still; they were a family. That which had chanced to tie them all up together from the start persisted irrevocably, far below consciousness, far beyond the divergences of the present, uniting them in a mysterious reality, independent of reason. As it was in the beginning, is now. . . . Only the vast central lighting-piece no longer stupefied the cloth with a white china glare. When the daughters came home, grown up to have ideas on becoming lighting, they had condemned it; and during their visits, four candles in elaborate Victorian silver candlesticks burned above the expanse of damask, around the silver fruit-bowl. The table floated, a stealthily-gleaming craft moored far from shore, between the beetling promontories of clock and sideboard, below the soaring lighthouse of grand-papa's portrait. Very restful and pleasant it was too, once you got used to the enormous areas of shade where anything might be happening: though Violet was a worry, always tripping up at the door with the tray: on purpose, Kate said. . . . How young, how pretty Kate looked; no more than a girl; and Olivia too, softened, glowing, as she always used to be . . . and I too helped, no doubt, more as I would like . . . as I was, before these wrinkles. . . . Mrs. Curtis finished her glass of claret. Delicious, reviving. . . . The girls had insisted; and certainly it had made a difference,—just for once. . . .

"I needn't go up just yet," she said happily, as they rose from table. "He's all settled for the night and Nurse is there. Isn't it a blessing he's taken such a fancy to her? There's something about her tickles him, though I can't see anything funny myself. . . . Let's sit in the drawing-room."

The fire blazed and the lights stared behind thin, white silk, rose-wreathed shades. Olivia stretched herself upon the white wool hearthrug, between Kate and her mother, facing each other in their arm-chairs. They knitted. Stockings for the children, jumpers for the children, babies' night-vests, coats, bootees—there was never an end. Kate had taken on and elaborated the theme unfolded in her own infancy by Mrs. Curtis. The little tables either side of the fireplace were choked now with photographs of the grandchildren at all stages:

straight-fringed, neat-featured, hygienic-looking. A number of the more rococo pre-war likenesses of Mrs. Curtis's own young—plumes, curls, ribbons, frothing frills—had been put away to make room for them. From time to time Kate laid down her needles and studied them closely, with a searching frown. From time to time Mrs. Curtis's hands dropped and she heaved a sigh: her vast unconscious sigh. But nowadays this no longer cast a blight upon her daughters. Olivia smoked, looked at the *Illustrated London News*. Over her head the two pairs of hands resumed their busy conspiracy, the two voices droned peacefully on. . . . The children, the servants, the children, Rob, Dad, James, the children. . . .

At ten o'clock the telephone rang in the hall.

"Now who can that be?" said Mrs. Curtis. "At this hour?"

"I'll go." Olivia sprang up with a sudden tingling surmise. "Hallo?"

"Could I—er—speak to—er—Miss Olivia Curtis possibly . . ."

"Speaking." Yes. It was.

"Oh, hallo, good-evening!" He sounded relieved. "This is Rollo Spencer."

"Oh, yes! Good-evening. . . ."

"I hope I'm not an awful bore ringing up. I wanted to ask how—if—how your father is. . . ."

"It's frightfully nice of you, Rollo. He's better—really better. We *think* he's turned the corner."

"Oh, I'm terribly glad to hear that—terribly glad." Warm, delighted voice.

"It is sweet of you to ring up."

"Not at all. I wanted to, I've been wondering a lot. . . . I didn't want to be a nuisance. Mummy'll be terribly glad, she was awfully sorry when she heard. . . . She wants to say a word to you. . . ."

"Oh, does she? . . ." Alarming. "How are you?"

"I'm extremely well, thank you."

"Are you, really?"

"Yes, truly. How are you?"

"Oh . . . in my usual rude health. . . ."

They laughed, waited doubtfully, embarrassed.

"Hang on a moment, will you," he said finally. "Mummy wants to speak to you. Hang on. I'll give her a shout."

"Right you are. I'll hang on."

Gone. That was all. Full, strong lazy voice, trailing away, inconclusive; nothing said one could fasten on to, or remember; current expressions of superficial sympathy. . . . Only the voice, promising something, raising an expectation. . . . Oh, well, that was that: finished with. All the Spencers had good manners.

"Is that Olivia?" Incisive ringing tones filled the earpiece.

"Yes, Lady Spencer." At once she felt meek and gratified, nestling under a wing: as of old.

"My dear, Rollo's told me the good news. I do *so* rejoice! We've been so concerned since Rollo saw you. I hardly *liked* to ring up but I've thought of you all so much. Do tell your mother this with my love. *What* an anxious time, poor dear. How is she?"

"Oh, she's very well. A little bit tired, but really marvellously well."

"*Is* she? How splendid. She must take care of herself—she'll feel the strain now the anxiety is less."

"Yes, I expect she will."

"Now, my dear, *are* we going to be able to get a glimpse of you, I wonder?"

"Oh. . . . I don't know, Lady Spencer. I'd love to. It's ages. . . ."

"I know. *Far* too long. Do you think your mother could possibly spare you to us for an evening?"

"I'm sure she could."

"That would be delightful. Well, now, we've got Rollo and Marigold with us till Monday—and they're *so* anxious to see you. In that case it would have to be *to-morrow* evening, wouldn't it? Would that suit you?"

"To-morrow evening would be perfect."

"It would? How delightful. Marigold will be so enchanted. Is Kate there?"

"Yes, Kate's here."

"Dear Kate. Give her my love." The voice fell a tone or two, seemed to reflect a trifle doubtfully. "Would she come too?"

"I don't know. If you wouldn't mind holding on, I'll ask."

Back to the drawing-room she flew, gave rapid messages.

"How kind of her." Mrs. Curtis was gracious, appreciative. No more than one's due, but thoughtful all the same.

"I won't go," said Kate quickly. "I'd truly rather not."

"Do go, Kate, dear, why not? It'll do you good."

"No, I don't want to. Go on, Livia, rush. I'll lend you my white. Tell her you'll come, but not me."

Back she flew.

"Kate is so sorry, Lady Spencer. . . ."

"I quite understand," cut in the voice vigorously, with sympathetic approval. "I felt perhaps your mother wouldn't *quite* like to spare you both. Well, dear, we shall expect you to-morrow then. Benson will be there at 7.30. . . . But of course, nonsense, I insist. . . . And we shall all look forward so *very* much to seeing you. Good-bye, dear."

V

BENSON drew up beside the portico, hopped out and pulled the bell while she waited inside the car. Stiff, ageing as he was, his limbs still moved not at their own pace but as if under an old persisting mechanical compulsion to look sharp now, look alive, bustle up for orders at a moment's notice. A lifetime of service, said his patient figure, standing on the steps, waiting: the last, no doubt, to wish to change his station; deploring each successive stage in the breakdown of the social scale; yet a man of intelligence, of dignity.

The heavy doors were flung open, the lights of the hall blazed out, the footman faintly returned her faint smile, she stepped inside.

"I'll just leave my coat here." Assume my image is still the one I saw in my bedroom glass: satisfactory enough. Another view might shake my equilibrium. She slipped off her mother's fur coat into the footman's hands, and gave a touch or two to the white dress. Floating, transparent and fragile, swathing itself lightly over breast, waist and thigh and sweeping backwards and out in a wide flaring line, it was a romantic, pretty, waltz-like frock. Inside it she felt drastically transformed, yet at home with it, able to suit it.

"There you see," Kate had said scoldingly. "In spite of you choosing to adopt the Bohemian consumptive style nowadays, the fact remains that this looks entirely apt on you, whereas on me it's on the kittenish side." She pulled in and tied the long flying airy bow in the back of the waist. "Look." She marshalled her to the long glass.

It was true. She looked a young girl, and a pretty one.

"You'd better stick to it," said Kate. "I fell for it in the sales, but I can't wear this sort of thing any more."

"Oh, you can. . . ."

"And may it be a lesson to you," said Kate.

Olivia followed the young footman's spruce, swinging, glittering back across the pillared spaces of the hall, down a corridor lined obscurely with supernumerary specimens of family portraiture—here a legal wig, red robes; there the dulled splendour of ancient regimentals; here a pink satin gown, a smirk, a rose, a long neck, a white hand and breast, there a towering Victorian group, exaggeratedly fertile-domestic-blissful. Now they were in the drawing-room. Empty. I'm too early.

"Her ladyship will be down in a few moments." He swung briskly away.

She went and stood by the fire where the logs blazed and

whispered rosily in the wide carved marble grate. She looked round. There it all was, not changed at all: the long elegantly proportioned prospect of white, of gold, of green brocade, the panels of glass, the screen, the Aubusson carpet, the subdued gleam of porcelain and crystal, the piano painted with light faint-coloured wreaths and sprays. Chrysanthemums, white, bronze, and rose-coloured, outsize, professional-looking, were massed in Chinese bowls, in vases and stands. The oval mirror above the mantelpiece gave her back a muted reflection; for the chandeliers were unlit and, except for the narrowly radiating wall-lights in triple-branched gold brackets, the only suffusion of light came from two tall porcelain reading-lamps by the fireplace. . . . Yes, and the Gainsborough ancestress was lit, the Romney boy and girl.

This was the scene—huge, flashing, stripped, a hall of ice in memory—of the children's parties years ago; of that last dance for Marigold's coming-out. After that, the parties had been in London: and we weren't invited. She left the fire, crossed over and craned her neck at the Gainsborough. Feet make no noise on the passage carpet. The room might be filling up behind me. . . .

"Hallo!" A voice from the door.

Rollo came towards her, alert and pleased-looking.

"Hallo. . . ."

He took her hand and held it, looking down at her with head held up, lids lowered, in a characteristic way. "This is a good idea."

"I'm awfully early, I'm afraid. Benson was so prompt."

"Benson is a very punctual man. Well, all the better."

"I'm glad you're first. I'm so frightened."

"Nonsense. Mummy's thrilled to see you again. So's Marigold."

"So am I thrilled, but—Is there a party?"

"Not my idea of a party." He laughed. "Not a lot of party spirit."

"But people?"

"A few."

"God!"

"Don't worry. I'll look after you." Their eyes met, smiling, acknowledging a secret united front. "Come by the fire," he said. "Have a cigarette. Have a drink. Shall I make a cocktail?"

He busied himself over a tray of bottles and decanters on the piano, and brought back two brimming glasses.

"Goodness, what a size," she said. "I shall be dreamy after this."

"Will you? But you're always dreamy, aren't you?"

She looked at him, slightly startled.

"Yes, I suppose I am. Is it so awfully noticeable?"

"Only to a close observer."

"Oh. . . ." She raised her eyebrows, glanced sidelong: an adaptation to his technique. "Well, when I'm really tight I get dreamier and dreamier. I do everything in slow motion. I lean and lean about and my words trail off and I smile and smile. . . ."

"It sounds rather attractive. Come on, drink up. Here's luck!" He drained his glass and scrutinised her again, attentively. "You're looking very well to-night. . . . I'm most awfully glad, you know, about your father."

"Yes, thank you so much. It's grand."

"I told you it would be all right, didn't I?"

"Yes, you did. I'm afraid I didn't believe you."

"Ah, you see, you should. Poor dear, you did look so small-faced. I couldn't make out what was bothering you. I didn't like it."

"It was nice of you. . . ."

"I hate gloom, don't you? For myself or any one else. . . . It's so uncomfortable."

"Yes, it is." She laughed. "I can't do with it at all."

"Yet some people enjoy it. It's a fact. I know someone who does." He made a rueful grimace and she said in mock surprise:

"You don't really, do you?"

"Yes. My mother-in-law. You wouldn't credit what a lugubrious woman she is. Give her a really large-scale disaster in the morning papers and she's renewed like that bird. Not to speak of private croakings and prognostications of doom."

"I know the type."

"Do you? I suppose it's fairly common." He looked a little depressed.

She said rapidly:

"I had a mother-in-law. She was just the same."

"Ah!..." He hesitated. "You had. I *have*. ... Has yours passed away?"

"Far from it. They never pass away. But—but we're dead to one another, as you might say. At least I hope so. Worse than dead, I suppose I am to her. Though it's what she always worked for."

He nodded, sighed dolefully.

"My case is different," he said. "We are far, far from dead to one another. We meet with outstanding frequency . . . in my house. . . . I suppose we always, always shall. . . ."

"Can't you make a stand?"

He said after a moment of silence:

"No, I can't. I'm a weak selfish easy-going character, and all I want is a quiet life." He glanced at her with a smile. "Don't you?"

"It's not *all* I want. . . ."

He shrugged his shoulders and looked away, whistling softly between his teeth.

"However," he said, " let's not dwell on unwholesome subjects. Have another drink."

"No, thanks."

"Why not?"

"I don't need any more support. I feel fine now."

His eyes travelled intently over her and he smiled to himself. She looked up at him. Yes, all was well. For this evening some illusion was being breathed out, some reflection thrown back of a power as mystic, as capricious in its comings and goings as it was recognisable when it came. No need for anxiety now: it would carry her through. I shall enjoy myself.

"Well, I need a good deal more support myself." He strolled over to the piano and mixed himself another drink.

"Who'd have thought it?"

He looked handsome, fresher than ever in a plum-coloured velvet smoking jacket; and the prosperous aroma clung to him: cigars, expensive stuff on his hair, good soap, clean linen . . . a rich mixture.

"You're right," he said. "I don't feel too unhealthy, and that's a fact. Two days hoofing it in the open air—blown some of the cobwebs away. Shooting's not among the more intellectual of my recreations, but it suits me quite well all the same."

"Do you think I might be sitting next to you at dinner?"

"I do think so. I've reserved you."

"Oh, good!"

She beamed on him whole-heartedly.

"Olivia! It is!"

Lady Spencer was in the doorway, was bearing down, full-rigged, confined in an ample severity of black, with diamonds, with heroic shoulders bare, with white, austerely sculptured cheeks and hair, with both hands outstretched. "My dear! This is delightful!" She kissed her warmly on both cheeks. "We all felt we *had* to see you—when Rollo told us of your meeting. . . . Let me look at you. . . . Yes, it's our same Olivia. But thin! . . . Naughty girl." She gave her a loving, scolding pat on the hip; then laid a hand on Rollo's shoulder.

"I am so glad to see you. . . ." Olivia felt the tears prick under her lids. . . . Absurd. . . .

"Dear. . . ." Lady Spencer looked affectionately absent, musing. There was something. . . . Ah, yes. . . . "And your father is *really* on the mend? That does make me so happy. . . . Do tell your dear mother . . . Jack!" she called: for Sir John himself had entered, had creaked down the room to join the group . . . and she was calling out to him in reassurance,

to cover his entrance . . . because there was something wrong
with it; because one couldn't help watching, with faint uneasiness, his ponderous leaden-footed progress. . . .

"Hallo, Daddy!" said Rollo.

"Hallo, m'boy. . . ."

"Jack, dear, you remember our friend Olivia?"

"Who?"

"Olivia Curtis, Marigold's friend, you remember?"

Lady Spencer addressed him with a careful encouraging
firmness that spoke of habit, her eyes made blank, long ago
refusing to consider impatience or acknowledge dismay.

"Ah, yes, yes! How are you? Very glad to see you."

His hand was dry and stiff.

"Olivia's come over from Little Compton to dine with us."

"Very friendly of her. Some good shooting round Little
Compton. Nice spot. . . . Know it well?"

"You remember Mr. Curtis, Jack, Olivia's father, at Little
Compton. . . . We used all to meet in the old days—more than
we do now, I'm afraid."

"Curtis? Are you the daughter of my old friend Charlie
Curtis?"

"Yes, I am."

"Bless my soul! How is he? Haven't seen him in years. . . ."
For a moment the look she remembered broke across the thick
inflexible surface of his face—the mastiff look, kindly, amused,
mildly titillated. "So you're Charlie Curtis's girl. . . ."

His mouth dropped open, he looked vaguely round the
room. "Er . . ."

"Where are the dogs, Daddy?"

"Shut them in the library. They're all right. Both got their
baskets." He smiled at Rollo, the expression of faint bewilderment smoothed out.

"That reminds me, I must have left Lucy in my room. She's
probably cooking up a deadly grievance under the bed, waiting
for me to kneel down and implore her to come out. . . . Shan't
be a moment."

Laboriously his father's gaze went after him, clung to him as he strode out of the room. Yes, Sir John was altered. He was so slow, so heavy, standing beside his wife, she seemed somehow to be supporting his dead weight. Both had aged; her hair was white, her face hollowed under the cheekbones, the delicate skin scored with innumerable fine papery lines, the Queen Mary curves had lost perhaps the ultimate edge of opulence; but she was erect, imposing as ever, and an ageless vitality flashed from the pale blue, enigmatic, clear-gazing jewel-like iris. But he had gone old irrevocably. Below his smooth forehead and thick brown young-man's hair, the spark was extinct in the bloodshot eyes and the broken-veined dusky cheeks; and though his frame still carried him upright, broad and tall, it seemed embedded in some petrifying semi-solid material; as if too much of earth, too little of live flowing blood informed it.

People were coming in now. Almost perceptibly the energy began to well up in Lady Spencer. She began to draw them all towards her, to relinquish them with care and set them in motion towards one another. For the millionth time in this drawing-room, by such a fire, effortlessly, she was designing the social process, and nothing should be left to chance: no one left out, no one obtruded.

"My sister, Lady Clark-Matthew—Blanchie, I wonder if you remember our neighbour, Olivia Curtis, such an old friend of Marigold? . . . Do see to this hook for me, there's a dear, Doris always misses it. . . . My niece, Lady Mary Denham. . . . Mary, dear, I looked out that address you asked me for—*and* the recipe: remind me to give it you. . . . Mr. Denham: Harry, did you get a game of billiards? . . . Sir Ronald Clark-Matthew . . . Ronnie, have you pronounced yet on the Wilsons? Jack was going to ask your advice—weren't you, Jack? . . . Mr. Bassett, Miss Curtis. . . . Well, George? Did you have a nice nap? . . . Oh, yes, you did, my dear, it was quite audible. Never mind, we're all apt to drop off now and then as we grow older. . . . *Henriette!*"—stooping to shout in the ear of an apparition

newly arrived upon the hearth, shapeless and formidable in a
casing of lilac and silver brocade with trailing skirts, festooned
like a Christmas tree with chains and bracelets, head wrapped
in black lace shadowing a mad frizzle of frosty fringe and two
dark star-pierced pits of eyes ringed with smudges of mascara.
. . . "Ma chère! Je voudrais te présenter une jeune amie. . . ."

"Qu'est ce qu'elle me dit-là!" . . . Toneless croak of interruption, addressed to nobody in particular.

Once more, *fortissimo*:

"Une bien chère amie, Olivia Curtis. . . . Marigold's dear
godmother, Olivia, Madame de Varenne. . . ." *Sotto voce*: "She's
rather deaf. . . ."

"D'où donc arrive-t-elle celle-là?"

Again the remark hung on the air, in utter detachment,
like a statement picked up on the wireless.

"Now where's that bad girl? Late as usual, I suppose. . . ."

"She was in her bath a few moments ago," said the one who
was to have the recipe. "I heard her singing. I just gave a tap
on the door and called out the time, but I didn't get any
answer."

"I dare say not." Rollo was back, followed self-consciously
by Lucy, had come straight to stand beside Olivia, smiling at
her, conspiratorial. "I dare say the singing got louder, didn't
it, Mary?"

Mary gave him a pained, slight, patient smile, and turned
away.

Olivia bent to pat Lucy, who winced away, hostile and
cringing.

"She doesn't like me."

"That's odd."

"She hated me on sight in the train. Is she always like this
with strangers?"

"Not always—she has an unerring instinct."

"That sounds rather impolite."

He laughed.

"I don't think you quite follow me." He gave the woolly

body a soft push, saying: "She sets up to be my conscience, you see. . . ."

"Well, we won't wait," said Lady Spencer, turning from conversation with the tall, spare, rosy, white-moustached pronouncer-on-Wilsons, and putting a finger on the bell.

Expectation sharpened perceptibly in the air. Ha! A good meal coming, another good dinner: one of hundreds before, hundreds to come—anywhere, any time they liked. Not one grain of doubt, ever, about the quality, quantity, time and place of their food and drink. . . . In prime condition they all looked: no boils or blackheads here, no corns, callouses, chilblains or bunions. No struggle about underclothes and stockings. Birthright of leisure and privilege, of deputed washing, mending. . . . Can they sniff out an alien upon this hearth? Or is it disguise enough, simply to be here, in an evening-dress?

Marigold . . .? Where is Marigold?

"Dinner is served," pronounced an official voice.

They started to file out, through the double doors, across a space of hall towards the dining-room: Olivia last, with Rollo.

Someone was running down the spiralling, shallow staircase. Out of sight still; round and round; would be swept out on it into the hall in a moment, just behind us. . . . A figure swayed round the last curve of the balustrade, and came arrowing down the last flight in one straight skim, ran silently to her side, caught her and clutched her hand at the dining-room door.

"Marigold!"

"Olivia!"

She said rapidly, panting a little, barely glancing at her:

"You haven't changed a bit. Oh, I'm so glad. . . . How's Kate? I've changed, haven't I? Hell, I did mean not to be late. Nannie would wuffle on, and make me change my stockings. . . . Are you all right?"

"Yes. . . . Marigold." They still held hands, tightly, half-inclined to laugh, to cry. She was so different. She was exactly the same. "You do look wonderful. . . ." Her hair, her mouth, her neck and shoulders . . . and such a dress. . . .

"Do I? D'you like my fringe? It's new. Darling, I'm so pleased to see you. . . . I've got two children. . . . Can you imagine? . . . Oh, you *have* changed, as a matter of fact. You're lovely, and you weren't. Kate was. Is she still? P'raps not. . . . She is lovely, isn't she, Rollo?"

"She is . . ." said Rollo. He was watching them both with an absorbed expression, smiling and narrowing his eyes. They had the same eyes, though with variations—longish with full lids, the pupils dilated, the iris deep, peculiarly blue, electric-looking.

"D'you remember the Dance of the Wood Nymphs?—with shot chiffon scarves? And Monsieur Berton's ear-trumpet? And the passion he had for you?"

"And Miss Baynes drinking tea all through our music lessons?"

"I wonder if it *was* tea? She used to get awfully hazy and mop her eyes a lot after a cup or two. . . . How eccentric everything was, wasn't it? Every one of our instructors cracky. No wonder I'm backward!" She gave a high shout of laughter. "But you're not. But then you were clever, you and Kate. . . . Oh, look, they're all beginning to masticate. . . . Where are we at this dismal board? Miles apart, I suppose. Never mind, we'll talk afterwards. You're over there, by Rollo. Good-bye."

She waved her hand in the remembered gesture as she left them, and ran to slip into her place.

Now the scene had shifted on to another plane, unrealistic, strange and familiar. It was as if Marigold's appearance had somehow co-ordinated diverse ordinary objects, actions, characters, and transmuted them all together into a pattern, a dramatic creation.

Now all was presented as in a film or a play in which one is at one and the same time actor and infinitely detached spectator. The round table with its surface like dark gleaming ice, its silver and glass, its five-branched Georgian candlesticks, the faces, the hands, the silent, swift circulating forms of butler and footman, the light clash and clatter, the mingling voices . . . all existed at one remove, yet with a closeness and meaning almost painfully exciting. This element I am perfectly at home in. Now all would unfold itself not haphazard but as it must, with complex inevitability.

Rollo on one side, Sir Ronald on the other. Whom had Rollo on his other hand? The one called Mary . . . and Sir Ronald had the Wicked Fairy. He was leaning towards her ear speaking French with an accomplished Foreign Office accent, scarcely raising his voice. She could hear now all right; she looked lively, rejuvenated, disconcertingly intelligent. Marigold was diagonally opposite, sitting beside her father: no doubt—with the aid of Aunt Blanche on his other side—to spare him social effort. Her hand was laid on his, she stooped forward with a soft rounded thrust of bare shoulders, curving her neck towards him, towards George on her left, animating them both, seeming to caress them, talking with the old mobile lip movements, screwing her eyes up. Her dress was made of some curious thick silk stuff, faintly striped and flecked, greenish whitish, with a gold thread in it, plain and clinging, taken back in a sort of bustle and cut right off the shoulders. Two white magnolias in the front of the bodice touched the table as she leaned out over it.

Drinking clear soup, she said to Rollo:

"It is exciting to see her again."

"Marigold?"

"Yes. It's so nice when the years haven't made a person dim out. I was a tiny bit afraid she might have. You never can tell with those uncertain, shifting faces. Sometimes it's all over in no time. They just bloom out tentatively and wither off. I suppose it depends what happens inside them. . . . She's more extraordinary than ever. She's really beautiful."

"Beautiful?" He looked across at her. "Could you say that

quite? It's such a funny little snouty face—indiarubbery—isn't it?"

"Well—it all depends what you like, I suppose . . . what you look for."

"What do you like?"

She said ardently:

"I like what's uncertain—what's imperfect. I like what—what breaks out behind the features and is suddenly there and gone again. I like a face to warm up and expand, and collapse and be different every day and night and from every angle . . . and not be above looking ugly or comic sometimes. . . ."

"I see. . . . It sounds interesting—but not awfully restful."

Nicola was the other kind, of course—flawless, unimpeachable.

"Is your wife still as lovely as she used to be?"

"Nicola?—Yes, I suppose she is." His voice was rather flat. "She hasn't altered much. But she's not what you so eloquently describe, you know. She doesn't give you surprises every half-hour."

"Seeing her once was a lovely surprise."

"Was it? That's nice. You didn't meet her properly, did you? You must some day." He was silent, his mouth falling into a heavy line. He added abruptly: "It's a bore when people aren't strong. . . ."

"Isn't she strong?"

"No. . . . Always seems to have something wrong with her, poor dear. She's always taking—having to take to her bed."

"I'm so sorry. How wretched for you."

"It is. . . ." His expression was grateful. "You see, she's awfully—I don't know—highly strung, I suppose. At least, so her mother tells me. . . . It's a thousand pities, isn't it?"

"It is."

"One's apt to feel such an insensitive brute—always being with a highly-strung person."

"I don't suppose for a moment you need to feel that . . ."

Was that going further—saying something a little less in

the fencing style—than was expected? She felt a qualm. But he said, in the same doubtful, depressed voice:

"Well, I don't know. . . ." He helped himself to fish before saying with a rueful twist of an eyebrow: "I can't bear women to cry. I do deplore it."

"Yes, it's a bad habit."

He said quickly:

"That's what I think——" checked himself; added vaguely: "No. . . ."

"What does it make you feel when people cry?" she asked lightly. "Sorry? Irritated? or what? Does it melt you, or freeze you?"

He thought a moment.

"Donno. A mixture, I suppose. Damned uncomfortable anyway. I want to rush off *miles*. . . ." He made a grimace, sighed. "It's a very sad thing how much men make women cry." His voice became personal again, light, flirtatious.

"Do they?"

"Don't they?"

"Well. . . ." She hesitated. . . . Oh, yes! . . . Memory flashed *mal à propos*, all out of key. . . . Far back, in the early love-making days with Ivor: so far away, so almost unremembered. And he'd cried too, had needed to be comforted. . . . But that was to be buried. . . .

"Perhaps I'm not much of a crier. . . ."

"Oh, but it's such a luxury!" he exclaimed with that curious sensual mockery and harshness she had noticed before. "Don't you know what a luxury tears can be?"

"Well. . . ." She felt at a loss. "P'raps I've still to find out."

"Are you a puritan?"

"No."

"No, I don't think you are. . . ."

"So what?" She met his eyes.

"I'm not sure. . . . You don't give away much, do you? Wise woman."

"No, I'm not that."

"Don't tell me there's nothing to give away. . . ."

"It's just that my life's . . . not peculiar, I don't mean, or mysterious . . . just rather unexplainable. . . ."

"Is it? Try."

"But it's not like *any* kind of life!" she cried out, in a kind of helplessness and distressed reluctance. "Not like any that comes your way, I'm sure."

"How d'you know what comes my way?"

Not that kind of waking anyway, and getting on a bus, and mornings with Anna; not bed-sitting-rooms and studios of that sort; not that drifting about for inexpensive meals; not always the cheapest seats in movies; not that kind of conversation, those catch phrases; not those parties and that particular sort of dressing, drinking, dancing. . . . Most particularly not those evenings alone in Etty's box of a house, waging the unrewarding, everlasting war on grubbiness—rinsing out, mending stockings for to-morrow, washing brush and comb, cleaning stained linings of handbags; hearing the telephone ring: for Etty again; and the ring before, and the next ring. . . . Not the book taken up, the book laid down, aghast, because of the traffic's sadness, which was time, lamenting and pouring away down all the streets for ever; because of the lives passing up and down outside with steps and voices of futile purpose and forlorn commotion: draining out my life, out of the window, in their echoing wake, leaving me dry, stranded, sterile, bound solitary to the room's minute respectability, the gas-fire, the cigarette, the awaited bell, the gramophone's idiot companionship, the unyielding arm-chair, the narrow bed, the hot-water bottles I must fill, the sleep I must sleep. . . .

"Should I be shocked?" he asked with a comic look of hope.

She burst out laughing.

"No, I'm afraid not. . . . No. I don't mean to sound interesting. There's nothing to tell. It isn't anything."

She cast about in her mind. . . . Amorphous, insubstantial. . . . Leaning against Etty's mantelpiece, head pressed down on the edge, till forehead and wood seemed part of one another, thinking: Do I exist? Where is my place? What is this travesty I am fixed in? How do I get out? Is this, after all, what was always going to be? . . . One couldn't explain that to him.

"Let's take it step by step," he said. "What do you do in the mornings?"

"In the mornings I go to work. . . . But that gives a wrong, busy impression. I help a friend who's a photographer. Her name's Anna Cory. She's very good. I'm a sort of secretary; and sometimes I help her with sitters, when she's tired or bored."

"Sounds interesting," he said conventionally.

"Occasionally it is, but often it isn't. Nobody comes, or Anna gets sick of the faces and won't take any trouble. . . ." And is so casual, not to say contemptuous, that they go away flustered, bridling, and do not recommend her to their friends. "She's a painter, really, a good one, only she says not good enough; and she's only interested in beautiful people."

"She sounds rather petulant and exacting. I don't think I'd like her to take my photograph."

"I've made her sound awful, but she's nice. And you should see her when she *is* interested. She'll take endless trouble. Only of course it isn't a commercial way of going on. I expect it'll come to an end soon."

"And what'll you do then?"

"Don't know. Look for something else, I suppose—goodness knows what. I shan't be snapped up." He looked faintly disturbed and she added gaily: "The rest of the time I mooch about and go to the pictures, and see people and play the gramophone and talk. . . . Just like other people, in fact. So there really is nothing to tell, you see. What I enjoy most in the world is my hot bath. I'd stay in one all day if it weren't so debilitating."

"What a horrible confession."

"What do you enjoy most in the world?"

He considered, raising his eyebrows:

"I really only like one thing." He said it in a momentary general silence; laughed to himself and added: "Tell me where you live."

"I live in the house of my cousin, Etty Somers. P'raps you remember her?"

"Lord, yes, I remember Etty Somers. We were debs together. What's happened to her? Hasn't she married?"

"No, she never married. She still floats about—just the same. Does some little odd jobs and goes lunching and dining and night-clubbing. . . ."

"She was very attractive."

"Yes. She is still: only she's got a bit teeny-looking—shrunken. And somehow she doesn't fit these earnest down-to-bedrock days. She's a pre-war model left over, really. She says garden parties and parasols and blue velvet snoods, and a stall at society bazaars and Lily Elsie . . . and the *Dolly Dialogues* and airs and graces. Poor little Ett! Though I don't know why I say poor. She seems quite safe and happy. . . ." She had her own money, and people with a bit of money were all right. "She never wanted to marry. She could have a dozen times over."

"I see," he said. He was looking at her closely, amused. . . . Wondering about me. She said on a sudden impulse, flushing:

"I married years ago—I'm really Mrs. Ivor Craig. It didn't work. We separated two years ago. . . . However, perhaps you know all that by now."

"Bad luck," he said quietly.

"Oh, no. Stupidity. Only myself to blame."

"Oh, don't do that," he said quickly. "Don't blame yourself. Or any one else. I never do." He was serious, saying something he meant. "People do what they must," he said, staring at his plate.

"Yes," she said, with a kind of internal start. "I think that too."

It was like a surrender. She felt acquiescent, supported. Now he's the person who's said that to me.

As if some obstacle to general sight and hearing had suddenly been removed, she became aware again of the room and its other occupants. Voices, faces by candlelight opened out on her once more. She saw Marigold shaking with laughter, heard her talking shrilly, rapidly, down the table to George and beyond George to her mother, to the man called Denham on her mother's further side. They seemed to be chaffing Lady Spencer. All were turned laughing towards her, and she was countering their sallies with a quick tongue and a sparkling eye. Dear, dear Lady Spencer, enjoying herself, being teased. . . . Even George looked almost lively. He doesn't remember me. He looked quite blank when I murmured we'd met . . . as if he couldn't have heard aright. He hasn't changed much . . . a little less of the flat brown hair on the small round, unintellectual head; frame a little heavier, expression a trifle more stunned, opaque. . . . "D'you remember, Mr. Basset, when you were obliged to correct me for calling pink coats red coats? . . ." Oh, dear, the mortification. . . . The one called Denham's got a horrid face. And so has his wife. A coupling of monsters. . . . Rollo ought to talk to her now, she looks constricted, conveying: "Don't mind me. Being ignored doesn't upset me in the slightest. I have my own thoughts. . . . Nowadays of course one's used to bad manners. . . ." Plump, buttoned-up face, baby-blue eyes close-set, turned-up nose, banal obstinate mouth in grooves. . . . Beyond her, the impassive, steadily-chewing macaw's profile of Aunt Blanche. . . .

Now for Sir Ronald. She turned towards him, breaking the ice with a radiant beam. He said in a surprisingly high, feminine register:

"I feared vis uvverwise delightful meal was going to slip by in vain proximity."

"I feared so too." She continued to beam, disarming him. In case he thinks because he's old . . . or because I'm too engrossed. . . .

"Better late van never," he said. His eyes were as limpid, as innocent as a couple of dew-washed periwinkles: the girlish eyes of the British general, the Imperial administrator, the pioneer explorer. . . . He gave a jerk of his head towards his other neighbour, and murmured: "Wonderful creature. . . ."

"She must be. Such an appearance. It's fabulous, isn't it?"

"Ve wittiest woman I ever knew," he pronounced solemnly, "and ve most truly cosmopolitan. And what a musician! . . . What a musician! . . ."

Olivia took a look across him at the gaunt aquiline profile set in a dark remotely-brooding immobility, neither eating, drinking, looking nor listening.

"She seems to embody Gothic grandeur. . . ."

He considered this.

"I fink raver of ve great French style," he said. "Zélide. . . ."

"Ah yes. Zélide. . . ." To reassure him about the extent of my culture.

"In vese days," he sighed, "a glorious anachronism . . . a blessed anachronism. . . ."

"Ah, yes." Time to change the tone. Culture will fail me. "No pudding?" She raised her eyebrows at his empty plate.

"No. . . . No . . ." he said doubtfully, rather anxiously. He stuck his eyeglass in and eyed the pink-and-white cherry-scattered *volupté* she was engaged upon. "No, I fink not."

"It's so good,—you can't imagine. Angel's food."

"Between you and me," he murmured, leaning towards her confidentially. "I don't care much for sweets. Never did. I shall reserve my forces for ve savoury . . . I suppose vere is a savoury?" He looked anxious again. "I can't read ve menu at vis distance."

"'Croûtes aux champignons à la crême,'" she read encouragingly.

"Ah! Yes—good. Croûtes aux champignons à la crême. Always delicious in vis house. Vey've had veir cook close on twenty years here—did you know? I fink I must be acquainted wiv the whole of her extensive repertoire. She's a wonderful creature. Of course, she has her weak spots like all artists.

But she has a way of doing veal. . . ." He cast his eyes up. "It's like nuffing I ever tasted in vis country. . . . Croûtes aux champignons à la crême. I shall reserve my forces for vat and enjoy vis course vicariously."

"I love puddings," she said, in the style of pretty confession. "In fact, I love food altogether."

"Excellent! So do I. I like to hear a lady admitting to a healthy appetite. From what I gavver, it's rare in vese degenerate days." His eyes travelled mildly over her, and his thought was plain: Not that these curves are as they should be. . . . Tastes formed in the Edwardian heyday, when Aunt Blanche had, presumably, dazzled him with her upholstery, revolted from modern concavity. Ah, Blanche and Millicent Venables, notable pair of sisters, graceful, witty, majestic! . . . And all the others. . . . Alas! a mould discarded. These contemporary silhouettes, not only unalluring but disquieting, like so many other symptoms in the sexes nowadays. . . .

"My very dear sister-in-law, Millicent Spencer," he went on, polishing his eyeglass, "has always understood to a remarkable degree ve art of living . . . somefing of a lost art nowadays, to my mind . . . decidedly a lost art. It includes, I need hardly say, a forough understanding of ve principles of gastronomy . . . a forough understanding. . . . Her table is still one of ve best in England . . . one of ve best." He turned round in his chair and sniffed yearningly towards the serving-table. Still no savoury?

"I adore her," said Olivia, gazing at her hostess. "I've known her since I was a child. Marigold and I did lessons together."

"Did you indeed . . . did you?" That sends me up a place or two. "What a charming child she was! Dear me, yes; exquisite. . . ." He stuck his eyeglass in, and blew out a reminiscent sigh. "But she'll never be what her mother was. Never."

"No, I suppose not. The scale's entirely different for one thing, isn't it?—the difference between—say a lyric and an

ode: an Elizabethan lyric and a grand rolling Miltonic ode."
Another blow for culture, at a venture.

"Precisely. Very apt." He was pleased. "Both rare and
precious in veir degree—in veir degree—— Or, to make a more
general comparison, let us say between ve romantic and ve
classical. My personal taste has always leaned towards ve
classical. Particularly nowadays," he added mildly, "as I
descend gradually towards ve brink of total decrepitude, do I
find its austerities and formalities a consolation. . . . But in
youf," he added, smiling with charm, "in youf we can afford
to dally wiv caprice and irregularity."

"Reason has moons . . . you know," she cooed, feeling more
and more exquisite.

"What is vat? It seems unfamiliar. . . ."
She continued to quote in a dainty voice:

> Reason has moons, but moons not hers
> Lie mirrored on her sea,
> Confounding her astronomers,
> But oh! delighting me!

"Delighting me too, I'm afraid." She gave him a slightly
wistful smile.

"Ah!" He meditated, surveying her, owing to the monocle,
with one libertine's orb, and one seraphic one. "A very pretty
little case for it. Whevver or no we subscribe to ve doctrine
. . . whevver or no. . . ." He sighed. "Even a horny old
crustacean like myself is capable of a sharp unmefodical twinge
on spring or autumn evenings . . . or in ve company of ve
young and fair." Another old-world smile. "*Le cœur a ses
raisons*. . . . I often fink of vat. It's one of ve trufs we haven't
outgrown yet . . . not yet."

No end to the tossing back and forth of this fragrant
nostalgic æsthetical cowslip-ball. . . . In what career had he
doubtless distinguished himself—lisp, monocle and all? The
aura of authority was around him; drawing-rooms of taste,

cultured evening parties seemed his obvious setting; upper-class Egerias his natural companions: all gracefully, spaciously, securely à la recherche du temps perdu. Connoisseur of . . . collector of . . . He suggested that sort of thing.

The savoury was before him now, rich, succulent. He was respecting it with silent gravity and concentration.

"What a pretty room this is." Deep sea-blue walls, panelled, picked out in gold leaf, elaborate moulding, ceiling a slight finely turned vault, painted with tumbling sea-nymphs, and glowing wreaths, shells, tritons, and Venus emerging among it all. "It's such a nice shape."

"A gem," he said with satisfaction. "Unique, I should judge. Although of course vere's Holkhurst—know Holkhurst? . . . Ah, you ought to go to Holkhurst. Glorious place. I was vere last week-end. Now, ve dining-room vere—ve small dining-room not ve large one—is after ve same style. Fought to be a copy. Ve detail is distinctly coarser—distinctly coarser." He spared a moment to stick his monocle in and survey the ceiling; continued: "I sometimes ask myself whevver ve work doesn't show traces of more van one hand. It's uneven. Ve painting of ve right-hand group in ve corner, for instance. . . . Vat's always seemed to me a *fought* crude. . . ."

"Yes." She examined a few wantoning nymphs. "I see what you mean . . ."

"Ah, vese treasures are a goodly heritage!" He shot out his monocle with an elastic flick, wiped his moustache and squeaked with sudden violence: "And what's to happen to vem all? Look at Holkhurst! Look at Hilton! Closed free-quarters of ve year!"

She hazarded tentatively:

"I suppose it's the end of a chapter . . .?"

"Yes, ve end of a chapter! Ve end of all æsfetic standards! I ask myself: who'll care a hundred years from now for art and letters . . .? I ask myself who. . . ."

"More people perhaps?" Careful now, careful. . . . His eye

was glinting with a fixed fanatical inward spark. . . . Soothe him. ". . . with more leisure, better education . . .?"

"Ach . . . !" He controlled himself, swallowed, brought his voice down an octave. "Potted! Re-hashed! Distributed cheap to all consumers. Yes, yes, yes. . . . No doubt. Museums plentiful as blackberries. Ve long gallery at Holkhurst railed off wiv greasy ropes, guides in attendance, ve cheap excursions disgorging at ve gates and shuffling frough. . . ." Overcome yet assuaged by the drama of the conjured vision, he added with quiet and mournful solemnity: "Yes. Sometimes when I look round I tell myself: Yes, all I care for's well-nigh had its day, and so have I, fank God. . . ."

It was best to smile deprecatingly, sympathetically. One more false step and he might leave the table; or at best awake with indigestion in the night.

He continued with nobility:

"One must try to take ve long view—ve historical perspective. . . . But what goes to my heart"—he leaned towards her, and muttered—"is to see *vem* so hard up. It does indeed. Ve worry tells on vem. Vey put a brave face on it but ve worry tells. It's told on him." He jerked his monocle in the direction of Sir John.

"I'm afraid it has. . . . An estate like this must be a terrible problem these days."

"Parting wiv ve Rembrandt was a terrible blow. And heaven knows what'll have to go next!" Another jerk, towards Rollo. "What's to happen in his time I can't imagine. Unless he contrives to make some money. He's very able—oh, very able. . . . Of course, a—an advantageous marriage would have helped matters, but vere it is. . . . We couldn't wish vat uvverwise. Wiv a young man of his mettle, ve highest fings come first. . . . Dear Nicky. . . . Do you know his wife, his Nicola?"

"Only by sight."

"Beautiful creature, charming creature. . . . Ve most devoted couple. . . . No, one cannot wish vat uvverwise. . . .

Only"—he sank his voice to a mutter—"one could wish her stronger."

"Is she so very delicate?"

"Raver delicate, I fear. Very poor helf. Poor dear. Hmm. Pity." He cleared his throat and continued in stronger tones: "Ah, but when I call to mind ve way life was lived once here! . . . in ve old days . . . before ve War. . . . What happy times we had, to be sure! Everybody came here in vose days. Veir week-end parties were famous. . . . She had vat extraordinary knack of getting ve best out of everybody. . . ." It was like reading a *Times* obituary notice. "Ah dear!" He laughed wistfully. "I shall never forget some of ve charades. Quite elaborate dramatic performances vey used to develop into: everybody used to dress up and have a part: even ve butler and ve ladies' maids. Dear me! I remember a maid of my wife's wiv ve most remarkable soprano—untrained, of course, but really charming. Vere was some idea of paying for her training. . . . I don't fink anyfing came of it. . . . I was always called upon to provide ve musical accompaniment. Hours I spent at ve piano . . . very small beer, you know—I was never a composer—but it served, —it served. My wife and Millicent—Lady Spencer, you know— bof had pretty musical voices, trained voices, and vey used to sing duets. . . . Why does nobody sing nowadays?"

The image came up sharp to her mind's eye: Blanche and Millicent, in white, with hour-glass waists and rosebuds sewn all over their flounces, standing up together by the piano, all splendid curves and sparkle, opening their unpainted lips and warbling out duets. Dear me! . . . And there sat one of them, opposite, elderly, powerful and sober, frowning a little, giving some view with obvious trenchancy: practical farming perhaps or the housing committee; the other, a few places up, cracking a walnut with deliberation, unwieldy, rather torpid, stertorous-looking: both in black. Dear me! . . .

"I remember so well—little Guy, as Eros, in a classical charade—wiv his little winged cap, and a bow . . . and nuffing else on . . . how enchanting he looked. . . . How it shocked

some of ve neighbours.... Dear oh dear! Did you know Guy?
What a dear handsome boy he was!..."

"No, I never saw Guy. I suppose I was just too young."

"Yes, yes, of course. I was forgetting. Yes. Of course. It
was long before your time...."

"I've seen his portrait often. He looks wonderful."

The charcoal head of him as a boy, by Sargent: an Edwardian dream-child with romantic hair, and one of those
long necks in an open cricket shirt....

"Ve flower of ve flock...."

But he died for England: going over the top, at the head of
his men, shot through the heart.... All as it should be. And
they'd done what could be done: worn white for mourning;
put a memorial window in the church; collected his letters
and poems and all the tributes to him, had them printed for
private circulation. All bore witness—nurses, governesses,
schoolmasters, broken-hearted friends—all said the same: gay,
brilliant, winning, virtuous, brave Guy: pattern of the eldest
son....

"I remember—a very handsome boy, a cousin—called
Archie——" she hazarded. For of course he must be Archie's
father: yet one never knew: Archie might have died, or turned
out a problem or a disgrace....

"Ah, you knew Archie, did you? My young hopeful....
Young scamp vat he was...." His voice seemed to lose
warmth, to suggest dissatisfaction, perhaps reluctance. "Yes,
he spent a good deal of his time here as a schoolboy. His aunt
was extraordinarily good to him... extraordinarily good. She
had a weakness for him...." He shook his head. It was clear
that Archie was no part of the pink sunset glow of the past.
"We had no settled home in England ven of course.... It was
during my last governorship...."

"Oh, yes, of course...." So that was it. But where? Where
are Governors?...

Sir Ronald turned to his other neighbour.

"Cigarette, Olivia?"

"Thank you." She turned joyfully to Rollo. The way he said "Olivia" sounded pleasant and strange, setting up a kind of echo in her ears. She met his eye, ironical, over the lighter he held out to her.

"The point is," she murmured, "nothing is as good as it was before we knew about it."

"And any one dead is automatically superior to any one alive. . . . All the same, if he was telling you what a much better person Guy was than me, you can believe him. It happens to be the truth. Dear old Guy, he was a good chap, he really was. He had that dead right touch. . . ."

"Do you miss him very much?"

"I did once. Mostly I forget him now." He relit his cigar. "Occasionally I still feel a vague impersonal annoyance when I reflect on the waste . . . and the inferior article's aptitude for survival. Mine I mean."

She said nothing. After a bit he went on in the same colourlessly reflective voice:

"He loathed the war, it shocked him, he believed in God. I'm never shocked. I dare say I'd have taken very kindly to the war. . . . Dash it all, most people did, didn't they?"

"I suppose it was easy to get apathetic. . . . One can't keep up horror and indignation. . . . They're too wearing."

"They're no good anyway."

"Why not?" There he goes again. . . . "Surely one must believe *something's* some good?"

"Oh, rather. . . ." He puffed away at his cigar, narrowing his eyes; then continued: "What I should like is to be able to keep my head—sort of on the sly—wouldn't you?—whatever I found myself involved in . . . I feel that might be some good."

"Some satisfaction, you mean. Awfully superior feeling."

"Well, no." He nibbled his forefinger, frowning a little. "It's a *kind* of belief, really. . . ."

"Living privately—no matter how publicly . . .?"

"Something of that, perhaps. . . ."

Marigold called across the table:

"Rollo, *haven't* you got a foul temper?"

"Foul."

"Mummy's saying none of her children ever quarrelled. Did you ever! I can remember when I was about four, looking down from the top landing and seeing you and Archie trying to throw each other over the banisters."

"Marigold, what nonsense."

"Well, I did. Didn't I, Rollo?"

"Don't remember. I dare say you did, though."

"I was thrilled."

"It was a game, you silly girl," said Lady Spencer, almost annoyed.

"Well, it wasn't. Because they didn't make any noise at all. It was like a fight in a film. That's how I suddenly realised they meant it. I've never forgotten it."

"You dreamt it."

"Well, fancy not wanting us to have tempers," said Marigold, subsiding with a pout. "We're not eunuchs."

There was laughter; and the table broke up again, into separate pieces.

"What's happened to Archie?" said Olivia, low to Rollo.

"Oh, he hangs around. . . . When did you last see him?"

"At Marigold's coming-out party. He made rather an impression."

"Oh, did he?" Rather harsh, hostile voice.

"He was the beautifullest young man I'd ever seen."

"Was he? He's gone off a bit, I fear. He's put on a tummy and his hair's a bit thin."

"Oh, how sad."

"Terribly sad. I'm afraid he's worried."

"Also he was the first drunk person I'd ever talked to. It was a shock."

"Oh, was he a bore?"

"It wasn't so much that. It was something more general—more important. About people changing and forgetting—and not meaning what they said. . . . It turned life suddenly into such a *black* problem—too much to go through with almost. When one's young and gets a knock, all humanity seems involved. . . . As a matter of fact that was why I went out on the terrace. . . ."

"Where I also had gone for a breath of air. . . ." He stared at a wine-glass, turning it in his hand. "Very odd."

They were silent. . . . And when we came in again, Archie was shouting for Nicola. Rollo shouldered him out of his way, it was clear then, the impact of their dislike and jealousy. . . . Nicola came down the stairs and held her hand up.

"And ever since then," he said, "I've wanted to see you again."

She looked quickly away from him, round the table. It sounded preposterous—like a voice in a dream.

"So have I. . . ."

Change was in the air. The wheels were running down. Lady Spencer and Aunt Blanche were on their feet. Rollo stood up and pulled her chair back without looking at her at all. Lady Spencer held out a hand affectionately as she passed and drew her on into the doorway.

Replete, at ease, smoothing their hips, warming their backs, the ladies stood round the drawing-room fire. . . . Now Marigold and I will talk. . . . But no. Marigold, wandering absently, touching things with vague fingers, sketching fragmentary smiles, powdering her nose without looking at it, said suddenly:

"Mummy, I must dash up and see Nannie. I promised I would. She's got hurt feelings because we haven't had a heart-to-heart, and you know what that means . . . purple patches on her neck and hell for the housemaids. I shan't be longer than I can help."

She darted out of the room without so much as a glance in Olivia's direction. As if she'd forgotten my existence. Nothing could have been more disconcertingly typical. She hadn't changed at all; still restlessly appearing and disappearing, suddenly attentive, suddenly remote; like a cat.

"Poor old Nannie." Lady Spencer looked thoughtful. "She's getting very difficult. She's *so* rheumatic and crotchety and trying with the young servants. . . . But what's one to do?"

"Can't you pension her off?" said Aunt Blanche.

"That's what I'd like to do, but where's she to go? She's hardly got any relations left—only one old married sister somewhere in Wales, and they don't get on. And she won't just take it easy here and potter about. It would break her heart to feel she's not useful any more. And of course she *lives* for the children's visits. Marigold's so sweet to her."

"I often think," said Cousin Mary, sitting down and drawing a piece of tapestry work from a large black silk bag, "what a sad life it is to be a Nannie. I'm sure I don't know what I'm going to do with mine. John goes to school next term and the guvvie will take on both girls in the schoolroom. There'll really be nothing for the poor dear to do. I suppose I might keep her on for sewing. She's very clever at loose covers and so forth. But Harry thinks we shouldn't afford it." She sighed complacently, threading a needle.

"And then of course you do so much sewing yourself." Aunt Blanche sat down with a heave and a creak, knees spread, legs planted foursquare on a pair of incongruously elegant narrow feet.

"I make most of the girl's clothes, of course," said Mary, in a modest voice.

"Marvellous."

"It's a saving, of course."

"What's that you're on now?" Aunt Blanche put up a lorgnette and leaned forward tremendously to peer. "Jolly colours."

"Do you like it?" Mary smoothed out the canvas, appearing to deprecate it. "It *is* rather a nice design. Tudor."

"Mary always did lovely work," sighed Lady Spencer. "Do

you remember, dear, the cushion you did for me, years ago?
It's in my boudoir to this day."

"Oh, that!" She looked scornful. "Quilted. I remember.
It wasn't a bad pattern."

"I wish I was clever with my fingers."

"I can't bear having idle hands," Mary confessed gently.
"I got the children's winter jumpers finished, and stockings
for John, so I thought to myself, well, why shouldn't I give
myself a treat and do something in the ornamental line for
a change."

"What's it going to be, dear?"

"Oh, it's just for a chair. I'm doing a set of eight for the
dining-room."

"*What* a labour for you?"

"I think it will be gay," she said meekly, holding up
the square with her dear little old-fashioned head on one
side.

Nothing you did or conceived of could ever be gay; and
do your children know yet they hate you?

"What's *your* masterpiece, Blanche?" inquired Lady Spencer
as her sister also opened a work-bag, a massive and handsome
one of crimson damask, and drew from it a stout pair of wooden
knitting pins, a ball of violet wool and a curious knitted oblong
to match.

"Oh, my dear, it's just a garment. For my needlework
guild. You know—everybody makes two and the things go
to the Workhouse for Christmas. It's a sort of bed-jacket, I
think." She looked at it in a brooding, doubtful way.

"It'll be nice and cheerful," said Mary with gracious
interest, conscious of superior powers. "What's the stitch,
Aunt Blanche?"

"Oh, my dear, just plain. Purl's too much for my feeble
brain."

"You'll never finish it, Blanche."

"Not a hope, my dear. Tucker'll have to unpick it all, I
expect, and knit it up again. Still. . . . I thought I'd start it.

Poor old dears, they do so appreciate it if they know one's made the things oneself."

Olivia sat down on a low stool beside Aunt Blanche.

"What a gorgeous bag," she said. The look of it lying richly on that bursting lap made her feel weak, yielding and protected. Aunt Blanche looked down at her in a plethoric kindly way from under her full, fowl's lid.

"Rather jolly, isn't it? I got it at that Blind place in London. Do you ever go there?"

"Oh, yes, I know," said Mary. "They do wonderful work. I always make a point of doing my Christmas shopping there. Only, of course, they're so dreadfully expensive. . . ."

What's the Blind place. . . . What's become of the blind man. . . . Timmy his name was; and he and his wife kept hens, and he had a child called Elizabeth. . . . Sharply she remembered him in this room, ten years ago: waltzing round and round with him to the Blue Danube, his fingers quivering; . . . feeling him listen for Marigold hour after hour. . . .

"Do you do needlework, Olivia dear?"

"No, I'm afraid I don't. It's as much as I can face to mend my stockings. Kate was always such a natural-born sewer, I felt defeated at the starting post and never bothered."

"Dear Kate, how is she? I always admired her so much. Has she still got that exquisite skin and hair?"

"Yes, still very good."

"Olivia's sister," explained Lady Spencer, "had the most exquisite fair skin and hair."

"Kate's exactly the same," said Olivia. "Only of course quite different."

Mary uttered a deprecating tinkle.

"Like all of us." Lady Spencer smiled with a sigh. "And is she happy, dear Kate?"

"Yes, I think she is. I think she'd say she was happy on the whole."

"She was always such a splendid capable girl." The sensible sister . . . the one who'd avoid getting into trouble:

so different from the younger one. . . . "And *how* many children is it?"

"Four. Beautifully spaced out."

"Four! How delightful. The ideal number for a family. I hope they look like her?"

"No, they don't. They look like their Pa, but they're quite nice. Three girls and a boy. The youngest a baby."

An extraordinary bleating sound, something between a gasp, a groan and a coo, came from Mary.

"Oo-o-oh! *How* old?"

"About eight months, I think. I can't remember."

"Eight months! The *lamb*! How I do envy her. Every time I hear of any one with a tiny baby I feel quite *green* with envy. Oh dear! If *only* they'd stay wee and cuddly and *never* grow up. Personally I think up to a month old is the sweetest time of all. . . . Oh dear, when I think of mine, the great long-legged things!—I can't bear it."

"Can't you really?" said Olivia. "I should have thought the only point about producing them was to encourage their growth. Or isn't it like gardening?"

Mary ran an eye over her. . . . Ringless hands, flat hips and stomach. . . .

"I don't think it's quite the same," she said with cold firm amused gentleness, making allowances. "Not for mothers anyway."

"Of course I've never had any," said Olivia clearly, "so I can't tell."

"I always found their companionship such a joy as they grew older," said Lady Spencer, breaking in with tact. "But of course, one misses the babies too."

"Personally I always disliked babies," said Aunt Blanche, struggling with a dropped stitch. "All the same, I do wish Archie would marry a nice girl and make a grandmother of me. I find I quite yearn to be a grandmother, Millicent. I suppose it's old age."

"It's very pleasant," sighed Lady Spencer. "Marigold's two

are such darlings. Of course grandmothers have to know their place, and *never* give advice or interfere."

"You must find that a little difficult, dearest."

"Not as difficult as you'd find it, love."

"Are you the mother of Archie?" said Olivia, playing with the ball of wool. "I remember him. We used to dance together at the children's parties." She smiled up at Lady Spencer. "I remember teaching him the baby polka and he thought it was so funny. He simply stood still and cackled with laughter. I couldn't think why. And once I said to him: ' What lovely blue eyes you've got,' and he said, ' Oh, d'you think so? Yours are brown, aren't they? I do prefer blue myself.'"

Aunt Blanche shook to the depths with a chuckle. "The wretch!" She was, delighted. "I hope you snubbed him."

"Not I. I was much too madly in love with him. I was a fearfully amorous child. But even at that, I think he must have been irresistible."

Mary gave a trifling laugh in the top of her nose: deploring the tone. . . . I must always have been a nasty-minded girl.

"He's always been very good to his old Ma," said Aunt Blanche. She gave Olivia an approving, it seemed almost a grateful look. She likes me anyway. . . . Without a word said, it was all plain: Archie, far from satisfactory, on bad terms with his father, tapping secret supplies of money, of love, comfort and indulgence from his foolish mother. . . .

"He's a dear boy," said Lady Spencer, looking unusually abstracted.

"Do you see much of him these days?" inquired Aunt Blanche, a touch of something in her voice,—embarrassment, apology. . . . "He's got so many friends, I really don't know. . . . He's out so much. . . ."

"Oh, no, I haven't seen him for years. He'd never remember me. We're in quite different worlds now."

Lady Spencer broke in quickly:

"What is it exactly you're busy at nowadays, dear? Your mother did tell me——"

"I work in London." It seemed a futile effort to explain it all again; but she did so, briefly.

"How interesting," said Lady Spencer, approving the principle of labour. "It sounds delightful work."

"You must give me the address," said Aunt Blanche. "Not for myself—God forbid!—But I do think Archie ought to be done. I haven't got anything nice of him since Eton. Don't you think Archie ought to be done, Millicent?"

"What sort of prices do you run?" said Mary.

"Absolutely top prices."

"Oh, really? What a pity! I mean I do think it's rather a pity not to come down these days when everybody's coming down—don't you? I mean everybody's so badly off. . . . It sort of keeps people away, doesn't it?"

"Oh, yes, it does keep people away." This is the personal touch in salesmanship—counts for so much: dine out in the best houses, use your charm, and the rest's child's play.

A dance orchestra flooded the room suddenly, noisily.

"Gracious! Where can that come from on a Sunday?" said Mary.

"Some low foreign station," said Olivia.

Silently, Marigold came back through the open doors from the ante-room, and stood in front of the fire, listening, nibbling her fingers—the same trick as Rollo.

"What a jolly tune," said Aunt Blanche.

"Couldn't you turn it down just a little, dear?" said Lady Spencer. "We can't hear ourselves speak."

"No, no," said Aunt Blanche. "It's cheerful. Makes me want to dance." She tapped her feet and swayed about from the hips in her arm-chair, humming loudly.

"I haven't danced for years," sighed Mary. "Harry just won't go out in the evenings. He's getting *such* an old stick-in-the-mud. I tell him he's just letting himself get middle-aged—and me too. We'll soon be just a dull old stay-at-home couple, sitting over the fire." She made a pretty, girlish *moue*. "And I do so *love* dancing."

"Why don't you find a boy-friend and go on the tiles?" said Marigold.

"Oh, Marigold!" Mary bridled and tinkled. "Aunt Millicent, isn't she awful? What next?"

Marigold dropped suddenly on her knees by Olivia's stool and leaned a cheek against her shoulder.

"What next? What next?" she murmured.

After a moment she moved away lightly and knelt by the fire, staring into it. Something seemed to happen in the room. Beneath the incongruous assault of drum and saxophone it appeared frozen suddenly in a gleaming fixity. The group by the fire had a static quality, as if anæsthetised. The needles paused. The ladies leaned their heads upon their hands, stared in front of them.

Only Lady Spencer stood up erect, majestic, upon the hearthrug: as if to stand thus were her sole purpose and function: as if the pose were an heroic assertion. Time drew a circle round the scene. It was now: it was a hundred, two hundred years ago. . . .

Nothing essential is changed yet. . . .

"What a lousy din," said Marigold suddenly. She sprang up, seizing Olivia by the hand, and led her rapidly away through the doors into the ante-room.

She switched off the wireless, flung herself on the sofa and pulled Olivia down beside her.

In the ensuing vacuum of silence Aunt Blanche's unrepressed voice rang out, clearly audible from the other end of the next room.

"What an attractive gel, Millie. Where did you get her over from?"

Olivia kicked her legs towards the door, kissed both hands with a flourish.

" *We can—hee-ee-ar you!* " Marigold trumpeted through her fists in a loud ribald whisper. They giggled.

A low murmur was going on from the inner sanctuary, inaudible now. . . . Laying fingers to lips, raising eyebrows,

nodding. . . . *Most unfortunate.* . . . *Really?* . . . *Who was he?* . . .
And is she . . .? Dear, dear! . . . Pity. . . .

Discreet, guardedly regretful.

Marigold sprang up again.

"Oh, come on."

Olivia caught her up in the corridor among the dark
bloodshot pictures.

"Let them cackle their heads off," said Marigold. "God,
how I do hate women. That Mary needs a bomb under her—
and I wish I could be the one to set it off. . . . Olivia. . . ." She
stopped short and gave her a hug. "I'm *extraordinarily* glad.
. . . Why don't I ever see you? Why haven't you ever looked
me up in London? You are a pig. I think of you so often—
you and Kate. Oh dear! How we used to laugh! Didn't we?
Mm? D'you remember?"

"Yes, I do."

I suppose we laughed. . . . Yes, we did. . . . Only what I
remember seems much more complicated: exciting, emotional
—melancholy, somehow, on the whole. . . .

"Such fun. . . ." She went on walking apparently at random down one passage and at right angles into another.
"You must tell me all about you. My dear, I've got two
children. Did you know? Can you imagine? I've done my
duty, haven't I? They're rather sweet. Oh, and I remember
you wrote me a divine letter when I had Iris, and I don't
believe I ever answered."

"It doesn't matter. It didn't need an answer."

"Oh, but I meant to! Only I'm so hopeless about letters.
I don't know what comes over me. I *can't*. And there were so
many," she added vaguely.

She opened a door at the far end of the passage: they were
in a wing of the house Olivia had never penetrated before.
She switched on a light and they went into a small, close
uneasy-shaped room with red walls and dark red curtains and
heavy Victorian furniture. Various antlers, foxes' brushes,
heads of animals were nailed about the walls; and in a case

on the table was a stuffed otter, snarling on a rock among greenery, with bared teeth and scarlet tongue. Silver cups and other athletic trophies adorned the mantelshelf; and above them hung photographs of horses and fish, and sporting and school groups. A thick smell of polish and green baize pervaded the room.

"Ugh! How murky." Marigold wrinkled her nostrils. "Never mind. It's sequestered anyway. They'll never guess where we are. I must telephone." She closed the door behind them, switched on a stark rail of electric fire in the grate, and looked about her. "My God! What a nightmare of a room. I never noticed before. Its name is the telephone room. It's a secret extension known only to the family and you, and everybody comes here to put their secret calls through. The footman mostly, I should think, judging by the smell." She took up the receiver from an old-fashioned instrument screwed to the wall behind the door, and gave a London number. "Sit down, Livia. Make yourself at home. I promised to ring up Sam. You don't mind, do you?"

"Shan't I go away?"

"No, of course not. It isn't private. . . . Beside I want to talk to you." She leaned against the wall, holding the receiver in a vague half-hearted way. "Livia. . . . It *was* fun Rollo running into you like that. He was so thrilled. Isn't he a darling? . . . I do love him. . . ." She stiffened suddenly and said: "Hallo! . . . Oh, Lang? . . . It's me. . . . Tell his lordship, will you, please? . . . Not there? . . . Oh. . . . Wasn't he expected? I thought he said he'd be dining to-night. . . . I see. . . . Yes, p'raps he did. . . . No, no message. At least . . . No, never mind. Good-bye, Lang."

She hung up with a crash and stood gnawing at her fingers, her eyes very narrow beneath the fringe. "His lordship telephoned at seven o'clock to say he'd been unavoidably detained in the country," she quoted. "Just—as—I—thought. Damn his eyes. The fur *will* be in the fire. . . . Well, he can stew." Her eyes darted, looking at nothing.

"What's the matter?"

"Oh, nothing really. . . . Only he'd arranged to dine in London to-night with his aged parents. It was all fixed up. He was going to do the clean breast and ask for some money. We're so in debt. And they're so touchy, they'll be furious and bitterly wounded and everything, I suppose. Bang goes our last hope. He *never* does what he says he will. *Never.* I've never known him to." She laughed. "Oh, well. . . . What the hell? . . . It doesn't make much odds. We've been bust for years, but we seem to go on in comparative afflatus, not to say luxury, like everybody else. . . . Sam's fantastic about money. You wouldn't believe. And I'm not awfully economical either. . . . What's to be done? . . . I wonder if Mr. Ponds would like to put me in his harem. . . . What, jib at a couple of double gins?—not Lady Britton. . . . Shall I offer myself for five hundred?" She began to walk up and down, fingering and shifting objects. "You know, I wouldn't a *bit* mind being poor. I truly wouldn't. I know I wouldn't. It's one of the few things I'm certain of . . . though everybody laughs if I say it. I mean —if I was in love with a person—and we wanted perhaps to go off together—I wouldn't mind *one scrap* if he hadn't a bean— it would never occur to me to be refrained by that. *Heaps* of women I know, quite nice ones, simply say, ' No money, no go, my boy '—and that's that. But personally I'd be glad . . . yes . . . I'm almost sure I'd prefer it. It 'ud make one feel one was doing something *real* . . . wouldn't it? I often think about living in a little house and doing the cooking and saving up for treats and——"

"Oh, Marigold! *What* a day-dream!"

"Why?" She reflected, seeming to be taken aback. "Are you poor, Olivia?"

"Pretty poor."

"I know, someone told me." Her eyes flew over Olivia from top to toe; and the latter said, smiling:

"Don't I look it?"

"No, you look marvellous. But then you always did, you and Kate. It's your figures, I suppose."

"It isn't amusing to be poor, darling. You wouldn't like it, honestly. Unless you mean something different from what I mean. I expect you do. . . ." Well on the safe side of the line, with somebody to fall back on and a guaranteed overdraft. . . .

"I don't know what I mean. Never do. I suppose I'm talking through my cocked hat, as usual. But I just feel anything would be better than this frittering futile. . . . I'd like to have to work—have my day filled up from start to finish and come home too weary not to be peaceful." She leaned against the mantelpiece, brooding. "Tell me, Livia, do you ever feel as if you weren't real?"

"Often."

"Oh, do you ? I shouldn't have thought you would. It's a beastly feeling. Everybody has a solid real life except oneself. One's a sort of fraud . . . empty." She spoke the last word with a slow lingering emphasis. "I thought having babies would cure me: it's one of the few things you can't pretend about all the way through. However prettily and unsickly you start, you're jolly well for it in the end. But I don't know. . . . It turned out to be another sort of dream. They gave me so much dope I sailed through the worst of it as if it wasn't me. And there I was again: the young mother. Touching. Money for jam for the photographers." She laughed suddenly.

"I'd love to see your children."

"Oh, yes, you must! They're divine." Her voice was vague. After a moment she went on, differently: "I adore them, of course, but I must admit I'm simply *amazed* every time I see them, wondering where on earth they came from and why they've taken up their abode in the house. And then . . . Bennie's so frightfully naughty and unbridled—absolutely a *gangster*. When I see him in one of his moods I think to myself —*look* what you've done . . . and I simply *long* to abolish him. It seems the only way out."

Olivia burst out laughing; and Marigold's rapt ferociously

frowning expression relaxed gradually into a look of puzzled, faintly amused relief.

"I suppose it'll work out all right," she said vaguely; adding after a pause: "I wonder if dying'll be a sort of dream too? Don't you? I can't believe it'll seem like *me*, *me* dying. . . . Ugh! Have I really got to?" She opened her eyes to their widest, and they looked blank and blind with their dilated pupils, like eyes made of glass. "I get moments when it sweeps over me—in the middle of the night or when I'm by myself in the house—and depressed. It's like dropping through a trap-door unexpectedly."

She turned round and leaned her arms along the mantel-piece and her head down sideways on her arms. Her curls tumbled over out of their sophisticated dressing, and looked irresponsible, childish. What the years had done to her looks became suddenly evident. The face, that sketch in a few light lines, had acquired not precision exactly, not an adult cast, but a curious clarifying and definition of each one of the old tentative ambiguities and contradictions. Enthralling, para-doxical interplay of planes and surfaces seen momentarily in repose: cold, sensual, tender, adamant . . . transparent, dissimu-lating . . . moving romantic creature. . . . Sinister creature. *Mad, bad, and* . . . No, what nonsense! . . .

"Are you often by yourself and depressed?"

She lifted her head and looked round at Olivia out of the corners of her eyes.

"No, no, not I." She looked slightly sheepish, slightly mocking, as she used to look in the Shakespeare class when they caught her drawing rude Skinny Gingers. "I'm practically never alone and I enjoy myself *frightfully* practically always. Don't you? It's so silly not to, don't you think? . . . Livia, darlin', tell me more about yourself. I've been talking too much about me. Why *did* you go and drop out of my life? I wish people wouldn't do that. I hate it. I was so excited when Rollo told me. . . . He was quite determined you were to be got to come—not that he needed to be determined, because

of course we all wanted. . . . Only it was funny of Rollo, he
doesn't often. . . . I was so glad. I do hope you like him. Poor
sweet, it's time he had a break."

"Why? Does he need one?"

"*I* think he does. He's just *wasted*. Only he's so kind and
easy-going it 'ud never occur to him. Between you and me,
and any one else who cares to listen, that Nicola's no damn'
good." She made a grimace, and came and flung herself down
in one of the leather arm-chairs opposite Olivia. "There! That
clinches it: this chair smells of Albert's hair-oil. I suppose
he wantons in it with the housemaid. I always thought this
room had a sort of lustful atmosphere."

"Why do you say she's no good?"

"Who? Oh, Nicola? Oh, she's a bitch. She loathes me and
I loathe her. She's jealous. Mummy can't do with her either,
only of course wild horses wouldn't drag it out of her. . . . All
this family bunk! Of course, Rollo won't hear a *word*. . . . He
adores her—or he thinks he does. My only hope is that somebody'll enlighten him one of these days."

"You mean you don't think he does really?"

"No, it's only he's so loyal. . . . She doesn't give him a
thing. . . ."

"I don't believe that makes much difference. . . . In fact,
quite the contrary sometimes." Why do I go on? Why feel
embarrassed—almost guilty? . . . and pleased as well? "Is she
double-crossing him or something?"

"Oh, no, not that! She'd never have the guts. . . . If only
she *would* do something definite, like have a lover or take to
drugs, there might be some hope. Oh, I don't know. There
never was such a witless die-away ninny. And not an ounce
of humour. She had a miscarriage once, quite an ordinary
one, at least two years ago, and instead of going ahead and
trying again she's decided she's an invalid—or her mother has.
Her mother's a proper sabre-toothed tiger. I bet she's told
Rollo Nicola's too delicate to take any risks with and he mustn't
go to bed with her. She's always lying on sofas and if she's

crossed she cries and her mother says her nervous system's ruined. . . . Poor old Rollo. . . ." She took up a tiny silver-framed snapshot from the table beside her and examined it through screwed-up eyes. "Who's that pursy infant? One of us, I suppose." She put it down again, thrust out her gold-sandalled feet and examined them, wriggling her toes. "The point is . . . she's awfully sweet in some ways. She's just an infant, a spoilt one. And of course she's quite, quite lovely. One can't help rather cherishing her. There's no vice in the girl. . . . Not like Sam, he's full of it. Livia, you must meet Sam. You'd like him. Women always do. He's terribly attractive and he's rather sweet too, only he's got a lousy temper, specially when he's a bit tight. . . .

"He's sort of unexpected too: he's very musical and he goes to concerts by himself . . . and he gets worked up about Ireland: he's Irish, you know, so of course he's got the gift of the gab and he's not awfully reliable." She sprang up again, looking restless and undecided. "I must say I'd like to know what he's been up to this week-end. . . . I *thought* there was something in the wind: he was so emphatic about being bored to death where he was going. . . . Shall I ring him up and give him a glorious surprise? Shall I? Now?"

"If you like."

She looked at Olivia in a vague yet insistent way. . . . Ringing up Sam an act of hostility to which I'm to lend support. . . .

"I jolly well will." She started towards the telephone, stopped. "No, I won't. . . . I don't know where he is, and that's a fact. I meant to ask him, but I forgot." She went off into one of her silent laughing fits. "Livia, marriage is the devil, isn't it? It's too degradating. . . . It suits me all right though, really." She looked suddenly sobered: remembering my ambiguous state. "Livia . . ." she said with affectionate vagueness.

"Mine turned out to be a non-starter. My marriage, I mean." Olivia coloured and giggled.

"You laugh just like you used to. . . . Darlin', I'm sorry. It's a gamble and no mistake, to put it in an entirely original way." She spoke uncertainly, as if wondering what to say.

"Oh, it can't be helped. I shouldn't have married him. . . . I dare say I'm not particularly suitable to marriage."

"Aren't you? Why not? Come to that I don't know who is, on the face of it. Perhaps Mary. Marriage or murder. . . . I know which I'd put her down for. . . . God, what a week-end, really! They make such a point of my coming down, and of course I do love to—only *why* will Ma collect all these specimens—rattling their bones and reeking of moth ball? Talk of feasting with skeletons! . . . Tante Henriette's all right—the French one—she's got some kick left—she's a devil—only she's deaf and ill. . . . But as for the others! Can you imagine when you're old wanting to sit round like they do and track down all your relations and relations by marriage, known and unknown, all ages and generations, and whether they've inherited the family squint or hammer-toes or whatever it is? . . ."

"I know. My mother's just the same. I suppose it makes them feel safer . . . as if they weren't going to disappear altogether."

"I suppose so." She looked sober. "Poor darlings. What with Daddy being so ga-ga. . . . I don't think they feel awfully cheerful any more. Everything falls flat. Have you noticed he's not frightfully bright? It is a shame. There's nothing to be done. He's best with old friends that don't notice him."

"I expect he's quite happy really, you know. He doesn't notice. He looks very peaceful."

She said with grateful eagerness: "Yes, he does, doesn't he? He didn't when he first got ill, he looked so melancholy I couldn't. . . . But now he's quite serene. And he still makes his little jokes, and he can do a bit of fishing and let off his gun. . . . Only there must be moments when——" She stood and stared. "He really was rather a good person. I'll tell you what he was—magnanimous. People aren't often." Suddenly she put out a foot and switched off the electric fire. "What

are we doing in this most unprepossessive room? Let's go
back." She drew Olivia close to her, an arm round her waist.
"Darlin' Olivia, it's lovely talking to you again. How thin
you are. Like a boy. Are you all right?"

"As right as rain."

They leaned against one another. Marigold said abruptly,
her voice pitched at its highest: "Do you know any queer
people?"

"Lots." Olivia laughed. "Nothing but . . ."

"What I meant was—you know—what d'you call 'em—
Lesbians and things. . . ."

"Oh, I see." Olivia made a slight involuntary movement
away. "Oh, a few, I s'pose."

"Do they fall for you?"

"No—not particularly. . . ."

"I wonder what it would be like. . . . I don't *think* I should
like it. I've never felt inclined that way . . . but I once knew
someone who was. You never know. . . . Lots of people are,
aren't they? Far more than one realises. . . ."

"I expect so."

"Have you ever felt attracted like that?"

"No, I never have."

"I bet if I were like that I'd make a pass at you." She patted
and stroked Olivia's hip with a light clinging touch.

"Thank you. The same to you." Olivia put up a hand and
ran it quickly over the curls. . . . But I feel foolish, uneasy. . . .

"D'you remember that time you stayed the week-end and
we slept in the same bed and pretended to be a married couple?
How old were we, I wonder? About fourteen? . . . Innocent
fun. . . ."

"I remember."

A silence fell. The smell, the weight, the darkness of plush,
mahogany and leather seemed to Olivia to swell out around
them, closing them in suffocatingly. What's she driving at?
She turned and looked at Marigold and said: "But that's not
why my marriage didn't work."

"No, of course. . . . I didn't meant that. . . ."

Oh, didn't you. . . . But why? My looks? A rumour? A sudden, reckless shot of her own at random?

"Not a lover of any sort," said Olivia, laughing. "Nothing romantic. It was more like getting on and off a moving bus very clumsily with the wrong foot and being left sprawling in the road with your hat crooked and your stockings muddy, feeling a fool. . . . For weeks I wasn't sure whether to go back or not. But I just didn't. I drifted away somehow. There wasn't what's known as a clean break."

"Well, I think it was frightfully brave of you," said Marigold vaguely, losing interest. "I'd never dare. . . ."

She pushed her hair back carelessly with one hand and it fell once more into its apparently careless, inevitable arrangement of curls. She took a few steps towards the middle of the room and stood still again, with the dull yellow light from the ceiling full on her fresh silvery skin and greenish gold-shot dress. In this claustrophobic lugubriously human room she looked strange, nymph-like, imprisoned. Her unfathomable individuality of appearance belonged to no period of fashion in looks, seemed independent of care, effort and artifice. She hasn't once glanced in a mirror or fussed with her frock the whole evening. . . . What's she thinking about?

"I s'pose we must rejoin the giddy throng," she said finally.

She sighed deeply, slipped her hand through Olivia's arm, and walked with her up the long empty passage, humming softly. They said nothing more. There was not another word to say.

She's rather bored with me, after all. . . . She made a false step with me. So she's finished; indifferent now. It's ten years ago, and these efforts to recapture . . . a mistake, really. She'd like to yawn. It's been a failure, she won't try again.

This is the last time we'll ever be alone together.

The gentlemen had rejoined the ladies in the drawing-room.

Rollo. . . . He was leaning against the mantelpiece, talking to George. Directly they came in he glanced towards them, glanced away again, went on talking with apparent absorption. The other men were standing about: the evening had not settled down yet. Lady Spencer was sitting opposite Aunt Blanche at the backgammon table, in the middle of the room. Busily they rattled their dice, not looking up. This is the first time I've seen her relaxed, absorbed in a private diversion, not on the *qui vive*, not ready aye ready, official and in control. She looked less old and worn now, her pale face had smiles beneath it. She's beating Aunt Blanche.

Madame de Varenne was in the room again now; sitting in an upright, high-backed chair, not far from Mary, smoking a small cigar and staring at the fire.

Rollo? . . . Surely he hasn't finished with me for the evening. . . . The old familiar sense of loss, of insecurity swept over her.

"Oh, there you are!" cried Mary, laying down her work and staring at them. Her face with its prettyish, loose, trivial moulding seemed to reach out like a sea anemone. "I thought you'd been spirited away."

"Did you?" said Marigold, with marked languor, taking up *Country Life* and examining a page of properties for sale.

"Up to mischief?"

"Mm, rather. We've been arranging a murder, haven't we, Livia? I've often thought I should make a first-class murderess. It's all a question of selecting a victim. And I *think*—I *think* . . . I—have selected—mine. . . ."

Rollo, still leaning against the mantelpiece, turned his head slightly, as if listening. Olivia caught his eye; he smiled, almost imperceptibly. The French eyes had shifted too, were resting on Olivia and Marigold, but there was no flicker in their blackness. Could she hear? Was she observing?

"Marigold! Rollo!" called Lady Spencer from her table, shooting a casual arrow of duty without looking up. "Does any one want to play bridge? . . . Double."

"Does any one want to play bridge?" repeated Marigold gloomily. "Hands up for not on your life," she added in a mutter to Olivia, flinging up an arm in a ribald waving gesture.

"Yes, now, who's game for a rubber?" called out Mary, looking hopeful. "Harry'll play if he's needed, won't you, Harry? Who else is feeling energetic?" There was no answer, and she added winningly: "Who'll be my partner?" She put her head on one side and looked up at Rollo.

He detached himself from his support and lounged across to Olivia's side.

"Play bridge?" he said.

"No, I don't. Don't know how. But don't bother about me. I shall be quite happy."

"With a photograph album," said Marigold.

"Must I play bridge with Mary?" groaned Rollo under his breath.

"No." Marigold leaned against him, fingering his studs, looking dreamy. After a moment she said: "Stay and talk to Olivia and seem as if you weren't paying attention to anything else in the room. Don't take your eyes off her, and if Mary calls out, be deaf."

"I can do all that."

She left them rapidly and went over to the fireplace.

"She'll manage it," said Rollo. He turned his back on the company, and leaning an elbow on the piano, bent an amused unwinking gaze upon Olivia. "Please look as if we were discussing philosophy . . . or something. . . . Olivia, are you enjoying yourself?"

"Yes, Rollo."

"Tell me something else. Shall we meet in London?"

"Yes, Rollo. Yes."

"Good. Good. Now ask me something."

"Where's Lucy?"

"You've got that dog on your mind. Sh! Asleep in her maiden basket behind the sofa. She turns in at ten sharp, thank

God, no matter what's happening. So after the hour has struck, I can range at will."

"I noticed you seemed freer."

"Much freer. Is anybody noticing us?"

"Your father. He looks as if he'd like to talk to you."

He turned quickly at that, and Sir John who had come to a halt in his slow walk towards them, as if uncertain of his welcome, now trod ponderously forward again and joined them.

"Hallo, Daddy."

"Hallo, my boy." He stood in front of them, creaking, breathing deeply.

"What you going to do with yourself?"

"Absent me . . . absent me from felicity." The last word was almost imperceptibly blurred.

"I should."

"I might go and smoke a pipe in the library. Then bed, I think, eh?"

"That's right, Daddy. Cut along. I'll look in on you later."

Affection flowed between them, warmly, as in the old days, but now its quality was changed; was protective, indulgent, tender in Rollo, and in his father tinged with a sort of doubt and appeal, as if he felt a bit lost, liked simply to be near Rollo.

He stood as if weighted down into the carpet.

"We were discussing the Polish question," said Rollo.

"Ah," said Sir John. "Ticklish . . ." and the melancholy inert mass of his face lost its fixity, lifted and became mobile with amusement over its whole surface. Now they smiled all together, feeling at ease, intimate, making an isolated, conspiratorial ring in the room. If Mary had noticed, she'd have called out: "What's the joke?"

Sir John said, without warning: "Do you like heliotrope?"

"Very much."

"So do I."

"I don't seem to see it often nowadays."

"Nor do I. I don't know how it is. Old-fashioned taste, I suppose. . . . We bring forth this sort of thing by the ton." He jerked his head towards a large tub of chrysanthemum and poinsettia. "Elaborate vegetation . . . Not flowers to my mind."

"Well, I admire them awfully. Only perhaps a bit too prosperous. . . ."

They laughed.

"A bit too prosperous." Indistinct again. "Yes," Sir John meditated, his eyes on her. . . . Wondering where on earth I've sprung from, if he knows me. . . . What about the women in *his* life? He must have been a handsome man, virile, well set-up, like Rollo. What memories were shut in his head, or what had he forgotten? *Dear dead women with such hair too.* . . . What old once-battering secrets between him and her alone? Or was it all plain sailing?—a straightforward uneventful history of monogamy, duty, fatherhood . . .? It was all nearly over. His time was past.

Answering her smile he said finally: "Know this part of the world?"

"She's a neighbour, Daddy." Patient voice. "Little Compton she lives."

"Ah, yes. Little Compton. . . . So you live at Little Compton. I don't often have occasion to go that direction nowadays. If I remember rightly, my old friend Charles Curtis had a house there."

"Yes. He still has. He's my father."

"What, you Charles Curtis's girl? . . . Bless my soul, how time flies. Well. . . . Very nice for my old friend Charles Curtis."

"Thank you." She gave the correct smile.

"Very able man . . . and what's better and rarer, a very witty man. Used to be. Sorry to hear not so fit as he was."

"No. Poor darling, he's a great invalid these days."

"Ah, very sorry indeed to hear that. Hard luck for an active fellow like him. Can he—can he get about pretty well, eh?"

"No. Not very well. Not just now, anyway."

He shook his head in melancholy. "Poor fellow. You give him my greetings. . . . Mm."

"I will indeed."

He was thinking: I'm still active on my feet: not like Charlie Curtis.

He laid a large lean vein-corded hand on Rollo's shoulder and said:

"What about a ride to-morrow?"

"Yes, Daddy, thanks. I rather thought of a short one before breakfast if the weather holds up."

"Good. I'll get a message to Naylor."

"I did, Dad. Save you trouble."

Sir John nodded.

"Wish I could come with you." His face puckered into a smile, unconscious of pathos. "Think I won't, though."

"I shouldn't. I wouldn't be so hearty myself, only I must get back to London by lunch-time."

"Must you? Hoped you could stay over to-morrow. Sure?"

"Afraid it's impossible, Daddy. I've got an appointment."

"Pity. Ah, well. . . ."

Sir John nodded again and raised a hand, sketching an awkward gesture of farewell. His face drooped again; carefully he set himself in motion and disappeared through the double doors.

Marigold caught Rollo's eye and made a reassuring grimace; and he and Olivia went back to the fireplace. Mary was stitching away, her eyes bent on her work, her mouth pressed in a sour twist. Marigold was lying on the arm of her godmother's chair, one arm flung across the lean purple-brocaded shoulders. The cigar was puffing furiously. Sir Ronald was in the act of dropping his monocle and putting on a pair of glasses to examine the Gainsborough—a long-necked young woman in rose-coloured satin, with high arching brows and protuberant slanting eyes; graceful, lively, fragile.

"Beautiful bit of painting," he murmured. His large up-turned pink-moon face looked beatific. "You know, Rollo, m'boy, I consider vis the finest fing in the house—one of ve finest examples in England, what's more. On a small scale, but it's masterly. I'm not sure vough—I'm not altogevver sure it's hung in ve right place. I've never been sure it does itself ve highest justice here. I've an idea I'd like it on ve end wall vere between ve cabinets. . . . I've an idea I would. . . ."

"Would you?" said Rollo politely.

"By Jove!" cried Harry, with awestruck frantic zest, "I do believe you're right."

He stared first at the picture, then at the wall, then at the company, his jaw dropping with the intensity of his interest. But his enthusiasm fell flat into a disregarding silence. He continued to stand and stare, straddled on his little thick legs, stretching up his short red neck until the roll of fat above his collar swelled out like inflated rubber.

Scenting collapse, mistrusting her children, Lady Spencer now called once more through the click of counters: "No bridge to-night?"

"Not to-night, Mum. Everybody's lazy," called Marigold quickly; adding, to deflect attention: "Who's winning over there?"

"Your mother," said Aunt Blanche, with bitterness. "She's had every scrap of the luck. I never saw anything like it."

"*Luck*, dear?" said Lady Spencer sweetly, shifting and discarding with intent glee.

"You always were *revolting* at games."

"How pretty it looks," said Olivia, looking across at the board with its long narrow red and black triangles and piled shining counters.

Marigold leaned forward and pulled her down beside her on the broad chair-arm. Madame de Varenne turned her head and, through the faint smoke-screen of the cigar between her teeth, scrutinised her unwinkingly. After a few moments she remarked in a harsh crackling monotone:

"C'est un visage assez bien fait."

"N'est ce pas?" cried Marigold, nodding vigorously.

"Mais l'autre là bas. . . ." She jerked her cigar towards Mary. "Je la trouve assommante, hein?"

Again Marigold nodded, her eyes dancing. She put her lips to her ear and said:

"Specimène très mal réussi."

"Quelle banalité. . . . Mon Dieu!" She removed her cigar, and a long sigh, as of unutterable scorn and boredom, stirred her shrunken, padded-looking breast. After a moment she continued:

"Mais qu'est-ce qu'elle vient donc faire ici, cette petite?"

"Aha! Aha! Voilà!" cried Marigold, leaning on her god-mother's shoulder, playing with one of her ornaments, a heavy cross of diamonds and topaz. "Voilà ce que je me demande!"

She laughed at Olivia out of the corners of her eyes. . . . Not saying: She is my friend of childhood. . . . Not including me in her laughter . . . leaning away, remote, mocking, estranged. . . . Now she looks like a pretty rat.

A cold menacing wind blew round the hearth. These people are not my people. I don't want to come here any more. . . . Rollo. . . . I'll tell him I must go. . . .

Harry had buttonholed him and was saying cheerily:

"I say, old man, you know all about these things . . . be a good chap and give me a tip. . . ." Something about a shooting syndicate. . . . But Rollo was cool, off-hand.

Poor Harry, he wasn't at ease either in this house. Looks of indifference, of suppressed irritation, well-mannered rebuffs appeared his lot. Was he aware? Did he complain in the bed-room, over the collar studs, the black tie; worry away on his side of the double bed? Did Mary rally him, comfort him?— or snub him impatiently, with scorn, deploring her mate, wishing in her heart for another face upon the pillow? . . . A natural bore: every gesture and intonation revealed him pure-bred, true blue; but something more separated him from the rest of them: something deeper: Harry was not out of the

top drawer. . . . Mary—possibly a little past her first hopeful
bloom—had married out of, say, the third drawer down: her
father's agent?—her brother's tutor?—her mother's secretary?
. . . Relatives had turned the smooth public face of acceptance
upon her choice, for the sake of the family, for dear Mary's
sake . . . ?

He didn't look a happy man, but on the whole he looked
more assertive, more gratified than anxious. Tufts of sandy
hair sprouted out of his ears and nostrils; and his thin lips
stretched smirkingly beneath the bags of his cheeks and the
pink beaky little nose. . . . What could it be like to go to bed
with him? . . . Something tough, reptilian, was in him, something scaly and resilient, something between a turtle and a
salmon. . . . He and she had the same light blue eyes, pouchy,
rapacious.

"Il est beau, Rollo, hein?" croaked an abstract voice behind
her ear.

"Très beau."

"En voilà un au moins qui n'a rien d'ignoble de sa personne.
A votre âge il m'aurait fait faire des folies."

Olivia looked at her, dubious, smiling; and all at once she
smiled back, an irresistibly moving smile, spontaneous,
friendly, humorous, lighting her face, her past. . . .

"Elle est gentille," she remarked to Marigold after a pause,
making the bare statement.

Olivia put out her hand and gave hers with its long fingers
and encrusted rings and bracelets a quick pressure.

Warmth started to creep in again round the hearth. It was
all right after all. Only one of those moments. . . .

"Comme on est triste ce soir!" Her voice was lively,
taunting. "Ronald, viens donc ici me raconter quelque-chose.
. . . Et toi, Rollo, qu'est-ce que tu fais là a te gratter le menton?
Voici une demoiselle qui s'ennuye horriblement auprès de moi.
Tu n'a rien a lui proposer?"

"Mais beaucoup de choses. . . ."

Ceasing to yawn and rub his shoulders against the mantelpiece he leaned forward and pulled Olivia to her feet, keeping his hand through her arm.

"Zero hour," said Marigold.

She jumped up suddenly and went to George, saying:

"Darling George, come and see the kittens."

"Kittens?" said George. "Rather, Marigold."

"Nothing jollier than a two-months old kitten," said Harry.

"Oh, these haven't got their eyes open," said Marigold. "They're not worth seeing, only George loves kittens."

"Harry," broke in Mary sharply, "you might fetch me my jacket from my room, will you? The black velvet one. It's in the wardrobe. I feel a bit chilly. I don't know if there's a draught or what. I may have caught a chill this afternoon. I got my feet so wet in that long grass, and I always get a chill if I get my feet wet."

"Better turn in with a hot-water bottle," suggested Harry.

"No." Peevish. "I'll be all right. Just fetch my jacket."

"Right."

Dutifully, without alacrity, Harry made off.

"Try a hot lemon and whisky," said George kindly. "Nothing like it."

"Ugh! no." She made a face of disgust. "Lemon always upsets me, and I simply can't *touch* whisky. It makes me sick."

"Who's got a cold?" called Lady Spencer from her table, not looking up. "Ammoniated quinine. . . ."

"Oh, come on," said Marigold, still with her arm through George's. "We don't want to keep the poor kittens up till midnight."

"Are you interested in kittens?" said Rollo to Olivia.

"Very interested."

"They're only ordinary little tabby ones," said Marigold, "but you shall see them."

Mary followed the departing procession with a goggling stare.

"Oh, what time is it?" said Marigold yawning, collapsing

on a chair in the ante-room. "It feels like three o'clock. I want to go to bed and pick my toes."

"I must go home," said Olivia.

"No, no," said Rollo quickly. "Marigold's remarks were purely rhetorical, weren't they, Maggie? Now we've managed to shed the husks at last, we can start the evening."

"Then I must have a drink," said Marigold, with her eyes shut. She's so bored she could die. Hopeless, all of them. . . .

"Where are the kittens?" asked George.

"The kittens? . . . Oh, the kittens!" Marigold sat up, looking tragic. "Oh, George! There was such a disaster. I didn't like to tell you before. Those poor little darlings . . . ten of them . . . they were all born dead."

"Good God!" said George, shocked, fond of animals.

"It was for the best, George."

"The fact is, George," said Rollo, "they didn't really come to anything, poor devils."

George looked blank, then his face cleared.

"Oh, I get there. . . ." He broke into a slow prolonged guffaw. "Aaah, ha, ha, ha, ha, ha, ha! Subterfuge, eh?"

"Aren't we ones?" cried Marigold. She got up and gave him a hug. But when he tried to keep his arm round her, rapidly she detached herself.

Olivia said to him: "Do you still hunt?"

"Me?" He looked surprised. "Oh . . . off and on, you know. . . . Whenever I can."

"George is a man of affairs nowadays," said Rollo. "Sport's loss has been the city's gain."

"And the fox's opportunity," said Marigold.

"You don't remember me." Olivia beamed on him.

A spasm went over his face. He gathered himself together suspiciously, stubborn, alarmed.

"N-no. . . . I'm afraid. . . . I car't say I do."

"Never mind. I'm glad. Because the last time we met you were obliged to correct me. You did it very kindly considering. I've never forgotten."

"Good Lord! . . . Me? . . . You must be thinking of some other bloke, eh?"

"George never spoke harshly to a woman in his life," said Rollo, "unless she'd done something unpardonable in the hunting-field."

"This was in the hunting-field. A bad toss."

"Another leg-pull, eh?" George's face cleared, ready for a laugh.

"What are you talking about?" said Marigold with another yawn. "I want a drink. Drinks in the hall."

She sprang up, opened the lid of the wireless cabinet, turned knobs, swooped through a range of snarls, whoops, wails, and opened out full blast on a jazz band.

"Hamburg."

She floated out in front of them, pausing for a second on her way to snatch up a large, smiling, plump débutante's photograph of herself and whisk it face to the wall.

In the hall, among the antlers and skin rugs, the Spanish chests and chairs, the music beat insistently through the open door. Marigold began to hum and sway, glass in hand; then draining it and setting it down, put both hands on George's shoulders and danced him off.

Drinking a whisky and soda, Rollo watched her a minute or two, standing beside Olivia. Then:

"Dance," he said, putting an arm round her.

After a turn or two he gave a sigh, as if weary or impatient.

"Why do you sigh?"

"Did I? Sorry. Bad habit."

He went on turning and swaying with the soft, subtle balance and rhythm of a good dancer. After a bit he said suddenly:

"Let's get away . . . mm?"

It sounded so rapid, toneless, odd, in spite of the questioning inflection—as if it had slipped out unawares, unconsciously almost. . . .

"Get away. . . . Do you want to?"

"Do you?" He looked down at her, not smiling. Uncertain, disturbed, she hesitated; and after a moment he gave a brief laugh.

"No. Never mind. Don't know what I'm talking about. . . . One can't, anyway, can one?"

"I suppose not." I'm not helping him, I'm stuck. . . . "At least I suppose one can . . . a bit . . . if one wants." . . . Careful, be careful. . . . But he's waiting. I must say something. "It depends if one has ties—that are going to stop one. . . ."

"*That* depends on oneself, doesn't it?" he said quickly. "Whether one's going to let 'em. . . . They needn't. . . ."

"Needn't they . . . ?"

"There are occasions—very rare ones—when I personally shouldn't let them. . . . It would be all right, absolutely, from my point of view. . . . What about you?"

"Well, I can't judge. I haven't any ties."

"None?"

"I'm on my own—entirely."

"You're lucky."

"I don't always think so. *You* are. . . ."

"I'm not sure."

"Why not?"

"Well, I want something—and I'm not sure if I'm going to be able to get it."

"I expect you get most things you want."

The voices were so light, quick, toneless, answering each other, they might have been repeating something trivial learnt by heart. They went on dancing, mechanically, not looking at each other now. She felt her heart beating and his hand just quivering. What's happened? All's been said. Hush, put it away now, not another word. It's not to be true yet.

Presently he said in a drowsy peaceful voice:

"People do manage to come across each other once in a blue moon. . . . It beats me how, considering the population of the globe."

She laughed, feeling happy suddenly, peaceful too.

"The whole thing beats me," he said. "It isn't as if one went about sort of looking for it in a business-like way. . . . One had given up worrying too much about all that—given up feeling young and excitable and all that. . . . Put the stopper on. Told oneself to lock up and turn in."

"Who's one?"

He laughed. His words, his new soft easy alarming manner burrowed and lodged, hiding in her mind, too insinuating—decisive—too . . .

"I ought to go now."

"Yes. I'll take you home now."

"Are you going to take me?"

"Of course I am."

So it's going to be true. I can't stop it.

She became aware again of Marigold and George. They were at the drinks table and Marigold was saying in a quarrelsome, insistent way:

"Why shouldn't I? I'm not tight. What makes you think I'm tight? George keeping an eye on my drinks! I like that, I must say! I should hide the next one or pour it away. Save me, George, save me! The demon drink's got me!" She drank off a stiff whisky and soda and said more peaceably: "I am a bit tight—but no more. I wish I was blind—and I would be if I was anywhere but in my own home. There's something about the roof-tree that makes it impossible to get absolutely roaring. I must confess to you, George, I've had enough to make me, what with one nip and another—but it's working the wrong way or something. I'll be sick if I go on or start to boo-hoo and you'll have to put me to bed. And you'd hate that, wouldn't you, George?"

"I wouldn't mind," he said.

"Well, I would. I don't want to be beastly, but I *really* would. You *are* one of my oldest, dearest friends, George, but I simply would *hate* to be put to bed by you. Oh dear! I don't feel a bit witty or exulting or anything. . . . Don't let's dance any more, for God's sake. It's *too* idiotic padding round and round and round . . . like those two. . . . Oh, no, they're not any more." She handed her glass to Rollo. "Give me another, Rollo, darlin'."

Rollo took the glass.

"Just a minute," he said mildly. "Olivia wants one."

"Sorry, sorry, Livia! . . . Manners." She shook her head.

"I don't want anything, thank you," said Olivia.

"Try a drop of this," said Rollo, firmly, pouring out Irish whisky. "Good for you. Warm you up for your drive. Look, I'll mix it with a dash of ginger ale and you'll love it."

"Gimme the same," said Marigold, sitting in a high-backed arm-chair, with her eyes shut.

"Right."

He poured out half a glass of neat ginger ale. "Here."

She took it, drank it, waited a moment and suddenly laughed.

"You old stoat," she said. "You're enough to make a cat laugh."

"Marigold, I must go now."

"Is Rollo going to take you?"

"Yes, I am."

"If it isn't too much bore."

Marigold lay back again, eyes shut, rolling her head to and fro on the chair back.

"Oh, *no*, it's not a *bore* for Rollo. He's looking forward to it. And you'll be *perfectly* safe with him because he's *dead* sober—and never does anything he oughtn't. He's so tactful too—quite extraordinarily tactful and temp—temp—what's the word?"

"Temperamental," said Rollo. "Tempestuous."

"No. Not that. That's petticoats."

She opened her eyes, sat up and smiled sweetly at all their watching faces.

"Well, I don't give a hoot," she said, "you're a lot of old

cows. You ought to wear caps and mittens. I don't want a drink anyway. And when I do I'll have one."

She sat there smiling to herself, curving and lifting her spine, her long full neck, serpentine, secretive—like a smooth-fleshed strong serpentine white and green plant—indescribably shrouded and somnolent-looking—like an arum lily. . . .

"Must you really go, darlin'?" She got up, stumbled a little and giggled. "I wish you wouldn't go."

"I'll just look in on Daddy," said Rollo, "and bring the car round. While you do the good-byes."

"Don't hurry the girl," said Marigold. She put an arm round Olivia. They were the same height, dark and blonde. "We'll go entwined," she said, "like two dearest female friends —as we are, as we are. Livia, you might keep your arm round me unob—unobstentatiously. I don't want to fall down at Ma's feet. Do I reek? Give me a cigarette. There now." She went off into helpless laughter. "*Don't* look so helpful and understanding. I'm as sober as an owl. Good-bye, George! The party honestly is over, darlin', and you might as well stagger off to bed."

"Right you are," said George equably. "Good-night. Just help myself to a night-cap."

"My aim is to lose George," murmured Marigold, glancing backward as they left the hall.

He looked lonely all by himself, receding at the other end of the enormous room, his simple round oil-sleeked head gleaming, his stiff shirt stark and blank, his neat shoulders rigid above the table, patiently squirting a siphon—expecting nothing after all these years of being in love with Marigold; waiting for nothing but his drink.

In the drawing-room, Sir Ronald was playing a gentle Scarlatti tinkle upon the piano. Madame de Varenne had gone and so had Mary. The sisters were still at the backgammon board, but play was over. They were piling and putting away counters, and talking in low sisterly gossiping tones.

"Olivia's come to say good-bye," said Marigold.

"Oh! . . . Olivia dear. . . ." Lady Spencer got up and took Olivia's hand in both her own. "My dear, this has been such a very great pleasure. Now we've found you we're not going to lose sight of you again so easily—are we, Marigold? Next time Marigold's with us we must try and arrange . . . we must telephone. . . ." She looked a little vague. "I expect you'll be coming down quite often, won't you, dear—to see your father?"

"Yes, I shall try."

"That's good. Your mother must be so glad to have you within reach. I know what a difference it can make. . . . Now I wonder if the car . . . Marigold, does Benson know, dear?"

Marigold, leaning on the piano, absorbedly watching her uncle's hands, was deaf, and Olivia said, with some loss of confidence:

"I think—Rollo said very kindly—he'd take me home."

"Ah! . . . Rollo's taking you. . . . *That's* all right then."

But did it quite do? . . . Not quite. Barely perceptible, the contraction of tone, the addition of emphasis to simple cordiality. . . . Or is it my guilt?

"I do hope he doesn't mind. It seems such a bore for him."

"Oh, no, I'm *sure* it's not. Rollo so enjoys a spin . . . and then I dare say he thought. . . . Dear old Benson, he's getting old. He's been with us thirty years. . . it's hard to realise. . . . Rollo's so considerate."

So considerate. . . . All the same if there weren't something not quite . . . not quite about me—something that's such a pity and explains why I'm not living with my husband—I'd have shaken hands all round in grateful affection and been removed according to formula by the chauffeur.

"How I wish," said Lady Spencer, "you could have met our dear Nicola."

Rollo came in, looking large and powerful with his overcoat on; and she said, laying her firm, strong white hand on his shoulders:

"I was just saying, dear, if only Nicola could have been with us. I should so have liked her and Olivia to meet."

"Yes," said Rollo, in a filial uncoloured way.

"She has such horrid headaches," Lady Spencer sighed. "I want her to see this new Austrian doctor Aunt Blanche has been telling me about."

"Oh, really?" said Rollo pleasantly. "I should think she'd love to. . . . Seeing new doctors is Nicky's pet hobby."

"I hear he's done some wonderful cures. He does all these modern scientific tests, you know. I always feel they *must* be on the right lines. I think they'd give her confidence. Well, Olivia dear——" She bent forward and bestowed a kiss briskly, closing that unfruitful passage. "My love to your mother— and dear Kate."

"Look me up in London some time, do," said Aunt Blanche. "Be jolly to see you."

"Tell Parr not to wait up for me," said Rollo to his mother. "I'll let myself in and lock up."

Marigold, murmuring "Wait for me in the hall," darted ahead and vanished.

Olivia went out with Rollo at her side. Glancing back for a moment at the door (but Lady Spencer was not looking, not sending after her a last smile), she took in the scene once more as in a painting—static: interior with figures. Now I've fixed it, to remember. In case this is the last of it for me.

"Marigold said wait," said Olivia by the front door.

"What for?" said Rollo. "This your coat?" He took up her mother's musquash from the settee where it lay folded. "It goes against the grain to extinguish you," he said, holding it, staring at her. "I love white. Dark ladies in white dresses."

He helped her into the heavy unyielding old coat and wrapped it round her.

"I wonder how one acquires these tastes," he said. "They seem to get into one's system unawares."

"I expect you once had a nice dark nurse in a white apron."

"I never thought of that. . . . Of course, that explains it."

Nicola wore white satin . . . with her knot of dark polished hair.

Marigold came running downstairs, wrapped in a long mink coat, the broad full circular collar turned up over her curls in a kind of hood. She called out hurriedly as she ran, to counteract Rollo's look of unwelcoming surprise:

"Rollo, will you go out by the south gate and drop me?"

"Drop you where?"

"Just a little way on. I'll tell you."

Avoiding their eyes she came on and opened the front door.

"What d'you want to do? Go for a walk or something?" He was annoyed.

"No. I want to see somebody."

"Who?"

She turned on him irritably. "Oh, can't you do what I ask without—— It isn't much to ask." She went down the steps, got into the back of the car, and said from within, reluctantly but more quietly, "As a matter of fact I want to see Timmy. Now come on, do."

"Get in, Olivia." He settled himself behind the steering-wheel, started the engine running, and said, still crossly: "Who on earth's Timmy?"

"Blind?" said Olivia.

"Yes." Her voice was grateful. "Olivia remembers. You know he's ill, I suppose—or didn't it penetrate?"

"Oh, Lord, yes. The chap they were talking about at lunch to-day."

"Yes."

He said more mildly: "But, Marigold, surely you can't go visiting an invalid at this hour?"

"Yes, I *can*!" she cried in a frenzy. "You don't suppose he *sleeps*, do you?—with a cough like he's got. . . ."

"Is he expecting you?"

She flung herself back in rigid screaming silence; and in silence they started off.

The moon was near the full, the night was windless, clouded, grey, with a smell of mist in the air, and decaying leaves.

Through the park, out by the south lodge, then between hedgerows along a narrow winding road.

"Stop here," said Marigold suddenly.

He slowed down and pulled up.

"This doesn't seem to be anywhere."

"Yes, there's a stile, look, and a path through the field into the side of the garden. I don't want to stop with a flourish at the front door, do I?—and blow the horn?"

"All right, all right."

She got out of the car and stood in the road.

"What a queer night. . . ."

She lifted her head, breathed out a great sigh. Above the frame of fur her face floated insubstantial, a livid papery disc, phosphorescent-looking, marked in with black stains for eyes, lips, nostrils. . . .

"I don't know yet if I'll go," she said. "I don't quite know what I'll do. I'll just see. . . . I might not feel like seeing him after all. You go on."

"Do you want to be picked up again?"

"No, I don't. I want to walk home."

Their voices dropped out flat on to the air, answering each other in the distilled, impersonal, mourning way of human voices at night. Still looking upwards, Marigold called absently:

"Good-night, Olivia."

"Good-night, Marigold."

He put the clutch in and slowly, softly drew away from her. She stood by the roadside, not moving, and the corner hid her.

"What'll she do?" said Olivia.

"God knows. . . . There's the house in there."

They saw a light burning in what appeared to be a kind of wooden hut or shelter on the lawn, and farther back the white shape of a small square house, half-concealed by fruit-trees.

"There's a light."

"I saw him once, I remember him very well. He came to that dance, and I danced with him. What's the matter with him?"

"Lungs. Started about a year ago. They're frightfully badly off. Mother tried to get him to let her send him to Switzerland—or a sanatorium somewhere, but he refused point-blank. He won't move. She had the hut built for him and he just lies there. Won't be nursed or let anybody do anything for him. Won't see his child and keeps his wife away as much as he can."

"Doesn't he want to get better?"

"Doesn't sound like it." He made a movement of discomfort. "He's pretty bad, I believe. Poor devil. I never saw much of him, but he seemed an awfully nice chap. . . . I don't suppose he clings madly to life. . . . Though you're always told the blind are so cheerful."

"And consumptives so hopeful."

"I didn't know she knew him as well as that. . . ."

"I don't know how well she knows him. . . ."

No one would ever know.

A sudden impulse? . . . a deliberated plan! . . . Out of love? . . . pity? . . . curiosity? . . . No one would ever know what had been, what was between them. Emotional images, fragments of dialogue came to mind. "Timmy, it's me. . . ." "Marigold! I knew you'd come." "Of course I came." "I wouldn't let them move me, in case you did. . . ." "Timmy, darling, I love you, you're not to die. . . ." That kind of thing? Or was she hurrying away now, panic-stricken, from his death, from the destructive element? . . .—which is hers too, which she'll never escape, which they recognised in each other, long ago, dancing and joking. . . .

"What a witless thing to do, though," muttered Rollo.

"Probably finish him." He was silent, than added, "I'll say for my sister, she knows how to make herself felt."

"What can it be like to be married to her?"

"What indeed? Beats me how any one had the nerve to take it on. Plenty of quite sensible people seemed to want to though. . . ."

"Of course. Everybody would want to. You see, it's the illusion she gives. . . ."

"What illusion?"

"Of being free, I suppose. Escaping, getting free. People see she's got loose, she's off. . . . They want to run after her, make a grab to catch her. . . ."

"You've been reading *The Green Hat*," he said after reflection. "Though I see what you mean . . . All the same she won't really come a cropper. She's a jolly sight too clever. Besides, she likes Sam. They hit it off, more or less. Couple of lunatics. . . ."

"Are the children nice?"

"The children are divine," he said briefly.

Easy to imagine Rollo as favourite uncle—tossing them up, stuffing their money-boxes, generally indulging them. Surely not Rollo's choice, or fault, being childless? An obvious begetter. . . . He doesn't want to talk of Marigold any more. Dwindling now, she still obstructed them; left a vacuum they could not fill. They hung separated, cold and light—hollow people.

Down into the valley. Far below to the left, a sprinkling of late lights still spoke in the mist, from village windows. On the right, the beech coppice ran down steeply to the road: when Kate and I used to come on our bikes with a picnic tea, and sometimes the Martins came; or Marigold was allowed to meet us, riding over on her pony. We cut our initials with a penknife, each choosing a different tree, and said we'll come back to look in twenty years. . . . And I climbed, and Kate dug up plants—she never cared for climbing; and we brought our books and ate nut-milk bars and turned somersaults over the railings, and free-wheeled home again down the hill in the evening with primrose and white violet roots in our bicycle baskets, and dead leaves stuck to our backs and stockings; and the sunset going on, different every time, the other side of the valley. . . .

. . . All that was important: had made an experience of emotion more complex, penetrating and profound, yes, than getting married. . . .

Round the corner on the hill known in the family circle as The Bad Turn: perennial object of foreboding and suspicion to Mother, though innocent still of disaster. Down, past the first cottages, round past grandpapa's houses—those triple-fronted stucco eyesores. In the middle top window a light— the usual light that burned all night—the window of the youngest Miss Robinson. She was in there, hare's face, soft, narrow, ignoble, peering perhaps from behind the lace curtain with her wild, full, harmless eye, or lying flat on her back, whispering to the ceiling; or pacing up and down her room, laughing, crying by turns. Not dangerous at all: only very trying turns. She wouldn't do her hair or bother to dress. Go out, even for a second into the back garden, she would not; and write anonymous letters she occasionally did; only the post office Miss Robinson was generally able to intercept them: not obscene, but calvinistic, minatory, or in the style of warnings—straight tips from God's confidential agent: certain damnation pronounced on Winnie Pratt, the stationmaster's daughter, fornicatress; a message from the Lord to the young milkman; a hint, no more, to the vicar about Miss Sibley, his housekeeper, instrument of Satan. . . . Also they'd had to lock up the piano with its rose-silk fluted bodice, she made such a din on it in the middle of the night, at dawn—waking the neighbours. She'd cried bitterly at that—oh! how she'd cried! They'd thought of doing away altogether with the piano to spare her feelings, only it had always been there like in Dad's time and his father's before him: the place would seem funny without it. . . . Then she wasn't to be trusted with scissors—

not that she'd do herself a harm, but seemed as if she had to lay about with them on any bit of stuff—slicing, snipping, shredding—romping through the length and breadth of it. In fact it was with the cutting-out scissors the crisis had exploded five years back: Mrs. Uniack's new black moracain victimised all of a sudden one morning, just after the second fitting; Miss Robinson's professional career brought to an abrupt full stop. ... But she ate well: oh, yes, she enjoyed her food. Some days she felt a king.

Dark crouched the two old cottages facing the green, housing on the one hand Miss Toomer and Miss Mivart, sleeping light, never quite warm enough in bed, poking their noses up at the sound of a late car (what faces if they could see one coming back at midnight with Rollo); empty on the other of Major and Mrs. Skinner.

Oh, dear, awful Major Skinner, you're under the earth, you were never allowed to teach Kate or me to play golf. We never went to tea in your cottage among Mrs. Skinner's gold and purple cushions. . . . Brazen Winnie, scornful, ruthless girl, finished him off—sapping his means and strength with trips to Tulverton—shops, movies, cafés, movies, shops. Seeing her home late on foggy winter evenings was what got him down at last. The chill settled in his kidneys. "Rubbish: fit as a fiddle," he'd said the first week. "Cracked up, done for, good run for m' money, look after the dogs," he'd said the second; and during the third, Mrs. Skinner unostentatiously buried him, and vanished from Little Compton, leaving dozens of empty whisky bottles in the kitchen.

Nearly there now. . . . Is this all? Can't we get back to each other? Isn't it to be true after all?

"Straight on?" said Rollo, his voice sounding brusque after the long silence. He slowed down at the cross-roads.

"Yes, and then the next drive on the left, where all that shrubbery is. You won't drive in, will you?"

He drew up close to the fencing, under the laurel hedge; switched off the headlights.

"There. . . ." She waited a moment. "Good-night, Rollo. Thank you so much for bringing me. . . . It was a lovely evening. . . ."

He sat still and said nothing. He took out his case and lit a cigarette with deliberate movements. Then he said:

"When shall I see you again?"

"When do you want to?"

Answering him, with fingers already on the door-handle, she felt unwillingly flippant, rather shrill. He put his hand out and snatched hers back into her lap, saying with a hint of roughness:

"As soon as possible."

Overtaken, caught, punished. . . .

"All right," she said at last, sighing it out.

She turned slightly to look at him—the dark bulk beside her, head in profile, staring straight ahead, the short, high-bridged nose, small thick moustache, full rounded chin; the hand shadowy on his knee, holding a cigarette. The smoke wreathed up. Slowly he stubbed it out into the ash-tray. He said:

"Do you want to see me again?"

"Yes." I suppose so. . . .

"That's all right then." He took her twisting hand in his warm dry firm-clasping one. "You remember what I said—that I wanted something I wasn't sure I was going to get?"

"Yes, I remember."

His voice was so quiet, so calm-sounding, one had to listen, answer in the same way. . . . Think, think. . . . But there aren't any thoughts.

"Well, shall I?"

"Yes. . . . At least. . . . If you're sure. . . ."

"I'm sure. But you must be too."

I must be, too. . . . I must be sure. . . . What's the answer? . . . He said, more hesitatingly:

"Do you think you might be able—to like me a bit?"

"Oh, *yes*. . . ."

He whispered, "Oh . . . *darling* . . ." and pulled her towards him and began to kiss her.

Self-conscious . . . reluctant . . . appalled: Rollo Spencer, married man, Nicola's husband, stranger practically, Rollo *Spencer*. . . . What'll they say—Lady Spencer, Sir John . . . Mother, Dad, Kate. . . . All watching. . . . Wrong, disgusting —naughty girl, leading him on, a married man. . . . An enemy. . . . Ivor wasn't. . . . Why do I think of, stop thinking of Ivor . . . ?

He went on kissing her, whispering to her, floating her away. Names, faces, times and places slipped off the reel into darkness. Only his voice, face, hands, unknown—recognised—remained.

Head on his shoulder, as if it was all quite natural, quite suitable. . . . Dumb.

"You're so *young*," he said. "I never knew anything so young." His voice was full of pleasure. "You're like a young, young girl. . . ."

What did he expect? . . . A woman on my own, I said, not so young in years. . . . A woman of experience? . . . What did he suppose? Anxiety brushed her, the faintest breath, there and gone again. . . . He's not young. . . . So certain, so un-diffident. . . . Expert.

"I must go in now." Still my own voice.

"I'll see you to the door."

They got out of the car. He took her arm, keeping her close, and walked with her along the drive, his step on the gravel crunching out loud and firm. At the bend in the shrubbery, where the house came into view, he halted, looking towards the square solid shape of brick outlined with its stout neat chimneys in the moon.

"Is that your home?"

"That's my home."

He stood and looked at it. The bushes gave a momentary shallow stir and twitch, and an owl hooted.

"I'll say good-night to you here."

He pulled her gently out of range of her home's blank

square rows of eyes, put his hands along her cheeks and tilted her face up.

"What are you thinking about?"

"Nothing. I can't think."

"You're not afraid, are you?"

"No." She sighed.

"What then?" He had a kind, safe voice.

"I suppose I just can't believe it."

He smiled.

"You will soon, you know. You'll believe it in no time— I'll see that you do—and then you'll be used to it . . . and then perhaps you'll be tired of it. . . ."

"Don't say that. . . . Why do you say that?" She felt quickened, awake suddenly.

"It does happen, you know. . . . You might get bored with me in no time. . . ."

"So might you with me. . . ."

They kissed each other, in sad voluptuous disbelief, denial, acknowledgment.

"When did you think of this?" she said, smiling for the first time.

"As soon as I saw you." He smiled too.

"What d'you mean?"

"In the train. Just as I'd finished ordering the sausages—— No, before that, to be honest."

"When?"

"The first time we met. At that famous dance."

"I don't believe it!"

"Yes. On the terrace. I nearly kissed you then."

"Oh! You didn't! What nonsense!"

"Well, I certainly toyed with the idea. . . . I did think you were rather sweet."

"I'd as soon have thought of being visited by the Holy Ghost."

"Now who's talking nonsense?"

"Well, it *may—just*—have occurred to me it would be nice.

. . . But entirely on the Gary Cooper level. . . ." Laughter, confidence came easy now. "Specially as I was so peculiar that evening—so in a flux. . . . Seeing myself in dozens of distorting mirrors. . . ."

"You looked all right to me. You seemed like something cool and kind." His voice was serious, almost unhappy. "Like the wind on the terrace. Restful. . . ."

"Darling. . . ." Incredible, miraculous words.

"What's more, after that I even thought about you—definitely thought about you. Not often. Say twice a year. For no reason at all. Getting into the tube—or shaving—or talking rot to my neighbour at dinner. . . . You'd pop into my head and I'd think: 'I'd like to see her again. . . .'"

"I thought about you too. I always knew I should meet you again. It was like feeling excited suddenly in the middle of a sunny day—or a wet one—for no reason you can think of. . . . It's queer—this doesn't seem sudden a bit to me—does it to you?"

He laughed.

"Not in the least."

"We don't quite know *where* we're going now—do we?"

She waited. . . . Say: She doesn't count, she wouldn't care, that's over, I'm free for you. . . . But all he did was to shake his head quickly, faintly.

She said hurriedly:

"It doesn't matter." She had a pang of love for him. It was the shake of the head, helpless-looking.

"You see——"

What? He stopped, lifted her hand up and kissed it instead. Leave it alone.

"Are you happy?" she said.

He turned her hand over and kissed the palm; nodded.

"Of course I am."

"I always meant to be happy," she said. "I always thought some day I would be. I believed in it. . . ."

He took out his pocket-book and by the light of the match

she held, wrote down her London address and telephone number.

"I'll write to you," he said. "And if you want to get hold of me——" He scribbled on a blank page, tore it out and gave it to her. "That's my office. . . . Ring up there if you want me, will you?"

She took the paper. He means: there, not my home. Don't speak to me at my home.

"Lots of other engagements, I see." She smiled, seeing various jottings as he flicked the pages.

"They're nothing. They can all be scrapped. Nearly all." He shut the book. "My memory's rotten, I have to write everything down."

Nicola tells him what dinners and things to put down. She gave him his little book. A full social life, of course, lots of engagements—not like me. She dropped the match.

They kissed again. She listened to his step going tramping back again down the drive, so loud, collected, unconscience-stricken; waited for his car to start away; ran back into the house.

There was the awaited envelope, sitting on the hall table. *Put chain on door and remember landing light.* The variations had been slight, all these years. The jar of biscuits, the plate of apples and bananas. Only no thermos now, except when James was home. He liked Ovaltine, but the girls wouldn't touch it. A nice cup of cocoa then? Hot milk? . . . So good for you. . . . No, thank you, Mum. Not even Horlick's, which Olivia used to be really greedy for, which had so undoubtedly helped her to pass her Oxford exams. with flying colours. Of course, neither of them did much brainwork now. A pity, particularly in Olivia's case. A married woman with children has plenty to occupy her without improving her mind; but a pity all the same that neither of them appeared to take any interest in politics or the deeper kind of thought: still preferring Pip, Squeak and Wilfred, or that ridiculous Beachcomber, or any gossip column, to *The Times* leader or the foreign news. Pity. They were both girls with plenty of brains, if they cared to use them. Mrs. Curtis herself and Aunt May, too, had always believed in keeping abreast of the times in the broadest sense.

His hat, his cap and muffler on their pegs: no longer dumb creatures in pain, but homely symbols, their virtue restored, dozing peacefully, guarding the hall.

Nibbling a biscuit. . . . Around me the furniture frozen into night silence, friendly, estranged. . . . Kate, Mother, Dad, the maids asleep upstairs, the nurse, too, dozing in her chair probably—all of them unconscious of me, unconscious of the male step in the garden, the alien form by the shrubbery, deaf to branch listening, gravel speaking; to the two forms murmuring, clasping; to me hurrying away alone; flying from him, back to my home, back to myself, away from the two shapes in shadow; leaving them there: to be there now for ever, clasped, as I dreamed in the beginning they would one night be. This is with whom it was to be, and this is the night. Now I am back at the beginning, now begins what I dreamed was to be.

My own bedroom waiting, awake for me. . . . Peep in on Kate. Then a hot bath: float in water, warm water, softly dissolve; without one thought sink into sleep.

But something rustled on the landing: nurse going by on heelless slippered feet with a stir of starched skirts. . . . Without seeing she saw the broad haunches, brisk and trim, swinging down the passage, the broad short feet going hard down, flap flap on the heels in those blue bedroom slippers, trimmed beads and black fur.

She switched off the hall light, went softly upstairs, along the passage. At his door stood the white figure, waiting.

"Hallo! Had a nice time?"

"Lovely, thank you."

"That's right. It's nice to have a little change—good for you." The blue stone eye scanned Olivia up and down. . . .

Probably heard the car stop when it did, start again how long afterwards? . . . goodness knows. A good hour . . . perhaps two? And my face must be different. . . .

"How is he?" Anxious suddenly.

"Oh, all right. He's just had a little drink of hot milk with a drop of brandy. . . . He's been asking for you."

"Has he? Oh! Since when? Shall I go in?"

"Yes, I should. Just pop in for a tick. He'll settle off better."

The lamp, muffled with mother's dark green silk scarf, shone on the table by the fire. The bed in shadow. He lay on his back, propped on three pillows, eyes closed, exhausted. She went and stood beside him.

"Hallo, Dad——"

His eyelids lifted with an effort.

"Oh, it's you, is it?"

"I've been out to dinner—just back."

"Thought you'd gone away. . . ."

"No, no. Just to Meldon—to the Spencers. They sent you heaps of messages. They're so glad you're better."

"Hm. Jack Spencer. . . . Sick man. . . . Hm. . . ."

His unfamiliar grizzled sprouting jaws worked a little. . . . Presently he said, with his eyes shut:

"Let me see now. . . . How many children has Kate?"

"Four. Nice ones. I don't think you've seen the baby yet, have you?"

"No, I have not. . . . At least, I think not. . . . That husband of hers . . . he's all right, isn't he?"

"Yes, Rob's all right. He suits Kate. They understand each other, and get on."

He breathed out a deep sigh between his slack thin lips. Presently he said:

"Are you all right?"

"Yes, Dad. Of course I am." Still on his mind. "Don't you worry about me. I'm fine."

After a pause, he said with extreme diffidence:

"I forget for the moment what the exact position is. . . ."

He's been leading up to this.

"Between me and Ivor, you mean, Dad? Well, you know I don't live with Ivor any longer. It's all over. We separated —some time ago."

"No chance," he said apologetically, "of coming together again?"

"No. It was a bad mistake. We're best apart."

"Pity."

"Yes."

"To the best of my recollection he was a decent young chap. . . ." His voice was very weak.

"Yes, he was." Dad had taken to him, the few times they'd met. "Only we oughtn't to have married, that's all."

"I dare say you know best." Another sigh. "It seems unsatisfactory though. I wish . . ."

"Don't worry, darling. It'll work out. I'm awfully sorry to have been such a nuisance to you."

He waited; made a statement:

"I want you to be happy."

"I mean to be," she said quickly, moved. "Get better, and I'll be perfectly happy."

"Oh! . . ." He sighed irritably. "What's that got . . ." Soothing him, putting him off; when he was so tired too, when it was such an effort to say anything. . .

She bent down and said carefully:

"Listen. I will be happy. I promise you."

His eyelids moved slightly, as if in approval. He said, in a blurred way—rather like the other, like Rollo's father:

"No need to go regretting . . . suffering for things. Morbid. Remorse's nasty habit. Bad pol'cy. All make mistakes. You've got 'r life b'fore you."

"Yes, I know I have." Oh, yes! . . .

He tried again; but his mind, a burden painfully sustained on a bare knife-edge, began to topple. He couldn't quite finish. Feebly pompous, he pronounced:

"You can r'ly 'pon my co-operation. . . . Should've informed you sooner. . . . But I pr'cras'nate. . . ."

"Thank you, Dad. I'll remember. Good-night. Go to sleep now."

She kissed his forehead. . . . What a different kind of kiss . . . went out, closing the door noiselessly. He did not stir.

In the dressing-room adjoining, the white poised wing-spread of cap in the arm-chair by the fire. A tray with sandwiches, a thermos beside her. A book, the papers.

"Got all you want?" Olivia stood in front of the gorgeous fire and warmed the backs of her legs. . . . "She doesn't stint herself of coal; I must speak to her," said Mother. "Surely *half* the quantity these mild nights . . .?"

"Yes, thanks, I'm all right."

"I can't think how you manage to keep awake."

"Oh, well, you get used to it, you know. I do get a bit yawny-like towards morning. But I have a wee doze now and then. He doesn't need very much seeing to now."

"How is he, do you think?"

"Oh, he's all right. He's doing quite nicely."

"He's awfully patient."

"Oh, yes, he's quite good. I always say I'd rather nurse men when it comes to anything bad."

"He's so terribly weak."

"Oh, well, he would be that, of course. I dare say he'll pull up gradually. He'll have to go slow, of course, and take it easy. He won't ever be what he was before, I don't suppose."

"He looks much iller now than he did. But I suppose that's natural at this stage. . . ."

"M'm. . . ." That was enough about the patient. Anxiety in relations was natural, but a little went a long way. He was all right, she'd said so. "What a noise those owls do make here at night."

"Yes, we've always had a lot of owls—ever since I can remember. Don't you like them?"

"Can't say I do. Creepy sort of noise. I suppose you'd have nightingales here too, would you?"

"We once had a nightingale.... Every May, in the shrubbery by the drive." ... Just at that place. ... "But he doesn't come any more now. I don't know why. I suppose it's getting too suburban."

"M'm. Suburban you call this, do you?" She uttered a brief sharp laugh. "Of course, the country's all right for a bit—but I shouldn't care for it for long. My goodness, I should get blue! Specially in winter. I couldn't stick it. Give me London in winter. I love London."

"Do you? It's exciting, of course, but I don't love it. I'd far rather live in the country. Most of all in winter."

Oh, stop, awful voices, glib words rubbing, rattling against each other without hope, without illumination. ... Is it true, can it be true, what was said, felt, half an hour ago? Are the shapes still there, perfect as we left them, in the November night, in the garden just beyond these windows? Is the night still beautiful as it seemed—penetrated with moon, with warm leaf smell, cold smell of mist, secretly dying and living? Is it all nothing? Can it be defaced, deformed, made squalid by a voice? Could it be seen in some other way—in her way, not mine? ...

"I hope my next case will be in London."

"I do hope so. It must be dreadfully boring for you here."

"Oh, it's all in the day's work. You can't pick and choose."

"I suppose not."

"That's a nice frock. Suits you, that long line. I like white. Not that I wear it myself—get enough of it on duty—white, white, white—so I always go for a colour. But I always think white looks distinguished. You always notice a woman in white—I mean a well-dressed woman."

"I'm glad you like it." Oh, enough, enough. ... She yawned elaborately, stretched. "I'm sleepy, I must go to bed. Good-night, nurse."

"Want to undress here and warm your toes a bit?"

"Oh, thank you so much—it's sweet of you—but my sister told me to look in on her."

"I see."

The blue eye screwed down, cold, speculative, obscene. . . . Now what have *you* been up to? You're not the stand-offish sort, I know you. Come on now: no flies on me either. *Men!* *We* know 'em. . . . All after the one thing. I could tell you some spicy bits. . . .

Wasn't it what I thought? Was it coarse, furtive? Was it making myself cheap and allowing liberties? Was it a passing lust that he indulged, was it something with obscene words for it?

Quick, quick, get away. . . .

"Well, good-night, nurse. Have you got everything you want?" Ingratiating smile.

"Yes, thanks. Night-night."

The eyes stared, dropped, fastening quickly on the news-paper. . . . Baulked.

Kate.

She turned the handle and looked in. The bedside lamp was switched on, but Kate was fast asleep. She'd meant to stay awake, but sleep overcame her. She lay curled up on her side, the bedclothes tucked well round her, her face pink, childish, peaceful, pressed into the pillow, squashing her nose a little.

Why is she so touching—what makes her so adorable?

Nowadays, away from her own home, Kate slept soundly, taking a rest. In the bosom of her family, the broken nights, nights of light sleep—tremulous, full of queries: Did a child call out? Was it a night bird? Cattle lowing? Would that car starting up, those late loud voices wake the teething baby? . . . Yes? No? . . . Prepared to leap up in a flash, assuming calm alertness. . . . Yes? No? . . . falling into thin sleep again.

All the same she won't like it in the morning when she finds she succumbed unawares and left the light on; and that

I came in and switched it off without waking her. She'll think there's been a mean march stolen: she won't like it at all.

What luck she was asleep—married, innocent Kate. To-morrow I shall have grown a more solid mask, there won't be a crack in it.

My own bedroom, my bed. She stretched out her limbs, relaxed, heavy from the hot bath. One blessing about Dad's illness: the boiler got a late stoking, the water stayed hot all night. Safe, alone at last. Now, can I think about him, can I see what it is, what it will be? . . . Is he in yet, out of the dark? Is he falling asleep too, and thinking? . . . One or two images floated up, sharp, and gone again, bewildering: as if one had been shocked into paralysis, recovering now slowly, making a tentative sequence little by little. Or like coming round from an anæsthetic, repossessing by degrees one's identity. . . . Springs, long dry, beginning to stir, to flow again; the blood beginning to assert its life again; after years of unsharingness, of thinking: It isn't so important; no hardship to do without and not feel starved, repressed . . . at least, not often. . . .

Rollo, I haven't had a lover. There was nobody I fell in love with, I didn't try experiments: it was never worth it. Not because I'm cold, only because of love—because I believe in it, because I thought I'd wait for it, although they said schoolgirlish, neurotic, unfriendly. . . . It was because of you. . . .

I shall tell him all that. I'll tell him. . . . He'll say: I feel the same, it's worth not spoiling. . . . He'll say: Darling, I'm so glad. . . . If he were here now. . . . I want him here. . . . Once Ivor . . . I don't want to think of Ivor. . . . Once we stayed out very late on the river, we took off our clothes and bathed from the punt, he said how lovely you are, you're so smooth and white; it was the first time seeing each other naked. . . . Afterwards he cried a bit, why did he, it was a failure for him somehow, I had to comfort him. . . . I won't think about Ivor. . . . Once I went to bed early and he came up late from reading, and when I opened my eyes there he was looking at me: his face so moved, and sort of pitying, tender, watching me sleep, and I held my arms out. . . . We were married. Rollo's married to Nicola. . . .

Why do I, I don't want to, I won't think about Ivor. . . .

Rollo'll write me a letter. I'll find the envelope in London, and it'll be true, it'll be from Rollo. What sort of writing does his hand make, will it be speaking in his voice; saying darling, saying Olivia, darling, will you. . . .

Yes, I'll say. . . . Yes. Anything you say. Yes.

PART TWO

IT WAS THEN THE TIME BEGAN WHEN THERE WASN'T ANY TIME.
The journey was in the dark, going on without end or beginning, without landmarks, bearings lost: asleep? . . . waking?
. . . Time whirled, throwing up in paradoxical slow motion a
sign, a scene, sharp, startling, lingering as a blow over the
heart. A look flared, urgently meaning something, stamping
itself for ever, ever, ever. . . . Gone, flashed away, a face in a
train passing, not ever to be recovered. A voice called out,
saying words—going on, on, on, eternally reverberating . . .
fading out, a voice of tin, a hollow voice, the plain meaning
lost, the echo meaningless. A voice calling out by night in a
foreign station where the night train draws through, not
stopping. . . .

There was this inward double living under amorphous
impacts of dark and light mixed: that was when we were
together. . . . Not being together was a vacuum. It was an
unborn place in the shadow of the time before and the time
to come. It was remembering and looking forward, drawn
out painfully both ways, taut like a bit of elastic. . . . Wearing. . . .

There were no questions in this time. All was agreeing,
answer after answer melting, lapsing into one another: "Yes";
"Yes, darling"; "Yes"—smiling, accepting, kissing, dismissing.
. . . No argument, no discussion. No separate character any
more to judge, test, learn by degrees. He was like breathing,
like the heart beating—unknown, essential, mysterious. He
was like the dark. . . .

Well, I know what it is to be in love all right. . . . What
happened to the person I was beginning to know before—
going home that time, going to dine with the family at
Meldon? . . . Suddenly, the connection snapped. . . . I remember
him well: agreeable, easy-mannered, with a kind of class-

144

flavour to his flirtatiousness and wit; friendly: and then not friendly: hostile, obstinate, on his guard. . . . Does being in love create a new person? Did I know him then, and not now? Have I swallowed him up? *Vénus toute entière.* . . . No, no! Nobody could say Rollo was a victim. . . . Could they? . . . Except that he's a bit weak and in a muddle. . . .

Beyond the glass casing I was in, was the weather, were the winter streets in rain, wind, fog, in the fine frosty days and nights, the mild, damp grey ones. Pictures of London winter the other side of the glass—not reaching the body; no wet ankles, muddy stockings, blown hair, cold-aching cheeks, fog-smarting eyes, throat, nose . . . not my usual bus-taking London winter. It was always indoors or in taxis or in his warm car; it was mostly in the safe dark, or in half-light in the deepest corner of the restaurant, as out of sight as possible. Drawn curtains, shaded lamp, or only the fire. . . .

In this time there was no sequence, no development. Each time was new, was different, existing without relation to before and after; all the times were one and the same.

The telephone rang in the morning. I was just going out.

"Look here." He always said that on the telephone. "What are you doing to-night?" He was always guarded on the telephone, crisp, off-hand, he never spoke for long—only to make quick arrangements. He never said anything nice.

"Well, I was having dinner with some people, and going to a film or something."

"I see."

"But I could get out of going——"

"Well, I've got to dine in myself."

He was always like that on the telephone—non-committal —grudging it sounded: rather putting-off till I got accustomed and could tease.

"Oh. . . . It doesn't seem much use then. . . ."

"I was rather wondering if we could meet afterwards? I

can get away by ten. We might have supper or something?
Unless you're fixed up?"

"I'm not fixed up. That'll be fine."

It was a funny sort of half-hearted-sounding invitation. . . .

"Shall I pick you up somewhere or what?"

"Well, I don't quite know where I'll be. I'll have dinner
with my people, you see, and not go to the film. . . . Of course
I don't mind a bit, I've seen three films this week." I had—it
was all I could do. "The best thing'll be if I come back here. . . ."
Quickly planning it all. "Call for me here."

"Right, I will. Ten o'clock then."

It sounded so very ordinary and above-board—a bleak-
sounding sort of date. I couldn't think at all or feel excited—
not consciously. The only thing in my mind was Etty would
be out; I'd have the flat to myself.

It was supper in Simon's studio, which is one of the things
I like best. Simon cooked and Anna helped, they know about
cooking like most painters. I brought some of those little
cigars, they were pleased. It turned into a kind of celebration,
I don't know why; every one in good form, amusing and a
bit light-headed. Adrian brought a new discovery, Ed, a boxer,
very handsome and mild, with beautiful manners, absolutely
charming, we all said, a fascinating character, we said. We
all took Adrian aside and congratulated him on Ed; and
Adrian said, the point is, my dear, his extraordinary shrewdness and capacity for irony, we must hear his stories about life
in the ring. He did say a few things, a clipped mutter up in
his nose, we all said absolutely fascinating. . . . I've forgotten
them. I got on well very with dear Ed, we held hands towards
the end, very kindly, not desirously. I thought: he's like Rollo,
somehow—the power, the goodness sealed up dark in them,
an unknown quantity, exciting—not spilled about all over the
place, or thinned off, gone through the tops of their heads with
taking little samples so often for public analysis and discussion.
I saw Rollo through Ed, clear, for a moment; their separation

from, magnetism for women. . . . No comradeship there. . . .

Every mouthful of food and drink tasted sharp and good, and all their faces, movements vivid, absorbing, and I noticed things in the room I'd never noticed before—not really to take them in: the design on the hand-blocked grey linen curtains, a cushion worked not very well in bright wools—a pattern of shells; a small lead figure of a woman high up on a shelf, a painted jug with Woolworth flowers stuck in it, a joking sketch of Simon examining his cactuses, one or two small paintings, still lives, I'd never noticed before, a mask Colin must have done during his mask period—wherever the eye fell some mark of liveliness, some kind of wit, selection, invention—the vitality of shape, pattern, colour making an æsthetic unity—the creative hand, the individual mind mattering—the dirt, untidiness, poor materials not mattering at all. Thinking: the room lives; their rooms are dead, full of dead objects. I meant Meldon. Wondering what would Rollo think of it, what kind of rooms Nicola'd made, and Marigold. . . .

Colin hadn't shaved for days, he had a butcher-blue shirt and a red scarf round his neck, no collar, he looked more like a miner, a stoker, than ever with his muscular neck, haggard pronounced features and jutting forehead with the lock of hair over it. He was explaining to us about music in relation to painting and writing, and then explaining why it was impossible to explain it. Anna was beaming quietly, her mouth open a little showing her front teeth like she always does when she's happy, running backwards and forwards to the kitchen trying to do everything for Simon and wait on every one. . . Simon was very white, his eyes incandescent—flitting, darting about, then sitting in that noiseless light way of his . . . as if he'd been checked, as if he was patient, waiting to be gone again. . . .

Sometimes when I see Simon going about, he seems the only person who *moves*, other people fumble. I've noticed it coming out of cinemas. We linger and jostle down the stairs, jammed in the crowd, talking, stopping, caught up with all the other lumpish bodies and clumsy slow limbs; but Simon always goes straight forward, threading his course delicately through the jumble, and you find him standing waiting on the edge of the pavement, looking ahead of him. It's as if he'd one of those flexible steel measuring rods slipped into his back, keeping him so upright, sheer without rigidity, balanced so neatly. . . .

It was nine when they said what about a film? And Anna said there's a French film at the Academy I want to see, and I got up and said, "I must go, dears." There was expostulation, and I said, "My cousin that none of you believe in is in bed with a feverish cold, and I swore I'd come back at nine and look after her." Soon we were all out in the street, Simon, Colin, Adrian puffing at their cigars, Adrian in his new, enormous, black felt hat from Paris. Ed said:

"You don't have to go, do you?"

"I wish I didn't have to." Mournfully looking at him.

"Be a cad," said Simon.

"Shall I? Shall I? No, I can't, I can't."

"She can't, it's her trouble," said Colin.

Calling, "Good-bye, dears," taking to my heels in the opposite direction. In the square I hopped into a taxi, panicky, I might be late, Simon's clock slow, I might not have time to prepare, do things to my face. . . . I was back at half-past nine.

Ten. Ten-past ten. Ten-fifteen. Twenty-past ten, and a car came round into the street and stopped, and next moment the bell rang. Starting up weak in the bowels from waiting, starting downstairs in a flurry, then making myself go slow, in a calm way, opening—and there he was on the doorstep. His long, big, black car seemed to stretch from here to the pub on the corner, a notable vehicle, not one to come covering one's tracks in.

"Hallo! May I come in?"

He stepped into the midget hall, his voice sounded so loud in it, sonorous, his shoulders blocked it, his head grazed Etty's phony little chandelier. He took off his overcoat and hung it up, genial, easy, deliberate in all his movements; at home wherever he goes. He was in a dinner-jacket with a soft shirt, pleated silk, rather a shock, I had the black studio dress on.

"How are you?" he said, going up the little stairs. "You're looking awfully well. Sorry I'm late. This residential area is most baffling. I've been up and down half a dozen little streets I've never heard of."

"It is rather mythical," I said. "It's every taxi's Waterloo."

He went into the sitting-room. "Very nice," he said, looking round. He walked up and down, looking amused rather, looked out of the window, picked up a pink crystal elephant on the mantelpiece.

"It's rather a snug little nest, I'm afraid. This is all Etty's. I just have a room upstairs. Etty's out somewhere."

"Etty's out, is she?" he said vaguely, looking at the huge, signed, fuzzy photograph on the writing-table, to Darling Et love Mona in a round fat female hand with a flourish—Etty's dearest girl-friend. That signature gets me down sometimes, but Mona's not bad, you never could mistake her for anything but what she is, a good-lookingish Englishwoman about thirty-five in the right hat worn not quite right, and small string of pearls, who's divorced a husband and has one little girl called Averil. She's always very friendly if I look in when she's come to tea with Etty—she's interested in Bohemian life. She once had a flutter with a Russian count, an artist. . . .

"Cigarette?" I said.

"Thanks so much. I've got masses on me. Have one of mine. I'm afraid it's a queer sort of time to call," he said. "I had to dine with Marigold. She had a party and I promised to do host, Sam's away. I do hope it wasn't a bore my coming at this hour. . . ."

"Not a bit. I couldn't have dined, anyway. I was dining out too. I've just got back." He wasn't to think I'd been sitting waiting. . . .

"They've gone on to some Charity Ball affair or other. I had her permission to sneak off. I can't stand these galas and festivals any more." He always had rather an ornamental special style of talk.

"You look very smart. . . ." It was all I could think of; and not able to look at him quite, feeling stiff, self-conscious, awful . . . wondering: Is it a ghastly mistake? . . .

"Sorry about that too," he said. "I had to. I hate this formal clothes business, don't you? It's such rot. . . . All the same it's rather nice after the city, you know—get out of your office suit and have a bath, and feel a bit cleaner. . . ."

"I like changing for dinner," I said. "At least, I should like it if I ever had occasion to. . . . I'd like to make a long ceremonious *toilette* every night and appear looking fancy as the Pope. I hardly ever see the inside of an evening-dress nowadays. . . ."

"People don't dress up like they used to," he said vaguely. "At theatres and things, I mean—do they? . . . Much more sensible. . . ."

"When I came to Meldon last week was my first full-dress event for—oh, months!"

"Was it? That was fun, that evening. . . ." Catching each other's eye, not knowing whether to laugh or what, looking away again. . . . Fun indeed!

"What you been doing since then?" I said quickly.

"Oh, nothing much. . . . As a matter of fact, I seem to have had rather a full week. Don't quite know what it's all been about. Nothing particular. It's always the same in London, isn't it? It's appalling, really, if you stop and think about it."

"It is."

He came to the fireplace where I was standing—standing up straight as always when I'm in a stew—threw his cigarette on the fire—electric fire—treating it like a coal one. He stood beside me, an elbow on the mantelpiece, played with the elephant and the three ivory monkeys and the cloisonné box, fiddling like Marigold. A stranger. It was all heavy, laborious, flinty, it was like having to break stones . . . wondering: Has he come to unsay it, call it off?

"Rollo, will you have a drink?" And my voice cold, sharp, smooth. "I'm afraid there isn't much in the house. There's some beer . . . or some gin?"

"No, thanks awfully. I really won't just now."

I sat down on the stool. "I say, how's your father?" he said.

"*Much* better, thank you. Sitting up in bed and eating more and stronger. I rang up this evening."

"Oh, excellent. I'm so glad. . . ."

Being with Rollo, even thinking about him at that time always made me start worrying about Dad, feeling guilty. I'd had to ring up twice that day. Mother'd been pleased but a bit bracing the second time—an extravagance, unnecessary now.

"Are you going away this week-end again?" I said.

"I think I am. Are you?"

"I'm not quite sure."

"Nicola went down to Cornwall last night—to her mother. I may go down and join her—just for the week-end—get a bit of shooting. . . ."

"Oh, will you?" Hell of a way for two nights, I thought— the expense—but that's nothing to him. . . . I thought: How devoted-sounding.

"She's going to stay a bit," he said. "I'll be a grass-widower."

"Oh, will you?"

Suddenly he said: "I came as soon as I could. . . ." Trying to break down something, making an appeal; as if saying: I had to wait till she'd gone, surely you see. . . .

"Thank you for your letter. . . ." Able to say that now, look at him with a bit of smile unfrozen.

"Not much of a one, I'm afraid."

"It was very nice." By the last post Monday night, and this was Thursday . . . three lines in his small, thick writing, un- even and not too legible, running downwards on the page;

saying, "Darling, I've been so happy all day, you were so
sweet to me. How do you feel? I'll ring up as soon as I
can.—R."

Read and reread. . . .

Getting up from my stool to take another cigarette,
nervouser and nervouser. . . . He struck a match for me, saying
very softly, in a funny, diffident, plaintive voice: "I've thought
about that evening such a lot."

"So've I." Looking at the cigarette, puffing furiously.

He put his head down suddenly to give me a light, quick
kiss on the cheek. No good. What can break this down? How
to melt, how to start? . . . Because here he is, he's come for
what I promised, it's got to be made to be . . . standing up side
by side in Etty's crammed room. . . .

"Darling, are you glad to see me?" Coaxing. . . .

"Yes, Rollo."

"Don't be frightened," he said.

It was all over before now, it could still be nothing, never
happen. . . . I don't know how, there wasn't one moment, but
he made it all come easy and right as he always did, saying:
"She won't be coming in, will she?"

"Not before midnight, anyway. . . ."

His head looked round the room quickly, over my head.
"Not here," I said. If it had to be it must be where it was me,
not Etty. . . . It must be more serious and important. . . .
"Wait. I'll call."

Running upstairs, one flight, past Etty's bedroom, another
flight, my bedroom, my own things. That was better. Bed,
books, dressing-table, arm-chair, my picture of people sitting
on park chairs under a plane-tree, sun-dappled—a woman with
a pram, another with a red sunshade—my picture I bought
with Ivor at the London group, with a wedding cheque, and
was so excited, that was still all right to live with, though
not so good as I'd thought. I turned up the gas-fire and
switched on the bedside lamp with the shade Anna did. I
thought: He must think everything nice, not tartish, un-

dressing quickly, and my red silk dressing-gown on, tied tightly, it had to be wonderful, not sordid, thinking: This tremendous step, I must tell him, explain. . . . But it was already the space in between where no deciding is, and no emotion. . . . His loud step came up the stairs, he came in quickly as if he knew the room. "I couldn't stay down there any longer." Not looking round, but only at me. That's the thing about him, it always was, from the beginning—his directness—no constraint, awkwardness or head-doubts about what he wants, acting on a kind of smooth, warm impetus, making it all so right and easy. . . . Saying: "Oh, darling, I knew you'd be beautiful." Delighted. . . . "It's rather a step," I tried to say, but already it wasn't any more.

Then it was afterwards. He said, whispering:
"I'm your lover. . . ."
I thought about it. I had a lover. But nothing seemed changed. It wasn't disappointing exactly. . . . The word is: unmomentous. . . . Not wonderful—yet. . . . I couldn't quite look at him, but it was friendly and smiling. His cheek looked coarse-grained in the light from the lamp. I saw the hairs in his nostrils. . . . I was afraid I'd been disappointing for him. . . . Thinking: Aren't I in love with him after all then? . . . We hadn't said love once, either of us. . . . Thinking: It's happened too quickly, perhaps, this'll be the end. . . . I thought of Simon, of Anna and the others at the cinema, seeing them so clearly, thinking: What a contrast: a different make of face even, a different race altogether. Where was I between the two? Rollo with Anna would be unimaginable. Simon and I . . . I love Simon; but that's different again, never to sleep together, that's certain. . . . All the same, just then I thought: I love Simon, not Rollo—thinking I'd done something against Simon, somehow . . . it was mad of course . . . thinking it was siding with Etty and Mona and people like that, against Anna and her kind of feelings about love, to have Rollo for my lover. . . .

He said: "Isn't it nice being all quiet and peaceful afterwards?" He was so kind and gentle.

"Yes," I said . . . thinking how one's alone again directly afterwards.

"What time is it?"

I hadn't an idea. It might have been half an hour, two hours. . . . He looked at his wrist-watch.

"Half-past eleven."

"I'm so afraid Etty may be back sooner than she said."

"Oh, Lord, that wouldn't do, would it?"

I said, "I'm hungry." We laughed. "Let's go out and have something to eat." I dressed. He sat on the bed and smoked a cigarette, seeming quite at home. I thought: Has he done this sort of thing before, then?

"Nice room," he said. He was taken with the lamp-shade, thinking the horseback-riding ladies lewd and funny. He said he'd like one like it for his dressing-room. He walked about in his way, and smoothed his hair with my brush, stooping to peer into the mirror. It felt so domestic. . . . Being married to Rollo, which would never be. . . . Thinking that was the worst of my marriage; not enough money to have privacy, places of one's own; Ivor's clothes and comb and toothbrush mixed up with mine, Ivor lying in bed, bored, watching me dress. . . . Rollo and Nicola wouldn't know what that was like, did they have separate bedrooms or what? . . . I smoothed out the bedclothes and pillow, which amused him, and tidied everything, opened the window to let out the smell of his cigarettes—to blow it all away. Turn down the fire, switch off the lamp. There! He's vanished. Hypocrite room, deny it all! At the door he put his arms round me and kissed me—a different kiss from any yet—tender, grateful and protective.

"Darling," he said.

We went downstairs and put out all the lights. Then we went out into the empty street, into the car, and we drove away.

Rules's was rather empty that night. There were a few theatre people vaguely familiar, and an unaccountable party of stout thick people with indistinct standard faces, women by Derry and Toms with artificial sprays pinned on, and big, black, leather handbags with fierce clasps and handles; men with thinning, sleeked hair, stiff collars, face and neck in one; all with false teeth; all silent or speaking in undertones. No one we knew. We went through into the farther part and got the corner table, and sat on the red plush side by side. Opposite us were two young men, blonds, smoothing their hair and saying rather elaborately: "The point is . . ." They didn't take much notice of us. When they left, with a toss of their heads, settling their ties, we were alone behind the partition and we held hands. All the junk round us, the prints, the marble busts, oil-paintings, the negress with the lamp, the plush, the rather murky yellow light, the general stuffiness— all this made an atmosphere of a sort of sensuality and romantic titillation—the kind that lurks and lingers in curiosity shops and old-fashioned music-halls; the harsh, dark, intimate exhalation of hundreds of people's indoor objects and sensations, unaired, choked up pell-mell for years with no outlet. . . . It was just right then. . . .

We ordered sausages, and Rollo a lager and I a big cup of coffee. He felt in his breast pocket and took out a coin and showed it me on his palm. "I told you I'd hold you to it," he said.

"To what?"

"This cup of coffee."

"Is that my shilling?"

"It is."

"D'you mean to say you really kept it?"

"I did."

"We didn't imagine this sort of cup of coffee, did we?"

"I did," he said. "I've got lots of imagination. . . ." Thinking to himself *then*: I will too? . . . flipping, pocketing my shilling—planning the joke? . . .

"You're very business-like," I said. "Do you always get on so swimmingly?"

"Ah, now don't," he said, coaxing, plaintive. "Don't say things like that, will you, darling? I'm the luckiest man in the world. You don't know how proud I feel. You don't know what you've done for me. I'm so grateful and so proud...." We held hands and smiled into each other's eyes; it was all tender, relaxed now, drowsy and smiling, the last of the bars fixed so stiff against him gone, and all of me acceptance, pleasure, like floating in warm lit water.

He said, "My God, I was nervous when I walked into your house to-night."

"You concealed it," I said.

He said, "You were like a statue. I thought I'd never be able to bring you to life."

"I was afraid you wouldn't too," I said. "But you made it all right for me."

He said, "You feel all right about it now, don't you, my sweet?" His voice has a particular way with endearments—irresistible.

"It was *wonderful*," I said; I seemed to realise suddenly ... wishing we were back now in the room, and it could all be again and me different, more welcoming ... I did wish it.

We went on talking softly, saying it had to happen, didn't it? We were always to have this kind of meeting. . . . At least I said so, he agreed. We could have sat on all night, but we didn't stay so very long. It was just as easy to part. . . . He was going down to Cornwall to Nicola next morning, but that didn't matter at all; just then it didn't seem particularly important to arrange for our next meeting; everything would glide on without our worrying and be all right. . . . It's strange how incurious, unpossessive we both were then. It might have finished that night. It might have been enough ... or couldn't it have been, really? . . .

We dropped the shilling into the vase of scratchy, dry chrysanthemums on the table, so that we'd never know what happened to it next. I went home in a taxi by myself. I didn't want the car announcing me sensationally in the tiny street, in case of running into Etty. . . . Darling, *whose pluto*cratic auto? . . . We waved good-bye through the taxi window, and I kissed my hand to him on the pavement looking at me, and drove off. I was home before Etty after all. I was glad, it took away the last bit of fear of her noticing something different in the house. . . .

He used to say: "I don't believe you'd ever make a scene." He said that often in that time. "You're the only woman who doesn't go on about things. You leave people alone. It's so refreshing. . . ." "But of course," I'd say. "That's not odd, is it? Unusual?" "You don't know how odd it is," he'd say, wrinkling his forehead. . . . But what have I got to go on about? I used to think then. I've got everything. . . . He's my lover. . . . It was enough. Enough belongs to me. . . . Perhaps not possessive like some women, I'd think, smug. Congratulating myself, saying: "I don't think I've ever been very jealous. I suppose it's not my line." . . . The time I said that he shook me, saying: "I'd like to make you then" . . . and making love, we played a game of jealousy, saying things to provoke and tantalise, and in the game I was pierced for a moment as if truly pierced with jealous rage. I saw what it was like . . . but only till it was afterwards, and then it all slipped away among the words and feelings of that plane, so disconnected from the everyday ones, one hardly can imagine them. I only thought it had been exciting. . . . He was always giving me to understand he was a jealous person. "My God yes!" he said; and I thought, Nicola?—and I couldn't ask. In that time Nicola was hardly mentioned. We kept his life apart from me separate, we suppressed it; or it didn't seem to matter. Yet often she was why he couldn't meet me, or had to get home early. . . . I was incurious—or I made myself so—or I thought I did. . . . "Now I've got you," he'd say, "nothing else matters—all the things I *couldn't* see how to cope with.

. . ." Always very vague, but I felt he'd been sad or dissatisfied for a long time in his private life and I wanted to comfort him without asking too much. . . . It was enough he put his head down on my breast. . . . I wonder how long that time lasted. . . . Perhaps not long at all . . . a few weeks perhaps. . . .

It was understood when she was in London it was difficult to meet, but that winter she was away a lot. She went to Germany to see a doctor, or else she went down to her mother. I got a picture of someone perfectly helpless, with a maid to do everything, and every one gentle to her, and trays in bed, and wonderful nightdresses and wraps—the kind in Givan's window or the Ladies' Royal Needlework place. I saw her under a white satin quilted bedspread with pink and apricot satin cushions, monogrammed, propping her head, and a blue satin and lace wrap on, being visited by assiduous doctors exuding that restrained pervasive hygienic sex-appeal that is so telling. . . . I put her like that, a wax figure immune in a show case, to account for her, to make her harmless. . . .

I wouldn't let him give me clothes, though I longed for new things to wear for him. He wanted to buy me frocks, but I said no. It was partly not liking to dwell on how much I needed them, would like them—he couldn't bear to feel I was poor and had to work—partly the impossibility of appearing suddenly in new things and everybody wondering, guessing; but also it was pride. I wouldn't be a kept woman. He seemed surprised about this, but he partly liked it too, saying, "You're such a frugal little thing." . . . Though he was so generous, lavish, he was pleased I didn't want to spend his money. . . . I thought indignantly: He's got bills enough, paying for her négligées. . . . But he gave me wonderful stockings, and flowers, and all the books I wanted. I suppose I thought nobody would notice these. I don't know if anybody did or not. . . . Then of course the ring on my birthday—a square emerald set in platinum, deep, flawless. God knows what it must have cost. I was aghast. I looked and looked at it, and it said Nicola, Marigold, not Olivia. It said nothing about us, just brilliant, unimpeachable, a public ring, saying only with what degree of luxury he could afford to stamp a woman. . . . I didn't know what to say. He said, "I did so want to give you an emerald, darling, because I love emeralds. Do you?"

"I do. Oh, I do," I said.

"Look," he said suddenly, "I thought this looked like you. I don't know why—I had to get it too."

He put it in my hand, and it was the ring I wanted, our ring—a ring for the little finger, early Victorian, I think, a peridot set round with little pearls, in a thin elaborately turned gold setting. Made by hand and special. I loved it at once. "I'll wear it always," I said, "and the important one I'll wear at night alone, or when we dine together at the Ritz—when you want to flaunt me." I put it away in my jewel-case in the top right-hand drawer of my dressing-table and there it is now. Sometimes I look at it, thinking: that's an expensive thing. I'm worth something now if I'm ever in a fix. . . . I haven't even looked at it for weeks now. I suppose it's still there. . . . My darling little ring, I never take it off. I said to Etty and Anna it belonged to my grandmother, and to Kate and mother, Anna gave it me, it was her grandmother's.

The white lacquer and onyx cigarette case with the marcasite mount was his Christmas present. "Love" engraved inside it in his small crooked writing . . . but it never seems mine in spite of the inscription. I use it when I'm with him or by myself, I don't think anybody's noticed it . . . though Kate's bound to spot it sooner or later. . . . It's nice, I must say, to go about with somebody well off for a change. I wonder how rich he is, there seems no limit to what he can spend, yet they're all supposed to be badly off nowadays. It's all relative, I suppose. . . . People like him can overdraw and no questions asked.

No one must ask questions, no one must find out. It dashed me a bit sometimes at first, Rollo being so cautious, always in a stew for fear he'd be seen, recognised; always saying safer not, better not go here, do this or that; not ring up too often at the office. . . . Quite soon I got infected with it. . . . At Christmas when he went away with Nicola he had some cheap yellow office envelopes typed with his name and address, and gave them to me for my letters to him.

"Did you burn them at once?" I said.

"Yes, darling," plaintive. . . . I minded rather. . . . "I did adore them," he said coaxing. "Such lovely letters. . . ." I'd hoped he'd say, "I meant to burn them, but I couldn't. . . ."

I kept his. I had to. But I didn't tell him so. They weren't lovely long ones full of everything, like mine; they were slap-dash and sketchy, and about taking exercise with perhaps one little loving sentence at the end, shamefaced looking. . . .

I did think once or twice had he done something of this sort before and got into trouble, to be so afraid of being found out? . . . I suggested it, teasing, but he was upset: he said did he seem like an experienced seducer. . . .

"Well, I'm not sure," I said.

"No," he said seriously. "It's just that I could *not* bear it to be spoilt. The world's so bloody, people are so revolting—you're so precious."

I said once, "Tell me truly, does it make you feel miserable really to be practising a deceit? Do tell me, darling. It would me."

"I'm afraid it doesn't," he said in his funny rueful way. "What people don't know about can't hurt them, can it? I'm not hurting her as long as she doesn't find out, am I?"

"I suppose not," I said. "Only if it was me I think I might worry. I do see how difficult it is for you," I said, awfully understanding.

He said nothing. "You see——" he began, then stopped. After a bit he said differently: "Women are dreadful creatures. They will want to have their cake and eat it too. It's what they call being honest. If my wife had a lover I hope to God she wouldn't see fit to tell me so. I call this confession and all-above-board business indecent." Saying "my wife" it didn't seem like Nicola.

"That's because you'd feel it was such rotten luck for the other chap to be given away," I said. "You'd mind that almost as much as the unfaithfulness. It wouldn't be cricket. . . . You don't like women really, do you?"

"There's one or two things I quite like about them," he said in that beginning voice, kissing my ear. . . .

Searching back into that time, it seems confused with hiding, pretence and subterfuge, and covering our tracks . . . though it didn't seem to matter then. But now I see what an odd duality it gave to life; being in love with Rollo was all-important, the times with him the only reality; yet in another way they had no existence in reality. It must have been the same for him. Our lives were occupied, arranged without each other; the actual being together had to be fitted in, mostly with difficulty, carefully spaced out and always a time limit. Etty might come back or he had to go and dine, go away for the week-end, he was delayed at the office, I had to go and see Dad. . . . I thought once of our private debating society at Oxford—all of us b.fs. sitting on the floor in my room debating away sententiously without a ghost of a smile, the subject being: Love is the occupation of idle minds. I was against the motion. . . . But now I saw how busy people can be without love, and once or twice I got panic: Where is the time and place for this? Where is it? Supposing Rollo were to die, my outward life wouldn't alter one jot. Where, how should I do the crying? . . . I wonder how many women in England in such a situation. . . . Their lovers killed in an accident, or dying in hospitals or something, and nothing they can do, nobody ever knows. They go to work, they cut up the children's dinner, and choose their spring coats and go to movies with their husbands. . . . I was always thinking something awful would happen to Rollo, he'd be snatched away from me behind an official barricade of lawful friends and relations. . . . Because I loved him he was threatened—by life—by me—I don't know. . . .

Going into restaurants, one tried to be invisible; walking

with one's eyes fixed ahead, looking only at the table; then after a bit summoning courage to look round and about in a calm way. It's so sad, because I'm so proud to be with him, so fine and handsome, I wanted to be seen and envied. . . . I'd have liked to go to the smart places where people eat, and to theatres and dance places. He didn't want to. Of course it wouldn't do, he knows all those well-connected faces, they're his world. . . . He only wanted to be alone somewhere and make love. "Where can we go?" he'd say. "Can we go back to your room?" Sometimes I'd say, "No, I'm afraid not to-night. . . . Mrs. Banks is staying late; or Etty's gone without her latch-key, she'll be back early," rather than risk it; then he'd look gloomy, sulky nearly . . . cursing London and Mrs. Banks, and Etty and everybody else. . . . I told him he had only one idea in his head. . . . I said to tease what I wanted was a soul-mate. "You don't, do you?" he'd say, rueful, coaxing. "And, anyway," he'd say, "I do love talking to you. You know I do. You're such a clever young creature. . . . We have lovely talks, don't we?"

We did, of course, really, lovely talks—specially in the place we always lunched on Mondays. Every Monday, without fail. I was always early, so as to be sure to get our table right at the back, in the darkest corner, almost a separate little room. Coming from the city, he was often late. I sat and smoked and had a cocktail while I waited and read my book and looked at all the glinting wine bottles, all shapes and sizes, ranged round the room on a shelf. The darkness was the chief reason why we liked it, we felt safe; that and the emptiness. I can't think why it was so empty, considering the delicious food. Too expensive, I suppose—really beyond all bounds; but Rollo never cared what he spent on a good meal, he'd never eat anywhere inferior or female. He's a sybarite. There'd be one or two business men, motor-car people they looked like, and an occasional guards' officer and girl-friend, or an American, and some dark-skinned people, French, who'd come in late and lunch with the dark proprietor; friends or relations of his, I suppose, who got the left-over food. Our waiter was French, old, he looked like old Punch cartoons of Mr. Redmond, but wickeder. He called Rollo "milord." Rollo said, "Hallo, you old villain," and it was an understood thing the bill was roughly double what it should be, and Rollo would put the pencil through the total and pay something quite different, though still enormous. We were very happy together there, side by side at our table. Only once, just as we were going out, someone called "Rollo!" behind us, and Rollo turned and said in his easy way, "Hallo, old boy! Haven't seen you for ages. Where've you been lurking?" and I strolled on to the door to wait for him, after smiling a bit the way one should, seeing out of the corner of my eye a fair, rather stout young man with a pink face and a toothbrush moustache, and a quiet cool Scotch-looking girl with amused eyes and a short neck and silver fox furs. When we got into the taxi, "Who was it?" I said, and Rollo said, "A chap I was at school with. Dickie Vulliamy. That's his new wife. Rather nice, I thought." . . . I wonder why that made me so depressed . . . I felt left out. They were all safe except me, she was his new wife, not his new mistress, they were against me. . . .

Thursdays we lunched at another place, not a dark, voluptuous lunch, nice in another way. It was right off our ordinary beat, usually pretty full, but not with the people either of us knew; residential faces from S.W.1 and 3, youngish men with museum faces, one or two actors, the healthy publicschool type, actresses,—real ladies, with the minimum of make-up. One got a comforting feeling there of the world being liberal-minded, cultivated, unsuspicious. Men and women could lunch together and no insinuations. The waiters were impersonal and everybody else indifferent. . . . Even one's relations wouldn't have suspected one there. Behaviour was agreeable and sterilised. And good food. I thought a lot about food in that time, I was always hungry. It came nearer being a public relationship, a reality in the world there than

anywhere else. Almost, the split closed up. We talked about
the city and about our families. I told him stories about our
childhood to amuse him. He'd explode in a roar of laughter,
he liked my jokes. He asked questions about my friends, he
was always curious; he said he wished he knew them, they
sounded more sensible and interesting than the people he
knew; but he supposed they were too highbrow for him. He's
got the most awful nonsense in his head about painters and
writers; awe and suspicion and admiration, and envy and
contempt all mixed up. I spoke of Ivor, too; it was odd how
he seemed to understand how it had all come about—he's very
intuitive, and never will judge, never blame. He was sorry
for us both. . . . Oh, Rollo, you're so tender-hearted. . . .
Magnanimous. . . . Occasionally he spoke of Nicola too, but
in a semi-impersonal, detached way, indulgent—how much
she'd minded about the baby, such a blow for her, poor sweet
—things like that. . . . He seemed to assume nothing could be
expected of her after such a catastrophe, it excused any mood
or collapse. I didn't say why doesn't she pull herself together
and try again, of course, because of not being able to bear to
envisage that . . . him getting her with child . . . I preferred
to assume—I mean I assume—I'm sure—a child's out of the
question now, they don't sleep together any more, it's not a
marriage. . . . A beautiful protected doll is in his house, not
a wife. . . .

He never spoke of his own feelings about the baby, he never
has; just said once, of course it didn't affect a man in the same
way. . . . I don't think he knows himself how much he minds;
it's obvious to me. When I said once how I'd love a child of
his . . . I only said it once, never again, it made him worried
and depressed. "Oh, darling, it wouldn't do. . . ." His children
must be legitimate, they must have the orthodox upbringing
and inherit. . . .

Occasionally after lunch he'd decide he needn't go back to
the city, and we'd drive to Richmond Park. First he'd ring
up his house and get his car driven to the nearest parking place,

with Lucy in it. We'd come out after allowing enough time, and there would be the car and Lucy sitting inside, all perked up, knowing what was coming. It was a relief to see that shrewish, anxiety-gnawed female throw etiquette and responsibility to the winds, and re-dog herself and go screeching after rabbits. Even to me she relaxed her fixed antagonism and bounded up on to the seat afterwards beside me with quite an amiable indifference. We'd walk a bit over the grass, and see the deer in the spacious silent blue-misted drives; it was sunny and still the times we went; hoar-frost on the bracken.

Driving back he'd say: "Is there *nowhere* we can go?" . . . He suggested a hotel, and I wouldn't. Then he said couldn't we take a room, why didn't I let him rent a flat for me or something. But, no, I said, no. . . . In his heart of hearts I don't believe he wanted to either. I didn't want even the shadow of a situation the world recognises and tolerates as long as it's *sub rosa*, decent, discreet; that means a word in the ear, a wink, an eye at a keyhole. . . . My idea being we were too fine for the world, our love should have no dealings whatsoever with its coarseness, I'd spurn the least foothold. . . . What was my idea, what was it really? We must be honest. . . . Was it that thing he said women do . . . wanting to have their cake and eat it? . . . It may have been I wanted to assure myself I was in between still, not choosing more patently than I must against Simon. . . . Not that Simon would ever have known or ever minded in the least whom I chose, what I did. . . . How surprised he'd be to know he's a sort of mystical private touchstone to me of—of some perfectly indefinite indefinable kind of behaviour . . . spiritual, if the word can be whispered. . . . He wouldn't like it at all.

Of course I had dreams of being Rollo's wife. . . . Sometimes we'd say, "If we were married," but in a pretending way, or joking about how it would be. . . . He always knowing what he wanted and intended, I suppose; I being content, I suppose, with a kind of permanent dream, keeping it intact from interference by reality. . . . One must face facts. . . . I think that's how it was.

Lord, I was happy! . . . Never so happy. Happy for the first time in my life.

No. . . . It wasn't exactly being happy. . . . We asked each other so many times. . . . "Oh, *yes*. Are you?" "Yes, yes, of course I am." He didn't by any means always have a happy face . . . only just at moments, afterwards, peaceful, utterly relaxed; or when I made him laugh. . . . I see I was more actually happy than he . . . more capacity for it, I suppose; a happy nature, as they say. . . . Then of course I wasn't having a double life to deal with in the same way. What do people mean about being happy, there's so much talk about it, as if it was the one aim and motive—far from it; it doesn't affect anything, as far as I can see, it isn't the desire for happiness that moves people to do what they do. . . .

I suppose Simon's a happy person; not from trying to be —he never tries to be or do anything. . . . An inherent quality —a kind of unconscious living at the centre, a magnetism without aim or intellectual pretension. . . . Simon seems to cause an extremely delicate electric current to flow between people when he's there; they're all drawn in, but he's just one degree removed from it all, he doesn't need anything from anybody. . . . He's like Radox bath salts, diffusing oxygen, stimulating and refreshing. . . . Dear Simon.

He said more than once, "Darling, don't care too much about me, will you?"

"Don't you want me to love you then?" I said.

"Yes, yes, I do, terribly. Only you mustn't sort of think too much of me, will you? I'm not much good, and mind you remember it. Don't expect a lot of me, will you? I've never been any use to any one. . . ." He was always running himself down, warning me, not in an emotional way, quite matter-of-fact, laconic, almost—not exactly—evasive; as if he wanted to dismiss himself, shrug off the responsibility of being himself. . . .

Not like me. When he said so often, "You're the nicest person I've ever known," I thought, "I expect I am." I never contradicted . . . I did say once I was a coward, though.

When I try to think over it, the times we were alone together weren't so very many. After a bit I began to think the walls and windows were full of eyes when he came back to Etty's. There was his big car, and twice he put down cigarettes and forgot them, one burn on the sitting-room mantelpiece, one on the table by my bed. Mrs. Banks said what had come over me, was I in love . . . and then I began to suspect she didn't go home, but watched from the pub window on the corner. I dare say it was only my imagination, or even if it wasn't she'd never have breathed a word, she'd be delighted to encourage both Etty and me to have lovers, she's all for a good time and no Paul Prys or Mrs. Grundys, she thinks it's deplorable the half-hearted spinsterish finicky way we live. But all the same, I began to hate and fear her small sharp Cockney eye, I thought of her nosing in my room for signs. . . . The house always seemed to me so weighted after he'd gone with his strong male physical life. . . . I made more and more excuses for not taking him back.

He didn't come there any more, I don't think, after we'd had our week-end together. The week-end was the end of the first stage.

It must have been January. Extraordinary to think it wasn't till then we managed it. There was always some reason that prevented it; his week-ends were so booked, he's very popular. . . . And then Nicola of course. But in January she went off to Switzerland for three weeks. Marigold and Sam had gone too, and George and a good many of his circle. Altogether the air was less thick with his friends and relations and he felt

safer, had more time for me. . . . What a pity it was never the
other way about. I'm always accessible, waiting for him.

He called for me with the car on Saturday morning. Etty'd
gone away the evening before, I'd told Mrs. Banks not to bother
to come. The sun was coming out; it was mild weather, my
favourite kind. When he turned up about ten I was making
coffee. He poked about in the kitchen, very cheerful. He said he
was hungry so I sent him out for a couple of sausages and fried
them for him. That delighted him. "You are a domestic little
creature, aren't you?" I suppose he'd never seen a woman put
on a kettle or use a frying-pan in his life, it moved him: like
Marigold—romantic about the simple life . . . we sat on the
kitchen table together and drank our coffee and felt light-
hearted. It was a happy start. I felt specially well and pretty
that day, everything was without effort. We drove to his club
to get some money, and I sat outside the important-looking
door and felt it was quite all right, I belonged where I was,
I'd be equal to any one who came out down those steps. One
young man with an O.E. tie did come out, he glanced in at me,
I smiled at him, and he at me—recognising Rollo's car, I
thought—saying to himself, "She looks all right, wonder who
she is . . .?" Rollo came out, running down the steps—he
didn't often hurry, nearly always deliberate, on the heavy side,
and said, "Darling, come along in and have a drink. There's
nobody about." He took me to the room for the lady guests
of members and we sank in vieux rose brocade arm-chairs with
jade green walls panelled and decorated with plaster bunches of
trophies and gilt-framed mirrors around us, and the ceiling
above us bulging with fat moulding, and in the discreet expensive spaciousness we drank champagne cocktails and talked
in the kind of voices that come over people in clubs. I heard
the ping-tock of a game of squash going on somewhere
underneath.

"It's quite lively in this room round about six and onward,"
he said.

"*Really?*" I said. It didn't seem likely.

"Yes. You know—chaps and their girl-friends. . . ." I saw
wholesome young chaps and nice, well-brought-up pretty girls
sitting together, talking in their pleasant, arrogant, standard
voices about dances and horses and house-parties; temperately
smoking and drinking cocktails, mildly flirtatious or just jolly
good friends. . . . Well, why not? I was jealous, really. . . .

He ordered two more champagne cocktails and went to
cash a cheque. I looked at the *Bystander*.

He was rather a long time, and I began to feel muffled,
weighed down by thick stuffs and silence. I thought: He'll
never come back; and when he did his figure seemed to come
at me from very far away, dream-like and dwindled, making
his way back along a tunnel. . . . I dare say it was champagne
at eleven in the morning. I remember the waiter's face who
brought the drinks—pale, with high cheekbones and fine
features, faintly smiling, as if Rollo was a favourite.

It was such a heavenly day. We seemed to float out of
London on the sun—champagne again, I suppose. We had no
plans except to make for the coast and wander till we found
somewhere we liked. It was one of those days when all the
landscape seems built up of intersecting planes of light and
shadow; the tree trunks' silvery shafts wired with gold and
copper, violet transparency in between the boughs. The hills
looked insubstantial, as if you could put your hand through
them. The damp roads flashed kingfisher blue. I remember
a line of washing in a cottage garden—such colours, scarlet,
mustard, sky-blue shifts, petticoats—all worn under grey and
black clothes, I expect—extraordinary. I remember light
dazzling on rooks' wings as they flew up; and an ilex-grove
at a crossroads, and red brick Queen Anne houses on the outskirts of old villages—nothing more fitting, more serene, could
ever be invented. Oh, I was happy that day. I kept saying:
"Look! . . ." The air was like April. It smelt of primroses, I
said.

In the afternoon we came to the Dorset coast: through
Corfe and out along the road that goes to Swanage. He knew

where we could get down to the beach; we left the car and walked down, down, a long way, a rough, steep, scrambling winding path. In all that sunlit green immense descent we were the only people. The sun was getting low. I remember only the great space, the swelling green, the evening shadows folded in the hollows, the iron-dark cliffs, towering, tumbling in phantasmagoric outlines, the sea spread out below, and us going down, down, down. . . . It was half-tide and perfectly still, the narrow, grey waves collapsing with a light noise of summer. We walked along the beach, and he played ducks and drakes, and I picked up some shells and bits of agate, saying, "Look!" "Lovely, darling," he'd say in his indulgent voice, not much interested. We sat on a rock; and it got dusk, and cold. The big round pale stones of the beach were so cold. Our feet sank in, slipped about on them with a grating, harsh rattle and crunch—it gave one a dismaying futile feeling to toil through them. We walked up the cliff again, slowly, arms round each other, stopping to kiss. Oh, how wonderful! . . . Going up along together in the dusk, peaceful and safe, stopping to kiss. It's a terrific climb, and if there's one thing I hate it's that: but this was effortless: like being drawn up by ropes invisible . . . my breath came and went so easily, without strain. The gulls were crying. Near the top we stood and listened to them. "Hundreds," he said. . . . It was nearly dark. I can hear them now. It was too much suddenly, too much space, and too sad. We were threatened . . . we wanted to be indoors. Back in the warm car again, leaning against him, the rug tucked round, I felt better. We were hungry, we'd had only a snack at a roadhouse for lunch, wanting to get on. "I feel like a rattling good dinner and every comfort," he said. So did I. We got to Swanage, but it looked all gloomy and deserted, so we went on, past the lights of Poole Harbour, into Bournemouth. We asked an R.A.C. man the best place to dine, and he directed us through sandy roads among pines, past astonishing brick and stucco residences with towers, turrets, gables, battlements, balconies—every marine-Swiss-baronial fancy—to the new first-class modern hotel on the front. It was carpeted in pink, and there was an orchestra in the vast dining-room, and pink and gold chairs and rose-shaded lamps. The atmosphere was refined luxury, and the women dining looked expensive, flamboyant and respectable. The dinner was good, we enjoyed it very much. People looked at us, but there was nobody we knew, although Rollo had a qualm about the back of one man's head. After dinner, having coffee in the rectangular and zigzag chromium-fitted modern beige lounge, "Well, shall we hang up our hats?" he said. So he strolled away to the office where they were most eager and affable, I could see from my arm-chair, and he came back and said he'd booked a double room with a bath, was that all right? "I'd better go and put the car away and be done with it," he said. "You go up." And while I was standing waiting for the lift and the suit-cases, the frock-coated, brass-buttoned gentleman at the desk suggested most suavely I should sign the register now to save troubling us again. "Oh, yes," I said cordially. I took up the pen. For the life of me I couldn't think of a name on the spur of the moment. Every surname except Spencer went out of my head. It must begin with S because he had a huge R.B.S. on his suitcase. It wouldn't do to hesitate. I scribbled Mr. and Mrs. Spender, London, in a rush. The "d" came to me after I'd embarked on "Spen." "Thank you, madam," he said, and took a key and personally conducted me in the lift to the second floor. It was a grand room—gilt and cane twin beds with fat pink eiderdowns and a balcony overlooking the sea, and a bathroom next door with a smart built-in bath.

When he came up we laughed about the register. . . . We stood on the balcony for a bit in the mild, dark, starry night, and looked at the bay and the lights, and heard the sea whisper-ing. We felt calm and tender like the night. . . . I had a bath and went to bed. We were both a tiny bit embarrassed. I thought chiefly about my new nightdress, whether it would look nice enough. . . . It was queer seeing him in blue silk pyjamas, cutting a broken finger-nail with my scissors. But when we put the light out, all night we were quiet and gentle, as if we'd slept together for a long time. Not the kind of night I'd imagined, but lovely; and waking up in the morning was smiling and drowsy and close. We had breakfast in bed, and then I wanted to be up and gone. I didn't like the way I thought the waiter smirked when he brought the trays in. Rollo went down first in case of being spotted—we'd got that on our minds again—and paid the bill, a whacking one, I bet, and after a bit, when I thought the car would be round, I walked down by the staircase looking straight ahead, willing my form to be obliterated. . . . Doing that has become such a habit I don't think I'll ever get out of it. Very bad for my poise. . . .

"Did you run into any one?" I said when we were in the car.

"Faith an' I did," he said. "A big stiff called Podge Hayward I was at Sandhurst with. He appeared in the lounge with a very hot bit indeed—a redhead. Something told me he didn't want to be publicly acclaimed any more than I did, so we passed each other discreetly by. . . ."

"Podge," I said. "Etty had a great friend called that. She brought him to your dance. I'm sure it's the same. . . ." He would be here, I thought.

"Lucky you weren't with me, darling," said Rollo lightly, dismissing Podge as we drove away. But I couldn't. I remember his awful patronising laugh and bulging opaque eye . . . hearing him say to Etty, "That little cousin of yours is quite sweet, but she needs teaching. . . ." *Needs teaching*. . . . Why should he crop up again to blight me? I felt almost nausea to think he'd been there last night with a very hot bit indeed. I couldn't bear Rollo saying that. It turned love, passion to derision and lust and squalor. I thought: I'll remember him saying that more than I remember our night, so after about an hour of moroseness which he didn't notice, I told him the trouble, and he was astonished, but he made it all right, and we came cheerfully to Weymouth.

It clouded over at lunch and a soft misting rain began to fall. We turned inland after lunch, through a wild, open country of moor and gorse and heather, with patches of tawny grass and marshland, and groups of pine and birch. The noiseless thin rain went on blotting out the distance. I told him, *O Western wind when wilt thou blow? That the small rain down may rain,* and he adored it and said it after me till he knew it. The darling, he's so sentimental. I don't remember much about the day. We drove in a dream, he steered with one hand and held mine on his knee with the other. Once or twice we stopped and smoked a cigarette. In the evening we came to a town with a cathedral, and bells ringing. It must have been Salisbury. We had dinner at an hotel, and decided to stay there. We drank burgundy at dinner, and afterwards brandy; we drank a good deal to make up for the horrid food. I felt hot and dazed going upstairs. It was one of those country-town hotels with rambling, uneven passages and shallow staircases winding on to broad landings, with palms in stands, and a coloured print of King Edward, and sets of old prints and warming pans hung up along the passages and stairs, and objects of china and Indian brass and carved wood by the score on every available surface, and stuffed birds and fish in cases and pampas in giant vases, and dark-brown and olive paint, and a smell of hotel everywhere—dust and beer and cheese, and old carpets and polish. . . . I don't know what. . . . The bedroom was big and square and colourless and stuffy, with thick draped lace curtains and an enormous architectural suite of light-brown furniture, and a white honeycomb coverlet on the staring hard high double bed. We had a fire lit and put out the screaming light above the dressing-table and then it was better. The fire piled up high with coal made a curious glow over us in bed and over everything. . . . And the wine, and the queer frightening room, so unconnected with any kind of room we'd ever known, and the rain outside, sealing us in together. . . . Oh, Rollo! Who were we? . . . There wasn't ever another time like that. . . . Crazy. . . . Footsteps went up and down outside on the pavement all night it seemed; late cars passed and clocks in the town chimed every quarter and the fire was still yearning out red over the ceiling when I fell asleep at last.

We went back to London early next morning. He put me down at Hyde Park corner and went on to the city, and I took a taxi back to Etty's, dropped my suitcase and went on to the studio.

After that week-end things were different. I couldn't go back to those furtive snatched half-frustrated meetings. I couldn't think what to do, but we didn't worry just then— still nourished by the week-end. We met for lunch nearly every day and dined together twice too that week and went to cinemas. It was a peaceful week. I see us talking, smiling in warm, calm intimate affection, almost without desire. It seemed so easy! . . . Is that what's called halcyon days? . . . They didn't last. He went away next Saturday, a week-end he couldn't get out of, he said, so I went home. Mother was glad to see me, relieved because I had some colour and looked well. I told her stories about Etty and Mrs. Banks to amuse her, and asked her advice about clothes and pushed Dad round the garden in the bath chair and read to him for hours, he didn't take in much, he dropped off asleep all the time. That was the first time I realised he wouldn't get any better in mind or body. . . .

I didn't go back to London till Tuesday, the day of Simon's party. We were looking forward to it, there hadn't been a real party for ages. I'd arranged with Rollo to drive with him first and go to Cochran's new revue. For once it would be me going on to a date I couldn't miss, I was elated and excited. I even thought I might take him on with me. I wore the white frock, my lucky frock. I told Etty I was dining with Marigold and her husband—that Marigold had asked me. She was thrilled for me, and twittered about while I dressed and made me take her silver coat lined with green velvet. We dined at Boulestin's and felt very festive. Rollo looked so fine and

handsome, and it was romantic wearing the white dress again,
I could see from his eyes he was feeling in love with me. He
said he'd enjoyed his week-end in Wiltshire, he'd been in the
right mood to enjoy himself. "Thanks to you, darling," he
said. "You're so sweet to me and make me so happy."

"Were there any lovely girls to flirt with?" I said.

"Well, yes," he said, eyebrows up, coaxing and plaintive.
"There was one rather nice one, darling. She's a sort of distant
French cousin of mine—a great-niece of the old girl who was
at Meldon, d'you remember? . . . Very young and awfully
enthusiastic and spontaneous and unspoilt—and the prettiest
figure I've seen in months—bar yours, darling," he added. I
made a disbelieving grimace. "Honestly, truly, darling," he
coaxed. "She *was* nice, but nothing like as nice as you. I was
comparing you with her all the time to your advantage. I do
much prefer you, darling." He took my hand under the table-
cloth. I wasn't a bit jealous then. I asked some more questions
and agreed it was nice to meet a pretty French cousin unexpectedly. Attractive cousins were extremely advantageous—in
fact, the only possible kind of relative for pleasure. I'm sure
I didn't feel one jealous twinge at the time.

I enjoyed the revue madly, the brilliance and frivolity, and
sitting in the third row of stalls with Rollo and walking about
with him between the acts. There was no one he knew, except
one or two by sight. In the second half, just before the end,
there was a girl dancing with a partner—a swooping, whirling,
flying waltz. . . . I shall never forget. . . . She was terribly
exciting . . . her long blue chiffon skirts swirled out, clinging,
swirling—her long, slender legs showing and vanishing, her
long, white, serpentine hips and back twisting, bending backwards, her face drugged-looking, mysteriously smiling with
long, pointed lips and eyes under a standing-out cloud of
white-fair, short, crinkled hair. Her name on the programme
was Thalassa. That means the sea. She was enough to make
any one hold their breath; I did, and I could feel Rollo spell-
bound. He didn't say a word afterwards, but clapped and

clapped. I looked at him, smiling enthusiastically, and clapped too. But a terrible feeling came down to me . . . like sour thick carpet dust in my chest and windpipe. . . . The worst feeling of my life.

We went out with the crowd and found the car, and got in.

"My God, what a figure!" he said, moving out into the traffic.

"Yes," I said. I knew when he saw her he'd wanted her. After a bit I said in a bright thin voice, "You seem to have got figures rather on your mind to-night."

"I always have," he said; it seemed like a quick hit back, straight across the chest, a ghastly pang, but he thought we were laughing, he was quite unaware. . . . It's not the only time there's been a lag before he realised a change in atmosphere; in some ways he's not sensitive. . . . The blue shape played on by lights went on provocatively turning and smiling before my eyes. "Where now?" he said. I gave him the address in Fitzroy Square. I felt terrible, but I said nothing. We drew up and got out, still not having decided whether he should come or not. He wanted to rather. "Shall I?" he said. I felt too rigid, stifled to squeeze out more than a word or two, I couldn't say yes or no. I just went on in with a nod or a shrug —I don't know which—and he followed. We went in silence along the passage and met the blare and glare full blast in Simon's doorway. . . . Sailor trousers, shorts, berets, stoker's caps, scarves, grey flannels, peasant blouses, little velvet jackets, stark tailor-mades; Myra in pink satin and pale blue gloves, Mrs. Cunningham stately and noble in an ancestral frock of maroon velvet and old lace, ineffably posed against the wall, Gil Severn in tails and a monocle, Billy Meaker in a complete suit of white tights, his hair and eyebrows shaved off entirely, covered in wet white, and a white glazed cotton vine leaf, the smell of whisky and flesh and powder, and all, and all . . . the mixture as before, moving, struggling about in a mass blocking the doors—the party in full swing and no error.

"Coming?" I said, feeling less awful already, faced by the crowd.

"Good God!" he said, staring over my head; I thought for a minute it was horror at the party. "There's Marigold." I looked and it was; in a backless plain black frock and a wreath of metal flowers in her hair, dancing with David Cooke and looking pretty bemused. There's always a few of their kind at Simon's parties; one corner of his world slides over into Mayfair-Bohemia. It was a shock, I must say. Rollo was suddenly furious. "Who's that cad holding her up?"

I told him. "You know, the gossip-column person."

"He looks it," he said. "Dare say he'll give her a write-up. . . Give you all one, I expect. . . ." His jealousy evaporated mine, I felt nearly all right again. "I'm off," he said, hard, sullen. For a moment I thought I'd go too. But Anna dancing with Ed had just seen me and was waving, and I waved back, saying:

"Oh, there's Ed!"

At that he turned on his heel, and said, "Well, good-night," and went off down the passage. I debated a moment and then I had to run after him, he was going down the steps when I caught him up and took his arm.

"What are you going to do?" I said.

"Go home to bed, I suppose." He looked moody, wretched, childish.

"I won't stay long, I promise," I said. "Do let's meet afterwards, do!"

"Will you come along to my house then?" he said defiantly.

"All right," I said quickly.

"I'll wait up," he said, and I kissed him and went back in and swam straight into a nest of cronies all together round the drinks.

"You do look a lady," they said.

I said, "I've been dining with a wealthy benefactor."

I drank some gin and felt better; Ed put his arm round me to dance. We got on fine. He said:

"You're the quiet sort, aren't you, same as me. . . . I liked your style the first moment I clapped eyes on you."

"And I liked yours," I said.

"They're a funny lot," he said. "Funny idea of having a good time. . . . There'll be some nasty heads to-morrow." He cracked a quiet smile looking round. "Anna's very nice," he said. "I like her very much. Simon's very nice, too."

He picked me up and made a few remarks and lost me again at intervals for about an hour, then he went home. I looked for Marigold, but she'd disappeared. Simon was seeing to the gramophone and the drinks and everything, Anna helping him now and then; he was drunk, that means amused, deft, rapid, lightly caressing. He kissed me, saying, "I wish I saw you more." It didn't mean anything, but I was very pleased. Colin was dramatic-drunk, with a loud, wild, forced heartiness; his hair all over his forehead in heavy locks, his eyes glassy. He seemed to be flung from one person to the next, all supporting, embracing him. When he got to me he said the oak trees are cut away by the salt tide, the seaweed grows right under the cabbages and cornfields. "That's a symbol," he said, throwing the word at me as if I'd never heard it.

"I know."

"You don't. You're a woman. You know nothing about it."

"I know all about it," I said stupidly; he looked at me in a hostile way and laughed contemptuously.

"If you did," he said, "if you *did* . . . you'd understand the whole relationship of sex to life. . . . I could explain, I *could* explain, but I won't. You're a woman. You'd be *bored*. . . ."

I said, "Colin, I'm in love. . . ." But he tumbled on, shouting:

"Come on! Come on! Come on!"

Adrian bowed over me with a tumbler of whisky, portentously solemn, saying, "My dear, I'd very much like to have a word with you about Miles and Rachel. I hear they're *separating*. My God, how trying these couples are! Having at *last* found a real out-and-out bullying devilish character like Rachel, why can't he be content with her? After all, she *does* know how to spend his money...."

"Yes," I said, "we shall miss her...."

"My *dear*, yes," he said. "None more than I...." He saw me laughing and went away in a huff, saying, "You're a *beast* to laugh, Olivia." I heard him complain to a group with Colin in it: "My dear, Olivia *laughed* at me." And Colin cried out, "Olivia laughs at us all!" and he turned and fairly hissed at me. I moved away, feeling depressed and lonely, there seemed so much hostility about, and suspicion. There was a young man from Cambridge standing against the wall, looking aloof and self-conscious, he reminded me of Ivor, who wasn't there; he looked grateful when I went up to him, thinking I seemed one of the respectable ones, I suppose.

"How are you getting on?" I said. "Are you amused?"

"It seems to me desolating," he said, clipping his words, precise, soft and haughty.

"Perhaps," I said, "we should drink more. Then we'd stop watching and blend."

"Not necessarily," he said stiffly.

"Do you feel isolated?" I said.

"Don't we all?" he said with a slavic shrug. He looked suddenly amused and youthful, and said, watching Colin's antics, "Perhaps not Mr. Radford...."

Colin was shouting, "Lights! More lights!"

"Perhaps not," I said, thinking: You fool! Colin most of all.

Gil Severn came up and began talking about hotels in Spain. The young man knew all about them and after a few minutes I slipped away and left them talking, thinking: The lad won't feel his evening wasted, he'll have talked to the eminent critic, Gil Severn.... Desmond Fellowes was sitting on a sofa with an artistic-looking girl on his lap. She had ear-rings and a string of huge coloured beads round her short neck, and a little jacket with emerald and orange chenille flowers on it; she was plump and dark and springy and she had a kitten on her shoulder. He's always discovered sitting like that at parties, where does he get these girls, what do they talk about; they look so incongruous against his spare, fastidious, unrelaxingly intellectual-looking form, his beard and glasses. The kitten was the crowning touch. . . . Peter Jenkin turned up, of course, he's a hardy perennial, under a pile of sub-revellers, teeny actors and things, he didn't see me or wouldn't—more green-faced, spiteful, wizened than ever. To think of Oxford and the way he poisoned my first year—that note I got: "It's a pity you didn't think fit to save me, good-bye," in a shaky hand—and when I rushed round trembling faint to his rooms a cocktail party in full swing, and him drunk and perky, calling out, "Sorry you've been troubled, dearie. . . ." Billy was making odd noises dancing with voluptuous contortions by himself and snapping his fingers, he'd almost passed out, the wet white gone streaky, the vine leaf gone. Anna was wandering entwined with Mrs. Cunningham's beautiful son Peter, they were having long kisses. She's always adored him for his beauty, so I was delighted to see she'd got him for the evening, she looked quite pretty, flushed and sparkling. . . . Then suddenly Marigold was there again, with David Cooke. She was going round the room saying with earnest formal politeness, "Excuse me, have you seen half my bracelet? You haven't? . . . Thank you so much." David came up, sleek, black and flashing, and said:

"Olivia, my dear, if a section of old paste and ruby bracelet turns up it belongs to Lady Britton. . . ." How he did relish saying Lady Britton. "Can I rely on you to take charge of it? It's an heirloom, she so values it. I must take her home now."

"Yes, it's about time," I said.

He went away, and I looked down and round, and there it was just by my foot, under the piano. I picked it up and followed her into the passage; she was leaning up against the banisters, very pale, her eyes fixed.

"*There* you are, Livia," she said, looking cornered, evasive. "Why didn't you come and talk to me before?"

"You disappeared," I said.

"Oh, well . . ." she said. "There was such a noise and crowd. . . ."

"Here's your bit of bracelet." I put it in her bag.

"Thank God," she said. "I thought I'd left it upstairs, far, far up among all those twanging springs. . . . The day springs from on high. . . . Whose room was it, I wonder? *Too* extraordinary. . . ." She giggled suddenly and drew in a sharp breath, her eyes flew. "David's pocketed the other bit. I s'pose he's honest. Isn't he sweet, I adore him, don't you? Though he's been a bit of a broken sepulchre to-night. He's taking me home, that's a meretricious act, anyway. . . . He's just gone to fetch my coat. I really *could not* fetch it . . . Livia, what an awful party, isn't it? Or isn't it? I don't know how I got here. David brought me. Why do they wear such dirty clothes? Have you seen Rollo at all? You ought to ring him up. I know he'd love it. Nicky's in Switzerland, breathing the bracing mountain air."

"I thought you were too," I said, forgetting myself.

"So I was, but I came back," she said. "Sam's still there."

"I saw your photograph in the *Tatler*," I added hastily, but she didn't notice.

David came back with her mink coat, surprised, I saw, to find me talking to Lady Britton, specially when she said, "Good-night, darlin'," and gave me a lingering kiss with her arms round my neck, saying, "David, isn't Olivia sweet?" Then she said rather frantically, "For God's sake come on now, if you don't get me home soon I won't answer for me." He enveloped and surrounded her, soothing, important, and they started down the stairs. Half-way down she began to whimper, saying, "Oh. . . . Oh, David. . . . Oh. . . ." I wondered whether to go to her, but I thought better not; I heard him say: "It's all right, my dear, you'll be all right. . . . I've a

taxi waiting. . . ." I think he'd got more than he bargained
for taking Lady Britton out. He fairly swooped her out of
the door and into the taxi. It was one o'clock. I went back
to the party. The more repressed people were beginning to go,
the pot was boiling over nicely; people leaning and lying
about, and dancing in heavy stumbling groups, looking intent.
Dick had snitched that blonde called Muffet, Jasper's property—
he was glowering and glaring at Dick, his face working like
the villain in an old-fashioned film, it looked so faked I wanted
to laugh. Someone had been sick in the grate and someone
else said, "Rum on top of whisky. *Fatal*. . . ." Simon was
dealing with it, looking patient as Christ on the Cross. Fat
old Cora Maxwell had fallen down and cut her head open
somehow, there was a crowd round her bandaging and mopping. Simon came with a glass of water and put his arm
beneath her shoulders, holding her up to sip. . . . Her red,
congested face, the handkerchief tied crooked over one eye,
the knot sticking askew on her peroxide mop, her fat hips and
little legs prone on the floor, stumpy toes turned up, and
Simon stooping above her, pale and clear, his beautiful mouth
folded so gently, blinking a little, holding the glass to her
lips. . . . I found Jocelyn, he'd only just turned up from writing
late, we sat in a corner on top of a table and had a quiet
talk. He made a cool island in the room. He wrote down his
address in the Tyrol for me, he was just off for six months to
write his book; he said why didn't I come out and join him,
and do some writing too. He always thinks I could write,
since those sketches I showed him. He said too I could have
his room to work in after he'd gone, he wasn't letting it, he'd
post me the keys. . . . Dear Jocelyn, you're my friend, you make
me sit quiet and consider ideas—that injustice matters and
unemployment, and the power and hyprocrisy of rulers, and
revolutions, and Beethoven and Shakespeare and what poets
think and write. . . . Things like that, not individual relationships and other people's copulations and clothes and motor-cars,
and things. . . . Not that it lasts. . . . But Jasper came prowling

up and put his paw on my wrist, and drew me away reluctant
to dance. "The virgin," he announced, meaning my white
frock. After a bit of his usual style, clamped against him,
dancing around with deep swoops and squeezes, and sharp
stops, my frock clutched up at the back like when I was sixteen
and always got those hard-breathing, hot-handed partners who
showed the backs of one's knees, he looked at me under his
brows like a seer, more like a lecherous old bison and announced, "You've got a lover. . . ."

"Have I?" I said. How I loathe him—all that mystic
intuitive prophetic bunk and sententious blood-wisdom about
Women; fancy his parents calling him Jasper of all suitably
bogus names. . . . The worst is he does hit the nail on the
head by accident sometimes. . . . " Have I?" I said, raising my
eyebrows, innocently surprised; but suddenly I couldn't bear
it any longer, I must go to Rollo, there were cigarette stumps
and ash everywhere, and empty bottles and marks of dirty
shoes, and a pool of something on the oilcoth by the lavatory
door, and everybody still going through their dreary old paces.
I thought: I don't want them, I'm superior, I've got someone of my own, I haven't got to stay. I sent Jasper for a
drink and ran for my cloak. The last I saw was Billy with a
broom sweeping the rubbish, pulling down the paper decorations and making a heap of them in the middle of the floor
and putting a match to them, and Colin with an efficient level-
headed expression squirting at them with an empty soda-water
siphon. I suppose Simon saw to it. . . . Jasper loomed up
behind me as I went down the stairs, he started to follow me,
muttering—but I escaped and was in the street. It was two.
Would he have gone to bed? If I couldn't see him what was
I to do? I told the taxi to put me down at the corner of the
street where it led into the square. I'd only once been there
before, when I walked past his house out of curiosity. . . .
That part of residential London behind Bryanston Square is
unknown country. There was a cold wind blowing. I shivered.
There it was, Rollo's house, number two on the corner, the

hall light showing through the fan; lights in a room on the right of the door, the curtains parted a bit so that I could see in, and I saw him. Standing up by the mantelpiece, smoking a pipe. From outside the room looked warm, rich and snug— a first-class comfortable home. I saw that. . . . I leaned over the railings from the step and just managed to knock on the bulging Regency window. The taxi I'd left went past and stared at me. . . . Rollo, my darling, you opened the door and drew me in and shut the door again, and there we stood clasped in the hall of your house . . . murmuring: "Oh. . . . I did *so* want to get to you. . . ." And, "I nearly gave you up. I couldn't have borne it if you hadn't come. . . ." And, "Forgive me. I'm sorry. . . ." "It's all right now. . . ." Loving each other very much and both comforted. He took me into the room and I sat on his lap in the arm-chair by the fire to get warm.

"I mustn't stay here," I said.

"Well, I'm not going out into the streets with you at this time of night," he said. "What's there to worry about? Everybody's gone to bed hours ago. I'm all alone."

So I hid myself against him, hiding from his home. It wasn't a personal room we were in—more like a comfortable office with a big, manly desk with a telephone on it and an *ABC* and *Debrett* and *Who's Who* in a case and a high bookcase with a glass front and smart editions of the classics bound in calf behind it, and a dark-red and brown colour scheme. Over the mantelpiece was a shockingly bad pastel portrait of Nicola with a smirking bow mouth and an elongated goitrous neck— the kind they always seem to have of their wives in these houses: too meaningless to be upsetting. The first thing he asked was about Marigold; it had been such a shock to see her, thinking she was in Switzerland. I said I'd spoken to her for a minute, she was all right, only a little drunk, she'd left early.

"She told me to be sure and ring you up," I said. We laughed. "She seems to think it's time you had a fling."

"The fiend," he said. "It's not safe to tell her a thing. She's had this hunch you'd only got to persevere to compass my ruin ever since we met in the train."

"You don't think she knows about it, really, and isn't letting on?" I said.

"No," he said emphatically, after a second. "She can't possibly. Nobody knows. We've been so careful." And I saw him give a quick look round, as if thinking: This isn't careful. He asked if I'd enjoyed myself, and I said:

"Oh *no*, I hated it all. They all seemed so futile and drunk and squawky. . . ."

"I don't expect they were really," he said in that tranquil way he does when I make sweeping generalisations about people, putting me right without snubbing—although it always makes me feel accused of pettiness. . . . "They looked very cheerful. Fancy-dress party, wasn't it? I expect you weren't in a party mood."

"The fact is," I said, "one shouldn't go to parties when one's in love. . . . It makes one act aloof and superior and they distrust you."

"I dare say that's it," he agreed softly, stroking my shoulder. . . .

It was like a reunion after danger, a reconciliation without the soreness and recriminations of an actual word-quarrel to get over. . . . After a bit I said:

"She was wonderful, wasn't she?"

"Who?" he said.

"That girl, Thalassa—the dancer," I said. "I can't get her out of my head."

"Oh, yes. . . ." he said in an ordinary, almost vague voice. "Was that what she was called? . . . Yes, she was good at her stuff. . . ."

That's all we said about her. I didn't let on. . . . Seeing him in this new setting, which was his own, made him in a way a stranger again—undiscovered, terribly significant, as he seemed at Meldon; and wearing the white frock again—and

the lateness, the silence, the keyed-up mood we were both in
... it was like being back at the beginning again. ...

"This is a damned uncomfortable room," he said. "Come
upstairs."

We went up to the next floor—the stair carpet's chestnutty
brown and the paint deep tawny yellow, nice—and opened a
door, and switched some lights on.

"It's a lovely room of its kind, it really is. . . ." I exclaimed,
and he said:

"Yes, it's nice, isn't it? We knocked two rooms into one
to make it." That "we" was rather painful. I saw them
planning it, doing it together, to be a background for Nicola,
pleased with it together, showing it off to their friends—never
thinking I'd come and look at it. . . . I told myself rooms
made by a couple, joint possessions, don't matter, they're not
a real tie, not important. . . . But they are, they're powerful.
. . . The light came indirectly from three long shallow-scooped
niches in the walls, and these had tall white glazed pots in
them, elaborate Italian shapes, filled with artificial flowers—
brilliant, bright-coloured arrangements, formal but not stiff,
seeming to have a kind of rhythm in them. I thought: If
Nicola did these she can do something. . . . But I expect somebody in Fortnum's or somewhere did them. . . . The room
was long and empty and simple with cool luminous colours
like the insides of shells—the low, straight-lined, broad chairs
and sofas covered in white brocade, and the woodwork pinkish
grey. It really was a good modern room. There was only one
picture, a long, horizontal panel in the end wall, contemporary, though I can't be sure who did it—two seated
monumental figures of women on the seashore playing on
guitars, a group in the foreground lying with stretched
listening limbs, the colours rather pale, blues, browns and
greys. It surprised me, worried me rather. I liked it. But I
can't remember it clearly—or anything else; only the first
pang it all gave me, and a general impression of whiteness
and space. . . . We were there a long time. I lay on the sofa

with my eyes shut, sunk into the cushions, and heard the white clock ticking. . . .

"What's that?" I whispered suddenly.

He listened. "What?" he said.

"I thought I heard a creak . . . as if someone was outside? . . ."

"Couldn't be," he said. He got up and smoothed his hair and went softly over to the door and opened it. Nothing of course. The landing was empty, and I saw the empty staircase winding up. "Why are you so nervous?" he said, coming back. I sat up on the sofa with my feet tucked under me and saw Rollo walking about in his drawing-room, looking for a cigarette. Something was changed—far down, below all conscious layers. Yes, something began to change then. . . . It was that I began to lose my feeling of security. . . . Rollo had a nice house and a life of his own in it, and dependants, responsibilities. . . . I knew it after that. It's hard to face facts when they go against you.

I said, "I must go now."

"Next floor, darling, if you want to," he said. "Up two little steps and straight in front of you. I'll be downstairs." He gave me a kiss and I went up . . . thinking: the first door will be her bedroom. . . . I stood and waited by the first door on the right. . . . I remember the glass door-knob. The silence was dark, rigid. . . . I got a crazy feeling eyes were looking at me from above, looking over the banisters out of darkness. I opened the door of Nicola's bedroom, switched on a light, looked in . . . came out and shut the door again. Dust sheets over the quilt on the broad, low, silver-headed double bed, the mirror laid flat on the dressing-table under sheets of newspaper, pale-blue walls, blue curtains with a magnolia pattern, a drawing of Rollo, young, over the mantelpiece, two flower pictures, irises and pink lilies, pretty, a door leading into what must be Rollo's dressing-room. Shrouded, deserted. . . . The mistress of the house is away. . . . I went on into the bathroom and washed and dried my hands on her pale-pink towel, as soft

as silk, and saw her blue glass jars for bath salts and powder
and stuff, and saw Rollo's big bath-towel on the hot rail. The
farther door must lead into his dressing-room too. . . . A
married couple's suite . . . perfectly charming, extremely well
appointed, every convenience. . . . What have I done? Why did
I? How could I? . . . I didn't dream it would burn on, on, hot
and sullen . . . as if a dull gong had been struck that will go
on echoing for ever.

I ran down. Rollo was standing at the foot of the stairs,
a glass of beer in his hand, looking up. The light was on in
the dining-room, to the left of him—where he and she have
their meals together and have well-dressed dinner-parties.

"I've been foraging for refreshments," he said. "But all
the biscuits and fruit and things seem to have been put away,
and I'm blessed if I know where, though it is my own house.
. . ." My own house. . . . I wasn't hungry. I was shivering
again. He made me drink some beer from his glass, holding me
close to him. We went out and found a taxi on the rank and
he took me to Etty's door. It was five o'clock when I got to
bed. Dead beat. . . . I've seen Rollo tired, but never without his
warm, dry, vital hand, never without his clear eye and fresh
ruddy skin. His health is glorious. In his arms I feel an electric
glow pass from him to me. How can Nicola be an invalid,
living by such a warm source of vigour? If she slept with
him. . . . But she doesn't, of course—that's what it is. . . .
She won't. Poor Rollo. . . . But I comfort him, I always will.

Then came the next week-end, the last we could have
together for goodness knows how long; she'd be back the
week after. Etty was in, so he didn't call for me. I went with
my suitcase to Paddington and sat on a bench on Platform One,
and waited. He was half an hour late—a depressing start—A
man in a bowler hat and stiff collar with wet lips and eager
teeth sat down beside me and tried to engage me in conversation. He spat when he talked. An elderly crumpled woman
with a brown stole and pince-nez walked up and down eyeing

me, I got a mad idea she was the Girls' Friendly or the Rescue
and Preventive come for me; and when I saw Rollo at last I
went to meet him in a stiff flurry as if everybody was looking,
and guessing what we were up to. He only said, "Sorry I'm
late. I couldn't help it." I was prim with unuttered reproach.

What a day—dark, sodden, ruined with rain since early
morning. We drove west. There was something between us,
heavy, that wouldn't disperse. We lunched in Oxford at the
George; it was funny to go back there with Rollo. Afterwards
we went into Blackwell's and looked about. Rollo bought a
huge illustrated book about Greek art, and I ordered a volume
of poems by a new young man Jocelyn had told me about. We
went on through Stow on the Wold—on. . . . All that spacious
sad green country with its beech groves and stone walls was
beaten out by rain. It was like the end of the world; there
seemed no way to deny or disregard its declaration of catastrophe. We wanted not to go to an hotel this time. I couldn't
face the register, and hotel faces staring again, we got too
much attention. Rollo has the kind of English appearance and
manner that makes waiters and porters press forward wherever
he goes, expecting his tips to be liberal and his name quietly
distinguished. He could never look like a medium-price
standard traveller staying around with his wife. . . . Our plan
was to find a romantic little inn or a farmhouse that took in
guests, and have two wonderful peaceful nights in rustic
solitude, with perhaps cows and chickens and rural voices in
dialect to wake us, and rosy-cheeked open wholesome country
faces round us. . . . Blue remembered hills, and perhaps the
wood in trouble; never this infinite thick soup of rain. . . .
Oh, the rain!

When it began to be dark we were far out on a country
road the other side of Tewkesbury, the car began to splutter
and check, going on the wrong number of cylinders. We drew
up under trees and I held a torch in the rain while he did
things inside the engine for what seemed ages. Then he went
on; but soon she started to halt and cough again. "Poor dear,"

he said. "She's got a chill in her tummy. We'll just have to crawl to the nearest garage if we can." We crept on in low gear and after a mile or two we had the luck to find a lonely roadside wooden garage and workshop with a light on, and one man inside. We drove in under shelter and Rollo and the man poked about in the engine and fetched tools from the oily bench, and had a technical dialogue while I sat inside half in a stupor watching them stoop, straighten up in queer lights and shadows, seeing their lips move, hearing the hum of their voices like in a dream. He opened the door finally, and said:

"There's nothing for it, darling, we'll have to leave her here till to-morrow. There's quite a job of work to do on her, and he wants to knock off, it's his Saturday night." He spoke with indulgent regret; I knew he was quite pleased to be fussing with the engine, looking forward to more to-morrow. "He says there's a little pub place about two miles on where they'd put us up. He'll run us up in his tootler. He's a nice chap. Shall we go and see what it's like, darling? . . ."

The man's car smelt like Walker's taxi used to, going to Meldon or Tulverton parties. The pub looked all right in the nearly-dark—square and whitewashed with a low dim stuffy bar full of wrinkled, grizzled men with pipes on wooden benches, and two young chaps throwing darts. Women weren't allowed in the bar and I waited in the parlour beyond—a dun-coloured airless box with a table with a green plush cloth and an ash-tray on it saying "Smoke Player's," and a calendar for 1920 saying "Guinness" hung on the wall, and a pink egg-cup on the mantelpiece. Our man took charge for us in the bar, and there was a calling out into the kitchen and a consultation and a woman came in, and said doubtfully:

"We 'ave got a room. . . ."

So I asked to see it, and she showed me up. It wasn't too bad, just small and stuffy with a cottage smell, a mountainous iron bedstead and a tiny window looking out over fields. We'd be quite happy in it, I thought, with a fire and the window open. The woman had by no means an open apple-face, she was raw-boned and harsh and crooked, with untidy despairing hair-wisps and a pale long face both tense and vacant. The man came up from the bar and looked in—a little sharp man with false teeth and a cap on—and was familiar, perky, obsequious. Not a sympathetic couple. The dialect they spoke was Cockney.·... No bath, of course, I did long for one. When I went down again, Rollo was having a drink with his car chap in the bar, looking very cheerful and matey, so I went back to the awful parlour and waited. Soon I heard him say, "Well, good-night, and thanks so much. I'll be along to-morrow morning. . . ." And he came and joined me, and said again what a nice chap he was.

"I think we'll be all right here, darling, don't you?" he said coaxing, in case I might be going to grumble—of course I didn't, I never did with him. He often said I was the only woman who never did, his theory about women is they expect every damn' thing and complain without stopping. I wonder does Nicola nag. . . . How I loathe women who expect consideration because they're women and give nothing back; who insist on the chivalry and yet hoot about sex-equality. I suppose with Ivor . . . I did go on at Ivor sometimes. . . . Yes, I did. But there was tremendous provocation. ·. .

Rollo soon got things going, as he always did; a fire in the parlour and drinks and supper ordered. The woman said she supposed she could cook us something, the man said: "Anything you fancy, you've only to mention it." We had fried eggs and bacon, they tasted good with beer, Rollo had cold beef and pickles as well. I went up to bed, he stayed down and played darts with a local lad, making himself so popular with them all. . . . Affable condescension like his mother and the rest. . . . No, no, no, he's not like that—never. . . .

The bed was remarkable—appalling, the sheets made of thick cottony stuff—is it twill?—faintly hairy and with a special smell. They were a bit damp. Outside in the black night the rain went on teeming. . . .

I don't know what happened. I can't remember how it

started; I try, but I never shall. He was asleep long ago, I couldn't sleep, I was so uncomfortable, and the other side of the wall someone snored, snored, hour after hour, a dull rhythmic boom with now and then a choke. It sounded so difficult, destructive, hostile, as if someone coarse and angry were hating human sleep, defiling it. And the rain going on seemed to be piling up something irrevocable around us—a doom. Rollo slept on his side, soundly, turned away from me. . . . I started to cry, first quietly to myself, I was so on edge and tired—then sobbing and snuffling to wake him, he must comfort me. At last he turned over, and after a bit stirred and made a sleepy protesting noise, and murmured: "Oh, darling, don't. . . . What is it? I shouldn't cry. It's all right, you know. Go to sleep . . ." wanting not to hear, to be left in peace. I wondered if that's how he talks to Nicola. . . . I couldn't let him not hear, I sobbed louder.

Suddenly he woke right up, astonished, incredulous, horrified. Poor Rollo. It was the first time he'd seen me cry, except for a few voluptuous tears. . . . At Meldon he'd said so queerly: "Oh, but it's such a luxury! Don't you know that?" "Perhaps I'm not a crier," I'd said demurely. . . .

"What's the matter?" he said. "Why are you crying? Olivia!" He shook me. He never called me Olivia, always darling or something, the sound of it sobered me down. It all came out in a howling jumble—I couldn't go on like this— I couldn't—I loved him. . . . Why should I stand aside, why should I never count? I realised now what his life was. I was outside and had nothing. I should lose him. In spite of boo-hooing so madly I felt quite clear in my head, not saying things I didn't mean. Didn't he know what love was? I said. Did he think I was satisfied, as he apparently was, seeing him once a week by stealth—did he ever think of it from my point of view? . . . Sobbing into the pillow till it was soaked, part of me thinking all the time of that horrible couple awake perhaps, listening, nudging each other, whispering: "Something funny up. . . . I told you so. . . ."

Poor, poor old boy, he was appalled. "Stop, stop," he kept saying, trying to turn me over. He lit a candle and got up and fetched his hanky to blow my nose. I blew it, and then I saw his face by candlelight, calm, thoughtful, severe almost; and I stopped crying. Was it worse than I thought then? Had I said something final, irrevocable? Would his voice say: "If you feel like that we must stop?" I shrank up into myself, flat on my back, to receive the blow he'd deal.

"I must be very blind," he said. "I'd no idea you weren't happy, Olivia."

"I am—at least sometimes. . . ."

"I thought we were so happy."

"Perhaps we are really. . . ." Imbecile, wanting to unsay it all now. "I know we are really."

"Why didn't you tell me all this before?"

"I didn't know I felt it."

"Then what's happened?"

I couldn't say it. I couldn't. . . . Jealous. . . . I've seen your home, she's real, I'm jealous of her; having said always I'm not jealous, not possessive. I said, "I suppose it's been boiling up underneath. I've tried to suppress it, not worry you. . . . But I get so frightened. . . ." And I let out some more sobs.

"You see——" He stopped. He'd said it before once, just like that, and stopped. I waited, terrified. The snoring went on and he seemed to hear it all of a sudden for the first time. He listened, and said, "God!" and gave a laugh. So I did too. After that it was easier. He took my hand and started stroking it, speaking very quietly.

"Listen, darling. You know what my life is. . . ."

"Yes. . . ." It began to be like being spoken to for one's good by a kind firm elder, someone who expects you to be sensible enough to see their point of view, and there'll be no appeal. . . .

"I'm married."

I could have cried out, hearing him state it like that, bald and direct for the first time.

Anguish. I dug my nails into his hand, it must have hurt him, but he went on stroking.

"Yes. You're married."

"Well, there it is," he said after a pause, and we were silent. There it is, there it is. He's married. That was a fact when we started. . . . It'll teach you to get mixed up with a married man.

"I can't hurt her," he said.

"No." Why shouldn't she be hurt? I am. . . .

"And—whatever happens—as long as she wants me to stay —I couldn't leave her."

"No." She's his wife, she comes first. "She does want you to stay then?" . . . Torture, getting that out.

"Yes, she does."

"I see. . . ." Well, there it is. After a bit I wrenched out, "Have you—have you ever talked of *not*, then?"

Poor Rollo, he was suffering too. He didn't know what to say, he was in an awful fix.

"I suppose most married couples do some time or other . . . when they have difficulties. But she knows I never would— unless she wants it. And I don't think she . . . she may some day, but I don't think . . . She wants—she needs—to have someone she can count on. . . ."

"Yes, it's nice for her. . . ." I couldn't help saying.

We were silent. What was plain was what hadn't been said. Never once, not even in the joyful, grateful, amazing beginning days, had he . . . no, not once . . . put her second—broken a plan made for, by, with her to stay with me. . . . Not once. Nothing explicit said ever. Nothing crude or marital to hurt my feelings, but—well, there it is. . . . I should have thought of it all before, I should have gone on being content with a half-share. I shouldn't have gone to that house. . . . He sat on the edge of the bed, holding my hand, his shoulders drooping forward, his face set, heavy and mournful-looking in the candle-light. Perfectly exhausted now, bled white, wanting only to rest, I said what hadn't been said, knowing I wouldn't feel any more pain much:

"You love her."

"Yes, I do love her."

"Although she doesn't—although it doesn't work very well?"

"No, it doesn't work well at all."

He was struggling with things to say, not to say. It was agony for him, the whole thing, poor boy. He said:

"But I thought you knew—I thought you understood all this."

"I suppose I did. One doesn't think—tries not to. . . ."

He beat his fist in his hand, saying:

"I've been the most bloody selfish swine that ever . . . You made me so happy. I never dreamt . . . I suppose I took it for granted you were happy, it was all right for you too. . . . What am I to do?"

"Don't worry, I *am* all right. It doesn't matter. As long as you . . ." Stopping, in case it was forcing him to say what he couldn't say . . . what he did say.

"Olivia, I love you." Hardly ever saying it quietly like this. Often, "Darling, I *do* love you," making love, but that's quite different.

"You do believe it, don't you?" he said. "You must. Listen. I can't change anything. I can't change myself. I can't shatter her. But I love you, I expect I always shall. If it's worth it at all for you, don't quite leave me."

The misery and despair were draining away like smooth dark water pouring away noiseless, without check, into a tunnel, gone. . . . Life turned itself inside out again, like after a bad dream, showing its accustomed unsinister face. I thought I'd been mad. What on earth was the fuss?

"I'm terribly happy," I said. "If you love me nothing else matters. I can do without other things. And I promise," I said, "I'll never make a disturbance again." I said, "Forgive me."

"Some day," he said, "you won't want me any more. Why should you? You'll be fed up with me. Somebody will come along and marry you, and take you away from me. It'll be only natural." He was very sad. "You should marry again, I know you should. I tell myself so."

"It won't happen," I said.

"Yes, yes. It will. You should have a home, you should have children. It's such a waste you shouldn't." Terribly unhappy voice. "I'm so afraid of getting in the way of that. I dread it. You might want to marry and not like to tell me. *Promise* to tell me. . . ."

"Who on earth could I marry?" I smiled, pleased, he was feeling a qualm about losing me; it was that way round now.

"That Simon you're always talking about or someone. . . ."

I laughed out. He was jealous too. Why did he pick on Simon, I wonder? I hardly ever talk about Simon—more about Colin and the others if at all.

"*That* won't occur, I can guarantee. I could never persaude Simon to want to marry me, I'm afraid."

"Oh, I hope not!" Holding me. "I hope nobody will! I could *not* bear it. I wouldn't be any good at being noble and unselfish. I want you for myself."

So that was all right. I was exalted. The way he spoke of the future made it sound as if it was a thing going on till we were old: a woman on her own, I saw myself, with brave sad smiling eyes and a secret. Never any children. I thought I could manage. Rollo would die and I'd step forward afterwards and say I loved him too, and Nicola would turn to me for comfort, we'd set up together, I'd look after her. . . . God knows what muck went through my head. . . .

"Perhaps when we're very old," I said, "we can be together."

"On my seventieth birthday," he said, "we'll have a night together, for old times' sake. Is it a date?"

We laughed about that. He soaked my sponge in cold water from the jug and brought it and bathed my swollen face for

me. We lay with my head on his shoulder and went to sleep.
What I must, *must* know hadn't been said: I didn't say it till
next day. The threatening images faded and were harmless.
. . . But waking up was clouded, heavy. Of all things, I'd had
to go and dream about Ivor and his mother: I was at her
house and she came out of the front door to meet me, I was
propitiatory, full of plausible explanations about why
I'd left Ivor, she was friendly, and smiled a lot, I looked
for sinister thoughts behind the smile but found none. I
woke thinking: Well, I'm glad I've got that straight at last;
and there was Rollo, up, half-dressed, wanting to get to
his car.

He was kind, but a shade off-hand, his mind on the job of
work he was going to do. The rain had stopped, the day was
dark, grey, cold and gusty—one or two tattered blue holes
blown into the sky for a moment, then over-blown again. Flat
fields out of the window. The features were a shed of pink
corrugated iron, telegraph wires, some chicken coops and a
new yellow stucco bungalow. He told me to rest, I looked
pale. I took a look in my mirror; my God, I was a sight;
dead looking, no eyes, even my lips pale, puffy.

"Poor little one," he said, absent, soothing. "You'll be all
right later:" making it plain what a bad business I was. He
kissed me and went off cheerfully, saying he'd tell them to
bring my breakfast up. I bathed my face and got it a bit
deflated and put on rouge. After a bit the woman came in,
harsh, with her noisy raking stride, and plunked a great unappetising tray on my bed. She stayed a bit and gossiped, but
not in a friendly way—disgruntled, dyspeptic, whining. They'd
only been there a year, they were Londoners, she hated the
country. She was ugly, she made everything raw, strident,
ugly. I dozed a bit more, but one couldn't be comfortable in
that bed, I ached all over. I was just dressed at lunch-time when
Rollo came back, in good spirits, his hands black with oil. We'd
have the car by three, he said; it was more of a job than he'd
thought. We had a cut off the joint in the parlour, I could

scarcely taste, all my senses numbed; I remember noticing my own voice gone light and small, my movements inert, languid. I'd meant to walk with him back to the garage, but a storm of rain came on, he went off again alone. I dragged myself upstairs and lay on the bed, and looked at his Greek sculpture book. Nearer four than three I heard the car; he came up and sat on the bed, and asked how I felt.

What I *must* know I hadn't asked yet. I asked it then. I shouldn't have, but I had to. . . . Whether he and Nicola—ever nowadays . . . my arm over my face, very quick and calm. . . . He waited a moment, I didn't look at him, it seemed for ever before he said: "No."

That was all I wanted to know, my mind was at rest. At least more so. . . . I asked him to forgive me, I had no right, but I had to know.

He nodded his head, and lit a cigarette. I said: "Let's go," and jumped up and packed very energetically, wanting to get away. It was after five when we started, lugubrious swollen clouds rolling up from the west.

"Couple of sharks," he said, amused, annoyed, as he got in the car. But he wouldn't tell me what they'd rooked him; he never will let me see any bill. I didn't feel right: on edge, a crashing headache coming on. He wasn't in good form either —a bit morose and distant. We turned towards London again, not having any plans. About dinner-time we found ourselves in Oxford and stopped at the Mitre for a meal.

"Shall we stay?" he said afterwards. "Or push on to London?"

"Just as you like, darling."

"Well, I've got to be back so frightfully early to-morrow it 'ud really be better perhaps if we pushed on. Getting up at crack of dawn is so grim—one gets back feeling like hell. What do you think, though, darling?"

"Let's push on," I said. I don't remember caring particularly. What with all those tears and the rain and all, the week-end was submerged, finished. We couldn't have revived it.

He was tired too. We only wanted to be alone and sleep. We drove on to London.

It's funny, after that week-end there seems a gap for a long time. We didn't see each other much, I'm sure of that. The problem of where to go got more and more acute. The snatched snips and fragments had become hateful to me—though he didn't feel it in the same way, and once or twice went away sulking when I said no, impossible. It was getting on for spring, he gave me freesias, mimosa, tulips. It must have been in early March that Jocelyn sent me his keys as he'd promised, with a note saying he was just off to Austria, and wouldn't I try to come out for a bit later. I rang him up and said would he mind if I lived there say for a month, and tried to do some writing after studio hours. He was delighted—telling me where he kept his sheets and towels, and about the geyser; and did I want his charwoman to do breakfast for me? I said no, I'd look after myself, but she was to come in for an hour every morning while I was out. It's a lot of washing up that gets me down. I explained to Etty, saying I just needed a workroom of my own for a few weeks, I knew a publisher who was interested, she was thrilled of course; she's marvellously uninquisitive and unobservant, I must say. Mother was suspicious at first, but pleased on second thoughts. She always thinks it's such a pity I dropped Writing after being in print so much at Oxford. She thought at last I might be going to settle down and Do Something. Poor Mum; she doesn't trust Etty, or Anna—or me either for that matter. So my tangled web was nicely woven. I didn't say a word to Rollo. We lunched together the day I moved in. I said I'd something to show him, and directed him where to go in the car after lunch, opened the door with my own latch-key, walked him upstairs, very mystified, and ushered him in. A grand surprise. The sun was streaming in at the window, and he was so beautifully pleased and excited. I thought I'd be very happy there. I like that part of London too, off the Fulham road. After he'd gone, masses

of flowers arrived, and in the evening a great hamper from
Fortnum's, full of those delicacies—fruits in brandy, foie gras,
pickled figs and things—that are a bit of a worry really; one
never can decide at what meal to eat them, and it seems such
a shame to open the jars. A bottle of Calvados too. The sad
thing was he couldn't have dinner with me, he'd got to dine
out, he'd come round afterwards, if he possibly could. . . .
Sometimes I remember what he said that time I got a glimpse
of his engagement book: "They can all be scrapped." It wasn't
often they were. . . . He can't help it . . . I couldn't be bothered
to cook dinner for myself. I had a banana and a cup of coffee
and went out and saw a bad film at the Forum. I came back
and sat by the gas fire and waited. About midnight the bell
rang, he was there. He stayed with me an hour or two, it was
heavenly to feel secure against disturbance. He left and I heard
his step go down the uncarpeted stair. . . . I felt lonely then
and oppressed. The room seemed quite the wrong shape—too
high—square—what? . . . I don't like bed-sitting rooms,
specially at night. I can't sleep properly. The building seemed
utterly empty except for me. A German couple lived on the
ground floor, but in between me and them on the first floor,
were empty rooms. A painter had one, but he lived in the
country and only came up and used it if he had a portrait
commission. He didn't have one while I was there. . . . And
Jocelyn's windows, large, bald, vacant with his long dismal
unlined butcher-blue curtains, trailing down like a giant's
boiler-suit. . . . He hasn't any taste in decoration; not that he's
indifferent, he likes his room; he just hasn't any eye. Writing
young men often haven't. Not like painters: whatever the
mess and squalor their rooms are generally alive. But serious
young authors like Jocelyn are apt to live in impersonal apart-
ments with a good deal of brown and blue casement cloth, and
oak sideboards, and wicker chairs their mothers have let them
have from home. Not uncomfortable, or downright ugly;
undeveloped more, student-like. Not puritanical exactly, but,
anyway, a hint of a moral attitude. . . . Jocelyn being against

possessions at the moment, he'd given away a good many of his books, and the only things in the way of pictures were two photographs, one of Gaudier-Brzeska, one of D. H. Lawrence, cut out of books and framed in black passe-partout; and one lithograph, quite good—a nude. The walls were distempered in fawn, the bed had a Paisley shawl over it by day. . . . Even trimmed up with Rollo's flowers, that room never cracked a whole-hearted smile.

The thing is really, I don't like living alone. The wind gets up; or else I start wondering what the people were like who lived in the room before me; dead now, and soon I'll be dead and what's it all about? . . . I sit in a chair and do nothing, or lean against the mantelpiece. . . . I got to know Gaudier and Lawrence well, and the ugly bit of Victorian-Gothic church the window showed. I was alone in that room more than I thought I'd be. It was disappointing. Nicola stayed in London the whole of the time; I hadn't thought of her doing that. I used to think why didn't Rollo urge, persuade her to go away for a few days. He could have if he'd tried. I wanted him to spend a week-end there with me, or at least one whole night, and he wanted to too.

"But I *can't* suggest her going," he said rueful, his eyebrows up. "It seems so mean, doesn't it, darling? Don't you think it does?" It was one of the kind of little things he just can't do. . . . He told me she was much better, had more energy, wanted to go out so much more, and enjoyed things. I said I was so glad.

He was in such good spirits all that time, so sweet to me, I couldn't bear to let him see I wasn't in form myself. I'd promised I'd never complain or make a scene again; I never have. The Other Woman mustn't make too many demands: Rule the first. . . . Sometimes I thought—I still think—he was loving in a different way during that time. . . . What was it now? . . . More spoiling, more attentive. . . . As if he was apologising, wanting to make up to me. . . . I suppose because he wasn't seeing me as often as I'd hoped. . . .

He'd manage to come for dinner once a week. I cooked it in the tiny cupboard of a kitchen, and he laid the table, awfully pleased with himself. I shall never like cooking, I'm not talented enough, but it was nice cooking for him, he appreciated it so. I bought a stylish little new cookery book and dished up all sorts of mixtures. Sometimes when he couldn't have dinner with me, he'd ring the bell late, about one o'clock. I never stayed out anywhere after midnight in case he did. It was rather wearing, the waiting; often after one had struck, I'd listen for the half-hour, then two, then the half-hour again; still keyed up for the door-bell, the telephone, hearing in my brain his car come down the street and stop, sitting frozen in my chair—a listening machine. . . . I asked him how he explained when he came late. "I go to look up old George," he said. I knew George was an habitué of the house—Nicola's friend—it didn't seem safe; but he said George had had standing orders for the last ten years to provide an unhesitating alibi on all occasions with an element of doubt in them. George could be trusted. He was a very useful chap, never been known to ask a question.

His father and mother came to stay with them for a week during that time. Sir John was having some new sort of treatment from a specialist. That week I scarcely saw him, and when he did come he seemed to bring Lady Spencer with him—which was appalling. I thought: Her son. How dare I. . . . How wrong. . . . I thought how she'd disapprove, and I worried, thinking whoever Rollo can deceive he won't get past her. . . . Whenever the bell rang that week I had a mad fear it was Lady Spencer come to say all was discovered, I must give him up at once. I saw exactly what her hat would look like, I heard her voice ordering me off with majestic uncompromising finality—like the Queen at Ascot sacking improperly dressed ladies from the Royal Enclosure. My heart used to beat, going down to answer the bell. Dotty. . . . It just shows how guilty I really feel.

I did try to write now and then, I got about half a sketch

done, but I kept losing my way in it; and the listening and waiting interfered. A person in my state can't work. . . . Oh! Sometimes I wish . . . no . . . yes, sometimes I wish I could be free again, able to belong to myself. . . . The burden is too heavy, there's hardly a moment to fit in the happiness of loving. . . . And I would like to do something definite with my life. . . .

What it came to was that the evenings I knew for certain he wouldn't come were a kind of relief. Etty trotted round once or twice, and Anna, of course, and once Kate came up and spent the night. She took me to a theatre and I made her up a bed on the other divan and she enjoyed herself, though she criticised the geyser a good deal and got up horribly early and alert the next morning. . . . Having a love affair makes one very remote and useless to one's friends. I didn't care much at that time what happened to any of them.

I slept better the nights I knew he wouldn't come. Another trouble was the thought of his having to leave in the early hours and go out in the dark and cold right across London to his own home. It worried me more and more. We hadn't thought of that side of it; only of the peace and relief of his being able to stay late. Now that he did, I saw it was bad for him, it meant short broken nights, nervous strain. . . . I began to dread it for him. I thought he did too. I'd start quite soon saying, "You'd better go . . ." I'd follow him in my thoughts all the way, picturing his journey, timing it till I could imagine him home. It wasn't till I saw him undressed and in his own bed in that dressing-room that I could relax, and try to sleep. He caught a bad cold going back in a snowstorm one night, he gave it to me and it went on my chest. I couldn't shake it off. . . . Oh, God! There's no solution for a situation like ours. Whatever we try out, the clock defeats us, complacently advancing acknowledged claims, sure of our subservience, our docility. . . . Why should she be so protected, pitied? Why shouldn't she have one pang, one wet lace handkerchief? . . . Why shouldn't she lose him, why not? What's she done to deserve to keep him? Let her stand on her own; why not? It's what she needs. Make her grow up. Make her get out of bed and pull herself together. Shirker! Upper-class parasite! Hysterical little vampire!... *Stop!*

Once after lunch, taking me back to Jocelyn's in the car, he stopped at a flower shop in the Fulham Road, he'd seen some pink lilies in the window he wanted to get me. He says it with flowers all right.... White lilac too. He picked it out, branch by branch, and the girl packed it up, and the lilies too, in cherry-coloured paper. My arms were full. He wandered round as he always does, and then stood looking at some sprays of stephanotis, precious-looking, in a glass on the shelf. "I'll have these too," he said, curt. She lifted them out to wrap up and he said, "I want them sent, please. Give me a card." He scribbled down Mrs. R. Spencer and the address, no message. "See they go at once, will you?"

Outside he said, a little apologetic, "It's her favourite flower."

"It *is* heavenly," I said, cool and bright. My arms were crammed with lilies and lilac, I shouldn't have minded. I wanted to throw them all away. I thought of her thanking him for the charming thought when he got back—wearing them in her dress that night... little guessing who'd given them a dirty look before they reached her. It's the only time he's ever been obviously tactless. It must have been he hadn't quite got his grip after rather a heavy lunch.

One night the bell rang late; about midnight, down I flew thinking Rollo had come unexpectedly. I opened quickly and there on the doorstep was an unknown young man. As he saw me his expectant smile faded abruptly. "Is Jocelyn in?" he said uncertainly. He was hatless, with rough brown hair, he wore a shabby overcoat with the collar turned up. He had large brown shining eyes with clear-cut lids under a broad jutting forehead; and that worn look of dignity, stress, youth which sets the maternal instinct working, wanting to look into the question of his food and underwear.

THE WEATHER IN THE STREETS 205

"I'm so sorry," I said when I'd explained.

"It doesn't matter a bit." His voice was gentle. "I just looked in."

I wanted to do something about him, ask him in—but I didn't. He looked as if he'd walked a long way. He smiled in a friendly and charming way, and said good-night and went away. I don't know why the incident made such an impression, but it did. It still haunts me. I wonder who he was, what he's doing. . . . He was so different from the person I'd opened the door to let in. He should have been there, he should have come in—not Rollo. . . . I don't know. . . . It was wrong that he had to go away again.

I suppose I was there about six weeks altogether. I know it was April when the two things happened. One was, I got 'flu badly, the other, his trip to America. Two months; on the firm's business: alone, that was something. I think he told me the day I started to be ill. Anyway, when I try to think the two things are mixed up: a waste of waters, a liner, the New York sky-line churn in my mind with shivering and aches and throbbing and trying to get up and falling back in bed again. When Mrs. Crisp came as usual about ten to tidy, she found me. Her appearance was wrong for illness, but she went out and got me some more aspirin, I'd run out; then she did a bit of dusting and clattering and went away again. After she'd gone I managed to ring up Rollo at the office and tell him not to come; he had to sail in ten days. The day wore away, parched, dazed. I dozed and woke and poured down aspirin and dozed again. Late in the afternoon the bell rang. I staggered down and it was pink lilies and grapes and peaches with a note from Rollo. After that no one came or rang up. The night was terrible. Next morning was Saturday, Anna was away, Rollo away, I couldn't face the week-end alone in the flat. I didn't know, but I thought I must be pretty ill. When Mrs. Crisp arrived I told her to ring up Etty, and she came, and the doctor came, and I was bundled in blankets and taken back to Etty's in the doctor's own car. He was nice and good-looking, a personal friend of Etty's of course. I'd managed to scrawl a line to Rollo while Etty was ringing up Mrs. Banks to order my bed and hot-water bottle. I gave it to Mrs. Crisp to post. So that was the end of living in Jocelyn's room. I suppose Mrs. Crisp took away the lilies and peaches. When Etty kindly went back next day for the rest of my belongings they were gone.

Etty looked after me, and the doctor went on coming and I went on having a cough and temperature. I'd been in a low state for a long time, I suppose. The struggle to keep secretly in touch with Rollo was too much. I gave up, and let on in an airy amused way to Etty after the second load of hot-house blooms. . . . I suppose he thought flowers were uncompromising. . . . Of course she was enchanted, and after that brought me up bouquets even when they weren't from him—Simon sent some, and Anna—in a roguish triumphant way—and when he rang up once to inquire had a little conversation with him which she enjoyed very much.

"He's fearfully solicitous, darling. *Too* perfect."

I said, "It's only because I happened to be going to lunch with him—his wife's away—the day I got ill, and had to put him off. He's very prompt with little attentions— lavish. The kind of gentleman-friend who gives one prestige in nursing homes. I suppose he's well broken into it—his wife's ill a lot. . . . I don't wish to belittle," I said. "It makes a nice change for me, and I do appreciate it, but after all, sending flowers is an easy way to get people off one's mind."

"There's an easier way," she said. "Sending none."

"Not always," I said. . . . "You know, even if I hadn't known him nearly all my life," I said, "I don't think I'd ever have found him terribly attractive."

Luckily she agreed about that, he's not her type, she likes small un-English-looking dapper men.

"But, my dear, *some* women *rave* about him, I believe. Iris Mountford was *tremendously* smitten once—and that Hungarian wife of Ronnie Arkwright's. Ronnie had to take her round the world."

"When was that?" I said.

"Oh, *before* he married—years ago. I believe he's *most* circumspect and domestic now, isn't he?"

"Oh, yes," I said. "At least, as far as I know."

"You take care," she said, shaking her head archly. "Those virtuous husbands can be awful traps—*far* more insidious than the obvious flirts."

"Oh, my dear!" . . . I shrugged my shoulders, entering into the spirit. . . . "Not a hope." An utterly dreary feeling came on, thinking of the Hungarian wife, of his reputation as a virtuous husband, of Etty's typical light assumption that all married men were up to no good on the sly.

After a week I was much better, but the doctor made me go on staying in bed. I was thankful—I dare say my subconscious was seeing to it—it was easier to hide in bed; it meant I needn't face the business of living over the time of good-bye. He came to say good-bye one evening about six. I'd been having visitors the last two days, so it didn't seem too odd. Etty went out, arch and tactful. He brought a bottle of champagne, which saved the situation, suppressing the ghastly cobwebs and sawdust feeling in my inside, not to speak of the tears I'd felt sure I'd shed. I got quite cheerful and made him laugh, he was so relieved and pleased with me. I expect he'd dreaded a scene. He said I looked prettier than ever—much too tempting. I took his big blue and green silk handkerchief out of his pocket, to have something of him to take to bed every night. I did, too. He debated what to take of mine that would be intimate yet not compromising. My toothbrush, I suggested. Finally he took the ribbon off my nightdress and put it in a compartment of his manly note-case.

"One plain white satin ribbon, an inch wide, without laundry mark or initials," he said. "Non-identifiable in case of loss, accident or theft. . . . It's safe there. I shall take a peep

at it every night and morning . . . and possibly sometimes at
midday as well."

We kissed, he held me close; it isn't for long, we said, write
often, cable. . . . "A family dinner party to-night," he said.
"I shan't be able to ring up. Besides, you must go to sleep
early." There didn't seem one particular instant of his going,
but he'd gone. . . . And then he was gone. It was rather bad
then. . . . Late that evening half a dozen bottles of champagne
arrived of course. I must say they helped my convalescence. . . .
In the morning, before Etty was awake, I crept down to the
sitting-room and rang up his house: the first time of breaking
the rule. "Hallo!" I thought for a moment it was him—the
butler must imitate his voice. "Could I speak to Mr. Spencer,
please?" Everything was swimming. I shook all over.

"Mr. Spencer left for the United States, madam, twenty
minutes ago. Mrs. Spencer has accompanied him to Southampton and will be back to-night; would you care to leave
any message, please?"

Very nicely said; efficient, concise, polite. "*I* see . . ."
Emphatically casual. "No, no message, thank you. It doesn't
matter a bit. Thank you very much."

When I was better Anna told me she'd decided to give up
the studio, anyway for the summer, and try to do some painting again instead. She wasn't paying her way, she was sick of
it. She'd felt lately she must take to the brush again. She had
ideas about changing her technique and getting on better.
Simon was going to be in France all summer, he'd offered her
his cottage for two guineas a week. Why didn't I come too?
She wouldn't let me share the rent, but I could share other
expenses. She was worried, I knew, having to cut off my pound
a week, but also she wanted my company. So I said Yes. With
Rollo not there London was awful, anyway. Time enough
when he came back to see how he felt about my being out of
London, but easily reached by car. I thought myself I might
see him for longer times with more peace and leisure . . .

country summer evenings, I pictured, perhaps nights together in country pubs. Mother highly approved my leaving my unhealthy London life. . . . A year ago she'd have tried to make me come home and be looked after, but now with Dad and nurse to supervise, she seems to dismiss me more easily. She has enough. Violet and Ada have enough trays and hot drinks to see to. The last times I'd been home she'd only wanted me to gossip and amuse her. She'd seemed almost detached about James and his walking tours in France and his suddenly announced decision to take a room in Paris. As if she'd decided to say at last, "Oh, what the hell! Let them rip. . . ." She's tired. Home is narrowed down to an unalterable invalid routine.

May, June went by in the country. . . . There's no two ways about it, the early days are clearer—those first few weeks in the winter. . . . Now after May, right up till now, till August, there seems a slowing down of my vitality, impulse—a faint mist over every scene. Don't I feel so much? It's natural, I suppose. One can't keep up the pitch I started at, it wears one out. There comes a sharp break of separation. You feel at first it's not to be borne, but you bear it, you grow accustomed. . . . Longing sinks down and is silted over. . . . You never uncover it again in its first unearthly freshness. . . . That's what happened. Week after week of being irrevocably far away. Sitting up in bed in the nights, sending out the very utmost desperately-stretched feelers of thought quivering to find him wherever he was—I couldn't find him; though sometimes I kidded myself I did for a moment or two. . . . Perhaps one needs a mutual effort for successful telepathy; I'm sure he never tried. Of course there were letters. But as usual his letters were sketchy, they didn't make a lot of difference, though if they hadn't come, I suppose I'd have gone mad. . . . On the whole it was easier than I expected; being with Anna was what really helped, and in the country, and in Simon's house.

Simon's house is one to love, it's important, like a being with its own life and idiosyncrasies. It filled up a little of the emptiness, it got to be in some way a substitute for a part of Rollo: a channel for emotion. . . . Simon's house is poetic. Not pretty, sweet, quaint, old-world, anything like that. . . . When I think of it, I think of it as standing back a little from reality, like a small Victorian engraving of a house—a tail-piece in a book; or like something seen through the wrong end of a telescope. Yet one can pass dozens more or less like it on a motor drive; small white houses, prim, rather narrow, straight-fronted, green-shuttered, two pairs of windows, the lower pair longer, larger than the upper, a steep-sloping, slate-tiled roof, with two miniature dormer windows in it. I wonder who built it and when. . . . It's by no means an architectural gem—yet it's entirely special; I suppose it's the setting and the feeling of isolation. . . . And because it's Simon's. When Billy came down he said haunted, but he would. . . . The lay-out of garden is what's so queer. No flowers or flower-beds; all grass—trees—water. In front, the narrow length of rough lawn, edged all round with a ragged stout hawthorn hedge. . . Two rosemary bushes under the lower windows. Half-way down the lawn, a bit to one side, the pear-tree, tall and old, flings up with an astonishing sideways curve and lift—a dancer's pause. . . . Three elms at the end of the grass. The front door's in the right side; no gate, a gap in the hedge, a bit of grass and you come to it, painted green. Opposite it, the other side of the rutty cart-road leading to it, is a perfectly round black pond ringed with fine chestnut trees; and beyond, half-hidden by them, a barn, some cow-sheds, old brick and lichenous tile, tumbling down, disused this many a year. If you stare into the pond, the black mud basin goes down sheer —bottomless they say. The surface never stirs, but just beneath it goes on a myriad stirring of infinitesimal wriggling black pond life. . . . The cart road winds off at an angle through the field to join the hedgy lane to the village; and the way to the river is over a stile by the elms at the bottom of the lawn, over

a flat green meadow, another stile, another meadow, willow
hedges—then the river, with shallow broken earthy banks just
there, rushes, flags, meadow-sweet, willow-herb; a sort of
little beach in one place, where we picked up mussels when
we bathed.

Anna does love that house. She says one could paint all
one's life within a two-mile radius from the door. Morning,
afternoon, evening, she scuttled out with her easel—whenever
she wasn't cooking, in fact. She likes cooking, she did more
of it than me, I'm afraid. She had depressed times about her
painting, and scrapped two-thirds, but she thought she was
getting on better on the whole. All the rooms smelt of
turpentine and wet canvases. She was preoccupied at meals
and forgot to comb her hair, and had streaks of paint on her
face. Dear Anna, I do like her so much. She's so quiet. . . .
She's independent, her judgment is right, just on the sour side.
Though she's not at all serene or confident underneath—quite
the reverse—she makes no demands. When she's very low she
just gets quietly drunk. She lives an intensely concentrated
inner life of thought and feeling, but never highbrow, priggish
or pedantic; and when she's enjoying something—a picnic, a
drive, a party—she's almost ludicrously irresponsible, as unselfconsciously extrovert and simple as a child. A grotesque element
comes up in her—something there is in her of the clown of
the world. . . . The most unvulgar woman I've ever known. . . .
Colourless. . . . Unperspicacious people think dull, insipid;
they're wrong. If you break up white, there are all the colours.
. . . I wonder if she'll ever marry again or get properly fixed
up. . . . Poor Anna, she doesn't have much luck, she will choose
the most unlikely people. . . . I suppose the truth is, she doesn't
in her inmost heart want anybody to supplant Simon. . . .
He's absorbed her emotion . . . although I suppose whatever
the relationship once was—nobody seems to know exactly, she
never tells any one much—it's all quieted down now, worked
itself on to some sort of possible permanent friends basis. It
can never have been very satisfactory for her. It must always

be partly painful to love Simon. . . . I'm proud that Anna's fond of me. It's not only her being so much older makes me rely on her. . . . Integrity has become a debased word, sentimental, like purity, or I'd say Anna has integrity.

May, June. . . . May was wet and cold, June sunny from end to end, my legs and arms got brown, Anna's dusty hair bleached in stripes, her eyes looked brilliant blue in her dusty-brown face. In May the hawthorn hedge was soaking; after a windy night the elm flowers came down in drifted heaps at the end of the garden. How pretty they are; I'd never noticed: clusters of green discs with a clear, red stain in each. Being with Anna is what makes me remember such country details so precisely. Her visual sense is so sharp and penetrating, she helped me to see too; not just look and dream, half-remember, half-overlook and forget. Country walks with her make an experience in themselves, not an excuse for day-dreaming; or for banging along blindly, like Jocelyn, fiercely considering literature and the proletariat. She sees into hedges, seeing leaves and moths and beetles; she sees how a tree grows in a landscape.

In May there was a frost; it made the evening strange. The full-sailing, torch-loaded chestnuts were caught, islanded in the pale blue-green Arctic fields of sky. All over the earth was the flowering spring growth; in the sky was frail winter light. . . . *A dream of winter, sweet as spring.* . . . The living green, the fruit-blossom enclosed in a cold transparent lucent shell of light—brittle, perilous. . . . The cuckoo was strange, an icy note. I wanted Rollo terribly that evening. We were threatened.

After that frost, the weather softened out, the warm days came. The doors and windows stood wide open from morning to night, people came every week-end to stay; in the evenings we went down through the buttercups and willows to bathe in the river, and afterwards played darts and had drinks at the Dog and Duck. Or if somebody had a car, we motored in to Oxford. . . . It sounds an ideal life . . . it should have been. . . . I don't remember much apart from the sun, and waiting

for the post; and swimming in the river. . . . I was writing
a bit, but it didn't get on much; I planned three stories, each
with a different background of water—a river, a lake, a sea.
It sounds a good idea, but it won't get done. I took some jolly
fine notes though; all my writing energies went into doing
that—and into my letters to Rollo. Every three days I posted
off a fat envelope, a diary really. He loved them; so he ought.
Every single one of his letters was disappointing and precious.
. . . He seemed to be having such a good time; he said how he
missed me, but I don't see that he had a moment to miss me.
Parties, week-ends, gorgeous American girls. . . . Loads of
peaches, he wrote, nobody who's taken my fancy, darling. I
didn't always believe it. I saw him open to onslaught on every
side—flirting as he always must, saying the things he said to
me, starting an affair for the duration. . . . There'd be plenty
willing, and he loves sleeping with people—and what was to
stop him? Me? Nicola? Unfaithful to her with me, why not
to me with someone else? Ce n'est que le premier pas qui
côute—and he'd taken that with me. Why shouldn't he embark
on a career as lover, one affair within another, each secret, in a
water-tight compartment? . . . Perhaps he had already. . . . Of
course he had. I had bad moments. . . . Jealousy coming like
a bank of poison gas out of a clear sky, corrupting the face of
the earth. After one letter about a week-end on Long Island
I lay on my bed and tore his blue handkerchief, and hit my
head again and again on the bed-rail. I did. . . . I can't believe
it, but I did. . . . It was after that I couldn't stand it any more,
I told Anna that evening that he was my lover. That made it
more real, a load rolled off, I was happier. We talked about
him till very late, she said everything just right and cheered
me up. For one thing, she took it all for granted, accepted it
with her cool sympathy as a live, working relationship. And
she seemed to understand why it was, how it was; she illumined
the situation all over again for me, asking questions that
showed me him and myself. Trying to describe with absolute
sobriety and precision what he was like, what had happened,

made me detach him from the amorphous emotional fog and
observe him more objectively, as I did for a brief moment
before this started. She understood I was jealous. . . . I asked
her had she guessed what was going on and she said quietly,
Yes, but didn't like to ask questions. She *is* nice. I'm glad I
told her. I can trust her to be silent, and she won't criticise
or give advice. . . .

He sailed for England early in July. But he didn't land in
England; Nicola met him at Southampton and they went to
Cherbourg and landed, and spent a week in Paris. A reunion,
a holiday away from everybody; her idea, he said; he personally would rather have come straight back. I wonder what
. . . I wonder why . . . He didn't refer to Paris much to me,
except to say it had been looking nice, they'd had quite an
amusing time, but it was her idea; she hadn't been in such
good form for years, full of impulsive plans like that. I said
Good, I was glad, she must be feeling better. I wondered to
myself if she had a lover. . . .

It was the middle of the month when he got back and rang
up. I wanted to dash straight up to London, but he said better
not, he was so busy; he'd slip off the first moment he could
and get down for the day, anyway. He'd come home to a perfect
whirl. . . . He sounded busy and *distrait*. Two days later came
the telegram—meet him in Oxford, the Mitre, one o'clock. It
was a Friday, hot and sunny. I went in by the morning bus,
in my clean coral-pink linen dress, and the peasant straw hat
from the south of France, with a wreath of poppies and daisies
round it. I walked down Long Wall and the Broad, trying to
observe the architecture, looking into shops, but I was too
flustered. I shivered, my hands were icy-cold, sweating. At
one I walked into the Mitre. He was a quarter of an hour late,
he looked hot and Londony. . . . We had a couple of iced gin
fizzes, then it was better, we could look properly at each other
and smile. He said. "Oh, darling, you look about seventeen
in that hat!" He kept saying: "I *am* so pleased to see you,

darling. . . ." But he was—what was he?—a bit preoccupied . . . not evasive exactly, but skimming about on the surface, a shade imprecise, facile, hard to pin down. He didn't seem to be able to describe much of what he'd been doing all these weeks . . . but he never can give a clear account of his activities. He forgets, he says. . . . He told me it had been awfully difficult to get away—he'd had to tell the most complicated set of lies to get out of a family fixture that evening; there'd been considerable sickness; he'd had to invent something about seeing George off to the Continent, and he didn't see how he could stay the night; she'd accepted for a week-end party for him, they were due to drive down in the morning. . . . Yes, it wasn't just the natural awkwardness of re-meeting in a public place, he was different in some deeper way. . . . Perhaps I was too. . . . Perhaps it was simply the break and neither of us was the same—or ever has been since. . . . Naturally, relationships can't stand still, they must develop. . . .

We drove back to the house after lunch, I showed him everything. We had it to ourselves; Anna had gone out with Colin and the others on the river, we were to join them after tea for a bathe. The house delighted him, specially inside— the light bright mixtures of colour, the decorations on the walls and doors, the whole flavour of the house that is so strong and individual I can almost taste it in my mouth; every object, every bit of stuff chosen with an unfailing idiosyncratic eye—even to the water-jug, the salt-cellar—yet all quite valueless in terms of money; mostly faded, chipped, worn. . . . And the rooms in themselves aren't a good shape or size. He said he hadn't realised what one could do with a cottage. I don't think it was just the desire to be agreeably enthusiastic; Rollo's very quick and sensitive to places, he takes in a lot. He said, which is true, that though it's stimulating, there's something not quite cheerful. . . . He wished Marigold could see it. But she wouldn't like it, really—none of those people would; any more than Kate would. As for Mother, she'd deplore it. The fittings are distinctly casual;

queer mattresses, and a stormy, capricious plug, and a rough little bright-green bath in a blistered bathroom so small you soon can't see for steam. Personally, I like it—cosy and secretive—hardly able to see one's own legs. Back to the womb with a vengeance. Anna says if I could sublimate my bath-lust I might become adult. She's sublimated hers all right, if she ever had one. I had that bathroom practically to myself.

Alone together all the afternoon. Oh, at last! . . . It was so still, we heard the hot bees burning in the rosemary. The blind knocked, knocked. Through it the violent afternoon light was purple, almost black. "No, truly, darling," he whispered, coaxing, "I didn't find anybody else. . . . Not one. . . . I couldn't forget you. . . . I did miss you. . . ." I still can't help wondering sometimes though. . . . About five we came down, had tea and bread and honey in the kitchen where it was cool. Then we walked down across the field with our bathing things. . . . I'd been nervous about producing Rollo; all they knew—except Anna—was a friend down for the day; but now I didn't worry any more. I suppose it was because of feeling released, slack, peaceful after the afternoon. He was rather nervous. He kept saying: "What'll I talk to them about? I don't know about books and pictures, darling."

That evening was a riot. What fun it was! . . . A bathing party breaks ice among strangers quicker than anything else I know. Something about swimming together makes immediate intimacy. By the time we were out of the water, we were all old friends. Adrian had turned up with a German young man from Berlin, to whom he'd been showing Oxford. His name was Kurt, and he was very decorous-mannered, anxious for information, determined to be equal to any manifestation of English behaviour. He wore an amethyst ring and a stylish light cloth overcoat, elegantly buttoned in to his waist, never taking it off—except for bathing; and a few spots apart, he was attractive. Adrian had got bored with him and was neglecting him shamefully; and Anna was being nice to him. He was a beautiful swimmer, and justly proud of his torso. He added a curious, slightly unreal element.

The westering sun was spilled all over the water. A pleasure steamer went by, crowded, people were dancing on board to the gramophone. They waved as they passed. On the opposite bank some little girls, skirts pulled up to their waists, were dipping and splashing each other with shrieks; and two fat middle-aged couples in black clothes came and sat down close to where we undressed, and took off their boots and drank ginger beer, and ate out of paper bags and stared, munched, stared at us in silence. They must have been on an outing. Like a picture by Rousseau, they looked; all in a stiff row; the bourgeoisie under the aspect of eternity.

Colin and Rollo hit it off together from the word go. Colin was happy that day—giggling, cursing the horseflies, trying to turn somersaults and dive off Rollo's shoulders. They made such an odd contrast; Rollo, tall, broad-backed, narrow-loined, white-skinned, ruddy, giving out that sense of harmonious effortless privileged existence; Colin, small, thick, sunburnt, muscular, with his thin hair plastered down long, lank with wet, over his forehead, his face rough-modelled like a head in clay, all broad steep planes, thumbed into hollows at the temples, beneath the cheek-bones. Such a contrast. . . . But that evening Colin had thrown off the thoughts that furrow and corrode him. His face was alight, enjoying the moment, his voice quick and laughing, without its echoing, heavy note of melancholy. I longed to keep him like that always, bathing in sunny water, not thinking at all, just being. Afterwards, dressing, they stood in the sun by a thorn bush, towels round their waists, lighting cigarettes for each other, slipping their shirts vaguely over their roughened heads, their clear, hard, square-breasted chests—deep in talk, not hurrying, forgetting the rest of us. I see them now, so absorbed, so idle in the sun. . . . "What a fascinating character," said Anna quietly to me, as we sat on the bank. She never says anything she doesn't mean, so I was glad. She watched him, I could see she was delighted by his physical ease and charm. We went back and had supper. We needed more eggs for scrambling, and Rollo dashed me to the farm for them in his car. That was the only moment we had alone all evening. He was so cheerful, enchanted to find highbrows were quite ordinary and easy to get on with. He said Colin was a marvellous chap, wasn't he? What did he do? Studying nervous diseases at the moment, I said, and left it at that. The word psycho-analysis starts stubborn resistance in Rollo; the only time I tried to explain, he would go on saying surely people ought to be able to get themselves straight by themselves, and isn't it an excuse for gutlessness? . . . He didn't know anything about it, and he supposed there was a lot in it, but personally he couldn't imagine himself ever wanting to go and pour out his troubles to a perfect stranger. Why not be a Roman Catholic and go to confession once a week, and be done with it? In fact, he got distressed as well as fogged. . . . So I gave him quickly a list of all the jobs Colin has had in the past. "By Gum!" he said. "He must be versatile." It sounded so schoolboyish, I got a shock—admiring Colin for all the things he's tried and got sick of—teaching, translating, being a journalist, being secretary to a gallery, doing woodcuts, masks, hand-printed stuffs, market-gardening—none of which expresses Colin in the least—or rather only the crack right though him which makes everything sooner or later equally distasteful. "Too much in the brain-pan, I expect, to settle down," said Rollo comfortably—the silly. For the first time I realised it's no use telling him *really* what people are like. He doesn't care to inquire. . . . If I weren't in love with him, would this matter rather? Might I get irritated? Bored? . . .

"I *am* enjoying myself, darling," I said.

After supper we piled into his car and went rushing to a pub Adrian knew about, a few miles up the river. What was it called? . . . A pretty name. . . . The Wreath of May. Picturesque is the word for it—old, thatched, whitewashed, sagging, full of beams. We sat outside on a bench against the front of the house. The garden is quite big, long, running down to the river. The light was rich and still, standing in simple gold shapes among the shadows. Groups sat about on the lawn under apple trees, and the grass was brilliant, thick; there were a good many beds of cottage roses, red, white, pink, carefully tended. Two swans lurched up the path from the river. From the bar just behind our heads came men's laughter and clinking of glass. Chaps with Oxfordshire voices kept roaring up their motor-bikes and going away on them with ugly girls in crinoline straw hats and flowered frocks and high heels and twisted, peaky expressions in their calves, genteelly riding pillion. We drank ale out of mugs. Colin began to get drunk and talk about trees. . . . Staring at a grove of poplars, alders, willows, growing up high all together the other side of the road, picking out the variety of shape, colour, texture, depth in them. "Now why can't painters do anything about them? . . . Anna? You just scratch them in all exactly alike and think you're painting trees . . . even Simon . . ."

Anna just smiled. It began to grow dark, stars pricked the blue-iris air, a white owl swooped from the poplar out towards the river, and Colin leapt up excited, waving his arms, saying:

"Did you see? Did you see? That *meant* something! . . ." Kurt said, interested, "De oil is ein English symbolism, yes?" and down sat Colin, punctured; and then giggled. After a bit he sighed, and said:

"It's the first sign of madness when every object appears to contain a hidden meaning—that nothing's what it is. . . . In another moment you'll grasp what's going on behind the scenes, what everything's up to—but you never do. . . . Those children paddling this afternoon—they were tremendously significant, important in some cosmic scheme or other I thought I had a glimpse of. . . . It's wrong, it's bad. Mystic. . . . I find it extremely painful."

And he was silent, we all were. . . . We went indoors and had more drinks. We found an ancient piano in the bar, and Anna played, and we yelled songs, and Adrian did a mad dance with Colin. Kurt suddenly began to sing to himself; his voice was beautiful, he sang louder, alone, soon, German songs, and everybody came round to listen. Adrian borrowed my hanky to wipe his eyes, and wrung my hand with feeling too deep for words. . . . By the time we left we were all fairly drunk, with varying results. Anna seems to whisk, fly about on her thin legs like a cat, very quiet and amused. Nothing happens to Rollo except that he gets more so . . . seems to give out double strength, like an electric radiator switched on full from half. He beams and towers and is very much in control of his wits . . . luckily that night; it was a crazy car load, tearing through the lanes. The roof was open, and Colin stood up in the back, hailing every passer-by with free courtly gestures. Adrian found our straw shopping bags we'd brought stuffed with bathing things in case of another dip, and he put one on his head, one on Kurt's, the handles under their chins. God! they looked funny. . . . We had to stop once for them all to get out; Adrian made a wild rushing leap at a quick-set hedge and landed on top, stuck fast, his long limbs waving. We tried to drag him off, and he kept shouting, "I'm an eagle! I'm spread! I'm an eagle!" And Anna and I gave up hauling on his ankles and sank limp, tortured with laughter, on the bank. . . . Rollo seemed to assume the rôle of host or manager, I remember that, and looked after everybody, giving sudden bursts of laughter now and then to himself, shepherding them into the house. He started off for London about midnight with Adrian and Carl; they had to get back, Kurt was travelling back to Germany next day. They were getting subdued and sleepy, but Colin, who was with us for the week-end, was still going strong. I kissed Rollo good-night and he was embarrassed till he realised kissing was going on all round, and then he gave me a kiss and Anna one too, and Colin and he shook hands, both hands, for a considerable time.

"One *last* favour, my dear," said Adrian. "The gin." And he took the bottle and climbed into the car beside Kurt. They started, we waved . . . and suddenly Colin went off at a gallop down the road after them, took a spring on to the running-board and went head first in on top of them. We saw his feet sticking out as they rounded the corner, and that was the last of them. . . . He came down again by train next afternoon rather morose and yellow, and merely said the journey back had been successful. Rollo had upper-class charm, he said. . . . "Obviously madly neurotic. . . ." I was furious.

I suppose I saw him about five times in all the rest of that month. There wasn't any more fun. He snatched times and drove down. Never a night. I ate my heart out rather, as they say. . . . We sat in a cornfield once, and once or twice took a punt on the river. . . . It was towards the end of the month he was always moody, his high spirits were gone. He pretended not—but catching his face in repose, it was heavy, his mouth drooped; though when I asked, he said immediately, no, nothing. . . .

It was an absolute surprise, the sudden plan to go abroad together. I'd been thinking he and Nicola would be sure to be going off somewhere in August, wondering how I could possibly bear it, but I never mentioned it—dreading what I'd hear, I expect—deciding to scrape the money somehow and join Jocelyn, rather than stay alone, gnawing away, always being the planless left-behind one. Anna was going to the south of France for a bit with some others, she wanted to be near Simon. . . . She's still there, I suppose. . . . I'll hear when I get back. . . .

Why shouldn't we? He said, Why not? I'd never heard him speak like that—defiant, bitter-sounding; more as if his motive was to do something against the world than with me. Nicola wasn't well again, the brief improvement was over, I wasn't too shattered to hear, she wanted to go down to Cornwall, instead of the trip to Ireland they'd tentatively planned. "And I'm damned if I see why I should go with her," he said. I felt half-thrilled, half-alarmed, hearing him say it. He could only be away a fortnight, so we decided to fly to Vienna and pick up George's car and drive about in it. Dear George, always coming in so useful. He'd left his car in Vienna and wanted it driven home. We thought we might do that. It seemed too good to be true, coming unexpectedly like that, I hardly knew myself for joy. The only snag was telling Mother, I dreaded searching questions; but there was no trouble at all. When I went home for a night, she was busy preparing for Kate's children's visit, touching up the nostrils of the rocking-horse with red paint, and beyond a momentary attempt to arrange I should stop in France and see James and a warning about not losing my passport, she seemed quite satisfied I should be going out with friends to join friends. She likes people to go abroad and broaden their minds. She rummaged in her wardrobe and dug out for me a little canvas bag you're supposed to strap on round your waist under your skirt and keep money and valuables in. She'd worn it the time she went to Italy with Dad, twenty years ago. It was astonishingly obscene. I sent it to Anna with instructions. . . . She gave me five pounds, which was sweet of her, and I bought this nice coat in the sales.

It's strange I don't remember more deeply, vividly about this time. . . . Perhaps I will a bit later when the images have taken their place in the gallery, and I can stand back and look at them. Oh, what a beautiful holiday! . . . Will it ever happen again? What's going to come next? Nothing stays without development, growth or decay. The pause has gone on too long, the immobility. . . . Like August, the sinister pause in the year. . . . But August will go over, the year tip imperceptibly towards inevitable change. . . . I feel the change ahead, it must be, I know; I don't see what or when. . . .

My first flight, sitting beside him, among the other quiet, somehow ghost-like passengers turning their heads, raising, lowering papers; sun on the huge wings, our shadow far below us on the water; sun, heat all the way; coming down outside foreign towns, sweeping off again; the journey so smooth, sheltered, easy with Rollo—the unmistakable dependably-tipping English gentleman. A night and a day in Vienna; but it was too hot, and we found the car and motored off into the country where we could feel lost and safe. . . . Oh, it was peaceful. . . . We stayed always in little inexpensive places for fear of English tourists; not that we didn't see plenty, but not the ones he'd know. Never more than one night in any place. . . . The super-romantic obvious landscape—peaks, pinewoods, lakes, waterfalls, bright-green villages—not Anna's taste, or Simon's, I was sure—rivers rolling their turbulent, thick, grey snow-waters through Innsbrück, Salzburg; spacious white peasant houses with their painted fronts and shutters and rich wooden balconies covered with vines and geraniums; churches set high, with those white towers and green bulbous domes; the bare clean pinewood floors and furniture of our nightly bedrooms; the smiling, sociable Austrian faces with their open uncomplicated look of innocence and equability, their bursts of laughter and music in little cafés, their soft grüss gotts, bitte schöns, mahlzeits. . . . We did enjoy our meals too. I got plump in a week on eggs and meat and creamy vegetables, and coffee mit schlagen. We walked in the woods, we picked blueberries, we bathed, we got bitten by horseflies, and drank from mountain brooks. . . . Lord, what a rustic idyll. . . . The smell of the pines in the hot afternoon, while I read poetry aloud to him. Housman was what he liked best, and Wilfred Owen. . . . He bought me a peasant dress in Innsbrück—nice stuff, silver buttons on the bodice. I wore it every day, he liked it; it gave me a touch of disguise, of novelty and excitement for him. . . .

It wasn't long. Only ten days all told. It seems much longer—and yet nothing—a pause without even a breath. We never had a quarrel or an argument. More tender, more dream-like every day, not in the world at all.

One night we drove late, up in the mountains. No moon, but starlight made a muffled incandescence. . . . When I was a child I had more sense of infinity, of the universe, than I have now. I'd stare at the stars till gradually they began to be worlds to me, spinning immense in space, and under the awe and terror of them I'd sink away, dissolve. Now I don't generally bother to look at them, and when I do they remain points of light in the sky. . . . But that night the feeling came back. "Look, *look* at the stars!" They hung enormous over peak and valley.

"Good Lord! They are bright!" he said. "What are they so big for?"

He switched off the headlights and drew in to the roadside. It was cold in the mountains, he wrapped me in the rug, I put my head on his shoulder. What stillness it was. . . . I listened. How many sounds? Rollo, whistling softly, intermittently. One frog, very loud. The wind, a light gust, now and then. Cowbells, in the distance. A brook, striking a tiny, rapid chime. A little waterfall hush-hushing somewhere. The number of sounds was surprising; they seemed to help make up the enormous silence. . . . He sniffed up the air, and said:

"I wonder where we are? We can't be near the lake. I don't smell water."

I giggled. "Rollo, can you really smell water?"

"Of course," he said. " Can't you?"

It got too cold, we drove on. Round the next corner was the lake, big stars aching over it, breaking in it, misty. "There now, you *can't* smell water!"

And I remember, of course, the evening before the last. Stopping in the evening at a small gasthaus, set a little back from a narrow, dusty road edged with apple trees, leading to the village. There were tables and white chairs set about under chestnut trees, and a band was playing in a corner of the yard —three yellow-haired youths, that is, in leather shorts and green jackets and hats with feathers—two violins and an accordion, playing slightly ludicrous merry tunes, and sometimes singing. After a while they packed up and Rollo gave them some money, a good deal, I should think, from the way they beamed and bowed to us, and wished us luck; and then they took out their instruments and played us one more tune to honour us before they went away. We felt moved by that absurd sentimental little band. After a while, we were the only people left; we sat on under the trees, drinking a bottle of ice-cold yellow wine. . . . Oh, let me think about it all again, let me remember. . . . His eyes looked into my eyes, he was utterly in love with me then . . . at last . . . I knew he was.

"Listen," he said, "let's not go back. Why should we ever go back? I don't want anybody any more but you. Let's just go on being together—anywhere—round the world if you like. There'll never be anything so good as this again and why should we miss it?—break it off? Let's not go to Salzburg to-morrow for our letters. . . ." His voice, different from any voice of his I'd ever heard. . . .

"We must," I said.

"Listen," he said, "you can do anything with me. Only say. You choose. You say." Urgent, insisting almost harshly, throwing the onus on me, like in the beginning.

"Let's not think to-night," I said. "Let's wait. We may see what to do." Putting him off, he seemed so wild, so unlike himself. His voice was reaching to my marrow, I must keep my head. I felt such a glorious new burst of confidence I was able to counsel patience, prudence. Thinking: I've won! . . . Not caring much beyond that. "We'll go to Salzburg first and then see," I said.

"No, don't let's go," he said. "I don't want to, I don't want to be bothered with any damned stuff from England."

"You said this morning you'd have to get your letters," I said, gentle and reasonable. "Besides, I rather want mine." . . . Feeling we must go back to the world and touch it for luck, if only for an hour, in case some blow was being prepared, had been launched in the world against our unlawful, reprehensible life outside of life. . . . Feeling always Dad might have died, with me lost, ungetatable, condemned for ever. . . . He said no more, he was silent on the drive back to our *pension*; but at dinner he was the same as ever—more loving if anything that night. No more insistence on reckless schemes. All that was as if it had never been. Next morning we drove in to Salzburg and went to the post office for our letters. The streets were crowded, one saw *Tatler*-familiar faces there for the Festival, and a good many smart English cars. I had a letter from Jocelyn giving me his new address in the town, one from Kate, one from Mother. All was well. Nothing from Anna. Rollo had a great packet, he didn't open them then. We didn't dare stay and have a look round, we got into the car and went out to the Wolfgangsee. After lunch I went to my room to lie down, my head ached, there was thunder in the air. From my window I saw him sitting on the terrace by the lake at the table where we'd had coffee, under a scarlet sun-umbrella, reading his letters. I watched him a long time.

I must have dozed off. He came in at tea-time, and sat on my bed and took my hand, and said he must go back to England to-morrow. It wasn't a surprise, I knew it. . . . Some muddles about dates, he said, another partner wanting to start his holiday, he couldn't feel justified in taking more now, specially after America; besides, he wanted some of September off to shoot in Scotland. . . . We said never mind, it had been perfect, more than anybody could reasonably expect in a lifetime. . . . The best days of our lives, we'd never forget them. . . . I didn't feel any great pang of misery. . . . So brimful of contentment and satisfiedness, it seemed enough and to spare to keep me going through even a long separation. We considered for a moment whether I should drive back with him, it was very tempting, but he didn't urge me, and I didn't want to be back in England yet—Etty's house closed, Anna away, Kate and her family making too much work for the maids at home. I wanted to see Jocelyn—to have a week or so of a different kind of time while I was about it. . . . We looked out Rollo's route on maps, I wired to Jocelyn to expect me, we were quite cheerful and serene.

That night, just before dawn, the thunderstorm broke. I was afraid. I shall always be afraid of thunder. At the first tremendous peal he came in from his bath next door, saying,

"Don't be frightened." I did love him then. It was what one had always longed for, never expected to have—someone appearing quietly at need, saying that—someone for oneself. . . . The storm went away, the sun came up over the lake behind banks of shimmering splitting mist, the air was fresh and cold. We went to the window and looked out. He turned me to him, holding me by the shoulders, and said: "Remember I love you."

Remember I love you. . . .

I packed, and helped him pack. He made me take some money and come home comfortably, with a sleeper. God, I'm glad I did. . . . The dark smiling waitress brought us a bunch of dahlias and gladioli as a farewell offering. We drove on to Salzburg and left my suitcase at the station; I got out by the fountain of the horses, and said good-bye, and saw the car move on, out of the Platz, and then I was alone in Salzburg. I strolled about a bit and sat in the Mirabelle Gardens, and then I went to Jocelyn's hotel.

He was banging away on a typewriter in a cell of a bedroom, with a thick smell of cooking and drains coming up from the court, his clothes all over the bed; and he was pleased to see me. He was leaving that very afternoon to join some friends on the Attersee. We went out by the bus, it seemed to take hours. He sat hugging his typewriter and talking about his plans for starting a new review. I could hardly take it in, I suddenly felt exhausted; and I kept on seeing Rollo rushing away, farther and farther away, over strange roads, alone, my place beside him empty.

What a contrast, these last ten days. Jocelyn, everything he stands for, the whole colour and temper of his mind—politically indignant and convinced, bigoted, really, so much the reverse of complacent: Europe not England his country, his point of departure in argument and discussion; his rabid class-consciousness, his ill-fitting clothes, just clothes—necessities—unrelated to him inside them, his earnest, midnight-oilish,

physically arid look, his unemotional affection for me. . . .
What a contrast! . . . A kind of life I've never shared in before;
anti-luxurious, a bit antiseptic, a bit humourless . . . but cheerful, friendly, smoothly regulated. A life of belief—that's the
true difference. Jocelyn and his kind believe in themselves, in
their work, in a future they must contribute to. There's no
principle of belief in Colin, Anna and those, nor in Rollo. . . .
In Simon it's different again, an unconscious power, without
direction, or this awful moral fervour. It was a frugal life,
funds barely eked out, drinks and expeditions carefully communal. . . . No one got on anybody else's nerves. . . . Johann
and Willi, the Austrian friends, so neat and spotless with one
change of linen, so easily happy, sensitive, delicate-mannered;
so much the antithesis of what is coarse or oafish. . . . Willi
three years without work, Johann's elder brother shot in the
Vienna rising. . . . I should think more about such fates and
struggles. If I were free I would, perhaps. . . . Willi taught
me some German. He's charming, with his lazy blue eyes and
ravishing teeth. Pale Johann played in the evenings on the
café piano. Willi's plump Lisel from the village came boating
with us and fell in. . . . The tow-headed child at the villa where
we lodged, with his page's haircut, his white cat, his passion
for Jocelyn's typewriter. . . . Our long swims in that heavy
peacock-blue water, the pert, theatrical little steamers, the café
on the jetty, the moon on the water. . . . Rollo's heavenly
letter coming, far the nicest he's ever written, a poignant
letter. . . . I read it again and again, almost incredulous.
Jocelyn lent me books; I began to think again about writing.
. . . Took some notes for my lake story. I should have done
more if I hadn't begun to get worried. . . .

What are they all doing now, I wonder. . . . Sound asleep
beneath their *plumeaux*. . . . Good-bye, Jocelyn, Willi, Johann.
. . . You were good to me, I was happy . . . till I got worried.
Even after that of course; because, of course, there's no need
to worry. Six, seven days late . . . I'm worried. But it's happened
once before, the first year Ivor and I were married; over a

week then, I was beginning to be sure—but it was a false alarm. . . . That was in August too—so I expect it's the time of year, I'm sure I've heard it does happen sometimes; or all that long cold bathing, lake water's very cold, that might easily account for it . . . I'm worried. Falling for one, Mrs. Banks calls it. "When I fell for our Doris . . ." I feel a bit sick. Train-sick, I expect. I've never been train-sick in my life. This morning when I got up, suddenly retching as I began to wash. . . . Nerves. Lying down like this I feel fine. Be all right to-morrow. Sleep. Thank God for lying down, a sleeper to myself. Supposing I'm sick when I get up to-morrow. . . . That would clinch it. No, it wouldn't. A long journey like this often upsets people.

Switch on the blue light. No, off again—too mournful. The water-bottle rattles. Is the stopper out? The cupboard door unlatched? My hands are dry, I feel the smuts in my nails. . . .

Queer, how a train journey throws up images, applies some stimulus to memory and desire. . . .

The story unrolled from the beginning in a kind of rough sequence; like when a person's drowning, so they say. . . .

Ai, what a screech. . . . Into a tunnel, my ears thicken . . . out again. Nearer home, nearer Rollo. To-morrow, come quick . . . don't come. . . . Slowing down now. . . . Through a station, lights on the blind, under it, sharp flashes; rumble and clank; a man's voice calling out, what does the French voice say? . . . Cut off. . . . On again, faster now, gathering speed. . . .

Relax, go with the train's speed, give to its swaying. . . . Breathe, breathe easily. . . .

Sleep. . . .

PART THREE

I

DRIVING AWAY from Victoria, she thought: I can let myself
in, put cool sheets on the bed, be hidden, sleep for a few hours
anyway. Face facts to-morrow, see what to do . . . Get hold
of Rollo. But I don't want to . . . I don't want to see him or
think of him. How can this be, in twenty-four hours? Is it
a symptom, does it seal my fate? . . . The female, her body
used, made fertile, turning, resentful, in hostile untouchability,
from the male, the enemy victorious and malignant . . . Like
cats or bitches. . . . Ugh!

London in the scorched irritable airless end of day was an
extension of the mind's loathing and oppression. Petrol fumes
were nausea; the traffic a fatuous, reluctant, laborious progress
towards a pointless destination; the picture-houses, with mock-
oriental fronts, proclaiming within a blend of cool darkness
and hot passions, were tawdriness, satiety, cynical sham and
cheapness. The main thoroughfares looked empty and discouraged. Only in the by-streets, where mews and slum just
touch, just unaggressively nudge the more classy residential
quarters, groups of children, submerged in the fuller season,
had come up and overflown upon the pavements: London's
strident August undergrowth, existing like cactuses in water-
less stone; shouting, running, taking communal licks at ice-
cream cornets; deprecated by the charitable passer-by, wish-
transferred with spade and bucket to the seaside, where it
would be better for them to be. . . . But they look tough,
cheerful enough, perhaps some Fund is sending them soon,
one really should contribute. . . .

Outside the pub on the corner, a yellow mongrel lay
stretched on the stone in the shade, tongue dripping, teased by

flies. A couple of urchins in ragged bathing-suits were watering one another out of a watering-can. . . . Oh, to be under a fountain, sprinkled from head to foot with fresh reviving spray; to be dissolved in the crisp break of a cold salt green wave! . . .

Lifting heavy weights is a good thing to do. She dragged her suitcase to the second landing. Etty's bedroom door flew open, and who should appear but Etty, in her dressing-gown.

"*Darling!*"

"Etty! I didn't expect you'd be here." She pulled her face together to smile a delighted greeting. "I was just going to creep in for the night and collect a few things and go on home. What are *you* doing in London?"

Etty had come back, she explained, for two nights on the same errand: to refurbish her wardrobe before joining Mona and some others on a Mediterranean cruise.

"My dear, *Greece*! Isn't it too marvellous? I shall really *see* all that. I've been most *studiously* informing myself about the Acropolis and *all* those temples. They have *lec*turers on board, too—I shall come back a perfect *blue*-stocking."

"Etty, it is nice to find you."

It was: a comfort . . . possibly salvation. Etty'd be sure to know of someone, in case. . . . Everything would be all right. Of course. Already the nausea had let up a bit, retreated to manageable distance.

"Come and sit down and tell me *all* about it. I was just having a little rest." She went back and lay down on her bed again, and Olivia sank in the arm-chair, her back to the light. "Did you have a *mar*vellous time? Austria *is* a divine country, isn't it? There's something so *ador*able about it. You're *mar*vellously brown. Oh, how I *en*vy you!" She glanced in the mirror at her own white cheeks . . . which she would perish rather than permit to tan. "Look, over there, darling, there's some letters for you. I didn't know *where* to forward them."

Among a mixed lot, one fat one from Anna. Nothing from Rollo . . . though I told him to write here . . . I don't care.

"Darling, it's *too* unfortunate I'm dining *out* and there isn't a *bite* in the house. I never *dreamed* there was a *soul* left in London, but *Jack* rang up this morning, he's *stuck* in an office all this month. What *can* we do? It would be *too* unkind, wouldn't it, to desert him at the *last* minute? Shall I ring up and sug*gest* bringing you *too*?"

"God forbid! . . . No aspersions meant, darling, I'm sure he's divine."

"Well, he's *not* actually. He's quite sweet, but I'm afraid you *might* be rather bored."

" Is he mad about you?"

The expected formula of reply—familiar since the far days when Etty had dazzled her cousins with a flapper bow of black taffeta, high-heeled patent-leather slippers and corsets—tripped blandly, deprecatingly from her tongue.

"Well, *rather* enamoured. . . . He's not awfully *scintillating*, poor sweet, but he's a good *friend*." She added, in the new line of tart self-mockery which was growing on her: "And how we superfluous women do value that!"

Disquieting in Etty, unsuitable . . . as if nowadays something led her to consider, in secret, with distaste, the passage of time, and with dissatisfaction her own part in it.

"As a matter of fact, Ett, I think I'll go to bed. I don't want any food—except perhaps a biscuit. I'm a bit done in after the journey."

"Darling, what a *shame*. Of course you must be. Those sleepers always *finish* me."

"It's the heat. It was fearful."

"I can imagine! Too *ravaging*. I can't tell you what an *oven* London's been to-day. I'll make you a cocktail. Luckily there's a scrap of gin and grapefruit in the cupboard. I was just about to indulge in a di*min*utive doleful orgy on my own, just to *strengthen* me for Jack. Stay where you are."

She rolled busily off the bed. Olivia, on the point of saying, out of habit, "Let *me* . . ." gave it up, stayed where she was and opened Anna's thin French envelope. Anna's handwriting, small, nervous, spidering, half formed, her style, child-like, vivid, ingenuously eccentric, her punctuation, a few capricious commas, made up an obscure yet revealing commentary on her character.

Darling Olivia (she wrote) here we are in Villefranche now, and I personally never want to leave, although needs must shortly, having spent £100 what with one thing and another. That is the Last of the Profits of Photography and shortly comes the Winter of my total Beggary. It's gambling that's chiefly done me in, Simon's so reckless in every way, running the gamut of sensations and passing money like water. He's mostly in very good spirits and has collected a lot of remarkable friends. Arthur Menzies for one—do you remember the one his discarded mistress shot at and wounded?—poor man, he's more or less in hiding in his sumptuous villa, and has more or less persecution mania, which, of course, makes him persona grata to Colin. It was Peter Cunningham who discovered him; he took us all to call, and we won him round at once quite unintentionally by saying we'd come by bus. The result is we have the car sent round daily, in case we need it.

There are a few monsters with sketching utensils in the hotel we don't speak to, and one lovely Frenchwoman who looks like a South Sea Islander—I would like to paint her, but of course don't dare ask and anyway would make a muck of it. Besides, there hasn't been time to touch a brush. She has a superb two-seater roadster, she and her husband sit in the front in white linen motoring caps with clip-on ear-flaps. We sit in the dicky and drive at terrific speed to Juan-les-Pins, drop husband at the gambling rooms and go and dance rumbas with lovely negroes under the palm trees to lovely negro rumba music.

Our last evening cost the poor husband 9000 francs,

as we rushed from Juan to Cannes and completely forgot about him till 4 a.m. He'd gambled it all away waiting for us—made it during the first part of the evening, put it in his pocket and sat down to wait for us, when we didn't appear he got so bored he started to play again and lost the lot. We had a glorious drive back in the dawn, eating hot dogs from an American bar. I wish you could see some of the negresses in beach pyjamas, yachting caps and monocles.

I'm having a mixed time as regards emotion, but I am determined to go with the wind, bathe, drink and *not brood* till I get home. That will be soon for Mrs. Cunningham's turned up and is having an Effect on Peter, though she's in a different party, living in a fragrant literary ethereal upper-class way with Gil Severn, and not interfering. We met her walking in Cannes the other day with her hot-water bottle in a pink plush cover full of tepid water instead of her bag. She only seemed mildly surprised when we pointed it out, and what's more, even that didn't make her in the slightest degree a figure of fun, we all felt just as respectful.

Cora's turned up too, and haunts Simon night and day, which he suffers with patience unruffled. However futile my own predicament . . . (here two lines were barred and cross-barred out in thickest impenetrable black) I will let you know directly I get back. Simon says we can go on having his house for September, so I hope you will come there too. I do hope all is well, I do think of you. Personally I don't think I could be happy in Austria, I didn't like it when I went, it seemed awfully thick-skinned and uncivilised visually—no good—but I suppose this is a narrow exacting professional view. I can't remember any Austrian painters, but I suppose they say look at our music. Love A.

She folded away the letter, amused and depressed. It wasn't quite like Anna : so glib, external. She must be in a bad state over Peter. . . . How are we all to make the change-over quietly into winter? To what shall we look forward?

Etty came back with a glass of yellowish liquid in each hand.

"I just *popped* some sheets on your bed while I was about it," she said. "Then you can *cast* yourself between them whenever you feel like it."

"You are an angel, Ett."

She took up her glass. The chunk of ice from the frigidaire clinked temptingly, but the fumes of gin came up, overpowering. This is a test now: if I can swallow this . . . She sipped, and her mouth twisted. Sticky, sickening, unclean . . . Her jaw muscles tightened, fighting down nausea, hard-pressed . . . Thank God for the ice. She fished it out and sucked at it, said smiling:

"This is what I was longing for."

"Darling—you don't feel *sick*, do you?"

"Good lord, no. Just thirsty and sort of unfresh—you know how a journey makes you feel. I'll have a bath unless you want the bathroom, and sip this later in bed to cheer my solitary evening."

"It's rather a *me*lancholy little programme." Etty looked distressed.

"Far from it. Bed, book, drink—perfect."

Etty sighed.

"It's a *com*fort to think if the worst comes to the *worst* there *is* always bed and the bottle. I often feel I shall end my days in a *stupor* of debauchery."

She took her drink in little nips, throwing her head up between each, like a canary.

"Now have a bath, darling, and I'll tuck you into bed. I'm not dining till nine. I felt so *wilted* I wanted to do my packing quietly and have plenty of time for *collapse*."

Protesting against protest, she helped Olivia to carry up the heavy suitcase, straining her puny arm and shoulder with ineffectual stubbornness; then tripped down again and turned on the bath.

She got into bed and lay flat. That's better. The room was almost cool, the sun had left it hours ago. The picture looked back at her from above the mantelpiece—cool people sitting at peace in chequered shade. Rollo's cigarette burn on the table beside her. . . . Oh, be abolished, all signs and reminders of him, till I'm out of this mess. Rollo, I've started a baby, what shall we do. . .? No, I won't. Not yet, anyway.

She dozed for a few moments, lapped immediately in confused and violent half-dreams; was roused by Etty coming in with a plate of vita-wheat biscuits.

"Darling, *but* for these the cupboard is *bone* bare. I just had these and some orange juice for breakfast and I've been out *all* the rest of the day. I feel so *mortified*. *Do* let me run out and get you some fruit or eggs or something."

"No, my dear, thank you." (Eggs—fearful thought.) "This is just what I want."

She nibbled eagerly: good taste, dry, crisp, slightly salt.

"Ett . . . I've had a letter from a friend . . . Where is it? . . . Oh, I put it in my bag, never mind. She's in the most awful hole."

Etty, sitting on the end of the bed, presented a face of expectant sympathy.

"She's been having an affair with some man or other, married, I believe, and to her horror she finds she's started a baby."

"Oh, my *dear*, how *shattering*. . . ."

Was it imagination—one rapid, questioning glance from Etty?

"She wants to know if I can help her."

Etty reflected, serious.

"Has she tried pills?"

"She doesn't say. There are pills, are there? That really work? She'd try anything, I'm sure. Do chemists sell them?"

"I know of one who does. But I've never heard of them working if it's really the worst. . . . They may, of course."

Etty fell silent, adding, "They give you the most *stupe*fying diarrhœa, that I do know . . . Still, she might try."

"She sounds pretty desperate. You see, she's an actress, on tour. It would simply do in her career."

"Where is she?"

"Weymouth or somewhere—touring along the south coast." If Etty'd had suspicions they must surely be allayed: the story comes so pat, so plausible. "She says she could get up to London if she had to."

"Has she got any money?"

"No. . . . But I think . . . she says she could get some—a little—I don't know how—from the man perhaps."

"I do know someone . . ." said Etty uncertainly.

"In London?"

"Yes. Let me think . . . His name . . . It's ages since I . . . Tredeaven—that's it."

"Is he in the telephone-book?"

"Oh, yes. He's a what d'you call it—manipulator or something. . . . He's got a more or less respectable practice. This is a *side*-line."

"How could I get hold of him? Could I ring up and make an appointment for her? Or take her to see him?"

Etty was silent.

"He won't take any one unless he knows who's sent them," she said at last. "You see, it's *fear*fully dangerous for him. If you're caught it means prison . . . In spite of his being, of course, a public *bene*factor really. I suppose he's saved *regi*ments of unfortunate *err*ing women from *ru*in . . ."

"You mean," said Olivia, "he might refuse to do it—if she just went out of the blue?"

Silence again.

"You could give my name, I suppose. . . ." Etty stirred. Her slightly protruding eyes between curly doll's lashes became fixed with a certain wild blankness on her cousin. "Only it was so long ago. . . ."

"Did you go to him, Ett?"

"My dear, *once*. Wasn't it *shattering*?" The colour came up in her fragile egg-face, painfully, from neck to brow. She laughed, rather shakily. "The *wages* of *sin*, darling."

"Poor Ett."

Amazing. A shock, definitely. That narrow miniature body, that, too, trapped, subjected to the common risks and consequences of female humanity. It only showed, for the hundredth time, how little one knew about anybody, particularly one's nearest. . . . Seeing only Etty's marionette surface, allowing one's intuition and mere circumstantial evidence to decide that never—however much she might dally with preliminaries—would she have brought herself to face ultimate physical issues.

"I've never told a *soul*," said Etty, wiping her eyes. "I nearly *died* of it. *Never* breathe it, will you?"

"Of course I won't. When was it?"

"About five years ago. Oh dear! And he was *married* too. . . ."

"Were you awfully in love?"

"Well *no*, darling—*low* be it spoken—that was the *crowning* shame. It was just *once*. He was so impo*rtu*nate . . . I never *dreamed* . . . Oh, how *sordid*! . . . I *couldn't* tell him. I simply *loathed* him the *moment* after. I never wanted to *see* him again."

"Yes, I can imagine . . ." But, of course, not the same with me and Rollo: not sordid. I love him so much. I always wanted to have his child.

"Really," sighed Etty, examining her face in Olivia's hand-mirror, "these physical processes are too *treach*erous. *Why* should wretched females be so be*leag*uered? . . ." She dabbed on a little powder, came back and perched herself on the bed again; sitting there with her look of pathos, as if the sudden emotion had exhausted her. "I *swore never* again would I stray from the path of virtue." She glanced at Olivia, arch, faintly sly. "But one *does* forget, *doesn't* one?"

"One does."

"I must say it's a *com*fort to feel he exists. . . . Not that I *ever* intend to require his services *again*. . . ."

"Was it awful?"

"Not *really*—not too shattering. He was *divine* to me. He's a *lamb*. But of course I did feel *too* squalid."

"Did you go alone?"

"Well, *no*. Mona was a *saint*—she simply arranged *every*-thing. You see, *she'd* been to him *just* before, poor darling."

"Oh, had she?"

Mona too! Well, well . . . She began to feel fatally cosy and consoled, the seals of arduous secrecy, of solitary endurance melting, melting. . . . Not such a catastrophe after all: quite a common little predicament, distressing, of course, but soon over and no one the wiser. . . .

The fact is, Ett, it's me—I'm properly in the soup. I've been having an affair with Rollo Spencer. . . . Darling, how distraught you must have been feeling. But don't worry any more. You'll get put right in two twos. . . . Enter into the feminine conspiracy, be received with tact, sympathy, pills and hot-water bottles, we're all in the same boat, all unfortunate women caught out after a little indiscretion. Give up the big stuff. Betray him, yourself, what love conceived. What's love? You're not a servant girl, bound to produce illegitimately, apply for a paternity order, carry a lifelong stigma. . . . You can scrape up the money and go scot-free. Go on, go on. . . . She bit into her thumb. *I won't.* I can lie and lie; I can be alone.

"Do you know what he asks for doing it?"

"I'm not sure. He's not *cheap*, I'm afraid . . . but then he's safe. And I believe he varies according to what he thinks you can afford. I'm sure if your friend told him she was hard up he'd be kind."

"Could I really ring up and ask for an appointment for her, and say you sent me? . . . I'll have to see her through."

Etty considered.

"I know *what*. Give Mona's name. It 'ud *sound* better, as

she's married. I'm sure she wouldn't mind. It's at second-
hand, so to speak, but I suppose you can *vouch* for your friend
being *mum*. I'll look up his number before I go to-morrow,
if you remind me. He's in one of those little streets off Welbeck
Street—I forget which." She listened to a clock striking.
"Nine. I must go and do one or two *last* things. Good-*night*,
my pet. *Bless* you, sleep well. Drink up your drink. I'll be back
early, I've got a *bar*barously early start to-morrow. See you in
the morning. Ma Banks will be in, of course. Don't *stir*
unless you feel like it."

"Oh, I'll be fine to-morrow. I'll go home by the midday
train, I expect. Good-night, Ett, bless you. Have a nice time.
Give Jack a break."

Perhaps she will too. . . . Nobody thinks of anything else
in this beastly world.

She smiled at Etty, smiling in the doorway, kissing all her
carmine finger-tips. . . . Dear pretty Etty, familiar, mysterious
creature, unfailing girl-friend: ready to keep a secret, or
console by giving one away; amiable feather-pated rattle—
yet saying, knowing what?—to herself only, alone at night
or sitting by herself? Cool, brittle Etty, untouched by heat,
fresh to one's sick, contaminated eye and nose; comfortably
detached, yet known from the beginning. Saviour Etty.

Chemist's outfit first: probably work, I'm always lucky.
If not, Tredeaven, divine to one, a lamb, special terms if you're
hard up. . . .

When bell, voices, slam of the front door, departing car
successively had died away, she got up, poured the cocktail
down the wash-basin, went to the telephone. Giddy, bemused,
the motion of train and boat still swinging and spinning
through her, she lifted the receiver and gave the number of
Rollo's house; for the second time. . . . She heard the bell
cawing over and over again at the other end. . . .Not in, then.
Wait a little longer, just a little. . . . At last a voice . . .
"*Ull*-oah!" By no means the bland male voice of last time:
female, hot, cross, offended . . .

"Could I speak to Mr. Spencer?"

"E's not in." Under-housemaid or such, reluctant from the back door or the upper regions: Rollo living in a small way with depleted August staff.

"I suppose you don't know when he's likely to be in?"

"'E didn't say. 'E called back for 'is dog before dinner and went straight out again."

"I see. It doesn't matter. Thank you so much."

Down clapped the receiver at the other end. That settles that one, and D.V. no more of 'em to-night.

It doesn't matter, doesn't matter . . . Just as well. Somewhere, a mile or so away, Rollo's walking with Lucy.

She went back to bed, sank through another sharp trembling fit into heavy sleep.

She dreamed of green waves that never broke. Swinging, swinging, from one cool glassy bell of silence to the next, up and down, up . . . down . . . In her dream she cried to someone shadowy beside her, "Oh, this is *bliss*! I'm in bliss! . . . bliss. . . ."

II

THE bath-chair bowled briskly over the lawn. Grandpa sat in it with his eyes shut, carefully dressed in his old-fashioned light grey summer suit, his Panama hat placed by Grandma on top. Grandma was at the helm. Jane, aged six, Christopher, three and a half, dragged at the handle, steering a jerky erratic course from rose-bed to shrubbery, from shrubbery to walnut tree; over and across, up and down, as fast as possible, giving Grandpa a little airing in the cool of late afternoon. Grandma was tireless. In a blue linen frock, trimly belted, a little tight behind, she swung along at a girl's jaunty pace. She beamed and marched, occasionally shouting directions, warning or encouragement. The bath-chair amused the children. All was well.

Kate and Olivia sat under the walnut tree in deck-chairs.

Now and then Kate said, "Where's that child?"—got up, extracted the lurking baby from some nook, brought her back, sat down again.

"How old is she, Kate?"

"Nearly sixteen months."

"Surely she's very forward?"

"I don't think so." Kate let out a long sigh: almost one of mother's old sighs: certainly of the same genus. "They were all much of a muchness. They could all walk at a year —except Christopher, he was slow. . . . But he was the first to talk. In fact I never remember him *not* talking." She looked across the lawn at her son, narrowing her eyes, frowning faintly. "He's enough to drive anyone dotty."

"His style seems rather eccentric."

"Oh, he's a freak." Kate rubbed her eyes. "I don't know where he came from."

"I expect he takes after some of our side-lines."

"Yet he looks more like Rob than any of them."

"Only on the surface. There's something pretty tricky looking out from beneath: nothing Rob's responsible for, I'm sure."

Kate's frown relaxed: her nostrils dilated in half-apologetic amusement. It was nice talking to Olivia about the children. She was sensible. She treated them as curious specimens, was delighted when they quarrelled or were rude; and this caused a sense of lightening of one's responsibilities. One did forget to be scientific enough. . . .

"He really is rather extraordinary," she admitted, succumbing to pride.

"He reminds me of James," said Olivia, "though he couldn't be more unlike."

"I hope he won't go sour on us like James," said Kate, depressed by the comparison.

The likeness was generic, the unlikeness partly a period one. Little girls were women in embryo; little boys frequently seemed not fathers of themselves but some totally separate, unaccountable, disconcerting kind of animal. She attempted to explain this.

"Perhaps," said Kate. "I suppose what you really mean is boys don't play to the gallery. They don't care about making a good impression." She followed the bath-chair with her eyes. "His brain's too active," she said, worried again, abandoning theory. "It's quite a relief to see him gambolling and squawking round that bath-chair."

"He's all right," said Olivia.

"There's one thing," said Kate. "He's never been afraid of the dark. They're all quite tough in those ways. Jane's the only one who ever had to have a night light—after being frightened by some animal masks at some idiotic party Rob's mother took her to. It was only for a short time though."

"I think you manage very well."

It was one's rôle as childless aunt to replenish Kate's maternal confidence.

"As for the period question," said Kate, leaning back, "if you mean they don't know the meaning of the words filial respect, they don't. They cheek Rob and criticise me—at least not Priscilla so much, she's always been soppy about me—but Christopher even goes on about my clothes—can you imagine? ... He can't bear me in brown and he can't bear me in a taffeta frock I've got, and I'm not allowed to wear stockinette bloomers and I don't know what. Rob says he's bound to be one of those cissy dressmaking young men. He *won't* have a speck of dirt on his hands and the fuss that goes on about what he's to wear! I wish Jane and he would swap a bit of each other, she might be a tramp's child—— What's that you've got in your hand, Polly?" She broke off sharply, seizing the baby's paw in a firm and gentle grip. An unripe greenish-pink half-squashed mulberry lay revealed. "You haven't eaten any, have you?" She prized her jaws apart and investigated. "No, I don't think so. Polly not eat, good girl. Nasty, Polly, ugh!"

The baby attentively examined the mulberry upon her

cushioned palm. After a moment of trance she cried, "Away!" and as a bowler towards the wicket, plunged immediately into a gallop, swept her arm up and back, and hurled it from her. "Gone!" she announced. She began forthwith to search over the grass, croaking "Where? Where? Where?" in urgent reiteration.

"There it is," said Kate languidly, pointing with her toe.

"Dere tis," she cried rapturously. Knees flexed, she bent forward from the hips to examine it once more, then fell on it, stamped it to pulp, her face contorted with disgust, an eye on Kate. "Ach! Ach! Ach!" She was hoarse with loathing.

"She's very good about not putting things in her mouth," said Kate.

"She's terribly engaging." Olivia watched the legs, a couple of burstingly stuffed pegs, start off once more towards the mulberry tree.

"She's a bit overweight," said Kate, also watching. "I'm sure my clinic would condemn her. I can't see that it matters. Those weight charts are all bunk."

"She'll be the most attractive," said Olivia. "The crooked smile."

"That's like you!" cried Kate in triumph. "I told you she was like you. And the eyes too. Everybody says so—except Mother for some reason."

"I see what you mean." Deprecatory, flattered . . .

One could go on for ever. It was a drug, a substitute for thinking. *I can have a child too.* I'll take a cottage somewhere near Kate and have it without any fuss and bring it up with hers. I'll look after it myself, and plant sunflowers and holly-hocks in my garden, and have a wooden cradle on rockers, and sing it to sleep. Kate and I'll sit under the trees when they're all in bed and talk about them . . . She's going to light a cigarette. Don't do it, you brute, don't do it, why must you, you don't want it; who wants to smoke in this heat? . . . She turned her head away, receiving the first penetrating nauseous whiff, closed her eyes. The blood began to push up thick and scorching in her cheeks and neck, behind her ears. Getting on for the bad time of day; have to crawl upstairs soon and surreptitiously be sick: continue the interminable slow-motion struggle with Laocoön.

Kate stole a look at her. Hollow-cheeked, inert. . . . A ghastly colour, greyish beneath the make-up. Thinner than ever. Blast her . . . and she'd been looking so much better, so happy: in love obviously: somebody with money it seemed like—those silk stockings, those expensive flowers, that hand-bag. Who is he, has it gone wrong? Damn. Damn.

She said sharply:

"You haven't told me much about Austria. Did you enjoy it? What did you do?"

"I did enjoy it," Olivia opened her eyes, tried to think, to speak briskly. "It's so difficult to describe a holiday, isn't it? Unless you know the country."

"God knows when I shall get abroad again," said Kate bitterly. "Never, I shouldn't think. . . . Not since my honey-moon. And even then Rob didn't like it." She brooded.

"Some day we'll pop off together somewhere. We've always said we would. Not that I believe you'd ever bring yourself to leave the family."

"*Wouldn't* I!"

Perhaps when Christopher's gone to school. . . . When Priscilla's stopped minding my being out of reach. . . .

After a while Olivia said:

"Getting this blasted food-poisoning on the journey has sort of spoilt it all."

"How d'you feel now?"

"Oh . . . better . . . Only it still niggles on."

"Gripes?"

"M'm. Can't seem to keep much inside me. Still, as Mrs. Banks says, a good turn-out never did nobody any harm."

"Don't be idiotic," said Kate crossly, worried. "You've said that the last five days—ever since you've been here. You ought to see a doctor."

"Good God, no! It's nothing. Etty's doctor gave me some stuff. He said I'd be all right."

Time for the next dose . . . When will it work? "We've never had any complaints," said the rat-faced young man in the white linen coat, knowing, smooth, reassuring among the jars and bottles. "Of course, you must persevere." I'm persevering. Per ardua ad astra.

"For Pete's sake don't say anything to Ma about a doctor." Not Dr. Martin saying, "Well, young lady . . ." and peering through his glasses, grunting, saying, "Now are those cheeks your own, or are they not?"—remembering me as a child, when I was jollier. . . .

But Kate was looking round for Polly, and shouting at Jane and listening to Christopher. Her non-parental, undiluted moment of attention was over. She was dispersed again, split up with nervous alertness among them all.

No danger there.

"Now me!"

"No, *me!*"

"Get him out, Grandma."

"Please," said Kate.

Grandpa, a non-magical effigy, without the sinister power of a guy or a ventriloquist's doll, was hoisted out of his conveyance and placed in a *chaise-longue*. He opened one eye, closed it again. Christopher climbed into his place, Jane seized the handle, away went the bath-chair at a spanking pace, Christopher jigging and squealing inside, Jane rushing with a crimson face and grimaces of mad exertion.

"It's much better without Grandpa," shouted Jane.

"Look out for Polly, don't run her down," called Grandma indulgently. Really, the bath-chair was the greatest blessing; it kept them happy for hours.

"Now, Christopher, it's my turn. Get out, I want to try by myself down this hill."

The chair and Jane launched themselves from the top of

the mildly sloping terrace and, gathering impetus, ran down to the very end of the lawn, coming to rest with a bump against the kitchen-garden wall. Grandma started forward.

"Leave her alone," said Kate sharply. "Don't shout at her. She's much more likely to crash if you make her think she will."

"My border," said Mrs. Curtis doubtfully. "Still . . ." She sat back again. "Her nerves seem very strong. It's curious how much more fearless girls are. You and Olivia were just the same. James took twice as long with his bicycle."

They said all the things, it all went on and on. They were handed over lock, stock and barrel to the young.

"Kate, dear," said Mrs. Curtis smoothly, "I've asked Miss Mivart and Miss Toomer to look in for tea on Saturday. They're so longing to see the children."

"That'll test their nerves," murmured Olivia.

Kate groaned. But not now, as in the old days, did she object with scorn, argue with acrimony, make herself difficult. The old scarecrows could see the children if they wanted to.

"Well, keep Dad out of the way," was all she said. "You know Miss Mivart *will* try to shake hands with him and pass him the bread and butter and generally bring herself to his notice with tender tact and solicitude."

"Dad doesn't bother," said Mrs. Curtis comfortably. "He doesn't take any notice. She likes to do little things for him. She always admired him so very much."

"I wonder if she sees now why God in his infinite mercy didn't see fit to let her marry Dad."

Mr. Curtis lay back without stirring in his chair, pale, his jaw sunk, his lips blowing in and out as he lightly dozed.

The bath-chair stood abandoned in the herbaceous border beneath the wall, half-hidden in August perennials. Jane and Christopher were hurrying back.

"We're very very sorry, Grandma," began Jane from some distance. "We accidentally snapped off this." Flushed, anxiously honest, she held out a head of pink hollyhock.

248 THE WEATHER IN THE STREETS

"Oh, dear!" said Grandma, "what a pity. Poor hollyhock."

"We don't call them that," said Christopher.

"What do you call them?"

He considered a moment, his eyes blank, false.

"Mountains," he said casually.

Polly also had returned.

They stood in a row before their elders—the two solid, mouse-haired, unproblematic little girls, the frail-legged dangerous little boy.

"I wish we had our Priscilla here," said Mrs. Curtis, trying again, sparing a thought for her eldest grandchild, on a visit to her other grannie.

Jane and Christopher exhanged sly glances. "We don't," said Jane. They doubled up, cackling with laughter. "We don't! We don't!"

"Not want Priscilla? Oh, come now, why not?"

Christopher went on squawking, but Jane looked troubled, sighed, turned a negligent somersault before replying:

"Well, she's rather rude. She bites."

"She bites," said Christopher, "but she's not *rude*. I've met rude people. They smash flowers." He also turned a somersault, a poor one, continued: "I've met them in Scotland."

Grandma raised inquiring eyebrows at Kate, who shook her head.

"This is rude," said Christopher. He ran a few steps forward, stopped and stuck his bottom out towards them.

"What could be ruder?" said Olivia faintly. She covered her face with a handkerchief and her chair shook.

"Mabel said it was rude. Pip's rude sometimes. D'you know who Pip is? He's our dog. I call him Poodle. D'you know which he wears, fur or fevvers?"

"Fur, of course," said Jane with scorn. "Only birds wear feathers."

"Genklemen wear fur on their legs," said Christopher, rolling aimlessly on the ground. "Daddy does. Mabel does too, but she's not a man, she's a nursemaid."

"Mummy, Polly's got something in her hand, she won't give it up."

"Polly, show Mummy."

Another unripe mulberry. Jane pounced on it, and Polly shrieked. "It's a mulberry, Mummy."

"Throw it away," said Kate, rubbing her eyes.

"Can't I eat it?"

"No, it's too sour."

Jane bowed her head over the mulberry, murmured to it regretfully, "You're too sour," and threw it into the bushes. "It *was* a shame to pick it," she said regretfully.

Grandma started to croon, tossing the tearful Polly on her knee. "*There was—an old woman—tossed up in a blanket, seventeen times as high as the moon,*" she sang. Marvellous how the old rhymes came back to one. James had been the one for nursery rhymes. Ceasing to toss, starting to jig, she continued, "*Polly put the kettle on, Polly put the kettle on. . . .*"

"I don't care for your singing, Grandma," interrupted Christopher. "So please stop."

Mrs. Curtis stopped abruptly . . . No, *not* an attractive child. Spoilt, tiresome. His father spoils him. James was inclined once to have a phase like this, I soon got him round . . . It wouldn't do to appear to be noticing him. She started singing again, but in a suppressed way.

Christopher sat down on the arm of Grandpa's chair. The effigy behind him put out a hand and touched him, smiling faintly . . . the faintest hovering flicker . . . But all passed unnoticed. Christopher didn't even wince or wriggle. He seemed dreamy, gazing at the grown-ups each in turn with melancholy hazel eyes.

"What a nice smiling face you've got, Mummy," he said gently.

"Have I?" Kate shot him a sharp glance behind her smile.

"I like smiling faces. Daddy's got the best smiling face."

"Hasn't Grandma got a nice smiling face?" coaxed Mrs. Curtis, rushing as ever upon her fate.

"You've got a cow's face," he said casually. The pause was too long, nobody did anything whatever. He added, "You've got the best smiling cow's face."

"Mummy, Polly's wet," said Jane.

"Never mind," said Kate. "Here comes Mabel. Get up, Christopher, bed-time. I'll see to you. Mother, will you keep Jane? Mabel'll come for her after she's bathed Polly. Polly, say night-night, Grandma. Christopher, say good-night, give Grandma a kiss."

Jane sat in the swing, wound herself up and unwound again rapidly.

"What a pity they've all got such straight hair," said Mrs. Curtis to Olivia. "You had such lovely curls, every one of you. I believe it's all in the brushing. However, don't mention it to Kate." To Jane she said: "Don't make yourself giddy, dear. Wouldn't you like me to read?"

"No, thanks."

"It's funny they don't care to be read to. You all loved it so." To Jane: "Well, what about a little game then?"

"Yes, shall we climb the potting-shed roof?" Jane got down rapidly.

"Very well. Olivia, you'll stay by Dad, dear, won't you?" She took Mr. Curtis's handkerchief from his pocket, wiped his nose, tucked it back again. "Come then, Jane."

They went away hand in hand.

"How much can you do on it?" Olivia heard Jane ask. "Can you get to the top?"

Grandma was Jane's favourite person. "She's just what I was," said Grandma. Jane alone received Grandma's tomboy confidences: how when she was six she'd fallen out of an apple tree and left her skirt caught on the topmost bough; how she could jump high hedges and had beaten all the boys once vaulting a five-barred gate. . . .

"And when we were children," said Kate aggrieved, "she was so on her dignity she practically pretended she had no legs."

Was it Jane's influence, or the withdrawal of Dad's? . . .
Was a load lifted now she was freed, in all but elementary
impersonal ministrations—freed in her mind and speech—
from that ever incongruous-seeming union?

There he lay. Sometimes he knew one, sometimes he didn't.
On and off he muttered, mostly he was silent. Uncle Oswald's
visits seemed to revive him a little, but Uncle Oswald didn't
come so often now: Mrs. Curtis had never liked the little man.
He'd got quite fat too. His bird's face had a pouch beneath the
jaw, like a pelican's in embyro. Miracle: his asthma was gone.
Not a trace of it since his mind began to go to sleep. There
was a lot to be thankful for. He was obviously quite comfortable.

Only when he did those things . . . like putting his hand
out to touch Christopher . . . it was a bit upsetting. Otherwise
one took him for granted. After all he hadn't said—whatever
it was he should have said, had been on the point of saying.
He'd given up, let it slip; and now it didn't matter . . . even
to me . . . any more. What was left had gradually, imperceptibly lost power to disconcert, to move to love or sorrow.
. . . Only pity and a somewhat weary patience. . . . After he
dies I'll remember him again and weep . . . remember that he
said: I want you to be happy; and I said: I will be happy,
I promise.

His eyes were open now. He was leaning slightly to one
side, studying a small patch of sun that moved and flickered
on the grass, shadow-crossed in the light breeze. After a while
he looked at her, cocking one eye, amused.

"Never try to take away his bone," he said quite clearly.

"Not I, Dad. I wouldn't dare."

"Get your foot snapped off." He chuckled.

Simpkin the Pekinese, a handful of bones this many a year
beneath the mould and the primroses in the hazel grove at the
bottom of the garden, still revisited his master in glimpses of
sun or moon, as a shadow on the floor by the chair, a hump in
the eiderdown at the foot of the bed.

He closed his eyes again. Almost she leaned forward to say: "Dad, are you pretending?"—the notion was suddenly so strong that he was still there, that it was all assumed, out of perversity, laziness, disillusionment: as people decide to be deaf. But the moment passed. He was far out of earshot.

The loud deep voice of Jane floated over the garden from the potting-shed roof. She got up and crawled languidly over the lawn, down into the kitchen garden. She saw Jane's strong brown legs and scarlet-suited rear vigorously ascending the slope of the tiled moss-grown roof. Grandma on the path was adjusting a ladder and preparing to follow her.

Olivia called:

"Mother! I'm going in now. Dad's all right. He's dozed off." What an effort to raise one's voice. . . . Nearly fatal.

"Very well, dear."

"Do take care on that roof, Mother. Your skirt's too tight for climbing."

"I'm quite all right. I shan't go all the way up . . . Go on, Jane, Grandma's coming."

Vigorously Mrs. Curtis launched herself upon the ladder.

Olivia went briskly indoors, spurred on by the rising nausea.

Thank God . . . That's over for a bit.

Now I must, I really must force myself to write to Rollo. Probably he'd been ringing up Etty's every day, poor boy; and getting no answer. Sitting on her bed, she scribbled a note in pencil.

Darling, no word from you—or have you written and it's got stuck in this cul-de-sac of a month? I got back and thank God for your sleeper, for I began to feel ill on the journey and illish I've been ever since. So not wishing to show you a glum green face I made tracks for home to give my family the benefit. My plans are vague. Please let me know here, darling, if you're in London. I want to see you. Your O.

She put it in an envelope, sealed and addressed it; then

opened it again and scrawled under her signature: I *must* see you.

Something must be done, something . . .

Tell him, or not tell him?

I don't want to say it to him. I don't know him. . . . Far in the back of her mind persisted a loved, an almost abstract image, free of taint. Not to hate him she must think of him thus, by himself, unrelated to her, impersonal.

She took two pills, washed ; summoned the bare energy to make her face up carefully. I mustn't let myself go. If nobody else suspects, that damned nurse soon will. . . . She went down and slipped her letter into the middle of the pile—Kate's and mother's—lying ready for post on the pantry table. She began once more to think about prune juice, to yearn for it. Prune juice, prune juice . . . I must have it . . . She took a glass from the pantry shelf and went softly to the larder door. No one about. She heard the wireless going in the kitchen where Ada was cooking dinner. She went noiselessly into the larder, saw the basin of prunes, poured out a glassful of juice and drank it greedily. More. More. Must leave some . . . just a little. She stole out again, washed the glass under the pantry tap and put it back.

Kate called over the stairs.

"Liv, they want to say good-night. Can you be bothered?"

"Of course."

She went up with a show of alacrity. Jane in the camp-bed, Christopher in the old cot with headrails, sat up in Aertex sleeping suits, their bath-flushed faces tense and shining with self-conscious expectation.

Olivia sat down on Jane's bed and looked at her animals: a monkey, a teddy bear, a Doleful Desmond, and a rabbit in a suit of pyjamas.

"What are their names?"

"They haven't got names." She looked troubled. "They're my Annies."

"Short for animals," said Christopher.

"Have you got anything of the sort?" said Olivia.

"No, I wouldn't have *Annies*. I call everything names."

"He's got a *doll*," said Jane. "She's called Barriecasie."

"May I see Barriecasie?"

"I haven't got her to-night. I wanted something else instead." His hand crept under the pillow, his eyes, fixed on her, looked dangerous: *If you laugh I'll hack you up.*

"His new shoes," said Jane, bouncing in bed.

"May I see them?"

He drew forth a pair of scarlet sandals.

"How beautiful. No wonder you wanted to sleep with them."

"He always has to sleep with anything new," explained Jane, without scorn. "Last Christmas Father Christmas brought him a porter's hat."

"A real one," interrupted Christopher, making a quick peak-expressing shape with his hands.

"And he had to have it on to go to sleep. He went right to sleep with it on."

"It wasn't on when I woke up," said Christopher.

"I think we ought to lie down now," said Jane. They lay down. "But you needn't go yet," she added.

"What a blue sky," said Christopher, gazing out of the window. "Blue as bluebells. Blue as Percy's eyes. D'you know who Percy is? He's Mabel's friend."

"He mended my wheelbarrow," said Jane.

"Once we had tea on the lawn when Mummy was away, and Percy came to tea. He had tea with all of us. Did you think Mrs. Eccles had tea with us too? Well, she didn't. She was having a barf."

"Mrs. Eccles was a cook," said Jane. "She's gone now."

"Percy's very funny," said Christopher. "He said Mabel Mabel under the table." He burst into shrill laughter.

"He's got a motor-bike," said Jane.

"He said another thing. He said I'll have a shave and go to my grave." Christopher doubled up, convulsed.

"Do you ever make up poetry?" said Olivia.

"No," said Jane.

"I do," said Christopher.

"You don't."

"Do tell me one," said Olivia.

His face froze in an agony of concentration. A poem should come. He willed it. He said rapidly:

"The clouds pass and pass. Willy's lying in the grass."

"Very good," said Olivia. "Any more?"

He turned away his head, let his lids fall, muttered:

"I can't answer any more voices."

"I think we ought to go to sleep now," said Jane politely. "We've said our prayers. Will you pull down the blind?"

Speculating on Kate's reasons for bringing up her children in the strict letter of orthodoxy, Olivia did so, kissed them and went to the door. Jane said out of the yellowish twilight:

"If we go for a picnic to the woods to-morrow, will you come too?"

"Would you like me to?"

"Yes."

"Then I will."

"We didn't remember you very well," said Jane. "We thought your face would be like Auntie Ruth's."

"Are you glad it isn't?"

"Yes," said Jane.

Christopher sprang violently inside the sheet, and lay still.

"Kate, shall you ever have any more?"

"More what?"

Kate lay on her back in the copse, relaxed, staring into the beech tops. They had brought the children in the car to the old picnic wood.

"Children."

"Oh . . . No . . . Too much sweat."

"I suppose it is an awful sweat."

"I don't mind them once they're there—but it's the hell of a performance to go through four times. *Nothing* to be said for it."

"Did you feel awful when they were coming? I don't seem to remember."

"I felt sick at first, of course. Most people do."

"How long for?" I must know.

"Oh, I forget. It varied. Six weeks—eight weeks."

Kate rubbed her eyes, bored, on the verge of irritation, as always when her health was in question. Why go on about feeling sick? . . . She added with a sort of sour triumph: "I did everything just as usual, of course. Nobody ever knew I had a qualm. You don't want to go giving it away to everybody."

She can't have felt like me, she can't have. . . .

"But after the beginning, did you feel well?"

"I felt all right, more or less. One doesn't feel one's brightest."

I mustn't go on.

A little way away the children ran about, hunting for the initialled tree-trunks. Occasionally one or the other shouted, "Is it tea-time yet?"

"Yes," called Kate finally, sitting up. They came tearing back and she unpacked the tea basket, and spread out interesting white paper parcels.

"We call this jelly red," said Christopher, parting his sandwich. "Sometimes we call it pink. I call it a mixture."

"We had doughnuts when we went to tea with David," said Jane. "And do you know what his daddy said? He said: If I catch you calling your sister pig any more I'll spank you with a slipper, so he called her horse. David's older than me, a whole year, but I can lift him as easy as anything."

Christopher belched. He said in pride and surprise:

"Did you hear me make that turn?"

"When Mabel does it, she says beg pardon," said Jane.

"Do you know why I do it? It's because I'm a windbag."

He looked dreamy. "Men think it funny, but ladies don't care for it. . . . Mum?"

"Yes?"

"What man of all the men you know would you choose to make that noise for you?"

"You, I think."

He smiled secretively, flattered, self-conscious.

Replete, they ran about, each with an empty paper bag.

"Christopher, Christopher, there's a little baby in here."

He took a frantic peep.

"Shut it up! Shut it up!"

Screwing it tight at the mouth they rushed with it and poked it into a hollow place among beech-roots.

Christopher peered into his bag. His face was wild.

"Jane, there's a *giant* in mine!"

"A GIANT! . . . Shut it up, shut it up."

"Hide it so he can't see us."

"No, bury it, bury it, so he can't get out."

They ran about in a frenzy, squealing.

"What a remarkable game," said Olivia.

"Idiotic," said Kate.

She lay on her back again, unaware of the dropping around her of ripe plums for analysts. Suddenly she said in a different voice, a voice for Olivia:

"God, I wish they were all grown up! If I could have a wish that would be it. Grown up and—all right—independent —off my hands. . . . It seems such *years* before one can hope to feel they're all safely through . . . Perhaps one never will. . . . Supposing they're not happy . . . Sometimes when I get back from London or somewhere and smell eucalyptus coming from the bathroom *again* and know they'll *all* catch it and Christopher'll have a temperature and Priscilla a cough—I go quite . . . I feel what's the use, why not leave them out on the grass all night or something. . . ."

"I can imagine . . ."

Kate, darling, this is you, I know you, you're too vulnerable. Does Rob know you are? . . . I must have a child, to share this with her.

I'm going to have a child.

It was real for the first time, it was love and truth, she saw it with joy. A son, mine and Rollo's . . . Now I'll tell Kate, and then it will be irrevocable. Kate, listen . . .

She turned her head and looked down at the figure beside her—the pink, soft, firmly-modelled lips, slightly parted now, young-looking, the clear-water eyes looking up, abstracted, the wavy hair swept loosely backwards, the long supple body that had borne four. . . . Beautiful still; but where were those lyric lines, that astonishing grace really like a flower, a young tree? . . . She was the wife of Dr. Emery, living an ordinary middle-class family life, valued, successful, fairly contented. One saw her life running, peacefully, unsensationally now on its course, right on to the end: and why did this make one want to cry? Kate isn't wasted. But there should have been something else, I alone know her, some exaggeration. . . .

Kate, listen. . . . Madness. . . . Kate, I'm . . .

Staring up into the glowing black-ribbed roof of beech boughs Kate said suddenly:

"Who d'you think I saw when I went to the village this morning? Tony Heriot. Coming out of the post office as I went in."

"Speak to him?"

This was important. Their small cool voices betrayed them.

"No, I didn't. . . . He looked at me and sort of just lifted his hat-brim and went on and got into his car. Directly I saw that car I knew it was his. . . . I wonder how long he's home for. . . ."

"Was he embarrassed?"

"I don't know. . . . A bit, I think. Neither of us knew whether to stop or smile or what. . . ." She rolled her head sideways on the dead beech leaves, away from Olivia. She said with the ghost of a smile, "I nearly fainted."

"Kate . . . What did happen?" For not a word, through all those old hot-eyed, heavy days, had passed Kate's lips. Locked behind her stretched, harshly contracted, resigned, incredulous forehead, she had resisted them all. . . . Imprisoned me, too, far away from her. . . .

"Nothing," said Kate finally. "It wasn't anything. He was going to come to Paris and see me—it was all fixed up—and then he never came. Never wrote. Absolute fade-out. By the time I was back he'd gone off to India. . . . Oh, I don't know —it was all quite idiotic. I suppose he just thought better of it. . . . Or sometimes I feel certain his beastly parents interfered —thought he was getting involved . . . God knows."

"He married, didn't he?"

"M'm. About five years ago. I saw it in *The Times*." She relapsed into silence. The reversed angle of her head on its flat leaf pillow narrowed her eyes to shining slivers of green glass beneath the dropped lids. After a bit she said:

"I'm glad I've seen him again. It's always been something to get over. I've dreaded it." She turned her neck again and looked straight upwards. She said simply: "Whatever happens, nothing can be as bad as that again. The endless blankness and suspense . . . One can't put up any defences. . . ."

"You don't mind any more . . . do you, Kate?"

"No, I don't mind any more. One gets over everything in time."

Christopher came hurrying up from where he had been, out of sight somewhere. He sat down quickly beside his mother. After a bit he said:

"This wood's rather big, isn't it?"

"Fairly big, but not dark, is it? A friendly kind of wood."

"M'm." He leaned against her. "When will it be time to go home?"

Kate sighed, inaudibly.

"Now, I think," she said cheerfully, getting to her feet, holding his hand.

This before-dinner bout was the worst yet. The drive perhaps . . . or the emotion in the wood. It was all gone, the good feeling. Nothing now but the black miasma. The cold sweat broke out all over her. Faint . . . Get out of here. She found the lavatory door, unlocked it feverishly, got out along the passage—to the head of the stairs.

She cried out with all her strength:

"Mother!"

Mrs. Curtis was there at once, flying out from nowhere, her face opening with alarm, amazement. Olivia fell down with a crash at her feet.

Then she was lying on her bed with Mrs. Curtis holding smelling salts and nurse feeling her pulse.

"Hallo!" she said, "I feel fine." She pushed away the salts.

"That was a silly thing to do," said nurse, her eye cool, sharp, professional.

"It was . . . The heat always lays me out."

"Lie still," said her Mother.

"Like a drop of brandy?"

"No, thanks, I couldn't . . ."

"Cup of weak tea?"

"That would be lovely."

Nurse went away.

"Sorry, Mum. I don't know why I bellowed for you like that. . . ."

"Are you unwell?" Mrs. Curtis shook out eau-de-cologne on a handkerchief, and dabbed her forehead.

"That, and the tag-end of this rotten upset."

Kate came in with a cup of tea.

"You needn't have sent nurse," she said. "I'd got it already. Here, can you hold it? . . . A nice lump you were to carry."

She heard their voices bright and casual, saw their faces preoccupied, concerned. She repeated her explanation.

"I've never known you go off like that before," said Mrs. Curtis. "Kate used to be the one for faints."

"Oh, mayn't I too, please? Kate can't always have everything." She sat up and sipped the tea.

"I think I'll just ask Dr. Martin to look in." Come to think of it, she'd been a bad colour again lately . . . Tiresome girl . . . Eating well though. . . .

"Yes," said Kate sharply.

"Oh, Mum, don't be absurd. Just for a little faint. Besides, the poor old boy'll just be sitting down to his supper."

"Well——" Mrs. Curtis weakened. Dear old Dr. Martin, his well-earned rest, it did seem a shame. "If you're not better to-morrow . . ."

"But I shall be. There's nothing really wrong. I feel a king now, as Mrs. Banks would say."

"Well, stay where you are. I dare say a good night's rest is all you want. I'll send you up some nice fish and the sweet."

"She'd better get to bed," said Kate. "I'll see to her."

"Yes, do. I must give Dad his supper."

Mrs. Curtis went away; Kate stayed, keeping a rather silent fierce lookout while she undressed and got into bed. She rattled on, absurd jokes and tags of mimicry running glibly from her tongue: to make Kate laugh, to take that look off her face. . . . She was successful. By the time the gong sounded, Kate had relaxed, was wreathed in smiles.

When they were all safely in the dining-room, she got up, took the pills and the bottle from the back of the drawer—where I used to hide face powder, that other deadly secret—went to the bathroom, ran the basin tap and poured away everything. There, thank God. Those brews were poisoning me. I'll be better now.

I must go away to-morrow, say Anna's back, asks me to join her. They won't miss me. Not safe to stay here any longer, now they've all begun to watch . . . Send Rollo a telegram in the morning. She composed it in her head.

Leaving to-day, ring up or write London please. Liv.

III

"Is that Mr. Spencer's house?"

"Yes, madam."

"Could I speak to him, please?"

"Mr. Rollo—Mr. Spencer is out of town."

"Oh, is he? Could you tell me when he'll be back?"

"I couldn't exactly say, madam. Mr. Spencer has gone to Ireland. I fancy he goes on to Scotland until the middle of September."

"I see. . . . I suppose letters would be forwarded. . . ."

"Oh, yes, certainly, madam. Anything sent here would be forwarded at once."

"Thank you very much."

Third time of ringing up Rollo's house: third time unlucky. These voices speaking for him made him mythical, removed him far out of reach, guarding him like a public personage in an artificially important world. This time it was a different voice again: the muted voice, benevolent, of an old retainer . . . Familiar somehow, surely. . . . Who could it be?

There was nothing to do but wait for a letter. Surely he must write. Why hasn't he? . . . He'll write the moment he gets my letter, or, anyway, my wire. . . . Who forwarded that? Uncomfortable thought . . . signed *Liv*.

It doesn't matter.

His letter came the last day of August, by the same post as Anna's.

He wrote, darling, he wrote one page, saying sorry you've not been well, I got your wire and letter. I did ring up but got no answer, thought you were still enjoying yourself abroad, thought safer not to write till I knew you were back. London was so awful I couldn't stick it, he said. A pleasant house-party here but not exciting, some duck-shooting, Dickie Vulliamy and his new wife are here, she's a nice amusing woman. Not at the very top of his form, he said, but all right really: he'd be all right with some fresh air and exercise. Scotland next week, this is my Highland address, back about the middle of the month. Take care of yourself, darling, he said. You know I'm no good at letters, but I love you, darling.

He didn't mention Nicola.

Anna's letter was a scrawl on a torn-out page of a note-book, almost illegible. She'd been on the point of leaving, but now Simon wasn't well, a bad chill and to-day a temperature, and feeling awful. She was staying a few days longer, till he was better. She'd let Olivia know the moment she was back and they'd go down to Sallows. Simon sent his love.

To be alone, sick, in London in this dry, sterile, burnt-out end of summer, was to be abandoned in a pestilence-stricken town; was to live in a third-class waiting-room at a disused terminus among stains and smells, odds and ends of refuse and decay. She sank down and existed, without light, in the waste land. Sluggishly, reluctantly, the days ranged them-selves one after the other into a routine. Morning: wake heavy from heavy sleep, get up, one must be sick, go back to bed; nibble a biscuit, doze, half-stupefied till midday; force oneself then to dress, each item of the toilet laborious, distaste-ful, the body a hateful burden. Tidy the bedroom more or less, dust a bit in the sitting-room, let in what air there was: for Mrs. Banks was on holiday, there was no one to keep one up to the mark, no sharp eye and sharper tongue to brace one or contend against. Prepare to go out for lunch. Rouge, lipstick, powder . . . do what one might, it wasn't one's own face, it wasn't a face at all, it was a shoddy construction, a bad disguise. Walk down two side streets to the Bird Cage: morning coffee, light lunches, dainty teas, controlled by gentlewomen; blue tables, orange chairs.

She maintained in one compartment of her handbag a supply of salted almonds and these she chewed on the way . . . She kept on at them steadily till the mob-capped lady waitress set before her the first delicacy of her two-shilling three-course

ladies' lunch. At least there was no particular smell in the
Bird Cage, nobody smoked much or drank anything stronger
than orangeade. There was nothing to remind one of men.
The china was sweet and the menus came out of *Woman's World*.
She ate greedily through the courses, reading the *Daily Express*.
The waitress had a wry neck below the mob cap, and a check
dress with short puffed sleeves and a dainty apron. The
depressed angle of her head suggested mild suffering, feminine
patience and resignation. After the pudding she inquired
meekly, "The usual?"—and brought with a sad smile a portion
of mousetrap cheese, extra charge threepence, saying sometimes, not always, "You never get tired of cheese, do you?"
With answering deprecatory smiles, Olivia thanked her; and
when she had retired, ate a morsel, then secreted the remainder
in her bag. Necessity makes one cunning: she was never
surprised in the act. Such fellow fowls as patronised the Cage
—never more than two or three, every one was out of town—
appeared both cowed and famished, concentrating glassily upon
the food card, repudiating their helpings with light throat-
clearings and refined, difficult, swollen-cheeked pauses in
mastication.

Women eating by themselves look shockingly greedy.

After lunch, a bus to the park. She travelled on top, and
began to think about cheese. Cheese. *Cheese!* CHEESE!! The
lump in her bag seemed to shout it at her, her salivary glands
began to ache. Sometimes she mastered the craving till she got
to her bench in the park. Sometimes it was all gone before he'd
taken her penny and punched her ticket. And then, more . . .
more . . . MORE . . . began the clamour of her gnawing, perverse
palate. Once or twice it couldn't be endured, she went on up
as far as Selfridge's and bought some more.

She walked as far as one of the benches near the water; for
this was her one actively remaining pleasure: to see water.
This, too, was a craving, a demented appetite; not an æsthetic
pleasure. If not to be in sight of it, to dream of it by day
and by night, seeing it cool, willow-shaded, still at twilight;

or slipping polished, smooth-necked, obsidian-coloured over weirs to rise again beneath in a shudder of unearthly green-lit beaten-up whiteness. Oh, to lie in such waters of life, to watch the smooth column sliding down, down over one for ever, drowning one, dissolving all in that pure winnowed effervescence. . . . Fresh, fresh . . . to be fresh; to be washed clean, light as air. . . . To be a fish, cold in ribbony weeds. To swim far out, to cease from swimming and be rocked, cradled in soundless waves.

> *I come from haunts of coot and hern,*
> *I make a sudden sally,*
> *And sparkle out among the fern*
> *To bicker down a valley.*

Nice . . . nice . . . light and fresh. Brook: a nice word.

Dark brown is the river, golden is the sand . . . Dark brown good, merciful, washing the golden, sterile sand. *Pure ablution.* . . .

They fed her on pancakes of yellow tide foam. Oh, delicious. Airy mouthfuls, crisp and tasteless. If only I could taste them. . . .

She wore every day a plain dress of bluish-green crêpe. Red and yellow were lurid, scorching. She must be clothed in a colour like water, like the sea.

In the park the grass was brown and sere, the leaves dry, like leaves cut out of metal. Apart from the children, and the obvious but unaggressive foreign element—tourists up from the provinces, bareheaded student bands from Northern Europe—the park seemed populated by seasonal derelicts and eccentrics: muttering, bearded men, emaciated elderly women tripping on matchstick legs, in long full skirts with braid, Edwardian jackets, perched toques with Parma violets, fragments of feather boa; beings leading antique barrel-shaped asthmatic dogs; bearing parrots and cockatoos upon their shoulders; bird-headed creatures feeding the birds.

Sometimes she found an empty bench, sometimes she and the others sat side by side in silence, occasionally someone spoke to her, and once started was unable to stop; the dam of isolation down, the spate let loose.

One day it was a middle-aged man in a grey serge suit, stiff collar, black boots with bulbous toecaps. On his watch-chain hung some kind of club badge of brotherhood. His forehead was graven in savage furrows, and beneath its ploughed prominence a pair of small, deep-set, panic-stricken grey eyes scurried and hid under shuddering lids. He looked feeble, ill. After a few furtive blinks and glances he put his feet up violently on the bench and seemed to doze. Soon he jumped up as violently, sat down again, began to talk. A dead monotone poured compulsively, impersonally from his lips. After some time it became clear that his topic was motor-cars. Cars. Cars. Oil consumption, tyres, steering, accelerator, plugs . . . On and on he muttered, blinking, shuddering, glancing at her sideways, saying Riley, Wolseley, Austin, Ford, Vauxhall, saying engine trouble, saying . . .

"My nerves are bad," he said suddenly. "I've been advised to take a sea voyage. Now could one take a car to Egypt, for instance?" He stared at her in wild surmise. "But then," he said, "what about the passport difficulty?"

The passport difficulty. . . . She saw it looming mountainous, insuperable in his head, a mystic menace, blocking the light of reason. "Behold me!" implored his frantic eye. "Allow me to cast myself upon you."

After a while he became easier. His rigid lids relaxed, his voice took on a normal variation. He spoke of the bad times, deploring unemployment.

"One needs something to lean on nowadays," he said.

"I suppose one does."

"You look as if you'd had a lot of trouble."

"Oh, no, I don't think I have."

"Your face is young, but you've got some grey hairs, if I don't mistake; my sight's not very good." He moved closer.

Now I must get away, remove his spar.

"Personally," he said after a silence, "I've found religion a great consolation."

"Have you?" Now, at once . . . another second and it would be too late. She got up. "Well, I must be getting on."

He drew something swiftly from his pocket. "One moment," he said. "Please accept this. Yes, really. . . . I'd be pleased . . . I've plenty more. I frequently carry them about. . . . They're a great help, I find."

Half expecting some token of an embarrassingly symbolic nature, she looked at her palm and found a gun-metal penknife, thickly embossed with lettering and devices. Upon one side she read: *The Word of God is quick and powerful and sharper than any two-edged sword. Heb. 4-12*, above a representation of an open Bible. Upon the other side: *For what is a man profited if he shall gain the whole world and lose his own soul. Matt. 16-26*, and a picture of a globe.

"I came up to go to the Motor Show," he said, relapsing. "But I find I'm previous. I shall go next week. I shall look out for you there."

Another time a woman leading by the hand a pale child came and sat down beside her. He carried a little basket with some toys in it, and he was dressed in his best: a miniature coat and cap over a white pullover and white shorts, all home-made, neat and clean as a pin. He sat in silence beside the woman, holding the basket on his lap, not investigating it. From time to time the woman stooped forward and kissed him. He remained unresponsive. Only child, doubtless, one of those crushed into early apathy by the excessive embraces, bouncings, loud, wild crowings of relations: by the oppression of the crease in his pants, the damp brush concealed in a bag, whisked out at the corner to brush up his pretty curls; finicky over his food, segregated from common people's children. . . . There she was, taking off his cap, touching up his fine silvery curls with her fingers: just as I thought. At this he turned his head and looked up at her, but blankly. His large blue eyes travelled on and rested without inquiry on Olivia. Delicate-featured, beautiful almost. The woman watched him eagerly, looked at Olivia, smiled.

"How old is he?"

"He's three. . . . He doesn't know it, but he's going to the hospital." Composed, pleasant, superior, parlour-maidish voice. "He's got something the matter with his brain. Yes. Fits. Yes. Two a week he gets. Oh, yes, he suffers. He screams something cruel in the fits. Ever since he was fifteen months. The doctors are very interested in him, they want him in for observation. Only a miracle can save him, the doctors say. They say unless there's a miracle he can't live more than another year. Talk? Oh, yes, he can talk—says anything. But he doesn't care to talk. He's so good. When he's going to have one of his fits, he says to me, ' Mammie, I'll be dood.' Yes, he's taking his toys, but he doesn't care to play. He wants to be working all the time, if you see what I mean. He's too forward, that's his trouble. Oh, yes, he's my only one." Her voice continued conversational, her pleasant face seemed without stress or grief. "I'd like to have him home for Christmas," she said, "but I don't know . . . Oh, yes, thank you, of course, we hope so too."

Custom? Lack of imagination? Indifference? A noble reasonableness? Christian resignation? Was that it? . . . A little martyr in the home—soon to be a little angel in heaven? Not lost, but gone before, gone to the Better Home . . . A first-class cross, one with particular prestige attached. . . . And then, the doctors were so interested. . . . But then that way she had of watching him, of suddenly kissing him, not emotionally, but protectively: a helpless half-automatic gesture, it seemed, expressing—what?

Well, let's hope the doctors . . . Well, what can I do anyway? Offer a card, my address, do drop me a line. . . . Send a wreath later, *with deepest sympathy*? . . .

Nothing to be done. Merely one of millions of atoms,

doomed a little sooner than some millions of others . . . that was the way to look at it. It doesn't really matter. Human beings are all in a bad way, we are in a bad way. . . . It's to be expected.

"Good-bye."

"Good-bye, miss. Say bye-bye to the lady, dear."

To and fro near where she habitually sat passed a young man every day. Tall, gaunt, fair; shabby grey flannels, shirt unbuttoned at the neck, books under his arm. On he drove in a shambling, unconscious way, the wide world in his head confusing him, causing him to trip on the edges of pavements, to knock up against chairs and people. His fierce excitable eye poured unfocused light. A trial to friends, an anxiety to parents. He talked too much, he trusted everybody, incurably expecting from human nature some behaviour that would not occur; crying then, "Traitors! Swine!"; next turning cynic, thanking God with mirthless barks of laughter for a sense of humour. . . . Losing his way five times a day, forgetting errands; trying his eyes till the small hours in a wretched light; frying himself a sausage a day on the gas ring, his digestion suffering; tossing sleepless on his lodging-house bed. . . . When winter came he caught a bad cold. He drank the smutty milk out of the bottle on the doorstep and turned his face to the wall. When it was night he felt lonely. He got up, and having no dressing-gown wrapped himself in the plush tablecloth and looked out of the window at the lights of London. He thought about being unloved and about the sufferings of humanity, and wept. She bought him a muffler. "You must wrap up." So he did. He wore it always, right through the summer. She befriended him and he liked her, but soon he passed on, away from her: she was not what he sought. Nobody would be that. There was no comfort in him. He was of the breed of Jocelyn; of that one who came one night to Jocelyn's door. James was turning into something like that, walking through France, secretively filling up his copybook.... There seemed to be a good many of them striding about Europe, looking thin. Not safe, conformist young men. Perhaps more important than Dickie Vulliamy . . . or Rollo.

About five she left the park. On her way home she stopped at a snack bar and bought sandwiches for her supper. Sometimes she had a glass of ginger beer. Oh, delicious! More, more . . .

The evenings were bad, were very bad. She had a bath, washing with the cake of Wright's Coal Tar Soap she'd bought, because she remembered from childhood its pungent unsweet smell. The Martins had used it and smelt of it when they didn't smell of indiarubber, the guinea-pigs or bull's eyes. She went to bed, her sandwiches beside her. Ham was food. She never sickened of it. Oh, for a long savoury dinner! . . . Game . . . Welsh rarebit . . . If only there were someone to bring me iced soup; or one lamb cutlet. . . . Impossible to face cooking for oneself. . . .

She was no longer so thin: it must be growing, getting enough nourishment. Her breasts hurt. She fancied her figure changing perceptibly. When do one's clothes begin to get too tight? . . . She remembered Kate unfamiliar and touching in a grey maternity frock with white ruffles. Such dignities will not be for me. To be rid, to be rid, to be rid of this. . . . To be not sick . . . I should be hanging on doors, lifting wardrobes and pianos, trying to fall downstairs, doing everything I can. . . . Instead, day after day, inert, she rested, strolled, sank down in chairs, crawled to the bathroom, fell into bed again: protecting herself against her own designs against Nature, lowering herself unresistingly to a vegetable standard: A maggoty, spoiling vegetable. . . . I don't weep, I don't fret. I regulate my life; I hope only as a marrow might hope for sun and rain: a dull tenacious clinging.

In bed she read her old Oxford copies of Victorian novelists. *Vanity Fair, David Copperfield, Mansfield Park, Villette*—on, on . . . The characters so out of date, so vital, lived in her with a feverish, almost repellently heightened activity and importance, more real for their remoteness.

Sometimes a flash pierced her: I bear Rollo's child. Soon gone again. Or a good dream woke her exultant, haunting her with shapes and sounds of transcendental beauty. Nightly, the dreams crowded: voluptuous, or straightforwardly sensual dreams about Rollo—but not always Rollo; faces and fears from childhood or adolescence, long forgotten or suppressed; dramas in sequence, intricate conspiracies; those water images with swans and water-lilies; and a host more cloudy symbols. . . .

A fortnight went by alone in London. The telephone never rang, and Rollo didn't write again.

IV

A BAD afternoon. The park was airless. The sky was clouding from the west, saffron-tinged: the fine spell would have broken before night. There would be thunder and then the rain would come down. She was restless, waiting for the change, unable to breathe. Figures passing to and fro, or sitting on benches in the distance looked diminished, flat and lifeless in a sinister way, like figures in a nightmare. She left the dry railed spaces, the lurid trees, and hailed a taxi. Thank God, I needn't stint yet. Taxis, ginger beer, ham sandwiches— the remainder of Rollo's journey money supplied them all.

Too limp to climb as far as her own room, she lay down on the sofa in the sitting-room. *Alas, alack, my aching back is near to crack I feel so slack* . . . The tag rang in her head, over and over again. Invented hundreds of years ago, when we had measles, when I was ten. . . . The room looked unfresh, neglected. No flowers. Smuts on the window-sill; to-morrow I must pull myself together and dust properly. Must make a resolution to be more energetic. Another ten days and Etty would be back. Anna too, surely, soon. Anna'll be appalled at this fix. She never wanted a child. Even to discuss childbirth in a physical way upsets her. She's neurotic; she'd drown her-

self rather than face it. I must avoid her, or she'll avoid me.
There was a gulf fixed, and on one side of it were women with
child; on the other, men, childless women. She was alone on
the one side. On the other, Anna, Simon, Colin, all of them,
walked away from her with averted heads, estranged. . . .

The sharp ping of the front-door bell went through her,
twisting in her chest like a probe. . . . Who? . . . Was he back,
had he come? It rang again. She went down and opened the
door, and there was Lady Spencer.

"Lady Spencer . . ." Come for me.

"Ah, Olivia. . . . Something *told* me I should find you in."

Yes, there she was . . . looking just as I've always known
she would some time or other on my doorstep. A large hat of
thin black straw swept with grey ostrich feathers was attached
to the summit of her coiffure; her gown of black flowered
chiffon, broken up with chains, ruffles, pearls, flowed about
her ankles. Lavender kid gloves, a grey silk parasol. Her eyes
were steady, ice-blue: dictator's eyes, fanatically self-confident,
without appeal.

"Do come in." In spite of herself the conciliatory smile
beginning. "How lovely to——" No . . .

"*May* I come in? Just for a very short time." The tone was
pleasant, but all-concealing; the old cordial note one's ear was
tuned for absent.

"I'd no idea you were in London." Her guilty voice trailed
off. Unable to look anywhere, she led the way to the sitting-
room. Lady Spencer lowered herself in a stately way upon the
sofa. Olivia sat down on the edge of a chair. . . . Keep my
back to the light.

"Will you have a cigarette? Oh, I'm afraid there aren't
any. I think there are some upstairs. I'll just go. . . ."
And be alone for a minute, compose myself, dash a bit of
rouge on.

"No, no, I never smoke, thank you."

"Nor do I much." One whiff, you know, in my present
condition and I'm finished. . . .

"What a charming little house." Peeling off her lavender gloves, Lady Spencer looked about her.

"Yes, isn't it? Etty's abroad."

"Are you alone then?"

"Yes, for the moment. I'm going away in about another week, I expect."

"I suppose your work kept you?" For the first time a note of sympathy crept in: Lady Spencer's respect for the bread-winner.

"No, I'm not working really. . . ." Trapped, trapped. . . . She said rapidly, "Are you in London for long?"

"It's a little uncertain." Lady Spencer folded her gloves, looked away. "I brought my poor John up three weeks ago—for treatment. It's a horrid time to be in London, but we so *hope* it's doing him good—he's *such* a clever, charming man, we have such faith in him—and then it will be *well* worth while, won't it?" There was perceptible uncertainty behind her emphasis. She's really as muddled as Marigold. . . . She doesn't know how to begin. But she will, soon.

"I'm so sorry. I do hope it's nothing serious."

"Thank you, Olivia, we *hope* not. We don't know yet . . . but there seems *every* prospect of alleviation if not *cure* . . . so that's a lot to be thankful for, isn't it? Besides, we're *very* comfortable where we are. Rollo's so very sweetly lent us his lovely house."

"Oh, has he?" So that's who it was on the telephone: of course: the family butler: who used to give us pink throat pastilles when Marigold took us into the pantry.

"Rollo is away till the middle of the month."

"Is he? . . . They both are, I suppose."

"Yes, they both are."

"How's Marigold?"

"Marigold is well. She's just gone to Venice." Lady Britton basking on the Lido. . . .

Silence fell. The noise of her pulses seemed to Olivia to

drum in the room. Lady Spencer loosened a gold chain round her throat, as if oppressed.

"I came to see you, Olivia——"

"I suppose *not* a friendly call?" Olivia offered her a small weak smile.

"Friendly, I hope, Olivia. I do hope you will believe friendly. . . ."

That's as may be. I won't say anything. I won't be bamboozled: a good word that.

"I've hesitated a long time," said Lady Spencer, her clear eyes gazing ahead into space, heroic, calm, "before deciding to come. . . . You may think the fact of my being Rollo's mother doesn't warrant my interfering . . ." Olivia was dumb, and she added, still with the same alarming faith: "I must risk that."

"Has he told you then?"

She said quickly, with all her trenchancy: "Rollo has told me nothing."

That's something—that's a lot. Just guesswork. I must keep my head. She knows she can terrify: she counts on that, and worship.

"How did you know?"

Lady Spencer turned a curious expression on her for a moment . . . complicated . . . partly apologetic?

"You sent him a telegram."

"Oh, did you open it?"

"Yes. It was brought to me. Naturally," she added quickly, "it was sent on to him at once."

God, what bad luck, what a half-witted thing to have done. . . . with that silly intimate signature too—*Liv*—read, sent on by her. He must have been annoyed, fussed when he got it. His letter hadn't said so. . . . Sooner or later the criminal will be careless over a detail and betray himself.

"But of course," continued Lady Spencer, "I had known for some time."

Olivia stared at her, hypnotised.

"I should say—had guessed ..." Lady Spencer looked down, ever so slightly flustered.

"How?"

"It's hard to put in words. . . . I'm his mother. . . . Naturally one is sensitive to . . . He was changed." She coloured, very faintly.

"Happier," said Olivia.

She paused.

"He was different," she said. "Unlike himself. At least I thought so."

"You're very quick."

"Not particularly."

"He didn't feel ashamed—guilty. Why should he?"

Misplaced defiance, useless. . . . Its only effect to make one feel coarse-mannered. Lady Spencer said quietly:

"I never ask my children for confidences. But needless to say, I knew there were difficulties—in his married life, I mean." She went on with a touch of acerbity: "People of my generation may seem to you very ignorant and old-fashioned. You like to think we all wear blinkers and live in cotton-wool, but some of us know something of the world. I had long expected Rollo would take a mistress."

The sudden plain speaking and downright tone startled her, almost brought a blush. Unexpected . . .

"And after you came to dine with us that night at Meldon" —Lady Spencer nearly smiled—"I expected it would be you." She paused reflectively. "That sounds a little crude. I don't mean to imply there was anything in your behaviour. . . ." That means there was. I was more than etiquette expects: I knew it then . . . "You are an unusually attractive woman, and, well!—call it an intuition. . . ."

"Does everybody know then?"

"I don't know who everybody may be," she said sharply, "but as far as I am concerned, I have not discussed the matter."

"I wonder if Marigold knows. . . . She has intuitions too. Besides, she wanted it to happen."

Misplaced again. . . .

"I have no idea," interrupted Lady Spencer sharply again, "what Marigold wanted. In this case her wants are not of the slightest interest to me."

As if focusing headlights upon Olivia, she turned towards her, and summoning all her powers, said intensely:

"Olivia, do you love him?"

"Yes." Icy sweat burst out on her forehead. . . . Brutal. . . . Stop it, I'm ill. . . .

"I'm sure you do. Of course you do. Forgive me." She made a slight, rapid movement, as if suppressing the impulse to put out a hand, to show affection. She said gently, "Then will you give him up?"

"Why should I——?" Olivia shrank back in her chair, rigid, panic-stricken.

Lady Spencer sat still, giving them both time.

"I think he's unhappy," she said finally.

"Unhappy——?" A wave of blackness came over her. What do you know, you fiend?

"Lately, I have thought so. I'm sure of it."

"Why, has he complained?" . . . *Mummie, I'm so unhappy.* . . . *Tell me all about it, dear.* . . . The blackness kept on coming in waves. . . . The thing is, she's always right. . . .

"I've told you already he hasn't said one word. He never will." She fidgeted with her gloves, smoothing them. "I realise I am taking a lot upon myself. . . ."

"You are. Too much, I think." Insufferable, unwarrantable interference. . . . But I can't say that, I can't keep it up. She was trembling, breathing in long-drawn shallow breaths. I mustn't faint.

Lady Spencer allowed the rudeness to pass. She said simply:

"Something tells me he wants to bring it to an end." In the silence she added, "I don't think I'm wrong."

Not you. . . .

"If he did—he'd have told me. He's not a coward. We trust

each other. We know we can say——" We do, don't we, Rollo? . . . Do we? . . . He said by the window: Remember I love you.

"Yes. . . ." Lady Spencer looked a little embarrassed. "Only you can judge of that, of course. I'm sure Rollo would never —er—— He would never be selfish . . . light . . ."

Olivia laughed.

"I suppose you think I snared him."

"No, no. Why should I?" She does too. "I'm sure—I don't doubt—— But we won't enter into that."

The room had grown suddenly dark. Outside a thunder-shower broke sharply, rattling on the pavement. They listened to it for a few moments.

"If you think I don't know about *her* . . ." said Olivia. "I know he loves her. In fact, she's much the most important— I know that. He told me. I understand. . . ."

"Yes, he does love her," agreed Lady Spencer, unshaken, considering quietly.

"I know he'll never leave her for me, if that's what you——"

"No. No, never. . . ."

"I expect monogamy's a tradition in your family. . . ."

A show of it at least. . . . Façades of virtue and principle, as an example to the lower classes. Anything may go on underneath, because you're privileged. That Marigold's no good, she's a drunken tart. And what about old Sir John in his day, I wouldn't be too sure . . .

"Any break up in his marriage is unthinkable . . ." continued Lady Spencer, once more scoring for dignity. "Although of course things have been most unsatisfactory. . . . She is very much to blame . . . she and her . . ." Now she was a little flustered. "But I have every hope—that they—that their difficulties . . . that there may be adjustments . . . her health will improve . . . that she will make her duty her happiness . . . I'm sure she will. She is a dear child really. . . ." More than flustered, actually floundering; the *de haut en bas* impressiveness gone. Her hands moved restlessly on her lap.

She appealed: "You know him. You know that what he needs is a real home."

"Yes." Children . . . I won't say that for her.

"Olivia, will you be generous? Will you make a sacrifice for him? Will you give them a chance?"

Another blackout, a bad one. Don't give in. . . . She burst out with violent weakness:

"What's all this? What are you . . ." Her lids closed. "Has something happened I don't know about?" Rollo, where are you? How could you? . . . Tortured, and you don't care. . . .

Lady Spencer was silent. Outside the rain redoubled for a moment, then suddenly sighed itself out.

"Rollo is weak," continued the voice implacably. "I know it. . . . He can't bear to hurt. . . . Any—any sensitive man is bound to be weak in such a position. . . . Believe me if you can, Olivia, I am here as your friend. . . ." Rot. Here as a blackmailer, here to smell out my game, see how dangerous I am . . . to buy me off with sentiments: pity for you you can't suggest a cheque. . . . "Olivia, will you help him?"

"I do help him. I give him everything I can. I've made him happy—he said so. . . . You ought to be glad."

Silence again. And the furniture listening. . . . This is the room it began in. Can she see our kisses?

"Perhaps," said Lady Spencer with sorrowful rebuking gentleness, "we must agree to differ on that point. Perhaps our ideals of happiness . . . *true* happiness . . . But we won't embark on such a wide question. . . . I only wish to say that I think Rollo at least will never find peace—shall we say—in a divided allegiance? That if you continue this—this"—intrigue she'd like to say, doesn't quite dare—"you will do him a terrible injury. There, I've spoken plainly. It's the least I can do. That is my view. I may be mistaken. . . ."

But you're damn sure you're not.

"Well, there's nothing more to say, is there?"

Stalemate? Not a victory for her, anyway. I haven't given her much change: managed to keep my end up. . . .

Suddenly she said in a cross voice, as if irritated by a bit of bad management:

"You appear to have been remarkably indiscreet."

"How do you mean . . . ?" She heard her own voice weak, guilty, apprehensive. What's she going to spring now . . . ?

"I should have thought it would have been wiser to avoid a town populated by half London for the Festival."

Good God!

"Were we seen?"

"You were."

"We didn't think we had been." This is awful. . . . "Who saw us?"

"I don't propose to mention any names," said Lady Spencer crushingly, pressing her lips together, looking like a head-mistress.

"We were so careful . . . we never stayed in towns. . . . It was only about a week. . . ." Feebler and feebler: excuse, apology, embarrassment. . . . Oh, God! It was in ruins. It had seemed so beautiful—such pure escape and flight. Oh, God! Toad faces, rat eyes of the world. Where had been the eye bulging in the crowd, the gloating nostril? . . . We thought we were so wary, going about always as if with feelers all over us, back and front and sides, quivering, on the lookout. . . . Except when we said good-bye in the square, by the fountain of the horses . . . that was the only time I forgot the crowds, forgot to be on the alert. . . . Was it then?

"Luckily," said Lady Spencer, "my informant is *unimpeach-ably* discreet." The emphasis had come back. "I can *count* on its not going any further." She jerked her head, looking both imperious and complacent. . . . Somebody under her thumb. . . . A relation. Suddenly, in a spasm like a flashlight photo-graph, it was Mary Denham . . . who hated me so that night— my enemy. . . . It would be. She would go to Salzburg for the Festival. . . . It was the right thing to do this year. . . . She would spot us, and gleefully post off to Aunt Millicent with the news, importantly vow absolute eternal secrecy, for the sake of the family. What a break for her. . . . Pure supposition, of course, utterly illogical, probably nonsense. . . . But the image of that face, trivial and gluttonous, peering and pouncing unseen from a car? a café? from the sidewalk?—was fixed now.

"How beastly. . . ." She sighed deeply.

"I merely wished to point out that you don't go about wearing a cloak of invisibility," said Lady Spencer. Her voice rose, hardened. "Rollo must have been mad to—Think of the risk! You might at least. . . . The scandal! Did you ever think of that—for *him*? What right have you—even if you're prepared to sacrifice your own reputation—to endanger—other people's? Supposing it had come to *her* ears. . . . It's a miracle it didn't. . . . I hardly like to think——"

"Oh, don't you? *I* can think of it without swooning! Why shouldn't she have a bit of trouble like everybody else? Do her good!"—Coarse, hostile, scolding like a couple of scolds, me and Lady Spencer, how awful—"What's the matter with her? What's this thing about her? Is she dying? Just because she hasn't even the guts to put her own stockings on—she's to be treated like a Ming vase. You think it's all right to behave like her—she's so well-bred and ladylike—she must be protected. And it doesn't matter what happens to inferior people like me—we can be ill—we can be worn down—and badgered and attacked—and dropped overboard—so long as *you're* . . ."

The blackness came over again, and settled. Now I needn't hear any more. Needn't answer. What a relief. This isn't a faint, am I pretending? She was aware of herself slumped down sideways in her chair, her head on the arm. Quite comfortable. Can't move.

From far away she heard an exclamation, rustling movements. A voice said:

"Olivia . . ."

"It's all right," she said earnestly, not moving.

"Shall I get you some water?"

"No, thank you."

Presently she sat up. Lady Spencer was bending over her, rather red and anxious. Their eyes met, dwelling full, searchingly, on each other. . . . Time started again. Lady Spencer straightened herself.

"How do you feel?"

"Better. I'm sorry. I haven't been feeling up to much." Two tears ran down her cheeks. She brushed them off and two more ran down.

"You should have told me."

"It's the weather, I expect. Thunder always does me in."

"Are you having proper meals? Who's looking after you?"

"I look after myself. There's nobody left in London—except you and me." She smiled. "I'm all right really. This is enough to upset any one, isn't it?"

"I'm so very sorry to have upset you. I feel so distressed. . . ." Her voice faltered, a spasm twitched her face. She didn't think I was so sensitive. . . .

"Please don't be. I'm sure you came because you felt you must."

"Some day you may feel more inclined to believe I have acted for the best." She looked away, a wrinkled old woman. "So far as I could judge of it," she added.

"Yes. . . . I just think families are too awful, that's all."

She stood erect, gazing towards the window. After a while she said:

"This is not perhaps the time to speak of one's own feelings, but I've always been fond of you, Olivia." Her voice was unemotional but convincing.

"And I of you. More than fond." In love with the whole lot of them.

"I've always so admired you and Kate. It seems such a pity—I felt so grieved when your marriage—I should so rejoice to see you with a happy home of your own."

"I should be less of a menace, shouldn't I?"

"Don't be bitter," she said with mournful dignity. "After

all these years I hoped—you would have been able to judge less
cynically of my motives. I have been fortunate myself—happy
in my marriage—but I don't for that reason suppose marriage
is the solution for every woman. But for you—it's what should
be. . . ."

"That's what he said too. . . ." She got up and stood with
her elbows on the mantelpiece and her chin propped on her
hands.

"Don't waste yourself," said Lady Spencer earnestly.

The old feeling came surging up. Lady Spencer, I'm in
trouble, help me. You know everything. Beloved benefactress,
infallible . . . Punish and forgive me, approve of me again.
Say: I knew my Olivia wouldn't fail me.

"I can't give you any promise or anything. . . . When I
see him, if I really think he wants . . . I'll know when I see
him."

"Truth is all that matters. We see eye to eye there at least,
don't we?" She smiled sadly, encouragingly. "Make it easy
for him. You're not weak."

"I am."

She began to draw on her gloves.

"I can rely on you—not a word to him of this conversation?"

"No. I promise."

"You needn't fear that I shall trouble you again, Olivia.
Think of me as out of the picture *definitely*, for ever. Unless,
of course, you should wish to see me. . . . I shall always be
glad. . . . Otherwise we may not meet again."

Never again the cordial greeting, the warm kiss, the sympathetic inquiry. . . . How sad. . . .

Settling her chains and ruffles, giving a touch to her hat,
she pronounced:

"People must manage their own lives."

"I always knew you'd come," said Olivia. "I've been expecting you for nearly a year."

As if wondering what to make of this, Lady Spencer shot
her a dubious glance, paused; decided to let it pass.

"I must be getting back," she said. "He frets if I'm away too long."

They went down the stairs together.

"I'm so sorry about him. I do hope he'll get much better."

"Thank you, my dear. I'm afraid we can't really hope for very much. But so far he's had no pain. If he can be spared that, I must try not to complain." Olivia opened the front door, and she stood on the threshold, her strong, noble profile lifted towards the street. "He has a full, happy life behind him," she said. "We both have. It shouldn't be too hard to find oneself at the end."

How sad, how sad: they had come to the end. . . . His full, happy life must close in peace; she would fight for that, see to it: no breath of doubt, no shadow of distress about his only son should trouble his last days.

"The rain's over, isn't it?" She peered out, short-sighted.

"Yes. The air's fresher, I think."

"Delicious. *Blessed* rain." She turned, holding her hand out. "Good-bye, Olivia. God bless you. Take care of yourself."

Her gaze dwelt on Olivia standing at close range with the light full on her. Suddenly the smile froze, the blue eyes flew open wide, fixed in unmistakable panic. "You don't look at all well," she said. The dusky red came right up to her forehead.

She's guessed.

"Why . . .? I'm all right." Steady now, steady. . . .

"Are you in any trouble?"

What it cost her to say that, in a level voice, was written all over her. She had turned as white as the handkerchief she held to her lips. Her eyes were sunk to tiny black pits.

"No. Why should I be? . . . What do you mean?" I do sound guilty. . . . She summoned a laugh. "Do you mean—like kitchenmaids?"

"I think you understand me." Her voice dragged.

"You're very suspicious." Try icy dignity.

"I don't mean to be. I . . . After all, such things do happen."

She pressed her unsteady mouth with the square of lawn. "I should be so sorry. . . . It would be so terrible for you. . . ."

"I'm not going to have a baby, if that's what you think."

She went on as if she hadn't heard:

"Rollo could never. . . . An illegitimate child would be quite out of the—quite unthinkable. . . ."

"What would he do? Would you think he ought to marry me?"

"Please say no more. I'm very sorry to have—— It was a sudden—— You must forgive me. I must——" In agitation she looked up and down the street. "I'd better take a taxi."

"Shall I ring up for one?"

"Thank you, no; I'll walk and pick one up."

"There's generally one just round the corner."

"Yes——"

She started off down the street, hurrying, her back erect, yet with a look of strain. . . .

She was gone.

She didn't look at me once after that look. She didn't dare.

How did she guess? Is it so plain in my face? A kind of telepathy, or intuition? Did I convince her?

Well, I've seen her once knocked cock-eyed, utterly reduced to chaos. . . . The oddest likeness to Marigold had slipped out in her disarrayed face: Marigold's look of being cornered, of desperate shift and stratagem.

What an awful thing, what a shattering way to part.

I'm not going to have a baby, if that's what you think.

I'm not going to have a baby.

She went upstairs and was sick and then lay down.

Now, let's face facts.

He said, Remember I love you. That was after he'd read his letters: because of something in one of the letters? . . . meaning: remember what I meant at best? . . . meaning: in case from now on there's a falling-off? . . .

The words tolled now with a dirge-like note.

And he hasn't written, he didn't wait in London for me.

It doesn't matter. I don't feel anything whatsoever.

Only I'm in the hell of a mess.

Rollo, where are you? Help me.

No, I must get out of it by myself. Because he's not going to say: Oh, *darling* . . . tender, pitying, comforting, overcome; he won't say, like in books, "Our child." . . . Of course he won't. He'll say, "Christ! Are you sure? How awful. What are you going to do?"

An illegitimate child would be quite out of the question.

I must get out of it before he comes back. *All be as before, love.* . . .

She got up and went down to the sitting-room, and looked up Tredeaven, W.P., in the telephone book.

"Mr. Tredeaven's secretary speaking. Mr. Tredeaven is away on holiday."

"Oh. . . . When will he be back?"

"He's expected back next week. Did you want an appointment?"

"Yes, I did."

"May I make a provisional appointment for you? Tuesday next at twelve? What name is it, please?"

"Mrs. Craig."

By the last post that night came a letter from Rollo: a scrawl, one side of a big thin sheet, from a Highland address.

Darling, I do hope you're better. Your letter didn't say. This is a pleasant party, and eight hours of fresh air per day have blown some of the cobwebs away. (He always says that.) I'm staying in an old castle—walls feet thick—everything panelled in oak—no curtains or papers. Secret doors leading to secret passages—just what romantic you would love. Life is simple, drink and eats plentiful, and sport consists of a few grouse, partridges, black game, snipe, etc.—the usual rough Scottish shoot. It is all so feudal, all I need is a bonny lass to share my couch—I know who, in fact. I feel so fit. I think I could retire here and be a hermit for the rest of my days quite happily. Perhaps I couldn't. Anyway I can't! I'll be back about the 15th, darling, and hope to see you soon after that, or will you be at your cottage? It was lovely our day there, wasn't it? I loathe the thought of coming back, except for seeing you.

Next day Anna's letter said Simon was still in bed. His temperature swung up higher every day, he was feeling ill. It might be something worse than a chill. She'd got worried thinking she wasn't nursing him properly and she'd called the doctor who'd had him moved to the British hospital, but wouldn't say anything yet. She went to see him every day. She couldn't come home yet. He said to send his love.

V

"No, my husband's not here, he's abroad," she said. "He sailed for India last month, and I'm to join him at Christmas. So you see, it couldn't be more unfortunate. I *can't* undertake that long voyage alone in this state. I'm being so awfully sick, otherwise I wouldn't mind so much. But anyway, the sort of life we'll be leading the next year or so—quite in the wilds—I don't see *how* we could cope with a baby."

"Quite. Quite," said Mr. Tredeaven, folding his hands.

She sat in his arm-chair twisting the ring on her marriage finger: Rollo's emerald, unearthed from the back of the drawer . . . to look a person of consequence.

"It would upset all our plans."

"Quite."

"Of course, we want one later . . . when we're settled. It's only just now——"

"Quite. These accidents will happen. Nature's a wily dame."

"No, no. You need have no fears. My treatment is absolutely harmless—absolutely simple."

He leaned back, tapped his fingers together. The light from the window gleamed on his egg-bald pate, trimmed round with an unprepossessing semicircle of lank, sparse mousy hair. He wore a morning suit and a high stiff old-fashioned collar with broad wings. His face was broad, bland, hairless, secretive, with full eyelids and a slight puffiness about the jowls, the eyes opaque, set on the surface and widely spaced, the lips long, pale, stretched-looking. There was something about him of a Methodist preacher; something of a professional conjurer.

"Don't worry, Mrs. Craig, we'll fix you up."

"Thank you so much...." She fidgeted with her bag. "And about—I'm not quite sure—what it is you charge—about your fee...."

"My fee is a hundred——" Mr. Tredeaven crossed his knees. "Pounds, not guineas," he added with a reassuring smile.

"I see."

Silence fell heavily. . . . A body blow. . . . Mr. Tredeaven took up his fountain-pen from beside the blotter, unscrewed it, turned it about, replaced the top.

"It's a bit difficult," she said. Her heart beat thickly. What did I imagine? Twenty at the outside. Has the emerald put my price up?

He tapped his nose with the pen.

"Well, I don't want to be hard on you," he said at last. "Say eighty."

Her straining ears caught or fancied the faint cooling-off in his voice, the slightest withdrawal of affability. Disappointed in me.

"I can manage eighty...." If I bargain he'll throw me out. What'll the emerald fetch?

"That's agreed then."

"Thank you very much." For his tone suggested magnanimity. "When do you want it? Before? Now?"

"No, no, no." He chided gently. Come, come now, tact, dear lady! . . . "There's no such desperate hurry." He opened his appointment book. "Suit you to bring it with you when you come?"

"Yes, I can do that."

He said sauvely:

"Preferably not a cheque, if you don't mind."

"Notes?"

"If it's not giving you too much trouble. Just in an envelope, you know."

"All right, I'll do that. On Friday at three, then." She got up.

"Friday at three." He, too, rose. He held out his hand; strong, plump, manipulative fingers with cushiony tips.

"Is it painful?" she said.

"What a lot of worries!" He shook his head, chiding again paternally, half playful, still holding her hand.

"I'm not afraid. I only wanted to know."

"You needn't worry," he said. "Don't think about it. A few days taking it easy afterwards and your troubles will all be over."

"I'll be glad."

"I'm sure you will." He nodded, sympathetic, understanding. "Poor dear. . . If you ask me, Nature hasn't given women a square deal—I've always said so—not by any means a square deal, poor things." He patted her shoulder. "Now cheer up, Mrs. Craig. My advice to you is: forget about yourself. Get hold of a pal and fix up something cheerful. What about a theatre—eh?"

Conducting her to the door he paused by the mantelpiece and said: "Care for pretty things?"

"Yes." . . . Oh, rather.

"I thought you did. What do you think of these?" He indicated a couple of bronzes—female figures, semi-nude, with drapery, holding torches aloft. "I picked them up the other day. Nice, aren't they? Empire . . ."

"Lovely." She looked at them. Meaningless, expensive, repulsive objects. "It's not a period I know much about."

"I like to pick up a piece here and there when it takes my fancy." He fingered them with his notable white hands.

Whose envelope paid for those? What'll he buy with the next one?

"I don't go in for being a connoisseur," he said, relinquishing them, opening the door.

VI

THE gentleman in the morning coat with the pearl tie-pin came back, ring in hand, from the inner sanctuary and leaning across the plate-glass counter, said confidentially:

"We should say seventy."

"I see. Thank you. I'm afraid I couldn't possibly let it go for that." She took the ring from him and held it up, staring at it. Green, glowing, flawless.... A bit of green stone. "You see, I know it's worth a great deal more than that."

"It may have cost more, madam." He shrugged. "The market for this class of stone fluctuates. It *may* have—I don't say it didn't—but between you and me if it *did* . . . I should be inclined to say . . . well . . ." His shoulders expressed regret, discreet contempt. "Perhaps just a *lit*tle more was paid for it than *we* should have felt justified in asking. . . ."

Rollo, darling, I'm sorry, what a shame—your gorgeous present . . . I can't help it, Rollo.

"I suppose you wouldn't know where it was purchased?" he asked, drumming lightly with his fingers on the plate-glass. He wore a handsome signet ring.

"No, I don't." She went on staring at it. "It's a perfect emerald, isn't it?"

"It's a good stone . . . quite a good stone." We are always scrupulously fair here. "I shouldn't go so far as to say *perfect*. The colour's just a trifle harsh. Now, if you'd like to compare it . . . let me just show you a few. . . ."

"Well, no, thank you. I won't bother." Slowly she pushed

it back in its red morocco case. I must try somewhere else. I must get eighty. . . . Supposing no one will give me that?

The jeweller picked up the case and examined the ring again. "Say seventy-five," he said.

"All right, then . . . seventy-five."

I can't bother any more, too ill. . . . I want to get home. To-morrow I'll pawn the cigarette case, it ought to fetch a fiver.

Baleful, reproachful upon its black velvet pillow, the green eye stared at her for the last time. He snapped down the lid of the box.

I wonder how much I've been swindled. Never mind. Value is only relative.

She touched the ring on her little finger. Still there. As long as I have that. . . .

Ten pounds for the cigarette case: a pleasant surprise. Obviously a very superior article. Handing it over was quite painful.

Eighty pounds in an envelope; and five pounds over. Very acceptable: Rollo's journey money had come to an end.

VII

"STAY where you are, Mrs. Craig," he said softly. "There now. Quite comfy? That's right. Don't worry. All over. Wasn't too bad, was it, eh?"

"No, thank you."

He put a cushion under her head, threw a light rug over her. She lay flat on the hard surgical couch and closed her eyes. Several tears ran down her face and dried there.

"Relax, Mrs. Craig."

"Yes." She smiled blindly, obedient, behaving meekly, a good patient. He slipped a hot-water bottle under the rug, close in to her side.

"Thank you." I'm cold—funny in this weather—glad of it.

He moved about softly, busy with something the other side of the room, his natty back turned to her. She opened her eyes. In spite of the September afternoon sun the room was in twilight. The buff blinds were lowered; and besides this, curtains of wine-coloured net across the windows diffused a lurid murkiness. From where she lay she could see an arm-chair upholstered in purple brocade, a black-and-gold lacquered screen half-concealing a two-tiered surgical wheeled table; his big desk with papers on it, one or two silver-framed photographs. There was a smell of antiseptics.

Presently he came back.

"All right, Mrs. Craig?"

"Yes, thank you." She smiled up at him faintly, meekly. His face loomed over her, broad and bland. The high-winged old-world collar carried on the motif of his pointed prominent ears.

My deliverer. Your victim, here I lie. . . . "Bit shaky still, though."

He went away, came back with a glass.

"Drink this."

She drank. It was sal volatile.

"I might be sick."

He placed an enamel kidney bowl beside her chin; and soon she was sick.

"Tt-tt-tt. . . ." Sympathetically he removed the bowl. "Poor dear. You won't be troubled with this much longer."

She sat up, swung her legs slowly over the side of the couch, did up her stockings, combed her hair.

"I'll tell my man to get you a taxi." He touched the bell.

"I don't like your man." Black eyes with a cast, memorising her face in one sharp furtive glance, taciturn, noiselessly showing her up. "He frightens me."

He glanced at her as if he thought she might be wandering; laughed.

"Why? He's quite harmless. A most trustworthy chap. Been with me for years."

"I expect he's all right." She sighed. "I don't like his face."

"We can't all be attractive young women," he said casually.

There seemed to her to be a dreadful intimacy between them: sexual, without desire: conspirators, bound together in reluctant inevitable loyalty. She bent down to look at the photographs on the desk: a rather good-looking women in evening dress, with a pre-war plait of hair round her head; two children, girl and boy, grinning, in party socks and pumps.

"Those are my two," he said, picking up the photographs.

"They look very nice." The sights those kids must have grinned at. . . .

"Jolly little pair." He scanned them with an indulgent eye. "That was taken some years ago. The boy's just gone to Harrow." He can afford, of course, to give them an expensive education. "That's my wife. . . ."

"Charming. . . ." Does she know where the dough comes from?

He picked up an enlarged snapshot: a man in waders, with a tweed hat, holding up a dead salmon.

"Recognise that?" he said rather coyly. "Me. . . . That was in 1928. Biggest I ever landed, he was: thirty-pounder. Game old boy, too: gave me the tussle of my life. Played him for four hours. Between you and me I thought I'd pass out before he did." Simple pride and pleasure warmed his voice. He put down the snapshot, sighed: not sinister at all, rather wistful; playing salmon more to his taste than performing abortions. "Fishing's a grand sport," he said. "Ever do any?"

"Not often," she said regretfully. "I don't often get the chance."

She opened her bag, extracted the envelope and gave it to him.

"Oh, thanks, thanks very much." He whisked it into a drawer.

"When will it begin?"

"Oh—sometime within the next twelve hours."

"I see."

"Good-bye, Mrs. Craig." He shook hands. "Best of luck on your travels."

"Thank you so much. Good-bye."

They stood and looked at each other. Never to meet again, please God.

"I should trot home now and go straight to bed with a book. Something cheerful. There's nothing to worry about. If you *should* want to ring me up, you can. But you understand—no messages. . . . You quite understand?"

"I quite understand. I won't ring up."

He put an arm lightly across her shoulders and led her to the door. On the other side of it, in the dark hall, waited the manservant. He opened the front door for her, and there in the quiet sunny street waited the ordinary taxi.

She went to bed and read *Pride and Prejudice.*

About eight she got up again and dressed and went out and took a bus to Leicester Square. An hour or so of oblivion at the Empire, and all may be well.

It was an American crook film, not first-class, but snappy enough, absorbing. . . . Packed humanity weighed down the dark above, below her. She felt a tingle of consciousness: as if someone she knew were somewhere quite near in the darkness. . . . I don't seem to mind the smoke smell so much: a good sign?

She leaned back and plunged into a film-trance.

It was before the end that the discomfort hoveringly began. Pain? Yes, surely. . . . But I'll sit it out. Just before the lights went on she slipped away, avoiding "God Save the King." A few others were straggling out too. In the glare of the entrance hall she saw Ivor ahead of her, walking slowly through one of the doors into the street.

He was held up at the first crossing and she came level with him and stood beside him. He was looking at the traffic.

"Hallo, Ivor."

He turned his head and saw her.

"Hallo!"

"I saw you come out of there."

"Oh, were you in there?"

"Yes." He didn't seem surprised: but he never did. "Not really quite good enough, was it? I suppose our palate's jaded."

"M'm."

He looked pale and puffy, his eyes without lustre . . . the way they always went when his digestion was out of order. His white shirt, grey flannels and navy blue jacket had a seedy look. . . . Down on his luck. . . .

They walked along side by side towards Piccadilly.

"What are you doing in London, Ivor? I thought you were abroad."

"I have been. I was in Brittany all summer. I'm just back."

"With what's-her-name?"

"With Marda," he amended with dignity. "She's got a house near Quimper. I've been writing a book."

"Finished it?"

"Not quite. I got stuck, and Marda thought I'd better put it aside for a bit and have a change. She thought I'd been overworking."

Got sick of him probably and kicked him out. . . .

"Besides," he said, drawing up his shoulders and frowning in an important, theatrical-ferocious way she remembered, "I've got a new job in the offing."

"What?"

"Well, nothing's fixed yet. I'd rather not say too much about it." However, after a few moments of walking shoulder to shoulder in silence, he said: "As a matter of fact, Halkin's half promised me something in films."

"Who's Halkin?"

"You must have heard of Halkin. He's one of our biggest directors."

"What are you going to do—act?"

"No—on the production side. Halkin's got ideas. It ought to be interesting working for him. I know if I once got a break in films I could do something. . . . I've always wanted to get in on them."

They waited together on the edge of the Circus, then crossed towards the Criterion; then across again into Piccadilly.

Extraordinary, depressing, how the old relationship re-established itself at once pat and neat, without a moment's embarrassment or uncertainty: oneself aloof, caustic, and cool, pricking every balloon as fast as he blew it up: a sadistic, conscientious governess; he resentful, aggressive, feebly jaunty, making a stand against yet wishing to collapse, to receive protection.

"Had supper?" He looked at her out of the corner of his eye.

"All I want."

"Where are you making for now?"

"Home. If you want to come along and forage in the kitchen you can. I can't offer you much—but I think there's a tin of tomato soup and some bread and cheese—perhaps a bit of ham."

"Thanks. I will if you don't mind."

His voice brightened. He's hungry. . . . He stepped out more jauntily with his short, cissyish, sideways-veering gait, one shoulder up, one down.

"Well, I can't walk any more," she said presently. "Get a taxi, will you?"

He hailed one opposite Burlington House. Pain. . . . The lights, the traffic swam and snapped in her head as she waited. *Pain.* . . .

In the taxi she huddled in a corner. After a bit she burst out laughing. "This is a rum start," she said.

"I suppose it is," he said absently. He was leaning forward to watch the clock.

"It's all right, I've got half a crown."

"Though I don't know . . ." he said. "It doesn't seem out-standingly odd to me. Rather pleasant . . .?"

She didn't answer; and presently he noticed that she seemed to have been taken ill.

VIII

SHE turned over and saw him standing by her bed.

"How are you now?" he said.

She said through clenched teeth:

"Pain. . . ."

"Was it you making that noise just now?"

"What noise?"

"Calling out or something. . . ."

"It might have been. There's no cat."

"Where's the pain?"

"In my stomach."

"Got any brandy?"

"No."

"What's wrong, do you suppose?" He looked perplexed, bothered.

"Nothing. I'm very ill." The vice temporarily slackened and she said, "Have you had enough to eat?"

"Yes, thanks. I enjoyed it. Hadn't had any dinner."

"You might fill my hot-water bottle."

"I will. Where is it?"

"Hanging up on a hook behind the kitchen door. . . . Kettle on the stove. . . ."

He trotted off, noiseless, glad to be of use. He was always a good nurse . . . tactful, deft. He poured out my medicine five times a day when I had 'flu, and changed me twice the night my temperature came down with a whizz. I was always seeing him shaking the thermometer. . . .

She heard Ivor moving about below in the kitchen. After a while he came running up.

"Here you are," he said.

She didn't move, and after a startled pause he slipped the bottle between the sheets, stood looking down at her, at a loss, then took up her wrist and felt for the pulse. At the bottom of the pit she had a twinge of amusement, thinking: wrong place, anyway. . . . He said loudly:

"Olivia!"

She heard herself say clearly:

"I'm having a miscarriage."

"Shall I get a doctor?"

"Yes. . . . Quick."

He went hurtling down the stairs. She cried out on a tag-end of breath:

"Don't be long!"

He wouldn't have heard.

From some unknown level deeper than sleep she floated up, and saw Ivor looking down at her.

"Hallo!" she said. "How long have you been away?"

His face altered in relief.

"I don't know. I had to tear up and down streets knocking up people with brass plates. Then I couldn't make him hear."

"Who?"

"The doctor."

"Has he gone?"

"No, he's gone down to his car for something."

"What's he been doing?"

"He's been holding something under your nose."

"Oh. . . ." That's all, is it? "Well, I'm better." Pain only a faint dying echo. "What time is it?"

The doctor came in rapidly, carrying a small case. He had a black beard trimmed to a point, and steel-rimmed pince-nez. A beard—good gracious! . . . She smiled winningly. He put an arm under her head, gave her something in a medicine glass, laid her back. Sal volatile again. This time I'll keep it down and that's just the difference.

"I'm all right now."

He took her pulse.

"Well, young lady," he said, "you gave your husband a fright."

"Sorry."

She caught Ivor's eye; they exchanged rather sheepish smiles.

"She'll be all right now," he said to Ivor.

"I bathed too long yesterday. I must have caught a chill."

"You must be more careful at these times," he said severely, refusing to be melted. "Athleticism is all very well, but you young women should have more sense. If you're not more careful you'll ruin your health."

"I know," she said meekly. "I will be."

When she looked at him she wanted to laugh. He'd got out of bed in a hurry, and one long pointed prawn's-whisker eyebrow was pushed rakishly over one eye. He had a stiff collar on, but no tie or waistcoat, and this informality combined with his beard, glasses, black suit and paunch, gave him an invented appearance, like the distressed bourgeois character in a Rene Clair film. He looked far from young: a locum probably, unearthed from his retirement. What a shame to get him out of bed.

"I'm terribly sorry to have dragged you out," she said. "I feel an awful fraud."

She couldn't stop smiling. Serenely, weakly, she floated at her ease in the pellucid element of resurrection.

"Don't worry about that," he said, less grudging. "All in the day's work. Any pain now?"

"Just a niggle only."

"These will help." He took a pill-box from his case, and sent Ivor for a glass of water. Directly Ivor was gone, he said evenly, rearranging and closing his case with slow rather fumbling movements:

"You haven't been taking anything, have you?"

"Oh, *no*. . . ."

Too quick, too emphatic, understanding too well. . . . But he was old, tired, he wanted to get back to bed. All he said was:

"That's right. Never monkey about with yourself. Your heart seems a bit flabby. Been overdoing it?"

"I have been doing a good deal lately. I've had to be very busy. . . ."

"How long have you been married?"

"Not very long——"

"You'll want children later——"

"Oh, yes."

"Well, don't be foolish. Don't overstrain yourself. You can't play about too much with Nature without paying for it."

Been hearing a lot lately about Nature's character: nothing to her credit. . . . more spiteful than God. . . .

Ivor had come back with the water. She swallowed the pill. The doctor said:

"Give her another of these in four hours' time if the pain goes on. She'd better stay where she is for a few days. Keep quiet and eat plenty of nourishing food. You're thin. Been going in for this slimming craze?"

"No. It's just natural. . . ." It's no good, he doesn't like me. . . .

"Well, don't. If you want me to look in again, give me a ring."

"Thank you so much. I don't expect it will be necessary."

Ivor started to follow him out; she pointed violently towards her handbag on the dressing-table.

"Pay him," she whispered.

Swiftly he took out the notecase and ran downstairs after the doctor.

"Well, that's that." Ivor came back and sat himself down in the little oak arm-chair. He stroked his hair back into position. He was always very particular about the set of his thick soft wavy dark hair.

"I'm sorry, Ivor. I've been a hellish nuisance."

He said cheerfully:

"That's all right. Rather a good thing on the whole I ran into you, wasn't it?"

"It certainly was. . . ." She added casually. "What did you tell him?"

"I said you had a pain."

"You didn't say anything else . . . ?"

"No, I didn't."

"I seem to remember yelling out something in a mad way. . . ."

"Yes, you did. I didn't know what to make of that, so I left it alone."

He spoke apparently with perfect simplicity, incuriosity. Typical.

"I suppose you said I was your wife."

"Well, yes. It seemed less trouble than stating the exact position. Besides, it's true, I presume, isn't it?"

"I suppose it is."

They laughed.

"His *beard*," she said. "I thought I must be dreaming."

"I know. Superb."

"I should have thought a beard like that would interfere with his practice."

"Not in his heyday—I dare say it was an asset."

"It's very odd: he's *exactly*—in every respect—how I always imagined Dr. Fell."

They laughed again.

"Comfy?" he said.

"Yes, thanks."

"I think I'll sit up here for a bit in case you want anything, and read the paper. If I'm not in your way."

"Not a bit."

"I bought it hours ago and I was going to take it home to read in bed." He pulled the *Evening Standard* out of his pocket.

"Where are you staying?"

"Well, Marda's lent me her flat for a week or so—just till I can find something of my own. She's still abroad."

Scenting danger, he rapidly unfolded his paper, and concealed himself behind it.

"Move the light if you like. . . ." It's not for me to pry into his parasitic little arrangements.

He turned his chair round, pulled the lamp—Anna's lamp that always amused Rollo—closer to him, tilting up its shade.

"Anna do this?" he said.

"M'm."

"Rather witty. . . ." He jerked his head in the direction of the Park chairs picture. "Not unpleasant to see that again. It doesn't wear too badly." He screwed up his eyes professionally.

"I like it still. I always shall. Partly for the wrong reasons, I suspect—literary ones. And then it helps me to preserve the line of continuity. . . ." She closed her eyes, sighed with fatigue. "Which is sometimes hard to hang on to when one looks back. . . ."

She fell into a light doze, thinking of Rollo: nebulous thoughts and images, not sad. Ivor sat quietly, reading, rustling the paper now and then.

"Mind a pipe?" he said presently.

She woke up and said no.

He lit it. The first whiff she caught smelt odd—not quite right yet, but not nauseating. The sickness is over. I shan't be sick any more. I can go about anywhere, talk to people, look at them with nothing to hide, eat, drink, smoke. Oh . . . how wonderful! It's over. . . . Really the things one goes through. . . . But it's over. I always just manage somehow. . . . Lucky Livia. . . . I can be human and have thoughts again. My face will come back, I'll get a new frock with the money left over, to look pretty for Rollo. . . .

She turned her head towards Ivor. There he sat again, puffing at his pipe: clenching it between his side teeth, occasionally stretching his mouth and drawing in a hissing breath, exactly as he always used to. . . . She studied his profile. Oh,

Ivor, you've changed, how sad! . . . The lines of nose and lips had coarsened, the sweetness was gone. There was a fold of flabby flesh beneath the soft, full curve of his chin. . . . Did he drink? What's going to happen to him?

She dozed again. When she reopened her eyes, Ivor's head was sunk on his chest. She stirred and he roused himself, started up.

"How d'you feel?" he said half-mechanically, confused with drowsiness.

"Grand. That pill seems to have done the trick. I wonder what it was. I should have thought he'd set himself against any form of female alleviation. . . . What time is it?"

"Two o'clock."

"I'm hungry." Ravenous: not the morbid lugubrious craving, but real fresh elementary hunger. "I could eat the *Evening Standard.*"

He jumped to his feet, alert, excited.

"I could do with a bite myself. Shall I make some chocolate? I saw the tin."

"Hot chocolate! Oh, yes, and there's some milk." She had bought a pint on the way back from the purple room that afternoon, vaguely conjecturing she might be glad of a hot drink in the night. "But that won't be enough." She sat up straight in bed. "I want something solid. I tell you what —a mixed grill—— Oh!" She yearned at the thought of it. "Is there *nothing* in this blinking house? Some bread, I suppose. . . . Would any shops be open?" *Fool* not to have replenished the wretched store cupboard, got in eggs, bacon, cream, every sort of thing.

"I know what I did see: a tin of beans."

"Baked beans!—are you sure?"

"Yes—alongside the soup."

"And I never knew! Oh, God bless Mrs. Banks! She always has one in reserve for when Etty goes to bed early with a tray. It's Etty's favourite delicacy. Baked beans would be *perfect.*" She laughed with excitement. "Do hurry, there's a good chap."

"I'll be as quick as I can."

Off he trotted, delighted; a midnight spread! . . . He's awfully willing and domesticated. He'd be happy if he could live like this always: with someone or other for company— someone just in practical control but shelved as an exacting aggressive individual—someone being agreeable, not picking on him. He'd be a treasure to a lady invalid with cultured tastes. He'd push her chair round and round the garden, and take an interest in the bulbs, and they'd have hot scones for tea.

He came back with a loaded tray.

"I made myself a cup, too, while I was about it," he said.

"Good. Have a few beans as well—just a few."

"Well, I don't mind if I do."

"Go on."

Perhaps he also had days of lean fare to make up for. But he was always greedy. She recalled his questing eye over other people's tables; his furtive glance round always, as the next course came in.

He had arranged the beans nicely on squares of toast: a tempting dish. The chocolate was rich, steaming hot. Oh, good, *good*! . . . Moment of sharpest pleasure of my life.

"Sorry there's no beer," she said.

"I prefer chocolate," he said simply.

"What was the name of the man who did the detective in the film to-night? I've never seen him before."

"Harry Wallace? You must have."

"He's jolly attractive. The girl was good too—hideous figure, but good. I call it the phenomenon of the age—the brilliance of the acting in these wise-cracking American tough pictures."

They chatted about films.

She finished her drink, lay down again. She began to whistle, repetitively, rather flat, lackadaisically: *We won't go home till morning*. . . . Not getting further than the second line. . . .

"We'd better go to sleep now," she said after a bit. "Where do you propose to extend your limbs?"

"Anywhere you like," he said amenably. "I can sleep anywhere."

"I know you can. There's Etty's bed. I suppose you could have that. Only it isn't made up or anything."

"I don't mind sleeping in blankets. I'll hop off back to the flat if you'd rather, but I think I'd better stay in case you want anything."

"I shan't—but all right."

Impossible not to be ungracious. He was so jaunty, so unaware of undercurrents. He's lit on a free lodging, he'll dig himself in, I know he will. . . . He'll hog away in Etty's bed all to-morrow unless I kick him out. . . . Remembering his capacity for leaden sleep stirred up an old wave of exasperation.

"You can stay just to-night," she said, turning over, composing herself for sleep. "The maid'll be back to-morrow or the day after to clean up against Etty's return, and I don't want her to find me harbouring you. She's a tigress about Etty's belongings—she'd send for the police. Mind you take your shoes off and don't knock your pipe out on the electric fire or anything."

He said amiably:

"I won't. Good-night."

"Good-night."

Contrary to expectations, he appeared by her bedside before ten—just as she began to wake up. He must have made a terrific effort: must have had me on his mind.

"How are you?"

"Very well." Exhausted, peaceful, clear-headed.

In the light of the morning, he looked a trifle squalid—unshaven, pale, swollen-lidded.

"I'm hungry," she said.

"So am I."

She gave him money and sent him out to buy coffee, rolls, eggs, marmalade, butter.

About eleven he brought up a delicious meal on two trays. They ate it, in silence, concentrating on food.

He went out for a walk and she slept again.

The day trickled by, languid, animal—sleeping, eating.

It was evening again.

"I've been trying all day to find Brian," he said, sitting in the oak arm-chair, lighting a pipe. "He more or less promised he'd run me down to see Halkin."

"Who's Brian?"

"Carruthers. You remember. . . ."

"Oh, *him*. . . . D'you still see that lot?"

"What lot?" His voice was stubborn. She made no answer, and, deciding not to press the point, he went on placidly. "I thought he might be in the old Café. He often is. I looked in about lunch-time and again about six, but I couldn't spot him."

"Perhaps you ought to look in again."

"I might. . . . a bit later perhaps. He often turns up about midnight."

He sat and smoked his pipe.

"Do you ever write poetry now?" she said presently.

"Now and then." He sounded evasive. "I did a thing last year—a sort of satire. Marda liked it. I showed the beginning of it to Beckett Adye—he liked it very much. He said when I finished it he'd publish it, but you know he's left the *Clarion*. It was rather bad luck. I've been meaning to polish it off and send it to *New Poetry*. . . . Don't know if they'd take it."

"Do try. I'd like to read it." He might write quite a good small-scale satire. He had some wit, and a shrewd detached turn of his own.

"I'll send it along to you to look at when I've finished it," he said, looking pleased. "I wouldn't mind having your opinion."

He unfolded his *Evening Standard*.

"This is a curious situation," she said, after a long silence.

"What?" he said, looking over the top of his paper. "You mean us being here?"

"M'm."

"Rather amusing, isn't it? Still, I don't see why not, do you? I mean—we never quarrelled or anything, did we?"

"No, we never quarrelled."

"I don't really see any reason why we shouldn't occasionally see each other, do you? As a matter of fact, I've often felt I'd like to ring you up, or drop in. . . . I didn't quite like to."

His manner was wary, tentative, waiting for a lead.

"Well—it's a bit squalid, the whole thing, really." She whistled a few vague rather dreary bars. "It would be best as a satire. . . ."

Everything seemed to be on a knavish, rotten level. The seamy side. . . . Reaction, I suppose. Him turning up again, cool, unperturbed, to cap it all. . . . As if the past we shared wasn't worth, to either of us, even one moment's tremulousness, tenderness, remorse. . . . There is no health in us.

Ignoring or missing any implication, he added:

"I presumed, of course, you were perfectly friendly disposed——"

"Of course, Ivor."

"Still, one feels a bit chary of butting in."

A marvel he hadn't done so on one of Rollo's nights. . . . He puffed away at his pipe. Presently he said, looking at her obliquely, a funny look:

"Marda's always asking me why I don't get a divorce."

"Has she asked you lately?"

"Well, not very lately. Last year she was always on about it. I remained non-committal. It didn't appear to me to be really her business."

Still the edge of cautious propitiatory inquiry . . . combined now with a most peculiar hollow pomposity: like a parliamentary candidate attempting a declaration of policy upon a subject insufficiently studied and of no interest to him: yet upon which a strong opinion is obviously expected of him.

"I suppose she wants to make it her business."

"She seems to think I ought to be free . . ." he said dubiously.

"Oh, she does, does she? Does she propose to marry you?"

"I'm not sure."

"Do you want to marry her?"

His mouth dropped slightly open. He looked perfectly blank.

"I don't altogether think I do," he said at last.

"I wouldn't. It's not my business in the slightest degree, but honestly I wouldn't."

"No, I don't think I will." She detected relief; though his manner continued lofty and judicial.

"She's too old, Ivor. I don't mean that's necessarily fatal, but I think in this case it might be. Besides, that black varnished fringe would get on your nerves. I don't mean to be rude. . . ."

"No, no, I know." He brooded. "She's an intelligent woman, you know. Got a mind like a man's. . . . Sympathetic too. She was awfully kind after——"

"After what?"

"Well, the bereavement," he said, embarrassed, jocular. "You know—Mamma. . . ."

"Your mother?"

"Yes. She died nearly a year ago. November last to be precise. You didn't know then?"

"Good God! I'd no idea." She broke out into a sweat. I can't stand shocks in my weak state. . . .

"Well, I thought if it *had* happened to catch your eye you'd probably have written me a line. . . . As a matter of fact, I nearly wrote to you—just to let you know—but then I thought I wouldn't bother you."

"I'd like to have known."

Might have been spared some bad, guilty dreams. . . . Or would the dreams go on just the same, till I die too? . . . Last November: about the time it started with Rollo. . . . She remembered the conversation at Meldon about mothers-in-law: "Has yours passed away?" "Far from it. . . ."

"I'm so sorry, Ivor."

"It was pretty bloody," he admitted, sheepish. "She didn't have too pleasant a time. Cancer."

"You were living with her, weren't you?"

"Yes," he said in the familiar defensive-aggressive way. "She took a little flat in Knightsbridge after—after we separated. I had my own room—quite independent, but of course it wasn't an ideal arrangement from my point of view. Still, it seemed the easiest thing to do for the moment. . . . I'm afraid she didn't particularly like living in London. She was lonely . . . though I tried . . ." His voice trailed off, flat, dejected. . . .

All at once Ivor's mother lost her power, her venom; appeared as one of hundreds of harmless elderly middle-class widows dying with resignation of cancer. . . . In a minute I shall boo-hoo because I was a beast to her and she hated me and we weren't reconciled on her deathbed.

"She loathed me," she said shakily. An enemy's death is simply awful.

Troubled, at a loss, he drummed on the arms of his chair, looking blank.

"She never mentioned you afterwards," he finally ventured, uncertain. "She knew I wouldn't stand for any—well—you know what she was—attacks." He added resolutely: "I made her understand that once and for all, the first time she started."

"That was nice of you." More than I did for him. . . .

"She wasn't an outstandingly rational woman." He relit his pipe. "As you know, I was the only person who counted. I dare say that didn't do *me* much good. Still . . ."

"I'm glad you had Marda."

"Yes, it was something," he said meditatively.

Ivor an orphan. . . . It wasn't quite suitable. Somebody ought to be responsible. But somebody would be; he'd be all right; if not Marda, another mother. The world was packed with them. He was tenacious and he still had some looks; and that charm, with its curious, cold, somehow diminutive, somehow abstract flavour.

After a silence he said cautiously:

"What about you—as regards divorce?"

"Oh . . . I don't really mind one way or the other. It seems perhaps a pointless extravagance—unless one were proposing to remarry."

"And you're not?"

"No, not at the moment. Had you heard I was?"

"Oh no. . . ."

Had he or not? You could never be sure with Ivor. Might he be up to some funny business on the sly?—as Kate had once suggested. He was tricky. A dark horse. If Marda decided on detectives, and put up the money—would he need much persuading? She said, her voice rising a semitone:

"I'm afraid I can't oblige with any evidence just at present." As she said this, she suddenly saw light. "Besides, even if I could, it would be no go now, would it?"

"How do you mean?"

"Well, you see, we've just spent a night under the same roof. That's what's known as condoning, I believe. You've condoned anything I might have done up till now."

"Oh, have I?" he said simply. "I see."

"With Dr. Fell as witness."

"That's torn it, then," he said . . . humorously? . . . His face was totally expressionless, as it frequently was. You couldn't quite put anything past Ivor.

"I don't wish to stand in your way," she said.

"You don't," he said. "Not in the least."

He took his pipe out of his mouth and examined the bowl.

"I'd very much rather you didn't tell Marda about last night," she said.

"No, no, I won't."

"Is she jealous?"

"Apt to be . . . I'd certainly better not mention it."

He could be relied on there, anyway.

He eyed her, looked away again, straight ahead of him. She was conscious of his turning some scheme or other over in his mind. Presently he said:

"I don't know about you, but it seems to me remarkably natural being together again."

"Everything seems to me remarkably natural," she said. "My eye's right out."

"We never got on too badly, did we?"

"Not badly enough, really."

He hesitated: passed that over.

"When two more or less civilised people have roughly the same point of view they ought logically speaking to be able to hit it off."

"The hypothesis seems sound. . . ." She sighed. "But I feel there's a flaw."

Puffing away, looking perfectly blankly towards the opposite wall, he said:

"What would you say to another shot?"

"What, you and me?"

"Yes." She was silent, and he went on, warming to the proposition, "I take it you're more or less a free agent. . . . We might try it out, anyway. Of course, it would cause a certain amount of back-chat and gossip, but I don't suppose either of us minds that. I'll get this job—at least I see no reason why I shouldn't. . . . I ought to get quite a decent screw—these film people are rolling. And I suppose you've got just a bit. It wouldn't be penury like the last time—that's what got us down, to my mind. . . . What about it?"

She said painfully, apologetic but vehement:

"I couldn't, Ivor. Not possibly. You see, I've made my own life. I don't want to change."

"Right," he said immediately, in a hearty voice, not a flicker on his face.

She lay still, feeling upset. Just what I expected. . . .

"Sorry," she said.

He said equably:

"It was merely a suggestion."

What does he see, know, feel? Anything? . . . Impenetrable as agate. . . .

"You'd better go now, Ivor," she said. "I'm afraid you truly can't stay to-night. Mrs. Banks turns up to-morrow at eight. We don't want to be compromised any further, do we?"

"No, rather not." He got up briskly, folded the paper and rammed it into his pocket. "Mind if I take this? I haven't quite finished it."

"No, take it."

He set his hair with careful touches.

"I couldn't touch you for ten bob, I suppose? Just till I get this fixed up. I'm rather low."

"How much do you want?" He saw the notes in my bag.

"Well, if you could make it a couple of quid. . . . I'll pay you back."

"Take them," she said. "Leave me the rest. I may have to live on it for a considerable time."

"There's over two pounds left," he said after inspection, closing the bag.

"I had a little windfall."

"Lucky."

"It was."

"Well, so long. I might look in to-morrow to see how you are."

"I'll be all right. I shall get up to-morrow. Good-night, Ivor. Thank you for all you've done."

"Not at all." He paused by the door. "We might have a meal together occasionally . . . if you're going to be in London."

"I expect I'll be going back to the country soon. Still, we might."

"Good-night."

"Good-night."

When she heard the front door close, she got up and went down to the floor below to remove all traces of his occupation.

The kitchen was beautifully tidy. He'd washed up, hung up the cups, the jug, ranged the plates, put away the food in the cupboard. On Etty's bed the uncovered pillows looked faintly dented and disordered. . . . Oh, the queer little man, he'd lain there all last night, bounded in his stone nutshell. . . . We fell in love, we told ourselves to each other, kissed, shared a narrower bed than this. . . . Unimaginable. What did we tell each other? . . . Surely he wasn't agate then? . . . Have I done something to him? . . .

She plumped up the pillows, smoothed out the blankets and bedspread, went upstairs again and got into bed.

Depressed.

Soon I'll be out of this slough, I'll live again.

The slow blood goes on passing away . . . cleansing me. I shall look at Rollo with clear-washed eyes, I shall see truth.

I shall be washed whiter than snow.

Not next morning, but the one after, just before twelve, he came round. She was packing a suitcase to go down to Kate: Kate surprised, excited, on the telephone, almost emotional in her pleasure. . . . The door bell pinged. Mrs. Banks called huskily up the stairs:

"Expectin' any one?"

"No."

"Well, are you in, or aren't you?"

She slipped down to Etty's room and peeped out through the gold net curtains. There he was on the doorstep, looking down the street, his hands in his coat pockets. She could see his blunt, pale, puppyish profile.

She called down softly:

"Say I've gone away to the country. If he asks for how long, say you don't know."

She heard the front door open, voices, the latch clicking shut again. Now he'd be going away down the street, disappointed, jaunty, feeling snubbed perhaps. . . . Oh, bother!

Presently Mrs. Banks came creaking up.

"'E's gorn," she said. "I don't know what 'e came after. 'E arsked when you'd be back so I told 'im what you told me to. I said would 'e leave his name, but 'e said no, it wasn't of no consequence, 'e'd call again."

"I wonder who it was. . . ."

"Not a bad-lookin' young chap. Long 'air. Ar-tis-tic lookin'—you know. Un'ealthy. I should say 'e suffered from 'is stomach. Or it might be drink." She gave a flick to the lamp with her duster. "Anyway, if 'e does come again 'e does, I suppose." Hoping he will. . . . More inquisitive than usual. Concerned about him. And she's no sentimentalist.

Oh, he'll be all right.

PART FOUR

I

THEY motored down from London in the early afternoon, called at the Dog and Duck for the keys, and drove on to Simon's house.

The moment she opened the door, the new smell met her; not the familiar one of Simon's house—penetrating, exciting somehow, earthy, like ferns or mushrooms—something different—damp, sour, pervasive; something that had taken possession; a threatening smell. . . . She threw back the shutters in the sitting-room, opened the windows. Standing behind her shoulder, Rollo was silent. They looked out at the stretch of lawn, the elms, dry looking, shrivelling up, the pear-tree already shedding pale brown and grey leaves. The weather was dull, gusty, with clouds and wind coming up.

"What's the date?" she said.

"The twenty-fifth of September."

"It's autumn."

"M'm. Depressing idea." He gave a rapid start and shiver, as if suddenly chilled.

"The grass needs mowing. I wonder if I ought to get somebody to see to it."

Extraordinary how neglect could encroach in less than two months. It seemed abnormal. Simon's house had become an empty house. . . . It doesn't feel as if anybody would ever live here again.

"It looked awfully different last time," he said. "That *was* fun that evening, wasn't it, darling?"

"Oh, *wasn't* it fun?"

"This Simon's a myth to me. You all talk about him, and I'm told this is his house, but I don't really believe he exists."

"That's his portrait."

314

He went slowly over to the fireplace and looked at the head of Simon hanging above it. Billy had done it years ago, in black outline, and tones of green and yellow.

"It's not really the kind of portrait I understand, darling, but I'm sure he's a fascinating chap."

"It's exactly like him." She crossed the room and stood beside him and stared up at it. "He's ill," she said.

"Badly?"

"Yes, very badly. Typhoid fever. Still, he's better. I had a card from Anna yesterday—they're in the South of France. She says his temperature's gone down. As soon as he can travel, she's going to bring him here to convalesce."

An exciting thing to look forward to—living in his own house with Simon, helping to look after him, getting to know him better. He would be the necessary, the sufficient focus, the stepping-stone over into autumn. He would shift this deadlock, this meaninglessness. *After he comes, I shall see what to do.* . . .

"Will you be here?" said Rollo, looking away.

"I expect so—for a bit, anyway." The thought of Simon always made him oddly sulky, depressed, suspicious. "It's *some*thing to look forward to." He was silent, staring at the window, his mouth moodily pouting. She added: "But I suppose I must think about trying for another job soon. I'm sure I don't know what."

He looked miserable.

"What shall I do, Rollo? Try for a job in the chorus? Too old—and I can't sing or dance. I might be a mannequin perhaps—if I had any influence. . . . I suppose you don't know any smart society dressmakers with a vacancy?"

Where is the crystal element we were to bathe in without fear? Rollo, look at me! . . . I planned it to be beautiful and simple: a night together in this house where we were once so happy; the last perhaps; but that was to be revealed to us. . . .

"Or I might get a walk-on in a film. I saw Ivor about a

fortnight ago—did I tell you? He seemed to think he was in with some film magnate. He might give me an introduction."

Propped on top of the long, low, yellow-painted bookshelf was a picture of Anna's, unfinished; hay-cart, field, elms, the spire in the distance; a summer landscape. A long time ago, an old story. . . . Will she finish it in the winter? She never can finish things.

He was wandering about all over the room. Restless. Something on his mind.

Remember I love you.

"Rollo darling, if you'd like me to be in London I will be. I needn't be here when they come back. I'd rather be near you than anything, of course. But it's not as if you—as if we managed to be together very often, is it? And I haven't much life of my own in between—now—to fill up." I've given up seeing most people; they all think of me as remote now, under a glass case, not mingling with them. They're bored with me. "At least," she added, "if Anna and Simon weren't there."

But less than a year ago these fragments flowed over from such richness and fullness that no emptiness existed, not one empty cranny.

He went on pacing about, not coming near her.

"Darling, you must do as you like," he said heavily . . . as if I were badgering him.

Oh, stop walking about! . . . She straightened herself with a jerk, said briskly:

"Let's go up and open the bedroom windows. Try and get this stuffiness out."

She slipped her hand through his arm as they went upstairs. Melt, melt, come close, look at me, give me one kiss, then I can speak.

A high, thin, street-corner soprano started again in her head, going on as it if had all day: *Let our affair—be a gay thing. . . .*

"Oh, my precious," she said rapidly, "I have missed you."

"Have you, darling?" He gripped her close to him for a second. "So have I."

But when they got upstairs he loosened his arm, her hand dropped down ... or I took it away.

They went first into her bedroom. She threw up the window, looked about her. In the corner was the low, narrow, rather tumble-down bed with its red and white cotton patchwork quilt. She said, smiling:

"We couldn't share it all night with much comfort. You'll have to have the spare room next door."

"I don't mind where I sleep," he said agreeably.

He said that. The accommodating guest.

She said quickly:

"It doesn't seem so stuffy in here."

"No, I don't think it does."

"Why does everything look so bleak? Is it just a mood?"

She leaned her elbows on the window sill and looked out. Anything rather than see this different room with the different person standing in it, dejected, unresponsive; where we stood, in the dark light, that hot afternoon, blind tapping, bees burning in the rosemary. She lowered her eyes to the straggling grey bushes growing under the sitting-room windows. Two blue-tits were threading noiselessly in and out of them, pecking and flitting.

"It's a rotten sort of day," he said. "Liverish, I think."

A peevish weather, hostile to man. . . . I'm back in the blind alley again, where the fresh air can't blow; where vagrants nose in the dust-bins, drag out the cods' heads. . . . What's to be done? How can we stay here?

"What about a walk?" she said, turning round to look at him.

He exclaimed under his breath, took a sudden step towards her, and said:

"Why are you pale?"

"Am I? I'm always pale."

"No . . . you're different."

"I'm sorry I don't look pretty for you." She rubbed her cheeks, laughed shakily. "I meant to . . . I haven't been feeling too lively."

She felt him stiffen, refusing a demand on sympathy—suspecting blame attached.

"But you're all right now, aren't you?"

"Oh, yes, I'm fine."

"Please to be."

He has enough illness with that creature. . . .

"Everybody seems to be a bit sickly. It's a sign of the times."

"Oh, don't be biblical!" he said plaintive, irritable. "I can't bear that sort of thing."

An ordinary plain-thinking chap. . . . She laughed briefly, saying:

"*You're* all right, anyway, aren't you? You haven't lost your Austrian tan. I suppose all the open air you've had since ground it in nicely."

"Yes, I feel remarkably fit, I must say. I've had a jolly good summer, really . . ." He broke off, added, "As regards——" Stopped uncertainly.

"Look," she said. "You can just see the river. I don't think we'll walk that way, though, do you? It looks so chilly."

"It does, rather."

"Do you remember that night on the mountains when you could smell water?"

She smiled at him.

"Yes." He smiled too; put his arm round her. "That was a lovely night, wasn't it, darling?"

He aims at tenderness. . . . They leaned together. Now . . . Rollo, don't go away again. She tried to speak. Rollo, listen. . . . Her throat closed, aching. Not a word would come. He gave her a little pat and dropped his arm again. Lady Spencer who had momentarily dwindled, presided once more, as she had all day. . . . He didn't let me know he was back for nearly a week.

"Shall I make a fire in the sitting-room? That would make it perk up, wouldn't it?"

He loved a blazing fire.

"Olivia . . ." He looked round the room, as if trapped. "Let's not stay here."

"All right," she said quickly, quickly. "D'you mean—go back to London?" A pit seemed to open in her diaphragm.

"No. No. I want us to be together. At least if you do. Only not here. It's so incredibly uncheerful. There's something wrong with it."

"How do you mean wrong?" He feels it too, then. . . . But it's nonsense—Simon's getting better.

"It's got a funny sort of feeling, hasn't it? I noticed it before—a sort of feeling I wouldn't like to be alone in it. I suppose it's all bunk, but one does get like that sometimes about places. I'm sorry, darling, if it's a disappointment. Let's go somewhere not gloomy. D'you mind?"

"Where would you like to go?"

"I can't think of anywhere. Can you?"

"No. I can't think of anywhere not gloomy."

She began closing the shutters.

"What about that little pub place where we went and had drinks that night—where that German chap sang? That seemed nice, didn't it? Shall we go and see what it looks like to-day?"

"The Wreath of May," she said. "Yes, it seemed cosy. All right, let's try there."

She fastened the green wooden shutters. The little square room sank into sad monochrome. They went downstairs, locked up the house, went out. The car was under the chestnut trees by the pond.

"That's not a very appetising bit of water," he said.

They got in, backed and drove away down the rutty track. She looked back. It was a small white house with green shutters and a leaded roof, set in a piece of neglected lawn: dismal, unwelcoming. Nothing special about it except the ragged thorn hedge all round. The shrine was broken, the genius had departed.

There was nobody about at the Wreath of May. They went into the garden by the wooden gate. Ghosts of the summer evening haunted her: motor bikes roaring up, stopping, roaring away again, the groups beneath the apple trees, the cheerful, loud, male voices from the bar. Now all was deserted. There was a ladder set up against the apple tree, three or four mongrel chickens pecking in the damp grass, a blue-painted, peeling garden table with a pool of wet on it; still a few roses on the neat standard bushes. She looked across the hedge at the tall plantation of poplars, alders and willows growing all together—where the owl had flown out; and Colin held forth about trees. . . . When she looked at the house, she noticed things she hadn't noticed before: only one wing was old, the rest was shoddy pseudo-old-world, with thin, poor thatching. Rollo pulled open a glass-panelled garden door in the side of the old wing, and stooping they went into a dark musty parlour with thick sagging beams in the low ceiling. He was just able to stand upright on the hearth.

"But I couldn't anywhere else," he said. "Look."

He went and stood under the middle beam, his head bowed; he seemed to be bearing the weight of the ceiling on his nape. They laughed.

"What a smell! . . . Damp? Mice?"

He strolled about with his head down, set a tiny child's rocking-chair rocking, tapped on the oak panelling.

"Seems solid," he said. "Fearfully old, I suppose. Shall we have tea, darling?"

"I don't think tea would be very nice here, do you?"

"Plenty of seating accommodation, anyway."

The tenebrous space was choked up with hard-looking brown arm-chairs; probably a cheap lot bought up all together in a sale. He pulled two forward in front of the fireplace. A sallow, thin woman wearing a white blouse and a choker of large pink pearl beads appeared suddenly in the doorway from the garden, looking startled and suspicious.

"Do you want anything?" she said.

"Bring me twenty Player's, would you, please?" he said in his easy take-your-orders way. "And I'd like this fire lit."

She looked stubborn, hostile.

"We don't generally light fires at this time of year. Not unless visitors ask specially."

"I am asking specially," he said slightly raising his voice. "Will you please have this fire lit? We may be staying the night or we may not."

Without another word she disappeared. Now we've antagonised her. A horrid beginning.

"Bloody woman," he said. "God, these British inn-keepers. . . ."

Presently a large plump country wench in bedraggled black uniform and cap appeared from another door with cigarettes. She knelt down, put a match to the sticks, blew on it, her hips and haunches swelling out immense as she bent forward. When she got up again, Olivia said, smiling at her: "Thank you so much." Somebody here must be on our side. . . .

She said huskily in broad Oxfordshire:

"Please would you like tea?"

"No, thank you."

She continued ploddingly, carrying out instructions:

"Please, will you be taking dinner?"

"What could you give us if we did?" said Rollo, amused.

"Don't know, sir."

"Could you catch us some nice trout?"

"No, sir." She began to wriggle and squirm, her face congested, dementedly coy. "She says you can 'ave a chicking roasted if you arst now," she whispered.

"We'll stay for dinner," said Rollo, lighting a cigarette.

"Shall we, darling? We'll have a chicken. Mind it's a nice fat one."

She vanished with a sidelong lurch.

Olivia met his smiling eye, and smiled. He'd had to win over the girl, to right the balance. He must have friends around him, devotion, eager service.

The fire burned up brightly. He put on a few lumps of coal from the scuttle.

"This isn't too bad, is it, darling?" he said. "We'll have a drink soon."

They could hear the girl loudly singing and stumping about in some room the other side of the wall. He got up and locked the garden door, drew a short checked cotton curtain across the glass, opened a narrow inside door, saw that it led into a brick-paved bit of passage, shut it again.

"There," he said. "If anybody wants to come in they'll have to come that way and we'll hear their fairy footfall."

He came back, sat down, pulled her out of her chair on to his knee.

"Oh, darling, this is nice," he said, sighing. He began to kiss her.

Was it all to be as before then, after all? Dismissing, agreeing, accepting . . . the apt, familiar, responsive bodies smoothing all out, lubricating the stiff opposing heads? . . . Would the block of misery begin to dissolve into rich slackness, to drain away like noiseless smooth dark water into a tunnel? . . . All as before, the recipe unfailing, as before. . . . She murmured:

"Rollo, there's so much to say."

"Don't say it now."

"You do know what a lot there is to say?"

He sighed. "Yes," burying his face against her breast. "Perhaps. . . . Is there? I don't know. Oh, darling, I have wanted you."

But presently he stopped kissing her. My fault, I can't. . . . She slid down from his knee on to the dirty black wool rug in front of the fire, fed the flames with another coal or two.

He felt in his pocket and drew out a little box.

"Darling, I saw this somewhere yesterday. I thought you might fancy it. . . ."

It was a platinum bracelet watch with a minute oblong face set in diamonds.

"Oh, how exquisite!" another present for Nicola. "Rollo, you shouldn't . . ."

"You haven't got one, have you, darling?"

"No, indeed." She slipped it on. "It's much too grand for me. I don't know myself."

"Don't be silly."

She stared at it, elegant and expensive on her wrist. What would this have fetched? . . .

"Is it a good-bye present?" she said, staring.

"What do you mean?" His voice was flat, guarded.

"I don't know—it looks like one. . . ." But she laughed quickly, as if laughing off a foolish slip of the tongue. It wasn't the right way to begin.

"Now," she said, "I'll tell you the time by my beautiful new watch. It's just on six. What about a drink? You go and have one—and bring me one back. A gin and lime. Double."

He got up and unlocked the door, and went away.

She sat on by the fire, and was clear in her mind.

We mustn't remember *Remember I love you*—we mustn't speak on that scale. When we were in that world we were not in the world. When he spoke such truth, under the chestnuts at the Gasthaus table, standing by the lake-watching window, seeing light and water mingle, then he was not true to himself. We all say things at times we don't mean: or even if we mean, can never manage to adapt to our fixed arrangements: unwieldy shapes, looming too large, impracticable, best put away entirely. . . . It would be a shame to hold him to all that. We must face facts: he was beyond himself: we were translated. Life in the world is what must go on; not that other life. If we went back we wouldn't find the rocket, but the sodden end of burnt-out stick.

He's an ordinary chap, he insists, and he likes a quiet life. He's afraid of me now, because I had a victory. I got too far ... like taking advantage of a person when he's drunk. He's been thinking the best thing to do is to avoid me for a bit, till things have settled down. *All be as before love* . . .

Perhaps an evening, even a night, together now and then, when it's not too difficult. Because that's turned out a most satisfactory arrangement. . . .

We don't live by lakes and under clipped chestnuts, but in the streets where the eyes, ambushed, come out on stalks as we pass; in the illicit rooms where eyes are glued to keyholes.

Well, that's how it is.

Lady Spencer, your son. . . . I mustn't let you down.

He came back with a whisky and soda in one hand and her drink in the other. He looked much more lively.

"Sorry I've been so long, darling. There was a comic commercial traveller bloke in the bar, and we had one together. Funny life these chaps have—rather interesting—I wouldn't mind it at all. . . . The old girl's quite amiable now. Once she got a double gin inside her she cheered up no end. She's not so bad, really." Genial, expansive patronage. . . . Why not be jolly? "Drink up your little drink, darling, and have another. You'll feel better."

He sat down, leaned forward to stroke her cheek and neck. Presently he said, coaxingly: "We *were* morbid this afternoon, weren't we, darling? I was in rotten form—I'm so sorry. Fancy spoiling our first time together after such ages. . . . What do you say to staying here? Let's! I slipped upstairs just now and had a peep into one or two bedrooms. They might be a lot worse."

"Oh, good. Let's stay then."

It was all to be as before. Leave out one or two moments of recklessness and indiscretion and carry straight on. . . .

She sipped her drink.

"I like this funny room," he said. "What a lot of funny rooms we've been in together, haven't we, darling?"

"Yes. . . . The unlikely fires we've lit! . . . Do you realise it's nearly a year?"

They began to say do you remember—remembering the first week-end, the night of Cochran's revue, other times: not the lake and the chestnuts. She moved closer, clung against his knee. . . .

Everything's all right, what was the fuss about?

"How's your father, Rollo?"

His smile faded, he looked troubled.

"Oh, poor Daddy—he's no better. He's having injections and things, but they can't cure him. If he'd let 'em operate six months ago he might have had a chance, but he wouldn't. And now they can't, his heart's too dicky. They've been in London."

"Oh, have they? For treatment, I suppose."

"Yes. I lent them the house while we were away. But he wanted to get back to Meldon, so they've gone. He's restless."

"Your poor mother."

"Yes, isn't it wretched for her? She's marvellous of course." He brooded. "You ought to have looked them up—they'd have been pleased. You were always a favourite."

Look them up! . . . Take it easy; keep things comfortable all round; what people don't know about can't worry them. Cover your tracks and what's the harm in anything? It's a little deception here, a little there, that makes the world go round.

"I couldn't see them now. I can't keep things separate like you. I suppose I've got a worse conscience. I should want to break down and confess all." She added vehemently, emotionally, "I'll never see them again—never!"

So be off with you, Lady Spencer, Goddess of Morality, sententious, interfering old woman. . . . Don't you listen to this—this is between somebody you don't understand—as usual—and another person you know nothing about. If you only knew what I'm going to tell him. . . .

He had glanced at her, startled, saying mildly: ·"All right, darling." He put his fingers through her hair, lifting it lightly back, caressing her. She buried her eyes against his thigh.

"Rollo, darling, shall I tell you what happened?"

He'll be so tender, so sorry for me; think me so brave. We shall be so close. . . . Nobody was as good as he at comforting words.

She began to tell him about what had happened.

He seemed too dumbfounded, too appalled to speak; that is, except for exclaiming "God!" under his breath, again and again.

"But it's all right now. It's over . . ." She caught him by the arm, insisting, trying to make him look at her.

"Why didn't you tell me . . ." he said at last. But not reproachfully, with indignant love and distress for keeping herself from him, not allowing him to help, to share; more as if—yes, as if trying to suppress the extreme of revulsion and dismay. And quickly he took away his hands.

"You seemed so far away," she said, panic-stricken, struggling for words to explain, to put it right for him. "I couldn't get near you. After a bit—almost at once really—I felt so awful—I didn't want you to see me like that. And then I got into the state where you *can't* make any effort, not even to write a letter. The only thing that mattered was to get through each day somehow and go to sleep again. And of course not to let anybody know. . . ."

"*Does* anybody know?"

"Not a soul—except the man who did it. I didn't see anybody at all, so as to make sure. I lived in a wilderness—on a desert island. . . ."

"Christ!" He propped his head on his hands, ruffled his hair up wildly. "Was he awful? Didn't he want the hell of a packet? They always do, don't they?"

"It wasn't too bad. I had enough. I borrowed a little from Kate. . . ."

"You should have let me—you must let me pay for it. . . ."

"No, no! Don't let's *think* about it even any more."

"Please! For God's sake! Surely it's the least——"

She cried, stopping her ears:

"*You did!* . . . I sold your ring."

He was silent at that, then said quietly:

"What, the emerald?"

"Yes." She burst into tears. "I'm sorry. I did mind. What could I do? I couldn't go on. He sprang it on me—I had to find the money at once. I couldn't write to you for it—I've never asked you for . . . And I couldn't explain why in a letter, I couldn't. I couldn't bear to bother you. I thought I'd better get through it by myself as quick as possible. Because you see, I *knew* . . . it was no good—we couldn't have it. . . . You'd never—you always said never, it wouldn't do. . . . I *knew*. . . . I thought—well, it'll make it a little better to do it by myself —it'll redeem it a little—because *I'm* the one to mind—I wanted it. . . . You didn't. For you it would be just a tiresome mistake, but for me it was a grief . . . so I must bear it by myself. I told myself—all through the worst, it was for *you*. . . . I said your name. That helped. Something to do for you. Not sordidly getting rid of something not wanted. Oh, I *did!* I did want it. I wish I'd never told you now. I'm sorry about the ring. I minded too. And I'm sure I didn't get nearly enough . . ."

"Hush! *Stop!*" He took her by the shoulders and shook her, not roughly, but not gently. "As if it mattered about the blasted ring. I'm glad it's gone—if it was some use. . . . Only it's the idea of you——" His voice failed. ". . . Going through that by yourself. . . . I feel such a——"

"You needn't feel anything—anything. It's finished."

"But are you sure you're all right?"

"Quite all right." She dried her eyes, blew her nose. The storm of tears had eased her, and she felt calm now, clear-headed. "Perhaps it wasn't quite like I said. I didn't mind with the whole of me at the time—far from it. My chief idea was to stop being sick—and the *relief* when I did! It's really since—I've never stopped minding—and longing for it. I suppose it's Dame Nature's revenge; one's body cheated. . . ."

"What a shame," he said helplessly. "Oh, darling, what bad luck."

"Sometimes I laid the craziest plans for going through with it—going away somewhere abroad to have it, and then coming back in a year and presenting you with the finished article. I thought you'd get such a thrill when you saw it, you'd be glad after all, you'd . . . I don't know. I suppose it would never have worked out."

He shook his head slightly, plunged it in his hands again, drew in his breath.

"I don't honestly think it would. I'm rather glad you didn't. . . . I should have been awfully——"

An extraordinary sound burst out of him—a kind of groan —almost a laugh.

"I know it was a wonderful ring—but I didn't love it like this one." She turned the cat's eye on her little finger. "As long as I've got this. . . . This is our ring, isn't it?"

He smiled briefly, took up her hand and kissed it, let it fall again. He said nothing.

Steps sounded on the brick passage. The woman in the white blouse came in, amiably smiling, carrying an oil lamp with a white glass shade. She set it down on the table in the middle of some green plush and woollen fringe, and struck a match.

"Thought this would brighten things up a bit," she said. "It does get late early and no mistake, as the saying goes. This room's no artist's studio when it comes to light at the best of times. Still, visitors seem to like it. It's old, you know— genuine—that's what appeals to them. That's why we didn't have the electric light put in this part—more in keeping like. I don't care for antiques myself—can't see the point. You

don't go to make a show of a lot of senile old crocks in bath-
chairs, so why anything else old? It doesn't make sense to
me." She uttered a high, harsh thrill of laughter. "Oh, dear!
Winter's coming on. I'm rheumaticky already. Last year we
had the floods right up the garden. It's enough to give any one
the pip.... There! Quite comfy? Fire all right? What time
d'you want your dinner? Eight? Righty-ho."

He suggested a stroll before supper, and they walked arm
in arm along the willow-bordered road as far as the lock. They
leaned over the parapet of the bridge and watched the weir
plunge dizzily and boil below them. The sound of it bemused
them, breathing its eternal monotone into the noise of the
wind and the rainy murmur of the poplars behind the lock-
keeper's cottage.

"Why is water so fascinating?" he said. "I could watch it
for ever."

They said it would be nice to be a lock-keeper. They
admired the old bridge of rose-coloured brick with its long
smooth-curving span and Gothic arches. They strolled back
again, down through the inn garden beneath a straggling
pergola to the bank of the river, where there was a raft, and
a skiff tied up, and a punt with a green canvas shelter over it.
On the farther bank, opposite them, the bank rose abruptly
into broken knolls clothed with woods and crowned with a
square grey church tower: an un-English looking outline.
With sunset a deep glow had come into the sky. Dark fire-
fringed masses of cloud raced along the west, splitting around
a perilous intense green core of light. Earth, sky and water
reflected one another in one unifying, clear, liquid element.
A short way out a fleet of white ducks lay at anchor, bobbing
and dipping with soft, creaking, gossiping noises. Two swans
sailed out round the bend heading for the middle of the river,
taking the full, living and dying, light-and-wind-shaken, mid-
stream current with round full breasts of peace. They stood
on the bank watching the swans float away downstream.

"Look!"

It was seeing too much. She turned away her head and looked at him instead.

What's to come next?

Oh, I see! . . . An illumination went through her, sharp, piercing and gone again; what I've been waiting for. All the pieces fell together . . . like the broken-up bits in James's kaleidoscope we used to look through, exclaiming at the patterns.

"Oh, I see. . . ."

She was scarcely aware of saying it aloud until she saw his unconscious lips move, murmuring some vague word of query or endearment.

But it's nothing to do with him. . . . We are born, we die entirely alone; I've seen how it will be. To suffer such dissolution and resurrection in one moment of time was an experience magnificent enough in itself. It was far above the level even of the lake, the chestnuts. It should have no sequel.

Everything went away again. . . . There it is: a fact in the world that must be acted on. . . .

"Look at those creatures," he said presently.

She strolled with him to the fence and looked over. On the step of a thatched cottage an old woman in a black print dress was setting down saucers of milk for three ginger cats.

"I've always wanted a ginger cat."

"Shall I give you one, darling?"

They strolled up again, arm in arm, beneath the ramshackle pergola.

The transfiguring light was gone, and it was dark and cold now, blowing up for rain.

The dining-room was in the new wing: a long, dreary, pallid room with curtains of pink casement cloth, and big tables with white cloths, and a number of palms in stands. It was lit by three electric lamps hanging from the ceiling beneath ornamental orange-tinted shades of bogus marble. Built

doubtless to accommodate summer parties from steamers or
charabancs, it contained that evening only one other couple,
silently masticating at opposite sides of an expanse of table
at the farther end. A youngish, flat, pinched pair of weather-
beaten holiday makers. The male wore grey flannel trousers
and a blazer, the female a royal blue stockinette frock with a
crochet neck. Both had long indefinite noses and brownish eyes
set close together.

"Campers; out of that punt with the shelter, I bet."

"Come in for a hot meal and a night's lodging, I suppose."

"That means it *must* be going to be a dirty night. I'm sure
they're very nearly waterproof."

Tinned apricots followed the stringy, over-roasted chicken,
and then a sour and tepid cup of coffee. Afterwards the sallow
and now servile woman conducted them to a narrow brittle-
looking bedroom with an art frieze of black, blue and orange
leaves, and narrow twin beds with orange art bedspreads. The
fireplace had a fan of paper in it. It was too meanly proportioned and grudging to hold a fire worth lighting. After she
had left them he made a wry face.

"I'm sorry, darling. I must have been tight when I saw
it before. The sun was streaming in and it didn't look too
bad."

"These beds look a close-fisted respectable pair, I must say.
. . . Made for people like those campers. Of all the art specimens
this frieze takes the cake. . . ."

"The walls are made of cardboard. The campers are next
door, I'm afraid. I saw the chap prancing in with a haver-
sack."

"We shall hear them brushing their plates."

"I don't somehow feel we'll hear much else, do you?"

"What do you suppose he says to her?"

Flippancy, foolish jokes had never come easier; she'd made
him laugh all through dinner. We're hollow people, and
our words are so light and grotesque. . . . Clown's patter. I
could always make him laugh. . . . The laugh's on me. . . .

"I *am* sorry it isn't nicer, darling. I feel I've let you in for it."

"Never mind. It doesn't matter."

Because I suppose I shan't sleep here with him, after what's going to be. How, where shall I go? Will I stay out all night somewhere, walk about or lie in a ditch or get a lift in a lorry to London or what? It's all very awkward. It's a cold night. Could he possibly make it unnecessary for me to go away? . . . If only he could. He's so ingenious. . . .

"We'll try and manage to forget about it, won't we, darling?" He put his arm round her. She twisted herself lightly away, moving as if to look at herself in the glass above the dressing-table. He glanced at her. She felt him shrink under the snub, taken aback, puzzled. He's so sensitive in those ways. What's he thinking? "Is she going to turn touchy too? . . ." That look on his face—somebody else caused it long ago, has seen it often. . . . It was so immediate, it must come from an old wound.

"Have you signed the register?" she said brightly, powdering her nose.

"Not yet. Who shall we be this time?" His heaviness lifted; anxious, as always, to be comfortable. . . .

They giggled, remembering or inventing names.

"Shall we go down for a bit by the fire, darling? I've booked the old oak parlour:" Thinking, "She'll soon come round. . . ."

"Oh, good!"

He thought of everything.

The room was overpoweringly close, its former complex smell submerged beneath the single smell of oil lamp. She threw open the garden door and drew the dark plush curtain across. Now if I must I can get out that way. They stood together on the hearth lighting cigarettes. Now it was like the first time, in Etty's house—standing up side by side saying thank you for matches, stubbornly resisting the pressure, like grindstones, that was already irresistibly bearing in on them, forcing them together. Already they couldn't see each other any more; their eyes were blank, too close.

Olivia said:

"Where is she?"

"She's still in the country. But she'll be back morrow."

"How is she?"

He said in his rueful half absent-minded way:

"Well, apparently she's all right now. Never been better. I went down last week-end."

"Some people do feel their best at these times—specially quite often the delicate ones."

He seemed to grow heavier, blanker where he stood; and he kept his eyes fixed on a point above and beyond her head," She said:

"She's going to have a baby?"

He said yes, and then it was said. It had long been a fact. There was no change between the moment before and the moment after saying it. Nothing could have been simpler.

"Who told you?" he said.

"Nobody. . . ." Your mother told me clear as a factory whistle. I didn't listen. . . . "When?"

He gave a kind of stifled groan under his breath—as if saying, must we talk about it? . . .

"Sometime next spring. I'm not quite—April, I suppose."

Let's see. . . . Last July then. . . .

"But how exciting! I suppose everybody's thrilled . . . all the friends and relations? . . ." Guarding her, cherishing her so carefully now that she was justifying herself: the precious vessel for the heir. Imagine any scandal coming to her ears— at such a time. . . . Unthinkable.

"I suppose so," he said sullenly. "They haven't said much to me."

"I do hope for everybody's sake all will go swimmingly this time." Talking like in a modern play: slick irony: almost enjoying it—feeling nothing. "Let's hope it's a boy."

He turned away. His broad-backed figure blocked the garden exit, the escape. He said:

"How did you guess?"

"Oh. . . . I have visitations, you know. . . . Messengers from the beyond to lay bare mysteries. . . . Voices and great lights."

"Was it when we were down by the river?"

"Yes, it was." So he'd been aware of that much.

"I thought something happened," he said. "I couldn't think what."

Sometimes he did get on to a thing quick like that. . . . Intuitive. . . . Secretive too—not giving a sign. . . .

"I can't explain," she said. "Everything fell together." The moment when the catch slips at last and the jack-in-the-box flies out. "Watching water always makes me psychic. . . . There was a sort of annunciation—by proxy." She laughed. "Most extraordinary. Women do sometimes seem to appear in a sort of foreshadowing aura of pregnancy. I've never known it happen to an expectant papa."

His shoulders went up. After a silence, she said:

"Were you going to tell me? Or was I to have a glorious surprise?"

"I did mean to tell you," he muttered, still with his back to her. "I was going to—of course. But when I saw you I didn't know how to. Especially after you'd told me——"

"About my own little attempt. Very awkward for you, I do see." She was shaken with a moment's violent laughter. "Poor Rollo! A bit more than you'd bargained for."

He turned round on her with a furious suppressed shout: "Don't!" And again there was silence.

"You must admit I'm making it easy for you," she said. "I always hoped I would."

He sat down suddenly in the arm-chair, put his head in his hands, looked helpless; got up again. She said:

"It's not my business, but did you know before we went abroad?"

"No, I didn't."

"But you knew the day you left me."

"Yes."

That, of course, was the letter he'd read by the lake, under the red sun-umbrella. . . . What did she say? How did she put it?

"So you felt you must hurry back to her."

"She didn't ask me to." He hunched his big, heavy shoulders in sullen defensiveness like an animal. "She said not to think of coming home on her account. . . . She'd got to be in bed for a bit as a precaution—it would be so dull for me. . . . She did hope I was having a lovely holiday. . . ." The harsh struggle in his voice shocked her: self-contempt, bitterness, rage, appeal. . . . Poor Rollo. . . . It's not my place to pity him. . . .

"What a good thing you took my advice and went to Salzburg for your letters."

He said stiffly:

"It was."

"How wonderfully you mask your emotions! What did you actually feel when you left me?"

"I don't know. I just felt I'd got to get away."

She burst out laughing.

"Hurrah! It's a safe bet—men feeling they've got to get away." Women prefer to stick around and make something happen next. "What *did* you do? Dash to her bedside?"

He waited before answering. He'd like to strangle me.

"I went to see her, yes. I left her down there at her home—she wasn't allowed to move for a bit. . . . Then I came back to London." He sank down again in the chair, pushing his hair up with both hands. In contrast with his usual well-groomed appearance he looked startlingly dishevelled. Everything's comparative: Simon's always dishevelled. "I meant to stay in London," he said helplessly; "but I couldn't. I went off to Ireland. I tried to write to you. . . ."

She sat down too, leaning forward in her chair, staring at the fire. The scene looked cosy and domestic. She said:

"Well, it's all worked out like they tell you in *Woman's World*. A husband may stray, but home ties are strongest, and if you hang on he'll come back. It's the Other Woman who gets had for a mug."

He drew in a painful breath. He's really in torture—almost more than he can bear. . . . Though I'm not making a scene.

"I must tell you another funny thing," she said. "That night I told you about—I ran into Ivor. He was with me all the time. Wasn't it killing. I didn't actually explain the situation, but he was tremendously tactful and helpful. And at the end of it all, what do you think? He suggested setting up together again."

He got up violently and strode two steps to the window. Feeling he must get away. . . . He pulled apart the curtain. . . . He's going to . . . dropped it again. He came back, and said flatly, utterly embracing his inadequacy:

"I'm sorry."

"Don't apologise. It's so much better to get things straight. It's been so ludicrously pointless for ages, really, hasn't it?"

"Has it?" he said in the same voice.

"Well, I mean the only point was——" Her throat closed. What was swelling in her frightened her—so black, so boiling and gigantic. "The only point for *you* was—wasn't it?— difficulties which one must presume are over." She went on more and more rapidly, in a high-pitched voice: "It'll be rather a relief, don't you think? One does prefer to be blame- less—it's so much less trouble. It gets so wearing, always the worry of being found out. It isn't worth it—honestly, is it? I'm sure you agree. You never know who'll find out and start a bit of blackmail or something."

He stared at her, his eyes fixed and bright, dangerous. But he can't stop me. "One would simply hate her to find out in her present state. Supposing somebody sent her an anonymous letter or something——"

"Oh, rot!" he said angrily. Making a bid for temperance

. . . not liking sweeping statements ever, always pulling me up. . . . She cried furiously:

"It isn't rot and how dare you say so! The world's full of blackmailers and don't I know it! I'm going to steer clear of you!"

He made a blind, bull-like half-turn again. He's off—I'll stop his game.

"Good-bye!" she said insanely. She pushed past him, pushing him roughly with all her weight, made a dash for the curtain, and was on the dark slippery path, running.

Where shall I go? Which way shall I start off? This way was the river . . . and that . . . and along there, beyond the field. The river was everywhere. He'll think I've gone to throw myself in, what a predicament for him. . . . How dark, I can't find the road; the wind, what a wind, a gale, I hadn't noticed; the wind from the Atlantic, the equinoctial gale. When it died down for a moment a sound came after it like giant tumbrils rolling and snarling in caverns in the sky. What a night to be out, how pathetic, a heroine's night in a film: *Way Down East*, Lilian Gish to the rapids. . . . Well, I might. . . . Into the boiling plunge of the weir pool. . . . But I won't. Do I walk all night or what? I've got no money, will he stumble after me, shouting my name? . . .

She started to walk along the road. Growing accustomed now to the moonless dark she began to distinguish outlines of objects—the lines of pollarded willows bordering the road, a five-barred gate in the hedge. She climbed up and sat on the top bar. The wind rushing against her blew her head clean and empty, clean and thin as a sieve. She jumped down from the gate on the farther side, and set off across the meadow, but aimlessly now, knowing that after a bit she would go back. A dark object loomed up in her path. It moved sideways. A horse. Good gracious. I can't go running into horses. What's it like to be a horse, standing up and breathing in the dark for hours? The field grew full of large quadrupeds advancing unseen upon her. She turned and hurried back towards the gate, lost it, went up and down in panic along the hedge looking for it. Her foot slipped, she went down heavily, sprawling in the ditch. Icy water gripped her ankles.

I've fallen down in a muddy wet ditch, I've twisted my leg, my stockings are soaked, the mud's on my knees, in my nails. . . .

She thought she heard a shout. My name. . . . Or did I fancy it? . . .

Next moment she found she was an arm's length from the gate. She got over. Rollo was on the other side.

"Is that you?" he said.

"Yes."

He took her by the shoulders, holding her hard, not lovingly. He said hoarsely:

"You shouldn't have done that." He was trembling. He took out a handkerchief and wiped his face.

"I don't know what to do. . . ." She began to weep.

"Come back."

"I ran into a horse. . . ."

He put his hand through her arm. Bending their heads forward against the wind, they began to walk back together down the road.

The woman in the blouse came out from somewhere and met them at the foot of the staircase, saying:

"Been for a blow?"

"Yes," they said, smiling.

"Not an extra special night for a stroll. Still, it freshens you up. . . . Could I trouble you to sign the register, if it's not troubling you. . . ."

"Oh, yes," he said; and to Olivia: "You go on up."

She went upstairs and down the passage. He caught her up by the bedroom door.

"What name did you sign?"

"Smith," he said. "Disappointment for her."

She sat down on the bed and he took off her mud-caked

soaking stockings and rubbed her feet. She examined the dirty hem of her frock and took it off and hung it up.

"Better let it dry and brush it off to-morrow."

She went over to the washstand, poured out warm water from the can and washed her hands. The water became stained pale-brown and she stood and held her hands in it, staring at them, stock-still, her head sunk over the basin.

He went on sitting on the bed, bowed forward with his palms propping his forehead. After a bit he looked up and saw her standing the other side of the room, bowed over the wash-basin, in her white slip, with bare legs and arms. He got up quickly, with a stifled exclamation, and came over and led her away.

"You'd better get to bed," he said.

"All right."

"Where's your nightdress?"

"In my suitcase."

He got it out and slipped it on over her head. He said not to bother about her teeth, and turned back the bedclothes, and she got into the cold bed and lay down.

"Could we have separate rooms?" she said.

He was silent; then said miserably.:

"All right—if you like. Only it's a bit awkward now going and asking. . . . Still, I will. . . ."

"No, don't, never mind, you couldn't. . . ."

They spoke very low, because of the noiseless couple the other side of the wall.

"Do you mind too horribly me being here?" he said in a broken voice.

"No."

"Anyway, we've got separate beds." A brief laugh came out of him.

"Yes. It's all right."

He sat down on the other bed, facing her. Dead beat he looks; poor Rollo.

After a while he said bitterly:

"Well, I always told you I wasn't any good, didn't I? I told you I'd let you down."

"I'll get over it. It's my own fault for taking things too seriously. And for believing what you said. I just feel a fool. If I'd had the sense of a mouse I'd have known it couldn't be true."

"What couldn't be true?" he said hesitatingly.

They went on speaking very quietly, not raising their voices at all.

"I suppose I had no business to ask, anyway—and you thought a lie would be easier. Keep me quiet. Anything for a quiet life!" She smiled. He was looking at her in an uneasy, doubtful way. . . . *He doesn't even know what I'm talking about. . . .*"I mean when I asked you if you and she . . . and you said, no, never now."

He exclaimed again under his breath, in that helpless hard-pressed way.

"But it was true," he wrenched out. "When I said it, it was true. I don't think I'd have told you a lie about that. . . . I was always more or less honest when you asked me things. . . . Only how could I come panting up to tell you——" He stopped, struggling painfully. "I mean—when it stopped being true, I couldn't exactly come posting to tell you. . . ."

"When did it stop being true?"

"Oh. . . . I don't know. . . . After that . . ."

"About the time I went to live in Jocelyn's flat?"

"Yes—perhaps. . . . I suppose so. About then."

About the time he was in such tremendous spirits—so loving to me in that new way I noticed: more spoiling, more attentive. And yet, somehow remote. In fact, just as husbands are supposed to behave to their wives when they're up to no good on the sly. Probably the way he'd behaved to Nicola when he started the affair with me. Playing a double game both ways: a ticklish position. Only an equable voluptuous non-moral temperament such as his could have coped with so successfully.

"I see," she said.

"I couldn't very well come dashing along to tell you," he repeated.

"I see it was awkward for you." Poor Rollo, what an embarrassing conversation for him, really in ghastly taste. "I know what you feel about telling being indecent. And then I suppose your maxim came in useful—'what people don't know about can't hurt them.'"

He shook his head.

"You see . . ." he began, stopped, his breath sighing out slowly.

"What?" This was the third time he'd begun like that and stopped. It had always been when the talk turned on Nicola.

"I don't know," he said. "She changed. When we married," he said with a great effort, "she wasn't in love with me. I knew it. She'd always been in love with another chap."

"Archie?"

"Yes, Archie . . . how did you know? . . . He went all out after her and then . . . he sort of backed out. It's a favourite little trick of his." His voice grew harsh, as it had at Meldon, talking of his cousin. "She had the hell of a time. . . . She takes things terribly to heart . . . and she can't sort of express herself. . . . She agreed to marry me on the understanding—I'd sort of be there—you know—she could rely on me. . . . As long as she wanted me about I wouldn't snap out of it. It worked fairly well for a bit . . . and then——" He stopped, swallowed. "Then there was this baby business. It sort of upset her, you know. Everything seemed a failure all round . . . she got into a sort of state——"

"Poor girl. . . ." Yes, I see. . . . Now one must accept her as real, as human and suffering.

"Well, then—I got a bit gloomy myself. I'd sort of hoped she'd. . . . I didn't see what to do. . . . And then I met you, and all that started. . . . I thought it wouldn't make any difference to her one way or another, whether she knew or not. I

honestly didn't. But I don't know . . . gradually it did seem
to make a difference. . . ."

"You mean she knows?"

"No, no. At least—you know—sort of subconscious business perhaps. I was different, I suppose." He looked embarrassed. "She may have felt I was—sort of moving away from
her and that made her—sort of want me not to. I suppose
she'd never thought I would. . . . Anyway," he said, horribly
uncomfortable, "she began to want to try again. . . ."

"She fell in love with you."

"I suppose she did—a bit. It sort of seemed like it." His
embarrassment was profound. He added: "One does sort of
hear of it happening, doesn't one?"

"It was what you'd always wanted and longed for."

"Yes." But that was tactless, he saw. He tried again. "But
. . ." He gave it up.

"And that's why you were so happy last spring?"

"I wasn't happy. At least——"

"Didn't I tell you you had a lucky life?"

Once during that time he'd said in soft, grateful amazement: "*Everything* seems to come my way. . . ." That's what
he'd meant. Two women in love with him. Two separate
intimacies not overlapping at all, both successful: it was what
he needed—what suited best his virility and secretiveness. It
was all quite clear.

Well, that's how it is, there it is. . . .

"Then things suddenly went wrong again—with her," he
said. "At least I thought so—but the reason was this thing
starting—the baby. You know, it sort of makes women close
up inside themselves, doesn't it? I didn't realise, and she
wouldn't tell me till she was sure. . . ."

That was when he'd been so moody and dispirited.

"When she wanted to go home instead of going to Ireland
with you?"

"Yes."

And that's why we went to Austria. . . .

"I didn't know what to do," he said, ruffling his hair up, sighing heavily. "You may not believe it, but I loathed playing this sort of double game. I couldn't give you up, I simply couldn't. I knew I ought to. . . . A year before—I'd have said it was the only thing I wanted—to get things right with her. . . . But you went and got so terribly important. . . ." His voice shook.

Well, that's something, of course. . . .

He said, overcome:

"And all I've done is to muck you up."

"Oh, well . . ." she said. "It can't be helped. It's just one of those things. . . . As a matter of fact, I really did have it in mind to suggest to you we'd better—bring it to an end. I couldn't see any future for us—it seemed to be a blind-alley after all—and I didn't want it to get messy and fag-endish. Only it seemed so difficult to say it. . . . I meant to have a different kind of parting. I'm sorry about that. I didn't mean it to be hideous. I really do want you to be happy—and have a nice baby."

"You mean, you don't want ever to see me again?"

She said in a light, simple way:

"I really don't think I could, you know." What with Nicola having him and a child, and a home and everything. . . . The contrast would be too denuding; I should behave badly.

After a long time, he said slowly:

"I see. . . . Very well, then."

There was nothing more to say in quiet voices in this bedroom. She turned over and lay with her face to the wall. He undid his suitcase and got out his pyjamas and sponge-bag, and undressed and switched off the light, and got into bed. Everything he did was done in a resigned, noiseless way like a child who is in disgrace and attempts by obedient, unobtrusive behaviour to reinstate itself.

They lay quietly in their beds, not hearing each other breathe. He stirred one or twice, then turned over on his side. She knew he was turned towards her.

He'll soon be asleep.

But she listened and knew he was going on being awake. He was usually such a quick, peaceful, easy sleeper. It brought home the fact that he was unhappy, and she felt distressed. Finally she whispered:

"Go to sleep."

His hand came out, feeling over her bed to find her. She pushed hers out from under the bedclothes, and he grasped it and held on tightly.

"I love you," he whispered. "You don't believe me, but it's true."

"I do believe you."

Yes, it was true. It was only that the word love was capable of so many different interpretations. It could perfectly well be nothing to do with exaltations, with the lake and the chestnuts, or with going up the darkening cliff-face stopping to kiss, seeing the mauve sea below. hearing the gulls. For another person it could just as well be I do love you, you're so sweet, such a delicious person to be with and so attractive. We do make each other happy, don't we, darling? . . . It was what he'd always said, from the beginning: Let's make each other happy. There'd been no deception: only two people.

Soon after, she heard him fall asleep.

They got up early next morning. He drove her to Oxford Station and left her there; going back to London together was too much to face. He bought her a ticket and the morning paper, and then he went away, and got into his car, and drove off.

In the afternoon she went to a cinema. She sat the programme twice round, and then she went back to Etty's house. Etty had just come in, with a copy of the *Evening Standard.*

"Oh, darling," she said. "Isn't this horrid? I didn't know if you'd have seen it."

This was a headline saying, Baronet's Son in Car Crash. There wasn't much other news that day, so they let themselves go over it. Mr. Rollo Spencer, only son of Sir John Spencer, Bart., had been injured that morning in a collision with a motor lorry on the London road, between Henley and Maidenhead. He had been removed to Maidenhead Cottage Hospital, suffering from grave leg and head injuries. His car had been completely wrecked, and the lorry seriously damaged, the driver escaping with a severe shaking. The exact cause of the accident was not yet known, but eye-witnesses including the lorry driver state that Mr. Spencer, apparently miscalculating his powers of acceleration, passed another private car just before a deep bend in the road, and subsequently found himself unable to cross completely to his left side before the bend, where he met the lorry—also travelling somewhat too close to the crown of the road—in a head-on collision. The surface of the road appears to have been somewhat slippery at the time and this was undoubtedly a contributive factor.

There followed a brief biography.

"Isn't it too *devas*tating?" wailed Etty. "I was so afraid you'd see it before I could *break* the shock. It's on some of the *placards* too. I know how devoted you are to them *all*. Oh, dear, let's *hope* for the best. I ex*pect* he'll be all right. It's *mar*vellous how people *do* recover. . . ."

The telephone rang. Etty answered it and after a moment said:

"Yes, *would* you hold on, please? . . . Darling, it's for *you*. I don't know who."

She handed over the receiver and went discreetly out of the room to change for dinner.

"Is that Olivia?"

"Yes, Lady Spencer. Yes—yes——?"

"I thought I must get in touch with you—in case you've seen these tiresome evening papers." Strong, crisp, invigorating voice, unimpaired.

"Yes. I just have——"

"He's all right."

"*Oh! . . .*"

"*Quite* conscious and as comfortable as can be expected. We can't *altogether* say he's out of danger, but we *hope* and *believe* with his splendid constitution he'll pull through."

"How bad——?"

"A broken jaw, poor dear, and a rather horrid smashed leg, I'm afraid. . . ."

"Pain?"

"Well—he's under morphia. . . . Everything's being done that can be done. We got hold of Slade-Murray at *once*—you know he's such a brilliant surgeon. . . . And he's in a nice room, and they all seem so capable and anxious to do everything possible."

"Can I see him?"

There was a split second of silence. Shocked. . . .

"No, I'm afraid that's out of the question." The voice was firm, on the indignant side. ". . . At present," it added, less uncompromisingly.

"But I must. Don't you see? It's my fault."

"What do you mean?" The voice froze alarmingly.

"I'd just said good-bye to him. . . . I upset him. He was being careless, I'm sure, he'd *never* have . . . He's such a good driver. . . ."

Nothing occurred in the receiver; until at last the voice said in a new, muffled way:

"I wondered where . . ." But almost immediately resuming sharp control. "Pull yourself together now, my dear. What nonsense! As if there were the *slightest* reason to blame yourself. . . . It seems to have been one of those *unfortunate* accidents when the fault, if you can call it fault, was on *both* sides. Rollo insists on taking most the of blame— he told me at once it was his fault, but you know what he is— so generous."

"He does talk then?"

"Well, of course we don't allow him to—more than a few words. I was going to tell you that the lorry driver called *personally* to inquire this evening—most distressed, poor man.

I thought it was so nice of him. It's always so horrid when there's bad feeling afterwards. . . ."

"Is she with him?"

"Yes, she's with him now."

"How is she?"

"She's being quite splendid—so quiet and sensible. I'm *delighted* with her. We were a little afraid for her—the shock —but I don't think we need have been. She's pulled herself together wonderfully and thinking *only* of him—I've just driven up to collect a few things and then I shall go straight down again. Now listen, Olivia. I shall keep you informed— do you understand? Every day. I will ring up or write you a line *without fail*. You can trust me. . . . I will also take the first opportunity of telling *him* you have inquired and that I *myself* spoke to you."

"Thank you. . . . He might worry. . . . Thank you. . . . If you just mention me along with a lot of other names —he won't think anything. . . . I mean . . . naturally I *would* inquire, wouldn't I? Being friends, that is, we *were* friends. . . ."

"Of course, my dear, *such* old friends. . . ." Kindly, pitying. . . .

"Thank you, Lady Spencer."

"Good-bye, Olivia." Wishing to cut off as quick as possible.

"Good-bye. Thank you more than I can say. I'm so terribly grateful. . . ." Don't cut off, don't leave me alone in outer darkness. . . .

But the receiver had been hung up. She didn't want my thanks, or any of my emotions. It was not to pass beyond the limits she imposed. Her magnanimity, her perfect behaviour made subjection a moral obligation.

Oh, she's wonderful! . . . Lady Spencer, you've won. I am beholden.

She went upstairs. Etty was in the bath, and called through the door that she must fly, she'd be half an hour late.

She went on up to her own room.

This is what I always knew would happen, this is the punishment. I foresaw it—an accident, his relatives round the bed and me outside. What I didn't foresee was the clemency even of one. . . .

She's sitting by his bed, so quiet and sensible, thinking only of him, I'm delighted with her, let's hope she won't have a miscarriage. He's bandaged, he's under morphia. He's not out of danger. If he dies, I did it. He wouldn't mean to kill himself, but I meant it. I corrupted his confidence and destroyed his happiness. I accused and condemned him; I put death in him.

Where's that handkerchief. . . . She began to search frantically, terror-struck, pulling open drawers and throwing things about. There it was, at last, in the place where she'd looked first—the blue and green silk handkerchief crumpled and neglected—torn too, where I tore it. . . . She wrapped it round her wrist and tied it tightly. There. And never take the ring off for one moment day or night. Charms. And I will keep awake all night, holding on to him, without one moment's relaxation. . . . I'll save him. . . . I shall do it—not her, or any of them. . . . Will he know . . . will he think of me? . . .

Start now.

Anna! If Anna where here I could go and be in the same room as her. If I could see Simon. . . .

It's no good, they're far away.

Start now.

II

MRS. CUNNINGHAM's November party for Amanda was an outstanding event. Amanda herself was supposed to have selected her guests, but as it turned out the ingredients were fundamentally the old familiar ones, with a sprinkling on top of Amanda's contempories—the word friends would give the wrong impression, she had none—striplings and virgins still obscure and folded in the bud: a decoration or flourish, like the nuts and cherries on top of a pudding.

To be Mrs. Cunningham's daughter was to be situated from birth upwards in a paradoxical position—concealed yet public, beneath a responsible wing of sorts, yet so overpowering and magnificent a one as rather to dazzle and dismay than shelter its peering infant object. It might be that Amanda, like other little English girls of gentle birth, had received the attentions of a reliable Nannie, had hung up her stocking, learnt to ride a bicycle, worn a school hat and a gymn tunic, done fractions and the exports of Australia, played lacrosse, been taken to the pantomime—gone, in short, with the throng; but if it were so, it had not interfered with Amanda's development. To be Mrs. Cunningham's daughter set a problem in comparison with which all other interests and activities were negligible. She had solved it by being what nobody considering her parentage could logically have expected: a tricky, doubtful proposition, take it or leave it; the antithesis incarnate of the Victorian-heroic-statuesque; a nymph, tall, willowy, graceful, capriciously fascinating, with a cloud of ash-blonde hair floating to her shoulders, describing an aureole round a pale, indefinite smudge of a face with slanting half-shut eyes; not so much of delicate appearance as downright ill-looking; melancholy, emotional but unaffectionate, self-centred but disorganised, with a taste for art and theatricals and for inventing æsthetic gestures and poses to unlikely modern music. No doubt the heritage of will and shrewdness from her parents was greater than superficially appeared.

At seventeen her future as unpredictable. She'd lead them a dance, was the expression which, looking at her, rose to one's lips. How she herself would emerge, if at all, from the mixture of Celtic twilight and Aubrey Beardsley décor which at present enshrouded her, was another question.

Meanwhile, putting a dab of vermilion on her long mouth to heighten the greenish pallor of her complexion, she chose to attend a school of acting and miming; and to celebrate her coming out by a festival which was to include charades, and three original dances by Amanda.

The entertainment, charming and touching though it was, designed and executed entirely by Amanda and a tender troupe of associates, chiefly from the Slade and the dramatic school, rather interfered with the free development of the party spirit. After the clapping and cheering had subsided and Amanda had reappeared among her guests, gliding sidelong, rapt and speechless, in a dress of white brocade with a hoop—her great-grandmother's—and a nosegay of moss rosebuds in her bosom —the crowd began to overflow the two connecting classical-cum-contemporary rooms which had hitherto congestedly contained it. Mrs. Cunningham stood in the double doorway, in black velvet with a deep fichu of cream lace, receiving with a smile of the lips, but not of the hollowed *mater dolorosa* eyes, congratulations upon Amanda. Not far off stood Mr. Cunningham, florid, Roman, stockbroking, incongruous; as usual an unaccountable addition to the party: yet there he was, always, at every one of the parties, quite affable and imperturbable; and no one knew what to say to him; and what the position, what the relationship was, no one could do more than conjecture. He provided the money, some said, and was proud of his artistic wife and children, and discreetly looked after his own interests by keeping a mistress in a little house in John Street. They were a devoted couple, said others; she relied on him absolutely, there had never been any unfaithfulness. . . .

But she was worn, white, this evening; she had aged. In her heart was locked away the image of Simon. She would never speak of him again. She had loved him for eighteen years. . . .

Now we shall get on without him, we shall make do with imitations of him. Peter, she thought, watching her son across the room, was an imitation. At twenty-five he had something of the look Simon had had as a young man: the merest superficial resemblance though: the quality wasn't there. There was nobody left in the world like Simon, who had died in September. Naturally one would go on giving parties, going to the ballet, the opera, going abroad, filling the house, filling the days. Life was perfectly full, one saw to that; one could manage without Simon who had never been a practical part of any of it. There was scarcely anything tangible—scarcely a letter or a snapshot —to remember: anything, that is, of a private nature. His pictures hung on the walls. She had started buying them on Desmond Fellowes' advice when Simon was unknown and twenty-one. She now owned the best of them. These would shortly be lent to a memorial exhibition. He wasn't a great painter, but he might have been. It was in his nature, she thought, to be great; never to narrow or to crystallise in mediocrity. It was the richness and variety of his temperament which had hindered a straightforward development; so that at thirty-eight he was still half-promise, half-fulfilment. He hadn't entirely found himself. A painter of charm, of intense individuality, not a great painter. . . . I helped him, I gave him a splendid start. . . . Oh, Simon! . . . You've left me nothing for myself. My portrait by you wasn't done for me, it didn't spring from our intimacy; which existed only by my will to which you were never subject. . . .

"Clara, my dear, it was charming." Gil Severn came up and took her hand and kissed it. He stuck his monocle in and sighed.

"It was rather moving," she said, smiling faintly.

"Touching," he said. "Lyrical creature. . . ."

"She hasn't much talent," said Mrs. Cunningham, in the way that caused her friends, her children especially, to consider her severe, alarming, cold. "Just that she's got youth, and there's a grace . . ."

"Exquisite," he agreed with enthusiasm, suppressing, his private emendation: no talent at all.

The fact is I don't know what to do with her, thought her mother, gazing beneath marble lids towards where Amanda was, unfortunately, dancing with Jasper, handsome and

swarthy, bending his magnetic eyes, his wide, square brow
upon her, exerting wizardry. Successfully or not? Amanda
looked fugitive, innocent. . . . Well, she must look after herself.
The death of Simon had been her first grief. She'd known him
all her life. It had disorientated her, made her distraught,
rebellious for a day; vowing never, never . . . crying out why,
why? . . . Spurning comfort. Then she had put him away
from her. At least it seemed so. In youth these things go
over. . . . Though I know nothing about her. She was undoubtedly at her best with Simon; happy and unaffected.
She'll miss him.

Olivia joined Adrian downstairs in a small back room, a
kind of study.

"Hallo, darling," she said. "Who are you prowling after?"

"My dear, the relief of finding you." . . . He seemed
tearful.

"You haven't found me. You weren't even looking. Adrian,
will Anna come, d'you suppose?"

"I think so. Colin rang up from Sallows about four. He
said she'd practically decided to appear—and if he could
manage to keep her to it he was motoring her up almost
at once."

"It's time she was here."

Her heart turned over in her chest. The first time since
Simon died. . . . When I see her it'll be true. Nobody had seen
her so far, except Colin: she'd suddenly asked him down to
Sallows last week to help go through Simon's things. Simon
had left her his house, and she'd been there ever since she came
back after burying him.

"My dear, a word to the wise. I have a strong feeling the
whisky will run out before long. It's apt to at these respectable
festas. Should we make sure of more than our share?"

"Upstairs again?"

"Yes, upstairs." He was looking about him in a vague yet
preoccupied way. Something on his mind. . . .

They emerged into the hall, and met Anna and Colin, just arrived, at the foot of the staircase.

"Hallo! . . . You've missed the performance." Olivia gave Anna a hug, speaking with off-hand brightness. For one must be natural, deny any change, any ghost in attendance. . . .

"Should we regret it?" said Anna, quietly smiling, just like herself.

"Between ourselves," said Adrian loudly, "it was the most witless, arty, boring performance I've ever attended. Never was such a lack of any idea of anything paraded."

"Amanda looked rather divine in her tunic," said Olivia.

"Did Peter perform?" said Anna.

"Peter was very good indeed to my mind as the front part of the bull in the charade—or was it the back part?"

"The back," said Adrian. "I've been trying in vain to discover the front ever since they doffed their disguise. Does anybody know who he is?"

"I didn't notice him," said Olivia.

"He was one of those absolutely charming pug faces. . . . Don't you remember, Olivia, when he peeped out through the hole in the neck at the end?" His eye roved anxiously round. "I distinctly saw him come downstairs, but my pursuit was impeded and he vanished. I wonder if he's slipped up again."

"Take care you don't slip up," said Anna, just like herself, starting to ascend the wide, shallow, curving staircase. But just at the turn she stopped, seemed to shrink back. "I suppose it's a respectable party," she said uncertainly.

"On the well-conducted side. There's a perfectly devilish array of young. Hurry if you want a drink."

"I love your dress, Anna," said Olivia. It was made of stiff, dull, rich prune-coloured stuff, high in the neck, with long sleeves and a fitted waist, perfectly plain.

"Oh. . . . It's French stuff," said Anna, still hanging back. "Simon gave it to me. I don't like it on me. It's too important."

"Nonsense!"

"I've never seen you in such a good dress," said Colin.

"I quite agree, my dear Anna," said Adrian.

"It ought to be yours," said Anna, gripping Olivia's arm. "I shall give it to you." Her eyes started to fix, in panic and revulsion: seeing through and opposing the attempt to support her upwards into the throng with a show of bright normal behaviour. They all stood still, unnerved, guiltily meeting each other's eyes; Olivia by her side, the others behind her. It was one of those moments in a party when there is no coming and going; when, arriving late, listening in alarm, you think you have mistaken the night, for the house seems deserted.

But next noment, as if they had been momentarily deaf and hearing was now restored, voices, movement, laughter opened out on them above. Two or three young people came bounding down the stairs, brushing past them without a look. Anna went quietly on, saying in a murmur to Olivia:

"How is he?"

"Better. Much. Moved to London. I get only an occasional bulletin now."

"His mother?"

"M'm. . . . I'm to be allowed to see him soon—just once, when she can arrange it."

"Good!"

Wanting to say: But none of that matters, for God's sake don't think of me, don't sympathise—it's not of the least importance. . . . Forgive me for my letter. . . . The letter dashed off in frenzy the night of Rollo's accident had crossed the one from Anna saying Simon died peacefully at two this morning. Hers was so calm, restrained, and when she got my yell she sent a pre-paid telegram saying so distressed wire news at once. She'd behaved too well. Oh, Anna! . . . If she wouldn't look at us as if we were shadows.

They reached the broad first-floor landing and met the hubbub and the brilliant light. Peter Cunningham appeared on the threshold, pale, handsome, his blue crystal eyes burning, slightly drunk, holding a plate and a glass. He cried, "Anna!" with such warmth of welcome that his cry seemed to draw her forward to join him. He encircled her with the arm that held the glass and made her drink. They heard him say: "This was for old Cora, but we'll get her some more perhaps. Don't leave my side. Anna darling, you look marvellous and I am so pleased to see you." They drifted off together.

Yes, he was a bit like Simon—the colouring, the shape of the face. If he was going to make a fuss of her, she'd be all right. He wasn't of intrinsic importance, she'd see that now: but one went on feeling emotional about people long after one had seen through them; and he might help to link her on to living again—blow up a spark in her perfectly indifferent, faintly smiling face.

"You managed to get her here," said Olivia to Colin: for one *must* force oneself to speak of her and Simon sensibly, without this anguished chest; discuss ways and means, what's best to do for her; practically, dispassionately. It's not my tragedy. I'm right outside. It was my day-dream, loving Simon.

"Yes," said Colin, staring at the party. "She was acquiescent. Agreed it was time to start seeing people again—and a party was the easiest way. I made her tight after tea and dashed her up and took her to the Palladium. She enjoyed that. I've never seen her laugh more."

"Does she talk about him?"

"Yes. A good deal. She's been going through old papers of his all day—burning a lot—and sorting his clothes and things. She wants to distribute them and be done with them. She's quite calm. I don't think she sleeps. But last night I made her take a drug."

"Good. . . ." Well, we shall all get used to it in time. . . . "Come and find a drink."

Adrian had disappeared. Soon Colin, acclaimed and surrounded, vanished too. One thing about having had a lot of trouble—I don't mind any more being stranded at a party.

The tide's going away from me, carrying them all on its crest; my dress is an old boring one; I can't say I care.

At the buffet in the farther room, a large young man in a dark suit that needed pressing, elbowed her in an effort to reach the galantine. He turned out to be her brother James. She said:

"I was wondering where I'd seen you before."

He looked at her under his eyelids. She noticed he had that look of a bird of prey . . . a wild or untamed version of Dad's and Uncle Oswald's look of a queer bird. A notable young man, alarming.

"Have some of this," he said. "It's remarkably good."

"When did you get back?"

"A few days ago."

"Been home?"

He looked at her quizzically.

"Not yet. I'm going to-morrow perhaps—or next week. It depends."

His voice was cool, slightly ironic. You leave me alone, it said. I'll go home when I like.

"It seems very odd to find you in this galère. How did you get here?"

"Through the back door," he said. "I'm friendly with the second footman."

He doesn't trust me. . . . I don't blame him. . . . He used to trust me when he was a child.

"It's terribly nice to see you, James. You look awfully well."

"So do you," he said. . . .

I don't. . . . But he wouldn't notice.

"You seem to have grown enormously and filled out, or something."

"Yes, I have," he said. "My chest measurement's a good two inches up on last year."

"Splendid. . . . Thank you for all your post cards."

"Can't thank you for yours," he said.

"I know—I'm a hopeless correspondent. I did mean to . . ."

"You might have sent me one line, I do think."

He sounded injured. She thought: Can I win him then?

"I've thought of you a lot. Only I felt out of touch. . . . I thought anything I wrote might seem unreal . . . or unwarranted." Taking the plate of galantine from him, she added quickly but casually: "Any plans?"

"Nothing definite. I shall go back to Paris soon, I think, for the winter, and then do a bit more wandering. I want to go to Central Europe, and then perhaps eastward a bit—Russia—Persia."

"I see." It sounded an impressive, expensive programme. But one must be careful to take it for granted he was sole master of his movements. "You like living abroad?"

"I do."

"Got friends?"

"Some."

Among that young, unknown group, perhaps, swarming in and over the settee, looking confident and lively.

"Have you been writing?"

"Yes." He glanced at her; then seeming suddenly to decide to trust her, said: "*New Poetry* has taken two. Look out for them if you're interested. I've got a sort of play in verse too. . . . I'll show you some of the stuff one day. If you like."

"I should indeed like. How exciting."

She thought: He'll do something, and I never shall. Achievement-to-come sat on his brow, it seemed to her, as it had in his childhood. He had his eyes again, and they were the same but different; he'd struggled a good deal, suffered. . . . He looked twenty-five rather than eighteen: twenty-five and five years old mixed. Something's happened to him that didn't happen to his sisters. . . . He's broken the mould entirely which we were all cast in. Kate might have but she wouldn't—doubting herself and her rebellion, deciding the discipline of ordinary ways was best. I might have, but I couldn't: meeting everybody half-way, a foot all over the place, slipping up here and there; in a flux, or thinking things funny. But he won't do that.

"How's the old man?" he said.

"Just the same. There he sits. Sometimes he makes a remark and Mother marvels at his brilliance and quotes it to everybody—like a parent with a child just beginning to talk."

He brooded.

"I rather wish I'd known him," he said.

"I wish you had. He was . . ." No good going into that now. Still, it was curiously consoling, James saying that.

"Is Mother still sore about the mill?" he said.

"No, I'm sure she's not. She's changed, I think—or gone back to something. Now she's alone so much she seems to turn things over in her mind. She makes pronouncements which fairly make one sit up; about education being no use and one can overdo self-control, and there's a lot in this new psychology, and trying to direct other people's lives is unpardonable. . . . All the old manner but such different matter I feel quite shocked. What d'you think she said last time I was there? Out of the blue: ' Your Grandpapa lived much too long—he ruined his children's lives.' Think! *Grandpapa!*"

Smiling together, seeing in mind's eye Grandpapa's imperial expanse of waistcoat and watch-chain, his magician's beard and dome of baldness guarding the sideboard, they were brother and sister.

"Poor Mother——" he said regretfully, well disposed but detached, unfilial sounding. "I'm glad she feels like that about the career question. Because I don't intend to settle down and be a credit."

"How about money?"

"I'm all right."

"A hundred and fifty doesn't go very far," she said, carefully casual.

He looked at her under lowered lids, debating within himself. "Of course," he said, colouring, looking youthful, "I hope to be able to earn a trifle by my writing. But apart from that. . . . I tap another source, you know."

"No, I didn't know," she said mildly.

"Uncle Oswald."

That was a startler and no mistake. But she managed to say with no more than the slightest lift of the eyebrows:

"I'd no idea . . ."

"Isn't it amazing?" he said, appeased by her equable front. "He started it about a year ago—just before I was packed off to Fontainebleau. He just wrote and told me he'd made arrangements for me to have a hundred a year from him—to help me do what I wanted—so that I needn't be pushed into anything for lack of funds."

"But he's got nothing himself. . . . Two or three hundred . . ."

"He said he had enough—more than he needed. Anyway, when I saw him just before I went, and said he mustn't, he got into one of those moods—you know, when he whisks down all the blinds and shrinks up to a little monkey-nut."

"I know."

They both fell silent, contemplating afresh the fact, which had been from the beginning, of Uncle Oswald's secretive nobility about possessions. All my life he's worn the same threadbare overcoat; frayed linen, grease spots on his suit; he lives in one dark room and hasn't enough to eat and gives his money away in the streets. Once, on my birthday, I put my hand out to shake hands and he slipped ten shillings into it, pretending not to know he'd done it. . . . The only purely disinterested character I've ever met. . . . Not quite right in the head, the freak of the family . . . a bit sinister, too—not altogether attractive. . . .

"It never occurred to me he knew what was going on," said James. "He never appears to register, does he? He didn't say one word to me. For some reason I couldn't stand the sight of him just then. I tell you what. I've an idea he pinched the key of my desk one day and read my journal. I knew some-body'd been at it." He laughed. For a moment his expression had the oddest resemblance to Uncle Oswald's: knowing, ambiguous, humorously sly.

"Please, it wasn't me." Though I wanted to. . . .

"I never suspected you," he said, "of as much interest in my affairs as that."

Now, was that meant to be a crack?

He put his plate down and said pleasantly:

"Why don't you come out to Paris for a bit this winter? I could show you a side of it you probably don't know."

"I might, James." She was gratified. "I'd like to."

"Well, think about it," he said.

He's not a bit interested in me, doesn't wonder what my life is. Not that I mind at all, it's rather a comfort. We might manage to get on, I shouldn't wonder. He'd be delighted to show me round, instruct me. . . .

He was scrutinising a picture of Simon's hanging just above their heads; a Provençal landscape.

"Is that by that man Cassidy?"

"Yes, Simon Cassidy. Those panels are his too—and that portrait." I can tell him something too.

"Extraordinarily competent," he said after a pause; "but on the sentimental side, isn't it? Nasty pink." He had the kind of dominating nose and curling lip that seem to scorn whatever they observe. "He's dead, isn't he?"

"Yes, he died nearly two months ago. He was a great friend of mine."

He nodded, not interested; strolled away—by design?—as Adrian bore down upon them.

"My dear," said Adrian, "between you and me, I feel profoundly uneasy. The younger generation's fairly hammering at the door—what do you feel? Who was that eagle you were engaged with?"

"My brother."

"Good God! I didn't know you had one. Is he nice?"

"Not exactly. He rouses pride in me, but also dismay."

THE WEATHER IN THE STREETS 361

"Why?"

"Well, I don't know. . . . Something to do with feeling his principles might oblige him to shoot us in the revolution."

"Good God! How beastly." Adrian had become a good deal tipsier in the last half-hour. "He looks to me an absolutely cold-blooded beast. I'm sorry—he's your brother, Olivia—but I must say it. Now, don't let's think about him any more. I come to you, my dear, with a personal request." He took her hand. His lower lip trembled.

"What, Adrian?"

"You *are* my friend, aren't you, Olivia? There's nobody else I can turn to. The only being besides myself who believes in disinterested affection." He burst into tears. "You're not laughing at me, are you?"

"Of course I'm not."

"You see that boy over there? The one who took the front part of the bull. . . ."

"Yes?"

"I *know* it's no good. I simply *know* he'll dislike me and be disagreeable—but to avoid the humiliation, my dear, of being an instantaneous object of suspicion—because *all* I want—which I *know* he won't believe, or his parents won't—is to offer him my friendship and affection . . . which at *my* age, my dear, is absolutely all one wants. . . ."

"I know, Adrian. Shall we go and talk to him?"

"That's precisely what I was about to suggest. If you'd support me, my dear—break the ice with a few light friendly words— I leave it to you. . . ."

They crossed the room, went out on to the landing and approached a fair-crested, attractive youth with a natural look of dissipation. He was standing alone upon the landing, leaning against the headpost of the banisters. She said to him with all the light amiability at her command:

"Do tell me, were you the front part of the bull or the back part?"

"The back part," he said simply.

"There, Adrian!" She looked encouragingly at Adrian; adding to the youth: "We've been having an argument about you."

Nervous, wistful, a bowed column of wincing, tender susceptibilities, Adrian uttered a hollow laugh, and said:

"I was absolutely convinced you were the front part."

"Were you?" said the youth. He seemed very sleepy, and didn't look more than fifteen. He looked vaguely away, then at his feet. Silence fell.

"You were frightfully good," said Olivia, losing ground.

"Did you think so?" he said politely.

"Wasn't it awfully hot under those great thick rugs?"

"Not particularly; I had a little hole to breathe through."

"It was frightfully amusing," said Adrian. "When you suddenly emerged at the end. . . . U—uh—huh—huh—huh—huh!" What a laugh—he oughtn't to attempt it. . . .

"Did you think so?"

Well, I can't do any more. . . . She slipped away. Out of the tail of her eye she saw Adrian take a feeble step forward, saying with an unnerved swallow:

"*Which* was it you said you were—the front part or the back part?"

"The back part."

Jasper kissed her hand with old-world courtesy, gazed deeply beneath his brows upon her, said intensely: "Yes . . ." nodding his head with slow and cryptic significance. But soon he passed on. I can't be bothered to-night and nor can he. He's other fish to fry. Fresh, palpitating young virgins to mould and subjugate. I'm in a black dress, drab and sober, unalluring; an old stager with a totally undistinguished walking-on part. . . . It's Rollo's fault, and Simon's. . . . Something with resentment, defiance, bitter, stirred inside her. I must be attractive again. I shall find another lover, Rollo. . . . Simon, I shall stop weeping for you. You make my face as dead as you are.

The party was splitting up and evaporating. One room was

now almost entirely occupied by a noisy huddle dancing and stamping in a ring—Lancers, judging from the shouting of contradictory orders, and the passing and repassing in different directions. Colin's face flashed up, sharply defined upon a background of more or less amorphous entities: frantic, he looked, with dilated eyes, one arm round the waist of Amanda, and the other encircling a plump, appealing young creature with a mop of dark curls and a dewy skin. Amanda was flushed, laughing—enjoying herself; she looked peaceful, dissolved into the noise and rhythm.

"Grand Chain!" shouted someone; and Olivia flung herself forward to join them, seizing and seized at random, whirled round, carried off her feet. . . . Mingling at last . . . for the first time this evening: laughing back into laughing faces. . . . But only for a few minutes. Soon it all petered out, broke up and drifted away . . . as if I'd broken it up. . . . She was left among a mixed group of drunken acquaintances, secondary figures; and David Cooke said:

"I hear Jocelyn's gone to China."

"Yes."

It would have been a drop of comfort to have Jocelyn in England.

Then he said:

"My dear, how's Rollo? It was too shattering, that accident. Marigold was beside herself—I happened to be dining with her that night."

"Rollo Spencer? Oh, he's all right now, I think. I heard he'd made a marvellous recovery."

She moved away and went downstairs.

In the small back room on the ground floor she saw James leaning up against the mantelpiece deep in conversation with another young man, absorbed and grave. Something clicked in her head, photographing them: James on his own, in his own world. He didn't see her, and she went upstairs again.

She saw Anna sitting quietly in a corner talking to her old friend, Desmond Fellowes. She was all right still. Everybody was looking after her, being kind and tactful. . . . She doesn't look well: faded, parchment-coloured, not a bit young any more, not pretty at all. She hadn't bothered to have her hair washed or properly cut; it looked dull and ragged. . . . Was it merely one's own knowledge of her suffering which seemed to remove and isolate her; or would a stranger also see her as it were behind a veil, scarcely in the room at all?

Colin came up with a tankard in his hand.

"Smell this," he said. His lock of hair was over his eyes. "Gin."

"It smells of thyme. Do you notice? Did you know gin smelt of thyme?"

He went away, carrying the tankard round the room, holding it under people's noses, saying, "Did you know gin smelt of thyme?"

Presently he came back, and said:

"There's been a mistake. Have you noticed?"

"What mistake?" He looks quite mad.

"He's not dead, I've discovered. He was in this room a moment ago, didn't you see him?" He gave a sudden loud shout of "Simon!"

She stood paralysed.

"No, Colin, no . . ."

"A resurrection," he said. "I must let them know."

He went on, but next moment his purpose seemed to desert him. He turned on his heel and disappeared down the stairs.

Adrian joined her. The anguish left by Colin began to relax, and she said, smiling:

"Well, was it any good?"

He said a little mournfully, amused at himself:

"Not an unequivocal success, I must admit." He wasn't nearly so drunk now. "The distressing thing is, my dear, he was really very boring as it turned out. A moron. I've noticed it goes with those eyelids."

"The young seem to have taken charge to-night, don't they? Although they're in a marked minority. I feel like a chorus of elders. I keep on wanting to say things like, Gather ye roses, and si jeunesse savait. . . ."

"I'm renouncing parties," he said. "I'm thirty-three. It's time to think of one's dignity."

"We're in an awkward patch again, I suppose. Just on the turn. . . ."

He looked across the room at the ebullient group still swarming on and over the settee or reclining upon the floor.

"How extraordinarily self-centred they seem," he said, with a note of indignation. "Does that strike you? Entirely wrapped up in themselves."

"They're beginning to fall in love and get biffs on their egos, and that sort of thing. . . . It *is* very absorbing." . . . She watched them. "I don't know if it's a delusion, but they seem much more vigorous and confident than we were. Happier."

"I loathe the young," he said grumpily. "Selfish, silly little beasts. I'm damned if I see why they should make one feel inferior."

Amanda came swimming up to him, her head on one side, holding her arms out towards him—affected, ingenuous, coaxing.

"Adrian, dance with me. . . ."

"With the greatest of pleasure, my dear Amanda."

I never knew Adrian could blush.

He put his arm round her and side-stepped off with her. Olivia heard her say in her sweet, fluting voice:

"I like dancing with you, Adrian. You're just the right height for me."

"Yes, my dear, yes, it's perfectly charming."

"I adore dancing, don't you?"

"I adore it, my dear. Just a second . . . I can't quite catch the tune. . . . Ah! . . . Here we go."

Bashfully smirking, holding her gingerly, he lunged into the stream of dancers; gradually assuming a softened bland expression, on the foolish side, but happy. A nestling look stole over them, as a couple.

Desmond Fellowes touched her arm, and said:

"Anna sent me to fetch you."

He disappeared, and she went to Anna: still sitting smiling in her corner. Anna said:

"I'd like to go now. I'm a bit tired. Will you come back with me?"

"To the flat?"

"No. To Sallows. I don't want to stay in London. I must go back. Colin said earlier on he'd drive me, but I doubt if he's fit to. . . . I'll drive. Could you come?"

"Of course, Anna. I'd love to. If you'd stop a second at Etty's and let me pick up a thing or two."

"Pick up several things, in case you feel like staying on some time. . . . Would you try and collect Colin? I must say a word to Mrs. Cunningham."

She went away to find Colin, her heart lifting in relief and anticipation, in spite of dread.

Now I shall be made to feel again. . . . An operation without anæsthetic is going to take place. Going back to Sallows. You're quite tough enough, you can stand it. . . . Anna's asked something at last.

After the first shock, there'd been no forward movement, nothing to disperse the element like a pea-soup fog that had come down and covered all. When the news came, like ghosts they had all drifted together for a bit, wandering about from place to place all over London, keeping together so as not to be alone, now and then letting fall a word, casually, about Simon, more often saying ordinary things. In fact, we talked a lot—even more than usual; not wishing to be too long silent. There wasn't any difference in the things we said. . . . I only had one collapse, when Colin came round. . . . Clinging to each other. . . . After that we blew our noses and went out to join Adrian at a pub for lunch. . . . Out of kindness, Colin had rung up old Cora Maxwell, and asked her to join them. They'd sat in the pub, and Billy had joined them too, and then Ed. In the evening they all went on in a party to the Plaza.

The next few days had rather overpoweringly starred Cora and featured Billy—Cora bedraggled and shaky, her orange hair flaunting incongruously above her ruined hulk of a face; Billy outstandingly drunk, making intricate symbolic maps and diagrams in red and blue chalk on the tablecloth. But Cora went on the water wagon for two days as a gesture to Simon. Her grief was tremendous and grotesque. Having to deal with her and Billy added a surrealist dream element, and sometimes they laughed a lot.

A few abnormal days and they then settled back. Everybody made careful preparations for managing without Simon. After all, he'd never been very close to any of them, never a familiar figure in daily life, so there was no great wrench or necessity for practical reorganisation. Colin wired to Anna should he come out, but she wired back, No. He had the key of Simon's studio, and he went and looked through the unfinished canvasses and stacked them tidily. Nearly everybody remembered owing Simon money.

III

ANNA drove, and Adrian, who had turned up and jumped into the car at the last minute, sat beside her. Olivia and Colin were in the back. The more the merrier. We'll break in all together on Simon's house.

A cold sleety rain began to fall as they came out of London. Colin's old car was draughty. Adrian was now in bubbling spirits, at the height of talkative amiability. Olivia saw Anna glance round at him once in affectionate amusement, grateful to him for being exactly the same as ever. Probably that was one of the worst hardships of her state—everybody putting on a behaviour for her. Even not to do so, which was one's own aim, involved something of effort and self-consciousness, obvious to her no doubt. But Adrian remained himself, whether Simon was in the world or no. He'd do Anna good.

"I see *no* reason, my dear," he was saying, "for not falling in love with her. She's attractive, intelligent, amusing—and obviously pretty keen on me, my dear. She simply came up to me and made the most charming, graceful, spontaneous advances—didn't she, Olivia? Olivia can bear witness."

"She's a fascinating character," said Anna, quietly smiling.

Adrian said she had one of those ravishing slightly pug faces, if you know what I mean, my dear. . . . As for her figure! . . . they went on talking about Amanda.

Flattened in a corner with his coat-collar turned up to his nose, Colin woke perfectly clear again in the head from a brief stupor and broke in:

"Can't you *see* she's no good? Can't you see? Doomed. In despair already. No hope for her." His deep musical voice with its echoing note seemed to toll Amanda's fate. "Now, that other one," he continued, "Pamela, Desmond's niece—do you *understand* how wonderful she is?—do you? I suppose you don't. . . ."

"Did you give her a kiss, Colin?" said Adrian.

"She does look a pet, I must say," said Olivia soothingly.

"*Pet!*" He snorted. "Now *there* is a really happy character! . . . Something developed without a trace of damage in the process. A freak, if you like: but what a miracle! Don't you see it? Don't you admire it? No! How sweet, we'll all say, what a nice friendly girl. . . . And we'll all fall in love with that grisly Amanda, designed to hate us and make us wretched."

"She doesn't hate me," said Adrian tenderly. He went on: "The point is, my dear, my conception of love differs from that of most people, and I should very much like to explain it to her, because I've a feeling I should strike a kindred chord. 'Amanda, my dear, I'm different.' . . . Rather a ticklish thing to say. . . ."

"In the gentlemanly style," said Anna. "but perhaps just

a shade banal." One could tell her broad delighted grin was stretching from ear to ear in the dark.

"Now, my dear Anna, you mustn't laugh if I say my conception is idyllic. What I should very much like to do, my dear, is to offer her my friendship and affection. I'll tell you roughly the kind of thing I had in mind. To begin with, a light but delicious lunch, possibly at the Ritz, my dear—then hire something absolutely slap-up from the Daimler hire and simply motor out into the country. Possibly holding hands under the rug. . . . Tea, my dear, at some country house with charming friends—possibly *your* house, Anna. In fact, I think almost certainly. . . . Then towards evening we should undoubtedly arrive at some Cathedral town——"

"I did that once," called out Olivia.

"If you did, Olivia, I dare swear your experience was not what ours would be. We'd stroll in the Close, Anna—look at the west door, I dare say—possibly sit down on a bench, and have just a little quite ordinary conversation. Between you and me, my dear, I'm not absolutely sure conversation's her strong suit, but I shouldn't mind that in the least. For instance, I might say: Look at that funny old woman with a string bag, Amanda—remarks of that, to reassure her."

"I see," said Anna gravely.

"What does she need reassuring about?" said Colin.

"Supper," continued Adrian. "Well, you can imagine supper. I dare say we would wash it down with a bottle of burgundy, or something of that sort. . . . After that we'd begin to feel deliciously sleepy from the long drive. We'd go upstairs. I'd have quietly booked an excellent bedroom for her and a small very uncomfortable dressing-room for myself. 'Amanda, my dear, good-night, God bless you,' I'd say, raising her hand to my lips. . . ." He paused: added uncertainly, "What do you suppose she'd say?"

"Adrian, don't go," pleaded Anna.

"In the event, my dear, of her saying that, I'd simply say, 'Oh, Amanda. . . .' and slip into bed beside her without another word. We should fall asleep almost as soon as our heads touched the pillow."

"Like two children."

"Exactly, my dear."

Suddenly Anna gave a choke, a snort; her shoulders shook; she burst into a deep, prolonged chuckle. Peals of laughter went up all round the car, Adrian joining in after a moment.

We can still laugh, still have good times.

They were far into the country now. The cold rain was left behind, and they travelled under a high travelling sky of intense freezing starlight and dark cloud patches edged with incandescence from a waning brilliant moon. An Arctic sky.

"Another twenty minutes and we'll be there," murmured Colin.

"Yes."

He put out his hand and took hers in a reassuring grasp. She moved closer to him.

"It'll be all right," he said. "It's just the same."

She nodded, unable to trust herself with words. *Dying's a part of living*, Colin had said when he came round to find me: *remember that. Not its utter cancellation. . . . Besides, see things in proportion, do: another trick of time and our dust, ours too, will be blowing away with his.*

They lay back silent, leaning close together; and soon Anna turned off the road down the winding lane; then the halt while Adrian got out and opened the white gate; the awkward turn through on to the cart road, the bumpy quarter of a mile. Anna drove the car into the barn, and they got out and went into Simon's house, where everything was exactly the same.

IV

ANNA knelt down and blew up the embers in the sitting-room grate. The logs came to life in a moment.

"I told Mrs. Woodley to come in and see to it as late as possible," she said. "*Also* to stoke up the boiler."

"D'you mean I can have a bath?" said Olivia. "Good egg."

"I knew you'd want to stew yourself before you got into bed," said Anna.

Then she'd planned it, I was expected.

"My dear," said Adrian, "would it be etiquette to ask one favour?"

"Gin and whisky in the usual place," said Anna. "You might put the kettle on. I'll make a hot toddy. What about you, Olivia? I'm chilly."

She whisked out of the room upstairs; came down again with an old coat of Simon's over her shoulders—a shepherd's jacket, lined with fleece, he'd brought back years ago from Palestine or somewhere.

They sat in front of the fire and ate bread and cheese and nuts and bananas and drank their drinks and talked about the party.

He was there and not there, for everybody, for nobody, as he always had been.

It was past five o'clock when they went up to bed.

Anna got sheets and Olivia helped her make up the camp-bed for Adrian in Colin's room. Olivia's own bed was already prepared, with the stone hot-water bottle in it. She had a bath in the tiny green-blistered bathroom in the middle of the steam, among the hissing, snorting pipes and the towels frayed and yellow with age and bad washing, and the cracked shaving mirror with the frame made by Anna of South of France shells.

She went to her own room, drew aside the thin linen curtain —Colin's first attempt during his far-off hand-blocked fabrics period—and looked out of the window. There was the pear tree, quite bare, its wide, curving aerial leap silhouetted dramatically in moonlight. A wind of the upper air, hollow-sounding, vast yet without menace, swung all the elm tops together. A queer night. . . . Where the uncut grass lipped the patch of shaven lawn was a line of light, like phosphorus from a breaking wave. We stood here and Rollo said, "Let's go away, there's something wrong": the day Simon was dying. Was it Rollo's mood or Simon's death that had made the dark oppression that day, the sense of virtue draining away? It wasn't so any more, in spite of cold and darkness: all was restored.

What he gave us can never be taken away. He so enriched us that we can but be the happier. We must value life more because he lived. Think that. . . .

There was a tap on the door, and Colin came in.

"Are you all right now?" he said.

"Yes, thank you."

"Do you see it's all right?"

She nodded.

Since that time when Colin came round he had been solicitous for her. They had shared a new intimacy. It was impossible to imagine being closer to a human being. I'll never be uneasy with him any more; he won't ever say again with hostile bitterness and contempt: "Olivia laughs at us all." . . . This is the best one can have probably: affection, confidence, understanding like iron; this willing, exact, unemotional giving of oneself away. Yet we shall never particularly want to be together. . . .

He came over to the window and stood beside her, looking out.

"Dying's so insidious," he said, speaking softly out towards the night. "It's so easy. Death's catching. We must steer clear of it. . . . Look at us all going about breathing it in at every pore because he caught it. . . . Carrying death about with us."

This is a lecture. He thinks I'm pretty rocky still—need watching. It's because of what I said when he came round— the thing he said was unpardonable, which he made me swear to unthink . . . that Simon was the sacrifice. . . . Meaning all the guilt and corruption, the sickness. . . . Dad, Rollo . . . me. . . . We didn't die—not us: it was Simon, the innocent one. . . . I was overwrought.

"We've all got too much death in us," he said. "A sight too much without him helping."

"He was more alive than any one, wasn't he?" she said eagerly. "Nearer the source. . . ."

He brooded, his face dark and bony, marked with pits of shadow in the light of the one lamp.

"He was," he said at last. "But not of life. Though they're so mixed. . . ." He fell silent again.

She waited for what he would say next, hearing the shriek and rumble of a goods train from across the valley, the other side of the river.

"He separated himself," said Colin, "long ago. I don't see what went wrong, but he chose the other thing. That's why he'd never have been a great man—only a person of genius. There was always something hectic about him, wasn't there? . . . hunted. To me he was like a being rapt away in an endless feverish dream. . . ."

He said that in his slow mournful voice; and all at once her resistance began to slacken. Was that the clue? . . . She saw Simon threading so light and swift through crowds, as if direct towards some narrow mastering purpose; as if impatiently saying to himself, "Is it time? It must be time now" . . . stopping dead on the pavement's edge, flitting back then to the room's threshold, peering out of the window, standing alone in the throng, chain-lighting another cigarette; sitting on the chair's edge, his eyes brilliant, vacant (with that look that made people say, did he drug?—but he didn't), checked again, thwarted in his flight.

"He was more completely remote than any one I've ever

known," said Colin. "*Nobody* was to know him. If you tried to get near him he hated you . . . as I found out. He was very dangerous—surely you could see that. . . . He was only interested in being loved. . . ." He added, "Anna knew it. . . ."

Was that why he knelt on the floor beside ignoble Cora, supporting her, binding her cut forehead, holding water to her lips . . . compassion itself. . .? Was that why he released that warning, delicate current of happy stimulus?—lent people money that would never be paid back?—clowned, as he sometimes did, in that inimitable way?—and all the rest? . . . Surely one couldn't explain him away with text-book statements. Things were more mixed than that—motives and results—inextricable. Colin himself said so. One could lay out all the ingredients one could think of, yet still the vital element was missing, and Simon as himself eluded one.

"Wasn't he happy, then?" she said.

"Happy?" he cried as if astounded; as if no one in their senses could have asked that. "Simon?"

He thinks it's better for Simon to have died.

He turned away from the window, said affectionately: "Good-night, Olivia," kissed her cheek and went to his own room.

Adrian was in bed, asleep already, but Anna was still moving about below in the kitchen. Olivia called over the banisters: "What are you up to?" and she came running upstairs again.

"I was just laying breakfast," she said. "Then we can all sleep on. Everything's done now."

"You would steal a march. Why didn't you call me? You're a thoroughly hostile character."

"Well, I wasn't sleepy."

She went on into her bedroom, which was Simon's, Olivia following her.

A ramshackle old trunk stood open in the corner, piled with his clothes. They stood and looked at them.

"I don't know who could wear them," she said. "He was so long and slight. . . . What shall I send back to his mother?"

"Has he got a mother?"

"Yes. She came out. We spent quite a lot of time together."

"What's she like?"

"A little grey body with glasses and wrinkles." Anna smiled. "Nice. She'd never been abroad before."

"Does she want his things?"

"She said she'd be glad of any little odds and ends." She smiled again. "She said he had his grandfather's gold watch but I can't find it. I'm awfully afraid he must have popped it—or just lost it. There are some rings and coins and things in this box . . . studs: Woolworth. She doesn't care much for his pictures, and she's not one for book-reading. Perhaps some of the photographs I took last year. . . . Only I don't think she'll like them." She picked up a Moroccan belt sewn with blue, white and red beads, dropped it again. "You must have something," she said, sighing vaguely. "What would you like?"

"Not now, Anna—please. Later, perhaps. . . ." Thick tears began to drip down. It was this sort of thing that took advantage of one—legacies, relics and mementoes of the departed.

"I know he'd like you to have something," said Anna.

She was so self-possessed standing there looking around at his things. The person who's been by the deathbed always is, they say.

"Simon was very fond of you," she said, looking at Olivia with blue fatigue-sunken eyes. "He said one day when he was ill he wished you'd walk in. You were refreshing."

"*Oh!* . . . I loved him. . . ."

Anna knelt down by the trunk and folded a mulberry-coloured shirt, not looking at her, giving her time to recover. After a minute Olivia managed to say:

"Did you know he was going to die?"

Anna considered.

"I'm not quite sure. Perhaps half-way through he had it

on his mind. . . . But not at the end. He tried very hard for quite a long time to live—and then he just didn't try any more. He got too weak."

"Did he talk much? Say anything?"

"Not very much." Anna sat back on her heels. "At first he liked being read to, but later on he couldn't concentrate—it worried him. We used to play word games, very simple ones—and invent names and conversations and life histories for his nurses—really ludicrous games. He made up rhymes too, and said over poetry to himself . . . He joked a lot. The nurses were mad about him. . . . He didn't ever seem distressed in his mind—although he had so much discomfort—except once when he said he'd never been able quite to understand how the telephone worked—and I couldn't remember either." She smiled.

No last words then. . . .

"I've burnt all his letters—letters to him, I mean," said Anna, still sitting on her heels. "I know he'd have wanted me to. There wasn't much. He never accumulated."

"What are you going to do, Anna? Have you made any plans?"

"I shall stay on here. I suppose you know he left it to me?"

"Yes, I do know."

"He actually made a sort of will last spring before he went abroad. I can't think why. Just on a half-sheet of paper—but Colin happened to come in while he was doing it so he told him, and showed him which drawer he was putting it in, so everything's all right and there'll be no trouble."

"That's lucky. . . . I'm so glad he left you the house."

"I often wonder," said Anna meditatively, "whether he had a hunch he was going to die."

"Did it seem as if he had?"

"I don't know. He never said anything. I've never seen him in such tearing spirits as he was this summer: enjoying everything quite extravagantly. Of course he always did, but . . ."

She pulled the lid of the trunk down slowly, and got up. "Have *you* any plans?" she said.

"Well, no. I'm a bit nebulous still, I'm afraid." Say it cheerfully, don't bother Anna with your totally blank future. "I've had an invitation to Paris. But I'm not sure if I'll go."

"I hope you'll come here tremendously often. I hope everybody will."

"Thank you, Anna, how lovely. . . . I must think about a job, I suppose. Turn a penny somehow."

"Oh, about that," said Anna. "I meant to write but I didn't: Simon left me some money—wasn't it angelic of him? Four hundred a year. It's more than I want and you're to have half. I'm arranging it. I know he'd be pleased. The letter said I was to do exactly what I wanted with it, but keep half anyway —so that means he knew I'd rather share it." She began to unbutton her stiff silk dress.

No words came.

"Get along to bed," said Anna, looking up, smiling. "You look like nothing on earth."

She held out her arms and gave Olivia a quick hug, saying: "It's nice to have you here."

She let her arms drop again; stood a moment staring in front of her.

"After he died," she said. "I made him a wreath of bay. He looked so triumphant."

V

As she rang the bell of number two, she thought she saw the family car, with Benson at the wheel, disappear round the corner at the far end of the square. Imagination, of course. Lady Spencer would never have cut it so fine. "Calling at two-forty," she'd said, "to take Nicola for a drive and a little shopping. Be there yourself at three," she'd said, "not before:

that will be safe. Be gone by four at the latest. I depend on
you. . . ." "Thank you so much, Lady Spencer, it is kind of
you. . . ." "Good-bye, Olivia." She hung up briskly, having
kept her promise: you shall see Rollo once. (Alone. But under
my auspices. I need say no more, I'm sure: you are on your
honour.)

The front door was opened.

"Oh, I called to inquire for Mr. Spencer."

"Mr. Spencer is going on very nicely, thank you, madam.
He's up—in an arm-chair, that is. We hope to get him downstairs and out for a drive next week." Owner of telephone voice
number one: young, pleasant, reassuring, disillusioned-
looking.

"I *am* so glad. It's been a terribly long time, hasn't it?"

"It has, madam. A very nasty time indeed for all. But
Mr. Spencer he's a wonderful patient. So cheerful. That's
what's helped him most."

"I'm sure it has. Would you give him this note, please? If
I might wait for an answer. . . ."

He ushered her into Rollo's study. She stood on the hearthrug—where I saw Rollo standing that night—looking at
nothing till the door opened noiselessly and he returned.

"Mr. Spencer says would you please come straight up,
madam."

Up they went on the chestnut-brown carpet, past the shut
drawing-room door, round, up another flight, next landing,
up two little steps and second door on the right.

Rollo said, "Come in," and he held aside the door for her
and shut it again noiselessly after her.

The afternoon was dark, inclined to fog. At first it was
difficult to distinguish much more than the outline of Rollo
sitting in an arm-chair by the fire with his back to the light,
one leg propped up on low stools and pillows.

"Darling!" he said softly.

"Hallo, Rollo." She saw her note open on his lap. He was
wearing a stylish navy-blue dressing-gown. Then she saw a

crumpled white fur head pop up shrewishly from a basket by the chair: Lucy.

"Darling, it *was* a glorious thought to come." He put his hand out, and when she gave him hers, held on to it. "And the most incredible luck—I'm quite alone. How did you know?"

"A little bird told me." She sat down in the arm-chair opposite him. "As a matter of fact, she added, "I didn't see why anybody should look at me old-fashioned if I did come to inquire after such a discreet interval. After all, I'm an old family friend, aren't I?"

"You are, but thank God the family are out. They've gone shopping or something."

Gone to look at cots or baby clothes perhaps, or to be fitted for her special tea-gowns, with tactful saleswomen to offer chairs in the right departments, and relatives to say take care, holding her arm down awkward steps or on slippery pavements. All the pleasantly important flags and garlands would be hung for her over the rooted, the appalling, the ultimately-unshroud-able rock.

She sat and smoked and asked the proper questions. He felt as fit as a fiddle, he said—pretty bored, that's all. Only the leg hadn't quite mended according to plan. However, next week he was to start massage. He had a nurse still, a boring woman, quite pleasant, he didn't really need her, but they insisted. . . . Now she could look at him less waveringly, she saw scars on his nose and forehead. He was thinner too; not pale, but the ruddy look was gone. His present complexion suited him.

Silence fell.

"I didn't bring you anything," she said apologetically, looking round at the stacks of fresh library books and weeklies, the bowls of flowers, the plate of fruit—everything for the sick-room. His bed with its quilted dark-patterned cretonne head was turned back and piled with pillows all ready for him to get back. Nurse would support him, and Lady Spencer would call out injunctions, and Nicola would plump up the pillow if she hadn't gone to lie down—and he'd hop back and rag the nurse and heave himself on to the mattress and say thank you darling to his wife. . . .

Go on thinking of things to say now. Carry it off with a high hand. It was bad luck to be the one facing the light. She bent down to pat Lucy, who winced away.

"She's still there, I see."

"Still there. And I'm completely at her mercy. Who said the monstrous regiment of women?" His eyebrow went up ruefully. "You've no idea how awfully well looked after I am."

"There's nothing like family life," she said.

"It's a funny thing," he said, gazing at her with embarrassing warmth, "when they—when I knew I was going to be alone this afternoon I as near as anything—I wanted terribly to ring you up and ask you. . . . I didn't like to. . . ."

"It must have been telepathy," she said smiling, aloof.

"I've wanted to so often. Only I didn't know if you were still angry with me." He lowered his voice, coaxing, plaintive.

A feeling of unreality began to float her away. Really, the things he said! . . . She made no answer, and he went on with a sudden emotional break in his voice:

"I thought I was never going to see you again."

"I had to come once." She swallowed nervously. "I had to ask you—I had to know if it was my fault you—had the accident——"

"*Your* fault?" He was astonished. "How could it be your fault?" She hadn't seized the wheel or been the driver of the lorry or anything. . . . Or did she mean . . .? "If you mean was I trying to bump myself off, I wasn't," he said with that rough, almost brutal contradictory note. "If I ever wanted to do anything of that sort, I'd choose a less messy way and not drag poor innocent lorry-drivers into it." He was quite indignant. "Good God, what an idea!"

"I only meant—perhaps you weren't being so careful— you'd been upset—and that was my fault. . . ."

Oh, give it up, what's the use, we don't understand one another. . . . The unreality was encroaching everywhere, blurring every outline. She was conscious now of nothing but him sitting there, bulking so large, almost touching her: Rollo, his face, his hands, his voice again. . . .

"What's the time?" she said.

"Half-past three."

"Will any one else come?"

"No. Don't worry. I told William not to show any one else up."

He always thought of everything.

"I must go in a minute."

"Not yet. They won't be back till four, they said so. Sit back and relax. Tell me what you've been doing, darling."

He will go on saying darling—as if everything was the same.

"Nothing very interesting. I've been in the country lately —with Anna. Simon's dead, you know. He got typhoid and died in September."

"Good God, he didn't really, did he? Poor chap—I'm most awfully sorry."

He looked away, with a funny sort of petulant sigh: meaning, I know it's awful and you've had a beastly time, but I have too, I'm not quite fit, I oughtn't to be made to dwell on miserable things.

After a pause he said softly:

"You've got it still then."

"What?"

"Our ring."

"Oh, yes." She looked down at it as if in surprise. "It's got to be such a part of me, I couldn't not wear it."

"I'm glad." He looked at her with meaning, trying to make her meet his eyes.

"I've got the wrist-watch too," she said. "But it doesn't seem to keep very good time. I think it must need regulating."

"Oh, send it back to me," he said, "and I'll get it overhauled."

"Oh no, don't bother. I'll see to it."

Lucy scratched at the cushion, turned round three times and settled down to sulky sleep with her nose tucked into her flank.

"Darling, you do look sweet," he said softly.

She got up.

"I must go now. I'm nervous about people coming."

"Will you come again if I ring up?" His voice hardened, obstinately pleading.

"No, Rollo, I can't."

He held out his hand, stretching it so that the fine familiar lines of wrist, palm, fingers, showed startlingly.

"Come here."

She put her hand in his and took a step closer.

"Kiss me," he said.

She bent down and he kissed her on the lips, a long kiss. He held her face down and whispered in her ear:

"I'm your lover, aren't I?"

She raised herself, flushed, the blood gone to her head, feeling dismayed, acutely self-conscious. *This isn't what she meant—what I had leave for. . . . Breaking my trust. . . .*

He said with determination:

"We're going to see each other again, aren't we?"

"I shouldn't think so."

"One day!"

She shook her head.

"Say perhaps!"

"Perhaps." *No harm in saying that. He'll forget again. It's only that he's feeling hemmed in, bored, over-domesticated. . . .*

"I think we'll see each other again," he said, staring at her fixedly.

"Rollo, you are an awful man. . . ."

"Let's not be final and desperate, darling." Coaxing, stroking her palm. "It's so silly, isn't it? We've had such lovely times, haven't we? Life's so short. When two people get on so well together, it's so stupid to say never again. Don't you agree?"

"Yes . . . perhaps. . . ."

So stupid, to make a fuss. A little rift, an unfortunate misunderstanding—over now. One must see things in proportion.

"I should so terribly miss our lunches," he was saying with soft persistence.

So should I. They were so pleasant.

"Our drives. . . ."

Oh, yes, the drives, they were so pleasant. Why not a lunch, a drive, if he wanted to, very discreetly, now and then? . . . It was all so pleasant. . . .

"Do you remember our drives in the mountains?" he was saying. "And the heavenly places where we stayed? The little inns? Do you remember that queer one under the chestnut trees?—with the funny little band? . . . It *was* fun, wasn't it, darling?"

THE END

FROST IN MAY

ANTONIA WHITE

(1899-1980) was born in London, and educated at the Convent of the Sacred Heart, Roehampton and St Paul's Girls' School, London. She trained as an actress at the Royal Academy of Dramatic Art, working for her living as a freelance copywriter and contributing short stories to a variety of magazines. In 1924 she joined the staff of W. S. Crawford as a copywriter, became Assistant Editor of *Life and Letters* in 1928, theatre critic of *Time and Tide* in 1934, and was the Fashion Editor of the *Daily Mirror* and then the *Sunday Pictorial* until the outbreak of the Second World War. During the war Antonia White worked first in the BBC and then in the French Section of the Political Intelligence Department of the Foreign Office.

Antonia White published four novels: *Frost in May* (1933), *The Lost Traveller* (1950), *The Sugar House* (1952), and *Beyond the Glass* (1954), which were televised by the BBC in 1982. Her other published work includes a volume of short stories, *Strangers* (1954), and an autobiographical account of her reconversion to the Catholic faith, *The Hound and the Falcon* (1965). All these works are published by Virago Press.

Antonia White translated over thirty novels from the French, and was awarded the Clairouin Prize for her first one, Maupassant's *Une Vie*, in 1950. She translated Eveline Mahyère's novel, *I Will Not Serve*, which is also published by Virago, and also translated many of the works of Colette. Like Colette, Antonia White was devoted to cats and wrote two books about her own – *Minka and Curdy* and *Living With Minka and Curdy*. She was married three times and had two daughters and four grandchildren. She lived most of her life in London and died in Sussex, where her father and many generations of her family were born and bred.

INTRODUCTION

FROST IN MAY is a girls' school story. It is not the only school story to be a classic; but I can think of no other that is a work of art. What, it may be wondered, is the distinction? A major classic is necessarily also a work of art. But a book may come to be recognised as a minor classic by right of virtues making for durability—vigour, wideness, kindness, manifest truth to life. Such a book gathers something more, as the years go on, from the affection that has attached to it—no question of its æsthetic value need be raised. A work of art, on the other hand, may and sometimes does show deficiency in some of the qualities of the minor classic—most often kindness. As against this, it brings into being unprecedented moments; it sets up sensation of a unique and troubling kind.

School stories may be divided and subdivided. There is the school story proper, written for school-age children; and the school novel, written for the grown-up. There is the pro-school school story and the anti-school—recently almost all school novels have fallen into the latter class. *Tom Brown's Schooldays* has a host of dimmer descendants, all written to inculcate manliness and show that virtue pays. *Stalky and Co.* fits into no classificaton: one might call it an early gangster tale in a school setting. The Edwardian novelist's talent for glamorising any kind of society was turned by E. F. Benson and H. A. Vachell on two of the greater English public schools. The anti-school school novel emerged when, after the first world war, intellectuals captured, and continued to hold, key positions along the front of fiction.

387

A few, too few, show a sublime disinfectedness that makes for comedy, or at least satire. In the main, though, the hero of the anti-school novel is the sombre dissentient and the sufferer. He is in the right: the school, and the system behind it, is wrong. From the point of view of art, which should be imperturbable, such novels are marred by a fractious or plangent note. Stephen Spender's *The Backward Son,* not thus marred, is a work of art; but I should not call it strictly a school novel—primarily it is a study of temperament.

To return to the school story proper (written for young people), those for boys are infinitely better than those for girls. The curl-tossing tomboys of the Fourth at St. Dithering's are manifestly and insultingly unreal to any girl child who has left the nursery; as against this, almost all young schoolgirls devour boys' school books, and young boys, apparently, do not scorn them. For my own part, I can think of only one girls' school story I read with pleasure when young, and can re-read now—Susan Coolidge's *What Katy Did at School.* As a girls' school *novel* (other than *Frost in May*) I can only think of Colette's *Claudine à l'École.*

I began by calling *Frost in May* a school story. By subsequent definition it is a school novel—that is to say, it is written for grown-ups. But—which is interesting—Antonia White has adopted the form and sublimated, without complicating, the language of the school story proper. *Frost in May* could be read with relish, interest and excitement by an intelligent child of twelve years old. The heroine, Nanda Grey, is nine when she goes to Lippington, thirteen when, catastrophically, she leaves. She is in no way the born "victim" type—she is quick-witted, pleasing, resilient, normally rather than morbidly sensitive. Call her the high-average "ordinary" little girl. She is not even, and is not intended to be, outstandingly sympathetic to the reader: the scales are not weighted on her behalf. We have Nanda's arrival at Lippington, first impressions, subsequent adaptations, apparent success and, finally, head-on crash. *Frost in May* deviates from the school-story formula only in not having a happy ending. We are shown the school only through Nanda's eyes—there is no scene from which she is off stage. At the same time there is no impressionistic blurring, none of the distortions of subjectivity: Lippington is presented with cool exactness. Antonia White's style as a story-teller is as precise, clear and unweighty as Jane Austen's. Without a lapse from this style Antonia White traverses passages of which the only analogy is to be found in Joyce's *Portrait of the Artist as a Young Man*.

The subject of this novel is in its title—*Frost in May*. Nanda shows, at the start, the prim, hardy pink-and-white of a young bud. What is to happen to her—and how, or why?

Of the two other girls' school books named, one is American and the other French. *Frost in May* is English —but English by right only of its author's birth and its geographic setting. Lippington is at the edge of London. But it is a convent school—of a Roman Catholic Order which Antonia White calls "the Five Wounds." Its climate is its own; its atmosphere is, in our parlance, international. Or, more properly, as one of the girls put it, "Catholicism isn't a religion, it's a nationality." A Lippington girl is a Child of the Five Wounds; she may by birth be French, German, Spanish or English, but that is secondary. Also the girls here show a sort of family likeness: they are the daughters of old, great Catholic families, the frontierless aristocracy of Europe;

they have in common breeding as well as faith. From Spanish Rosario, Irish Hilary and French-German Léonie the rawness of English Protestant middle-class youth is missing. Initially, Nanda is at a twofold disadvantage, never quite overcome. Her father is a convert; she herself was received into the Catholic Church only a year before her arrival at Lippington. And, she is middle-class, her home is in Earl's Court. There is one Protestant here, but she is aristocratic; there are two other middle-class girls, but they come of Catholic stock.

Lippington is a world in itself—hermetic to a degree possible for no lay school. It contains, is contained in, and represents absolute, and absolutely conclusive, authority. Towards what aim is that authority exercised? On the eve of the holiday that is to celebrate the canonisation of the foundress of the Order, the Mistress of Discipline addresses the school. "*'Some of that severity which to the world seems harshness is bound up in the school rule which you are privileged to follow. . . . We work today to turn out, not accomplished young women, nor agreeable wives, but soldiers of Christ, accustomed to hardship and ridicule and ingratitude.'*" What are the methods? *"As in the Jesuit Order every child was under constant observation, and the results of this observation were made known by secret weekly reports to Mother Radcliffe and the Superior. . . ."* How did one child, Nanda, react to this? *"Nanda's rebelliousness, such as it was, was directed entirely against the Lippington methods. Her faith in the Catholic Church was not affected in the least. If anything, it became more robust."* None the less, when, at thirteen, Nanda is faced by her father with the suggestion that she should leave Lippington to receive a more workaday education elsewhere, her reaction is this: *"She was overwhelmed. . . .*

Even now, in the shock of the revelation of her depend-
ence, she did not realise how thoroughly Lippington had
done its work. But she felt blindly she could only live in
that rare, intense element; the bluff, breezy air of that
'really good High School' would kill her." And, elsewhere: *"In its* [Lippington's] *cold, clear atmosphere*
everything had a sharper outline than in the comfort-
able, shapeless, scrambling life outside."

That atmosphere and that outline, their nature, and
the nature of their power over one being, Nanda, are at
once the stuff and the study of *Frost in May.* They are
shown and felt. The result has been something intense,
sensuous, troubling, semi-miraculous—a work of art. In
the biting crystal air of the book the children and the
nuns stand out like early morning mountains. In this
frigid, authoritarian, anti-romantic Catholic climate
every romantic vibration from "character" is, in effect,
trebled. *Frost in May* could, for instance, go down to
time on the strength, alone, of Léonie de Wesseldorf—
introduced, in parenthesis almost, but living from the
first phrase, on page 78. Momentum gathers round
each sequence of happenings and each event—the First
Communion, the retreat, the canonisation holiday,
Mother Francis's death, the play for the cardinal, the
measles idyll. . . . Lyricism—pagan in the bonfire scene,
sombre on the funeral morning—gains in its pure force
from the very infrequency of its play. . . . Art, at any
rate in a novel, must be indissolubly linked with craft:
in *Frost in May* the author's handling of time is a
technical triumph—but, too, a poetic one.

The *interest* of the book is strong, though secondary;
it is so strong that that it should be secondary is amazing. If you care for controversy, the matter of *Frost in*
May is controversial. There exists in the mind of a

number of English readers an inherited dormant violence of anti-Popery: to one type of mind *Frost in May*
may seem a gift too good to be true—it is. Some passages
are written with an effrontery that will make the Protestant blink—we are very naïve. As a school Lippington
does, of course, run counter to the whole trend of English
liberal education: to the detached mind this is in itself
fascinating. The child-psychologist will be outraged by
the Lippington attitude to sex and class. Nanda's fate—
one might almost feel, Nanda's doom—raises questions·
that cannot be disposed of easily, or perhaps at all. This
book is intimidating. Like all classics, it acquires further
meaning with the passage of time. It was first published
in 1933: between then and now our values, subconscious
as well as conscious, have been profoundly changed. I
think it not unlikely that *Frost in May* may be more
comprehensible now than it was at first.

ELIZABETH BOWEN

To
H. T. HOPKINSON

CHAPTER I

NANDA was on her way to the Convent of the Five Wounds. She sat very upright on the slippery seat of the one-horse bus, her tightly-gaitered legs dangling in the straw, and her cold hands squeezed into an opossum muff. A fog screened every window, clouding the yellow light that shone on the faces of the three passengers as they jolted slowly along invisible streets.

After several sociable but unheeded coughs, the third occupant could bear the silence no longer and began to speak to Nanda's father. She wore a dusty velvet tam o' shanter and a man's tweed coat, and Nanda could tell from her voice that she was Irish. "Excuse me, sir," she asked, "but could you tell me if we are anywhere near Lippington village yet?"

"I'm afraid I can't tell you," Mr. Grey answered in his rich, pleasant voice, "all I *do* know is that we haven't got to the Convent yet, because the driver is putting us down there. The village is further on up the lane."

"The Convent?" exclaimed the Irishwoman, "would that be the Convent of the Five Wounds now?"

"Yes," said Nanda's father. "I'm just taking my little daughter to school there."

The Irishwoman beamed.

"Now isn't that beautiful?" she said, "you're a Catholic, then, sir?" She pronounced it 'Cartholic.'

"I am indeed," Mr. Grey assented.

"Isn't that wonderful now? To think of the three of us in this omnibus in a Protestant country and everyone of us Catholics."

"I'm a convert," Mr. Grey explained. "I was only received into the Church a year ago."

"To think of that!" said the Irishwoman. "The grace of God is a glorious thing. Indeed it is. I wonder if the little lady knows what a grace has been given to her to have a father that's been called to the Faith?"

She leant over and put her face close to Nanda's.

"And so you're going to the holy nuns at the Five Wounds, my dear? Isn't it the lucky young lady you are? The saints must have watched over your cradle. There's no holier religious anywhere in the world than the nuns of the Five Wounds. I've a cousin meself . . . Mary Cassidy . . . that's one of their lay-sisters in Armagh. She'll be taking her final vows in February . . . the Feast of the Purification. Do you know when that is, my dear?"

"The second of February," Nanda risked shyly.

The Irishwoman rolled her eyes in admiration.

"Glory be to God, did you ever hear the like?" she asked Mr. Grey. "Are you telling me that young lady's not born and bred a Catholic?"

Nanda's father looked pleased.

"No. She was received only last year, when she was eight. But she's been having instruction and learning her catechism."

"It's wonderful, so it is," the Irishwoman assured him, "and it's a sign of special grace, I'll be bound. Perhaps she'll be called on to do great things in the service of God, who knows? I wouldn't be surprised if she had a vocation later on."

"Oh, it's early days to think of that," smiled Mr. Grey.

Nanda began to feel a little uncomfortable. She had heard a good deal about vocations and she wasn't at all sure that she wanted one.

"They say God speaks to them very early," said the

Irishwoman mysteriously, "and that they hear Him best
in the innocence of their hearts. Look at St. Aloysius
now. And St. Stanislas Kostka. And St. Theresa herself
that would have been a martyr for the love of God when
she was but three years old. And wouldn't it be a beautiful thing now if she was to offer her life to God as a
thanksgiving for the great blessing of your own conversion, sir?"

Nanda began to like the conversation less and less.
She was an only child and she had taken to her new
religion with a rather precocious fervour. Already she
had absorbed enough of the Catholic point of view to
see how very appropriate such a sacrifice would be. But
although she had already privately dedicated herself to
perpetual virginity, and had seriously considered devot-
ing her life to the lepers at Molokai, she did not entirely
relish the idea of cutting off her hair and living in a cell
and never seeing her home again. She was relieved when
the bus stopped and the driver came round and tapped
at the window.

"This must be the Convent," said Mr. Grey. "We get
down here. Lippington village is a little way further
on."

"God bless you both," said the Irishwoman. "Good-
bye, little lady. Say a prayer every morning to thank
God and his saints for bringing you to the holy faith.
And say a prayer sometimes for poor old Bridget Mulli-
gan, for the prayers of children have great power with
the Almighty. I'll say five decades for you this very
night that you may grow up a good Catholic and a
comfort to your father."

As they passed out of the omnibus, Mr. Grey pressed
something into the ragged woman's hand.

"God bless you, sir," she called after them. "It was the

holy mother of God sent you to me to-day. St. Bridget
and all the saints guard you and watch over you and
your family."

After the omnibus had lurched away into the fog,
Nanda and her father waited several minutes on the
Convent doorstep before the flap behind the grill blinked
up and down. After much rattling of chains and bolts
the door was opened and a lay-sister portress beckoned
them in.

"Will you wait in the lodge, Mr. Grey?" she said in a
very quiet voice. "I'll go and fetch Mother Radcliffe."

While they waited for Mother Radcliffe, Nanda took
in her surroundings. Her smarting eyes were soothed by
a long stretch of white-washed walls and red-tiled floor.
At the end of the corridor stood a statue of Our Lord in
white robes wearing a red, thorn-circled heart on his
breast like an order. The bent head with its pale brown
hair and beard was girlish and gentle; the brass halo
had been polished till it winked and reflected each flicker
of the little glass lamp that burned on the pedestal.
Never in her life had Nanda seen anything so clean and
bare as that corridor. It smelt of yellow soap and beeswax, mixed with a faint, sweetish scent that she recognised as incense.

Outside the portress' little room, which bore the notice
"No admittance for seculars," hung a printed card,
punched with a double row of holes and adorned with
two cribbage pegs. Over the top was written "Mother
Radcliffe"; the left-hand row of holes was headed "Is"
and the right-hand one "Is wanted." In the middle was
a list of all the places where Mother Radcliffe might
conceivably be or be wanted, such as "at meditation,"
"in the garden," "in the school," "with the novices," "at
the farm," "in the parlour," and "at recreation." When

Nanda drew her father's attention to this, he was much pleased at the ingenuity of the device.

"They're wonderfully business-like, nuns," he told her. "It's all nonsense about their being dreamy and unpractical and out of touch with the world. Every minute of their day is filled up with something useful. If you only learnt one thing from them, Nanda, I should be satisfied."

"What one thing, Daddy?"

"Never to waste time, my dear."

In spite of the ingenious card, it seemed to take the lay-sister a very long time to find Mother Radcliffe. But at last she appeared round the angle of the corridor. She came towards them with the step Nanda was to come to know so well, the characteristic walk of all the nuns of the Five Wounds, smooth and sliding, never slow, never hurried. She advanced smiling, but never quickening her pace, her hands folded in her black sleeves. Her pale face was so narrow that her goffered white bonnet sloped to a point under her chin. This bonnet scratched Nanda's face when Mother Radcliffe bent down to kiss her.

"So this is Fernanda," she said in a kind voice. "I am so glad to see you, dear child. Will you say good-bye to your father now, or would you like to go to the parlour for a little first?"

Nanda hesitated, but Mr. Grey looked at his watch.

"What do you think, Nanda? It's late and Mother will be waiting. But I'll stay if you like."

"It's all right, Daddy," said Nanda mechanically. She suddenly felt lonely and frightened. A great longing came over her for small shabby rooms and coal fires and the comfortable smells of tobacco and buttered toast. But she was one of those children who cannot help behaving well.

"That's a brave girl," said Mother Radcliffe approvingly.

Her father gave her an affectionate squeeze and tucked a bright half-crown into her muff.

"Good-bye, Nanda. Shall I tell Mother you're quite happy? We'll be down on Sunday. Only five days more."

"Good-bye, Daddy."

Mother Radcliffe was tactful. She seemed to understand that Nanda did not want to hear the clang of the nail-studded front door behind her father. She led her quickly along the red-tiled passage, talking all the way. Round the corner, outside an oak door, Mother Radcliffe paused in her walk, genuflected swiftly and made the sign of the cross. Nanda, with her hand clasped in the nun's, was taken by surprise, but managed to bob awkwardly. Not liking to remove her right hand from Mother Radcliffe's, she contrived to sign herself with her left, and hoped the nun would not notice. But, in spite of the jutting bonnet which hid her profile, Mother Radcliffe saw everything.

"Come, Nanda," she said, "that's not the way little Catholic children make the sign of the cross. It's not reverent, dear." Nanda felt hot with shame. But the next turn of the passage provided so much interest that she forgot her lapse.

"This is the school corridor," Mother Radcliffe explained, "and here are some of the other children. You mustn't be shy; there are plenty of new ones this term."

At the end of the passage hung a large oil painting of Our Lord, showing his five wounds.

"See, there is Our Lord welcoming you," said the nun. "If ever you feel a little bit homesick, just remember that home for a Catholic is wherever Our Lord is."

Instead of answering, Nanda tightened her clasp of

Mother Radcliffe's cool, dry hand. Thinking about religion was a secret, delicious joy, but talking about it still made her uncomfortable and self-conscious. She was a very raw convert.

To her relief, a door burst open and a red-haired, blue-bloused girl dashed out of it. Seeing the nun, she pulled up short and made a very sketchy curtsey.

"Gently, Joyce," smiled Mother Radcliffe, "I thought you were having deportment lessons this term."

"Sorry, Mother," said Joyce gruffly. Nanda liked her. She had freckles and a pleasant grin which showed very white teeth. Being two years older, she took no notice of Nanda beyond a quick, amused stare.

More doors opened and girls of all ages and complexions came hurrying out. Nearly all wore the uniform striped blouse and dark skirt, but here and there a velvet frock, a gold chain or a head stiff with American bows marked a newcomer. Nanda was thankful that her own home clothes were inconspicuous enough to pass without attracting attention. The older girls seemed quite alarmingly grown-up with their huge puffs and side combs. She wondered if she would ever dare to speak to such majestic creatures. Even the fourteen-year-olds looked at least twenty with their long skirts and their neat, small waists strapped in leather belts. There were curtsies all along the passage as Mother Radcliffe passed. Most were no more than quick, springy bobs, but some were deep and slow and wonderful to watch. They must be very difficult to execute, Nanda thought, sighing at her own abysmal ignorance.

A bell began to clang. Still more girls poured out from the glass-fronted doors. Two dark-skinned, graceful creatures with gold rings in their ears slid past, both talking Spanish at the tops of their voices.

Presently Mother Radcliffe stopped a tall girl with a plait reaching to her waist, and a wide blue ribbon slung across her handsome bosom.

"Madeleine," said the nun, "this is a new child, Fernanda Grey. Would you take her up to the Junior School?"

"Yes, Mother," said Madeleine graciously. Keeping her long back erect, she swept a slow and admirable curtsey. The nun inclined her head.

"I shall see you in the morning, Nanda. If there's anything you want, you can always come to my room. The one marked Mistress of Discipline."

Nanda attempted a curtsey which was not a great success, and which Madeleine's cold blue stare seemed to make still more inadequate. As soon as Mother Radcliffe's back was turned, this new guide inquired haughtily: "Have you been to Our Lady of Perpetual Succour, yet?"

"I don't think so," said the bewildered Nanda.

"Well, if you're not sure, you'd better come with me now," said Madeleine, bored but resigned.

She pushed open the door of a large room filled with excited and chattering children changing into their uniforms. A harassed Irish nun pounced on Nanda and peering at her with short-sighted eyes, asked anxiously:

"Are you Nora Wiggin?"

"No, I'm Fernanda Grey."

"Number thirty-six are you, dear child?"

"Yes, Mother."

"There's not a uniform for you. You'll have to wear your home clothes for a few days. Now what can have happened to Nora Wiggin? She was due here at six. I hope she's not lost in the fog. You'd better leave your hat and coat on the chair, there, Fernanda. Tidily, there's a good child. And pin a piece of paper to them with your number."

"Yes, Mother," said Nanda, carrying out these instructions.

"There's a good girl. You'd better go up to Mother Frances now."

"I was just taking her, Mother," said the righteous Madeleine.

As she trotted up the stone staircase behind Madeleine, Nanda ventured to remark: "I didn't see Our Lady of Perpetual Succour."

"Our Lady of Perpetual Succour is the name of the room we were in just now. All the rooms at Lippington are named after a saint. Didn't you know?" Madeleine answered.

Nanda found this very confusing at first. But she was soon to get used to it. By the end of the week she could perfectly understand the situation when someone said: "I was just rushing into St. Mary Magdalene without my gloves when Mother Prisca came out of St. Peter Claver and caught me."

She had no breath now for more questions. The stone stairs stretched up flight after flight and Madeleine's long legs strode on remorselessly. Nanda's own small ones ached, as if someone had tied a tight knot behind each knee, but she dared not ask the queenly Madeleine to go more slowly. By the time they had reached a lighted door at the very top of the building, Nanda was crimson in the face and quite sick with fatigue.

"Here's a new child for you, Mother Frances," announced Madeleine, pushing Nanda down three steps into a large room and towards a tall and very handsome nun. This nun was surrounded by a group of children of Nanda's own age, who all stared very hard at her.

"We've been expecting you," said Mother Frances.

Having already met several nuns during her wander-ings, Nanda had begun to wonder how she was ever to identify them individually. In their black habits and white crimped bonnets, they all appeared exactly alike to her untrained eye. But looking at Mother Frances, she thought: "I certainly shan't forget *her*." The nun returned her look with a smile at once sweet and ironical. Her three-cornered face was white and transparent as a winter flower, and the long, very bright eyes that shone between the blackest of lashes were almost the colour of harebells. Yet all this beauty seemed even to Nanda to be touched with frost. Mother Frances looked too rare, too exquisite to be quite real. During the long, amused look the nun gave her, Nanda thought to herself first: "She's like the Snow Queen," and then: "I shall never be comfortable with her." Under those remarkable eyes, her courage left her. She felt very small and hot and homesick and common.

Mother Frances laid a cool hand on Nanda's flushed cheek and tucked a strand of hair behind her ear.

"You know Marjorie Appleyard, don't you?" she asked in a voice sweet and ironical, like her smile. Mar-jorie smiled with distant politeness as Mother Frances mentioned her name.

She was a pretty, china-faced little girl who lived near the Greys in Earl's Court, and whom Nanda privately thought an intolerable bore. But the fact that she had already been at Lippington a whole year made her worthy of respect. Nanda noticed that the dark blue of her uniform was relieved by a pink ribbon worn like Madeleine's blue one.

"You'll have to follow in Marjorie's footsteps," she told Nanda. "She got her pink ribbon in her first term, and she's never lost it yet." Mother Frances' tone implied that there was something meritorious but slightly ridiculous in possessing a pink ribbon.

"What is a pink ribbon for?" inquired another new child, a small, self-possessed foreigner in a tartan frock.

"It's a reward, Louise," said Mother Frances. "A reward for being almost unnaturally good for eight weeks on end."

Some of the children tittered, but uneasily. Mother Frances swept her amused look over the group.

"I'll have to find someone to take charge of Nanda for a few days until she knows her way about," she observed. "Which of you would like to take charge of Nanda Grey?"

There was a chorus of "Me, please, Mother." One or two even held up their hands. Mother Frances surveyed these with distaste and the hands dropped like plummets.

"We don't hold up our hands at Lippington," she said coldly. "This is not a High School."

She swooped on a plain, sallow child who had not volunteered for the task.

"Why, Mildred, what a wonderful chance for you," she said in her sweetest voice, "and what a chance for Nanda. You're the eldest in the Junior School, and you've been here longer than any of the others."

"Yes, Mother," admitted Mildred, wriggling unhappily.

"That's not a very good example for Nanda, is it? I want to teach her a lot of things, but I don't want to teach her to squirm when she's spoken to. Nanda will think this is the original school where they taught reeling and writhing and fainting in coils."

"Oh, Mother Frances," squirmed Mildred, while the others, including Nanda, laughed.

"Do you know where that comes from?" Mother Frances flashed at Nanda.

"*Alice in Wonderland*," Nanda flashed back.

"Good child."

It was Nanda's first triumph. But Mother Frances spoilt it by telling the others: "You'll find Nanda's read a great deal, I expect. She's an only child and she's got a very clever father. None of you do Latin yet, but Nanda's going to do a Latin exercise every day and send it to her father. So if we can't understand any Latin in church, we'll have to get Nanda to translate it for us."

Poor Nanda reviled the Latin which had dogged her from the age of seven. Her father believed strongly in the importance of a classical education, and his one misgiving about Lippington had been that no Greek was taught there. Nanda blushed over her parent's eccentricity and felt a wild impulse to run away from the group of grinning little girls whose fathers did not insist on teaching them Latin.

But Mother Frances had not finished with her yet. She had kept her cruellest shot for the last.

"You'll have to get up very early, Mildred, if Nanda isn't to be late for mass. You see, Nanda's father wants her to have a cold bath every morning. So she'll have to be up a quarter of an hour before the others."

This had even more success than the Latin exercises. Nanda felt she had been branded for life. Never, never would she live down this shame. But Mother Frances, like some expert torturer, seemed to have decided that she had had enough.

"Your desk's the last one down there on the right," she told Nanda in her sweetest voice, and gave here a smile as if they shared some delicate joke together. "Just under the pink angel."

Nanda gratefully accepted this dismissal. Her desk was at the end of a long line, far away from the mistress' rostrum. Between the lines stood a statue of Our Lady, supported on each side by angels with folded wings and flying girdles. Nanda felt it was a privilege to be so near this holy company. Her desk was empty but for a small picture of the Sacred Heart gummed inside the lid and a square of black lace whose use she could not guess. She examined this, wondering if by chance it belonged to another child, but her number was neatly sewn on the hem in Cash's woven letters. She was still marvelling at this and at the exquisite *ronde* hand-writing on her name card, when far away in the depths of the building a bell began to clang.

She looked up to find Mildred, to whom she had already taken a mild dislike, at her elbow.

"Shut your desk," ordered Mildred. "Whenever a bell rings, you have to stop doing whatever you are doing. That's for supper. Get into the file, quick."

The other children had stopped talking and fallen into line. Mildred pushed her into a vacant place and pinched her to make her stand straight. Mother Frances, holding a small wooden object like a tiny book, eyed the ranks like a bored but efficient officer. The little wooden book snapped with a loud click and the file moved forward. Down the flights of stone stairs, passing files of older children, the Junior School moved like a compact regiment. In the refectory the regiment was broken up. One or two members were allotted to each table and the complement was made up of bigger girls. Each table had a "president" and a "sub-president" of responsible years, whose functions were to carve, to maintain order and to

see that the last scraps of abhorred fat were eaten up by
their juniors. The long ranks stretched from end to end
of the big refectory: a hundred and twenty children
stood behind their chairs waiting for the signal for grace.
Nanda absent-mindedly sat down, but rose again,
covered with shame, at a pinch from the horrified
Mildred. A tall girl at a centre table muttered: "Bless
us, O Lord, and these Thy gifts which we are about to
receive from Thy bountiful hands, through Christ our
Lord," and there was a loud "Amen" from the whole
school. A bell tinkled; the children drew out their chairs
with a noise like thunder and sat down. A few voices
rang out and were instantly hushed. At last came the
bell for "talking" and babel broke out. Nanda was too
bewildered to talk. She was taking in the large, long
room with its peacock blue walls, its raised platform and
reading desk and its various pictures. "I never thought
there were so many holy pictures in the world," she
thought to herself. Every room she had entered since
she had arrived at the Convent of the Five Wounds had
had its picture or statue. The refectory was especially
well provided. Right across one wall sprawled a huge
reproduction of Murillo's Assumption. Over the reading
desk hung a painting of the Holy Child, clad in white
and yellow (the Papal colours, as Nanda proudly remembered), standing on a sunlit hill. The Child stood with
outstretched arms which made a shadow behind Him
like a large, black cross, and in the background was an
apple-tree in full blossom with a serpent coiled round
its trunk.

Lastly, on a shelf above the dais was a statue of a
young man in a white pleated surplice, gazing at a
crucifix, whom Nanda took at first to be St. Aloysius
Gonzaga and later discovered to be St. Stanislaus Kostka.

Supper consisted of stewed meat and rice, cabbage drowned in vinegar, and sweet tea, already mixed with milk, poured from enormous white metal urns. Nanda did not feel hungry; the combination of foods sickened her, but the President of her table, the irreproachable Madeleine, was adamant. She would not even let her off the cabbage, though the sub-president, a pleasant Irish girl, pleaded for a little relaxation of discipline for a new child on her first night.

"You've got to learn to do things you don't like," Madeleine assured her. "You can't begin too quickly."

And she found time to outline to Nanda all the awful consequences, temporal and eternal, which might result from Nanda's allowing herself to become self-indulgent in the matter of food.

"If you give way to yourself in little things, you'll give way to yourself in big ones later on. Perhaps one day when you are grown up, you'll be faced with a really grave temptation . . . a temptation to *mortal* sin. If you've learnt to control yourself in small ways, you'll have got the habit of saying 'no' to the devil at once. The devil's a coward, you know. If you say 'no' the first time, he's often too frightened to try again."

But the more immediate consequence of Nanda's not eating her cabbage seemed to be that she might, if she were not careful, lose her "exemption."

"What is an exemption?" she asked, puzzled.

But no one took the trouble to enlighten her beyond saying: "You'll see on Saturday night."

The others had so many other and more interesting things to discuss that Nanda was content to listen fascinated to their chatter. But she realised dimly that there were such things as country houses and deer-parks and children who had ponies of their very own. She had read about such marvels in Stead's Books for the Bairns, of whose twopenny pink paper volumes she already possessed a considerable library. Now it seemed that she was actually sitting at the same table with the inhabitants of this dazzling world. Hilary, the pretty Irish sub-president, was talking of house-parties and the boredom of the summer when there was nothing to do but play tennis.

"And to think," she sighed, "that they'll be starting cubbing in a fortnight and I'll be in this wretched place."

Even Madeleine smiled sympathetically, although she remembered her moral mission a moment later and reminded her sub-president of "loyalty."

"Daddy's promised me a hunter next Christmas, if I get my blue ribbon next Immaculate Conception," went on Hilary, who was flat-shouldered and narrow-waisted, with a shapely little head. It was easy to imagine her in a riding habit, sitting that hunter to perfection.

"I wonder if you ever think of anything but horses," smiled Madeleine.

"They're the only things worth thinking about."

"Hilary!" said the scandalised Madeleine.

"Oh, I only meant they're more worth while than human beings," drawled Hilary. There was something about her voice and her air that reminded Nanda of Mother Frances.

"Hilary!" insisted Madeleine, scandalised still more.

But Hilary was already deep in a technical discussion with another expert. Nanda would have given anything to have been able to slip in one remark to show that she appreciated this glorious conversation. But, though she was good at guessing, she was too unsure of her ground, and she knew that this was a sacred subject where one blunder might betray one for ever as one of the uninitiated. So she listened, wide-eyed, wishing desperately that she were quite certain of the difference between a piebald and a skewbald, and wondering what colour a strawberry roan could possibly be. No one could trip Nanda up on the difference between Corinthian and Ionic columns. Mr. Grey had taught her to distinguish between these on her first visit, at the age of five, to the British Museum. How she wished that he had also or even instead, taught her to distinguish between a bay and a chestnut.

The kindly Hilary noticed Nanda's breathless attention.

"Fond of horses?"

"Oh, yes," whispered Nanda.

"I suppose you've got a pony, haven't you?"

"Well, n-not yet," she had the presence of mind to stammer. "Not a pony of my *own*. But there's an old white one that I'm sometimes allowed . . ."

"White . . . I suppose you mean grey?" said Hilary, and returned to the infallible Margaret.

Nanda was crushed. But she had to admit to herself that she deserved to be. It wasn't her fault that she didn't know that only Arabs and circus horses are called "white," but it served her right for dragging in that pony at all. For it was only a very old and fat and wheezy one that the rector sometimes lent Mr. Grey to mow his croquet lawn and which had never been saddled since it was foaled. Nanda often caught herself making slight exaggerations of this kind during the years she spent at Lippington. It was not snobbishness; it seldom even was the desire to show off; it was nearly always that agonising wish to be like everyone else, known only to children at boarding-schools, that made

her soften and enlarge the outlines of her home life.
When everyone else had butlers, it seemed ridiculous to
have a mere parlourmaid, and she got used to referring
with fine carelessness to "our butler." Also the cottage in
Sussex grew by imperceptible degrees to "our place in
the country," though she wisely alluded to this as
seldom as possible.

Madeleine let the hunting conversation have its head
for a few minutes before she turned it into more edifying channels. One of the duties of a president, as laid
down by the Foundress in the School Rule, is to prevent
the conversation from being too emphatic, too worldly,
or too much confined to certain members of the table.

"Of course, the winter holidays are very nice, with
Christmas and so on," she announced, "but there is
something very special about the long summer holidays.
They give us a chance of knowing our parents, giving
them pleasure by our company."

Nanda couldn't help wondering if Madeleine's parents
really did get very much pleasure from her society.
There was something in Madeleine's blamelessness
which reminded her of certain heroines she had read
about on Sunday afternoons in her Protestant days.

"And then there are some lovely feasts," Madeleine
went on. "The Feast of the Assumption first of all, of
course. We had such a beautiful day. Father Whitby
came over from Stonyhurst and celebrated mass in our
own little chapel. And my little sister Philomena made
her First Communion. She is only eight years old, but
Father Whitby said she was *quite* ready to receive Our
Lord." Madeleine kept Nanda well in the tail of her eye
during this speech to make sure that she was listening.
There was a murmur of admiration from the table.

"Eight, why she's quite a baby," said Hilary. "Some

of the Senior School haven't made theirs yet, though they're eleven and twelve."

"I believe the present Pope likes children to make their First Communion young," put in a girl who had not yet spoken. "I shouldn't be surprised if the age was lowered officially."

"Well perhaps His Holiness will send for you for a private audience to tell you when he does," said Madeleine with heavy humour. "It's not for us to guess what His Holiness will do and what he will not do," she added, reverting to her normal tone.

The bell rang for grace. Madeleine, while crossing herself with the utmost reverence and propriety, contrived to keep an eye on the deportment of her table.

Section by section, the children filed out, the Junior School last.

Mother Frances was waiting for them in the corridor.

"As it's the first night and you're tired," she said, "there'll be no evening recreation to-night. You'll say your prayers and go straight to bed."

There were a few protesting wails of "Oh, *Mother*," but a look from Mother Frances silenced them.

"Go upstairs quickly and quietly and fetch your veils," she commanded, "and then we'll go and say our night prayers in the Sacred Heart chapel."

Nanda was glad to discover the use of the square of black lace she had found in her desk. She followed the example of the others and draped it over her head. In another corner she found a pair of dark blue lisle gloves, and thus gloved and hooded, she filed with the others along the red-tiled corridor where she had walked with Mother Radcliffe, and through the nail-studded door outside which she had disgraced herself by making the sign of the cross with her left hand.

The children clustered together in the little ante-chapel of the Sacred Heart. Through an iron screen, they could see the red sanctuary lamps of the high altar. Behind the empty tabernacle with its mother-of-pearl door rose a huge white stone carving of Our Lord revealing His Sacred Heart to Blessed Margaret Mary Alacoque. Nanda liked this chapel; it was cool to the eye after the glare and heat of the peacock blue refectory. She liked, too, the faint scent of chrysanthemums and incense that drifted through the grille from the high altar, and the newly familiar smell of beeswax given out by the small, light-coloured benches.

"Marjorie will say prayers," Mother Frances said in a low voice. "I think we will whisper them to-night, in case Reverend Mother is in the big chapel."

The prayers sounded new and intimate recited like this in small, sibilant whispers. Nanda felt a wave of piety overwhelm her as she knelt very upright in her bench, her lisle-gloved hands clasped on the ledge in front of her. "Oh dear Lord," she said fervently in her mind, "thank you for letting me come here. I will try to like it if You will help me. Help me to be good and make me a proper Catholic like the others."

Marjorie was whispering the Litany of Loretto.

"*Turris Eburnea,*" she murmured.

"*Ora pro nobis,*" whispered twenty voices.

"*Turris Davidica.*"

"*Domus Aurea.*"

"*Foederis Arca.*"

"*Janua Cœli.*"

Nanda tried to put more and more of her heart into each "*Ora pro nobis.*" She was flooded with a feeling that was half passionate love of Our Lady and half delight in the beauty of the words, pronounced, not in her father's harsh English accent, but with an Italian softness.

In the last prayer the children whispered together, she could not yet join though it was soon to become as familiar as the Hail Mary itself.

"We fly to Thy protection, oh Holy Mother of God," began Marjorie, and the others took up: "Despise not our prayers in our necessities, but deliver us from all dangers, oh ever glorious and blessed Virgin."

Nanda would have liked to stay on indefinitely in the quiet chapel, but there came the businesslike click of Mother Frances' "signal." Already she was learning to obey. She rose briskly and, with a genuflection towards the high altar, followed the others out.

The Junior School slept in the Nazareth dormitory at the very top of the house, a flight further up than their school-room. Nanda whose knowledge of dormitories was derived from books, where they always looked terrifyingly naked and communal, was much relieved to find that each child had a tiny white-curtained cubicle to sleep in. When the curtains were drawn, there was just room for her to stand or kneel by her bed. Mildred showed her the use of the solitary chair which was there, not to be sat upon, but to hold her clothes during the night. The chair, with the clothes folded neatly and according to a definite prescription, was to be placed outside the cubicle. If she wanted a drink, she might place her glass on the chair too, and it would be filled with water by a child told off for this special duty. Stockings were ordinarily hung over the back of the chair, but Nanda found that it was a fashion among the more pious to spread them over the top of their clothes in the form of a cross.

The possession of looking-glasses was forbidden. Instead, each cubicle contained a white china picture of the Immaculate Conception and the Five Wounds and a small red flannel badge of the Sacred Heart. These, Nanda learnt, could be supplemented by private Holy Pictures or the photos of very near relatives.

"You undress inside," whispered Mildred, "but you put on your dressing-gown and come outside to do your hair."

By the time Nanda reappeared, hairbrush in hand, Mildred was already torturing her own lank, dark locks into a very business-like plait.

"Aren't you going to plait yours?" Mildred asked severely through a mouthful of tape.

Nanda's hair had never been plaited in her life, but she dared not admit it. Instead she answered weakly.

"I don't know how to."

"Baby," said Mildred scornfully. "I'll do it for you to-night. Turn round."

Nanda submitted while Mildred pulled her hair back and twisted it into an agonisingly tight rope. The efficient bony fingers tied it tighter still, until Nanda's eyes felt as if they would start from her head.

A bell rang.

"Get into bed quick," whispered Mildred, and Nanda thankfully obeyed.

Again the bell tinkled. There was a scrambling of children jumping into bed and much noisy pulling-to of curtains. Then a voice, not Mother Frances', but an old voice with a foreign accent, said:

"Precious Blood of Our Lord Jesus Christ," And twenty shrill voices answered from the cubicles: "Wash away my sins." Complete silence followed.

The gas was turned low. Nanda, huddled on her pillow, watched the huge bonnetted figure of a nun move across the ceiling. After a few minutes, the shadow came near her cubicle; then stopped and vanished. The curtains parted and a nun with black glasses came in. She held something towards Nanda.

"Well, my child?" said the nun, after a pause. She was still holding out the dim object towards Nanda.

"Are you perhaps a new child?" she inquired.

"Yes, mother," whispered Nanda.

"This is holy water, dear child."

Nanda stretched out two fingers, wetted them in the sponge of the little stoup and crossed herself.

"Now, lie down," said the nun kindly, "you were not, by any chance, crying when I came in?"

"No, mother," said Nanda decidedly.

"That is good. But you were lying in such a strange way. Did your mother never tell you at home to lie upon your back?"

"No, mother."

"But it is more becoming that you should."

Nanda straightened herself out from her comfortable ball, turned her back and thrust her feet bravely down into the cold sheets.

"So, it is better," said the nun gently, "and now the hands."

She took Nanda's hands and crossed them over her breast.

"Now, *ma petite*," she said, "if the dear Lord were to call you to Himself during the night, you would be ready to meet Him as a Catholic should. Good night, little one, and remember to let the holy Name of Jesus be the last word on your lips."

She passed silently out of the cubicle.

Nanda retained her new position rigidly for a few minutes.

"I shall never get to sleep," she thought miserably, as she heard the outdoor clock strike eight. But even as she thought it her lids grew heavy and her crossed hands began to uncurl. She had just time to remember to whisper "Jesus" before she was fast asleep.

CHAPTER II

NANDA found it very difficult to believe when, on the next Sunday afternoon, a lay-sister told her she was wanted in the parlour, that it was only five days since she had seen her parents. She felt so immeasurably older; so much unpicked and resewn and made over to a different pattern, that, as she trotted sedately behind the lay-sister, wearing her school uniform for the first time, she even wondered if her family would recognise her in all this new dignity. Her hair, which she had learnt to twist into the regulation plait, was drawn smoothly and tightly back from her forehead without a single straying curl, and crowned with a stiff, dark blue bow. Her pinafore was laid aside and she wore the ceremonial gloves without which no Lippington child was permitted to enter parlour or chapel.

The parlour, which lay in the older main part of the house, had begun life as an eighteenth-century ballroom, and still had a faintly secular air with its pale blue walls and velvet curtains. Sallow gilt mouldings of pipes and lutes adorned the pillars, and the parquet was polished to a most conscientious slipperiness. As Nanda entered, she caught sight of her father and mother sitting in a window seat at the far end. Her primness left her and she was on the point of skating recklessly over the waxed floor to fling herself upon them, when someone laid a restraining hand on her sleeve. It was the nun in charge of the parlour. At Lippington one did not meet even one's nearest relatives without *surveillance*.

"Gently, my child," whispered the nun. "There are others in the room. You must make a curtsey to them. And do not forget to curtsey to your parents before you embrace them. And it is also customary, a little formality only, to curtsey to the *surveillante* also." Nanda looked puzzled, but the nun added kindly: "Only when I am in the parlour. You don't have to curtsey if you meet me outside. Now, go to your dear parents."

The *surveillante's* name was Mother Pascoe. Like Mother Frances, she was easy to recognise, but for the very different reason that she limped always on a rubber-shod stick. She was one of the few nuns whom one could imagine transplanted into the outside world; she would look, Nanda thought, just like an ordinary aunt, with a pile of greying brown hair and perhaps a black velvet band round her neck. All the same, a sort of romance clung to Mother Pascoe. The frightened look in her pleasant, faded eyes had another source besides the almost constant pain she suffered from a broken ankle clumsily set by the community doctor. It was an open secret at Lippington that Mother Pascoe had seen a ghost. Sometimes, on very special feast days, she would tell some of the privileged older children the whole story, versions of which filtered through to the horrified and delighted ears of the Junior School.

Mr. Grey stood up to greet Nanda, but her mother quite spoilt her careful curtsey by pouncing on her and kissing her.

At the same time, Mrs. Grey said quite loudly: "But, darling, what have they done to your lovely hair?"

"Oh, Mother, *please*," muttered Nanda; "someone might hear you."

Indeed, the military-looking father of the red-haired Joyce was actually smiling in their direction.

"But it looked so pretty the way I used to do it for you," pursued Mrs. Grey in the same ringing and un-self-conscious voice. Nanda felt herself turn scarlet. This time Joyce was staring too. Nanda had been long enough at Lippington to know that personal vanity was the most contemptible of all the sins. Suppose, by some awful chance, Joyce should say to Marjorie Appleyard, whose cousin she was, that Nanda Grey thought herself good-looking?

"Shall we go in the garden?" gasped Nanda, drowning in seas of shame. Mercifully, Mrs. Grey had already thought how pretty the garden looked from the windows and Nanda steered her parents out of doors without any further disasters. The three of them paced up and down on the terrace which on Sundays and Thursdays was barricaded at either end by a notice saying "Visitors are not allowed beyond this board." Nanda had some difficulty in restraining her mother from darting away down various forbidden alleys, but, helped by her father, she kept her in fairly good order.

"I *never* saw a place with so many rules and regulations," wailed Mrs. Grey. "I'm sure we waited at *least* half an hour for you, darling child, didn't we, John?"

"Several minutes, certainly," said Mr. Grey, "but I expect Nanda was a long way away."

"Yes," said Nanda spotlessly, "and I had to do my hair and put on my gloves." She felt remote and self-possessed.

"Quite right," approved Mr. Grey. "I like all these little formalities and traditions. I was so glad to see you make that nice curtsey when you came in, Nanda. I felt quite like a French aristocrat coming to see his beautiful young daughter."

He gave her his rather rare smile and Nanda began to thaw into a human being. She was very fond of her father.

"Those dreadful gloves," wailed Mrs. Grey. "They make you look as if you bit your nails or something. And you've got the sweetest little hands. Just like mine at your age."

"The ones that bite their nails have to wear *white* gloves," said Nanda haughtily, "and Mildred has to wear black *bags* on her hands sometimes. She pinches, you see."

"That nice nun . . . Mother Pascoe, isn't it? . . . tells me you've made quite a good beginning with your work and so on. I'm very pleased," declared her father.

"I didn't lose my exemption," said Nanda. "But then, they say hardly anybody does the first week unless they do something really awful."

"Exemption?" asked her mother. "Exemption from what, darling?"

"Not from anything," explained Nanda patiently. "That's its name, you know. We have Exemptions on Saturday nights in here, and the whole school sits round and Reverend Mother is here and some of the school nuns. And they read out the names of the whole school two by two, and if you haven't lost your exemption . . ."

"Exemption from what?" said Mrs. Grey helplessly.

But Nanda swept her aside. "You get a little pale blue card with 'Very Good' on it. And if you've got one or two bad marks, say for talking or being late, you get a dark blue card with 'Good' on it. And if you've been very naughty, you get a yellow one with 'Indifferent,' and Reverend Mother doesn't smile at you. But if you've been really awful and done something serious, you get a sort of dirty green one marked 'Bad.' They're very rare of course. And Reverend Mother doesn't even hand it you; she just puts it on the table and you have to pick it up. And if anyone's done anything really frightful they don't get a card at all, but Mother Radcliffe just reads out, 'So and so . . . *No Note*,' and they say the person always cries. Of course, people are often expelled after they've had 'No Note.' "

"Now, that's very interesting," said Mr. Grey. "I like all this order and method. I shall be very pleased if you never get anything worse than 'Good,' Nanda."

But Mrs. Grey, bored, was poking her umbrella into a flower-bed.

"I think it's very untidy and unmethodical to call them exemptions," she persisted. "Exemption means something quite different."

"I'm sorry, Mummy," said Nanda politely, "but Reverend Mother is awfully particular about those beds."

"The nuns have lovely flowers here," said Mrs. Grey romantically. "I suppose they feel they must have *some* light and colour in their lives." She went on poking the bed.

"We've got a Scotch gardener," Nanda told her father. "His name's MacAlister. Mother Frances says he gets up in the middle of the night to curl the petals of the chrysanthemums."

The school bell began to ring.

"I must go," sang out Nanda, with a kind of relief. "That's for Benediction."

"Good gracious, I nearly forgot this," said Mr. Grey, fumbling in the pocket of his overcoat and producing a parcel. "I met Mrs. Appleyard the other day, and she happened to say that it was Marjorie's birthday next week. So I thought perhaps it would be nice for you to give her a present."

"Thank you, Daddy. Yes, I'd like to," said Nanda, though she had certain misgivings.

The present turned out to be a rather nicely illustrated edition of *Dream Days,* a book which Nanda had not read. The pictures of castles and dragons looked exciting; she wondered whether she could somehow manage to skim through it herself before handing it on to Marjorie, who wouldn't, she was pretty sure, think much of it.

"It looks a lovely book," she said rather sadly.

"I'll give you one in your Christmas stocking if you like," Mr. Grey promised.

"You *are* a dear, Daddy," Nanda muttered, fervently kissing him good-bye. "I must simply fly or I'll be late. Good-bye, Mummy."

The others were already lined up by the time she arrived breathlessly in the Junior schoolroom; there was only just time to slip *Dream Days* into her desk and snatch up her veil before Mother Frances gave the signal to advance.

After Benediction on Sundays, the Junior School were allowed to read for an hour before supper. Their library consisted of three shelves of Lives of the Saints and Letters from Missionaries of the early nineteenth century. In a small locked case there were some more frivolous works, including several volumes of Andrew Lang's fairy tales, some Little Folks annuals, *Alice in Wonderland*, and the works of Edward Lear. But these were story-books, only doled out for an hour or two on the major holidays that occurred two or three times a term. Nanda's own choice for the week, not entirely a free one, since Mildred was the librarian, was a small red *Lives of the English Martyrs*. Being a very quick reader, she came to the end of it while there was still half an hour of "free study" to be filled. She did not want to go over the martyrdoms again, having supped full enough of hangings and drawings and quarterings. In fact, the account of the pressing to death of the Blessed Margaret Clitheroe had nearly turned her sturdy stomach. The exciting green volume of *Dream Days* seemed to burn through her desk; she felt she *must* look at it or go mad. But on the other hand, it was quite obviously a story-book. Probably she had no right to have it in her possession at all; in any case, she ought to ask Mother Frances' permission before actually reading it. She temporised. At any rate, there could be no harm in writing Marjorie's name in it. She took the book out and wrote laboriously on the flyleaf: "Marjorie Apple-yard. With best wishes for her birthday. From Fernanda Grey." Her desk was conveniently far from Mother Frances' table, and Mother Frances herself seemed deeply absorbed in correcting exercise books.

Nanda had sternly meant to put *Dream Days* away at once. But somehow page after page slipped over, and before she knew it she was hopelessly enmeshed. She woke with a gasp as a thin, shapely hand blotted out the page in front of her.

"Very interesting, Nanda," said Mother Frances, smoothly. "Is this your library book?"

"No, Mother."

"It's a story-book, isn't it? Did your parents give it you in the parlour?"

"Yes. . . . I mean no, Mother."

"Be truthful, my good child. Which do you mean, yes or no?"

"Well, it was given me to give someone else."

"*Oh,* indeed," said Mother Frances very softly, opening her harebell eyes surprisingly wide. "Hasn't Mildred told you that we don't take things in the parlour either for ourselves or for other people?"

"Yes, I did, Mother," piped the odious Mildred, who had screwed round on her chair and was fairly goggling with curiosity. "I did, only Nanda was so excited she didn't listen."

"That was a pity, wasn't it, Nanda?" said Mother Frances, sweetly. "I'm afraid perhaps I'll have to take your exemption to remind you about that. And of course, I'll have to take the book as well." As she shut up *Dream Days* she saw the writing on the flyleaf. "Marjorie Appleyard," she mused. "Let's see . . . Marjorie's not *related* to you, is she, Nanda?"

"No, Mother," said Nanda, a little sullenly.

"Just remember, will you, that at Lippington we do not give presents, even birthday presents, except to relatives. We do not encourage particular friendships among little girls."

Nanda was conscious of a hot sense of injustice as Mother Frances moved gracefully away with the offending book under her arm. Her eyes pricked, and she felt horribly homesick. To stop herself from crying, she tried to concentrate once more on the sufferings of Blessed Margaret. "As she lay on the scaffold," she read stubbornly, "with a smile of heavenly patience on her face, the executioners lowered an heavy oaken door on to her prostrate form. On this door they piled a mass of great weights, and, to cause her still more exquisite torment, they" . . . but the rest of the passage was obscured by a fog of tears.

Two days later, Mother Frances called Nanda up to her table. In front of her lay the wretched copy of *Dream Days*.

"Look, Nanda," she said amiably, "I have managed to take Marjorie's name out quite well." The flyleaf, indeed, showed only the faintest ghost of yellow letters. "But I just wanted to say this to you. You are a new child and a convert, and you have not quite got into our ways yet. It is not for me to criticise what your father considers suitable reading matter for you . . . in the holidays, that is. This book will remain in your trunk till you go home for Christmas. But I think that you ought to know that the *tone* of this book is not at all the kind of thing we like at Lippington. Apart from its being by a non-Catholic writer, it is morbid, rather unwholesome and just a *little* vulgar." Mother Frances gave her a chilling smile. "That is all, dear child." Nanda turned to fly. Her ears were red-hot.

"Oh, Nanda," said the musical voice.

"Yes, Mother?"

"I think your stocking's coming down. The left one."

The Junior School day was modelled on the same ritual pattern as that of the Senior School and the community itself. As soon as the Rising Bell had clanged through the cold dormitory, each child publicly dedicated the day to the service of God, in the words: "O Jesus, wounded on the cross for me, help me to become crucified to self for love of Thee." A basin of hot water was allowed, but it was considered more mortified and hence more in the spirit of the Order, to wash in cold. Nanda's zeal went as far as denying herself the warm water, but as the days drew on towards December, her neck was apt to look rather grey against the whiteness of her painfully starched collar. She learnt the elaborate technique of dressing according to Christian modesty so that at no time, even in the privacy of her cubicle, was she ever entirely naked. The whole day was punctuated by prayers. Besides the morning and evening devotions and the thrice-recurring Angelus, every lesson began with an invocation to the Holy Ghost and ended with a recommendation to Our Lady. Before supper, the whole school assembled to recite five decades of the rosary, and there was usually a novena in preparation for an important feast or a special intention to add some extra petitions to the list. The day ended with prayers in the chapel, and an elaborate examination of conscience under the heading of sins against God, against one's neighbour and against oneself. The offence to which Nanda had to own herself guilty night after night was that of "wasting time in idle day dreaming." On Saturdays every child in the school went to confession and, in the evening, after "Exemptions," there were special devotions in the vestibule of Our Lady of Good Success. Here stood a silver-crowned statue of Our Lady, a replica of the one which had miraculously arrived at Aberdeen in a stone boat without sail or rudder, which was honoured as the special help of students. There were always little red lamps burning before it on behalf of brothers with imminent exams. On Sundays all the children heard two masses and a sermon in the morning and went to Benediction in the afternoon.

As a result of all this, Nanda developed a nice sense of piety. She really did begin to live all day long in the presence of the court of heaven. God the Father and God the Holy Ghost remained awe-inspiring conceptions, Presences who could only be addressed in set words and with one's mind, as it were, properly gloved and veiled. But to Our Lady and the Holy Child and the saints she spoke as naturally as to her friends. She learnt to smooth a place on her pillow for her Guardian Angel to sit during the night, to promise St. Anthony a creed or some pennies for his poor in return for finding her lost property, to jump out of bed at the first beat of the bell to help the Holy Souls in purgatory. She learnt, too, to recognise all round her the signs of heaven on earth. The donkey in the paddock reminded her that all donkeys have crosses on their backs since the day Our Lord rode into Jerusalem; the robin's breast was red because one of his ancestors had splashed his feathers with the Precious Blood trying to peck away the crown of thorns. The clover and the shamrock were a symbol of the Blessed Trinity, the sunflower was a saint turning always towards God, the speedwell had been white till Our Lady's blue mantle brushed it as she walked in the fields of Nazareth. When Nanda heard a cock crow, it cried: *"Christus natus est"*; the cows lowed *"Ubi? Ubi?"* and the lambs down at the community farm bleated "Be-e-thlehem."

Among her most revered possessions was a small white bean whose brown markings, to a seeing eye, showed the rough shape of a monstrance. This had been given her by Mother Radcliffe as a reward for good conduct. It was a bean with history. During the clerical persecutions in France, a parish priest, fearing for the safety of the sacred vessels, had buried them in a bean field. But when the danger had passed and he went to dig them up again, he could not remember in which of many fields he had hidden them. When the crop was gathered in, a certain field produced beans with a curious brown mark, just like a monstrance. The field was searched and all the holy vessels discovered intact.

The great repository of stories and guardian of pious traditions was old Mother Poitier, the French nun who taught Nanda how to go to sleep like a Christian. Nanda looked forward every day to the afternoon recreation, when, instead of playing organised games under the merciless eye of Mother Frances, the Junior School trotted up and down the long alley under the plane-trees, munching bread and jam and listening to Mother Poitier. Black-spectacled and comfortably shawled and goloshed, with her fingers always occupied with some grey, un-specified knitting, the gentle old nun always reminded Nanda of the sheep in *Through the Looking-glass*. Mother Poitier must have known as many stories as Scheherezade herself. There were stories of saints and angels and animals, of good children who died on the day of their First Communion, of Jews who stole the Blessed Sacrament, of atheists who were converted on their death-beds, and, most often and most impressively told of all, stories of Blessed Mother Guillemin, the foundress of the Order of the Five Wounds.

But this agreeable recreation only lasted twenty minutes. The serious playtime at midday was an hour of unmitigated penance to Nanda. She was extremely bad at games, partly from natural clumsiness, partly because Mr. Grey had a scholarly hatred of any amuse-ment which involved running about and making a noise. The daily baseball showed her up as a short-winded runner and a butter-fingered catch. Mother Frances, who caught and shied like a boy, was fond of sending her up swift, impossible balls for the fun of seeing her wince and paw the air wildly with her woolly gloves.

"*Poor* Nanda," Mother Frances would mock. "She's

afraid of spoiling her looks. What *would* her father say if we sent her home with a dear little Roman nose?"

And Marjorie Appleyard, who played sturdily and reliably, would titter politely. Even the despicable Mildred shone at baseball; her black, spidery legs fairly twinkled from base to base. The wretched Nanda would long passionately to bring off just one sensational catch, or even to be really badly hurt so as to have a chance of being brave about it, but the next ball would invariably find her fast asleep and up would fly her treacherous hands before she had time to stop them.

After the first intolerably slow one, the weeks ran quickly. Nanda found that being good was surprisingly easy; there seemed so little time to be anything else. Before she realised it, she had won the pale blue card of "Very Good" seven weeks running. One more would bring her a pink ribbon like Marjorie Appleyard's. She was a little excited; a pink ribbon was an enviable possession, with special privileges attached to it. Moreover, her father would be delighted if she secured it. So she began her eighth week in a spirit of the most rigid virtue.

It seemed to Nanda that Mother Frances was keeping a particularly vigilant eye on her. Evidently, she was waiting for a chance to pounce on some lapse and take Nanda's exemption. But she was determined to defy Mother Frances. Whenever she felt her mistress' sarcastic gaze on her, she behaved more exasperatingly well than ever. On Friday morning, when there was only one more day to hold out, Mother Frances called her to her desk.

"How many very goods have you had, Nanda?"

"Seven, Mother Frances."

Mother Frances considered her, with her head on one

side. Lately, she had had a very bad cough and the bright flush it had brought to her cheeks gave her an unnatural, painted look. Her eyes shone bright as glass, and the hand she put over Nanda's was dry and hot.

"And so I suppose you think you're a model little girl?"

Nanda did not answer.

"There's goodness *and* goodness, you know. I've known children who were the despair of everyone turn into real saints later on . . . all the more real because they'd had difficult natures to fight with. Look at the Saints themselves. Most of them were very far from being just bread-and-butter good when they were young. Think of St. Ignatius and St. Augustine and St. Mary Magdalen . . . they were sinners before they were saints. The trouble with you, my dear, is that you don't seem to have any normal healthy, natural naughtiness about you. God doesn't care about namby-pamby goodness, you know; he wants the real hard goodness that comes from conquering real hard faults. I don't mean that you haven't got faults. The trouble about your faults is that they don't show. You're obstinate, you're independent, and if a child of nine can be said to have spiritual pride, spiritual pride is your ruling vice. One of these days, if you're not careful, you'll be setting up your own con-conceited little judgment against the wisdom of the Church, which is the wisdom of God himself."

A few weeks ago, Nanda would have wept at such criticism, but to her own surprise, she found she was growing a hard little protective shell. She merely bit her lip and stared at Mother Frances.

Mother Frances smiled:

"Well, I suppose I can't take your exemption for

spiritual pride," she admitted, "only don't mistake a pink ribbon for a halo, that's all."

In spite of her outward calm, Nanda was in a tumult. Mother Frances' speech had pierced the protective shell after all. She hadn't, until the last week, even made any special effort to be good; she had merely tried to avoid being conspicuously naughty. Her father had always demanded a high standard of quietness and obedience, and these virtues had become second nature to her. But now she was faced with the horrid thought that perhaps she was one of those spineless and spiritless creatures who are incapable of anything but a sort of negative primness. After all, she had never actually proved to herself that she wasn't. She remembered her pitiful displays on the baseball field. Obviously, she must be a physical coward. Probably she was something still more contemptible . . . a moral one. She must find out as quickly as possible. The pink ribbon waved before her eyes, but she sternly blinked away its inviting image. "The very next lesson," she vowed, "I'll do something *really* bad."

Her chance came. The next lesson was history, and Friday was the day for the weekly history examination. Nanda was a favourite of mild, pink-faced Mother Patterson, who took the history class, and she usually got the highest marks in the test. According to her usual custom, Mother Patterson gave Nanda a written slip with the questions and told her to copy them on to the blackboard. Very neatly and carefully, knowing that there was no copy, she tore up the written slip. Her apprehension had gone; a high, cold excitement kept her up as, slowly and deliberately, she wiped every single question off the blackboard. There was a gasp of dismay from the history class, but as Nanda examined the row of faces, she saw something new and intoxicating written on them. She went through the day on a wave of exultation. Even the yellow card marked "Indifferent" handed her so coldly by Reverend Mother the following night and the ruined hopes of her pink ribbon could not entirely damp her sense of triumph. Her tears during the hymn to Our Lady of Good Success afterwards were quite perfunctory, the merest tribute to society. Through her fingers she could see some of the Senior School looking at her with interest. At supper, the admired Hilary talked to her quite a lot, and even let her off her cabbage.

For the first time in her life, Nanda was a success.

Towards the end of November, Nanda noticed in the chapel an elegant young lady of twenty or so, who knelt by herself at a prie-dieu at the head of the nuns' stalls. She was a source of great distraction to Nanda, for she was very pretty, with a mass of golden curls piled on the top of her small head. Her hair seemed to shine the brighter for the wisp of black net she wore as a veil and her soft dresses fitted her slim shape as Nanda had never seen dresses fit before. At night she sometimes appeared in the school corridor wearing silver shoes and a pearl necklace and a frock cut a little low round the neck. Once Nanda saw her talking to Hilary O'Byrne and plucked up the courage to ask Hilary who the lovely stranger could be.

"Oh, that's my cousin, Moira Palliser," said Hilary carelessly. "She was here two years ago. She's going to enter."

"What, become a nun?" exclaimed Nanda, aghast.

"Yes, if they'll have her," laughed Hilary. "She's been trying on and off since she left."

"You see, the Order has to be very careful," explained

Madeleine heavily. "They have to be very sure that she has a true vocation. You see, her father is an earl, and she will be a countess in her own right when he dies, and all the property will come to her. If she were to enter here, the estates would pass to the Order, and it would be a great responsibility for them. Moira Palliser has some very worldly relations—Protestants—who would like to make a scandal to prove that the Five Wounds are trying to force Moira to enter in order to get the money. Whereas, of course, it is just the other way round."

A few days later the whole school were asked to make a novena for a special intention. Nanda guessed that the intention had something to do with Moira Palliser. Soon after the novena ended, Reverend Mother told the children at Exemptions that their prayers had been answered. On the following Monday Lady Moira appeared in the chapel shorn of her soft silk frocks and wearing the hideous flannel blouse and serge skirt of a postulant. But her hair still shone through her veil in the same mass of beautifully rolled little curls. Nanda caught sight of her face; it looked gay, almost mischievous.

About a month afterwards came the ceremony of clothing. As the children filed into the chapel, the organ was playing soft, vaguely bridal music. The altar was ablaze with candles and so loaded with lilies that the air sickened with them. Two prie-dieu were set out on a red carpet in front of the altar gates, and these also were gay with candles and flowers. In the strangers' benches sat four or five very well-dressed people and a stout person in a tartan silk frock who wore a woollen shawl crossed over her chest, and an odd little cap of black net. This person alternately held a handkerchief to her eyes and recited her rosary in French in a very audible whisper.

Only two postulants were to make their first vows that day: Moira Palliser and her Breton maid. There was a flutter of excitement as they came up the aisle. Lady Moira looked pale and collected; she communicated a spiritual radiance to her secular white satin and pearls. Behind her walked the short figure of the red-cheeked, black-eyed Breton girl, encased in stiff muslin that stood out all round her in a huge bell. A little fichu of white silk came down to a point between her shoulders, and instead of a veil she wore a starched lace head-dress.

The sermon was preached by a lean and soldierly young Jesuit, who fidgeted all the time with the red marker of his missal.

He began, without preliminaries:

"St. Theresa said one day to her nuns: 'Sisters, let us go mad for the love of God.' That seems to us, perhaps, a Spanish exaggeration . . . something, in any case, more appropriate to the sixteenth century than the twentieth. And yet, we are here this morning to watch a young woman, who has everything a worldly person could desire, make a renunciation that must seem to nearly all her friends an act of sheer folly. Think of the good people at this moment playing golf at the club next door. You can imagine them saying to each other: 'Either the poor girl is hysterical, or, depend upon it, she has been entrapped by those wily Roman Catholics. No doubt, the Jesuits are at the bottom of it.' And they will shake their heads intelligently as they drive off from the tee. The trouble is, they don't go far enough. They should have taken the next step and said: 'Lady Moira Palliser is mad. Mad for the love of God.'"

By the end of the sermon, Nanda wanted to stuff her fingers in her ears. Yet Father Parry was only voicing the whole spirit of Lippington when he said that a voca-

tion was to be more ardently desired and more warmly
accepted than anything in the world. A secular life,
however pious, however happy, was only the wretched
crust with which Catholics who were not called to the
grace of religious life must nourish themselves as best
they could. A vocation followed was the supreme good;
a vocation rejected the supreme horror. Father Parry
spoke of people who led apparently beautiful lives, yet
who were devoured by the cancer of a rejected vocation
which made them loathsome in the sight of heaven. He
emphasised the extreme delicacy of the call . . . it was
the merest whisper easily drowned in the noises of the
world. It might come quite suddenly at a dance or in
the middle of a game of tennis. It might be a gradually
growing conviction, beginning in very early childhood.
To human thought it might seem capricious; often it
was withheld in spite of years of prayer, for the spirit of
God blew where it listed and often hovered over the
most unlikely people. But once the call had sounded, it
must be immediately and implicitly obeyed in the heart,
even though the actual dedication might not take place
till years later. Very seldom did it sound twice; God did
not force His lovers. But it was easier for a pagan
steeped in sin to enter heaven than for a practising
Catholic who had stopped his ears to Christ's secret
invitation.

Nanda could not decide which alternative was the
more frightening, the thought of being in danger of hell
or the prospect of having to be a nun. For she had an
uncomfortable feeling that perhaps she had a vocation.
She knew from Mother Poitier that the summons was
not always accompanied by a holy joy on the part of the
summoned. There were nuns who had fainted with fear
and horror when their vocation had been revealed to

them. Sometimes she found herself bargaining with God, saying: "I'll do *anything* else for You. I'll never marry, I'll be poor, I'll go and nurse lepers. Only let me live in the world and be *free*." But the chilly voice inside always answered: "The only thing that God wants is the thing you are afraid to offer."

She listened with painful attention as Lady Moira made her vows of poverty, chastity and obedience, and shuddered when Reverend Mother led her out of the chapel with the novice's thick, white veil flung over her orange blossom and tulle.

As the chapel door closed behind her, the nuns intoned a heavily stressed, unaccompanied psalm that beat on the nerves.

"*Sicut sagitta in mánu poténtis*," sang one side of the choir, and the other answered:

"*Ita fília excussórum*."

Mildred nudged Nanda's elbow.

"They're cutting her hair 'now," she whispered ghoulishly.

CHAPTER III

MOTHER POITIER was very old. As a child she had been at school at the first house of the Order at Vienne and had received her blue ribbon from Blessed Mother Guillemin herself. It was she who guarded the traditions of the saint in the young English house of Lippington, and who told Junior School after Junior School the story of Blessed Marie-Joseph's life. When one of the novices was set to painting a picture for the chapel in honour of Mother Guillemin's beatification, it was Mother Poitier who stood by the easel and jealously watched every stroke of the brush.

"You are making our Mother's habit too smart, sister," she would say. "Have you forgotten that she always wore an old habit out of humility?"

Or again: "You are making her hands too white. She was not a fine lady, but a peasant who worked in her father's fields before she worked in our Blessed Lord's vineyard. Our holy habit itself is only a copy of an old Burgundian peasant's dress."

Nanda found the official life of Mother Guillemin very dull indeed. It was printed in almost illegible type and illustrated with small, scratchy engravings of Five Wounds convents in different parts of the world. And, being written by a priest, it was full of long advisory letters from Mother Guillemin's confessor and literal transcriptions of papal encyclicals. In a fit of piety, she had prayed to win the two huge crimson volumes in a raffle in aid of the Society for the Propagation of the Faith, but by the time she had struggled through the first chapter, she wished she had prayed for the phonograph instead. It was so much more amusing to hear about Mother Guillemin from Mother Poitier, walking up and down the dusty alley under the plane-trees and munching thick slices of bread thinly spread with rhubarb jam.

"Our Holy Mother was so devout," Mother Poitier would say, beaming at the twenty attentive faces in their red woollen hoods, "that she would go into an ecstasy at her meditations. And one day I remember . . . it was very wicked of us, but we were young and naughty and only in the Junior School, as you are . . . we crept up behind her in her stall and scattered little pieces of

paper all over her habit. And when we came back, two
hours later, not a piece of paper had shifted. You can
think how very much ashamed we were of our own distractions at our prayers."

Another time it would be: "Our Mother was very ill
towards the end of her life, and hardly able to eat anything. The kitchen sister was always sending her little
special dishes to tempt her appetite, but the food would
come back almost untasted. But one day when she had
sent her in a little omelette, her plate came back empty.
Every scrap had been eaten. The sister was delighted.
The next day she sent her in a bigger omelette. Again
every scrap was eaten. The whole community was happy.
The third day she added a little bacon. Again the same
thing happened. But on the fourth day one of the
novices went into Mother Guillemin's room while she
was having her breakfast, and forgot to knock on the
door. What do you think she found? There was Mother
Guillemin sitting by an open window and talking to a
very dirty little boy from the village. And on the
window-sill was her breakfast tray and the little boy was
eating Mother Guillemin's omelette and her bacon and
her bread just as fast as he could. That was the secret of
our saint's wonderful new appetite. Mother Guillemin
was so spiritual and so mortified that it was as if her
body were glorified already and she would often eat
nothing all day but the wafer at Holy Communion,
although she worked harder than any man of affairs. She
had the greatest devotion to the Blessed Sacrament, and
she used often to say to us in the words of another
saint: 'So great is the virtue of this Sacrament that not
only the soul but the frail body also receiveth from it a
great increase of strength.'"

Off the parlour that had once been a ballroom lay a

circular vestibule that had been turned into a Lady chapel. Mass was only said there three or four times a year on special feasts, and the tabernacle was empty. The children used it for saying their rosary and for the special devotions to the patron saints of health, St. Philomena and St. Roch, which took place once a month. It was a gay little room, a little drawing-room with blue velvet curtains in the bow windows, that caught all the afternoon sunlight from the terrace outside. St. Roch and his plague-spot looked out of place beside the prim and dainty St. Philomena with her silver anchor and Our Lady with her distaff and work-basket. This picture of Our Lady was one for which all children of the Five Wounds had a very particular affection. The original had been painted by a novice of the Order in Rome and specially blessed by the Pope. It showed the Blessed Virgin as a girl of fourteen or so, sitting in a courtyard at her work. Instead of the conventional blue robes, she wore a bright pink dress with a laced bodice and a white hood which showed her hair done in neat Victorian ringlets.

Every new child at Lippington was told the story of *Mater Admirabilis*. It was from Mother Poitier, naturally, that Nanda heard it. She was walking with the others one November afternoon, up and down the terrace, and finding some difficulty in skipping backwards in front of Mother Poitier. Nuns are like royalty and one must never deliberately turn one's back to them.

"About the middle of last century," Mother Poitier began, "His Holiness wished to do Our Lady a special honour. Louise, you are not to give your *goûter* to the sparrows."

"But St. Catherine of Siena gave her dinner to the little cats," objected Louise.

"That may be. But you, my child, are not St. Catherine
of Siena. His Holiness, as I say, decided to add another
title to Our Lady's litany."

"May I say what it was, Mother?" asked Marjorie
Appleyard. Her china face was clear as a shell in the red
worsted hood.

"Well, child?"

"*Mater Admirabilis*," gasped Marjorie, just ahead of
half a dozen others.

"Yes, *Mater Admirabilis*. Well, our Holy Mother who
was in our house at Rome at the time, called her community together and asked, if they were to paint a
picture of Our Lady under this new title, how they
should show her. And one nun thought she should be
painted on her heavenly throne and another in her home
in Nazareth and another at the foot of the cross, and so
on. At last, Mother Guillemin asked a new, a very shy
novice, who had just arrived from Ireland. Who was
that novice, Josephine?"

"Mother O'Byrne, Mother."

"Yes, a great-aunt of Hilary O'Byrne in the Senior
School."

Nanda could not help hopping on one leg and crying:
"I know Hilary O'Byrne, Mother. I'm at Hilary's table,
Mother." And was promptly shamed by Mildred's con-
temptuous squeak: "Well, so does everybody know
Hilary O'Byrne. Snub to you."

But Mildred was silenced too, for Mother Poitier
turned her black spectacles, positively flashing with
reproof, on her.

"That is no way for an old child to speak to a new.
How often have I told you that a child of Five Wounds
is known by her courtesy? No more interruptions, children, or the bell will ring before I have finished. Now,

Mother O'Byrne was afraid to speak at first, for she was so young and could speak very little French. But at last she said that she thought of *Mater Admirabilis* as a young girl, still of school age, a little shy, but recollected and happy with her books and her needlework. And Mother Guillemin said: 'That is how I see her, too. Could you paint us such a picture?' And Mother O'Byrne was very much confused, for she had only painted little pictures of her horses and her dogs and the country round her home in Ireland, but she was bound by her obedience, and she said that, by the grace of God, she would do her best. So she began to paint her *Mater Admirabilis* on the walls of the children's study-room (it was during the long summer holiday) and the community was always coming in to see how the work was getting on. She was painting *in tempera*, and the older nuns began to laugh at her work, because the colours looked so much too crude and bright. And some of them went to our Holy Mother and said, quite scandalised: 'Sister O'Byrne is painting such a very strange picture of Our Lady. Why, she has even given her a pink dress instead of a blue one.' But Mother Guillemin only smiled and she forbade anyone to criticise the picture or even to look at it till it was finished. But she asked Mother O'Byrne in private about the pink dress, and the novice told her, very humbly, that her last new dress in the world had been just such a pink one, with a bodice laced with black, and that she had been immoderately fond of it, and had even had thoughts of it after she had entered and that she hoped, by making a present of it to Our Lady, as it were, to rid herself of such sinful temptations to vanity. At last, the day came when the picture was to be shown to the community. Poor Mother O'Byrne was very unhappy, because, though she had painted it a dozen times, she could not make the expression on Our Lady's face just what she wanted. But because of her humility and her vow of obedience, she would not ask for any more time to work on it. So she waited while Mother Guillemin drew the curtain, expecting to be shamed before all the nuns. And then . . ."

Mother Poitier turned her black glasses from face to face, smiling happily and expectantly.

"And then, as the curtain dropped, the whole community fell on their knees. For on Our Lady's face there was the most beautiful, the most heavenly look. And Mother O'Byrne said to Mother Guillemin: 'I did not paint it so. . . . I could not paint it so.' But Mother Guillemin blessed her and said: 'My child, I think Our Lady finished her picture herself.'"

There were sighs of satisfaction. The old ones smiled proudly at the new ones.

"There's a copy in every convent of the Five Wounds, isn't there?" asked Monica. Monica, bright-eyed and rough-haired, was the Junior School dunce. Though she was twelve, she still could not master enough of the catechism to qualify her for making her First Communion. Every time she did a paper on Christian Doctrine, she fell into the most dreadful heresies.

"My poor Monica," Mother Frances had said to her only last Saturday, "do you know you have fallen into the errors of the Jansenists, the Manicheans and the Albigenses all in the space of one hundred and fifty words?"

And Monica had, very naturally, burst into tears. She had only one talent, a great aptitude for drawing dogs. She could not draw anything else, but she really did draw dogs very well. Nanda thought it must be because

she looked so like a Scotch terrier herself, looking up
with bright, puzzled eyes through her mane of brown
hair.

"But they can never quite get Our Lady's expression
in the copies, can they?" insisted Marjorie.

"No," smiled the nun, "Our Lady might paint her
own portrait for her own friends, but she is much too
modest to have her photograph taken."

There was a chatter of dismay as a tall figure ran past,
a blue ribbon flying wildly behind her.

"That's Adela going to ring the bell," said Marjorie,
who never ignored the obvious. "She's late."

Hurrying to scramble into her place in the file, Nanda
dropped her bread and jam. She had been too much
excited by the story to remember to eat it. Mother
Poitier stooped and picked it up; then, extracting a rusty
penknife from her immense pocket, she carefully removed any actual pebbles from the bread and jam and
held it up with an inviting smile. The slice still looked
very dirty.

"Now, here is a nice little penance for someone," cried
Mother Poitier gaily. "Who would like to eat this nice
bread and jam? In the siege of Paris our Holy Mother
and her nuns ate bread even the rats would not touch.
Louise, you were wanting to imitate the saints a little
while ago. Here is your chance, dear."

Louise bit her red lip. She was the one, slim and dark
as an Indian, whom Nanda had noticed on the first
night. Then, with a shake of her plait that made the
tiny gold rings in her ears dance, she held out her hand
for the dirty bread. Her nose crinkled with disgust as she
swallowed, but she said nothing.

Mother Guillemin had laid down in the school rule
that, during their first years, the children were to be

gently coaxed into good and pious habits by a system of small rewards. She said quite frankly in the Letter to Superiors, which was read aloud at the beginning of every term, that if small children came to associate what was morally good with what was physically pleasant, the good habits would become fixed and remain in after years, when the sweets and extra bits of amusement were no longer forthcoming. The rewards varied from pink ribbons and silver crosses to trifles as small as a sweet wrapped in bright paper. But the ones most worth gaining were known as "Permissions." There were permissions of every sort and kind. Permission to go down to the farm and get in the eggs, to help in the bakehouse, to have talking in the refectory during lunch, to visit the printing loft, to go to the community mass at six o'clock, to have a story-book on a week-day. The permissions were written in an exquisite round hand on cream paper, twisted into a tiny scroll and tied with pink silk. Nanda was very much shocked when, at the fair on the Feast of the Immaculate Conception, she found a stall selling permissions at sixpence apiece.

The Feast of the Immaculate Conception in December was one of the great days of the year. Preparation for it began a fortnight beforehand, and included extra devotions to Our Lady, the learning of special songs and hymns by the whole school, and a Practice. Some particular virtue was chosen and had to be practised by the whole school. Nanda's first Practice was one of Courtesy. All the children were enrolled as Knights of the Blessed Virgin and given silver cardboard shields inscribed with the motto *Noblesse Oblige*. The Nuns and the blue ribbons were entitled to give good marks for outstanding examples of courtesy that they observed, and any case of really bad manners was punished by the loss of the

silver shield which could only be redeemed by heroic
acts of politeness. For a fortnight the air was tense with
courtesy. Nanda found her bitterest enemies kindly offering to tie her plait or button her pinafore. She was terribly embarrassed when the queenly Madeleine stooped
down and picked up a fork that she had dropped.
Madeleine wore stays that creaked and seemed to make
her condescension more fearfully regal than ever. There
was a heated debate as to whether Monica's idea of
giving the school cat the milk from her supper should
be praised as an act of courtesy to the cat or censured
as an act of discourtesy to her parents, who had provided
the milk. As the wretched Monica was known to prefer
cats to milk, the vote went against her. At the end of the
fortnight, on the eve of the feast, there was a solemn
offering to Reverend Mother of the fruits of the Practice. The name of each child, with the number of her
good and bad marks, was inscribed in an illuminated
book, copiously adorned with blue ribbons and silver
seals. The whole school assembled in the big hall, wearing their best white uniforms and proudly holding their
silver shields. Those who had lost them huddled in a
miserable group at the back, wearing their every-day
blue and not allowed even to join in the singing. A little
stage had been put up at the back and the curtains were
pulled up three times to reveal tableaux of special acts
of courtesy in the lives of the saints. There was St.
Martin, with Hilary O'Byrne looking boyish and handsome in gilt paper armour, dividing his cloak with the
beggar. There was St. Wenceslas cutting the corn with
his own hand to make the bread for the Blessed Sacrament. And there was a troop of angels preparing supper
for the friars, because St. Francis had fallen into an
ecstacy and forgotten to order any food for his brothers.

Nanda noticed with envy that the smallest angel, looking very angelic indeed, was Marjorie Appleyard.

Mother Frances had arranged for the Junior School to have a special offering of their own, so after the public ceremony, Reverend Mother was solemnly ushered up to the small room at the top of the house. The desks had been pushed back and a wonderful cave of brown paper and sparkling cotton wool erected at the end of the room. In the cave was the manger with the Holy Child and St. Joseph and Our Lady, and the shepherds. Each member of the Junior School was represented by a small wooden animal with her name tied round its neck. There were sheep and goats and deer and pigs. The child who had most good marks in the Practice—it was Marjorie, of course—had her animal nearest the crib; the others followed in order.

"That is a sheep for you, Marjorie," said Mother Frances, as she selected a very blameless lamb and planted it in place, "because you really are rather like a little sheep, aren't you? I think Louise must be a deer, because she has such long legs and runs so fast. And what shall we have for Nanda? I think a little pig, because pigs are the most obstinate animals in the world."

With a sweet smile she planted a stout pig in the very door of the stable.

"And now, what shall we have for Monica? I'm afraid Monica's animal will be a very long way from the Holy Child. Monica, can you tell us *yet* what the Immaculate Conception means?"

Monica turned crimson and twisted her hands in her skirt.

"It means that Our Lady was conceived immac—immaculate."

Mother Frances was still smiling.

"Just so. And what do those long words mean exactly?"

"That Our Lady . . . that Our Lord was born without . . . was born of a virgin."

"But that is the mystery of the Virgin Birth, not the Immaculate Conception. Don't you *really* know the difference between the two?"

Poor Monica wriggled.

"Oh, I do, Mother. Really, I do. Only I can't explain exactly."

"That's a pity, Monica, isn't it? That's like the Protestants, who can never explain exactly what *they* mean. Nanda had better tell you. Well, Nanda?"

Nanda mumbled.

"The Immaculate Conception means that Our Lady, alone of all human beings, received the grace of coming into the world without the stain of original sin."

"Alone of all human beings," mused Mother Frances. "What about Adam and Eve. Didn't they come into the world without original sin?"

"Oh, yes, Mother," piped Marjorie. "Original sin was the sin of Adam, the father of the human race, from whom we all inherit the primal stain."

"Just so. So, my dear Nanda, even you aren't quite a real Catholic yet. Still there's some excuse for you. But Monica comes from a good Catholic home and ought to know better. Here are we having a Practice of Courtesy in honour of Our Lady and Monica hasn't even the common politeness to Our Lady to know what the great grace of the Immaculate Conception, her proudest title, means. I am afraid that Monica must be this little black sheep that was lost on the way and never got near the crib at all."

On the day of the feast itself there was high holiday. The corridors were hung with garlands of evergreen and the children who had distinguished themselves in the Practice were allowed to help in the pleasant business of hanging red Chinese lanterns in perilous places. In the morning there were wild games of hide and seek all over the garden. Mother Frances, tireless as an amazon, with her habit looped up over her black petticoat, led a panting, racing band up and down the alleys. She was flushed and bright-eyed with running on a frosty morning, and she coughed as she leant against the winning post. But not one of the short-skirted children could keep up with her long strides. Then came the distribution of ribbons. Hilary's name was called out, and she almost ran up to Reverend Mother's table, sucking in the corners of her mouth to keep from laughing with pleasure. Nanda knew she was thinking not of the blue ribbon but of the hunter she had lassooed with it. Very much to her surprise, Nanda received a pink ribbon herself.

In the afternoon there was a grand reunion of Old Children. Nanda found them very fascinating. There were lovely creatures, incredibly grown up, who smelt sweet and wore big hats and spotted veils and had bunches of violets pinned to their sable muffs. Some of them displayed their Child of Mary medals hung on broad white ribbons over their beautiful worldly frocks. They giggled and chattered and rustled in and out of the study-rooms, calling out, "My *dear*" and "*Do* you remember?" and "How *perfectly* fascinating." And there were depressing ones who turned up year after year and who wore clothes as hideous as the postulants' flannel blouses and skirts, and of whom it was whispered: "She's tried to enter *everywhere* but they won't have her, and she's leading the *most* beautiful life out in the world; the poor *love* her."

At five o'clock came a solemn benediction, a benediction with more candles and lilies than Nanda had ever seen, and long hymns enriched by the ripe drawing-room voices of the Old Girls. The nuns' voices were thin and clear and remote, like wood wind, but the Old Girls' sounded like 'cellos played with a throbbing *vibrato*. The smell of violets and fur mixed with the smell of incense and hot wax; the air shimmered in waves of heat and sound. Out of the chapel they went two by two in their white veils, each girl carrying a lighted candle and a calico lily. They were singing the traditional hymn of the Immaculate Conception, the Old Children throwing back their heads and rolling their lace-collared necks in an ecstasy of reminiscence.

"*Sancta Maria Virgo Immaculata*
In conceptione, Immacula-ata
Immaculata, Immaculata, Ora pro nobis, Immaculata"

they shouted together, and the contraltos, striking deep into the bass, boomed alone, "*Immaculata*."

Two by two, shielding their candles from their neighbours' veils, they wound through the lantern-lit passages to the Lady chapel. Big baskets stood in front of the picture of *Mater Admirabilis*, and into the baskets each pair cast their calico lilies, murmuring:

"Oh, Mary, I give you the lily of my heart, be thou its guardian for ever."

Nanda dropped her lily with awe. It stood, she knew, for some mysterious possession . . . her Purity. What Purity was she was still uncertain, being too shy to ask, but she realised it was something very important. St. Aloysius Gonzaga had fainted when he heard an impure word. What could the word have been? Perhaps it was "belly," a word so dreadful that she only whispered it in her very worst, most defiant moments. She blushed and passionately begged Our Lady's pardon for even having thought of such a word in her presence.

Before they went to bed there was a great treat for the Junior School, one of Mother Poitier's "special stories." The lights were put out; the children huddled together in an exquisitely shivering group on the floor at the old nun's feet. Nanda was sitting next to Monica. She felt a hot, bony hand grasp hers imploringly and gave it a reassuring squeeze. It was nice to know someone was a little more frightened than she was herself.

"Once upon a time," came Mother Poitier's voice out of the blackness, "a large family of children lived in an old château in France. Their father and mother were very devout and the children received the best Catholic education of all, the education of a pious home. The father and mother had one great sorrow which they never told to their younger children. Their eldest daughter, on the very day of her marriage, had disappeared and never been heard of again. She and other young people had been playing hide-and-seek in the big gardens of the château and she had gone off to hide alone. Night came, and they were still searching for her. Every cupboard, every cellar was searched; the well in the garden was drained dry, and the pond dragged, but there was never a trace of the bride. Finally, her poor parents gave her up for dead, and prayed for her as for a soul in purgatory. The servants and the neighbours were forbidden to tell the story, lest it should frighten the younger ones; all they were told was that their eldest sister had died and that they must remember her in their prayers.

"Many years later, it was the birthday of their youngest daughter, who was a child of the Five Wounds. As her birthday came in the long summer holiday, her parents had allowed her to ask several of the children from the convent to help her to celebrate it. On the morning of her birthday she woke up so much excited at the thought of the fun she was going to have that, good child though she was, she forgot to say her prayers. She got up very early and called the other children together.

" 'What shall we play?' she asked them.

" 'Oh, let us play *cache-cache* like we do on holidays at school,' cried the others.

" 'Very well,' she said. 'And I will hide first, because it is my birthday. You are to hide your eyes for five minutes and then to come and look for me.'

"So she ran away to hide, full of high spirits. Below the garden there were some old underground cellars, in which the children were forbidden to play, but the little girl was so excited, thinking what a wonderful place they would be to hide in, that she forgot all her parents' commands. She crept down the old crumbling stairs that led to the cellars and at first she was frightened, it was so dark and cold down there. But she plucked up her courage and went on. She meant to go only a little way in and hide up the first turning, but it was so very black after the sunlight outside that she got nervous and lost her way. She took two or three turnings, but in the wrong direction. She could no longer see the light from the opening. She was hopelessly lost in the cold, dark cellars. For hours, it seemed to her, she wandered up and down in the dark, beating on the slimy stone walls and screaming for help, but no answer came back but the echo of her own little voice. Then, when she was nearly mad with terror, she saw something white in a corner, under a grating that let in a little greenish light from the garden above. She went towards it and saw that it was a young woman crouching down by the wall. The child spoke to her, but the young woman did not answer. She was wearing a beautiful white satin dress and a veil with flowers, but the flowers were all withered. The child went closer and touched her, and the young woman crumbled away into dust. There was nothing left but dust and some rags of silk. The little girl screamed and screamed. Then she remembered that God is never far away from all who are in a state of grace, and she knelt down and prayed. She asked God to forgive her for having forgotten her morning prayers in her desire for pleasure, and she promised that if He would get her out of this terrible place, she would say the fifteen decades of the rosary every day of her life for the holy souls in purgatory. Then she tied her handkerchief on to the bars of the grating and prayed that the others would see it there and come to look for her. Ten minutes later she heard footsteps along the cellars and her friends found her. She was very ill with brain fever after that, and when she recovered, although she was only eleven years old, her hair was as white as snow. But from that day to this she has never forgotten her prayers.

"Now, children, let us go quietly up to dormitory, thank God for this happy holiday, and go peacefully to sleep."

CHAPTER IV

IN the summer term that followed her eleventh birthday, Nanda began to prepare for her First Communion. She was in the Senior School now, where life was a sterner, more responsible affair, symbolised by a black serge apron instead of a blue pinafore. She got up for mass every morning at six o'clock and stayed up until nine at night. There were all kinds of new subjects to study . . . music, history, botany, German, mathematics, deportment, and Catholic Apologetics. The old days of learning the simpler pages of the catechism and the stories of the saints were succeeded by a study of the knottier points of dogma . . . a study to which she was to devote at least an hour a day for the next few years.

Rather to her surprise, Nanda found herself put in a higher class than any of the others who had been promoted from the Junior School. Joan and Monica and Louise and Mildred, who had been the chief figures in her life, became vague shadows whom she only saw in the chapel or at recreation. Mother Frances had disappeared from the school altogether; she was in the community infirmary in the last stages of consumption. Sometimes Nanda and the others would send up a letter to tell her that they had said the fifteen decades for her. Sometimes they would club together to have a mass said. And every time Nanda handed old Father Robertson the five shillings in an envelope, he would pat her head and say:

"Now, my dear little child, remember that this money does not *buy* the mass. No one can buy the Precious Blood of Our Lord. When you go out into the world,

Protestants may say to you: 'But you have paid money
to have this mass said.' Protestants are very easily
scandalised where Catholics are concerned. And they are
very clever, as ignorant people so often are, at getting
hold of the wrong end of the stick. This little offering
you make here is just to buy the matter of the Holy
Sacrifice . . . the actual bread and wine . . . and to
contribute a little to the support of the priest who says
the mass. Never forget that, my dear little child."

Whenever her old children sent her word that they
were praying specially for her, a little note would come
back from Mother Frances, scribbled on a piece of paper
neatly cut from an old exercise book. Nanda found these
notes hard to associate with the Mother Frances she had
known; they were so gentle and so humble. Once there
was even a lace-edged picture of the Sacred Heart inscribed "To dear little Nanda, in loving gratitude for
her prayers. Frances Page, s.c.v."

The mistress of Nanda's principal class nowadays was
a nun called Mother Percival. There was a good deal of
Mother Frances' old astringency about her, but not that
exquisite sense of one's tenderest vanities. Mother Percival was blunt and forceful; if she bullied, it was because she believed that bullying strengthens the
character. She was a firm believer in cold baths, hockey
and plenty of healthy laughter at one's own and other
people's failings. Had she not been a Catholic, Mother
Percival might very well have been a games mistress at
one of those Protestant high schools she so bitterly despised. In her own way, indeed, she was something of a
Protestant and a reformer. She represented the English
tradition against the French origins of Lippington. It
was due to Mother Percival that Nanda and the others
no longer had to have their bi-weekly baths clothed from

head to foot in long, white calico cloaks. But she made
no attempt to do away with the system of spying to
which all the children were subjected. Every letter
written by a child of the Five Wounds had to be left
open for the Mistress of Discipline to read and censure.
Even letters to parents were censored and sometimes
destroyed without the writer's knowing what had happened. Every incoming letter or parcel was opened and
examined and only given to the recipient at the Mistress
of Discipline's discretion. Occasionally a letter that was
considered particularly stupid or objectionable in tone
was read to the whole school and publicly criticised.

The preparations for her First Communion took up
much of Nanda's time, and nearly all her thought. The
First Communicants were a privileged band, set apart
from the others. They spent extra time in the chapel
and had daily interviews with Reverend Mother, besides
special religious instruction from a visiting Jesuit. They
were allowed to help in picking and arranging the
flowers for the altar and in looking after Father Robertson's vestments. When there were processions of the
Blessed Sacrament, before the great day of *Corpus
Christi* itself, they walked in white dresses in front of
the monstrance, strewing rose and peony petals from
silver baskets.

Nanda looked forward to her First Communion with
a mixture of awe and excitement. At mass and benediction she strained every nerve to concentrate on the
mystery of the Real Presence which, to a Catholic, is
even more profound and beautiful than the mystery of
the Incarnation. Mother Poitier had told her about a
little Protestant girl who had been taken to mass by a
Catholic friend and who, when her relations had told
her it was wicked to believe that the bread and wine was

changed into the actual body of our Lord, had exclaimed: "But when the bell rang I saw the priest holding up a beautiful little child." At the Elevation, Nanda would peer and peer until the candles swam before her eyes and she was almost sure she could see the outlines of a face in the white circle of the host. She listened greedily when Father Parry talked of how the Blessed Sacrament had been foretold all through the Old Testament and how even the pagan philosophers had had some dim vision of the mystery. Plato had said that if Divine Truth were ever manifested on earth, it would take the shape of a circle which symbolised eternity and the colour white, which was the sum and perfection of all colours. The day of one's First Communion was the happiest day of one's life; even the Emperor Napoleon, in the midst of his worldly triumphs, admitted that he had never known real happiness except on the morning he first received the Blessed Sacrament. Saints had died of ecstasy when the host first touched their tongue, and Mother Poitier was fond of saying that God could grant no greater grace than to die at the moment of one's First Communion. Sometimes, in moments of great fervour, Nanda would pray that she might die too, and she would leave the chapel with a queer, giddy feeling that after the tenth of June she would never see Lippington any more, never grow up or get married, never even go home for the summer holidays.

But, mixed with her devotion and longing for the great day was a fearful dread that something might go wrong, that, through her own fault, she might lose all the virtues of the Sacrament and even fall into mortal sin. There was a story in a pious book by a nun of another Order that she read over and over again with fascinated terror.

"Rose made all the preparations for her First Communion with the greatest fervour. At last the great day came. Rose and her companions were dressed in their white dresses and veils and made their way along the corridors to the chapel. Someone had carelessly dropped a sweet in the passage, and without thinking, Rose picked it up and put it in her mouth. No sooner had she swallowed it, than she realised what she had done. She had broken her fast and could not now receive Our Lord. Rose struggled with her conscience, but, alas, the terrible little devil of Human Respect won. She thought of the chapel all decorated in honour of the First Communicants, of her parents who had come from far away to see her and she had not the courage to take off her wreath and veil and say humbly: 'I have broken my fast and cannot make my Communion this morning.' So she went into the church with the others, and when they went up to the altar to receive our Lord, she went too, knowing that she was making a wicked mockery of the Holy Sacrament. Afterwards, she went to confession. All her days she bitterly regretted her wicked vanity and cowardice, but the tears of a lifetime could not undo the terrible fact that she had made her First Communion in mortal sin. Just think, dear children, had Rose died before she left the church that morning, she would have passed straight from God's holy table into the fires of hell."

Still worse was the fear that at some time she might have committed a mortal sin and forgotten to include it at confession. Years ago, fired by the example of many saints, Nanda had made a vow of perpetual virginity. At eight, this vow had not been difficult to make. But now that she was ten she could not help feeling that she was quite likely to want to get married some day.

Was her promise binding? She puzzled about it for a long time. Even the thought of going back on a promise to God might be a mortal sin. It took three things, she knew, to make a mortal sin: grave matter, full knowledge, and full consent. The matter was grave enough, certainly. And though she was not quite clear what virginity actually was, she knew, that with the one exception of Our Lady, one could not be a virgin and married as well. Besides, St. Joseph was always spoken of as Our Lady's spouse, so probably a spouse was not the same thing as a husband. As to full consent, she had been eight when she made the vow and seven is the age of reason. At last, she summoned up courage to mention the matter to Father Robertson when she made her usual Saturday afternoon confession.

The confessional opened on to Father Robertson's little parlour behind the chapel. Through the grating she could see his old, sleepy face quite clearly, and a little table on which his tea was waiting. She noticed that he had two pink sugar cakes, and wished that they sometimes had sugar cakes for *goûter* instead of stale bread and jam.

She shut her eyes and clenched her blue-gloved hands as she whispered as usual.

"It is a week since my last confession, Father, and since then I have been guilty of distractions at prayers and being uncharitable to my neighbour, and I've told a lie twice and I've been idle and jealous and disobedient and angry and conceited, Father."

"Very good, my child, very good," murmured Father Robertson. Whatever one's sins were, Father Robertson always murmured "Very good" in the same gentle, sleepy voice. There was a legend that once someone had confessed:

"Father, I have committed murder," and Father Robertson had answered:

"Very good, my child. And how many times?"

He was about to give her absolution when Nanda whispered breathlessly:

"Oh, Father, I'm afraid I've made a rash vow and I'm not sure that I really mean to keep it."

"And what was this vow, my child?"

"Perpetual virginity, Father."

"And how old were you when you made this vow?"

"Eight, Father."

"And were there any witnesses of this vow?"

"No, Father."

"Well, my child, I do not think that, in the circumstances, the dear Lord would hold you bound by it. You can reconsider the matter when you are twenty-one. Now, make a sincere act of contrition for these sins, and all the sins of your past life." He raised his voice and groaned: "Oh, my God."

When Nanda had first confessed to Father Robertson she had been very much alarmed by this "Oh, my God." She thought the priest was exclaiming in horror at her sins. But now she knew that it was only the beginning of the act of contrition, the rest of which he muttered below his breath. Greatly relieved, Nanda bent her head to receive absolution. Hardly waiting for Father Robertson to murmur "Bless you, my child, and pray for me," she fairly skipped out of the confessional.

Throughout each day, Nanda watched herself with the utmost scruple. She examined her conscience minutely every night, and made passionate acts of contrition for every fault. She gave up sugar in her tea and forced herself to eat the things she hated most to the very last scrap. Even the saintly Madeleine was impressed by her zeal and smiled approvingly as she gave her a second helping of particularly nasty cabbage. Having read somewhere of a Jesuit novice who mortified one of his senses every day, she tried to imitate him. On Monday she mortified her eyes by shutting her book at the most interesting place and not reading another word. On Tuesday, she stuffed her fingers in her ears while the organ played at benediction. On Wednesday, she refused to smell flowers and made herself sniff a particularly nauseating mixture of ink and liquorice powder. On Thursday, she put salt instead of sugar on her rhubarb to mortify her sense of taste. And on Friday, after much thought, she managed to penalise her sense of touch by scraping her finger-nails against the rough serge of her apron and putting burrs against her skin under her vest.

Among the First Communicants was a girl of twelve years old named Léonie de Wesseldorf. Léonie was half French and half German by birth; she belonged to a very old and very wealthy family whose name, to Catholic ears, had something of the glamour of Medici or Gonzaga. Nanda's private image of Léonie de Wesseldorf was of a young prince, pale and weary from a day's ride, with his lovelocks carelessly tied back in a frayed ribbon. Léonie wore a black uniform instead of a blue one, being in mourning for some ambassadorial uncle, and the dusty coat she wore in the garden had the name of Paquin on its torn lining. In her unfeminine, unchildish way, she was exceedingly handsome, yet her deeply cut mouth and beautiful shallow brows seemed like the stamp of a medal rather than the changing growth of a face. Her red, unformed hands did not seem to belong to the pale, haughty head. Nanda, always reverent towards the people she liked, looked at Léonie's hands as little as possible; they embarrassed her like a deformity. Her feeling for Léonie was one of pure admiration, the feeling of page for prince, too cold and absolute to be called love. It would not have mattered if Léonie had never spoken or even looked at her, provided Nanda could bind herself to her by a private allegiance. Léonie was invincibly lazy. She would let herself be beaten in arguments or work by Nanda or others far stupider, but every now and then she would say something startling or write a sentence so shapely and mature that the nuns would find it hard to believe she was not quoting. Her mind, like her face, seemed to have been handed down to her full-grown, a blade of old, finely tempered steel, that she carried as carelessly as her shabby Paquin coat.

Nanda and Léonie studied their catechism side by side for three weeks and were bracketed top of the test in Christian Doctrine which the First Communicants had to pass. Monica, with much difficulty, managed to obtain the necessary forty marks out of a hundred, though she was very shaky on the subject of Transubstantiation.

The day after the Christian Doctrine examination, while the band of First Communicants was walking round the inner garden, cutting flowers for the altar, Léonie dropped behind the rest and beckoned to Nanda. For a few minutes they strolled in silence, Léonie with her handsome chin in the air and her hands deep in her pockets. It was early summer, and the small, secluded garden, far away from the playgrounds, was spicy with the smell of azaleas. Nanda was glad that it was not Wednesday and that she need not stop her nose. The warmth playing on her skin made her feel quite dizzy with happiness; she wanted to tear off her thick serge and shake her hair loose from its plait. Léonie, who was always cold, huddled her smart, disreputable coat around her so tightly that it seams showed white in the sunshine.

"Well, Nanda, my child, what do you make of all this?"

"All what?"

"Oh, the Catholic Church, your First Communion, und so weiter."

Léonie had a very grown-up voice; husky and rather harsh but extremely attractive. When she sang, it cleared and sweetened, and its rich, coppery ring cleaved straight to the heart of the note.

Nanda knitted her eyebrows and did not answer. Léonie helped her.

"Do you really believe all the things in the catechism, for example?"

"Why, of course."

"You mean you want to believe them? Being a convert, you have to make an effort . . . more effort than I, for example. And so you come to believe them better than I."

"But don't you . . ."

"Believe them? I don't know. They're too much part of me. I shall never get away from them. I don't want to, even. The Catholic Church suits me much too well. But it's fun sometimes to see what a little needle-point the whole thing rests on."

Nanda's world was spinning round her.

"Léonie, what on earth do you mean?"

"Well, for example, there's no rational proof of the existence of God. Oh, I know there are four the Jesuits give you. But not one that would really hold water for a philosopher."

"But, Léonie, that's sheer blasphemy," said Nanda stoutly.

"Not necessarily. It doesn't affect the goodness of the beliefs one way or the other. After all, there's no rational proof that you exist yourself."

This had never occurred to Nanda. For quite fifty yards she walked in deep thought. Then she burst out:

"Good heavens . . . it's quite true. There isn't. Léonie, how awful."

"*I* think it's rather amusing," said Léonie, beginning to whistle.

A few days before *Corpus Christi* still another First Communicant joined the band, an overgrown, shy creature who was actually twelve but looked fifteen. Theresa Leighton was the last of a family who had been Catholics for five hundred years and of whom it was proudly said that they had never made one mixed marriage since the Reformation. Theresa was preternaturally stupid and preternaturally good-natured. She would sit with her great mild brown eyes staring agonisingly at Mother Percival as she tried to follow the simplest explanation, and then say:

"Oh, Mother, it's so *assy* of me, but would you mind saying it just once more."

Nanda was shocked to overhear Mother Percival say to another nun: "These old families, you know, they're like royalty. Too much intermarriage. Wonderful traditions, but not very much *here*," and she touched her black forehead band significantly.

But what Theresa Leighton lacked in intelligence, she made up in sweetness. Never was anyone so patient, so uncomplaining, so bewilderingly unselfish. She was so amazingly good that Nanda and the others were respectful, but embarrassed. In the chapel, her queer, mild face wore an extraordinary expression of ease and happiness, as if here at least she were completely at home.

When there was a tableau of the Annunciation, Theresa was naturally chosen for Our Lady, and Nanda, as the angel, was frightened by the look of strained, expectant ecstasy in Theresa's immense brown eyes.

Even when they practised receiving an unconsecrated wafer with closed eyes and outstretched tongues, it seemed to Nanda that at the moment of Communion itself, Theresa could not look more dazed with happiness.

The great day came at last. Every time she woke up during the night before, which was often, Nanda said, as she had been told to do:

"Even in the night have I desired thee, Lord. Come, Lord Jesus, come."

Everything she put on that morning was new and white. A white prayer-book and a mother-of-pearl rosary, a gift from Reverend Mother, lay beside her new veil, and the stiff wreath of white cotton roses that every First Communicant wore. They walked into the chapel two by two, pacing slowly up the aisle like twelve brides, to the sound of soft, lacy music. In front of the altar were twelve prie-dieu covered with white muslin and flowers, with a tall candle burning in front of each. At little stools at the side knelt the children from the Poor School, who were also making their First Communion. They had no candles, and their cotton frocks looked shabby.

Nanda tried to fix her attention on the mass, but she could not. She felt light-headed and empty, unable to pray or even to think. She stole a look at Léonie, whose pale, bent face was stiff and absorbed. She tried not to be conscious of the smell of Joan Appleyard's newly-washed hair above the lilies and the incense. Theresa Leighton's head was thrown back; she had closed her prayer-book and was gazing at the altar with a rapt, avid look, her mouth a little open. Nanda was horrified at her own detachment, she tried hard to concentrate on the great moment ahead of her, but her mind was blank. In a trance she heard the bell ring for the *Domine non sum dignus*, and heard the rustle as the others got up to go to the altar rails. In terror, she thought: "I haven't made a proper preparation. I've been distracted the whole time, to-day of all days. Dare I go up with them?" But almost without knowing, her body had moved with the rest, and she was kneeling at the rails with the others, holding the embroidered cloth under her chin. Under her almost closed eyelids, she could see the pattern of the altar carpet, and the thin, round hosts, like honesty leaves, in the ciborium. The priest was opposite her now; she raised her head and shut her eyes tight. She felt the wafer touch her tongue and waited for some extraordinary revelation, for death even. But she felt nothing.

Back at her prie-dieu, she kept her head bowed like the others. Above the noise in her ears she could hear the choir singing softly and dreamily:

"Ad quem diu suspiravi,
Jesu tandem habeo."

Over and over she told herself frantically:
"This is the greatest moment of my life. Our Lord Himself is actually present, in the flesh, inside my body. Why am I so numb and stupid? Why can't I think of anything to say?" She was relieved when the quarter of an hour's thanksgiving was over. As they filed out of the

chapel she looked at the faces of the other eleven, to see if they felt as she did. But every face was gay or recollected or content. Léonie's expression was grave and courteous; in spite of her stiff white dress and wreath, she seemed like a young soldier fresh from an audience with the king. She thought of Polish nobles who stand with drawn swords during the Credo, and wished she could be as much of the blood of this ancient faith as Léonie and Theresa. With all her efforts, all her devotion, there was something wrong with her. Perhaps a convert could never ring quite true. Perhaps real Catholics were right always to mistrust and despise them a little. For weeks she had been preparing herself, laying stick on stick and coal on coal, and now, at the supreme moment, she had not caught fire. Her First Communion had been a failure.

There was an impressive breakfast laid out for the First Communicants in the big parlour, with crisp new rolls, butter patted into swan-like shapes and a huge, bridal-looking cake. Against the walls stood twelve small tables laden with presents. Nanda's looked rather bare and dismal, for it only held a missal, a new rosary and a copy of the poems of Francis Thompson. She had no Catholic relatives to load her with gold medals, crucifixes, coloured statues, alabaster plaques and Imitations of Christ bound in voluptuous Russian leather. She had received quite a good number of holy pictures however, including one from Hilary O'Byrne, as handsome as a Christmas card, inscribed: "To dear Nanda, on the happiest day of her life, from Hilary E. de M."

The First Communicants, reacting after their two days of silent retreat, chattered like starlings. Reverend Mother looked in, with her glasses positively twinkling with benevolence, and even condescended to examine

everybody's presents and to exclaim politely over them.
But after a few minutes, she put up her hand for
silence.

"My very dear children," she said, "it is quite right
and proper for you all to be gay and happy on this day
of days. But not too much noise, remember. I would
like you all to be quiet and recollect yourselves for just
three minutes, while I tell you a little story . . . a true
one that happened this very morning. I am going to tell
you this because it shows what a true Catholic's spirit
should be all through life . . . that nothing is more
pleasing to God than suffering bravely borne for our
Lord's sake. I expect you noticed that there were some
children from the Poor School making their First Communion with you this morning. You must remember
that they do not come from good homes like you; they
are often quite pathetically ignorant. Well, one of the
nuns was helping them to put on their veils and their
wreaths, and one little girl called Molly had great difficulty with hers. So Mother Poitier fastened it on with a
big safety-pin, but, as you know, she does not see very
well, and she unfortunately put the pin right through
Molly's ear. The poor little girl was in great pain, but
she thought it was part of the ceremony, and she never
uttered a word of complaint. She thought of the terrible
suffering of Our Lord in wearing His crown of thorns
and bore it for His sake. I am sure Molly received a very
wonderful grace at her First Communion and I should
like to think that anyone here had such beautiful, unselfish devotion as that. She might have gone about all
day with that pin through her ear, if she had not fainted
just now at breakfast. Now, talk away again, children,
and be as happy as you can all day long. But even in
your happiness, never forget that a good Christian is

always ready to take up his cross and deny himself and unite himself to the passion of Our Blessed Lord."

There were no lessons that day. Nanda spent the morning walking about the garden with her father and mother. They could go wherever they liked, down to the farm or over to the orchard or right round the long walk that was called "The End of the World." Each First Communicant was surrounded by a chattering group of brothers and sisters and aunts and cousins and, not for the first time, Nanda wished that her parents had been Catholics long enough to support the tradition of having a very large family. Sometimes they would pass Léonie, pacing between a haughty-looking brother and an incredibly impressive mother, all black velvet and ermine. Léonie would wave energetically and Nanda would grin back shyly and wish her mother wouldn't talk quite so loud. For everything appeared so extremely odd to Mrs. Grey.

"What is that image, dear . . . the one of the young man in the lace-edged shirt? He's got such a beautiful face, I think."

"Not image, statue, *please*, Mother," begged the unhappy Nanda. "It's St. Aloysius and it's not a shirt, it's a surplice."

"And did you put those flowers there, darling?" Mrs. Grey would twitter. "I think it's such a pretty idea putting flowers in front of the images. But why must the saint be holding a skull? It's so morbid, isn't it?"

Down by the lake, half a dozen novices were playing ducks and drakes. Someone flipped a slate neatly; it bounced half a dozen times on the still water. The novice who had thrown it stood up and laughed. It was Lady Moira Palliser.

Mrs. Grey gave a little shriek of pity.

"John, *isn't* that pathetic? Those poor young women. Just think, they've given up *everything*, and there they are, throwing stones like little boys." She shifted her parasol on her shoulder, looking kindly at the nuns. Then, with an understanding smile she turned to Nanda: "Of course, there must be a kind of happiness in their lives. No responsibilities, you know."

CHAPTER V

ONE night, early in her third autumn term, when the Senior School were sitting at their evening preparation in the big study-room, the faint tinkle of a bell sounded in the passage outside. Mother Percival immediately rose from her desk on the dais, snapped her wooden signal, and announced to the eighty inquiring faces:

"Children, will you all very quietly and reverently kneel down beside your desk and pray for our dear Mother Frances, who is gravely ill? Father Robertson is taking the Last Sacraments to her now."

Nanda wrenched her mind from Boileau's *Art Poétique* which she was gabbling to herself in a whisper, and knelt down with the rest. The little bell sounded louder and louder; feet shuffled along the stone corridor; then the noise diminished, receded, was lost in the distance. Mother Percival's signal snapped again; the children resumed their seats, and Nanda tried to concentrate once more on Boileau. But the words no longer meant anything. She gave up looking at the book and

shut her eyes, repeating over and over to herself the few
lines she had learned, but the tiny stroke of the acolyte's
bell still rang in her ears. What was happening to
Mother Frances now? Were they already anointing her
eyes and ears and nostrils and hands with the holy oil,
symbolising the forgiveness of sins committed by each
unruly sense and member? How many blessed candles
had Mother Frances collected in her life to be lit round
her death-bed? Every year Nanda carefully laid by the
one she received on the Feast of the Purification for this
very purpose. It was distressing to think that she had
only three; her eight years of unwitting heresy had
robbed her of as many comforts in her last agony. Yet,
after all, why should twenty blessed candles be more
efficacious than one in keeping away evil spirits? It was
very puzzling. She tried to imagine the scene in the
community infirmary. But where was the community
infirmary? Somewhere in the building, there must be,
she knew, a hundred cells and a whole counterpart of
the school, libraries, classrooms, study-rooms and sick-
rooms, where no lay person except the nuns' doctor was
allowed to set foot. Even parents might not visit a dying
daughter there. But where did this house within a house
lie? She knew the forbidden stairs that led to the community's quarters, but that was all. How strange it was,
she thought, that living side by side with the nuns, the
children knew nothing of their lives. She had never seen
a nun eat or drink; she could not imagine Mother
Frances, even on her death-bed, dressed otherwise than
in her black and white habit. Did they wear night-
gowns? Did they have looking-glasses? It must be difficult to adjust those veils and wimples without them.
Yet even to imagine such things seemed to Nanda blasphemous. Someone touched her shoulder. She started,

and opened her eyes to find Mother Percival standing beside her.

"Well, Nanda, is this the way you do your preparation?"

"Sorry, Mother."

"There is still twenty minutes of your study time left. Do your work properly and offer up a good preparation for Mother Frances in her last agony. God likes a little dull duty well done better than the most elaborate prayers."

The next morning at breakfast, before the bell rang for talking, the Mistress of Discipline told them that Mother Frances had died during the night.

"A most beautiful and Christian death," said Mother Radcliffe, wiping her glasses on her sleeve. "I am sure that every nun and every child of the Five Wounds may feel she has a new friend in heaven this morning. Mother Frances is to lie to-day and to-morrow in the Lady chapel, and, as a great privilege, all those who were in the Junior School under her may say their rosary there to-night."

Nanda spent the day in alternate fear and excitement. She had never seen a dead person before. At last six o'clock came and she tiptoed into the chapel with the rest, feeling conspicuous in her Senior School uniform. Her nerve failed her at the last, and she closed her eyes, so that at first she was aware of nothing but the smell of lilies and melting wax. When she dared to look, there was Mother Frances lying uncoffined among trails of white flowers, looking hardly paler than in life, and still wearing her sweet, disdainful smile. Her habit and her crimped bonnet had taken on a stiff, carved look; her hands were carefully disposed, like a statue's, over the silver cross on her breast. She looked so secret, yet so defenceless, that Nanda could not help feeling it was an impertinence for them to peer at her dead face and to scatter beads of holy water on her body. The others, too, trod guiltily, as if fearing Mother Frances would wake, and she was half relieved when Monica cried out in a hysterical whisper: "She moved . . . I saw her move," and had to be taken out, sobbing and clinging to Mother Radcliffe's sleeve.

The morning of the funeral was wet and grey. As the whole school plodded slowly down the alleys to the cemetery, a fine rain hissed in their lighted candles and pearled the frieze of their black cloaks. The dead leaves, ankle-deep, whistled round their shoes, and the air seemed full of clammy, invisible cobwebs that clung to cheeks and hair. Across the path, Nanda watched Theresa Leighton patiently trudging; her rapt face up-turned to the rain, her veil half off, and her candle out. Was that how St. Theresa looked when she set off to find the Moors and martyrdom? She thought St. Theresa must have looked a little more intelligent, but crushed the idea as uncharitable. Theresa would certainly become a nun, and quite possibly a saint as well. She felt a pang of conscience that she did not seek Theresa's society more often, but, as she glanced further along the line and saw Léonie de Wesseldorf in her smart, shabby coat, clutching her candle as if she were presenting arms, Nanda forgot the very existence of Theresa Leighton.

In the cemetery, school and community formed a hollow square round the grave. It was raining in good earnest now; the flowers in the banked wreaths were becoming pulpy and transparent, and the grass struck up dankly through thin-soled shoes. At last the coffin, plain as a soldier's, was carried to the graveside by

Mother Frances' four tall brothers. The nuns' voices, intoning the *De Profundis*, sounded weakly through the heavy air, and even Father Robertson's rich notes had no ring in them as he prayed that all the angels and saints might come to meet the newly-arrived soul at the gates of heaven. Reverend Mother was crying a little, and Nanda felt her own eyes prick as, after long minutes of prayers, the tall young men payed out the bands and lowered the coffin into the spruce-lined pit. It was over, and the prospect of an ordinary day, however dull, seemed warm and comforting.

When midday recreation came, everyone was still rather subdued. As it was still very damp on the grass, games were abandoned in favour of walking round the garden in "trios." These trios were always selected by the nun in charge on the principle that, if two children were known to like each other's company, they must, at all costs, be kept apart. At no time at Lippington were any girls except sisters and first cousins allowed to walk in pairs; since, as they were frequently reminded, "When two are together, the devil loves to make a third." Nor were three of the same age permitted to make a trio; an older girl, usually a Child of Mary, was sent out with two juniors, in order that she might check their conversation while being wholesomely bored herself.

By some lucky oversight on the part of Mother Percival, Nanda and Léonie were put in the same trio, with Hilary O'Byrne as their chaperone. Nanda had not spoken to Hilary for many weeks. Since she had won her blue ribbon, she had a table of her own, and a dull German princess, who wore a flaxen wig and enormous shoes like leather boats was now Madeleine's vice-president. The princess had seriously upset Nanda's romantic notions of royalty, for she was plain, stupid, and addicted to violent colds in the head. All the same, she considered her an ideal table companion on account of her passionate fondness for the hateful, vinegar-soaked Lippington cabbage.

Hilary, thought Nanda, glancing up at the slender figure on which the serge uniform looked well-cut and almost elegant, would have made a much better princess. How pretty and grown-up she looked to-day, with her brown hair combed in a puff above a very white forehead. Even her blue ribbon and the silver chain of her Child of Mary medal had a decorative, secular air.

"Are you sorry you're leaving at Christmas?" Nanda asked her boldly.

Hilary smiled, curling her upper lip inwards in a way that would have been ugly in anyone else, but was charming in Hilary, who had teeth as white as a cat's.

"Not really sorry," she said thoughtfully. "Though I suppose I shall howl like the rest when it really comes to the point. It'll be heavenly not to miss any more hunting. And I'm going to be presented in May. Rather a bore, really, but I'm looking forward to it all the same."

"A ghastly bore," assented Léonie, looping a wet strand of hair ungracefully behind one ear. "Goodness knows how many times I'll have to go through it. London and Berlin for certain, and then Papa is sure to be sent to Vienna or Madrid, and I'll have to start all over again. I shall jolly well wear the same dreary white satin dress each time, and then I shall put it away for ten years while I sow my wild oats and produce it for one final appearance when I take the veil at Lippington."

Nanda giggled.

"I don't see you as a nun, Léonie," said Hilary. "You'd make a rotten, I mean a hopeless novice."

"A rotten novice, but a first-class Reverend Mother. And as a future Mistress of Discipline, my dear Hilary, may I remind you that there is a fine of sixpence for using the word rotten?"

But Nanda was not nearly ready to abandon the subject of courts and queens.

"Mother Frances was presented, wasn't she, before she entered?" she asked. "I wonder what she wore."

"A bustle, I should think," said Léonie scornfully.

"She was very beautiful," asserted Hilary. "My aunt, Moira's mother, said she made a tremendous sensation when she came out. I believe she had hundreds of proposals."

This was a new light on Mother Frances. But how, Nanda wondered, could any man have the courage even to mention the subject of marriage to anyone so proud and remote?

"It wasn't only that she looked so wonderful," went on Hilary. "My aunt said she'd never seen a girl who rode so straight to hounds. She was absolutely fearless. And she told me that when she left home to come to Lippington she was perfectly calm when she kissed all her family good-bye, but when the carriage came round to fetch her for the last time, Mother Frances couldn't be found anywhere. So they looked in the stables, and there she was, with her arms round the neck of her favourite hunter, crying her eyes out."

"I wonder why she entered?" said Nanda, with a shiver.

Hilary laughed.

"Oh, the usual reasons, I suppose. I've heard people say she promised to become a nun if one of her sisters whom she adored recovered from a bad accident. Her horse bolted and she was dragged half a mile over cobbles; they didn't have safety stirrups in those days, and she was terribly badly hurt."

"And did she recover?" asked Nanda.

"Yes, quite suddenly, when the doctors had given her up. It may have been a miracle. I don't know. But I don't believe it really had anything to do with Mother Frances becoming a nun."

"I can't imagine anything more awful than one's last night at home before one enters," said Nanda gloomily.

"That's because you were brought up a Protestant," Hilary explained kindly. "Protestants always have morbid ideas about nuns. Mother Frances made a gorgeous last night of it. The Pages gave a big ball for her and she danced every dance, Aunt Patricia said, looking too lovely in white satin and pearls and a wreath of camellias. And she was awfully particular about her hair, too. She had a man down from London, though the house was in Leicestershire, and she made him do it two or three times before she was satisfied."

"There are some things I'll never understand," said Nanda despairingly. "*I* think vocations are terrifying."

"You're a heretic to the backbone, young Nanda," said Léonie in her hoarse, amused voice. "Still, you'd better get over your childish terrors as at least twenty per cent. of us will certainly become nuns of one sort or another. I shall plump for the Five Wounds. At any rate, you don't have to sleep on a plank, like a Carmelite."

"Theresa Leighton wants to be a Carmelite," Nanda told her.

"Oh, Theresa Leighton," said Léonie contemptuously. "She's too holy to last. She'll marry some boring man and have fifteen strapping children. No, it's the unlikely ones like Hilary and me who end up in the community. Isn't it, dear Sister Hilary?"

But Hilary's face had taken on a cold, clouded look.

"It's fearfully chilly mooning about like this," she said suddenly. "Come on, infants, I'll race you down to Our Lady of the Lake."

Two days later, there was an outbreak of feverish colds all through the school. The infirmary was full and every classroom reeked of eucalyptus. The children who remained at work were alternately dosed with liquorice powder and cosseted with hot currant syrup, but in spite of these precautions, the sick list grew longer and longer. After three days of snuffling misery, Nanda gave in and presented herself at the infirmary. Her eyes felt like balls of lead and her cheeks scorched, though the rest of her body shivered. Mother Regan, the flustered Irish infirmarian, rolled her blue eyes despairingly as she thrust a thermometer into Nanda's mouth.

"I hope to goodness you're not running a temperature, child," she said. "I haven't a single free room."

But Nanda herself devoutly hoped she *was* running a temperature, for otherwise there was no hope of the blessed peace of a day in bed. She gripped her lips tightly, in case any precious degree of heat might be lost. Long before she felt the thermometer had had a fair chance, Mother Regan snatched it from her mouth. The nun frowned at it, held it up to the hissing gas for another look, then with a distrustful glance at Nanda, as if she and the thermometer were in league with each other, she beckoned the lay-sister who acted as nurse.

"It's a great nuisance, Sister," she said, "but I'll have to find this child a bed somehow. Is there anyone well enough to be moved?"

"There's Miss Theresa Leighton," said Sister Jones

doubtfully. "She's been here the longest. And she's normal to-day. But she's still not very well."

"What about Miss Marjorie Appleyard?"

"She's got a temperature still. And the doctor said all the others were to stay in bed, Mother Regan."

"Well, there's no help for it then. Theresa Leighton must go back to her dormitory to-night. Tell her she needn't get up till second rising, and she's not to go out of doors till I give her permission."

It was a good half-hour before Sister Jones returned to say that the room was ready. Now that she was in sight of her goal, Nanda began irrationally to feel much better. She wondered uncomfortably whether she ought not at least to make a show of refusing Theresa Leighton's bed. It had often been impressed on her that Theresa was very delicate. But supposing the offer were accepted? She doubted whether she had ever wanted anything as much as she wanted that bed, and the relief of being admittedly ill at last. She stared gloomily at the bottles of magnesia and gregory powder in the glass cupboard, quarrelling feebly with her conscience. Other snivelling victims arrived, but failing to pass the test of the thermometer, were dismissed with the cold comforts of quinine and Condy's fluid, till the bathroom next door resounded with the hollow noise of gargling. Nanda was just about to make a half-hearted protest when Mother Regan pounced on her.

"Good gracious, child. Go and fetch your things quickly. You don't think we keep a French maid here to look after your belongings, do you? Run along now. You can bring a lesson-book or two for the time when you'll be well enough to read."

The unsuccessful candidates for the sickroom tittered. Nanda with a sullen, "Yes, Mother," slouched off to

obey. She certainly wasn't going to be heroic and unselfish after *that*.

Feeling rather defiant, she stuffed the Francis Thompson that Léonie had given her for her First Communion
into the pocket of her dressing-gown. She was rather
surprised that it had not been confiscated long ago.
Wrapped in brown paper, it passed for an ordinary
school poetry book. Her conscience did not prick her
much, for Francis Thompson was, after all, a Catholic
poet, and she boldly scattered her essays with quotations
from his works. She quite understood the fuss that had
been made about Léonie's own copy of Shelley, for
Shelley was an atheist and there might be corruption
lurking in his most innocent poems. One day, Léonie
had broken away from the others at recreation and
strolled round the lake, reading *The Revolt of Islam*
quite openly and with an air of cynical detachment.
There had been a memorable scene in which Mother
Percival, pink with anger, had snatched the book from
Léonie, and Léonie, very politely, had taken back her
Shelley and flung it into the lake, saying: "If the book
is so scandalous, that it the best place for it. It can
hardly corrupt the little fishes." Strangely enough,
Léonie had not been punished.

The infirmary rooms at Lippington were bare and
dismal. There was plenty of space in each for two beds
at least, but in no circumstances were children allowed
to share a bedroom. The walls of Nanda's were painted
a dirty green, and the only decorations were a chipped
plaster crucifix, a shell, with a sponge as hard as cork,
that had once held holy water, and a spotty steel engraving of Leo XIII. Round the high, narrow bed ran a
curtain, whose rusty rings jangled at every movement
and effectively disturbed the patient's sleep. But to

Nanda the shabby room, with the grim, old-fashioned dentist's chair in the corner, the spluttering gas jet and the empty grate, looked like paradise.

She slept very badly the first night, waking at every bell that rang or clock that struck. How many bells there were; she did not know the meaning of half of them. She remembered that she ought to pray for the souls in purgatory every time the clock chimed. St. Theresa used to exclaim each time the hour struck: "An hour nearer to death. An hour nearer to heaven or hell." Curling and uncurling herself miserably on her hot, lumpy bed, Nanda began, quite naturally, to meditate on death. In the retreat given to the First Communicants in the summer there had been a colloquy on the last agony. In the afternoon silence of the sunlit chapel, with the leaves blowing across the windows and the birds cheeping outside, it had seemed too remote to be very terrible. But now in the dark, alone, feeling sick and aching, Nanda felt the words crowd back into her head with a horribly personal application. It was only a few days since they had buried Mother Frances. Her death had not made very much impression on Nanda at the time, but now it was real and terrifying as if a pain had begun to pierce the fog of an anæsthetic. Mother Frances had died, here in this house, only a week ago. She, Nanda, must die at some time, perhaps very soon. The words of Father Parry's colloquy came back as if they were printed on a gramophone record in her head. It was odd, because she had only half listened; she had been watching Léonie and trying to trace her profile with her finger on the flyleaf of her missal. "Transport yourself," Father Parry had said, in his quiet, convincing voice, "to the bedside of a dying person or beside a grave ready to receive a coffin. Ask Our Lord for a salutary fear of death and the grace to be prepared for it every day." Was she prepared for death? She had committed a sin against charity in not offering to let Theresa Leighton stay in this very room. It was not a mortal sin. But suppose Theresa had a relapse and died? It would be her fault. A good Catholic should always be ready and willing to die. Did she really love God? Would she rather go to heaven than spend the Christmas holidays with Léonie? She did not honestly feel she would.

"What is it, after all, to die?" Father Parry had said. "It is to say good-bye to everything in this world . . . to fortune, pleasures, friends . . . a sad, irrevocable good-bye. It is to leave your house for ever and to be thrown into a narrow pit with no clothes but a shroud and no society but reptiles and worms. It is to pass in the twinkling of an eye to the unknown region called eternity, where you will hear from the mouth of God Himself in what place you are to make that great retreat that lasts for ever: whether in heaven or in the depths of hell. Think of your friends who have gone before you. Young as you are, my dear children, there must be some who have preceded you into eternity. From the grave they cry out to you: 'Yesterday for me and to-day for thee.' Ever since the day of your birth you have been dying; every hour of play or study brings you a little nearer the end of your life. A good Catholic should live constantly in the spiritual presence of death. Now, my dear little sisters, I want each one of you to imagine that you are lying on your death-bed. A feeble lamp is burning; each familiar object in the room, the very chairs and tables seem to say to you: 'You are leaving us for ever.' You are in the throes of your last agony. At your side are the devils and the holy angels disputing for your soul. Above your own painful, suffocating breathing, you can hear the sobs of your mother, the voice of the priest saying the last prayers of the Church. 'Depart, Christian soul, in the Name of God the Father Almighty Who created thee, of Jesus Christ Who suffered for thee, of the Holy Ghost Who sanctified thee.' Imagine your own body at the point of dissolution, your icy feet, your rigid arms, your forehead cold with the sweat of death. Go further still, imagine your own funeral. Think of a few weeks later, of the terrible corruption of your own body after the soul has abandoned it. Think of the odour of your decayed flesh and realise that this is nothing to the odour exhaled by one sin in the nostrils of Almighty God. And think of your soul naked at the tribunal of the God whom perhaps it has never truly loved, that God now no longer a Friend but a terrible Judge."

Nanda felt a sweat break out on her own forehead. Was it the sweat of death? She jumped out and knelt on the cold boards, praying frantically and incoherently. A little calmed, she went back to bed and fell asleep, only to dream that Theresa Leighton was lying dead in Our Lady's chapel, wearing her First Communion dress and a gilt paper crown. As she looked at her, a worm came out of Theresa's mouth and Nanda woke up shrieking.

After the first day or two, Nanda began to feel well enough to enjoy life in the infirmary. Her temperature was still a little above normal, so that there was a comfortable justification for remaining in bed, but she was allowed to read and to do some old jig-saw puzzles that were very puzzling indeed, since about a third of the pieces were missing. The infirmary library included a few books that down in the school would have been classed as story-books and the competition for these was keen. Nanda was lucky; instead of back numbers of *Stella Maris* or *The Messenger of The Sacred Heart*, Sister Jones brought her a frivolous, secular work called *St. Winifred's or the World of School*. On the flyleaf of this was written in a nun's beautiful script: "Certain pages of this book have been cut out, as the matter they contain is both vulgar and distasteful to the mind of a modest reader. Their excision does not interfere with the plot of the story." The book had been still further censored. Several paragraphs were inked out, and wherever the word "blackguard" appeared, a careful hand had pasted a strip of thick, but unfortunately transparent paper over it. Nanda was a voracious reader. She devoured *St. Winifred's* so fast that by tea-time she had finished it. When Sister Jones appeared, bearing a tray with the unaccustomed luxury of hot buttered toast, Nanda begged for a fresh book. But Sister Jones was firm. "You'll not get another book till to-morrow, Miss Nanda," she assured her, "unless it's a lesson-book. There can't be much the matter with you if you can read that fast."

"But, Sister," Nanda implored her, "it's hours before you put the lights out."

"Then you can say your rosary, miss."

"Will you come back later and talk to me, then? It's so awfully dull here alone."

Sister Jones pursed her lips.

"Good gracious, child, do you think I've nothing else to do? You can say some of the prayers Mother Regan and I haven't time to say for ourselves, what with all this sickness in the house." She shut the door so smartly that Nanda half expected to hear a key turn in the lock. It would probably be two hours before anyone came in again. How was she going to get through such an eter-

nity of time? Sleep was impossible. And three slim bars
of toast, even if she counted ten between each nibble,
could hardly last more than a few minutes. Then she
remembered the Francis Thompson in her dressing-
gown pocket. In a few minutes she was stumbling
through *The Mistress of Vision* between gulps of sugary
tea.

> "Secret was the garden,
>   Set in the pathless awe
> Where no star its breath may draw.
>   Life that is its warden
> Sits behind the fosse of death.
>   Mine eyes saw not and I saw.
> It was a mazeful wonder,
>   Thrice threefold it was enwalled
> With an emerald
>   Sealéd so asunder,
> All its birds in middle air
>   Hung adream, their music thralled."

She read on and on, enraptured. She could not understand half, but it excited her oddly, like words in a
foreign language sung to a beautiful air. She followed
the poem vaguely as she followed the Latin in her
missal, guessing, inventing meanings for herself, intoxicated by the mere rush of words. And yet she felt
she did understand, not with her eyes or her brain, but
with some faculty she did not even know she possessed.
Something was happening to her, something that had
not happened when she made her First Communion.
She shut the book and tried to make out what it was.
But she could not think at all, she could only go on saying to herself some words that had once caught her
fancy and that now seemed to have a real meaning.
"Too late have I known thee, too late have I loved thee,
O Beauty ever ancient and ever new." But she did not
want to go on. She did not want to be led into prayers

and aspirations. This new feeling, whatever it was, had nothing to do with God.

The unexpected entry of Mother Percival made her feel hot and foolish. She clumsily tried to hide her Francis Thompson under the sheet, but it was too late. Mother Percival directed an unusually charitable smile at Nanda, but her eyes were on the book.

"Well, and how's Nanda?" she inquired affably. "Much better, by the look of her. Such red cheeks for an invalid."

"Oh, I'm nearly well," said Nanda feebly.

"Well enough to read, I see," smiled Mother Percival, seating herself by the bed. "A story-book, is it?"

"No, Mother," admitted Nanda. "It's just some poetry."

"Just some poetry, is it? I didn't know you had such a devotion to English literature. Perhaps you're learning something by heart to surprise me when you come back to class?"

She reached out a lean, capable hand for the book.

There was a silence while she opened it and scanned a few lines. Nanda felt the blood beating in her ears.

"Francis Thompson? That's not one of your school books is it? I didn't know there was a copy in the infirmary."

"It's my own. Léonie gave it me for my First Communion," Nanda said boldly.

"I see. Francis Thompson was a great Catholic poet, but he did not write for little girls of eleven. How much of this do you imagine you understand?"

"Quite a lot," said Nanda recklessly.

"That's very interesting. Let me see." She glanced at the page. "Now what, for instance, does 'cymar' mean? Or 'effluence'? Or 'vertiginous'? Or 'panoply'?"

"I don't know," Nanda admitted sullenly.

"I thought as much. Did you ever hear about the little pig that died of trying to grunt like a grown-up pig when it could really only say 'wee-wee'?"

Mother Percival shut the book and laughed wholesomely.

"Now, you see, my dear child, that you're being just a little bit silly, aren't you? Some day you'll see the very wonderful religious meaning that's hidden in all this. But not yet. Francis Thompson was a mystic and no one expects little girls to understand the secrets of the saints. Not that Francis Thompson was a saint. He was not always a Catholic, you know, and there is often something a little morbid, a little hysterical in his work. But some of his poems are very simple and beautiful. I was going to let the Fifth Form learn *To a Snowdrop* for the Christmas wishing. But I think it would be better for you to let older people judge what is best for your little understanding."

"Please let me keep the book, Mother," she begged.

Mother Percival smiled again and turned over some pages.

"Well, perhaps there's no harm in keeping a book you so obviously don't understand. I suppose you want the others to think what a clever little person this Nanda Grey is?"

Suddenly her eye was arrested by a verse. Over her shoulder in a poem she had never looked at before, Nanda read:

> "I shall never feel a girl's soft arms
> Without horror of the skin."

But she read no more. Mother Percival hastily shut the book. The geniality had gone out of her face.

"This book goes straight to your trunk, Nanda," she said in her coldest voice. "There are things in it which are not fit for any decent person to read. If I had my way it should be burnt."

Nanda was trembling with indignation, but before she had time to speak, Mother Regan burst open the door.

"I'll have to move you back to your dormitory, child," she said. "I must have a good-sized room at once. Theresa Leighton is very ill indeed."

CHAPTER VI

NEARLY two years after Theresa Leighton's death came the happiest summer Nanda had ever known. The weather was perfect. Every day dawned clear and soft and unfolded through hours of sunlight to long evenings smelling of hay and lime-trees. There was a kind of gaiety and relaxation in the air; hair hung more loosely and sleeves were rolled up unreproved over browning arms. Even the bells sounded less insistent; they chimed in a lazy, worldly voice like old stable clocks. It was good to come in, flushed from tennis, to the cool, sweet-smelling chapel; to sit in a weeping willow after supper surreptitiously learning La Nuit de Mai; to find a chestnut flower against one's skin when one undressed at night. The children spent nearly all day in the garden; lessons, like food, tasted better out of doors and even Christian Doctrine seemed to lose some of its harsher edge when one could blink up through the green meshes of a plane-tree and inquire, with earnest frivolity, whether caterpillars had the rudiments of a conscience. She and Léonie were in the same class now, for Léonie, whose parents cared nothing for reports, had deliberately failed in her exams in order that Nanda should catch her up in the Lower Third.

They were both attached, Nanda passionately and Léonie with her usual cool carelessness to two divinities in the Lower First. The two divinities were also inseparables, so that Nanda who was doing the eighth book of Virgil with her father, thought of herself and Léonie as favourite pages in the train of Nisus and Euryalus. Although Nanda devotedly admired Rosario de Palencia, she was too much dazzled by her to envy Léonie her intimacy. Whenever in after-life she wanted to imagine any heroine, Juliet or Laura or Anna Karenina, she always invested her with Rosario's looks. Never, she thought, could any creature be more exquisite than this tall Spanish girl of seventeen, with her honey-coloured hair and her warm skin, that was neither white nor pink nor brown, but faintly golden. Rosario's eyes were turquoise blue, her brows black and strongly marked; her nose, the critics said, too masculine and her mouth far too wide. Her sister Elita was the recognised beauty, but Elita's morbidly white skin and brilliant dark eyes made no appeal to Nanda. Elita was a woman. Those languid eyes said too unmistakably that she was bored here among all these dull little girls. She never played games, but sat at recreation under the limes making lace, and paid no attention to any lesson but singing. Sometimes she knelt beside Nanda at benediction, and her lazy, veiled contralto would make the *O Salutaris* sound like a love-song. The nuns shrugged their shoulders and disapproved; they scolded Elita, they reasoned with her, they laughed at her. But nothing could change her. She dawdled through the school days, sleepy and secret, and spent hours, Rosario said, sitting at the window of the private room they shared, combing her dark hair that smelt of Russian leather, and talking about love. But Rosario was different. She seemed to despise her own beauty, dragging her golden hair straight back from her face and slouching like Léonie with her hands plunged in the pockets of a black woollen jacket. She played tennis fiercely, forgetting sometimes to laugh when she was beaten, and then apologising with her charming, wide smile. She went out for riding lessons with Elita, and returned in the severest of grey habits, with her hair crushed under an unbecoming bowler. But she could never escape from her beauty; it clung to her like a mist, like a skin, so that she seemed to move in a haze of loveliness. Everything she touched, every word she used, took on this quality of grace; her very gloves and handkerchiefs were romantic.

Léonie and Rosario had known each other outside Lippington. There were Wesseldorfs and Palencias in every embassy in Europe. They had been brought down to dessert in white muslin and blue sashes at diplomatic dinners in Vienna and St. Petersburg, and had grimaced at each other when eminent old gentlemen patted their heads. Once or twice a term, they would go out together to a well-chaperoned tea at the Ritz, or a polo match at Ranelagh; Rosario exquisite in a blue dress the colour of her eyes, and Léonie incongruously arrayed in a military-looking coat chosen by herself and an absurd, daisy-trimmed hat her mother had bought in Paris.

Léonie rarely talked about her friend. Occasionally she wrote poems to her; frosty, elegant little eighteenth-century verses in which Rosario figured as Celia or Lucinda or Amaryllis. Sometimes, with a most unusual patience, she copied out music parts for their two violins or transposed a song to the compass of Rosario's voice. But if she never praised and seldom even mentioned Rosario, she would not suffer the least slight on her from anyone else. Once Marjorie Appleyard had said something contemptuous about Elita and Spaniards in general and Léonie, without a word, had shot out her fist and sent her sprawling.

There was no unearthly radiance about Clare Rockingham, but to Nanda she, too, seemed romantic. To begin with, she was a Protestant and had only managed to be sent to Lippington after incessant quarrels with her family. But after she had returned unannounced from Germany, having escaped from her governess at Basle, and had then proceeded to lame her father's best hunter by riding him without permission at a gymkhana, the Rockinghams had decided that there was something to be said for Lippington after all. They had, however, threatened to cut her off completely if she became a Catholic. This gave Clare the glamour of a secret sorrow. For days she would mock, with her wild, crowing laugh that could be heard all down the refectory, at the punctiliousness of Catholic doctrine. Then one evening she would be found in tears at benediction. She did not attend Religious Instruction, but she borrowed Rosario's catechism and read it during free study, to the delight of the whole Senior School, who were praying quite openly for her conversion. Once she even borrowed Nanda's rosary. Seeing Nanda looking a little doubtful, Clare tweaked her pigtail and asked:

"What is it, baby? Will it hurt your rosary to be used by a pagan?"

"I'll have to get it blessed again, that's all," Nanda explained.

Clare's eyes danced. They were odd eyes, green and, like her skin, freckled with brown.

"I say, am I as wicked as all that? Do I actually put a curse on everything I touch?"

"Of course not," said Nanda. "I'd have to get it blessed again if I lent it to anyone . . . even the Pope himself. You see, a rosary's only blessed for the person it belongs to, and so if anyone else uses it they don't get the indulgences and you don't either until it's been blessed again. Mine's blessed for a happy death, so I mustn't forget to have it done."

Clare threw up her hands and crowed with laughter. "What a fantastic idea, darling. Does it cost anything, having your beads blessed?"

"Of course not," said Nanda, profoundly shocked.

"Don't look so hurt, baby. I'm only a poor, inquiring heathen. But I always thought there was something called a sale of indulgences."

"Lots of Protestants think so," said Nanda kindly. "But it's quite untrue. They think that three hundred days' indulgence means that you get three hundred days off purgatory. But of course, that's quite impossible, because there isn't any time in purgatory."

"Well, what does it mean then?"

"It's rather a long explanation," Nanda told her.

"Go on. I'm fascinated."

"Well, it's like this. To begin with, every mortal sin has two sorts of punishment, temporal and eternal. If you die in mortal sin, you go straight to hell. But you're let off the eternal punishment if you confess your sin and get absolution."

"Then I should just go on sinning and being forgiven as often as I liked."

"Oh, no," said Nanda hastily, "because part of the

condition of getting absolution at all is that you have to have a sincere intention not to commit the sin again."

"I see," mused Clare. "By the way, how do I know when it *is* a mortal sin?"

"That's awfully easy. There's got to be grave matter, full knowledge and full consent. So if you kill someone by accident, it isn't a mortal sin. Unless you meant to hurt them badly, when of course it would be. Then take stealing. It's rather difficult to know just how much would constitute grave matter. But it's generally supposed to be about half a crown."

"So if I stole two and fivepence, it would only be a venial sin?"

"Ye-es," said Nanda a little doubtfully. "But, of course, if two and fivepence was all the person had, or if they were a widow or an orphan, or if you stole it from a church box, it would be mortal."

"And suppose it was a very dark night and I meant to steal a half-crown and it turned out to be two shillings, it would only be a venial sin?"

"Good gracious, no," said Nanda positively. "It would be a mortal sin because you had the *intention* of stealing half a crown."

"You Catholics are wonderfully definite about everything, aren't you? It must be a great comfort to know just where one is. But go on about indulgences."

"Sure I'm not boring you?"

"Not a bit, infant," smiled Clare, showing very white teeth that had crinkled edges like a small child's.

"Well, you're quite clear about eternal punishment and temporal punishment, aren't you? After the eternal punishment of a mortal sin has been remitted in confession, there's still the temporal punishment to be worked off in this life or in purgatory. Venial sins carry some temporal punishment, too, but not so much."

"I suppose there are heaps of venial sins?"

"Hundreds," said Nanda gloomily. "Almost everything's a venial sin, in fact. If I don't eat my cabbage, or if I have an extra helping of pudding when I'm not really hungry, or if I think my hair looks rather nice when it's just been washed . . . they're all venial sins. And then, as if one's own sins weren't enough, there are nine ways in which you can share in another person's."

"Good Lord," crowed Clare. "I bet you a holy picture you don't know 'em all."

Nanda shut her eyes and gabbled.

"By counsel, by command, by consent, by provocation, by praise or flattery, by being a partner in the sin, by silence, by defending the ill-done."

"It's amazing. How can all you babes reel them off like that?"

"Well, I've done catechism and Christian Doctrine for two hours a day for three years."

"Then tell me something. I was reading Rosario's catechism on Sunday, and I came across something very peculiar. It was one of the commandments . . . 'Thou shalt not commit adultery,' and it said it forbade fornication and all wilful pleasure in the irregular motions of the flesh. What does it mean?"

"I haven't the faintest idea," said Nanda coldly. "We don't do the sixth and ninth commandments. Mother Percival says they're not necessary for children. They're about some very disgusting sins, I believe, that only grown-up people commit."

She could not understand why Clare laughed so wildly that her green eyes brimmed over with tears.

Rather offended, Nanda said:

"I think we'd better be getting back to the others. I promised Léo to play tennis. And, besides, we're not really supposed to be about in twos."

"Nonsense, baby. Mother Percival has got us well in the tail of her stony eye. And besides, you may be converting me, who knows?"

"I shouldn't dream of trying, Clare," asserted Nanda, still hurt. "Catholics don't try and convert people like that. They just answer your questions and . . . and . . . pray for you."

Clare leaned over and touched Nanda's arm with a hot quivering hand that burned through her holland sleeve.

"Do you pray for me, baby?"

"Of course," said Nanda in a very matter-of-fact voice, but she blushed all the same. Clare's touch embarrassed and delighted her; it gave her the queerest shivering sensation in the roof of her mouth. Why was it that when everyone else seemed just face and hands, Clare always reminded one that there was a warm body under her uniform? For a minute her freckled eyes searched Nanda's, and then she laughed softly and shook her mane of wiry bronze-bright hair.

"Go on about indulgences, infant theologian."

Nanda was just explaining that in the old days people would perform penances for three hundred days in order to remit their temporal punishment, and that an indulgenced prayer was one which, if said with the right dispositions, entitled one to the merits such a penance would have gained, when an unexpected bell began to clamour excitedly.

Children were running from all directions towards the house; a nun appeared on the terrace, waving her arms.

Nanda forgot theology and seized Clare's hand.

"Come on, come on quick," she cried. "It's *Deo Gratias*, the holiday bell."

The nun on the terrace called to them as they passed: "Into the big study-room, children. Don't bother to change your shoes. Wonderful news for you."

Soon the whole school was assembled, panting and expectant. Scarcely had the last child scrambled into place before Reverend Mother and Mother Radcliffe came in, their faces rippling with smiles.

"Dear children," announced Reverend Mother, as they rose from their curtseys, "this is one of the greatest days in the history of our dear Order. I have just heard from Rome that His Holiness has consented to the canonisation of our beloved foundress, Blessed Marie-Joseph Guillemin. The ceremony will take place in a fortnight's time, on our own saint's feast."

There was a wild outbreak of cheering. Reverend Mother permitted the noise for several minutes, then, still smiling, she held up her hand for silence.

"Now, children, I want you all to join with me in singing the *Magnificat*. The rest of to-day will be a holiday. At five o'clock the school and the community will sing a solemn *Te Deum* in the chapel as a thanksgiving for this wonderful grace that God has bestowed upon us all."

She raised her old voice, a mere thin shell, but true in time and tune.

"Magnificat anima mea dominus"

and the whole school answered in a shout of delight:

"Et exaltavit spiritus meus"

Halfway through, Nanda stopped singing. In the rich web of sound she could trace two fibres, the silver soft-

ness of Rosario's voice and Léonie's coppery ring. Beside
Rosario, croaking dismally, but passionately, stood Clare
Rockingham, who had not the slightest ear for music
but professed to adore it because she adored Rosario.

The fortnight that followed was rich with a sense of
preparation. Lessons went on as usual but with an agreeable desultoriness. Nuns would appear at the door of a
classroom and beckon half the inmates away to rehearse
for a play, a tableau or a concert. The piano cells echoed
all day with people practising part songs. Mistresses in
charge of recreation stitched vigorously at secular
draperies of tulle and spangles; bands of helpers were
recruited to glue feathers on to angel's wings, and the
Guest House filled up with "Old Children," whose princess frocks and picture hats were a source of much
distraction in the chapel.

On the eve of the great day Mother Radcliffe summoned the whole school into the big parlour. The old
ones were there, too, proudly wearing their Child of
Mary medals over their pearl necklaces. Some of them
had fished out their former decorations, and Nanda was
enchanted by the sight of a stout Portuguese lady, the
mother of three children in the school, cheerfully dis-
playing a faded pink ribbon across her Poiret frock.
Mother Radcliffe's face, as she seated herself at the little
baize-covered table, announced that the occasion was to
be serious.

"My dear children, old and new," she began, "Reverend Mother has asked me to tell you something about
our saint and why the Church, after years of prayer and
searching for Divine guidance, has consented to raise
her from the high honours of beatification to the still
higher ones of canonisation. To-morrow, in St. Peter's,
her picture will be carried in procession, and she will be

publicly proclaimed a saint by the Holy Father himself. All of you know a little of the slow and difficult process of examination to which the Church submits her candidates for sainthood. You know that the body of the servant of God, if he or she has died a natural death, must be discovered after many years perfect and uncorrupted. You know that every written word is scrutinised, every remembered utterance weighed for the least taint of heresy or worldliness. The Pope appoints an official to act as the Devil's Advocate, whose duty it is to find any trace of evil, any departure from the highest, most heroic sanctity which might nullify the Cause of Beatification. And lastly, it must be conclusively proved, with medical testimony, that the Servant of God has worked major miracles of healing either through her direct intercession or through the touch of her holy relics. I want to tell you now of the three greatest miracles of the many our dear Mother wrought, cures which the doctors attending the cases, although many of them were not Catholics, could attribute to nothing but Divine intervention."

She proceeded to read out the details of the miraculous cures of an elderly nun, a girl of nineteen and a little boy suffering from meningitis. The nun had been at the point of death from a fibroid tumour; three novenas had been made to Our Lady and St. Joseph without result. But on being touched with a little bag containing some of the hair of Mother Guillemin, she had experienced a pain of burning. The swelling immediately subsided and the next day the doctors pronounced that there was no trace of the growth which had defied treatment for months. In the second case, the girl had been operated upon for appendicitis, and not only had gangrene set in, but a sinus had formed in the intestine. The doctors had given her up for lost, when a friend brought her a piece of the saint's habit and sewed it to the dying girl's nightgown. A novena was begun to Mother Guillemin, and on the second day the sinus suddenly healed up. By the ninth day the girl was not only out of danger, but able to get up for several hours a day. The little boy of five had been actually in his last agony with a very severe attack of meningitis. His mother, who had been sitting by his bed for two days and nights, had fallen asleep. When she woke, she was surprised to see a woman in a religious habit bending over her little son. The nun touched the boy's forehead and he smiled at her, instantly stopped moaning and lay quite still. In the morning the fever had left him and in a few weeks he was back at school and in perfect health. One day his mother saw a picture of Mother Guillemin and immediately exclaimed: "That is the face of the holy nun who cured my child."

Mother Radcliffe put down her sheaf of notes and smiled. There was something about her smile that reminded Nanda a little of Mother Frances. It had the same sweet disdain. Her face, like Mother Frances', was very pale and sloped down to a narrow chin, but her pallor was solid instead of being transparent, and her features handsome but rather thickly moulded. But her eyes, smallish and of a curious grey-green like lichen, searched one's face with a good deal of Mother Frances' cool penetration. "Physical wonders like these, my dear children," she said in her even voice, "are the things the world wants to hear about its saints." She had a habit of pausing between each word, as if words themselves, having been used by so many people, had a sort of uncleanness and must have the dust blown off them before they were fit for her use. "But for us, who are nearer to her heart, it is the small things, her silences, her mortifications, the secret signs of her spiritual growth that are so infinitely more precious. Our Mother had an ardent, even a passionate nature. She was generous to a fault. But her brother, who devoted his whole life to training her soul for God, mortified her even in her virtues. He knew that such fine metal could stand great heat. And some of that severity which to the world seems harshness is bound up in the school rule which you are privileged to follow. François Guillemin made our Holy Mother study long and hard without reward, without even a word of praise. Knowing that she was afraid of firearms, he would often fire revolvers in her presence to strengthen her courage. Her mother gave her a pretty shawl to wear to mass, and her brother tore it to shreds to mortify her vanity. And once, when she had lovingly embroidered him a pair of slippers for his feast day, he threw them in the fire without a word of thanks. And it is the same in the schools of the Five Wounds to-day. We work to-day to turn out, not accomplished young women, nor agreeable wives, but soldiers of Christ, accustomed to hardship and ridicule and ingratitude."

The morning of the feast day dawned clear and dewy, with a haze over the lake that promised great heat. Nanda was already awake when the *Deo Gratias* bell clamoured down the dormitory, and the Children of Mary, dressed up in serge aprons and white table napkins to look like nuns, came trooping in for the ceremonial "calling" with which all big holidays began.

Rosario, stately as an abbess, without one gilt hair straying under her black hood, read out the proclamation of the holiday from an enormous scroll hung with seals as big as saucers. Wherever possible, the pleasures of the day were to be related to the events of Mother

Guillemin's life. Thus the present awakening represented her vocation; hide and seek during the morning, her hidden life; boats on the lake, her voyage to America; the tableaux in the afternoon, her holy visions; a concert, the heavenly music she was often permitted to hear, and the bonfire and the fireworks with which the day was to end, the warmth of her charity and the illumination of her spirit.

After mass the children went out into the sunlit garden to breakfast in classes. As a great treat, they were allowed eggs with their bread and butter, and these eggs were gaily coloured as they were on Easter Sunday. Each child also received a picture of Mother Guillemin, with the motto "Pray that your hearts, like hers, may be made deep with humility and fiery with charity." It was the rule of these holiday breakfasts that the mistress should entertain her class, and to-day Mother Percival scored an unexpected success by a series of rhymes on the character of each of her pupils.

Léonie's was:

> "Gold under fire has a special charm
> But fire under gold may lead to harm,"

and Nanda, who had expected to be ridiculed, found herself unexpectedly flattered by a whole quatrain:

> "A rainbow swung in a morning sky
> Owes light and life to the sun on high
> So keep your eye fixed on heaven above
> And heaven and earth will give you love."

All the same, she was a little puzzled by it. Had Mother Percival noticed that lately she had been having odd fits of melancholy? Was there a warning concealed in it that she was too apt to consider any talents she had as her own property rather than as gifts lent her by God

for His own ends? She listened without much interest
to the rhymes about the others, though she was too well
trained not to join mechanically in the applause. What
was it that so often came over her nowadays and made
her so deeply and rather pleasurably sad for no particular reason? Sometimes, the melancholy began with
a phrase of music or a line of poetry, but often with far
less explicable things, such as the sound of cricket bats
on late summer evenings or the sight of a beautiful
stranger in the chapel. She was interested, as were all the
literary romantics of Lippington, in the mechanics of
sorrow. She starred her essays with quotations about
our sweetest songs being those that tell of saddest
thought, and the bitter taste of heaven's star-laden vine
and the poet's crown of laurel and thorns. She longed
passionately for a definite, solid grief which should give
this vague melancholy dignity and reason. When Léonie
occasionally looked coldly sad, she was worrying over
the fact that her father was threatened with cancer.
When Rosario's blue eyes filled with tears, she was thinking of her mother, who had died in the spring. When
Wanda Waleska, the fierce girl from Warsaw, clenched
her hands and bit her lips while Rosario played Chopin,
she was grieving for the slavery of Poland. And when
Clare sobbed violently in the chapel, she was sorrowing
because she was torn between the Catholic Church and
her own high-handed, exasperating, beloved family.
Only Nanda had no decent, acknowledged injury of her
own. For a time she tried to persuade herself that she
bore a secret and terrible share in the death of Theresa
Leighton. But her native honesty soon forced her to
admit that Theresa's death had moved her far less than
the death of the Duc de Reichstadt in *L'Aiglon*. Then
she tried to make *L'Aiglon* himself the noble object of

her melancholy. She wore a bunch of parma violets under her dress on the anniversary of his death, and, having a drop of Austrian blood in her, tried to persuade herself that one of her ancestresses had been in love with him. But even this image would grow papery and shrivelled long before her melancholy mood was exhausted.

However, to-day she was gloriously, irresponsibly happy. The stale rolls tasted delicious out here under the trees, the sun was warm on her hair, and a little bubble of pleasure burst in her throat every time Léonie grinned at her. Half the morning passed in long, exciting games of hide and seek; then came a heavenly hour in the hayfield. She and Léonie were pelting each other with armfuls of dried grass and meadowsweet, when Rosario came up to them. She wore an absurd white linen hat, like a plate, tilted forward over her rich hair, and her apron was kilted back over her skirt. Rosario was incapable even of making hay ungracefully; she moved in her haze of charm like Marie Antoinette playing at shepherdesses. But she was not smiling; her black eyebrows were drawn together and she looked both sad and angry.

"Have either of you seen Clare?" she asked.

Nanda and Léonie did not look at each other.

"No," said Nanda. "No, Rosario."

But Léonie answered:

"Yes. About half an hour ago. On the other side of the lake. She'd got her arm in a sling."

Rosario's golden skin paled a little, but she only said: "I'll go and look for her," and walked slowly away.

Nanda was hot with curiosity, but she waited for Léonie. "They've quarrelled," Léonie said presently.

"Clare's so frightfully sentimental. She won't let Rosario alone."

"I think Rosario's the loveliest person I've ever seen," said Nanda timidly.

"Yes," said Léonie judicially. She looked at Nanda for a minute; her face was pale and damp with sweat, a blue vein standing out in the middle of her forehead made her seem more than ever like a stern, handsome young man. Then she grinned.

"I suppose you want to convert Clare?"

Nanda blushed.

"Well, not exactly. But of course I should like her to be a Catholic."

Léonie propped her chin on her rake.

"I'd never advise anyone to *become* a Catholic," she said. "If you're one, you've got to be one. But you can't change people. Catholicism isn't a religion, it's a nationality."

"It's funny, Léo," mused Nanda. "You say the most extraordinary things; you're awfully slack about prayers and all that, you've even got a copy of *Candide* bound up as a missal, and I believe the nuns know, and yet you get away with everything. Yet if I do the slightest thing, I'm punished."

"Because they're not sure of you yet. You're a nicely washed and combed and baptised and confirmed little heathen, but you're a heathen all the same. But they're sure of me. In ten, twenty years I'll be exactly the same. It's in the blood. I'd as soon be a Hottentot as be anything but a Catholic. It may be nonsense, but it's the sort of nonsense I happen to like. And when I die, my great uncle Cardinal de Wesseldorf and my great-great aunt the Carmelite Abbess de Wesseldorf, who had an affair with Napoleon before she entered, will say to the recording angel: 'My dear sir, you can't seriously send a Wesseldorf to hell,' and into heaven I shall go."

But Nanda's mind had wandered to Clare. What had happened? Why was her arm in a sling? Clare was the sort of person who attracted accidents. She nearly always had a bandaged ankle or a cut finger. Perhaps that was one of the reasons why one was always so conscious of her body.

The bell for the next amusement interrupted Nanda's speculations. As they sauntered slowly towards the house, Clare herself joined them, with her free arm through Rosario's. She was laughing wildly; evidently they had made it up. But Rosario seemed worried.

"You must go to the infirmary, Clare," she imposed. "You're being ridiculous."

"Nonsense, darling. What's a little burn? I'm always damaging myself. Mother Regan hates the sight of me. I didn't go to the infirmary when I had rheumatism last week, and it was absolute agony."

"But this is different," Rosario appealed to the other two. "Clare burnt herself badly last night, goodness knows how, when she was lighting the gas in her room. She's just bandaged it up anyhow, but she ought to have it properly looked after."

"Well, let's see the burn," said Léonie sensibly.

She laid her hand on the arm in the sling, and Clare drew in a sharp breath of pain.

"No, I'm perfectly all right, silly child," she said bravely.

"I insist on looking," said Rosario. Her soft voice sounded dangerous.

Clare looked at her queerly for a minute, then burst into one of her crows of laughter. Suddenly she tore viciously at the knot of her sling with her free hand and her teeth.

"Then look, darling."

Her white, lightly-freckled arm was bare and un-scarred.

"Just a joke, darling. I so adore to see you looking angry and worried."

Rosario turned pale with rage for a second; then she laughed softly, but not altogether pleasantly.

Léonie caught Nanda's elbow.

"Come on. I'll race you to the house."

On the terrace Nanda said breathlessly:

"I don't understand Clare, do you?"

"She's just hysterical," panted Léonie. "One of these days she'll go off her head."

The golden day passed richly away. After the tableaux and the concert and the long benediction among a blaze of candles and azaleas, Nanda felt she could bear no more excitement. She felt tired and surfeited with the exuberance of the holiday; her head ached and her mouth was sore from eating too many sweets. At supper they served a weak, sickly wine that made her feel dizzy. It was a relief to go down to the big field by the lake and watch the bonfire and the rockets, and to know that soon there would be bed and sleep and an ordinary, blessedly dull to-morrow.

The great fire blazed and crackled; the whole school streamed round it in a wild eddy, singing and leaping. Jets of flame, hearts, scissors, tiny maps of England broke off from the main body and vanished into the clear, dark air. Faces showed red and strange, hair tossed away from ribbons, heads were flung back and mouths opened wide. Across the circle Nanda stared, fascinated, at Clare, who was dancing like a bacchante, her bronze hair flying, her face brilliant and wild, her body leaning back as if into invisible arms. Faster and faster they danced, until the strained, whirling loop broke and a dozen children fell in a heap, laughing and screaming. There was a thunder of fireworks, and the name of St. Marie-Joseph Guillemin slowly uncoiled itself in scarlet letters against the sky. Nanda felt Léonie give her arm a sharp jerk. The last burst of light from the rockets carved her face out clean against a net of leaves, pale and stern and beautiful.

"Come away," she said quietly.

Nanda followed her without speaking to the little clearing beside the lake. In the dimness, Léonie was only a dark shape, but Nanda could make out that her hands were clasped under her chin. Feeling suddenly shy, Nanda looked away from her at the quiet water where the mist was gathering. When Léonie spoke at last, it was in a deep, troubled voice, as if she were speaking to herself:

> "O Muse, spectre insatiable
> Ne m'en demandez pas si long
> L'homme n'ecrit rien sur le sable
> A l'heure où passe l'aquilon.
>
> J'ai vu le temps où ma jeunesse
> Sur mes lèvres était sans cesse
> Prête à chanter comme un oiseau—
> Mais j'ai souffert un dur martyre
> Et le moins que j'en pourrais dire
> Si je l'essayais sur ma lyre
> La briserait comme un roseau."

CHAPTER VII

AT the end of June came the annual retreat. Nanda
viewed the prospect of four days' complete silence
with mixed feelings. She had made retreats before, but
never one so long as this, and she knew that after the
novelty of the first few hours wore off, they were apt to
become oppressive. During a retreat, the children lived
like nuns; each one was given a classroom or a piano
cell to herself, in which she spent her time between the
four hour-long meditations in the chapel and the silent
meals and recreations. Recreation consisted of walking
up and down the alleys reading pious books or reciting
the rosary, and not a word was supposed to pass one's
lips after the first retreat bell had sounded. Even letters
were not allowed, so that the sense of being cut off from
the world was complete. Nanda entered into retreat with
the best intentions, determined to make the devotions
as wholeheartedly as possible and to offer them up for
the conversion of Clare Rockingham. The first day was
pleasant. Newly confessed and wearing clean clothes,
she had the sense of beginning life over again. She spent
a long time arranging flowers on the little alter of her
cell, polishing the brass crucifix and the candlesticks and
setting a nightlight in a blue dish in front of her statue
of Our Lady of Lourdes. Next, with an agreeable feeling
of travelling lightly and compactly on this spiritual
voyage, she set out the four books that were to be her
only companions: the *Watches of the Passion*, her
missal and *Imitation of Christ* and a stout new note-
book with a shiny cover in which she was to write out
her notes on Father Westlake's conferences and to make
pious observations of her own.

Léonie and Rosario were seasoned retreatants. They went into this solitary confinement with as little fuss as old soldiers going into camp. Rosario supplied herself with a great deal of delicate needlework of a vaguely devotional nature, while Léonie announced frankly that she was going to use her notebook to compose a blank verse tragedy on the death of Socrates. But Nanda had not yet lost her fear of the voices she might hear in the darkness. Her childish dread of a vocation reasserted itself, and she was by no means comforted when Father Westlake, in the course of the very first meditation, reminded them that in the silence of a retreat God had His chance to whisper his secret call to the soul to leave all and follow Him. Suppose that, in return for the conversion of Clare Rockingham, God should demand the dedication of her own life? Would she be equal to so heroic a sacrifice? And would it be, she asked herself in a moment of unheroic common sense, altogether fair of God to expect it, since Clare's conversion would presumably be to His own advantage? On the other hand, if eternity were everything, it was only logical to spend this life as unpleasantly as possible, in order to ensure permanent happiness in the next. But why had God made this world so attractive? It was so hard to keep one's eyes fixed on heaven when even the saints could give one no idea of what heaven would be like. If they were vague about heaven, they were very definite indeed about hell. Nanda felt a great deal more positive about the conditions of life in hell than in, say, the West of Scotland or Minneapolis. It was generally admitted, when they read the *Inferno* in class, that Dante had used a good deal of poetic licence in softening the outlines of the picture.

Nanda, full of her good resolutions, used the stout

notebook for its proper purpose. Every evening, after a meagre supper eaten to the accompaniment of Mother Percival's readings of the *Life of St. Francis Xavier*, she laboriously transcribed all that she could remember of the day's Meditations and Considerations. She did this partly for the benefit of Clare, who was not allowed to make the retreat, although she had done everything she could to persuade the nuns to let her. She had coaxed, she had wept, she had even tried to blackmail them by open rebellion, but they had remained firm. Poor Clare was forced to live through the entire school routine by herself. She attended all the usual classes as a solitary pupil, she played bumble-puppy sulkily on an empty playground, and did lonely preparations in the huge, deserted study-room. All this naturally tended to develop her mild flirtations with Catholicism into a hungry passion to be received into the Church. She read every pious book she could lay hands on, wept noisily and regularly in the chapel, and was constantly thrusting holy pictures into Nanda's missal, inscribed in her sprawling back-hand: "Pray hard, darling, for my great Intention."

So Nanda wrote out her notes as carefully as possible, with headings and sub-headings and neat underlinings and managed to slip the book into Clare's eager hands when she passed her in the garden.

And this is what Clare read.

NOTES ON MY RETREAT

Meditation I.

"Sink, sink into thyself and rally the good in the depths of thy soul." Examples of retreats in the Bible. Elija in the desert. St. John the Baptist. Jonah in the

whale's belly. Our Lord in the wilderness. St. Ignatius
in the Cave of Manresa. Importance of retreats when
one has gone out into the world. Devil hates them. Puts
difficulties in the way; social engagements, etc. Soul's
only engagement is with God. Opportunity to show
courtesy to God, to return His visits as St. Ignatius returned Our Lady's visits to him in visions by a pilgrimage to her shrine at Aranzazu. Opportunity to know
ourselves; to discover our faults without flinching, to set
right our accounts with God. Makes us realise that we
are solitary beings; naked came we into the world, etc.
No human friendship comparable to friendship of God.
Retreat a little death, making us see time and eternity
in their right proportions.

Meditation II. Sin.

Every human being tainted with original sin. Warped
instincts and passions like the beasts. Baptism remits
punishment due to original sin, but does not eradicate
results. Limited intellect, dull comprehension of Divine
things, etc. Unbaptised babies do not go to hell, but to
limbo, a sort of earthly paradise. Not comparable to real
paradise. One-third of angels became devils because they
were too proud to accept the idea of the Incarnation.
Human race will go on till vacant places in heaven are
filled. Devils' sins worse than ours; sinned with full
knowledge of God. Pride first and deadliest of sins.
Heresies all due to pride. Setting oneself up against
God's Divine revelation in the Church. Even children
have difficulties about religion. Ten thousand difficulties
do not make a doubt. Doubts are most apt to creep in
when moral fibre has been weakened. Vanity, self-indulgence, etc., lead to doubting God's law. Hence importance of mortification. Mortal sin makes the soul loath-

some in the sight of God. Saints could detect horrible
stench in presence of sinners. Soul dead to God. No good
work done in state of mortal sin counts, but God in His
mercy may take such works into account and hasten
grace of repentance. Sacrament of Penance restores these
lost merits. People make too light of venial sins, but
they weaken the soul's health and lead to mortal sins.
Venial sins punished in purgatory, a place as terrible as
hell, but not eternal. Souls in purgatory cannot help
themselves. Only prayers on earth can shorten their
sufferings. Better to be afflicted with the most appalling
disease than to commit one mortal sin. Disease a faint
type of sin. Mortal sins only forgiven in confession or by
an act of perfect contrition, *e.g.*, act of sincere penitence
from love of God alone, not from fear of punishment.
Fear of hell lowest reason for repentance. Always think
of having hurt God, not yourself.

Meditation III. Dangers of the World.

Worldly pleasures, business, etc., tend to interfere with
spiritual life. Things not in themselves harmful may be
harmful to soul. A saint said it was dangerous to walk
through a beautiful wood. Tendency to regard things
for their own sakes, rather than as manifestations of
Creator's power, wisdom, etc. Sermons in stones. Dangers
of nature-worship. Look for God in everything. Modern
Pantheism. Believing everything to be God. Idea that it
is better to go for country walk than attend mass. Dangerous nonsense and loose thinking. Devil responsible
for part of creation after fall. Thistles, weeds, etc. Trying to upset God's scheme. Nature only beneficial to
man before fall; now enemy. Even beauty often
poisoned. Choose friends for solid piety, not for superficial good looks or accomplishments. Give up a friend-

ship if it tends to hinder you in the practice of your religion. God hates exclusive personal loves. Mother love the highest of earthly loves, because essentially unselfish. Danger of idle conversation and frivolous reading. Never read books criticising Church. Priests must read them in order to refute them. Bad books do untold harm. Writer responsible for evil his books do; he shares in every sin occasioned by it. Cannot go to heaven until book has ceased to harm. Writer of bad book appeared in flames to saint. Tormented until last copy was destroyed. Oscar Wilde must now be suffering for untold evil done by his works. Books on the index. Kingsley, Macaulay, Huxley, etc. Abominable works exposed in Mayfair drawing-rooms. Zola, Anatole France, etc. Scientific works unsuitable for women. Puff up their vanity with ideas they only half understand. If science conflicts with religion, science must, by definition, be wrong. Garden of Eden a myth, perhaps; but true in essentials. Order of creation in Bible ratified even by modern scientists. Wrong to imagine Catholics not good scientists. Pasteur, Wassermann, etc. Jesuit astronomers. Read a spiritual book for every novel.

Meditation IV. Christian's Rule of Life.

Dedicate each day to God. Rise modestly, putting on clothes, remembering how much more important to clothe soul in virtue than body in fine raiment. Morning and night prayers. Mass and Communion whenever possible. When undressing, think of Christ stripped of His garments. St. Theresa rose to great heights of sanctity by always thinking of the Agony in the Garden last thing at night. Opportunities of mortification occur all day long. Pity looking-glasses were ever invented. Think how ugly you are when you look in them. Imagine old age, decay, etc. Encourage soul to look in mirror of lives of saints to learn its own defects. Christian marriage. Not for indulgence of selfish passions or even for exclusive affection. Object to provide Christian upbringing for children. Children always welcome to good Catholics. Take no thought for the morrow. God will provide. He sends little ones trooping down from heaven. Poverty does not matter. Saints came from large families. Essentials of life, Mass and the Sacraments are free to all. Wealth carries great responsibilities. Chokes spiritual growth. Rich and poor, however, a divine dispensation. Must not try to alter natural order of things. Abominations of socialism, freemasonry, etc. Trying to do God's work for Him. Women's votes unnecessary. Let her use her great influence in her own sphere. Modesty more effective than desire to shine. Our Lady had no vote and did not want one.

Meditation V. Death.

Every human being must die. Blasphemous scientist who said that death might one day be abolished by human agency. Must always be prepared for death; *e.g.*, be in a state of grace. Then it has no terrors. St. Charles Borromeo, when asked what he would do if the Last Trump sounded as he was playing chess, replied that he would go on with his game, since he had undertaken it to the glory of God. Even when body unconscious, soul might still be conscious. A strong presumption, though not article of faith, that God appears at the moment of death and gives the soul one last chance to accept or reject him. No one goes to hell except through their own fault. The Sacred Heart promised to Blessed Margaret Mary Alacoque that all who went to Communion on nine consecutive first Fridays should have the grace of final perseverance. All the same, it would be presumptuous to trust to that alone. Presumption and despair both sins against the Holy Ghost.

Meditation VI. Judgment.

Soul goes straight from death-bed to tribunal of God. Two judgments; that private one and the public one at the last day, when all one's sins and virtues will be publicly proclaimed in the valley of Jehosaphat. The soul condemned to hell would suffer only in the spirit until the last day, when the resurrected body would add to its agonies. Nearly everyone must spend some time in purgatory to cleanse away the last traces of sin. Souls in purgatory suffer, but are happy, knowing that they are sure of heaven. Sight of God makes the sinner horrible in his own sight; he longs for the cleansing fire. Dream of Gerontius. "Take me away and in the lowest deep there let me be . . . motionless and happy in my pain." No excuses at the Judgment Seat. No frantic pleas for mercy can alter the course of Divine justice. Decision is eternal, irrevocable.

Meditation VII. Hell.

But under this heading Nanda had written nothing but Eternally, Eternally, Eternally. It was not that she had forgotten what Father Westlake had said about hell. She remembered it all too clearly; she could have written down almost word for word his cool, accurate catalogue of the punishments of the damned. But she could not bring herself to write it down. Was it because Clare was to read her notes? Or because she wanted to forget? Or that she was superstitious and felt such things were better unwritten in case they should attract the very

horrors they described? But if there was no record of
the meditation on hell in her notebook, there was a
definite enough impression in her own mind. Body and
soul were to be tormented for ever and ever, with no
interruption of agony, no numbness of habit, no ray of
hope. Every sense would be revolted by filth and stench
and noise; every nerve exquisitely tortured by fire to
which mere earthly fire was as cool as water. The
damned suffered always from appalling thirst, their
swollen tongues were parched and cracked. They were
hungry and the devils in mockery offered them white-
hot coals to eat. They suffered still more from agony of
mind, from the separation of God, after Whom they
now so bitterly longed. They would gladly endure ten
thousand years of torment for the sake of one second of
earthly life in which they might repent and be reconciled to Him. Father Westlake had quoted a long passage
from Father Faber which was already sickeningly
familiar to Nanda. "With a cry that should be heard
creation through the lost soul rushes upon God and it
knocks itself, spirit as it is, against material terrors. It
clasps the shadow of God and lo, it embraces keen
flames. It runs up to Him, but it has encountered only
fearful demons. It leaps the length of its chain after
Him, but it has only dashed into an affrighting crowd
of lost and cursed souls. Thus, it is ever writhing under
the sense of being its own executioner. Thus, there is
not an hour of our summer sunshine, not a moment of
our sweet starlight, not a vibration of our moonlit
groves not an undulation of odorous air from our
flower-beds, not a pulse of delicious sound from music or
song to us, but that hapless, unpitiable soul is ever falling sick afresh of the overwhelming sense that all around
it is eternal." Even Léonie's observation that Father

Faber's style had a good deal in common with Mr. Pecksniff's could not quite rob the passage of its sting. It was not so much the thought of hell for herself that appalled Nanda, for after all, she knew the means of avoiding it, but she sometimes lay awake at night worrying miserably over the damned. For months she would forget all about them, then an account of a horrible accident or a sermon like this would remind her of them. She would pray frantically for them, forgetting that it was useless. In spite of this, she would go so far as to beg Our Lady to do something for them, clinging to some vague legend about their being allowed one day's respite in ten thousand years. Sometimes, she even doubted that their punishments were eternal, only to remember, horrified, that the eternity of hell was an article of faith, and that to doubt it endangered her own soul. Indeed, the eternity of hell was another proof of God's goodness, since the theologians agreed that annihilation would be a worse punishment than endless ages of fiery pain.

In spite of her good intentions, Nanda came out of retreat with a sense of relief, and a sense, too, that her four days had not been altogether a success. She had prayed and meditated as well as she knew how; she had often been rewarded by a real sense of pleasure in the spiritual company of Our Lord and Our Lady and the saints. But over and over again she encountered those arid patches where the whole of religious life seemed a monstrous and meaningless complication. The saints, who displayed, as she was always being told, so much delightful human diversity and personality in their lives, seemed all exactly alike and irritating at that. Even their early dissipations were tame, and all too soon the dreary tale of mortifications and hatred of the world

would begin. She liked some of their legends and their
miracles, but with the best will in the world, she could
not find their attitude to ordinary life anything but depressing and repulsive. She was frankly bored by the
ecstacies and the floweriness of the Little Flower, and
was disgusted with St. Francis, who is popular even with
Protestants, when she read that he laughed heartily
when Brother Juniper cut off a pig's foot out of excessive
charity to a greedy sick man. She liked the robuster
saints best, St. Theresa and St. Augustine and Blessed
Thomas More, but even these impressed her for the
wrong reasons. She enjoyed a sentence, a gesture, a touch
of gaiety or gallantry rather than the actual mechanics
of sanctity. But she was ready to admit that her own
ideas were entirely due to a perverse and worldly nature.
She accepted the Catholic Church whole-heartedly and
tried hard to mould herself into the proper shape of a
young Catholic girl. How could an institution be wrong
that was so evidently divinely inspired, that had survived
for nearly two thousand years in spite of persecution and
slander, that stood firm through scandals, heresies and
schisms? Had not her own father, whom she admired
more than anyone in the world, struggled for years
against conviction, and finally sacrificed his whole career
for the sake of what he felt to be the truth? She was
part of the Church now. She could never, she knew,
break away without a sense of mutilation. In her four
years at Lippington, it had grown into every fibre of her
nature; she could not eat or sleep or read or play without
relating every action to her secret life as a Christian and
a Catholic. She rejoiced in it and rebelled against it. She
tried to imagine what life would be like without it; how
she would feel if she were a savage blessedly ignorant of
the very existence of God. But it was as impossible as

imagining death or madness or blindness. Wherever she looked, it loomed in the background, like Fuji Yama in a Japanese print, massive, terrifying, beautiful and unescapable; the fortress of God, the house on the rock.

CHAPTER VIII

"I'VE had a glorious time, but it's heaven to be back," said Clare Rockingham. She squeezed Rosario's arm. "And how are you two infants?"

It was the first night of the autumn term, and the four had not seen each other for two months. Nanda felt shy of the others; traces of the holidays, of other worlds, still clung to them. Clare wore silk stockings and frivolous bronze shoes. Rosario had pearls in her ears; a wilted white bow drooped on Léonie's hair. She would not feel completely happy until to-morrow when they would all be subdued to the comforting impersonality of uniform.

"I did such heaps of things in Leipzig that I hardly scribbled a syllable even to Rosario," chattered Clare, her brown eyes more feverishly bright, more restless than ever. "I went to drawing classes for one thing. No one knows anything about art over here. I'm never going to draw one of Mother Roscoe's idiotic old plaster casts again. Do you know what a life class is? I never told my dismal chaperone, or she'd have had a fit. The models are quite naked; don't be shocked, Rosario darling. It's so fascinating drawing them that you forget all about that. Wouldn't it be fun to have a life class at Lippington? And wouldn't Nanda make the sweetest little nude?"

"Oh, shut up, Clare," said Nanda, blushing so much that her skin felt as if it would crack.

"Well, I'll tell you something edifying. I went to mass every single Sunday, and I fairly brandished my rosary in my chaperone's face. She was so busy writing home to my family about my shocking behaviour that she forgot to keep her eye on me half the time. You see, they sent me to Leipzig in the hopes that I'd forget all about this Catholic business."

"If they're so afraid of your becoming a papist, why don't they take you away from Lippington?" asked Léonie sensibly.

"Well, I've been to three schools before and run away from all of them. And they certainly don't want me at home yet.

"You see, they're trying to marry off Isabel, that's my eldest sister, and they don't want me in the way."

"For fear of spoiling her chances with your fatal beauty?" said Léonie.

"Good Lord, no. But men bore Isabel frightfully, and we get a lot of fun out of ragging her wretched *prétendants*. When we're together, we get much better ideas. Last Christmas there was a man quite dumb with admiration for Isabel, and he was awfully rich and appropriate and all that, but she couldn't stand him. So she made him eat some chocolates, though he didn't want to in the least, and we'd filled all the chocolates with cascara. He never came back."

Rosario withdrew her arm from Clare's.

"What barbarians you English are."

"But he was awful, Rosario, really he was. As red as a

radish and as stupid as a bull. Not in the least like . . ."
She paused and bit her lip. "No, I can't tell you that."

"A love affair in the holidays, I suppose," said Léonie
with an air of ineffable boredom. "Really, Clare, you're
too primitive."

"Not a love affair at all," said Clare, crossly. "I just
happened to meet a rather interesting Prussian painter
at the art school, that's all. We used to read Heine together and once we actually had a glass of beer at a café.
He was terribly intelligent, and there was none of that
nonsense of treating one like a schoolgirl."

"You'd better get him out of your mind," advised
Léonie, "because there's certainly going to be a war with
Germany within the next year or two. I was in Berlin
and Vienna in August, and there's a lot of talk about it.
So your precious artist will get conscripted and one of
your hearty brothers will probably put a bullet through
his cropped head."

"I love to hear little Léo talking about what goes on
behind the scenes in diplomacy," sneered Clare, trying
not very successfully to get her own back.

But Rosario flew to Léonie's defence.

"She knows a lot," she insisted in her soft, fierce voice.
"Papa has the greatest respect for her mind. He says
she should have been a man."

"I like old men best," said Léonie simply. "They are
so restful. And they often forget one is there after they
have patted one's head, and go on talking, and one
overhears the most interesting things."

"If there were a war with Germany," said Nanda
suddenly, "you would be an enemy, wouldn't you,
Léo?"

"I'm not sure," mused Léonie. "It depends whether
I went in with my German relations or my French ones.

In the Franco-Prussian war I had a great-uncle on each side."

"Your father's German, anyhow," persisted Clare.

"Hoch der Kaiser. Nationality is all rot, anyhow," said Léonie.

"How can you say that?" flamed Rosario. "I would rather be dead than be anything but Spanish. And however madly in love with anyone I might be, I wouldn't marry him unless he were Spanish to the backbone."

"What did you do with your holidays, beautiful savage?" asked Léonie.

"We were in Biarritz nearly all the time. It was very gay and amusing. There was a dance for Elita given by my aunt De Las Rojas, and I was not supposed to be going because I am not properly out yet. But the King himself saw me at a polo match in the afternoon, and asked Papa as a special favour that I should come."

"And did you dance with the King?" said Clare, touching her sleeve. "I wish I could have seen you."

"Yes, I danced with him. But I had no time to get a proper frock, and so I had to wear an old pink chiffon that is very *jeune fille*. But Elita looked wonderful. Papa was pleased, but my aunt was angry. She said: 'Why, the child's actually *made up*.'"

"And what did the King say?" asked Nanda.

"My aunt told me that he said Elita was a great beauty, but that he preferred the little wild Palencia."

"Meaning you?" smiled Clare.

"Yes," admitted Rosario with complete simplicity.

"Then you might be Queen of Spain one day, darling?"

Rosario turned a thunderous blue and black gaze on Clare.

"How can you be so utterly disloyal and . . . and so

utterly vulgar?" she flashed. Without another word, she
swung round, tossing her great golden plume of hair,
and strode away angrily, arms crossed and head thrust
forward.

Suddenly bold, Nanda caught Clare's wrist.

"Don't go after her," she begged. Léonie had already
sauntered off, whistling "Die Wacht am Rhein" with an
air of masculine indifference.

"But I must go," whispered Clare, her nostrils quivering and her eyes blind and bright as a hare's. "Must
go," she insisted, wrenching away from Nanda.

"I wish you'd be a little proud sometimes, Clare,"
said Nanda, in a small, cold, even voice.

But Clare, staggering a little on her high bronze
heels, was already running towards the corner where
Rosario had disappeared.

The term began peacefully enough. There was the
usual reshuffling of classes and a distribution of rewards
at which Nanda was agreeably surprised by being
awarded a green ribbon. Much elated, she wrote home
to her parents.

"I'm awfully glad, but I really didn't expect it.
The school and the nuns vote for it, you know. Of
course, the others tease me about it a good deal, and
so does Mother Percival. I've been moved up, but she
is still taking our class. I'm an Angel now, too. We've
got four congregations, you know, Holy Child, St.
Aloysius, Angels and Children of Mary. You wear
your medal on white ribbon on feast days and there
is a sort of secret meeting on Sunday evenings with
Mother Radcliffe, and you have a book of rules that
only other Angels may read. Léonie's uncle has given
her a horse and a violin. She has got the violin here,

but she is very angry that she can't have the horse too. She is going to play in the hockey match against the Five Wounds at Southsea, and we are all going to do penances all day so that we may win. Our table is going to put salt instead of sugar on the stewed fruit. I wonder if the Southsea children will do the same. Do pray hard that Clare may become a Catholic. I know she wants to really. I think she looks prettier than ever since she came back from Germany; most people look ugly with freckles, but hers suit her. I've never seen anyone with such bright eyes, either; they're brown, but if you look very closely they have little green rays like chips of emerald in them. Léo has given me an ivory card-case; it's Turkish, I think, all inlaid and lined with sandalwood which smells heavenly. I don't suppose I shall ever actually want a card-case, but it is lovely to have. There is a rumour that a cardinal is coming some time this term. I hope it's true, because it will mean a play and a holiday."

The next day, in the middle of a French lesson, a blue ribbon put her head officiously round the door and said: "Please, Mother, Nanda Grey is to see Mother Radcliffe at once."

With a palpitating heart, Nanda tore off her apron and fidgeted in her pocket for her gloves.

"Here, take mine," whispered Léonie, holding out a seedy pair, "and don't look so terrified. She can't hang you."

But this scarcely comforted Nanda as she stood knocking at Mother Radcliffe's door. As she knocked she feverishly but unsuccessfully examined her conscience for some misdeed. At last, after about half an hour, as it seemed to her, a cold sweet voice called: "Come in."

But when she entered, Mother Radcliffe did not look up. She went on entering figures in a beautiful square, upright hand in a large note-book. When she reached the end of the column, she went back and very carefully crossed all the tails of the sevens.

Nanda's heart was bumping so hard against her ribs that she thought Mother Radcliffe must hear it. To calm herself, she began to make an inventory of the room. One red carpet, one table covered with green serge, faded; one crucifix, no, two crucifixes; one portrait of Mother Guillemin; one portrait of Leo XIII; one statue of Our Lady of Lourdes; two chairs. Mother Radcliffe looked up suddenly and seemed to notice Nanda for the first time. Having noticed her, she looked at her with a polite, but increasing interest. She took off her glasses, polished them and replaced them, fixing her gaze, not on Nanda's face, but somewhere about her collar. At last, with a sudden smile, as if at last she recognised her, she said:

"Ah, Nanda Grey. Yes, I sent for you, Nanda, did I not? Sit down, child, and don't fidget so."

Nanda sat down on the edge of a chair. Mother Radcliffe's smile was wiped out suddenly as it had appeared. She stared at Nanda with a stern and puzzled air.

"Well, and what have you to say for yourself?"

"Please, Mother, I don't know why you wanted to see me," Nanda muttered.

"No?" said Mother Radcliffe very mildly.

With extreme deliberation, she opened a large file and extracted a sheet of notepaper. Nanda recognised her own handwriting.

"Perhaps you can guess now?" hazarded the nun.

"Did I forget to leave the envelope open?" suggested Nanda hopefully.

Mother Radcliffe made a little face at the letter as if it gave off an unpleasant smell. "No, you left it open," she admitted, "though I should not have been surprised had you wished to close it. Surely you realise, my dear, that the tone of this letter is not at all what we expect to find in the correspondence of a child of the Five Wounds?"

"Is it . . . is it the grammar?" asked Nanda in a parched voice.

"No. The grammar is slipshod enough. But it is the whole spirit of the contents to which I am objecting."

Mother Radcliffe peered again at the letter through her large, clear glasses. The glasses were steel-rimmed, and Nanda observed that they had been neatly mended with a bandage of black thread. Then she looked very thoughtfully at Nanda.

"You know quite well that the school rule does not approve of particular friendships. They are against charity, to begin with, and they lead moreover, to dangerous and unhealthy indulgence of feeling. I do not think your father and mother will share your rather morbid interest in Clare Rockingham's appearance. Chips of emerald. Really, Nanda. Aren't you rather ashamed at the sheer silliness of it?"

Nanda looked at her shoes.

"Yes, I suppose so," she muttered.

"Talking of green things," said Mother Radcliffe very blandly. "What about that ribbon you are wearing? I suppose you don't want by any chance to lose that particular chip of emerald, do you?"

"No, Mother."

"Your father will be so pleased to know about it. You

tell him in this unfortunate letter, I observe, but I have already written to him about it. So that if you lost it, he would be very disappointed indeed, would he not?"

"Yes, Mother," said Nanda. She was calming down now that she knew the worst, and beginning to feel bored and restless. Why, oh why, at Lippington, couldn't they go straight to a point and have done with it?

"Your father is a convert, is he not? Conversion is a great grace, but the Catholic outlook, Catholic breeding, shall we say, does not come in one generation, or even two, or three. So I suppose I must overlook this extraordinary lapse in your case, Nanda. Of course, I shall destroy this wretched letter; at least, I shall not send it. You will write another letter home during your midday recreation. And I hope that in future I shall see you about more with friends of your own age. There are girls such as Marjorie Appleyard and Monica Owen who are about your equals in years and in station of life. I think you would do well to cultivate their society. You may go."

With a very stiff curtsey, Nanda turned to the door. But instead of dropping her eyes, she looked very straight at Mother Radcliffe. The nun threw back her head and gave the merest ghost of a smile.

"You are very fond of your own way, aren't you, Nanda?"

"Yes, I suppose so, Mother."

"And do you know that no character is any good in this world unless that will has been broken completely? Broken and re-set in God's own way. I don't think your will has been quite broken, my dear child, do you?"

Although Nanda did not lose her green ribbon as a result of this interview, she was considerably shaken by it. For a time, she actually avoided Clare, and in spite of Léo's mockery, cultivated the society of Marjorie and Monica. The experiment was not a great success, for Marjorie and Nanda bored each other even more disastrously than they had three years ago, while the unexpected attention warmed Monica's dim friendliness into an embarrassing devotion. All the same, it did something to allay suspicion, and a severe bout of teasing by Mother Percival which had begun the very day after Nanda's talk with the Mistress of Discipline died down after a week into an occasional mild sarcasm. As in the Jesuit Order, every child was under constant observation, and the results of this observation were made known by secret weekly reports to Mother Radcliffe and the Superior. But how detailed such reports could be, covering not only the broad outlines of a character, but the minutest physical peculiarities and nervous habits, Nanda did not realise until she saw Mother Radcliffe play the famous Key Game. In the afternoon of some minor holiday, Mother Radcliffe summoned the whole Senior School into St. Stanislas Kostka, the assembly room. In her hands she held an ordinary door key. "I am going," she announced, "to play a rather unusual game which is played here from time to time, and which we call the Mistress of Discipline's game. There are about eighty of you here; all except the new ones, fairly well known to me. Better known, perhaps, than you realise. I shall go out of the room for a few minutes, and the head of the school, Rose Maclean, will give this key to anyone she chooses. No one is to speak while this is being done, and no names are to be spoken. Rose may keep the key herself if she likes. I think you will all trust me sufficiently not to think of Rose as a kind of conjuror's accomplice. She may give it to anyone in this room, but I ask her not to give it to any child who is actually new this term. When I come in again, you will all remain in complete silence while I try to discover, without asking any questions, which of you is hiding the key. When I think I know, I shall not say any name, but I shall give you indications by which you will all know whether or not I have guessed right."

She left the room and Rose, after a little thought, gave the key to Rosario de Palencia, who put it in her pocket. As Mother Radcliffe re-entered, every child composed her face into an unnatural blankness. The nun walked slowly down the rows of seated figures, peering into each face, skimming over some and gazing for nearly a minute at others. In front of Nanda she stopped for a long time, and, although she had not the key, Nanda felt herself blush guiltily. At Rosario she gave only a swift glance. After about a quarter of an hour of nervous tension, Mother Radcliffe returned to her table, and the whole school relaxed with a flutter of relief. Staring straight ahead of her, Mother Radcliffe began dreamily: "We have been at Lippington, I think, for some years. We have not any ribbon, though we are a Child of Mary, yet we are one of those personalities which are known to the whole school. We are not English; we come from a country where most of the inhabitants are dark, yet we have fair hair and do not conform to the usual habit of wearing that hair in a plait. We are courteous, but we are very proud, and perhaps we are rather passionate as well. We love the arts, especially music, and we have no great aptitude for mathematics. We are perhaps a little old for our age and have been out in the world more than an English girl of our age, which is about seventeen. Some months ago we suffered a great loss, a loss which we feel more than we admit." But she was interrupted by the muffled clapping of

eighty gloved hands. She smiled, as Rosario whipped the
key out of her pocket and waved it triumphantly.

Three more times Mother Radcliffe performed her
strange trick, but at the suggestion of a fourth attempt,
she shook her head. "This game is rather a strain," she
said, "and I think we will not have any more thought-
reading to-day." As she gave the signal for the gathering
to break up, Nanda noticed that she looked pinched and
whiter than usual, while the hand holding the signal
trembled.

"My dear, isn't it too uncanny?" shrieked Clare to
Léonie, as the school, chattering rather hysterically ran
out to the playgrounds.

"Rather beastly, I think," growled Léonie. "I hate
that sort of spiritual showing-off. If we had dossiers of
the community as they have of us, I daresay we could
bring off this Sherlock Holmes business just as successfully."

"Yes? But how did she do it? I watched Rosario's face
the whole time and she never blinked an eyelid."

"She probably noticed you, my dear Watson," said
Léonie. "There's a rational explanation of most
miracles."

Nanda, who was passing, caught the last words, and
exclaimed:

"Don't you believe in miracles, Léo?"

"Not entirely, my child. But I'm willing to enter into
the spirit of them. Like all the old men who bellow that
they believe in fairies when Tinkerbell is at her last
gasp."

"But you wrote such a lovely and convincing one for
your Christmas story," protested Nanda.

"I like the Catholic way of looking at things," said
Léo. "Any way of looking at life is a fairy story, and I

prefer mine with lots of improbable embellishments. I think angels and devils are much more amusing than microbes and Mr. Wells's noble scientists."

"But you're a pagan," asserted Clare in a shocked voice.

"So are hundreds of practising Catholics. I could tell you things about the Renaissance Popes that would make your hair stand on end."

"I'm beginning to think that there's something to be said for being a Protestant after all," said Clare.

"Oh, no, Clare," Nanda assured her, horrified at seeing the prospective convert wavering. "Don't you see it's just another proof that the Church really is divine and inspired? Any other institution would have been done for centuries ago with so much corruption in individual members. There really is something that keeps it going in spite of all that, and the gates of hell don't prevail in spite of all sorts of horrors."

"Go it, Nanda," mocked Léonie. "No one like a convert for getting up the subject good and strong. Yet I wouldn't mind betting that twenty years from now she's a red-hot, fool-proof rationalist while I'm a model Catholic mother with my children all festooned with scapulars and a pious sodality meeting every afternoon in my drawing-room."

She made a face and sauntered away, leaving the other two together for the first time for many weeks.

"One never sees you these days, infant," began Clare at once. "Are you afraid of being contaminated by poor heretics?"

"Of course not," said Nanda uncomfortably, "but Mother Percival is always herding us together to play hockey or something, and we hardly ever get a chance to speak to the other divisions."

"But even on holidays one never sees anything of you," persisted Clare. "I believe you've lost interest in me and don't care whether I ever become a Catholic or not."

"Oh, but I do," protested Nanda. "I want you to awfully. Really, Clare. Only there's nothing any of us can do but pray for you."

"Aren't you all kind?" said Clare sarcastically. "I suppose the truth is we're a little puffed up now we've got a green ribbon."

"Don't be a beast," Nanda flared. "You know that's got nothing whatever to do with it. Anyway, I'm pretty sure to lose it soon."

Clare changed her tone.

"I'm so awfully unhappy," she said softly, screwing up her bright eyes. "I don't suppose you can understand at your age. Besides, I don't believe fair people can really understand sorrow at any age."

Deeply offended, Nanda assured her that she understood every variety of suffering with the greatest sympathy.

"Really, I do, Clare," she said, nodding very sagely. "I can't show it because I haven't got the right sort of face. And if you knew how I loathed being fair and having idiotic dimples, you'd realise that there's quite a lot of suffering in that. It's as bad as being deformed, almost," she added gloomily.

Clare began to crow with laughter.

"You're adorable, baby," she cried.

But Nanda was by no means soothed. She edged away with great dignity as Clare attempted to tweak her ear. There was silence for a minute, then Clare said sadly:

"I don't really think of you as a baby at all. It's only

because you look such a child. You understand things wonderfully, you know. Poetry and all that. And some of your essays and things are really beautiful . . . more beautiful than you know. I often think that you must be one of those twice-born people. Your soul's so much older than your body."

Nanda softened visibly.

"Oh, nonsense, Clare," she said in a pleased voice.

"But I'm not only thinking of mental suffering," went on Clare, "though goodness knows I have enough of that. It's physical suffering too. I get the most frightful headaches."

"Well, why not see Mother Regan about them?" suggested Nanda helpfully.

"She wouldn't understand," Clare assured her. "I have spoken about them, but the fool doctor here says he can't find anything the matter. I'll just have to bear them, I suppose. Perhaps they'll help me to get converted. But I've got a queer feeling that they're a kind of warning. Perhaps I won't live long. Don't look so sad, darling. What does it matter, anyway? But I'd like to die a Catholic."

Nanda capitulated, but she was glad when the bell announced the end of the brief recreation, and of this rather embarrassing talk. But she forgot about Clare and her sorrows at the sight of Monica Owen, weeping loudly, being dragged towards the house by Mother Percival. As she passed Nanda, Monica managed to gasp out:

"Something frightful's happened. Pray for me."

For two or three days no one knew exactly what had happened to the unlucky Monica, but it was clearly something very serious. She appeared at no classes and her place was vacant in the refectory. When the others went into the chapel she was brought in by a lay-sister after everyone else and placed in a bench by herself at the back. As they filed out they could see her blank, pale face, almost unrecognisable from much crying, and speculate as to what her awful crime could be. Nanda was extremely worried. Although Monica was rather a nuisance, she had come to look upon her as a protégée, and she was genuinely sorry for her. She felt, too, that Monica was rather shabbily treated by the nuns, who made no secret of the fact that her father was a struggling doctor in a provincial town, and that her family could not afford the full fees at Lippington. True, they very rarely alluded to this openly, but they found a hundred ways of humiliating Monica. She was never given new lesson-books but had to be content with shabby copies blotted and torn by a former owner. Her uniform, too, had been made over from an elder sister's and shone lamentably at shoulders and elbows, while her gloves were darned at every finger. When the rest of the school was fitted out with new white dresses for feast days, Monica was forced to go on wearing her old nuns-veiling, yellow with age and of an antique and conspicuous pattern. Her seat was always the worst in every class, and she was grudged her very pencils and india-rubbers. Not very intelligent by nature, as Mother Frances had long ago discovered in her Junior School days, she had become duller still under this treatment. All her interest was concentrated in her passion for drawing dogs, and after some years of constant practice, she really did draw dogs with uncanny skill. And she was not allowed a sketch-book, she was forced to draw her mastiffs and terriers in the margin of her already battered lesson-books, a practice which kept her in almost constant hot water. But Monica, tearful and yielding in everything else, was obstinate in this. Every notebook was decorated with drawings of dogs of every age and in every attitude.

Many of Monica's dogs had oddly human faces. Nanda had laughed at a King Charles spaniel that bore a remarkable resemblance to Marjorie Appleyard, a collie with a distinct look of Clare, and a Saluki with Elita de Palencia's dark eyes and languid grace.

Out of various rumours about Monica's disgrace, Nanda at last sorted out one that had the air of authenticity. A notebook had been found in Monica's desk bearing the inscription, "European History." Instead of containing notes on the Holy Roman Empire, it was decorated with pictures of dogs, each dog a recognisable caricature of some member of the community. Nanda made many inquiries before she was finally convinced this was the true explanation. Satisfied that it was, she took great pains to discover what Monica's punishment was likely to be. But here she met with wise headshakings and gloomy prophecies. Some people went as far as to say that Monica had committed blasphemy in ridiculing the Brides of Christ, and one and all agreed that she would almost certainly be expelled. Nanda was so horrified at this that she went to Rose Maclean, the red-cheeked, amiable girl who had succeeded Madeleine as head of the school.

"Is it true that Monica Owen is going to be expelled?" she asked outright.

"I don't think that concerns any of us," said Rose uncomfortably.

"It certainly does if it's true," insisted Nanda angrily.

"Well, you'd better ask Mother Radcliffe," said Rose with a nervous giggle. "No doubt she's longing to take you into her confidence."

But Rose's mild sarcasm was lost on Nanda.

"I'll go this very minute," she said, white with rage. Two minutes later she was knocking at Mother Radcliffe's door. Summoned in, she found Mother Radcliffe busy writing letters.

"What is it, Nanda?" said the nun rather irritably. "I don't think I sent for you, did I?"

"No, Mother," said Nanda very quietly, though her knees were shaking with excitement.

"Then what is it? Be quick, please. I am very busy, as you see."

Anger and a hot sense of injustice had given Nanda a most unusual courage.

"It's about Monica Owen. Is she really going to be expelled?" she blurted out.

Mother Radcliffe dropped her pen with surprise.

"Really, Nanda, what a very odd question. I don't think that concerns you, does it? Is Monica another of these wonderful friends of yours?"

It was on the tip of Nanda's tongue to remind Mother Radcliffe of what she had said at their last interview, but she bit back the obvious retort. Still filled with her unnatural courage, she said in a cold and unreasonable voice:

"Because if you *are* going to, it's horribly unfair. Whatever Monica's done, she's been punished enough already. You know she's not quite like other people. She's not very clever, I mean. And people have always been rather unfair to her and laughed at her. There isn't an ounce of harm in Monica, everyone knows that. And if she is expelled, she's going to have a perfectly beastly time at home. She's got a very strict father and a stepmother who isn't any too nice to her in the ordinary way."

During this speech, Mother Radcliffe looked at Nanda with a blank amazement. If a cat had begun to talk, she could hardly have seemed more astonished. When Nanda stopped there was a strained silence, during which Mother Radcliffe's face slowly assumed an expression of sternness and distaste.

"Very interesting," she said at last. "I have not often been told my duty quite so clearly by a child of your age. Invaluable as your advice is, I am afraid I do not see my way to taking it. There are some things which are no doubt permitted in the high schools to which your Protestant friends are accustomed but they are not permitted at Lippington. Monica Owen has done something which cannot possibly be overlooked."

But even this did not deter Nanda.

"Monica hasn't spoken to a soul for three days," she said passionately. "She's been shut up in the retreat house all this time and only allowed into the chapel. She looks half dead with sheer misery. It's too much punishment for anyone. I thought Catholics were supposed to be charitable. Can't some of us go and see her just for five minutes . . . three minutes even?" she implored.

Mother Radcliffe picked up her pen, dipped it in the inkpot and began a new paragraph in her letter. Without looking up, she said:

"There is no question of that. Monica Owen was expelled from this house two hours ago."

CHAPTER IX

THE expulsion of Monica left a definite mark on
Nanda. A small core of rebelliousness which had
been growing secretly for four years seemed to have
hardened inside her. Outwardly her conduct was perfectly respectable; she no longer giggled or talked at
forbidden times, she worked fairly hard and generally
comported herself as a green ribbon should. But she
delighted in asking awkward questions in the Christian
Doctrine class and smiled with the complacent cynicism
of thirteen when her mistress was temporarily flustered.
Once she plunged into deeper waters than she knew
and without understanding the implications of her
remark brought a violent blush to Mother Percival's
prim cheek.

Mother Percival was explaining the circumstances
which could make a marriage invalid. If a couple did
not conform to certain regulations, they might be man
and wife according to the law of the country, but their
marriage would not be recognised by the Church.

"You mean to say that people might *think* they were
properly married, but they mightn't be married at all?"
asked Nanda.

"Exactly."

"Then how could they tell?" asked Marjorie Appleyard.

Without giving Mother Percival time to answer
Nanda called out briskly.

"It's quite simple, isn't it, Mother? If they had some
children they would know they were properly married,
and if they didn't they wouldn't have been. Only
married people can have children, can they?"

Nanda made this remarkable observation in all innocence, and for once she did not mean to be impertinent. But Mother Percival turned as red as a peony, and answered in a voice faint with horror.

"Really, Nanda, this is hardly a subject for discussion. No modest girl should have the remotest interest in the why or wherefore of such things. God gives children to whom He pleases and it is not for us to question his decisions. Marjorie, will you please give me a brief account of the origin of the Sacrament of Penance."

Nanda's rebelliousness, such as it was, was directed entirely against the Lippington methods. Her faith in the Catholic Church was not affected in the least. If anything, it became more robust. She went to Communion every morning and never again experienced the strange dryness and emptiness of her first approach. Outwardly, she was less emotional about her religion, and no longer lighted innumerable candles to St. Anthony, nor wrote *Ad Majorem Dei Gloriam* on the flyleaf of her lesson-books. The flowery ecstasies of the Garden of the Soul no longer satisfied her; she preferred the colder, more solid prayers of St. Augustine and St. Thomas Aquinas. But only very rarely and by extreme concentration could she ever obtain from any religious exercise the pure delight that poetry or music aroused without the least effort on her part. Quite sincerely, she tried to make religion the centre of her life, but to do so required constant watchfulness and direction of her will. She tried to persuade herself that her love of beauty was connected with God (how many pious and applauded essays she had written on "The Message of Beethoven," "The Message of Fra Angelico," "Whither was Browning Tending?", "Art, the Handmaid of Religion"), but some small, clear, irritating voice assured her that it was an independent growth. At other times, she forced herself to remember what she had so often heard, that conscious emotion was no part of religion, that it was a grace which God occasionally conferred but far more often withheld. Yet when she read the lives of the saints it seemed clear to her that their feeling at the thought of God was of the same kind as her own extreme delight when Léonie read Blake aloud, or Rosario sang Wolf. She was, of course, beginning to write herself and was alternately puffed up and disgusted by what she produced. For the most part, she wrote laboured little lyrics about spring and the sea, with a tardy reference to God in the last verse, and elaborate fairy-tales with saints for princes and devils for dragons. But now she was projecting something far more ambitious, nothing less than a full-length novel. The idea fascinated and alarmed her; she knew that religion must play a large part in it, but feared that too much piety would conflict with a really exciting plot. So she decided to describe a brilliant, wicked, worldly society, preferably composed of painters, musicians and peers, and to let all her characters be sensationally converted in the last chapter. She had already made several sketches for this great work, including one of Bohemian life, the material for which she had gathered during a half-hour's visit to the Café Royal, where Mr. Grey, rather surprisingly, used to play dominoes every Sunday night. But at thirteen, Nanda had not entirely decided where her talents lay. When the novel, scribbled in bed by the dim light of a low burning gas-jet outside her cubicle, went badly, as it usually did, she would turn to playwriting, only to realise; as the second act petered out half-way through, that she would never write anything half as good as Léonie's *Death of Socrates*. Often she thought she would like to be a painter, and, encouraged by Clare, who drew

remarkably well, she would turn out weak little land-
scapes of flat country with two or three poplar trees
grouped against acres of sky. However, the ultramarine
in her paint-box gave out so early in each term that she
usually fell back on music. Apart from the regular hour
each day, she would spend her free study in the piano
cells, playing Chopin's nocturnes with tremendous expression and more pedal than accuracy. But the sight of
Léonie making appalling faces at her through the
window had severely shaken her confidence and lately
her musical activities had taken the form of listening
admiringly while Léo drummed out Bach fugues with
great sternness and precision. In the background, of
course, there was acting. At Lippington, as at most
convent schools, there were plays and tableaux and
dramatic recitations every term, and after a small success as an English Martyr or Prince Arthur or Alice in
Wonderland, Nanda was usually ready to abandon all
her other pursuits for the stage.

All through this present autumn term there had been
rumours of a cardinal's visit and a play of hitherto
unheard-of elaboration and splendour. A new wing,
containing an ambitious theatre-room had just been
completed, and the cardinal had promised to open it.

Twice his visit had been announced and postponed,
but, towards the end of November, a notice was put up
saying that His Eminence would definitely arrive on
December 15th.

The whole school was in a ferment of excitement to
know what play could be considered worthy of such an
honour. There were old favourites which had been acted
year after year: *Thomas à Becket, Antigone, Joan of
Arc, The Ugly Duckling* and *The Rose and the Ring.*
Last year there had been a spectacular presentation of

King Arthur's Knights in a mild Lippington version
which left out all references to Guinevere, and Nanda
and Léonie had swaggered terrifically in cardboard
armour and horsehair plumes. But, immensely successful as it had been, no one felt that king Arthur was
equal to such an occasion as this. But when, at last, it
was announced that *The Vision of Dante* was to be performed, everyone agreed that Mother Castello, the
community's star producer, had risen magnificently to
the occasion.

At the first recreation after the notice had appeared,
there was no talk of anything but the great question of
casting. Even Mother Percival's breezy sarcasm could
not keep alive a listless game of hockey and the children
broke up into groups of earnest debaters. All the possible
Beatrices assumed expressions of extreme spirituality,
and when startled out of their dream, exclaimed
modestly: "Oh, I couldn't. Mother Castello would never
choose me. I expect I'll just be one of the lost souls or
noises off."

Léonie, having heard this remark for the seventh
time, observed:

"We'll need a good many damned, if we're going to
stick to the book. And there are some very ingenious
tortures. We'll have to hire a batch of heretics from
outside."

"Well, here's one all ready," said Clare winningly.

"There's an excellent torture for you," Léonie told
her. "You get shut in a fiery tomb for all eternity. The
lid's off now, but after the day of judgment they shut it
down and never take it off again."

"I think Catholics have some horrible ideas," shuddered Clare.

"Oh, well, Dante isn't dogma," Léonie grinned.

"That's one blessing," said Clare.

"All the same," admitted Léonie, "everyone agrees that he really drew it pretty mild. The early fathers thought of lots more revolting things than Dante ever did."

"I sometimes wonder," Clare said, "how Catholics can bear the thought of anyone, however wicked, being in a hell like that."

"Ah," said Léonie, "we've got you very neatly there. It's only a dogma that hell exists; it isn't a dogma that there's anybody in it."

Clare smiled.

"It sounds awfully like *Alice in Wonderland*."

"It is. Very," admitted Léonie.

"I do hope I'm in the play," Nanda broke in. "I don't honestly care what I am, but I do love rehearsals and things. And both of you and Rosario are sure to be in it."

"I don't know about me," said Clare; "but, of course, Rosario will be Beatrice. No one could look at her and hesitate. I wish they'd let me have a shot at Dante, but obviously, Léonie ought to play that. She's got the right voice and the right sort of noble head, and everything. If I can't be Dante, I'd like to be Paolo, and listen, wouldn't Nanda make a rather good Francesca?"

None of the three had noticed Mother Percival moving quietly up behind them, and they all started as she slid between Clare and Nanda and observed coldly :

"Those are names I never expected to hear mentioned in this school. No Christian woman, let alone a Catholic, who has any pretensions to decency, would sully her mind with such an episode as that."

She gave Nanda a penetrating look and moved away.

"So much for our greatest Catholic poet," said Léonie, wrinkling her handsome nose.

"I remember now," said Clare. "The Upper First are doing Dante this term in Cary's translation, and the whole of the fourth canto has been cut out of their books."

In a few days, the casting was known, and private disappointments were lost in public surprise. Contrary to everybody's expectations, Léonie was to play Beatrice and Rosario Dante. Clare was content to be Virgil, and Nanda delighted with the small part of Matilda of Tuscany. After recent events, she was delighted to be allowed to play anything so agreeable, for she had quite expected to be fobbed off with one of the prophets in paradise. Even plays at Lippington were apt to be run on disciplinary lines; parts which called for an attractive appearance were usually played by the most meek and mortified children of the school, while anyone suspected of thinking herself pretty was fairly sure to be cast for a hermit with prodigious wrinkles and a long beard.

Once the play was in rehearsal there were no more murmurs about the choice of Léo and Rosario for their respective parts. Rosario, to whom all languages came easily, spoke Italian particularly well, and her first reading proved that she would be an admirable Dante. All her softness dropped from her; she was grave, stern and passionate. Léonie, on the other hand, seemed to have borrowed all Rosario's former grace. No one had ever supposed that Léo, with her untidiness, her slouch, her masculine gestures and her bitter tongue, could be so delicate and moving a Beatrice. Her voice, usually hoarse and rough, took on the clear ring it had when she sang, as she spoke her lines. Even at rehearsals, standing on a sugar-box, with a lank lock drooping over her magnificent forehead and one hand tucked in her crumpled apron, she was impressive and beautiful. Mother Castello was in raptures. Her black eyes glittered with tears in her wizened, bilious little face, as she clapped energetically and cried: *"Bene, molto bene, fanciulla mia."*

The rest of the cast by no means lived up to this high level. Marjorie Appleyard wept regularly whenever she had to rehearse the ghostly embrace of Dante and Casella. Ten or twelve times, Mother Castello would make her go through it, but never with any success.

"But, Marjoree," she would scream, "Casella is a spirit . . . a spirit, not a great, clumsy human being. And when he cannot embrace Dante he should look sad and puzzled, not imbecile as if he had just dropped a cricket ball. Have you no feeling at all for poetry? *Ancora una volta.*"

Nanda fared a little better, but felt horribly self-conscious picking imaginary flowers among the benches which represented the earthly paradise, while Clare's Virgil, apart from being far too young and eager, was not too severely criticised, except when she gazed with such fond admiration at Dante that she forgot her cues.

The awkward stiffness of Anglo-Saxon gestures distressed Mother Castello so much that, after the first week, she begged that for the remainder of the time the play should be rehearsed in costume on the stage. Lights and dresses and scenery certainly did a good deal to loosen the agonised self-consciousness of the actresses, and to Nanda at least, the illusion of another world was complete. The new stage was equipped with machinery she had never dreamed of; there were trap-doors and spotlights, and even wires from which nervous but complacent angels could be suspended. The home-made dresses of spangles and sateen glistened magically under the coloured lights, and the dullest people looked suddenly beautiful.

Nanda, in blue and rose, felt every inch a duchess, and gathered her calico flowers with a quite convincing grace, while Rosario, in her scarlet mantle with her hair hidden under the peaked headdress, was the image of a young Dante who had never looked on hell. There was, indeed, no hell in the Lippington version of the *Divina Commedia*. It began with the meeting of Dante and Virgil outside the fatal gates, and proceeded to scenes in purgatory and paradise. Nanda's own part was so small that she had plenty of time to watch from the wings, following every movement till her eyes ached and whispering the lines till she knew everyone else's as well as her own. She loved the scene where the souls in purgatory dressed in thin grey draperies, glided in their boat, singing "*In exitu Israel de Egypto.*" It did not worry her in the least that the boat creaked rather than glided, and that the holy souls disembarked on to rocks of canvas-covered packing-cases. She was deeply impressed by the tableau of the Celestial Rose at the end, with the blessed in white sateen grouped gracefully and uncomfortably in the clouds round Our Lady. But the most wonderful moment of the play for her was when Beatrice appeared in her gilded car drawn by gryphons, and Léonie, pale, radiant and transfigured in her green cloak and flame-coloured dress, spoke her first words to Dante. Clare, who had just made her exit, would join her in the wings, and hand-in-hand, silent with ecstasy, they would listen to Léonie, saying gravely and sorrowfully:

> "*Dante, perchè Virgilio se ne vada*
> *Non pianger anco, non pianger ancora;*
> *Chè pianger ti convien per altra spada.*"

to the great moment when she lifted her veil and her
voice rang out triumphantly:

"Guardaci ben; ben sem, ben sem Beatrice."

About a week before the cardinal was due to arrive,
Mother Radcliffe announced her intention of being
present at one of these dress-rehearsals. She sat alone in
the large auditorium, a tall, inexpressive, black-and-
white presence, betraying no emotion, but occasionally
making notes by the light of a small electric torch. The
children were nervous, but, rather surprisingly, played
far better than usual. The excitement of a new audience,
even an audience of one, keyed them up to act with
more variety and less restraint. The stage mechanics,
too, surpassed themselves, and the boat sailed on real-
istically, Beatrice's chariot appeared without the least
hitch, and the lights glowed and dimmed in complete
accord with Mother Castello's loudly whispered directions. But the real glory of the evening lay with Dante
and Beatrice themselves. Rosario and Léonie shone like
the sun and moon in some element of their own. They
were no longer young girls, Nanda thought, in her lair
in the wings, but the very spirits of poetry. When the
curtain fell on Dante standing with uplifted arms, the
sound of the last lines was too much for Nanda's pent-
up feelings.

At the words:

"L'amor che move il sole e l'altre stelle"

her blood seemed to turn and run backwards through
her veins, and she burst into tears. Throwing off Clare's
consoling hand, she jumped up and ran blindly, stumbling over scenery, towards the door at the back of the
stage that led to the main school building. Her one

thought was to get away, to be by herself. The corridors were mercifully empty, and she ran panting and sobbing through doors and round corners, until she was in the deserted vestibule of Our Lady of Aberdeen. Here she flung herself on the prie-dieu, buried her head in her hands, and gave herself up entirely to convulsive tears. Her whole attitude was that of a penitent in the throes of remorse, she sobbed as if her heart would break, but her tears had nothing to do with sorrow or repentance. On the contrary, she felt blissfully happy, and the weeping she could not check was no more than an hysterical relief. How long she knelt there she did not know, but it seemed to her at least an hour. She was still sobbing, but more quietly and mechanically, when she felt a hand on her shoulder.

"Nanda, my dear child," said the voice of Mother Percival. "Whatever is the matter?"

"Nothing," choked Nanda without looking up.

"But one does not cry for nothing," insisted Mother Percival. "Look at me."

Very reluctantly, Nanda raised her head.

"But, my good child, your face is all swollen. Why, you've hardly any eyes left. You really must tell me what is the matter."

Nanda hesitated. After all, why was she crying? Did she really know? She could hardly say it was because Dante was so beautiful. She forced an unnecessary sob to gain time.

"Come now. I insist on knowing," said Mother Percival with her old asperity.

Desperately, Nanda groped for some respectable reason. At last she whispered:

"My . . . my mother's awfully ill."

To her great relief, this was accepted. Mrs. Grey was

known vaguely to be "delicate" and actually did spend a considerable time in nursing homes.

But as Mother Percival shepherded her up to the dormitory, with soothing promises of prayers and crumbs of advice on the duty of resignation, Nanda thought she looked at her rather oddly.

The next day's rehearsal was as flat as might be expected. It was made flatter still by the absence of Léonie, who had been called away to Mother Radcliffe immediately after lunch. Her part was read by Marjorie Appleyard, who had been given the understudy because there seemed not the least chance of her ever having to perform. Everyone knew that nothing short of death would keep Léonie away on the actual night. Nanda had been surprised and a little amused to see how much Léonie, usually so bored and casual, cared about the play. She was glad Léo could not hear Marjorie in her stolid British Italian, mangling the verse she loved so passionately. Faced with such a Beatrice, Rosario lost half her fire and recited her part in the most perfunctory way. Even Mother Castello seemed sad and indifferent, and only pulled Marjorie up when she ruined a line beyond recognition. There was something more in the air, Nanda felt, than the mere staleness of reaction; something gloomy, even ominous. Rosario looked sullen; Clare bit her lip as if to keep back a secret; a group was whispering warily in a corner. When the rehearsal broke up, there was none of the usual lingering chatter; the children dispersed quickly, almost guiltily, as if they had been doing something forbidden.

In the passage outside Mother Radcliffe's door, Nanda caught sight of Léonie. Running up to her, she pulled her by the sleeve, but Léonie swerved away and turned her head towards the wall, muttering: "For God's sake, leave me alone." She did not, however, turn quite quickly enough and Nanda saw enough of her face to know that she had been crying. Horrified, Nanda ran on as quickly as she could, without a backward glance at her friend. Never before had anyone seen Léonie cry.

During the geometry class that followed, Nanda could think of nothing but this episode. When the short evening recreation came, she plunged with unusual fervour into one of the dismal indoor ball games and strenuously avoided Léonie, who was leaning up against the parallel bars with an air of extreme boredom. But this time it was Léo who took the initiative. As the centre of the squealing game shifted to the other side of the room, she beckoned to Nanda, who promptly forgot all about her duties as goal-keeper and dashed to her friend's side.

"Forget all about this afternoon," said Léonie in her hoarsest voice. "I was so furious that I'd have pulled all the feathers out of an archangel if I'd met one at that moment."

Her eyes were tearless, though the lids still showed red, and her face even paler than usual. The vein in the centre of her forehead that always swelled when she was excited, stood out like a blue cord.

Nanda suffered at the sight of this strained, exposed face as she once had at the sight of Léonie's ugly hands. So she looked at her own shoes as she said:

"Oh, shut up, Léo. I understand."

"I thought you'd like to know what'd happened. It'll be all over the place anyhow, to-morrow. I've been chucked out of the play." Nanda gasped and stared at Léonie, whose face had relaxed now into its old amused expression, so that she could look at her without embarrassment.

"Nonsense," she said dizzily. "I simply don't believe it."

"It's true, anyhow."

"But, why on earth? You were so frightfully good. Everyone said so. You were simply marvellous."

"Ah, but, my child," said Léo in a pious snuffle. "Didn't you observe that I enjoyed myself? Didn't you observe that I took a wilful and sensuous pleasure in the performance? Had that pleasure anything to do with the glory of God or the honour of this sanctified school? No, my child, it hadn't."

"Surely they can't take away your part just because you liked playing it?"

"Good heavens, girl, haven't you been here long enough to know that it is the perfect Radcliffian reason? Have you forgotten that we are not here to acquire vain accomplishment but to form our characters? And don't you realise that there's nothing worse for the Catholic character than to do something it really enjoys? Oh, Mother Radcliffe was excessively affable. She even said I played Beatrice remarkably well, except that perhaps I emphasised the earthly side a leetle too much. For Beatrice, my dear child, was not the ghost of a woman whom Dante had loved in the human way, but the spirit of divine wisdom."

"Oh, I'm sick of all this beastly cant," burst out Nanda. "Why can't we for once do something for its own sake, instead of tacking everything on to our eternal salvation. One can't even get dressed or have a bath or eat one's bacon and eggs without keeping an eye on eternity. I'm prepared to be as devout as you like, if I can only have a little time to myself."

"Steady on," growled Léonie. "Sir Percival's got her steely eye on you."

But Nanda could not be checked. She stumbled and blundered on, talking much louder than she realised.

"It's impossible to think about God and Religion every minute of one's day. However fond one is of people, one doesn't think of them all the time. Even one's best friends. When I got so excited about the play the other night it hadn't anything to do with you or Rosario or God or anything. It was just the thing itself. I don't want poetry and pictures and things to be messages from God. I don't mind their being that as well, if you like, but not only that. Oh, I can't explain. I want them to be complete in themselves."

Mother Percival walked up to them.

"How often have I told you, Nanda," she remarked, "that you are not to stand about talking in twos at recreation? Will you kindly go outside with Marjorie Appleyard for a game of clumps?"

With the disappearance of Léonie from the cast of Dante, the play lost nearly all its life. Mother Castello coached Marjorie by the hour and did indeed manage to improve her accent, but failed entirely to infuse any spark of warmth or beauty into her performance. Rosario was too good an artist to speak her lines any less admirably than before, but the strange electricity that had flashed out that other night in her scenes with Beatrice never returned. At the end of the three weeks, everyone was heartily sick of the play and only longing for it to be decently buried and forgotten.

The cardinal did at last appear, and was received with due splendour. Every corridor was garlanded and hung with Japanese lanterns; the children went about for three whole days in their best white uniforms and the chapel blazed like a ballroom with hundreds of candles. The cardinal moved freely about the school, attended by his secretaries and Reverend Mother, and at any corner Nanda was liable to met his scarlet-robed figure. As she swept a nervous curtsey and kissed the huge amethyst on his finger, his handsome, peevish old face would nod to her and murmur a vague blessing.

The performance of the play on the third afternoon went off as well as could be expected. Marjorie looked as pretty as a musical comedy princess and delivered her lines in a weak, fluttering little voice. The cardinal sat throughout with his great chin resting on his scarlet bosom, and showed not the slightest trace of emotion. A special distribution of prizes and ribbons followed the performance. Baskets of wreaths were placed in front of him, and he roused himself sufficiently to place one on the head of each white-frocked winner. Nanda won a special prize for English and returned to her place with a large yellow calf copy of *Ancient Catholic Homes of Scotland* (which she had already received for geography the previous summer) and a crown of paper roses set askew on her fair hair. The glittering, tiresome day crawled slowly to its end with a blast of trumpets playing Handel's water music as the cardinal left the building, and the children, once more in their old blue dresses, filed into a supper that was at once an anticlimax and a relief.

There was no recreation that night, and they went straight from the refectory to the chapel. The cardinal's emblazoned chair was gone, the red carpet had been rolled away, and the altar too was back in its sober, everyday dress. The dimness, lit only by the two sanctuary lamps and a stray candle or two, was welcome to Nanda's eyes, tired by the pomp and glare of the last three days. Half asleep, she mumbled the response to the night prayers and made no effort to fight her distractions. In front of her knelt Léonie and Rosario with stern, peaceful faces: across the aisle she could see Clare with her head buried in her gloved hands. From the shaking of her shoulders, she knew that she was giving way to one of her fits of weeping. There had been a good deal of weeping during the last week at Lippington, she reflected. Everyone seemed a little excited and overwrought. She would be glad when the term was over.

CHAPTER X

NANDA'S father was so delighted about her green ribbon that the Christmas holidays passed even more agreeably than usual. There were extra treats, including a party with a conjurer, a visit to *The Blue Bird*, a concert and an afternoon at the Wallace Collection. Much as Nanda enjoyed these festivities, a little guilt was mingled with her pleasure. In her heart of hearts she realised that she held that green ribbon on very precarious terms. What would her father say if he knew of some of her recent interviews with Mother Radcliffe? She soothed her conscience, however, by making a fervent mental promise to behave irreproachably when she returned to school.

During these three weeks, Nanda and her father lived in a state of blissful companionship. Mrs. Grey was away at Bournemouth recovering from one of her mysterious indispositions, and the spate of private pupils which at all other times engulfed Mr. Grey's leisure, had shrunk to a mere trickle round about Christmas. Tea with cream buns to the sound of female quartets sobbing out the Indian Love Lyrics was as rare a treat to him as to Nanda, and there was a gay air of truancy about all their expeditions. To her great delight, her father had begun to treat her as a grown-up person. He dressed for dinner in her honour, asked her permission before he lit his pipe, and bought her pink carnations on the great gala nights when they dined out at a restaurant. For still further proof that he considered her a responsible being, he actually asked her advice in an important decision about her own future.

They dined at home that night; Nanda in last summer's white muslin and blue bows, and her father in his scrupulously brushed, green-black dinner jacket. Instead of going up to the drawing-room afterwards, he invited her into his study.

The study still had certain awful associations for Nanda. All family discussions, all upbraidings about over-spent pocket money and unsatisfactory reports, took place within its book-lined walls. A stale, but rather pleasant smell of tobacco pervaded every fold of its shabby serge curtains and green plush chairs; she could not open a book without inhaling the fumes of long dead pipes. The small space above the bookcases was papered with faded red and hung with photographs of Athens, while the shelves themselves were filled with volumes in the ugly bindings peculiar to classical works and commentaries. Among the rows of dull reds and liquorice browns stood out a cheerful regiment of fresh green-backed files. These were labellel in Mr. Grey's neat, upright hand: "Greek Prose," "Greek Unseens," "Tripos," "Greats," "Matric," and so on. Only four of these had any interest for Nanda; three containing the notes for Mr. Grey's important, but not yet written, pamphlet on the *Catalogue of Ships in the Iliad*, a work for which she had a most daughterly and ignorant reverence, and the fourth which bore the mysterious title *Haec Olim*. This last was a mine of fascinating records. It was stuffed to the brim with yellowed photographs of dead or dispersed Cambridge undergraduates of the early 'nineties; menus of huge, long-eaten dinners, a lock of her mother's hair, a tie of an obscure college club, and her own first letter to her father. She had spent many pleasant, stuffy Sunday evenings with its contents spread out before her, inventing stories about the stiff, elegant young men and tracing her father through successive incarnations, from a small boy in braided pantalettes to a young man in his third year at Emmanuel, surprisingly arrayed in a tiny bowler hat, a coat with the shortest possible lapels and an extremely fanciful waistcoat.

"I haven't looked at *Haec Olim* for years, Daddy," she exclaimed, catching sight of its reassuring back.

"No, my dear?" he smiled. "Well, it's old, faded, musty stuff. It's time we added something to it. When you leave Lippington, we'll put that green ribbon in with the rest."

"I'm afraid it'll be the last ribbon I'll ever get," said Nanda. Her father gave her a quick look over the top of his spectacles. "Why do you say that?"

"Well, I somehow cannot imagine myself as a blue ribbon. I don't believe if I stayed at Lippington till I was twenty they'd ever take me seriously enough for that."

"I see no reason why you should not have a blue ribbon one day . . . if you stayed on at the convent. It's about that I wanted to talk to you."

Nanda must have looked surprised, for Mr. Grey added hastily: "Now, my dear, don't be alarmed. Nothing's been decided. Nothing at all. And nothing shall be decided without your full consent."

"You mean you want me to leave Lippington?" She was conscious that her voice sounded far more sad and quavery than she meant it to. All the same, the idea was a severe shock.

"Not immediately. No, no. As I told you, I haven't decided anything at all. I wanted to know what you felt about it."

"But where would I go?" she asked helplessly.

"I've thought all that out, of course. But it's the merest suggestion. It's only your present and future happiness I have at heart, my dear."

Nanda had a horrible feeling that she was going to cry, but she managed to say in her coolest, grown-up voice: "What was your idea, Daddy?"

"Ever since I became a Catholic, I wanted more than anything that you should go to the Five Wounds and have a real knowledge in your Faith. I wanted you to have a real Catholic background of the kind I can't give you at home. Now, if I had been a rich man, and if I hadn't felt that at some time you must have a training that would enable you to earn your own living, nothing would have pleased me better than that you should stay on at Lippington till you were eighteen."

"But I won't even be fourteen until the Spring."

"I know, my dear. But you'll soon be of an age to take examinations such as the Cambridge Senior. And though I think the nuns teach you remarkably well, they don't profess to coach girls for exams. Have you ever thought what you would like to do when you're grown-up?"

"No, not really," said Nanda gloomily. The breath of

cold reality affected her like an east wind so that she actually shivered in her muslin frock.

"If you'll take my advice, you'll go in for teaching. I think you have all the right gifts for it, and with training, above all with a really good degree, I think you'd make a success. I could help you a good deal, you know."

"Oh, yes, I know, Daddy," she agreed tonelessly.

"So I had thought perhaps of your leaving the convent, say at the end of next summer. Then you could go to a really good High School and start working for your exams in real earnest. The longer you leave it, the harder it will be. I'm afraid the nuns have the haziest ideas of teaching Latin. And your mathematics are practically non-existent. Of course, your music is excellent and so are your languages and your literature. But what, after all, *are* literature and music?"

To her dismay, Nanda could keep back tears no longer. Three weeks ago, she had been bored and restless at Lippington, silently mutinous under its discipline, sick to death of its routine. Now, at the mere notion of leaving, she was overwhelmed with a passionate affection for the place. However much she might grumble and criticise, her roots were there. It was not only the possible loss of Clare and Léonie that horrified her. Day by day, for the last four years, she had been adapting herself to the Lippington standard, absorbing the Lippington atmosphere. Even now, in the shock of the revelation of her dependence, she did not realise how thoroughly Lippington had done its work. But she felt blindly she could only live in that rare, intense element; the bluff, breezy air of that "really good High School" would kill her.

Mr. Grey, alarmed and distressed at this unexpected outburst, patted her head and muttered:

"There, there, Nanda. Don't cry like that."

Nanda recovered herself a little, and he went on: "I'd no idea Lippington meant so much to you."

"Nor had I," sobbed Nanda. "I'm furious with myself for being so silly."

She was indeed furious with herself. She had, moreover, the oddest sense of having been tricked, betrayed. Her own nature saw the sense of her father's suggestion, even wanted to fall in with it. Yet here was some force she had never reckoned with bursting up in her mind, taking possession of her, driving her to protest with a violence she did not consciously feel.

"Listen, Nanda," said Mr. Grey comfortingly, "we won't talk about it any more. And please dry your eyes and stop crying, my dear little girl."

He pushed a large, clean handkerchief, that reminded Nanda of a nun's, into her limp hand. She blew her nose vigorously.

"I'm quite all right now," she said with difficulty. "Please let's go on talking."

"I only wanted to know how you felt about it," he said, sucking at his dead pipe. The familiar whistling noise did much to calm Nanda's nerves, and she even managed, with a watery smile, to hand him a matchbox.

"Thank you, my dear," he said gravely. Then, applying himself to the relighting of his pipe, he added: "Once upon a time I used to wish I had a son. But a daughter's a much better thing to have."

He did not look at Nanda, but she saw that his hands were shaking so that it took even more matches than usual to get the pipe going again.

When at last it was alight, he went on:

"I had thought that, having been at the convent for

four of the most receptive years of your life, the Catholic
impression was now strong enough in you not to be
effaced, and that it would do you no harm to make a
change. But I see you don't want it, so we'll forget all
about it. I'm very glad indeed to know that you're so
happy at Lippington. And I'm very pleased with your
record there, both for work and conduct. I hope you'll
go on as you've begun. If you do that, I shall always be
glad that we went by your wishes and not by my own
in this."

"I'll try, Daddy," said Nanda uncomfortably.

"Just one more thing, my dear. I hate even to mention it, but I think you ought to know. I'm not very
well off, and these nursing homes and doctors' bills for
your mother have been a great drain. Lippington is an
expensive school, but they are always willing to make
concessions to Catholics who cannot afford the full fees.
They have been very kind to me, but if you are to go on
there, I shall have to ask them to be kinder still."

"Oh, Daddy, I never realised that," Nanda burst out,
appalled. Thoughts of Monica Owen and the hundred
tiny humiliations which had preceded her final catastrophe rushed through her head.

"If things are like that," she went on eagerly, "please
forget all about my silliness to-night. I'll leave Lippington to-morrow, if you like. Really, Daddy, I will. I'd
rather."

But her father shook his head, smiling.

"Nonsense, my dear. It's very generous of you, but
I'm not going to let you sacrifice yourself like that. I've
no doubt something can be managed. There's only one
thing I would like to ask you, but I'm sure it will have
occurred to you already. If you do stay on at Lippington on those terms, you must go on doing as well, even

better, if possible, than you have done. That's the best way you can show your appreciation of what the nuns are doing for you."

Nanda nodded her head in silence. The clock on the mantelpiece, a reproduction of the Acropolis in black and green marble, struck ten.

"Good heavens," exclaimed Mr. Grey, "it's hours past your bedtime, my child. Up you go at once, and for goodness' sake, don't tell your mother I kept you up so late."

He held her for longer than usual as she kissed him good night, smoothing back her hair from her forehead, and looking into her eyes.

"I'm very proud of my daughter," he said. "We've always been the best of friends, haven't we?"

"Yes, Daddy."

"And we always shall be, shan't we? I've never believed all those dreary people who say that fathers and children can never see each other's point of view."

"It's nonsense, isn't it, Daddy?" she laughed, waving a last good night to him from the door.

In the hall she found a letter addressed to her. The envelope was thick and white, the stamp accurately placed, the writing familiar to her in a hundred exercise-book corrections. It was from Mother Percival.

Nanda sped upstairs to her room, her heart thumping with curiosity and misgiving. Why should Mother Percival write to her? She had never in her life received a letter from a nun. Tearing open the envelope, she read the following:

"MY DEAR NANDA,

"I daresay you will be surprised at receiving a letter from your class mistress while you are on your holiday, and thoughts of Lippington and lessons are probably the last things in your mind.

"All the same, it is not a bad thing that you should sometimes pause and look at yourself, not in the flattering mirror of young and perhaps not very wise friends, but in the eyes of one who, though your sincere well-wisher, is not so blind to your faults.

"I am purposely sending you this letter so that you you will receive it a few days before the reopening of classes in the hopes that you may be able to spare a few minutes from a doubtless continual round of holiday gaieties to meditate on its contents. I am not so optimistic as to suppose a child so independent as yourself will see fit to act on its advice at once, but I believe that one day you may be grateful for it.

"Now, my dear Nanda, God has seen fit to give you certain talents. He has given every human being on this earth talents of one kind or another, and I should like to remind you that the mere possession of a gift is no merit. It is the use you make of that gift which counts. Nor is there any superiority in possessing one kind of talent rather than another. It is a hundred times better to knit a pair of socks humbly for the glory of God than to write the finest poem or symphony for mere self-glorification. In fact, every talent carries its own responsibilities and its own temptations.

"It has struck me rather forcibly of late, from the tone of your essays and your conversation, that you are in danger of forgetting these important facts. A school is a little microcosm (I wonder if you understand that long word; if not, your father, with his knowledge of Greek, will explain it to you) of the great world outside. As a child behaves in her school days, so she will behave through life. Prizes are unimportant. In after life it is not the prize-winners, but those who have built up their characters by obedience and self-denial who make their influence felt for good.

"And I cannot help feeling, my dear Nanda, that you are not building up your character as you should; I notice that you choose your friends rather for such superficial attributes as cleverness and humour and even for the still more unworthy and frivolous reasons of mere 'good looks' and a social position above your own. Remember that the healthiest friendships are those between people who share the same background.

"These may seem hard words, but they are spoken in a spirit of sincere interest in your welfare. I do not mind hurting your vanity, but I do not want to hurt your feelings. Schoolgirls are notoriously uncritical and in the world you may find that Nanda Grey does not seem the clever, fascinating little person she appears to a small circle at Lippington.

"Well, I have lectured you enough, and I have enough faith in your honesty and good sense to hope you will take this in the spirit it was written. I shall be glad to see you back here next week. I think you will be interested in the new geography lessons we are to have next term. Mary Zulecca, an old child of the Five Wounds, who has been doing some splendid missionary work in Central Africa, has consented to give us three lantern lectures on the Congo.

"Remember me in your prayers as I remember you in mine.

"Yours in the charity of the Five Wounds,
"MARGARET PERCIVAL."

Nanda read this letter three times before she thoroughly mastered its contents. Then she tore it into very small pieces, put it in the grate and set fire to it with a match. She felt hurt and outraged, as if someone had struck her in the face. The world that five minutes before had been so warm, had turned unfriendly. Even the room that had been inviolably hers until now was polluted. There was no privacy anywhere. Why, oh why, hadn't she taken her chance and escaped from Lippington while there was yet time? She sat on the edge of her bed, clenching and unclenching her cold hands, and muttering to herself: "Unjust. Unjust."

Looking up, she caught sight of her face in the old, smeared glass. It looked pale and blank and ugly under the silly bows. Creeping closer to examine it, she remembered the letter again, hastily put out the light, and undressed in the dark.

She was very silent at breakfast the next morning. Never had she been so grateful for her father's unobserving eye. He evidently noticed nothing odd in her strained face and unbrushed hair.

For several minutes they sat without speaking, while Mr. Grey read the paper and Nanda cut her uneaten toast into smaller and still smaller cubes.

At last, reaching out mechanically for another cup of tea, her father said:

"Here's something that will interest you, my dear. You remember that Lady Moira Palliser, who entered your convent some years ago?"

Nanda gave him a toneless "Yes."

"Well, her father, the Earl of Kilmorden, died at Christmas, and she is now the Countess in her own right. It says that against her own wishes, but in obedience to the commands of her superiors, she is now returning to the world. They say it is her duty to go back and administer her estates. I think that shows great

wisdom on their part, though I expect it is a great
sorrow to her."

"She certainly wanted awfully to be a nun," assented
Nanda, a spark of life returning to her voice.

"I think it puts your Order in a most excellent light,"
said Mr. Grey heartily. "It's a magnificent reply to all
the people who accuse Catholics of being grasping."

"I suppose it does," Nanda agreed reluctantly, "but
she'll feel like a fish out of water in the world after all
these years. You can't get away from Lippington just by
growing your hair and putting on ordinary clothes."

Her father looked at her with an air of slight annoyance and returned to his paper. He did not speak again
until he was leaving the room. At the door he paused
and said a little coldly:

"You didn't happen to notice if there were any letters
in the hall when you went up to bed last night?"

"Were you expecting one?" she asked innocently.

"Yes. As a matter of fact, I was."

"No, there weren't any letters at all, Daddy," said
Nanda, bending over her plate, and slicing an infinitesimal corner off one of her cubes of toast.

It was the first direct lie she had ever told him.

CHAPTER XI

NEVER had Nanda returned to school so unwillingly
as she did at the beginning of her fifth Lent term.
Certainly, she had not enjoyed the last days of the
Christmas vacation, soured as they were by the taste of

Mother Percival's charitable advice, but they had at least not brought her face to face with the adviser. She did her best to postpone the hateful day, but without success. A promising cold, which she had tried hard to foster into pneumonia, betrayed her hopes by vanishing completely on the very morning of the reopening of classes, so that there was nothing for it but to pack her trunk and get ready. As it was, she dawdled so long over the process that she kept the cab waiting for twenty minutes and quite wore out her father's patience. Their drive together to Lippington was strained and almost silent, but Nanda wished it would last for ever. However, by some perversity, the cabman whipped up his old horse into the briskest of trots and, long before she had had time to compose herself, they were at the convent door.

To her surprise and discomfiture, Mother Percival herself was waiting at the portress' lodge. As Mr. Grey hastily kissed Nanda good-bye, the nun smiled at them with unusual friendliness. Nanda loitered a little in the corridor, expecting to be called back, but Mother Percival gave no sign, so she hastened along to the changing room with a slightly easier mind.

Léonie and Rosario had not yet arrived, but she found Clare and was comforted by the eagerness of her welcome.

"But you're not looking a bit well, infant," Clare said in her warm, quick voice. "Are you ill, or is something worrying you?"

"A bit. But I want to forget about it. Let's talk about you instead."

"I'm so glad to be back," said Clare with a gusty sigh. "I've had the most miserable holiday. My family were terribly difficult about letting me come back at all."

"Because of . . ." Nanda hesitated.

"Because of the Catholic business? Yes. They just can't understand that anyone should want a different religion from theirs. They've tried every argument from tears to threatening to cut me off entirely, but it's no good. Sooner or later I've got to be a Catholic. I know it quite clearly now."

"Did you tell them you had really made up your mind?"

"No. I begged for just a little more time to think it over. After all, nothing definite's been done. I'm not even having instruction or anything. The nuns won't take any responsibility about that."

"It's funny," mused Nanda. "People always imagine that tight-lipped nuns and wily Jesuits stand at street corners trying to entice people into becoming Catholics, whereas in actual fact they're rather discouraging if you do want to get converted."

"I know," agreed Clare. "I think that's why I managed to get back for just one more term. My father came up and had a long talk with Reverend Mother, and came away almost convinced that she, at any rate, would rather I stayed as I was."

"I wonder what she said."

"For one thing that I was much too young to know my own mind. Such nonsense. Why, I shall be eighteen in the Autumn. And another thing that simply infuriated me . . . that girls often get ideas of that kind into their heads and then they meet someone and get married and forget all about it."

"What did your father say to that?"

"Well, he said it might be a crazy religion, but there were some damn sensible women in convents, so I might as well stay here till Easter and then he'd give me a season in London to get all these schoolgirl fads out of my head."

"So you were very meek and grateful and all that?"

"Yes. But I was simply boiling inside. And nothing, absolutely *nothing* can change my conviction about Catholicism now. Reverend Mother and the whole lot of them can just wait and see."

Nanda frowned and bit her lip.

"I wonder why you want to be a Catholic so very much? Do you remember how you used to laugh when I told you about indulgences and purgatory and things? I must have been an awful little prig in those days."

Clare leant back and clasped her knee in her thin, over-sensitive hands.

"I may have laughed, but I never, never thought you a prig, infant. Secretly, I was terribly impressed. You looked such a baby, but you talked away so earnestly and used such long words, and so obviously understood it all and believed it all that I felt that there must be a tremendous amount in your religion. And it was just the same with Léo and Rosario and all the rest of you. You might joke about miracles and so on, but you had some wonderful secret, a real security. I was desperately curious about it. So I read everything I could lay hands on—the catechism, lives of the saints, anything. I've still got those retreat notes you copied out for me years ago. And sometimes I'd think it was all wonderful and at other times I'd be repelled by the whole idea. But it's just been slowly growing on me . . . the fact that I've got to be a Catholic or nothing."

"I see," nodded Nanda wisely. There was a moment's silence, and she stole a glance at Clare's face. Something about its bright, ecstatic eyes and half-open mouth reminded her of Theresa Leighton and touched her with a faint discomfort.

"If you really feel like that," she added in her most business-like voice, "you'll certainly get what you want, whatever happens. I'll pray for you all I know how."

Clare started and bent her wild, dreaming face towards Nanda. She was so pale with emotion that her freckles showed almost black.

"Darling, darling," she whispered quickly, and gave Nanda's hand a sudden squeeze.

Nanda jumped up. The room had been emptying as they talked, and they were now alone except for a snivelling new child who was changing into her uniform.

"Heavens, I forgot. I simply must take my home clothes up to the linen room before supper. See you at recreation, Clare."

The next day, Léo and Rosario returned. They had been spending their holidays in Paris, and the channel boat had been delayed by a storm. Léonie appeared during the early morning preparation, when talking was strictly forbidden, but she waved violently to Nanda and went through a masterly pantomime of sea-sickness and slow recovery.

In the brief mid-morning break, when the children were supposed to run briskly round the garden, she strolled up to Nanda and seized her by the pigtail.

"Don't paw the ground like that, as if you were going to break into a fiery canter. Aren't you glad to see your childhood's friend?"

"Jolly glad," said Nanda, "but the Percival's got her stop-watch out and she's timing me."

"Nonsense," said Léonie comfortably. "Let me tell you just how it was. You were just running at full speed when you saw Léonie de Wesseldorf, Mother, and

Léonie felt rather metagrobolised and dispericraniated after her dreadful crossing yesterday, and you sat down beside her and said: 'Léonie, my old friend and trusted confidante, can I do anything for you?' And Léonie said: 'Let us sit down on this rustic bench for ten minutes until the agony is somewhat abated, and then I shall be sufficiently recovered to be able to enjoy one of your incomparable geography lessons, Mother.' "

Nanda laughed. "You're just the same as ever, Léo."

"Well, why not?"

"I don't know. There's been something queer about these Christmas holidays. They've only lasted three weeks, yet I feel like a sort of Rip Van Winkle coming back after years and years."

"And you expected to find me in a bath-chair surrounded by troops of grand-children?"

"Idiot," said Nanda. She scraped the gravel with the toe of her shoe and added with a sigh: "I suppose you're horribly rich and all that, aren't you, Léo?"

"Horribly," assented Léonie with a grimace.

"I was afraid so," Nanda said gloomily.

"Why worry about it? You're not going to preach me a sermon on the appalling effects of riches on the character, are you?"

Nanda grinned but did not answer.

"Seriously, my dear, what are you getting at?" asked Léonie.

"Well, I've just realised that in three or four years we'll all be growing up and leaving school, and I'll probably never see any of you again."

"Why on earth not?"

"Oh, you'll see it all perfectly well if you'll just think a minute. I shall probably be teaching a howling mob of children and you'll be married to a duke, and I'll be lucky if I occasionally see a photograph of you in *The Tatler*."

"I never heard such nonsense in the whole of my life," said Léonie witheringly.

"It's true all the same," Nanda protested.

"Oh, for God's sake, shut up," Léonie broke out, with a ring of cold anger in her voice.

The bell rang for the end of the brief recreation and they moved towards the school, Léonie stalking ahead and Nanda deliberately hanging behind.

They seated themselves side by side in Mother Percival's class-room without exchanging a grimace or a whisper. Léonie began to arrange her books with elaborate care; Nanda stared moodily at the unrolled map of Africa. She felt Mother Percival's eye on her and was compelled after a few seconds to look up at the nun's face. To her surprise, instead of being disapproving, it seemed curiously softened and happy. The explanation came quickly.

Mother Percival clasped her hands on her desk, surveyed her class with a smile that suggested a shyness unusual to her usually straightforward, astringent nature, and said:

"I have some news for you which I wanted the Lower Third to be the first to hear. I shall be leaving you at the end of this week . . . leaving Lippington for some months."

"I knew it. She's going to get her ring," whispered Nanda's other neighbour triumphantly.

Nanda nodded absently. A wave of relief broke over her and washed away some of the barbs of that memorable letter. She was used to these sudden disappearances. After two years of novitiate and four of probation, the religious of the Five Wounds went to another house of the Order and made a six-months' retreat before professing their final vows and receiving the symbolic wedding-ring.

"I am going to Liège," Mother Percival went on, "and I think you will all know that I shall pray for each one of you while I am away. Mother Clement, who has recently arrived from one of our American houses, will take on my work, and I hope—I *know*—that you will all do your best to make things easy for her."

Her voice shook, and Nanda almost fancied she saw a tear in the unemotional grey eyes. But before she could be quite sure, Mother Percival had turned to the map of Africa, tapped it smartly with her pointer, and asked in her usual brisk, frosty manner:

"Hilda, could you *now* point out, with some faint degree of accuracy, the course of the Zambesi river?"

The rest of the day passed uneventfully. So quickly did the children slip into the orderly routine of a day chequered into sections varying from an hour to ten minutes that the homes they had left only yesterday already seemed ineffably remote. The punctual bells regulated every movement to class-room, to playground, refectory or chapel. They smoothed away some of the discomfort and bewilderment that had roughened the surface of Nanda's life for the last week. Except for the tension between herself and Léonie, she was almost happy. She looked at Lippington through fresher eyes, and was ashamed of her many disloyalties. After all, where would she find a place like it? In its cold, clear atmosphere everything had a sharper outline than in the comfortable, shapeless, scrambling life outside. The scrubbed boards and whitened walls and shining brasses reminded her of a ship. As in a ship, too, one had the scantiest of personal belongings stowed away in the smallest possible space; one wore a uniform, one obeyed orders. The simile rather pleased her, and she pushed it further, wondering whether, however much she might grumble and rebel against life on board, she did not secretly despise mere landsmen.

Half-past eight came, and night prayers in the chapel, where that mixed smell of incense and beeswax reminded her afresh of her first night at Lippington four years ago. Something in her softened, humble mood seemed to blow away the dust that had gathered on the familiar petitions she had repeated hundreds of times. They sounded as if newly improvised to fit her own needs. In the silence that followed, she found herself praying earnestly for friends and enemies alike, for Mother Percival and Léonie, above all for the conversion of Clare Rockingham. She was full of good resolutions. She would be kinder to stupid people and fierce only to her own vanity. She would break down that core of stubborn independence. She would think less of human friendships and more of Our Lady and the saints whom she had so neglected of late.

Outside the door, someone suddenly came abreast of her and thrust a piece of paper into her prayer-book. It was Léonie. But before Nanda had had time to do more than look astonished, she was gone again.

She was longing to look at the paper, but prudence warned her to wait until she was safe behind the curtains of her cubicle. There, in the faint glimmer from the gas-jet outside, she made out the well-known, cramped writing:

"You're an idiot but you are my best friend. So kindly shut up now and always.
"Léonie Magdalena Hedwig de Wesseldorf."

CHAPTER XII

FEBRUARY was wet and misty, with fogs hanging over the lake and puddles lying in the sodden playground. As Lent drew nearer, spirits became more and more depressed. There was an outburst of apparent cheerfulness on the two Shrove-tide half holidays, but with the austerities of Ash Wednesday just ahead, the gaiety was decidedly forced.

On Shrove Monday it was the custom for the lay-sisters to have a whole holiday from their heavy work, and for the children to take their places in kitchen and pantry. They scrubbed the passages and swept the dormitories, laid the tables in the refectory and actually cooked the meals. A band of younger ones was told off to entertain the Sisters, and shouts of applause greeted the appearance of old Sister Richter, who ruled the school cloakrooms with a military fierceness, driving up and down the alleys in the donkey-cart accompanied by the entire Junior School.

Sister Richter was one of the Lippington "characters," a focal point for the "My dear, *do* you remember's" of generations of old children. She was reported to be about ninety years old, and occasionally mixed past and present in her consciousness. Nanda and the rest had been delighted one day when she had scolded Mother Percival before a whole division for letting her pupils get their feet wet, and had ended up by saying: "I'm ashamed of you, Miss Margaret. I'll report you for this, and you will for certain lose your exemption."

She was very devout, and would often be discovered kneeling on a wooden work-box in the corner of the cloakroom, absorbed in prayer. But her devotions never interfered with her duties. She would leap up from her knees to pounce on any culprit who left a tap running or otherwise misdemeaned herself. "Vot a vicked extraffagance, my tear," she would mumble accusingly. "It is kvite unnecessary to use so much soap. And that peautiful hot vater! You vill haf to account to the tear Lort for effery trop you haf vasted."

It was so long since Sister Richter had entered that she could hardly remember her short life in the world. But she clung tenderly to the memory of her native village in Thuringia. If any German child came to the school, she would waylay her, and producing a faded picture postcard from her pocket, ask wistfully: "Do you know this? It is Behrenwald, the most peautiful fillage in Ghermany. I was porn there."

Léonie, who claimed actually to have visited Behrenwald, was her cherished favourite. Léonie might use hot water by the gallon, tear her towels to ribbons, or even use the precious soap for blowing bubbles; in Sister Richter's eyes she could do no wrong. Once, hearing her being scolded, she had planted herself in front of the mistress and declared: "You are kvite wrong, Mother. Miss Léonie is a good child. She knows my peautiful Behrenwald."

By Shrove Tuesday, the spirit of mortification had already set in. Several of the children voluntarily spent an extra half-hour in the chapel instead of playing hide and seek, to atone to the Blessed Sacrament for the sins committed during the carnival in Spain and Italy. Others gave up sweets or story-books for the same reason. The last moments of the holidays leaked swiftly away in tepid gaieties, and half-depressed, half-relieved, the school braced itself for the six weeks of penance.

Nanda had always hated Ash Wednesday. It had the gloom of Good Friday without its noble sorrows. The day began with the distribution of the holy ashes. The children knelt in long rows at the Communion rails, while Father Robertson walked to and fro smudging a cross on each forehead murmuring: "*Mememto, Homo,. quia pulvis es et in pulverem reverteris.*" Breakfast, eaten in complete silence, consisted of two thin slices of dry bread and a cup of tea without milk or sugar. The school kept the proper fast only on Good Friday, but the nuns, while going about their ordinary business, fasted every day except Sunday throughout Lent. They were allowed one good meal at midday, the only stipulation being that they might not eat both fish and meat; their supper consisted of a meagre collation of bread or cabbage. They abstained from milk and butter every day and from meat on Wednesdays and Fridays. But this was the least of their mortifications. Each member of the community had her private penances, spiritual and physical, at which Nanda could only guess. She remembered how horrified, yet impressed, she had been during her very first Lent at Lippington, when Mother Frances' sleeves had slipped back as she reached up to lift something from a high shelf, revealing small iron chains bound tightly round her arms. There were whispers of spiked belts and wire scourges, and when a mistress was sharper of tongue than usual during a class, the more charitable put it down to the fact that she was probably wearing a hair shirt that day.

However, the children were strongly discouraged from imitating such practices. Betka Winkenstahl was discovered wearing small pebbles in her shoes and forced to remove them before the whole school, and Vera Cooling-Brown was discouraged from drinking vine-

gar by being made to sit by herself in the middle of
the refectory while a lay-sister plied her with cups of
cocoa.

The Spring term in all boarding schools is usually
marked by the outbreak of infectious diseases. Two oppressive weeks of Lent had crawled by when a child,
having sickened for a day or so, retired to the infirmary,
and was later observed, wrapped in blankets, being
wheeled along the passage that led to the isolation wing.
Spirits revived magically. Epidemics were popular during
a dull term. For the lucky victims they meant not
merely the luxury of the infirmary, but a cheerful convalescence and a blissful quarantine free from regular
lessons and restrictions.

"I hope to heaven it isn't only chicken-pox or German measles," said Léonie to Nanda at the first opportunity. "I'd rather on the whole it weren't whooping-
cough, because it's such a barbaric disease. Anyhow,
whatever it is, I'm determined to catch it."

"Unless it's scarlet fever," said Nanda cheerfully, "in
which case, it's hardly worth the trouble, because we'll
all be sent home anyhow."

It turned out to be measles, and to everyone's delight,
three more cases were reported by the end of the week.
The infirmarian was busy with disinfectants, gargles and
liquorice powder, but the children were still busier trying to outwit her. Everyone with even a mild cold became an immediate object of interest and found herself
surrounded by people anxious to be in contact with her
and to borrow her possessions. In twenty-four hours,
Léonie, who always got what she wanted, was going
about with streaming eyes and a flushed face. Before she
went up to the infirmary, she drew Nanda aside and
croaked hoarsely:

"I've done it, my dear. Pains in the head and temperature rising every minute. Here is a precious legacy."

She produced a slightly grey handkerchief. "Perfectly clean," she added, as she gave it to Nanda; "it's only that colour because I did a bit of dusting with it. But it's been under my pillow all night, and with any luck, it should be swarming with germs by now."

Whether or not the handkerchief had anything to do with it, Nanda shortly found herself in the isolation wing. By great good fortune, Clare and Rosario also developed measles a day or two later. All four had the disease mildly enough to make a quick recovery, and they were soon thoroughly enjoying themselves in the convalescent stage. Among the dozen or so of the other patients they formed a compact and almost inseparable group, and their number freed them from the grave reproach of "going about in twos."

Never had Nanda enjoyed so free a life at Lippington. The only nun who visited them was a kind old Irishwoman who had not taught in the school for some years; for the rest, they were under the charge of two nurses, both of whom appeared to be iron disciplinarians until Léonie had the happy thought of ordering huge propitiatory boxes of sweets for them from Charbonnel & Walker. After that, the four did more or less what they pleased. No one disputed their right to the shabby armchairs by the fire in the convalescent sitting-room, and they were often allowed to sit up unchaperoned long after the others had been packed off to bed.

Léonie managed to smuggle in books by the dozen; Rosario had her guitar; Clare conjured up biscuits and chocolates and Nanda put in several hours of work on her much-neglected novel.

"I wish we could live like this for ever," sighed Clare

one night, as she pulled the faded serge curtains closer to shut out the sound of the March wind and rain.

"Oh, so do I," echoed Nanda. Léonie deep in the only really comfortable chair, with her legs flung ungracefully over its arm, merely grunted. Transferring a large caramel into one cheek, she said thickly:

"Sing something, Rosario."

Rosario, who was kneeling by the fire, smiled and shook her head. She had been washing her hair, and the thick fleecy gold hung in showers round her shoulders. Clare reached out her hand and drew one of the shining strands through her fingers.

"I've never seen such hair," she said. "It's like a fairy princess's. Really, you're too lovely to live, darling."

"Oh, *don't* be so silly," said Rosario crossly, jerking her head away.

"And don't be so fierce," laughed Clare. "I only said you had wonderful hair. And such yards of it."

"It's not as long as yours," insisted Rosario.

"Oh, but it is. Miles longer. Just look," said Clare. Her hands were busy with hairpins. In a minute the thick, doubled plait was unravelled and she shook down a great, coppery mane that reached nearly to her waist.

She leant her head against Rosario's and looked up with shining brown eyes at Nanda.

"Tell me, infant, aren't I right?"

Nanda frowned judicially.

"No, yours is longer, Clare. Quite two inches. But you do both look terribly beautiful to-night."

Léonie swallowed her caramel, shut her book with a bang, and yawned.

"When you've quite finished your beauty competition, you might get on with that singing."

"Oh, very well," laughed Rosario. "You always get your own way in the end."

She took down her gaily beribboned guitar from the wall and seated herself on a heap of cushions. As she tested the strings, Clare cried excitedly:

"Let's put out the lamps. The fire's heaps bright enough."

"What a one you are for the dramatic," observed Léonie. "If ever you have a young man, I don't suppose you'll ever let him kiss you unless the moon's out and there's a band playing *The Blue Danube* in the distance."

Clare pulled Léonie's brief and untidy plait, but she put out the lights all the same. Then she flung herself on the hearthrug at Rosario's feet.

"*Now* we're ready," she purred luxuriously. Rosario bent over her guitar. In the glow its belly had a ruddy shine. Her hair, as she continually tossed it back from her face, seemed to give off flakes of light, while Clare's red-brown head was frayed with gold at the edges. Nanda and Léonie drew back into the shadows; the latter huddled in her chair with her arms folded and her chin sunk on her chest.

Rosario strayed from song to song in her rich, soft voice that had none of the trailing languor of Elita's. She sang Spanish peasant songs and even love songs; she sang *The Rowan Tree* and *Funiculì, Funiculà,* in which the others joined guardedly in the chorus. At last she put down her guitar, shook back her hair, and said: "That's enough."

But Nanda and Clare begged for more. Rosario looked doubtful; then smiled as if an idea had struck her. She tightened the pegs of her guitar, struck a chord, and began to play a little prelude. Léonie shifted in her chair, and Rosario said through the music: "You don't mind, Léo?"

"No. Go on," answered Léonie gruffly. Rosario leant over the guitar again and sang almost in a whisper:

> "To a lovely myrtle bound
> Blossoms show'ring all around
> O, how sick and weary I
> Underneath my myrtle lie.
> Why should I be bound to thee,
> O my lovely myrtle tree?"

There was silence as she finished. After a minute she said:

"That's Léonie's setting, you know. I think it's most beautiful."

"But it's exquisite," burst out Clare, who could not hum the simplest tune.

"Did you really write the music, Léo?" asked Nanda with awe. She was deeply moved.

"Uhu," grunted Léonie in her most forbidding tone. Then she jumped up, and in spite of Clare's cries of protest, turned on the lights. The four blinked at each other with shy, apologetic smiles, their eyes bright and sleepy, with the pupils shrunk to mere specks.

"You are a heartless brute," said Clare. "I was so beautifully happy and comfortable."

"Well, go and be beautifully happy and comfortable in bed," grinned Léonie.

"Nonsense," Clare insisted. "Come and sit down and be sensible. We've got heaps of time still. I'm not going to leave this fire till I'm dragged away by main force."

Léonie rejoined the circle and they began to talk idly.

"I wonder where we shall all be in ten years' time?" began Clare romantically. It was one of her favourite themes.

"I shall be married," said Rosario, quietly but definitely.

"Why so certain, darling?" asked Clare. Rosario shrugged her elegant shoulders.

"Why not? Elita is engaged already, and she has only been out six months. My relations have several people in mind for me already."

"How can you be so matter-of-fact about it?" said Clare, shocked. "You can't fall in love to order."

"No, I know that."

"And so you mean to go through your whole life without ever really falling in love?"

"That doesn't follow at all."

"You mean, you'll fall in love with someone else after you've married your suitable person?"

"Of course not," said Rosario with great dignity. "Once I am married, I should never allow myself to do such a thing. It wouldn't be fair to my husband or my family. But I don't mean to marry until I am at least twenty-one. Until then, I consider I have a right to do as I please."

"What would you do if you were madly in love, Rosario?" asked Clare.

Rosario smiled and looked straight in front of her with enormous blue eyes.

"I should sit on the very top of the Pyrenees and read poetry and play the guitar."

"I don't suppose I shall ever marry," said Clare, busy with her own future. "But I shall be the most divine old maid, growing roses and things and driving about in a dog-cart and being the most marvellous aunt to all of your children. Of course, I'll be frightfully poor, because I'll be a Catholic and my family will have cut me off with an old bootlace."

"I shall have exactly two children," stated Léonie firmly, ignoring Clare's last remark. "One male and one female, and both incredibly talented and incredibly bad-tempered."

They all laughed and Clare said: "What about Nanda. We've left her out of all this?"

Léonie gave Nanda a glance of brotherly affection.

"Nanda's a dark horse," she declared.

CHAPTER XIII

ALL too soon, this slothful and delightful life came to an end. The school doctor arrived one day, inspected them, and told them that they might shortly return to school, since they were now perfectly well and there was no danger of their infecting the others. Léonie, as the first arrival, was the earliest to leave; it would be Nanda's turn next.

She spent her last two days in the isolation wing polishing up the fourth chapter of her novel. Surveying what she had written with as dispassionate an eye as possible, she decided that it really was rather good. Anyhow, it seemed to read remarkably like a real book. The heroine, who had "geranium red lips and hair of finest spun gold and huge, limpid violet eyes," might almost stand comparison with some of Mr. E. F. Benson's, whom she so greatly admired. In deference to her master, she also supplied her with a "tiny, tip-tilted nose" and furnished her background with a splendour drawn from

other works of fiction and occasional visits to the Troca-
dero. But most of her loving care had been lavished on
the hero, who was, she flattered herself, an entirely
original creation. To begin with, he was extremely ugly,
with an ugliness "redeemed only by a pair of brilliant
and marvellously penetrating eyes." He studied black
magic and wrote poetry "wrapped in a dressing-gown of
yellow oriental silk, wrought with strange symbols." In
the end he was to reject the love of the violet-eyed
heroine and to enter a Trappist monastery, but at this
early stage Nanda was only concerned with the difficult
business of making her characters as wicked as possible
in order that their conversion might be the more spectacular. The hero "frequented mysterious dens in China-
town, from which he might be observed issuing in the
early hours of the morning, still dazed with the fumes
of strange narcotics"; the heroine's life was one giddy
round of balls and flirtations. There was one moment
where the heroine's other admirer, after having
"swooned with her in the languid ecstasies of a waltz"
took her out on the balcony and "pressed a kiss of burning passion on her scarlet mouth, a kiss which had some
of the reckless intoxication of the music that throbbed
out from the Hungarian band they could hear in the
distance."

Clare and Rosario, watching her alternately biting her
pen and dashing it across the paper at breakneck speed,
often begged her to show them what she was writing.
But though she secretly longed for an audience, she
always said sternly: "No, you must wait till it's finished.
The whole point's the *end*, you see."

At last came the gloomy day of return to normal
life, a day which Nanda faced as unwillingly as a walk
in the east wind after an afternoon by the fire, and

which even the prospect of rejoining Léonie could not
brighten.

She was greeted carelessly and jealously by her class-
mates, for whom the rigours of Lent had had no miti-
gation.

"You're only just in time for Holy Week," grumbled
Marjorie Appleyard.

"Well, it's not *my* fault, is it?" said Nanda crossly.

"Of course, you didn't want to get measles, did you?"
sneered Marjorie. "And you didn't try to catch them?
Oh no."

And she bent virtuously over her exercise-book.

Léonie was more comforting. "It's nice to see a
human face again," she said. "One more day among
these sheep and I'd have been bleating myself. By the
way, I suppose you had to burn your manuscript?"

"What manuscript?"

"Why, your novel, or whatever it is. I had to make
a complete bonfire of all my most cherished possessions."

"Good Lord," said Nanda. "I forgot all about it. Nurse
Marsh told us to, and I burnt letters and so on, but I
forgot all about *that*."

"Well, don't let them know, that's all."

Holy Week arrived and proceeded on its majestic way.
Each year, however much she might have wavered in
her devotion or her unquestioning obedience, its slow,
magnificent rituals impressed on her afresh the beauty
and poetry of Catholicism. Each of the great days had
its special drama. After Palm Sunday every statue was
veiled with purple, the organ was silent, and the altar
bell replaced by a harsh wooden clapper. On the evenings of Tuesday, Wednesday and Thursday, the children
and the nuns sang the office of Tenebrae in the darkened

chapel. She was profoundly moved by the lamenting psalms with the recurrent, urgent cry *"Jerusalem, Jerusalem, convertere ad dominum Deum tuum."* At the end of each psalm, the sacristan nun extinguished one of the candles, until only one remained. This she took and placed behind the altar to symbolise the laying of Our Lord in the tomb. There was a brief silence; then a deep rumbling on the organ announced the resurrection; the candle was brought out from its hiding, and the office was over for the night.

Maundy Thursday came like a sad *Corpus Christi* with something funereal about the white flowers and lights round the Altar of Repose. The chapel, with all its lamps extinguished, and the door of the tabernacle opened wide was like an empty house. The Blessed Sacrament had been taken away; no one genuflected to-day before the deserted altar; even the holy water stoups were dry. The whole life of the Church had dwindled to its lowest pulse before the catastrophe of Good Friday.

The ordinary school routine on Holy Thursday served only as a background to the seven visits to the Holy Sepulchre, as they called the side-chapel where the host now reposed. At six o'clock came Tenebrae, the last and most sorrowful office of the *triduum*. Nanda noticed that the candles were being extinguished not by the usual sacristan nun, but by a postulant. At intervals her old fear of a vocation re-asserted itself so that the sight of any new aspirant always filled her with a certain discomfort. Supposing that one day one of those figures in ancient, borrowed skirts and dark flannel blouses should be herself? The chapel was too dim to make out the face of the newcomer, but she saw that she was tall and slender and moved with a rather awkward grace, as if

her natural motion were swifter. But when she carried
the last candle to its hiding place, its beam shone full
on her face, and Nanda recognised Hilary O'Byrne.

In the short recreation after their silent meal, Nanda
made straight for Léonie.

"Did you see her . . . the new postulant?"

"Hilary O'Byrne? Of course. I knew all about that
ages ago."

"I suppose I'll never be a proper Catholic," mused
Nanda, "but it does seem rather horrible, somehow. She
was so gay and all that."

"People who become nuns often are."

"Do you think," said Nanda romantically, "that it
was a sort of idea of atonement? I mean, because Moira
Palliser wanted to be a nun and they made her go back
to the world? Perhaps Hilary thought she ought to
make up for it by being a nun, though she didn't want
to?"

"Rubbish," declared Léonie with great firmness. "You
don't even try to be a nun unless you're pretty convinced
that you've got a vocation. You understand a lot of
things, but you simply don't understand that specific
Catholic something. I don't mean dogmas and all that.
No one can trip you up on those. I can't explain in the
least what I mean."

"You might try, anyhow," insisted Nanda.

"Well, I can just tell you the first example that occurs
to me. It's nothing whatever to do with this. I had an
old grandmother who lived in the country in France
and spent most of her time going to mass and playing
whist with the *curé* and doing endless knitting for the
poor. Well, she died last year at the age of eighty or so.
After she had received the Last Sacraments, she asked
for her knitting. Her maid was rather shocked: '*Mais*

Madame la Marquise a été administrée,' she exclaimed.
'Elle va mourir.' To which my grandmother replied:
*'Ma chère, ce n'est pas là une raison pour perdre son
temps.'* "

The nun in charge was looking at the clock. In a
minute the bell would ring.

"Hi, quick . . . before we're plunged into twenty-four
hours' silence," said Léonie urgently. "Lend me that
novel of yours to look at."

"But I can't," demurred Nanda. "It's nothing like
finished. Besides, I haven't shown it to a soul."

"I should hope not, if you haven't shown it to me."

"I'd much rather not, Léo," said Nanda.

Léonie fixed her with a cold, grey eye.

"Look here, are you my best friend or are you not?"
she demanded.

Nanda gave in.

"Oh, very well. I'll give it to you when we get our veils
for night prayers. But for heaven's sake don't let anybody see it—specially a nun."

"Do you think I'm a congenital idiot?" asked Léonie
acidly as the bell rang.

The children went to bed early that night to prepare
for the long day of fasting and prayer on the morrow.

There was no early mass, but at half-past seven they
had a silent breakfast of dry bread and milkless tea.
The entire morning was spent in the chapel for the Mass
of the Presanctified and the Adoration of the Cross. No
host is consecrated on Good Friday and the one the
priest receives is that brought back from the altar of
repose. The priest slowly unveiled the crucifix, and the
whole school and the community approached one by
one to kiss it, while two singers intoned the lamentations
and responses of the *Improperia*. The long, chanted gos-

pel of the Passion and the longer prayers for the whole world tired Nanda more than usual, so that by the time the altar was being silently stripped of its few clothes she felt quite faint.

After their lunch of salt fish and bread and water, the children returned to the chapel to watch there in spirit with Christ on the cross until three o'clock. There is a tradition that any prayer made as the clock strikes three on Good Friday will be granted. Nanda had long decided what her petition that year should be. On the first stroke of the clock she whispered urgently: "Whatever happens, dear Lord, please make Clare Rockingham a Catholic."

After they returned from this devotion, the tension relaxed a little. Although there were no lessons and they were not permitted to talk or to play games, the children could read pious books, sew, or tidy their desks. Nanda's class went for a walk in silence round the garden. When they returned to the study-room, they were greeted by the sight of many raised desk-lids.

During their absence, Mother Radcliffe had made one of her periodical visitations to see whether all was in order. Those whose desks were untidy were left open as a reproach, and usually lost their exemptions. Both Nanda's and Léonie's were open, as they usually were on these occasions. Léonie, with a click of annoyance, began rummaging in hers, throwing up holy pictures, broken crystal rosaries, letters with foreign stamps, snapshots, and biscuit crumbs from its amazing confusion. After two or three minutes, she turned to Nanda, looking paler than usual, and whispered:

"My God—it's gone."

"What's gone?" asked Nanda, also in a whisper.

"Your novel."

CHAPTER XIV

NANDA had seldom passed a worse night than she did that Good Friday. In the false security of the isolation wing, she had written on and on in a holiday spirit, with no idea that the eye of anyone in authority might fall on her work. The kind old Irish nun had never asked questions about it. She had even encouraged Nanda as she sat writing, patting her shoulder and occasionally observing: *"Laborare est orare,* my dear," or "The pen is mightier than the sword."

Nor, by the standards of the Mudie books that always lay about in the drawing-room at home, did her novel seem at all subversive. Certainly, it was rather "strong," so far, but the magnificent repentances and renunciations of the end would only make it all the more striking as propaganda for the Faith.

But, as she lay in the dark, sobered and shivering, she remembered passage after passage which would require a good deal of explanation in any nun's eyes; in Mother Radcliffe's most of all. She remembered the scene last term over her mildly silly letter about Clare. This time, Mother Radcliffe would be ruthless. She discarded the comforting hope that the manuscript might not, after all, have been in Léonie's desk. Léo was untidy, but trustworthy. She would never have taken the risk of leaving it lying about. Nor could she console herself with the thought that any other nun could have made the inspection, for Mother Radcliffe had appeared later in the day and delivered a lecture to the whole Senior School on the appalling disorder she had discovered in the course of her review. She had felt herself flush every time the Mistress of Discipline's eye had rested on her, but the nun had given no sign. For the remainder of the evening she had started every time the door opened, expecting to be called to Mother Radcliffe's room. She had not even been able to talk to Léonie about the disaster, for the rule of the Good Friday silence prevented any speech. As they sat sewing after supper, Léonie would only make guarded grimaces of remorse and consolation to which Nanda had responded with the ghastliest of smiles.

Where was the wretched book now? Did Mother Radcliffe already know the worst? Or was it still lying unread on her table? She had wild ideas of creeping down in her nightgown and abstracting the manuscript, but luckily, common sense told her that this would only aggravate her offence. True, the manuscript was not signed. But Mother Radcliffe knew the handwriting of every child in the school. There was nothing, absolutely nothing she could do.

Daylight came and she dressed herself slowly and miserably. Her head was aching and her eyes stung as if they were full of sand. At breakfast, she could only swallow a cup of milk. The bread and butter stuck in her throat. How was she ever going to get through the two and a half hour service in this agony of suspense? Should she rush now, uninvited, into Mother Radcliffe's room, and implore her to let her know the worst? Anything, anything would be better than this maddening uncertainty.

Half a dozen times during breakfast she was on the point of asking for permission to leave the refectory. Half a dozen times the opportunity slipped by. At last, the bell rang for grace and it was too late to do anything.

Never had the ceremonies of Holy Saturday seemed

so interminable. In other years they had been her favourites in the whole year's liturgy. They had once been celebrated at the very first dawning of Easter Sunday, and their whole tone was that of renewal and rejoicing. Even to-day her spirits flickered up a little when the priest brought in the newly-struck fire, and the paschal candle, with its five grains of incense symbolising the embalmed wounds of Christ, was solemnly kindled. But they flagged again during the twelve long prophecies, and her mind strayed back to Mother Radcliffe and her wretched book. She tried to calm her nerves and drive away the nagging distractions by following the service in her missal, but she could neither hear the words nor control her weary eyes. However hard she tried to restrain them, they were always at least a page ahead of the priest, so that the prayers seemed to crawl with ant-like slowness. The blessing of the font might have been an entire High mass; the petitions of the Litany of the Saints droned on unendingly. At last, the moment to which she had always looked forward approached. To-day, she only welcomed it because it brought the end of the office nearer. The purple veils were torn from the statues; the bells that had been silent for a week rang out all together; the organ pealed, and the priest, dressed now in the white vestments, intoned the first "Alleluia." Every other year, her heart had magically lightened at the sound of that "Alleluia," but to-day she felt no response. Her only thoughts were: "Has Mother Radcliffe read that book yet? What is she going to do when she has?"

An hour later the children, their chatter for once unchecked, ran noisily out into the garden. Everyone was already infected with the Easter spirit. The sun was out.

Lent was over. To-morrow would be Easter Sunday, and the last day of term. They rushed up and down the alleys like mad things, jumping over benches, pretending to give each other the kiss of peace and shouting: "Alleluia, Alleluia."

But Nanda only stayed there for a minute. Under cover of the noise, she slipped back into the house and tore off coat and apron and goloshes. As she did so, the sight of her green ribbon struck her as such a mockery that she nearly took that off as well. She would certainly lose it in a few hours' time. However, until she was officially deprived of it, she must go on wearing the wretched decoration.

Hastily smoothing her hair and pulling on her gloves, she presented herself outside the Mistress of Discipline's door. As she knocked, her knees trembled and she felt so violently sick that she was sure she was going to faint. Hardly waiting for the nun's "Come in," she wrenched the handle and almost fell into the room. The mild, spectacled face of Mother Bidford, the secretary, looked up from the desk with an air of surprise.

"Well, my child?"

"I want to speak to—— Will Mother Radcliffe be back soon?" Nanda stammered.

"No, my child. She will not be in the school all day. Is there anything I can do for you? It's Nanda Grey, isn't it?"

"No, it's all right, thank you, Mother," muttered Nanda and dashed from the room.

There was nothing for it but to rejoin the others in the garden. The fresh, bright air revived her a little. To her relief, she saw Léonie on the terrace. The latter waved to her, but approached slowly, hiding something under her coat.

"I saw you go in, and thought I'd hang about," said Léonie. "Here, drink this."

She produced a half-empty glass of milk with the strained smile of an amateur conjuror producing a rabbit.

"Some of it got spilt, I'm afraid. A great, clean-limbed hockey-playing blue ribbon cannoned into me. But there's a bit left."

Nanda drank it gratefully.

"Well, any news?" asked Léonie, throwing the empty glass into a laurel bush. "I'll never forgive myself to my dying day about this business," she added gloomily.

"You don't think there's any hope of its turning up?" said Nanda faintly.

"No. I know it was in my desk, folded up in a French-exercise book. That's gone, too. She must have been on the search for something. I believe that inspection was just a blind."

"It's just possible," admitted Nanda. "But what's she going to *do* about it? It's this hanging about not knowing that I can't stand."

"If she's any sense, she'll take the whole thing as a joke, make a few scathing remarks, and that'll be the end. But you never know with nuns."

"There were some pretty awful things in it," said Nanda uncomforted.

"Yes, but nothing blasphemous or seditious or even anti-Lippington. That's what flicks them on the raw. Besides, anyone with half an eye could see it was written by a perfect sucking-dove of innocence."

Nanda's vanity was far too deflated to resent the slight on the brilliant worldliness of those four chapters. Suddenly she began to laugh.

"It's pretty good irony, isn't it?" she said bitterly.

"What is, poor old devil?" asked Léonie, putting her hand on her shoulder.

"I've just remembered it's my birthday to-morrow."

The rest of the day passed without a sign.

Nanda mechanically darned stockings, went to the chapel, ate meals which tasted of sawdust, played rounders and read the life of St. Francis of Sales, until it was time to go to bed. To her surprise, she slept soundly and dreamlessly until the rising bell. She woke with her nerves a little soothed. Had she, after all, been working herself up into a state about nothing? She was further reassured when Mother Radcliffe appeared in the refectory as was customary on Easter Sunday, and handed each child a coloured egg. Nanda received the same cheerful smile as the others, and Mother Radcliffe even added: "It's your birthday, isn't it? Many happy returns." Perhaps things were not so bad after all.

But her misgivings awoke again as the afternoon approached. Her parents were coming to see her, she knew. Would Mother Radcliffe say anything to them?

Three o'clock came and she sat pretending to read in the study-room, fidgeting and jumping to her feet every time the parlour sister appeared at the door. Child after child was called away to see her friends or relations, but no summons came for Nanda. Impatience grew to foreboding, then to alarm. Her parents usually arrived most punctually at three. On her birthday, of all days, they would hardly be late without warning her. Half-past three came; four o'clock; a quarter past. At half-past four the bell rang, and Nanda went into the refectory to face the ghastly travesty of a birthday tea-party.

On the centre table stood her cake, with its fourteen candles, and the places of the six friends whom she was allowed to invite laid with crackers. Clare, Léonie and Rosario, with the three younger nonentities whom she had asked for prudence's sake, were waiting for her. She sat down absent-mindedly and had to be reminded by Rosario that she had not said grace. Léonie gave her a swift look, and seeing that she was dull and preoccupied, took the load of entertaining off her hands. She pulled crackers right and left, made the most out-rageous jokes, until Clare's loud crows and the flattering giggles of the nonentities nearly made the nun in charge ring for silence.

"Why, Nanda," said Rosario kindly, "you've forgotten to light your candles."

Someone produced a taper, and with a trembling hand, Nanda clumsily lit the nearest three. The taper went out, and no one offered her a match. She could see from their surprised faces that something was wrong. Looking round, she saw Mother Radcliffe standing behind her. She was not smiling now.

"I'm afraid you will have to leave your guests to finish the party without you," she said gently. "I want to speak to you."

Too stricken to say good-bye to the others, she followed Mother Radcliffe out into the passage.

"Your parents are here to see you," she said, still gently. "You will find them, not in the school parlour, but in the little community one. For reasons which you will understand presently, I thought it would be better to see them undisturbed."

Nanda's knees shook so that she could hardly walk. She was paralysed with terror and apprehension. In a few minutes, she would know the worst. Something in Mother Radcliffe's look told her that the worst was very bad indeed.

CHAPTER XV

HER father and mother were sitting at a plush-covered table in an austere and unfamiliar little room. They did not rise to greet her, though she heard her mother whisper: "After all, John, it *is* her birthday." But her father shook his head. Never, during the worst scolding had she seen his face like this. It was stiff as a death-mask, with all the colour drained away to a uniform greyish yellow. Her mother, too, looked stern, but there was none of that inhuman coldness in her air, and she fidgeted with her hand-bag as if not altogether associating herself with the scene. There was silence for a minute or two; then her father spoke in an icy voice whose edge Nanda felt like a physical hurt.

"And what, may I ask, have you to say for yourself?"

"About . . . about what, Daddy?" she gasped, forcing her voice out with immense effort as one tries to scream in a nightmare.

"I would rather you did not use that name, if you please."

She said nothing, but plaited the fringe of her green ribbon to try and calm herself.

"I have always believed in you and trusted you, Fernanda," went on the icy voice, "I even flattered myself that I knew something of your nature. In spite of many faults, I have always believed that fundamentally you were sweet and innocent—and good. Yesterday, if anyone had shown me the disgusting and vulgar filth that I have seen to-day in your own handwriting, I would have doubted my own eyes. To-day, with the evidence I have from Mother Radcliffe, I am forced to believe that you wrote it, and wrote it deliberately."

"But listen—listen," Nanda almost shrieked. "Let me explain."

"I do not want any explanation. I do not propose to discuss anything so vile and so degrading as the whole subject."

"John, really," put in her mother weakly. But her father ignored the interruption.

"I want to ask you one question. Until two hours ago I—wrongly, no doubt—believed you to be truthful. Until that, too, is disproved, I shall continue to hope so. Did you write this entirely of your own accord, without help or suggestion from any other person?"

"Yes," said Nanda, summoning up the dregs of her courage to look at him.

"No other girl bullied you into it?"

"No."

Mr. Grey brought his hand down with a thud on the table.

"Then I say that if a young girl's mind is such a sink of filth and impurity, I wish to God that I had never had a daughter."

Nanda's last thread of self-control snapped. She burst into a storm of convulsive, almost tearless sobs that wrenched all her muscles and brought no relief. The whole world had fallen away and left her stranded in this one spot alone for ever and ever with her father and those awful words. She felt her mother touch her sleeve and shook her off, blindly, mechanically, hardly knowing that she was there.

Her father was speaking again, but though she heard him distinctly, in spite of her sobbing, the words made no impression. All her consciousness was withdrawn into one burning centre of pain and misery, and the sounds merely beat on a numbed outer skin.

He was saying that she must leave Lippington for ever the next day. That though she was not officially expelled, her dismissal had all the stigma of expulsion. That Mother Radcliffe had even suggested that she might be removed to another house of the Order, but that he had refused to take the responsibility. She must go to some Protestant school where she was completely unknown and where, though he and she and her mother could never forget the scandal and shame of the whole affair, it could at least be kept from becoming public.

He seemed to talk for hours. At intervals, her mother interposed with a "But, John," or "I really can't help feeling——" but he did not even answer.

In time, from utter exhaustion, Nanda's breathless sobbing became quieter. She even looked up and dimly noticed the albums on the table, and a kid-gloved hand still fidgeting with the clasp of a bag. Then her eye caught the sight of a brown paper parcel only half-hidden by her mother's muff. She guessed at once that it contained her birthday present. Another wave of misery poured over her. A little while before, one sentence of her father's had torn right through every protective covering and shamed her to the very marrow. If he had stripped her naked and beaten her, she would not have felt more utterly humiliated. Never, never, could things be the same. Never again would he believe in her. Never again could she love him in the old way. But now, the sight of the absurd birthday parcel suddenly showed her all the small human losses included in that one great loss. She wept wildly for all the dear, silly things that were gone for ever; the happy tea times of the Christmas holidays, the talks in the study, the *Haec Olim* file to which she could never add her green ribbon.

In the midst of this fresh outburst, Mother Radcliffe

came in. Nanda, too given up to misery to move, saw her father stand up and make a stiff bow. She heard Mother Radcliffe say:

"I think Nanda has learnt her lesson now," and felt the nun's arm round her shoulders. She buried her face in her hands and seemed actually to lose consciousness for a little. Very far away, she heard people moving, heard someone whispering, heard a door shut. When at last she raised her head, she was alone with Mother Radcliffe. The nun sat down beside her and took her hands in her own cool, dry ones.

"There, my child," she said over and over again in a soothing, almost hypnotic voice. "There, my child."

They sat thus for a long time, until Nanda's tears were almost spent and she was conscious of nothing but an aching head and a feeling of shivering sickness.

Presently the nun said, still in the same gentle measured voice:

"Those are good tears, Nanda. I have waited for them and prayed for them. You understand very little yet, my dear child, but one day you will understand the significance of all this."

Nanda did not reply, and Mother Radcliffe went on:

"You are feeling that you have been unjustly treated —that no offence could deserve so great a punishment. Nanda, you must try and believe that all this is for your own good."

But Nanda could only mutter with dry and swollen lips:

"Daddy—Daddy."

The nun put her hand on her forehead.

"God asks very hard things from us," she said, "the sacrifice of what we love best and the sacrifice of our own wills. That is what it means to be a Christian. For years, I have been watching you, Nanda. I have seen you growing up, intelligent, warm-hearted, apparently everything a child should be. But I have watched something else growing in you, too—a hard little core of self-will and self-love. I told you once before that every will must be broken completely and re-set before it can be at one with God's will. And there is no other way. That is what true education, as we understand it here at Lippington, means. Real love is a hard taskmaster, and the love of God the hardest taskmaster of all. I am only acting as God's instrument in this. I had to break your will before your whole nature was deformed."

Nanda glanced at the nun's face. It was pale and controlled as usual, yet lighted with an extraordinary, quiet exaltation.

"Many things must have happened to you here at Lippington which have seemed unkind, unjust even. Very few of those things happened by accident. I am speaking to you now as if you were a grown-up person. Yours is a nature with a great capacity for good and evil; you are gifted but wayward; obstinate, yet easily led. You have one quality which I think will help you through life. I believe you are fundamentally honest. But there was a quality you needed more. We tried to teach you by easy ways, but to-day you have had to learn it by hard ones—the quality of humility."

"Mother—Mother—won't you give me one more chance?" Nanda begged suddenly. Her eyes were dry now, as if the last drop of moisture had been scorched out of her body.

The nun appeared to think a minute. Then very kindly she said:

"No, my dear. You must take your penance. I am not

going to talk about the wicked, foolish things you wrote. You have enough sense to see them now in their proper light. But there are many reasons why you should not stay here. For one thing, in some ways, we have no more to teach you. For another, I have a hundred other children to consider. There are some people, harmless in themselves, who can be a source of danger to others, as there are people healthy in themselves, who are what doctors call 'germ carriers.' But I want you always to think of yourself as one of us, as a child of the Five Wounds. Come back and see us often—write to us—pray for us, as we shall pray for you."

"But my friends—Léo and all of them——?" pleaded Nanda, and would have wept had she had a tear left.

"Give them up bravely, as part of your sacrifice. God will not forget. Remember, He never allows Himself to be outdone in generosity."

"It's too much," said Nanda quietly. "I'm not a . . . not a very strong sort of person."

The nun smiled and patted her hand. "We shall see. God sends us strength as we need it. And sometimes He sends us consolation when we least expect it. For many months, you and all of us have prayed for something that seemed hopeless. This afternoon, Reverend Mother gave me a letter about which no one else, even the child it concerns, as yet knows anything. It is from Clare Rockingham's father, giving his consent for Clare to be received into the Catholic faith."

A week ago it would have meant so much, but now Nanda hardly knew whether she were glad or not. She heard herself answer mechanically: "How wonderful," but no other words came.

Another long minute passed, then Mother Radcliffe said gently:

"It is seven o'clock, my dear child. I must leave you. Run and bathe your eyes before supper."

But at this Nanda's tears started afresh.

"I can't possibly go into the refectory," she sobbed.

"Very well, Nanda. Go up to the infirmary and ask Mother Regan to give you some supper there."

"No . . . please . . . I couldn't eat anything."

"I thought you were going to be obedient, Nanda," said Mother Radcliffe, with her old firmness.

Nanda stood up.

"Very well, Mother," she said firmly.

The nun smiled.

"That's right. Life's not all over at fourteen, my dear."

She took Nanda's arm and led her out into the passage.

"Perhaps you'd like to pay a little visit to the Blessed Sacrament?"

Nanda did not answer, but let Mother Radcliffe guide her to the chapel door. She went in alone and, forgetting to take holy water or even to genuflect, knelt down heavily in the nearest bench. From the smaller chapel came the sound of the Junior School saying their night prayers.

Everything was the same—the smell of beeswax, the red lights of the sanctuary, the words that the children were whispering beyond the altar screen. But Nanda knew that whatever might happen in the future, nothing for her would ever be the same again.

THE END

ALL PASSION SPENT

Vita Sackville West

INTRODUCTION

Vita Sackville-West began writing *All Passion Spent* in the spring of 1930. Her title could hardly be less applicable to her own situation at the time: at thirty-eight, she was at the height of her energies. She had just bought the romantic ruins of Sissinghurst Castle, though she and her husband Harold Nicolson were not to live there full-time for another couple of years; and she had just finished correcting the proofs of *The Edwardians*, which turned out to be a great popular success. In the year that she worked on her new novel she was spending all her spare time at Sissinghurst, clearing the rubble and rubbish of decades from what was to be the famous garden, and supervising the builders. She also wrote a long poem, 'Sissinghurst', which expressed the deep significance to her of this new commitment. Always a person for whom places were at least as important as people, and with this new passion for Sissinghurst dominating her daily life, it is not surprising that a house plays such a large part in *All Passion Spent*.

The novel was published by the Woolfs' Hogarth Press in May 1931. On 11 June, Virginia Woolf wrote to her that sales were '*very* good . . . Lord! What fun!'. Vita had been worried about the book when she saw it in proof—'it is quite, quite meaningless'—but became reconciled to it after publication as she never was to *The Edwardians*. She received a great many

607

letters about *All Passion Spent*, mainly from women who recognised their own situation in Lady Slane's, and this pleased her. Leonard Woolf, her publisher, said that this was her best novel, and she herself felt that it was 'a better book' than the more flamboyant *Edwardians*, compared with which it seems drawn in pastels.

This effect of anaemic, whimsical delicacy is misleading. Vita Sackville-West built into *All Passion Spent* much of her lifelong anger about the way society distorts and inhibits the individual, particularly if that individual is a woman. This unlikely alliance of manner and matter is the most curious thing about the novel and, artistically, its achievement.

She dedicated to 'Benedict and Nigel who are young this story of people who are old'. (Her sons were sixteen and thirteen at the time.) The dramatis personae of *All Passion Spent* are very old indeed. The Earl of Slane, after a distinguished career in public life, has just died aged ninety-four; his six children, none of them under sixty, are 'large and black and elderly, with grandchildren of their own'. When the story opens, these 'old black ravens' are discussing the future of their 88-year-old mother, Lady Slane. They do not foresee any difficulties with her; she has been the perfect wife: 'all her life long, gracious and gentle, she had been wholly submissive—an appendage.' They see her staying quietly with each of them in turn—like a Queen Lear, as one might say.

But this novel reverses the usual order of things. It is the children who are staid and narrow-minded, and their gentle aged mother who turns out to be revolutionary. She will live her own life, for the first time, according to her own inclinations and her own creeds, alone with her old French maid Genoux (the name of Vita Sackville-West's French maid in real life) in a small house in Hampstead she fell in love with thirty years before. She doesn't want her children to visit her, and she certainly does not want to see her grandchildren.

She finds the house empty, waiting for her; and here the author dwells lovingly on its spirit and character, 'an entity with a life of its own'. We know it is Georgian, red brick, and one of a row: from all the circumstantial evidence, I always imagine it to be in Church Row. Vita Sackville-West and Virginia Woolf, their romantic attachment no longer so urgent (for Vita at any rate) in its demands, sustained their friendship by means of excursions together. They went several times to Hampstead by Underground, as does Lady Slane; they walked on the Heath, like Lady Slane and Mr FitzGeorge; they visited Keats' house, described here as 'that little white box of strain and tragedy marooned among the dark green laurels'. And all the time they talked. There is a strong connection between the ideas of *All Passion Spent* and those of Virginia Woolf's two non-fiction books about women, *A Room of One's Own* (1929) and *Three Guineas*. Vita went with Virginia Woolf to Cambridge to hear her give the lectures that were the basis for the first book, and the second was conceived at the time of *All Passion Spent* though not published until 1938.

Lady Slane, from the triple vantage point of widowhood, old age, and tranquil Hampstead, surveys her marriage. Her indictment of the married state is softened by this indirect approach and by her gentle personality. She recalls her role as loving 'appendage'; she has been 'a lonely woman, at variance with the creeds to which she apparently conformed'—these passages echoing the descriptions of women submerging their own values 'in deference to the opinion of others' in *A Room of One's Own*.

There are on a first reading two unsatisfactory elements in the depiction of Lady Slane. Clearly a woman of sensibility and experience—an exvicereine—and on very familiar terms with the works of Shakespeare, she is nevertheless repeatedly called 'not clever'. So not-clever is she that she could not follow her husband's career, or 'know what people meant when they referred to the Irish Question or the Women's Movement, or to Free Trade and Protection'. She cannot understand the stock market; she cannot even make out a cheque properly. Why does she have to be so incapable?

What Vita Sackville-West was trying to do was to represent pure femininity. This she saw in terms of sheer impracticality, 'laces and softnesses', in opposition to the 'masculine' world of business, politics and visible achievement. Lady Slane realises that masculinity has been the 'keynote' of her husband's character: he craved a life of action, while she craved a life of contemplation. 'They were indeed two halves of one dissevered world.'

Virginia Woolf wrote in *A Room of One's Own* that a great mind was 'androgynous'. Vita herself was a masculine woman, and her husband a man with a strong feminine streak. Lady Slane's undiluted femininity, in Vita's eyes, is a disability as well as a grace. These themes, explored by both Vita and Virginia Woolf, were also discussed at much the same time, and with much the same conclusions, in Rebecca West's novel *Harriet Hume* (1928). The concensus on the masculine-feminine question in these three very different writers is striking, and a close reading of *Harriet Hume* and *All Passion Spent* reveals quite significant similarities.

The second apparently unsatisfactory element is that although the central frustration of Lady Slane's life is that marriage prevented her from following her vocation to be a painter, it seems clear that this ambition was never more than a dream: she never once set brush to canvas, so far as we know. This makes her frustration and sacrifice seem phoney, a vain whim. But Vita Sackville-West is making a point here as well. Talent, she writes later in the book, is beside the point. 'Achievement was good, but the spirit was better. To reckon by achievement was to make a concession to the prevailing system of the world.' Virginia Woolf developed this in *Three Guineas* when she argued

that the 'masculine' system of competition, rewards and hier-
archies led to the aggressiveness that made men start wars.

Lady Slane's three friends reinforce this philosophy. Mr
Bucktrout, Mr Gosheron and Mr FitzGeorge are all 'fond fan-
tastics', lovers of beauty, artists 'in appreciation', eccentric in
their disregard for success-values. The world is horrible, says Mr
Bucktrout, because it is based on competitive struggle, which
produces what men call 'civilisation', but which is not civilisation at all. *Three Guineas* makes the same point.

The conventional supremacy of masculine values had forced
Lady Slane on marriage to forego her separate existence—while
her husband continued 'to enjoy his free, varied, and masculine
life . . . It would not do, in such a world of assumptions, to
assume that she had equal rights with Henry.' To judge from all
this, *All Passion Spent* would seem an unequivocally femininist
novel.

Vita Sackville-West fought hard against the conventions that
made a wife an 'appendage'. Unlike Lady Slane, she declined to
be the 'diplomatic wife', and indeed persuaded her husband to
give up his career in diplomacy; apart from brief visits, she stayed
at home when he was *en poste* abroad. Her work came first. She
declined to be the 'politician's wife' when later he sat for Parliament. She used her own name; she was dismissive about the
domestic virtues; she did not think the pleasure of having children compensated for the resulting lack of personal freedom. She
railed against the bureaucracy that labelled her 'Mrs Harold
Nicolson' or 'housewife'; whenever she was defined as the wife
of her husband, she complained loudly. And yet she invariably
prefaced her complaints with the words 'You know I am no
feminist, but . . .'

It was not a question of women's rights, in her view, but of
human rights. (In *Three Guineas* Virginia Woolf too condemned
the word 'feminist' as 'a vicious and corrupt word that has done

much harm in its day'.) In *All Passion Spent* Vita Sackville-West redefines feminism negatively, to describe 'the freemasonry among women, which was always prying and personal and somehow a trifle obscene'. This claustrophobic female conspiracy was at its most potent before the wedding, in weeks 'dedicated wholly to the rites of a mysterious feminism' designed to deliver the bride over so that she might minister to a man. Seen in this light feminism, as separatism, is the deadest of dead ends.

Even though Lady Slane as a young woman felt defrauded of her chosen life by marriage, she did not blame her husband and, as the author writes in a key passage, 'she was no feminist'—using the word here in its more usual sense:

> She was too wise a woman to indulge in such luxuries as an imagined martyrdom. The rift between herself and life was not the rift between man and woman, but the rift between the worker and the dreamer. That she was a woman, and Henry a man, was really a matter of chance. She would go no further than to acknowledge that the fact of her being a woman made the situation a degree more difficult.

'Feminine' values are not confined to women: Lady Slane's semi-comic fellow-dreamers—Mr Bucktrout, Mr Gosheron and Mr FitzGeorge—are, after all, men; and the maid Genoux, Lady Slane's only female intimate, is a 'worker' to her worn fingerends.

It would be wrong to go away with the idea that the influence of Virginia Woolf's thinking, still less of Rebecca West's, was decisive in *All Passion Spent*. In her evocation of Lady Slane's past, Vita Sackville-West drew on her own experience; she was an excellent travel writer, as her *Passenger to Tehran* and *Twelve Days* attest, and the most vivid writing in this novel is about strange foreign scenes—such as the cloud of white and yellow butterflies that accompanied the Slanes on a desert road in Persia, exploited as an image for Lady Slane's 'irreverent, irrelevant thoughts'.

Years before she ever met Virginia Woolf, she had forcefully expressed—in her letters, fictions, and an unpublished play, 'Marriage'—her feelings about the way society repressed women's individuality. There are themes in *All Passion Spent* that are Vita's alone. The young girl's fantasy of escape from conventional girlhood to freedom in the guise of a young man were the young Vita's. Lady Slane's ideal of 'detachment' had been Vita's ever since her disastrous imbroglio with Violet Trefusis—even though, swinging between the extremes of passionate attachment and equally passionate reclusiveness, she never achieved it.

The question of compromise also exercised Vita. Mr Bucktrout says: 'Most people fall into the error of making their whole lives a fuzz, pleasing nobody, least of all themselves. Compromise is the very breath of negation.' Her characters, at the end of their lives, did not compromise; but she herself had to. In 1928 she wrote to her husband that she was 'not a good person for you to be married to'; life for both of them, she said, 'resolves itself into a compromise which is truly only satisfactory to neither'. She made the compromise because of love. 'But I love you, I can never cure myself of loving you, so what is to be done?' In *All Passion Spent*, into which she poured so many of her own ambivalent feelings, Lady Slane's love for her husband is 'a straight black line drawn right through her life. It had hurt her, it had damaged her, but she had been unable to curve away from it.'

Lady Slane's jewels, and her unexpected inheritance, also had a special significance for Vita Sackville-West, whose own lavish jewels—emeralds, diamonds, pearls—became hateful to her amid the general poverty of the Depression. The wealth that made the creation of Sissinghurst possible came from a vast legacy to her mother from her admirer Sir John Murray Scott—a legacy that her mother had not only welcomed avidly but fought in the courts to retain. Vita Sackville-West distrusted her mother's values profoundly but was unable to relinquish the money and valuables that made her own chosen life possible. Lady Slane, in her simplicity, did what Vita in her soul thought should be done. She was 'true to herself'—and for Vita, who was a complex person drawn to the great simplicities, the guiding motto for life was 'To thine own self be true.'

Lady Slane has the emotional energy, at the end, for only one last 'strange and lovely thing', which gives the book its optimistic and inspirational finale. For serene Lady Slane, 'Those days were gone when feeling burst its bounds and poured hot from the foundry, when the heart seemed likely to split with complex and contradictory desires'. Not so, for Vita Sackville-West. As she drew near the end of writing the book, she was overcome by irrational depression. She wrote to Virginia Woolf: 'If I, who am the most fortunate of women can ask What is life for? how can other people live at all?' A few days after completing the manuscript, she plunged into a new love affair and felt alive again. For she was still in the excitable 'middle years' that now meant nothing to her Lady Slane. What is more, to the end of her life Vita Sackville-West was to be to some extent 'split with complex and contradictory desires'. *All Passion Spent*, the theme and title of her best novel, was not to be her own epitaph.

Victoria Glendinning, Graveley, 1982

Part One

Henry Lyulph Holland, first Earl of Slane, had existed for so long that the public had begun to regard him as immortal. The public, as a whole, finds reassurance in longevity, and, after the necessary interlude of reaction, is disposed to recognise extreme old age as a sign of excellence. The long-liver has triumphed over at least one of man's initial handicaps: the brevity of life. To filch twenty years from eternal annihilation is to impose one's superiority on an allotted programme. So small is the scale upon which we arranged our values. It was thus with a start of real incredulity that City men, opening their papers in the train on a warm May morning, read that Lord Slane, at the age of ninety-four, had passed away suddenly after dinner on the previous evening. 'Heart failure,' they said sagaciously, though they were actually quoting from the papers; and then added with a sigh, 'Well, another old landmark gone.' That was the dominant feeling: another old landmark gone, another reminder of insecurity. All the events and progressions of Henry Holland's life were gathered up and recorded in a final burst of publicity by the papers; they were gathered together into a handful as hard as a cricket-ball, and flung in the faces of the public, from the days of his 'brilliant university career,' through the days when Mr. Holland, at an astonishingly early age, had occupied a seat in the Cabinet, to this very last day when as Earl of Slane, K.G.,

615

G.C.B., G.C.S.I., G.C.I.E., etc. etc.—his diminishing honours trailing away behind him like the tail of a comet—he had drooped in his chair after dinner, and the accumulation of ninety years had receded abruptly into history. Time seemed to have made a little jump forward, now that the figure of old Slane was no longer there with out-stretched arms to dam it back. For some fifteen years he had taken no very active part in public life, but he had been *there*, and on occasion the irrefutable suavity, common sense, and mockery of his eloquence in Parliament had disturbed, though it could not actually arrest, his more extreme colleagues upon the brink of folly. Such pronouncements had been rare, for Henry Holland had always been a man to appreciate the value of economy, but by their very rarity they produced a wholesome sense of uneasiness, since men knew them to be backed up by a legend of experience: if the old man, the octogenarian, the nonagenarian, could bestir himself to the extent of stalking down to Westminster and unburdening himself, in his incomparable way, of opinions carefully, soberly, but cynically gestated, then the Press and the public were compelled into attention. Nobody had ever seriously attacked Lord Slane. Nobody had ever accused Lord Slane of being a back-number. His humour, his charm, his languor, and his good sense, had rendered him sacrosanct to all generations and to all parties; of him alone among statesmen and politicians, perhaps, could that be said. Perhaps, because he seemed to have touched life on every side, and yet never seemed to have touched life, the common life, at all, by virtue of his proverbial detachment, he had never drawn upon himself the execration and mistrust commonly accorded to the mere expert. Hedonist, humanist, sportsman, philosopher, scholar, charmer, wit; one of those rare Englishmen whose fortune it is to be born equipped with a truly adult mind. His colleagues and his subordinates had been alternately delighted and infuriated by his assumed reluctance to deal with

any practical question. It was difficult to get a yes or a no out of
the man. The more important a question was, the more flipp-
antly he dealt with it. '*Yes*,' he would write at the bottom of a
memorandum setting forth the advantages of two opposite lines
of policy; and his myrmidons passed their hands over their
brows, distraught. He was destroyed as a statesman, they said,
because he always saw both sides of the case; but even as they
said it with exasperation, they did not mean it, for they knew
that on occasion, when finally pushed into a corner, he would be
more incisive, more deadly, than any man seated four-square and
full of importance at a governmental desk. He could cast his eye
over a report, and pick out its heart and its weakness before
another man had had time to read it through. In his exquisitely
courteous way, he would annihilate alike the optimism and the
myopia of his correspondent. Courteous always, and civilised,
he left his competitors dead.

His personal idiosyncrasies, too, were dear to the public as to
the caricaturists; his black satin stock, his eyeglass swung on
an extravagantly wide ribbon, the coral buttons to his evening
waistcoat, the private hansom he maintained long after motors
had come into fashion—by all this was he buttressed through the
confused justice and injustice of legend; and when, at the age of
eighty-five, he finally succeeded in winning the Derby, no man
ever received a greater ovation. His wife alone suspected how
closely those idiosyncrasies were associated with a settled policy.
The least cynical of people by nature, she had learned to lay a
veneer of cynicism over herself after seventy years' association
with Henry Holland. 'Dear old man,' said the City men in the
train; 'well, he's gone.'

He was gone indeed, very finally and irretrievably gone. So
thought his widow, looking down at him as he lay on his bed in
Elm Park Gardens. The blinds were not lowered, for he had
always stipulated that when he came to die the house should not

be darkened, and even after his death nobody would have dreamed of disobeying his orders. He lay there in the full sunlight, sparing the stone-mason the trouble of carving his effigy. His favourite great-grandchild, to whom everything was permitted, had often twitted him, saying that he would make a handsome corpse; and now that the joke had become a reality, the reality gained in impressiveness for having been anticipated by a joke. His was the type of face which, even in life, one associates prophetically with the high dignity of death. The bony architecture of nose, chin, and temples, stood out in greater relief for the slight sinking of the flesh; the lips took a firmer line, and a lifetime of wisdom lay sealed behind them. Moreover, and most importantly, Lord Slane looked as *soigné* in death as he had looked in life. 'Here,' you would say, even though the bedclothes covered him, 'is a dandy.'

Yet, for all its dignity, death brought a revelation. The face which had been so noble in life lost a trifle of its nobility in death; the lips which had been too humorous to be unpleasantly sardonic now betrayed their thinness; the carefully concealed ambition now revealed itself fully in the proud curve of the nostril. The hardness which had disguised itself under the charming manner now remained alone, robbed of the protection of a smile. He was beautiful, but he was less agreeable. Alone in the room his widow contemplated him, filled with thoughts that would greatly have surprised her children, could they but have read her mind.

Her children, however, were not there to observe her. They were collected in the drawing-room, all six of them; two wives and a husband bringing the number up to nine. A sufficiently formidable family gathering—old, black ravens, thought Edith, the youngest, who was always flustered and always trying to confine things into the shape of a phrase, like pouring water into a ewer, but great gouts of meaning and implication invariably ran over and slopped about and were lost. To attempt to recapture them after they had spilt was as hopeless as trying to hold the water in your hand. Perhaps, if one had a note-book and pencil always ready—but then the thought would be lost while one was looking for the right word; and, moreover, it would be difficult to use a note-book without everybody seeing. Shorthand?—but one must not let one's thoughts run on like this; one must discipline one's mind, keeping one's attention on the present matter, as other people seemed to do without any difficulty; though, to be sure, if one had not learnt that lesson by the time one was sixty, one was never likely to learn it. A formidable family gathering, thought Edith, coming back: Herbert, Carrie, Charles, William, and Kay; Mabel, Lavinia; Roland. They went in groups: the Hollands themselves, the sisters-in-law, the brother-in-law; then they sorted themselves differently: Herbert and Mabel, Carrie and Roland; Charles; William and Lavinia; and then Kay all by himself. It was not often that they all met together, none missing—curious, Edith thought, that Death should be the convener, as though all the living rushed instantly together for protection and mutual support. Dear me, how old we all are. Herbert must be sixty-eight, and I'm sixty; and Father was over ninety, and Mother is eighty-eight. Edith, who had begun making a sum of their total ages, surprised them all very much by asking, 'How old are you, Lavinia?' Thus taken aback, they rebuked Edith by their stare; but that was Edith all over, she never listened to what was being said, and then suddenly came out with some irrelevant remark. Edith could have told them that all her life she had been trying to say what she meant, and had never yet succeeded. Only too often, she said something precisely the opposite of what she wanted to say. Her terror was that she should one day use an indecent word by mistake. 'Isn't it splendid that Father is dead,' she might say, instead of, 'Isn't it terrible'; and there were other possibilities, even more appalling, by which one might use a really dreadful word, the sort of word that butcher-boys scrawled in pencil on the white-washed walls of the basement passage, and about which one had to speak, most evasively, to the cook. An unpleasant task; the sort of task that fell to Edith in Elm Park Gardens and to a thousand Ediths all over London. But of these preoccupations her family knew nothing.

They were gratified now to see that she blushed, and that her hands went up nervously to fiddle with the grey strands of her hair; the gesture implied that she had not spoken. Having reduced her to this confusion, they returned to their conversation, suitably hushed and mournful. Even the voices of Herbert and Carrie, habitually insistant, were lowered. Their father lay upstairs, and their mother was with him.

'Mother is wonderful.'

Over and over, thought Edith, they had reiterated that phrase. Surprise was in their accents, as though they had expected their mother to rant, rave, scream, give herself up for lost. Edith knew very well that her brothers and sister privately entertained a theory that their mother was rather a simpleton. From time to time she let fall remarks that could not be reconciled with ordinary sense; she had no grasp on the world as it was; she was apt to say impetuous things which, although uttered in English, made no more sense than had they been uttered in an outer-planetary language. Mother was a changeling, they had often said politely, in the bitter-sweet accents reserved for a family joke; but now in this emergency they found a new phrase: Mother is wonderful. It was the thing they were expected to say, so they said it, several times over, like a refrain coming periodically into their conversation and sweeping it upwards on to a higher level. Then it drooped again; became practical. Mother was wonderful, but what was to be done with Mother? Evidently, she could not go on being wonderful for the rest of her life. Somewhere, somehow, she must be allowed to break down, and then, after that was over, must be stowed away; housed, taken care of. Outside, in the streets, the posters might flare: DEATH OF LORD SLANE. The journalists might run up and down Fleet Street assembling their copy; they might pounce on the pigeon-holes—that macabre columbarium— where the obituary notices were stored in readiness; they might raid each other's information: 'I say, is it true that old Slane always carried his cash in coppers? wore crêpe soles? dipped his bread in his coffee?' Anything to make a good paragraph. Tele-graph-boys might ring the bell, propping their red bicycles against the kerb, delivering their brown messages of condolence, from all over the world, from all parts of the Empire, especially where Lord Slane had served his term of government. Florists might deliver their wreaths—already the narrow hall was full of them—'indecently soon,' said Herbert, peering jealously never-theless at the attached cards through his monocle. Old friends might call—'Herbert—so dreadfully sudden—of course, I didn't expect to see your dear Mother—' But obviously they had expected it, had expected to be the sole exception, and Herbert must turn them away, rather enjoying it: 'Mother, you understand, is naturally rather overcome; wonderful, I must say; but just at present, you'll understand, I'm sure, is seeing nobody but Us'; and so with many pressings of Herbert's hand they took their departure, having got no further than the hall or the doorstep. Reporters might loiter on the pavement, dangling cameras like black concertinas. All this might go on outside the house, but inside it, upstairs, Mother was with Father and the problem of her future lay heavy upon her sons and daughters.

Of course, she would not question the wisdom of any arrangements they might choose to make. Mother had no will of her own; all her life long, gracious and gentle, she had been wholly submissive—an appendage. It was assumed that she had not enough brain to be self-assertive. 'Thank goodness,' Herbert sometimes remarked, 'Mother is not one of those clever women.' That she might have ideas which she kept to herself never entered into their estimate. They anticipated no trouble with their mother. That she might turn round and play a trick on them—several tricks—after years of being merely a fluttering lovable presence amongst them, never entered into their calculations either. She was not a clever woman. She would be grateful to them for arranging her few remaining years.

They stood in the drawing-room in a group, uncomfortably shifting from one foot to the other, but it never occurred to them to sit down. They would have thought it disrespectful. For all their good solid sense, death, even an expected death, disconcerted them just a little. Around them hung that uneasy, unsettled air which attends those about to set out on a journey or those whose lives have been seriously disturbed. Edith would have liked to sit down, but dared not. How large they all were, she thought; large and black and elderly, with grandchildren of their own. How lucky, she thought, that we all wear so much black habitually, for we certainly could not have got our mourning yet, and how terrible it would have been for Carrie to arrive in a pink shirt. As it was, they were all black as crows, and Carrie's black gloves lay on the writing-table with her boa and her bag. The ladies of the Holland family still wore boas, high collars, and long skirts which they had to hold up when they crossed the road; any concession to fashion was, they felt, unbecoming to their age. Edith admired her sister Carrie. She did not love her, and she was frightened of her, but she admired and envied her tremendously. Carrie had inherited her father's eagle nose and commanding presence; she was tall, pale, and distinguished. Herbert, Charles, and William were tall and distinguished also; only Kay and Edith were dumpy. Edith's thoughts were straying again: we might belong to a different family, she thought, Kay and I. Kay in fact was a chubby little old gentleman, with bright blue eyes and a neat white beard; there, again, he differed from his brothers who were clean-shaven. What a queer thing appearance was, and how unfair. It dictated the terms of people's estimate throughout one's whole life. If one looked insignificant, one was set down as insignificant; yet, one probably didn't look insignificant unless one deserved it. But Kay seemed quite happy; he didn't worry about significance, or about anything else; his bachelor rooms, and his collection of compasses and astrolabes seemed to satisfy him quite as well as public esteem, or a wife and a more personal life. For he was the greatest living authority upon globes, compasses, astrolabes, and all kindred instruments; lucky Kay, thought Edith, to have concentrated so contentedly upon one little department. (Curious symbols to have chosen, though, for one who had never loved the sea or climbed a mountain; to him, they were collector's pieces, ranged and ticketed, but to Edith, the romantic, a vast dark world rose beyond their small brass and mahogany, their intricacy of pivots and gimbals, discs and circles, the guinea-gold brass and the nut-brown wood, the signs of the Zodiac and the dolphins spouting up the ocean; a vast dark world where nothing was charted on the maps but regions of danger and uncertainty, and ragged men chewed bullets to allay their thirst.) 'Then there is the question of income,' William was saying.

How characteristic of William to mix up Mother's future with questions of income; for to William and Lavinia parsimony was in itself a career. An apple bruised by falling prematurely from the tree must immediately be turned into a dumpling lest it be wasted. Waste was the bugbear of William's and Lavinia's life. The very newspaper must be rolled into spills to save the matches. They had a passion for getting something for nothing. Every blackberry in the hedgerow was an agony to Lavinia until she had bottled it. Living, as they did, at Godalming with two acres of ground, they spent painful-happy evenings in calculation as to whether a pig could be made to pay on the household scraps, and whether a dozen hens could out-balance their corn in eggs. Well, thought Edith, they must pass the time very absorbingly with such a constant preoccupation; but how miserable it must make them to think of all the sacks of gold squandered by them since their marriage. Let me see, thought Edith, William is the fourth, so he must be sixty-four; he must have been married for thirty years, so if they have spent fifteen hundred a year—what with the children's education and all—that makes forty-five thousand pounds; sacks and sacks of treasure, such as the divers are always looking for at Tobermory. But Herbert was saying something. Herbert was always full of information; and the surprising thing was, for such a stupid man, it was usually correct.

'I can tell you all about that.' He put two fingers inside his collar, adjusted it, jerking his chin upward, cleared his throat, and gave a preliminary glare at his relations. 'I can tell you all about that. I discussed it with Father—he took me, I may say, into his confidence. Ahem! Father, as you know, was not a rich man, and most of his income dies with him. Mother will be left with a net income of five hundred a year.'

They digested this fact. William and Lavinia exchanged glances, and it could be seen that their minds were involved in rapid and experienced calculations. Edith, who passed privately among her relations for a half-wit, could on occasions be surprisingly shrewd—she had a habit of seeing through people's words right down into their motives, and of stating her deductions with a frankness that was disconcerting rather than discreet. She knew now quite well what William was about to say, though for once she held her tongue. But she chuckled to herself as she heard him say it.

'I suppose Father didn't happen to mention the jewels in the course of his confidences, did he, Herbert?'

'He did. The jewels, as you know, form not the least valuable part of his estate. They were his private property, and he has seen fit to leave them unconditionally to Mother.'

That's a smack for Herbert and Mabel, thought Edith. I suppose they expected Father to leave the jewels, like heirlooms, to his eldest son. A glance at Mabel's face showed her, however, that the announcement came as no surprise. Evidently Herbert had already repeated his father's confidences to his wife—and Mabel had been lucky, thought Edith, if Herbert had betrayed no irritation against her for thus failing to turn him into a successful legatee.

'In that case,' said William decisviely—for although he and Lavinia had hoped for a portion of the jewels, it was pleasing to think that Herbert and Mabel also had been disappointed—'in that case Mother will certainly wish to sell them. And quite right too. Why should she keep a lot of useless jewellery lying in the bank? In my opinion the jewels should fetch from five to seven thousand pounds, properly handled.'

'But more important than the question of jewels or income,' Herbert proceeded, 'is the question of where Mother is to live. She cannot be left alone. In any case, she could not afford to keep on this house. It must be sold. Where, then, is she to go?' Another glare. 'Clearly, it is our duty to look after her. She must make her home among us.' It was like a set speech.

All these old people, thought Edith, disposing of a still older person! Still, it seemed inevitable. Mother would parcel out her year: three months with Herbert and Mabel, three with Carrie and Roland, three with Charles, three with William and Lavinia—then where did she herself and Kay come in? Rising once more to the surface of her reflections, she launched one of her sudden and ill-chosen remarks, 'But surely I ought to bear the brunt—I've always lived at home—I'm unmarried.'

'Brunt?' said Carrie, turning on her. Edith was instantly annihilated. 'Brunt? My dear Edith! Who spoke of brunt? I'm sure we shall all regard it as a joy—a privilege—to do our part in looking after Mother in these last sad years of her life—for sad they must be, deprived of the one thing she lived for. Brunt, I think, is scarcely the word, Edith.'

Edith subserviently agreed: it wasn't. Spoken like that, repeated several times over, without the support of its usual little phrase, it acquired a strange and uncouth semblance, like spick without span, hoity without toity, turvy without topsy. It became a rude and Saxon word, like woad, or witenagemot; brunt, blunt; a blunt word. And what did it mean, to bear the brunt? What was a brunt, anyhow? No, brunt was not the word. 'Well,' said Edith, 'I think I ought to live with Mother.'

She saw relief spread itself over Kay's face; he had been thinking, that was evident, of his snug little rooms and his collection. Herbert's voice had been as a trumpet threatening the walls of his Jericho. The others, also, considered Edith and the possibility she offered them. The unmarried daughter; she was the obvious solution. But the Hollands were not people to evade a duty, and the more irksome the duty, the less likely were they to evade it. Joy was a matter they seldom considered, but duty was ever present with them, seriously always and sometimes grimly. Their father's energy had passed on to them, turning a trifle sour on the way. Carrie spoke up for her relations. Carrie was good; but, like so many good people, she always managed to set everybody by the ears.

'There is certainly something in what Edith says. She has always lived at home, and the change would not be very great for her. I know, of course, that she has often wished for independence and a home of her own; dear Edith,' she said, with a digressive smile; 'but quite rightly, as I think,' she continued, 'she refused to leave Father and Mother so long as she could be of use to them. I feel now, however, that we ought all to take our share. We must not take advantage of Edith's unselfishness, or of Mother's. I am sure I speak for you too, Herbert, and for you, William. It would be greatly to Mother's benefit if, instead of embarking on a new house, she could make her home amongst us all in turn.'

'Quite so,' said Herbert approving, and again adjusting his collar; 'quite so, quite so.'

William and Lavinia again exchanged glances.

'Of course,' William began, 'in spite of our limited income Lavinia and I would always be happy to welcome Mother. At the same time I think some financial arrangement should be come to. So much more satisfactory for Mother. She would then feel no embarrassment. Two pounds a week, perhaps, or thirty-five shillings . . .'

'I entirely agree with William,' said Charles unexpectedly; 'speaking for myself, a general's pension is so absurdly inadequate that I should find an additional guest a serious drain on my resources. As you know, I live very modestly in a small flat. I have no spare bedroom. Of course, I have hopes that the question of pensions may some day be adjusted. I have written a long memorandum to the War Office about it, also a letter to *The Times*, which no doubt they are holding in reserve until a suitable occasion, as they have not yet printed it, though, I confess, I see very little hope of reform under this present miserable Government.' Charles snorted. He felt that that was rather a good speech, and looked round at his family for approval. He was not General Sir Charles Holland for nothing.

'Isn't it rather delicate . . .' began the new Lady Slane.

'Be quiet, Mabel,' said Herbert. He was seldom known to address any other phrase to his wife, nor did Mabel often succeed in getting beyond her four or five opening words. 'This is entirely a family matter, please. In any case, it cannot be discussed in any detail until after—h'm—poor Father's funeral. I do not quite know how this unpleasant subject has arisen. (That's one for William, thought Edith.) In the meantime Mother must, of course, be our first consideration. Anything which can be done to spare her feelings. . . . After all, we must remember that her life is shattered. You know that she lived only for Father. And we should be very seriously and rightly blamed if we were to abandon her now to her loneliness.'

Ah, that's it, thought Edith: what will people say? So they mean to combine people's good opinion with getting a little of poor Mother's money. Wrangle, wrangle, she thought—for she had had some previous taste of family discussions; they'll wrangle for weeks over Mother like dogs quarrelling over an old, a very old, bone. Only Kay will try to keep out of it. William and Lavinia will be the worst; they'll want to get Mother as a paying guest, and then look down their noses while their friends praise them. And Carrie will wear an air of high martyrdom. This is the sort of thing, she thought, which happens when people die. Then she discovered that underneath this current of thought was running another current, concerned with whether she would now be able to live independently; she saw the little flat which would be her own; the cheerful sitting-room; the one servant, and the latchkey; the evenings over the fire with a book. No more answering letters for Father; no more accompanying Mother when she went to open hospital wards; no more adding up the house-books; no more taking Father for a walk in the Park. And at last she would be able to have a canary. How could she help hoping that Herbert, Carrie, Charles, and William would divide Mother between them? Shocked though she was by their blatancy, she acknowledged inwardly that she was no better than the rest of her family.

*   *   *

Edith was frightened of being left in this strange house, alone with her living mother and her dead father. She could not own to her fear, but she did everything in her power to delay the departure of her brothers and sister. Even Carrie and Herbert, whom she rather disliked, and Charles and William, whom she rather despised, became desirable to her as presences and companions. She invented pretexts to keep them back, dreading the moment when the front door would shut finally behind them. Even Kay would have been better than nothing. But Kay slipped from her before the others. She fluttered after him on to the landing; he turned to see who was following him; turned, with his neat little white beard and his comfortable little paunch, crossed by a watch-chain. 'You're going, Kay?' He was annoyed, because he imagined a reproof in Edith's tone, where, really, he should have detected only an appeal. He was annoyed, because he already had a sense of guilt in his intention of keeping an engagement; ought he, rather, to have remained to dinner at Elm Park Gardens? Then he had consoled his conscience by reflecting that the servants must not be given any extra trouble. So, when Edith ran after him, he turned, looking as patiently annoyed as it was possible for him to look. 'You're going, Kay?'

Kay was going. He must get some dinner. He could come back later, if Edith thought it desirable. He added this, being cowardly though self-indulgent, and anxious to avoid unpleasantness at any cost. Fortunately for him, Edith was cowardly too, and immediately retracted any reproof or appeal her pursuit might have been intended to convey. 'Oh no, Kay, of course not; why should you come back? I'll look after Mother. You'll be coming in to-morrow morning?'

Yes, said Kay, relieved; he'd come in to-morrow morning. Early. They kissed. They had not kissed for many years; but that was one of the strange effects of death; elderly brothers and sisters pecked at one another's cheeks. Their noses, from lack of custom, got in the way. Both of them looked up the dark well of the staircase, after they had kissed, towards the floor where their father lay, and then in sudden embarrassment Kay scuttled off down the stairs. He felt a relief as he shut himself out into the street. A May evening; normal London; taxis passing in the King's Road; and FitzGeorge waiting for him at the club. He must not keep Fitz waiting. He would not go by bus. He would take a taxi.

FitzGeorge was his oldest, indeed his only, friend. Over twenty years of difference in age separated them, but after threescore such discrepancies begin to close up. The two old gentlemen had many tastes in common. They were both ardent collectors, the only difference between them being a difference of wealth. FitzGeorge was enormously rich; a millionaire. Kay Holland was poor—all the Hollands were comparatively poor, although their father had been Viceroy of India. FitzGeorge could buy anything he liked, but such was his eccentricity that he lived like a pauper in two rooms at the top of a house in Bernard Street, and took pleasure in a work of art only if it had been his own discovery and a bargain. Since he possessed an extraordinary instinct for discoveries and bargains—finding unsuspected Donatellos in the basement of large furniture shops in the Tottenham Court Road—he had amassed at small cost (to his own delight and to Kay Holland's envious but exasperated admiration) a miscellaneous collection coveted by the British and the South Kensington Museums alike. Nobody knew what he would do with his things. He was just as likely to bequeath them all to Kay Holland as to make a bonfire of them in Russell Square. Obvious heirs he had none, any more than he had obvious progenitors. Meanwhile he kept his treasures closely round him; the few people privileged to visit him in his two rooms came away with a tale of Ming figures rolled up in a pair

of socks, Leonardo drawings stacked in the bath, Elamite pot-
tery ranged upon the chairs. Certainly, during the visit one had
to remain standing, for there was no free chair to sit on; and jade
bowls must be cleared away before Mr. FitzGeorge could grud-
gingly offer one a cup of the cheapest tea, boiling the kettle
himself on a gas-ring. The only visitors to receive a second
invitation were those who had declined the tea.

Nearly everybody knew him by sight. When people saw his
square hat and old-fashioned frock-coat going into Christie's
they said, 'There's old Fitz.' Winter or summer, his costume
never varied; square hat, frock-coat, and usually a parcel carried
under his arm. What the parcel contained was never divulged; it
might be a Dresden cup, or a kipper for Mr. FitzGeorge's
supper. Londoners felt affectionately towards him, as one of
their genuine eccentrics, but no one, not even Kay Holland,
would have dreamed of calling him Fitz to his face, however
glibly they might say 'There's old Fitz' when they saw him
pass. It was said that the happiest event of his life was the death
of Lord Clanricarde; on that day, old Fitz had walked down St.
James's Street with a flower in his buttonhole, and all the other
gentlemen sitting in club windows had known perfectly well
why.

Although Mr. FitzGeorge and Kay Holland had been friends
for some thirty years, no personal intimacy existed between
them. When they sat at dinner together—a familiar spectacle in
Boodle's or the Thatched House Club, each paying his share,
and drinking barley-water—they discussed prices and catalogues
as inexhaustibly as lovers discuss their emotions, but beyond this
they nothing of each other whatsoever. Mr. FitzGeorge knew,
of course, that Kay was old Slane's son, but Kay knew no more
of Mr. FitzGeorge's parentage than anybody else. Quite possibly Mr. FitzGeorge himself knew nothing of it either; so
people said, basing their suspicions on the suggestive prefix to

his name. Certainly Kay had never asked him; had never even hinted at any curiosity on the subject. Their relationship was beautifully detached. This explains why Mr. FitzGeorge awaited Kay's arrival in some perturbation, uncomfortably aware that he ought to make some allusion to the Hollands' bereavement, but shrinking from this infringement of their tacit understanding. He felt vexed with Kay; it was inconsiderate of him to have lost his father, inconsiderate of him not to have cancelled their appointment; yet Mr. FitzGeorge knew quite well that a cancelled appointment was a crime he never forgave. Very cross, he watched for Kay's approach, drumming on the window at Boodle's. He must say something, he supposed; better to do it at once, and get it over. Surely Kay was not going to be late? He had never yet been late for an appointment, in thirty years; never been late, and never failed to turn up. Mr. FitzGeorge drew an enormous silver turnip, price five shillings, from his pocket and looked at the time. Seventeen minutes past eight. He compared it with the clock on St. James's Palace. Kay was late; two whole minutes.—But there he was, getting out of a taxi.

'Evening,' said Kay, coming into the room.

'Evening,' said Mr. FitzGeorge. 'You're late.'

'Dear me, so I am,' said Kay. 'Let us go in to dinner at once, shall we?'

During dinner they talked about a pair of Sèvres bowls which Mr. FitzGeorge alleged that he had discovered in the Fulham Road. Kay, who had seen them too, was of the opinion that they were fakes, and this divergence led to one of those discussions which both old gentlemen so thoroughly enjoyed. But this evening, Mr. FitzGeorge's pleasure was spoilt; he had not said what he intended to say, and every moment made the saying of it more awkward and more impossible. His irritation against Kay was increased. It was the first unsuccessful meal that

they had ever had together, and the disappointment made
Mr. FitzGeorge reflect that all friendship was a mistake; he
regretted crossly that he had ever allowed himself to become
involved with Kay; other people had always been kept at arm's
length, a most commendable system; it was a mistake, a great
mistake, to admit exceptions. He scowled across the table at
Kay, drinking his barley-water and carefully wiping his neat
little beard, unaware of the hostility he was arousing.

'Coffee?' said Mr. FitzGeorge.

'I think so—yes, coffee.'

Poor old chap, he looks tired, thought Mr. FitzGeorge suddenly; not quite so spruce as usual; he's drooping a little; he's
been making an effort to talk. 'Have a brandy?' he said.

Kay looked up, surprised. They never had brandy.

'No, thanks.'

'Yes. Waiter, give Mr. Holland a brandy. Put it down on my
bill.'

'I really . . .' began Kay.

'Nonsense. Waiter, the best brandy—the eighteen forty.
When all's said and done, Holland, I saw you in your cradle.
The eighteen forty brandy was only thirty years old or so then.
So don't make a fuss.'

Kay made no fuss, startled as he was by this sudden revelation
that old Fitz had seen him in his cradle. His mind flung itself
back wildly into time and space. Time: 1874; space: India. So
old Fitz must have been in India in 1874. 'You never told me
that you had been in Calcutta then,' said Kay, sipping his
brandy over his little Vandyck beard. 'Didn't I?' said old Fitz
negligently, as though it were of no importance; 'well, I was.
My guardians didn't approve of universities, and sent me round
the world instead. (Strange revelations! so old Fitz, in his adolescence, had been controlled by guardians?) Your parents were
very kind to me,' Mr. FitzGeorge proceeded; 'naturally, your

father as Viceroy hadn't much leisure, but your mother, I remember, was most gracious; most charming. She was young then; young, and very lovely. I remember thinking that she was the most lovely thing I had seen in India.—But you're wrong about those bowls all the same, Holland. You know nothing whatever about china—never did, never will. It's too fine a taste for you. You ought to confine yourself to junk like your astrolabes. That's all you're fit for. Setting yourself up as a judge of china, indeed! And against me, who have forgotten more about china than you ever learnt.'

Kay was well accustomed to such abuse; he liked being bullied by old Fitz; it gave him a little tremor of delight. He sat listening while old Fitz told him that he did not deserve the name of connoisseur, and would have done much better to go in for collecting stamps. He knew that Fitz did not mean a word of it, but enjoyed pecking at him like an old, pecking, courting pigeon, while Kay averted his head and dodged the blows, laughing a little meanwhile, ever so slightly arch, and looking down at the table-cloth, fingering the knives and forks. Their relations had miraculously got back to the normal, and so greatly did Mr. FitzGeorge's spirits rise at this re-establishment that he said presently he was dashed if he wouldn't have a brandy too. He had forgotten all about that difficult allusion he intended to make, or thought he had forgotten, but perhaps it had really been in his mind all the time, for when they came out of the club together, and stood on the steps preparing to part, while Kay pulled on his chamois-leather gloves—Mr. FitzGeorge had never owned a pair of gloves in his life, but Kay Holland was never seen without his hands gloved in butter-yellow—to his own surprise he heard himself growl out, 'Sorry to hear about your father, Holland.'

There, it was said, and St. James's Street had not opened to swallow him up. It was said; it had been quite easy, really. But what on earth was prompting him to go further to make the most incredible, unnecessary proposal?—'Perhaps some day you'll take me to call on Lady Slane.' Now what had possessed him to say that? Kay looked taken aback; and no wonder. 'Oh, yes—yes, certainly—if you'd care to come,' he said hurriedly. 'Well, good-night—good-night,' and he hurried away, while old Fitz stood staring after him, wondering whether he had made it impossible for himself ever to see Kay Holland again.

The house was strange—thus Edith pursued her thoughts— there was such a contrast between what went on inside and what went on outside. Outside it was all blare and glare and publicity, what with the posters, and the reporters still hanging about the area railings, and the talk of Westminster Abbey, and speeches in both Houses of Parliament. Inside it was all hushed and private, like a conspiracy; the servants whispered, people went soundlessly up and down stairs; and whenever Lady Slane came into the room everybody stopped talking, and stood up, and somebody was sure to go forward and lead her gently to a chair. They treated her rather as though she had had an accident, or had gone temporarily off her head. Yet Edith was sure her mother did not want to be led to chairs, or to be kissed so reverently and mutely, or to be asked if she was sure she wouldn't rather have dinner in her room. The only person to treat her in a normal way was Genoux, her old French maid, who was nearly as old as Lady Slane herself, and had been with her for the whole of her married life. Genoux moved about the house as noisily as ever, talking to herself as her custom was, muttering to herself about her next business in her extraordinary jumble of French and English; she still burst unceremoniously into the drawing-room in pursuit of her mistress, whoever might be there, and horrified the assembled family by asking, 'Pardon, miladi, est-ce que ça vaut la peine d'envoyer les shirts de

milord à la wash?' They all looked at Lady Slane as though
they expected her to fall instantly to pieces, like a vase after a
blow, but she replied in her usual quiet voice that yes, his
lordship's shirts must certainly be sent to the wash; and then,
turning to Herbert, said, 'I don't know what you would like
me to do with your father's things, Herbert; it seems a pity to
give them all to the butler, and anyway they wouldn't fit.'

Her mother and Genoux, Edith thought, alone refused to
adapt themselves to the strangeness of the house. She could read
disapproval in the eyes of Herbert, Carrie, Charles, and
William; but naturally no disapproval could be openly
expressed. They could only insist, implicitly, that their own
convention must be adopted: Mother's life was shattered,
Mother was bearing up wonderfully, Mother must be sheltered
within the privacy of her disaster, while the necessary business
was conducted, the necessary contact with the outside world
maintained, by her capable sons and her capable daughter. Edith,
poor thing, wasn't much use. Everybody knew that Edith
always said the wrong thing at the wrong moment, and left
undone everything that she was supposed to do, giving as her
excuse that she had been 'too busy'; nor was Kay of much use
either, but then he scarcely counted as a member of the family at
all. Herbert, Carrie, William, and Charles stood between their
mother and the outside world. From time to time, indeed, some
special rumour was allowed to creep past their barrier: the King
and Queen had sent a most affectionate message—Herbert could
scarcely be expected to keep that piece of news to himself.
Huddersfield, Lord Slane's native town, desired the approval of
the family for a memorial service. The King would be represented at the funeral by the Duke of Gloucester. The ladies of the
Royal School of Embroidery had worked—in a great hurry—a
pall. The Prime Minister would carry one corner of it; the
Leader of the Opposition another. The French Government

were sending a representative; and it was said that the Duke of Brabant might attend on behalf of the Belgian. These bits of information were imparted to his mother by Herbert in driblets and with caution; he was feeling his way to see how she would receive them. She received them with complete indifference. 'Very nice of them, to be sure,' she said; and once she said, 'So glad, dear, if you're pleased.' Herbert both relished and resented this remark. Any tribute paid to his father was paid to himself, in a way, as head of the family; yet his mother's place, rightfully, was in the centre of the picture; these three or four days between death and burial were, rightfully, her own. Herbert prided himself on his sense of fitnes. Plenty of time, afterwards, to assert himself as Lord Slane. Generation must tread upon the heels of generation—that was a law of nature; yet, so long as his father's physical presence remained in the house, his mother had the right to authority. By her indifference, she was abdicating her position unnecessarily, unbecomingly, soon. She ought, posthumously, for these three or four days, to rally supremely in honour of her husband's memory; any abrogation of her right was unseemly. So it ran in Herbert's code. But perhaps, chattered the imp in Edith, perhaps she was so thoroughly drained by Father in his lifetime that she can't now be bothered with his memory?

Certainly the house was strange, with a particular strangeness that had never invaded it before and could never invade it again. Father could not die twice. By his dying he had created this particular situation—a situation which, surely, he had never foreseen; the sort of situation which nobody would foresee until it came actually into being. Nobody could have foreseen that Father, so dominant always, so paramount, would by the mere act of dying turn Mother into the most prominent figure. Her prominence might last only for three or four days; but during that brief spell it must be absolute. Everybody must defer. She,

and she alone, must decide whether the doors of Westminster
Abbey should or should not revolve upon their hinges; a nation
must wait upon her decision, a Dean and Chapter truckle to her
wishes. Very gently, and cautiously, she must be consulted on
every point, and her views ascertained. It was very strange that
somebody so self-eclipsing should suddenly have turned into
somebody so important. It was like playing a game; it reminded
Edith of the days when Father in one of his gay moods would
come into the drawing-room after tea to find Mother with all
the children around her, reading to them perhaps out of a story-
book, and would clap the book shut and say that now they
would all play follow-my-leader all through the house, but that
Mother must lead. So they had gone, capering through silent
chanceries and over the parquet floors of ballrooms, where the
chandeliers hung in their holland bags, performing all kinds of
absurd antics on the way—for Mother had an inexhaustible
invention—and Father would follow last, bringing up the tail,
but always playing the clown and getting all his imitations
wrong, whereat the children would shriek with delight, pretending to put him right, and Mother would turn round with Kay
clinging on to her skirts, to say with assumed severity, 'Really,
Henry!' Many an Embassy and Government House had rung to
their evening laughter. But once, Edith remembered, Mother
(who was young then) had tumbled some papers in the archi-
vist's room out of a file, and, as the children had scrambled
joyfully to make the disorder worse, Father had darkened suddenly, he had conveyed displeasure in a grown-up way; his
gaiety and Mother's had collapsed together like a rose falling to
pieces; and the return to the drawing-room had been made in a
sort of scolded silence, as though Jove stooping from Olympus
had detected a mortal taking liberties in his pretended absence
with his high concerns.

But now Mother might play follow-my-leader as she would;

for three or four days Mother might play follow-my-leader, leading the dignitaries of Europe and of Empire some dance up to Golder's Green or Huddersfield as the fancy took her, instead of resigning herself to Westminster Abbey or Brompton Cemetery as was expected; but the disappointment—to the imp in Edith's mind—lay in Mother's refusal to take any lead at all. She simply agreed to everything that Herbert suggested. Just as well might Herbert, at the age of seven, playing follow-my-leader, have prompted her, 'Now let's romp through the kitchens;' her acquiescence to-day, when she was eighty-eight and Herbert sixty-eight, shocked Edith as something unfitting. It shocked Herbert too—though, true son of his father, he was flattered by womanly dependence. Only for these three or four days—since he was playing a game, subcribing to a convention—did he demand of his mother that she should hold opinions of her own. Yet at the same time, such was his masculine contrariness, he would have resented any decision running counter to his own ideas.

Herbert, then, became gentler and gentler as he saw his own ideas adopted and yet could persuade himself that they had originated with his mother and not with him. He came down from his mother's room to his brothers and sisters, again—continuously, as it seemed to Edith—assembled in the drawing-room. Mother wanted the Abbey; therefore the Abbey it must be. After all, Mother was doubtless right. All England's greatest sons were buried in the Abbey. He himself would have preferred the parish church at Huddersfield, he said, though Edith shrewdly estimated the honesty of this remark, and in speaking for himself he thought he might speak for them all; but Mother's wishes must be considered. They must bow to the publicity of the Abbey. After all, it was an honour—a great honour—the crowning honour of their father's life. Carrie, William, and Charles inclined their heads in silence at this solemn thought.

Edith, on the other hand, thought how much amused her father would have been, and at the same time how much gratified, though professing scornfulness, could he have watched himself being buried in the Abbey.

The pall worked by the ladies of the Royal School of Embroidery was undoubtedly very sumptuous. Heraldic emblems were embossed on violet plush. The Prime Minister duly carried his corner, becomingly serious, and so satisfactorily in character that no one seeing him could have hesitated to say, 'There goes a Prime, or at any rate a Cabinet, Minister of England.' The Leader of the Opposition kept step with the Prime Minister; for an hour they had buried their differences, which, indeed, were part of a game too, since under the tuition of a common responsibility they had both absorbed much the same lessons, though their adherents forbade them to repeat them in the same language. The two young princes, ushered hurriedly though respectfully to their seats, wondered, perhaps, why fate had isolated them from other young men, by condemning them to cut tapes across new arterial roads or to honour statesmen by attending their funerals. More probably, they took it all as part of the day's work.

But where, meanwhile, Edith wondered, was reality?

After the funeral was over, everything at Elm Park Gardens subtly changed. Consideration towards Lady Slane was still observed, but a note of impatience crept in, a note of domination, held rather insistently by Herbert and Carrie. Herbert had become, quite definitely, the head of the family, and Carrie his support. They were prepared to take a firm though kind line with their mother. She could still be led to a chair, and, once lowered into it, could still be patted on the shoulder with a kindly protective gesture, but she must be made to understand that the affairs of the world were waiting, and that this pause of concession to death could not go on for ever. Like the papers in Lord Slane's desk, Lady Slane must be cleared up; then Herbert and Carrie could get back to their business. Nothing not put actually into words could have been conveyed more plainly.

Very quiet, very distinguished, very old, very frail, Lady Slane sat looking at her sons and daughters. Her children, who were accustomed to her, took her appearance for granted, but strangers exclaimed in amazement that she could not be over seventy. She was a beautiful old woman. Tall, slender, and pale, she had never lost her grace or her carriage. Clothes upon her ceased to be clothes and became draperies; she had the secret of line. A fluid loveliness ran over all her limbs. Her eyes were grey and deeply set; her nose was short and straight; her tranquil hands the hands of a Vandyck; over her white hair fell a veil of black lace, highly becoming. Her gowns for years past had always been soft, indefinite, and of unrelieved black. Looking at her, one could believe that it was easy for a woman to be beautiful and gracious, as all works of genius persuade us that they were effortless of achievement. It was more difficult to believe in the activity that Lady Slane had learned to pack into her life. Duty, charity, children, social obligations, public appearances—with these had her days been filled; and whenever her name was mentioned, the corollary came quick and slick, 'Such a wonderful help to her husband in his career!' Oh yes, thought Edith, Mother is lovely; Mother, as Herbert says, is wonderful. But Herbert is clearing his throat. What's coming now?

'Mother, dear . . .' A form of address semi-childish, semi-conventional; Herbert putting his fingers into his collar. Yet she had once sat on the floor beside him, and shown him how to spin his top.

'Mother, dear. We have been discussing . . . we have, I mean, felt naturally troubled about your future. We know how devoted you were to Father, and we realise the blank that his loss must leave in your life. We have been wondering— and that is why we have asked you to meet us all here in the drawing-room before we separate again to our different homes—we have been wondering where and how you will choose to live?'

'But you have decided it already for me, Herbert, haven't you?' said Lady Slane with the utmost sweetness.

Herbert put his fingers into his collar and peeked and preened until Edith feared that he would choke.

'Well! decided it for you, Mother, dear! decided is scarcely the word. It is true that we have sketched out a little scheme, which we could submit for your approval. We have taken your tastes into consideration, and we have realised that you would not like to be parted from so many interests and occupations. At the same time . . .'

'One moment, Herbert,' said Lady Slane; 'what was that you said about interests and occupations?'

'Surely, Mother, dear,' said Carrie reproachfully, 'Herbert means all your committees, the Battersea Club for Poor Women, the Foundlings' Ward, the Unfortunate Sisters' Organisation, the . . .'

'Oh yes,' said Lady Slane; 'my interests and occupations. Quite. Go on, Herbert.'

'All these things,' said Carrie, 'would collapse without you. We realise that. You founded many of them. You have been the life of others. Naturally, you won't want to abandon them now.'

'Besides, dear Lady Slane,' said Lavinia—she had never unbent sufficiently to address her mother-in-law by any other name—'we realise how bored you would be with nothing to do. You so active, so energetic! Oh no, we couldn't visualise you anywhere but in London.'

Still Lady Slane said nothing. She looked from one to the

other with an expression that, in one so gentle, was surprisingly ironical.

'At the same time,' Herbert proceeded, reverting to his original speech whose interruption he had endured, patient though not pleased, 'your income will scarcely suffice for the expenses of a house such as you are entitled to expect. We propose, therefore . . .' and he outlined the scheme which we have already heard discussed, and may consequently spare ourselves the trouble of listening to again.

Lady Slane, however, listened. She had spent a great deal of her life listening, without making much comment, and now she listened to her eldest son without making any comment at all. He, for his part, was unperturbed by her silence. He knew that all her life she had been accustomed to have her comings and goings and stayings arranged for her, whether she was told to board a steamer for Capetown, Bombay, or Sydney; to transport her wardrobe and nursery to Downing Street; or to accompany her husband for the week-end to Windsor. On all these occasions she had obeyed her directions with efficiency and without surprise. Becomingly and suitably dressed, she had been ready at any moment to stand on quay or platform, waiting until fetched beside a pile of luggage. Herbert saw no reason now to doubt that his mother would dole out her time according to schedule in the spare bedrooms of her sons and daughters.

When he had finished, she said: 'That's very thoughtful of you, Herbert. It would be very kind of you to put this house in the agents' hands to-morrow.'

'Capital!' said Herbert; 'I'm so glad you agree. But you need not feel hurried. No doubt some little time must elapse before the house is sold. Mabel and I will expect you at your convenience.' And he stooped and patter her hand.

'Oh, but wait,' said Lady Slane, raising it. It was the first gesture she had made. 'You go too fast, Herbert. I don't agree.'

They all looked at her in consternation.

'You don't agree, Mother?'

'No,' said Lady Slane, smiling. 'I am not going to live with you, Herbert; nor with you, Carrie; nor with you, William; nor with you, Charles, kind though you all are. I am going to live by myself.'

'By yourself, Mother? It's impossible—and anyway, where would you live?'

'At Hampstead,' replied Lady Slane, nodding her head quietly, as though in response to an inner thought.

'At Hampstead?—but will you find a house that will suit you; convenient, and not too dear?—Really,' said Carrie, 'here we are discussing Mother's house as though everything were settled. It is absurd. I don't know what has come over us.'

'There is a house,' said Lady Slane, again nodding her head; 'I have seen it.'

'But, Mother, you haven't been to Hampstead.' This was intolerable. Carrie had known all her mother's movements day by day for the past fifteen years at least, and she revolted against the suggestion that her mother had visited Hampstead without her knowledge. Such a hint of independence was an outrage, almost a manifesto. There had always been so close and continuous a connection between Lady Slane and her eldest daughter; the plans for the day would always be arranged between them; Genoux would be sent round with a note in the morning; or they would telephone, at great length; or Carrie would come round to Elm Park Gardens after breakfast, tall, practical, rustling, self-important, equipped for the day with her gloves, her hat, and her boa, a shopping list slipped into her bag, and the agenda papers for the afternoon's committee, and the two elderly ladies would talk over the day's doings while Lady Slane went on with her knitting, and then they would go out together at about half-past eleven, two tall figures in black, familiar to the other old ladies of the neighbourhood; or if their business, for once, did not lie in the same direction, Carrie would at least drop into Elm Park Gardens for tea, and would learn exactly how her mother had spent her day. It was surely impossible that Lady Slane should have concealed an expedition to Hampstead.

'Thirty years ago,' said Lady Slane. 'I saw the house then.' She took a skein of wool from her work-basket and held it out to Kay. 'Hold it for me, please, Kay,' and after first carefully breaking the little loops she began to wind. She was the very incarnation of placidity. 'I am sure the house is still there,' she said, carefully winding, and Kay with the experience of long habit stood before her, moving his hands rhythmically up and down, so that the wool might slip off his fingers without catching. 'I am sure the house is still there,' she said, and her tone was a mixture between dreaminess and confidence, as though she had some secret understanding with the house, and it were waiting for her, patient, after thirty years; 'it was a convenient little house,' she added prosaically, 'not too small and not too large—Genoux could manage it single-handed I think, with perhaps a daily char to do the rough work—and there was a nice garden, with peaches against the wall, looking south. It was to be let when I saw it, but of course your father would not have liked that. I remember the name of the agent.'

'And what,' snapped Carrie, 'was the name of the agent?'

'It was a funny name,' said Lady Slane, 'perhaps that's why I remember it. Bucktrout. Gervase Bucktrout. It seemed to go so well with the house.'

'Oh,' said Mabel, clasping her hands, 'I think it sounds too delicious—peaches, and Bucktrout. . . .'

'Be quiet, Mabel,' said Herbert. 'Of course, my dear Mother, if you are set on this—ah—eccentric scheme, there is no more to be said about it. You are entirely your own mistress, after all. But will it not look a little odd in the eyes of the world, when you have so many devoted children, that you should elect to live alone in retirement at Hampstead? Far be it from me to wish to press you, of course.'

'I don't think so, Herbert,' said Lady Slane, and having come to the end of her winding, she said 'Thank you, Kay,' and making a loop on a long knitting needle she started on a fresh piece of knitting. 'Lots of old ladies live in retirement at Hampstead. Besides, I have considered the eyes of the world for so long that I think it is time I had a little holiday from them. If one is not to please oneself in old age, when is one to please oneself? There is so little time left!'

'Well,' said Carrie, making the best of a bad job, 'at least we shall see to it that you are never lonely. There are so many of us that we can easily arrange for you to have at least one visitor a day. Though, to be sure, Hampstead is a long way off, and it is not always easy to fit in the arrangements about the motor,' she added, looking meaningly at her small husband, who quailed. 'But there are always the great-grandchildren,' she said, brightening; 'you'd like to have them coming in and out, keeping you in touch; I know you wouldn't be happy without that.'

'On the contrary,' said Lady Slane, 'that is another thing about which I have made up my mind. You see, Carrie, I am going to become completely self-indulgent. I am going to wallow in old age. No grandchildren. They are too young. Not one of them has reached forty-five. No great-grandchildren either; that would be worse. I want no strenuous young people, who are not content with doing a thing, but must needs know why they do it. And I don't want them bringing their children to see me, for it would only remind me of the terrible effort the poor creatures will have to make before they reach the end of their lives in safety. I prefer to forget about them. I want no one about me except those who are nearer to their death than to their birth.'

Herbert, Carrie, Charles, and William decided that their mother must be mad. They took a step forward, and from having always thought her simple, decided that old age had definitely affected her brain. Her madness, however, was taking a harmless and even a convenient form. William might be thinking rather regretfully of the lost subsidy to his house-books, Carrie and Herbert might remain still a little dubious about the eyes of the world, but, on the whole, it was a relief to find their mother settling her own affairs. Kay gazed inquiringly at his mother. He had taken her so much for granted; they had all taken her so much for granted—her gentleness, her unselfishness, her impersonal activities—and now, for the first time in his life, it was becoming apparent to Kay that people could still hold surprises up their sleeves, however long one had known them. Edith alone frolicked in her mind. She thought her mother not mad, but most conspicuously sane. She was delighted to see Carrie and Herbert routed, by their mother quietly disentangling herself from their toils. Softly she clapped her hands together, and whispered 'Go on, Mother! go on!' Only a remnant of prudence prevented her from saying it out loud. She revelled in her mother's new-found eloquence—not the least of the surprises of that surprising morning, for Lady Slane habitually was reserved in speech, withholding her opinion, concealing even the expression on her face as she bent her head over her knitting or embroidery, when her occasional 'Yes, dear?' gave but little indication of what she was really thinking. It now dawned upon Edith that her mother might have lived a full private life, all these years, behind the shelter of her affectionate watchfulness. How much had she observed? noted? criticised? stored up? She was speaking again, rummaging meanwhile in her work-bag.

'I have taken the jewels out of the bank, Herbert. You and Mabel had better have them. I wanted to give them to Mabel years ago, but your father objected. However, here are some of them,' and as she spoke she turned the bag over and shook the contents out on to her lap, a careless assortment of leather cases, tissue paper, some loose stones, and skeins of wool. With her fine hands she began picking them over. 'Ring the bell for Genoux, Edith,' she said, glancing up. 'I never cared about jewels, you know,' she said, speaking to herself rather than to her family at large, 'and it seemed such a pity—such a waste— that so many should have come my way. Your father used to say that I must be able to deck myself out on Occasions. When we were in India, he used to buy back a lot of things at the Tash-i-Khane auctions. He had a theory that it pleased the princes to see me wearing their gifts, even though they knew perfectly well that we had bought them back. I dare say he was right. But it always seemed rather silly to me—such a farce. I had a big topaz once, a big bronze topaz, unset, cut into dozens of facets; I wonder if you children remember it? I used to make you look at the fire through it. It made hundreds of little flames; some went the right way up, and others upside down. When you came down after tea we used to sit in front of the fire looking through it, like Nero at the burning of Rome. Only it was brown fire, not green. I don't suppose you remember. That was sixty years ago. I lost it, of course; one always does lose the things one values most. I never lost any of the other things; perhaps because Genoux always had charge of them—and she used to invent the most extraordinary places to hide them in—she mistrusted safes, so she used to drop my diamonds into the cold water jug—no robber would think of looking for them there, she said. I often thought that if Genoux died suddenly I shouldn't know where to look for the jewels myself—but the topaz I used to carry in my pocket.' Here Lady Slane's dreamy reminiscences were cut short as Genoux came in, rustling like a snake in dry leaves, creaking like a saddle, for until May was out, Genoux would not abandon the layers of brown paper that reinforced her corsets and her combinations against the English climate. 'Miladi a sonné?'

Yes, thought Edith, there's nobody here for Genoux but Mother; only Mother can have rung the bell; only Mother can have an order to give, though we are all assembled: Herbert peeking over his collar, Carrie drawing herself up, outraged, Charles twisting his moustaches like somebody sharpening a pencil—though who cares for Charles? not even the War Office, and Charles knows it. They all know that nobody cares for them; that's why they talk so loud. Mother has never talked at all—until to-day; yet Genoux comes in as though Mother were the only person in the room, in the house, fit to give an order. Genoux knows where respect is due. Genoux takes no account of insistent voices. 'Miladi a sonné?'

'Genoux, vous avez les bijoux?'

'Mais bien sûr, miladi, que j'ai les bijoux. J'appelle ça le trésor. Miladi veut que j'aille chercher le trésor?'

'Please, Genoux,' said Lady Slane, determined, though Genoux sent a glance round the family circle as though Herbert, Carrie, Charles, William, Lavinia, and even the snubbed and innocuous Mabel were the very robbers against whose coming she had dropped the diamonds nightly into the jug of cold water. Indian verandahs and South African stoeps had, in the past, whispered in Genoux' imagination with the stealthy footsteps of robbers bent upon the viceregal jewels—'ces sales nègres;'—but now a more immediate, because a more legitimate and English, danger menaced these jealously guarded possessions. Miladi, so gentle, so vague, so detached, could never be trusted to look after herself or her belongings. Genoux was by nature a watchdog. 'Miladi se souviendra au moins que les bagues lui ont été très spécialement données par ce pauvre milord?'

Lady Slane looked down at her hands. They were, as the saying goes, loaded with rings. That saying means, in so far as any saying means anything at all—and every saying, every *cliché*, once meant something tightly related to some human experience—that the gems concerned were too weighty for the hands that bore them. Her hands were indeed loaded with rings. They had been thus loaded by Lord Slane—tokens of affection, certainly, but no less tokens of the embellishments proper to the hands of Lord Slane's wife. The great half-hoop of diamonds twisted round easily upon her finger. (Lord Slane had been wont to observe that his wife's hands were as soft as doves; which was true in a way, since they melted into nothing as one clasped them; and in another way was quite untrue, since to the outward eye they were fine, sculptural, and characteristic; but Lord Slane might be trusted to seize upon the more feminine aspect, and to ignore the subtler, less convenient, suggestion.) Lady Slane, then, looked down at her hands as though Genoux had for the first time drawn attention to them. For one's hands are the parts of one's body that one suddenly sees with the maximum of detachment; they are suddenly far off; and one observes their marvellous articulations, and miraculous response to the transmission of instantaneous messages, as though they belonged to another person, or to another piece of machinery; one observes even the oval of their nails, the pores of their skin, the wrinkles of their phalanges and knuckles, their smoothness or rugosities, with an estimating and interested eye; they have been one's servants, and yet one has not investigated their personality; a personality which, cheiromancy assures us, is so much bound up with our own. One sees them also, as the case may be, loaded with rings or rough with work. So did Lady Slane look down upon her hands. They had been with her all her life, those hands. They had grown with her from the chubby hands of a child to the ivory-smooth hands of an old woman. She twisted the half-hoop of diamonds, and the half-hoop of rubies, loosely and reminiscently. She had worn them for so long that they had become a part of her. 'No, Genoux,' she said, 'soyez sans crainte; I know the rings are mine.'

But the other things were not hers in the same way; and indeed she did not want them. Genoux produced them one after the other, and handed them over to Herbert, counting as a peasant might count out a clutch of eggs to the buyer. Herbert, for his part, received them and passed them on to Mabel much as a bricklayer passing on bricks to his mate. He had a sense of value, but none of beauty. Lady Slane sat by, watching. She had a sense of beauty, though none of value. The cost of these things, their marketable price, meant nothing to her. Their beauty meant much, though she felt no proprietary interest; and their associations meant much, representing as they did the whole background of her life in its most fantastic aspect. Those sceptres of jade, brought by the emissaries of the Tibetan Lama! how well she remembered the ceremony of their presentation, when the yellow-coated emissaries, squatting, had drawn howls of music from bones the length of a mammoth's thigh. And she remembered checking her amusement, even while she sat conformably beside the Viceroy in his Durbar Hall, checking it with the thought that it was on a par with the narrow English amusement at the unfamiliar collection of consonants in a Polish name. What, save their unfamiliarity, caused her to smile at the wails drawn from a Tibetan thigh-bone? Kubelik might equally cause a Tibetan lama to smile. Then the Indian princes had come with their gifts that now Genoux delivered over to Herbert, the heir, in Elm Park Gardens. The Indian princes had known very well that their gifts would be pooled in the Tash-i-Khane, to be bought back according to the Viceroy's purse and discretion. Knobbly pearls, and uncut emeralds, heavily flawed, passed now between

Genoux's resentful hands and Herbert's, decently avid. Red velvet cases opened to display bracelets and necklaces; 'tout est bien en ordre,' said Genoux, snapping the cases shut. A small table was quite covered with cases by the time they had finished. 'My dear Mabel,' said Lady Slane, 'I had better lend you a portmanteau.'

Loot. The eyes of William and Lavinia glittered. Lady Slane remained oblivious of their covetous glances, and of their resentment at this one-sided distribution. Not so much as a brooch for Lavinia! It had simply never occurred to Lady Slane that she ought to divide the things; that was obvious. Lavinia and Carrie watched in silent rage. Such simplicity amounted to imbecility. But Herbert was well aware, and—so amiable are our secret feelings—rejoiced. He enjoyed their discomfiture, and further to increase it addressed Mabel quite affectionately for once: 'Put on the pearls, my dear; I am sure they will be most becoming.' Becoming they were not, to Mabel's faded little face, for Mabel who had once been pretty had now faded, according to the penalty of fair people, so that her skin appeared to be darker than her hair, and her hair without lustre, the colour of dust. The pearls, which had once dripped their sheen among the laces and softnesses of Lady Slane, now hung in a dispirited way round Mabel's scraggy neck. 'Very nice, dear Mabel,' said Lavinia, putting up her lorgnon; 'but how odd it is, isn't it, that these Oriental presents should always be of such poor quality? Those pearls are quite yellow, really, now that I come to look at them—more like old piano keys. I never noticed that before, when your mother wore them.'

'About the house, Mother,' began Carrie. 'Would to-morrow suit you to see it? I think I have a free afternoon,' and she began to consult a small diary taken from her bag.

'Thank you, Carrie,' said Lady Slane, setting the crown upon the surprises she had already given them, 'but I have made an appointment to see the house to-morrow. And, although it is very nice of you to offer, I think I will go there alone.'

It was something of an adventure for Lady Slane to go alone to Hampstead, and she felt happier after safely changing trains at Charing Cross. An existence once limited only by the boundaries of Empire had shrunk since the era of Elm Park Gardens began. Or perhaps she was one of those people on whom a continuous acquaintance with strange countries makes little impression— they remain themselves to the end; or perhaps she was really getting old. At the age of eighty-eight one might be permitted to say it. This consciousness, this sensation, of age was curious and interesting. The mind was as alert as ever, perhaps more alert, sharpened by the sense of imminent final interruption, spurred by the necessity of making the most of remaining time; only the body was a little shaky, not very certain of its reliability, not quite certain even of its sense of direction, afraid of stumbling over a step, of spilling a cup of tea; nervous; aware that it must not be jostled, or hurried, for fear of betraying its frail inadequacy. Younger people did not always seem to notice or to make allowance; and when they did notice they were apt to display a slight irritability, dawdling rather too markedly in order to keep pace with the hesitant footsteps. For that reason Lady Slane had never much enjoyed her walks with Carrie to the corner where they caught the bus. Yet, going up to Hampstead alone, she did not feel old; she felt younger than she had felt for years, and the proof of it was that she accepted eagerly this start of a new lap in life, even though it be the last. Nor did she look her age, as she sat, swaying slightly with the rocking of the Underground train, very upright, clasping her umbrella and her bag, her ticket carefully pushed into the opening of her glove. It did not occur to her to wonder what her travelling companions would think, could they know that two days previously she had buried her husband in Westminster Abbey. She was more immediately concerned with the extraordinary sensation of being independent of Carrie.

(Leicester Square.)

How Henry's death had brought about this sudden emancipation she could not conceive. It was just another instance of what she had vaguely noted all her life: how certain events brought apparently irrelevant results in their train. She had once asked Henry whether the same phenomenon were observable in the realm of politics, but although he had accorded her (as always, and to everyone) the gravest courtesy of his attention, he had obviously failed to understand what she meant. Yet Henry rarely failed to pick up the meaning of what people said. On the contrary, he would let them talk, keeping his keen humorous eyes upon them all the while, and then he would pick out the central point of their meaning, however clumsily they had indicated it, and, catching it up between his hands, would toss it about as a juggler with golden balls, until from a poor poverty-stricken thing it became a spray, a fountain, full of glitter and significance under the play of his incomparable intelligence—for this was the remarkable, the attractive thing about Henry, the thing which made people call him the most charming man in the world: that he gave the best of his intelligence to everybody on the slightest demand, whether a Cabinet Minister at the council table, or an intimidated young woman sitting next to him at dinner. He was never dismissive, perfunctory, or contemptuous. He seized upon any subject, however trivial; and the further removed from his own work or interests the better. He would discuss balldresses with a débutante, polo ponies with a subaltern, or Beethoven with either. Thus he deluded legions of people into believing that they had really secured his interest.

(Tottenham Court Road.)

But, when his wife asked him that question about events and irrelevant results, he was not disposed to take the matter up, and had played instead with the rings on her fingers. She could see the rings now, making bumps under her black gloves. She sighed. Often she had pressed a tentative switch, and Henry's mind had failed to light up. She had accepted this at last, taking refuge in the thought that she was probably the only person in the world with whom he need not make an effort. It was perhaps an arid compliment, but a sincere one. She regretted it now: there were so many things she would have liked to discuss with Henry; impersonal things, nothing troublesome. She had had that unique opportunity, that potential privilege, for nearly seventy years, and now it was gone, flattened under the slabs of Westminster Abbey.

(Goodge Street.)

He would have been amused by her emancipation from Carrie. He had never liked Carrie; she doubted whether he had ever much liked any of his children. He never criticised anybody—that was one of his characteristics—but Lady Slane knew him well enough (although in a sense she did not know him at all) to know when he approved of a person and when he did not. His commendations were always measured; but, conversely, when withheld, their absence meant a great deal. She could not recollect one word of approval for Carrie, unless 'Damned efficient woman, my daughter,' could be counted as approval. The expression in his eye whenever he looked at Herbert had been unmistakable; nor had Charles ever succeeded in obtaining much sympathy from his father in his many grievances. (Euston.) Lord Slane had been apt to consider his son, the General, with an air of as-much-as-to-say, 'Now shall I bestir myself and give this rhetorical and peevish man my exact opinion of government offices, about which, after all, I know a great deal more than he does, or shall I not?' So far as Lady Slane knew he never had. He had preferred to endure in silence. William he quite markedly avoided, though Lady Slane, with dishonest loyalty for her own son, had always tried to attribute this avoidance to a dislike of Lavinia. 'My dear,' Henry had once said, under pressure of exhortation, 'I find it difficult to accommodate myself to the society of minds balanced like a ledger,' and Lady Slane had sighed, and had said yes, it must be admitted that Lavinia had done poor William's nature a certain amount of harm. At which Lord Slane had replied, 'Harm? they are two peas in a pod,' which, for him, was a tart rejoinder.

(Camden Town.)

For Edith he had had a somewhat selfish affection. She had remained at home; she had been obliging; she had taken him for walks; she had answered some of his letters. True, she had often muddled them; had sent them off unsigned, or, if signed, without an address, in which case they had been returned through the Dead Letter Office to 'Slane, Elm Park Gardens,' a contretemps which always caused Lord Slane more amusement than annoyance. Never had Lord Slane had occasion to call his daughter Edith a damned efficient woman. Lady Slane had sometimes been tempted to think that he liked Edith more for the opportunities she afforded him of teasing her than for the reliance he placed upon her well-intentioned service.

(Chalk Farm.)

Kay. But before Lady Slane could consider what Lord Slane had made of that curious problem Kay, before she could pull up yet another fish of memory on a long line, she recollected a restriction she had placed upon herself, namely, not to let her memory wander until the days of complete leisure should be come; not to luxuriate until she could luxuriate fully and freely. Her feast must not be spoiled by snippets of anticipation. The train itself came to her assistance, for, after jerking over points, it ran into yet another white-tiled station, where a line of red tiles framed the name: Hampstead. Lady Slane rose unsteadily to her feet, reaching out her hand for a helpful bar; it was on these occasions and these alone, when she must compete with the rush of mechanical life, that she betrayed herself for an old lady. She became then a little tremulous, a little afraid. It became apparent that in her frailty she dreaded being bustled. Yet, in her anxiety not to inconvenience others, she always took conductors at their word and hurried obediently when they shouted, 'Hurry along, please'; as, again, in her anxiety not to push herself forward, she always allowed others to board the train or the bus while she herself hung courteously back. Many a train and bus she had missed by this method, often to the exasperation of Carrie, who had invariably secured her own place, and was borne away, seeing her mother left standing on platform or pavement.

It was a wonder, arrived at Hampstead, that Lady Slane descended from the train in time, successfully clasping her umbrella, her bag, and her ticket inside her glove, but descend she did, and found herself standing in the warm summer air with the roofs of London beneath her. The passers-by ignored her, standing there, so well accustomed were they to the sight of old ladies in Hampstead. Setting out to walk, she wondered if she remembered the way; but Hampstead seemed scarcely a part of London, so sleepy and village-like, with its warm red-brick houses and vistas of trees and distance that reminded her pleasantly of Constable's paintings. She walked slowly but happily, and without anxiety, as in a friendly retreat, no longer thinking of Henry's opinion of his children, or indeed of anything but the necessity of finding the house, *her* house, which thirty years ago had been one of just such a red-brick row, with its garden behind it. It was curious to think that she would see it again, so imminently. Thirty years. Ten years longer than the span needed for a baby to grow up into full consciousness. Who could tell what might have happened to the house during that span? whether it had seen turmoil, desolation, or merely placidity?

The house had indeed been waiting several years for someone to come and inhabit it. It had been let once only since Lady Slane first saw it, thirty years ago, to a quiet old couple with no more history than the ordinary history of human beings—eventful enough, God knows, in their own eyes, but so usual as to merge unrecorded into the general sea of lives—a quiet old couple, their peripetias left behind them; they had come there to fade slowly, to drift gently out of existence, and so they had faded, so they had drifted; they had, in fact, both drawn their last breath in the bedroom facing south, above the peaches—so the caretaker told Lady Slane, by way of encouragement, snapping up the blinds and letting in the sun, in an off-hand way, talking meanwhile, and wiping a cobweb off the window-sill with a sweep of her lifted apron, and looking back at Lady Slane as much as to say, 'There, now, you can see what it's like—not much to look at—just a house to let—make up your mind quickly, for good- ness' sake, and let me get back to my tea.' But Lady Slane, standing in the deserted room, said quietly that she had an appointment with Mr. Bucktrout.

The caretaker might go, she said; there was no need for her to wait; and some note of viceregal authority must have lingered in her voice, for the caretaker's antagonism changed to a sort of bedraggled obsequiousness. All the same, she said, she must lock up. There were the keys. Day in, day out, she had unlocked the house, flicked it over with a hasty duster, and locked it up again, to return to its silence and the occasional fall of plaster from the walls. During the night the plaster had fallen, and must be swept up in the morning. It was terrible the state an unoccupied house got into. The very ivy came creeping in between the windows; Lady Slane looked at it, a pale young frond waving listlessly in the sunshine. Bits of straw blew about on the floor. An enor- mous spider scuttled quickly, ran up the wall, and vanished into a crevice. Yes, said Lady Slane, the caretaker might go, and no doubt Mr. Bucktrout would be so kind as to lock up.

The caretaker shrugged. After all, there was nothing in the

house for Lady Slane to steal, and she wanted her tea. Receiving a tip of half-a-crown, she went. Lady Slane was left alone in the house; she heard the front door slam as the caretaker went away. How wrongly caretakers were named: they took so little care. A perfunctory banging about with black water in a galvanised pail, a dirty clout smeared over the floor, and they thought their work was done. Small blame to them, perhaps, receiving a few shillings a week and expected to make their knuckles even more unsightly in the care of a house which, to them, was at best a job and at worst a nuisance. One could not demand of them that they should give the care which comes from the heart. Very few months of such toil would blunt one's zeal, and caretakers had a lifetime of it. Nor could one expect them to feel how strange a thing a house was, especially an empty house; not merely a systematic piling-up of brick on brick, regulated in the building by plumb-line and spirit-level, pierced at intervals by doors and casements, but an entity with a life of its own, as though some unifying breath were blown into the air confined within this square brick box, there to remain until the prisoning walls should fall away, exposing it to a general publicity. It was a very private thing, a house; private with a privacy irrespective of bolts and bars. And if this superstition seemed irrational, one might reply that man himself was but a collection of atoms, even as a house was but a collection of bricks, yet man laid claim to a soul, to a spirit, to a power of recording and of perception, which had no more to do with his restless atoms than had the house with its stationary bricks. Such beliefs were beyond rational explanation; one could not expect a caretaker to take them into account.

Lady Slane experienced the curious sensation common to all who remain alone for the first time in an empty house which may become their home. She gazed out of the first-floor window, but her mind ran up and down the stairs and peeped into rooms, for already, at this her first visit, the geography had impressed itself familiarly; that in itself was a sign that she and the house were in accord. It ran down even into the cellar, where she had not descended, but whose mossy steps she had seen; and she wondered idly whether fungi grew there—not the speckled orange sort but the bleached kind—unwholesome in a more unpleasant way. It seemed likely that fungi should be included among the invaders of the house, and this brought her back to the bare room in which she stood, with its impudent inhabitants blowing, waving, running, as they listed.

These things—the straw, the ivy frond, the spider—had had the house all to themselves for many days. They had paid no rent, yet they had made free with the floor, the window, and the walls, during a light and volatile existence. That was the kind of companionship that Lady Slane wanted; she had had enough of bustle, and of competition, and of one set of ambitions writhing to circumvent another. She wanted to merge with the things that drifted into an empty house, though unlike the spider she would weave no webs. She would be content to stir with the breeze and grow green in the light of the sun, and to drift down the passage of years, until death pushed her gently out and shut the door behind her. She wanted nothing but passivity while these outward things worked their will upon her. But, first of all, it was necessary to know whether she could have the house.

A slight sound downstairs—was it the opening of a door?— made her listen. Mr. Bucktrout? Her appointment with him was for half-past four, and the hour was already struck. She must see him, she supposed, though she hated business, and would have preferred to take possession of the house as the straw, the ivy, and the spider had taken possession, simply adding herself to their number. She sighed, foreseeing a lot of business before she could sit at peace in the garden; documents would have to be signed, orders given, curtains and carpets chosen, and various human beings set in motion, all provided with hammers, tin-tacks, needles, and thread, before she and her belongings could settle down after their last journey. Why could one not possess the ring of Aladdin? Simplify life as one might, one could not wholly escape its enormous complication.

The thought struck her that the Mr. Bucktrout whose name she had noted thirty years ago might well have been replaced by some efficient young son, and great was her relief when, peeping over the banisters, she saw, curiously foreshortened to her view, a safely old gentleman standing in the hall. She looked down on his bald patch; below that she saw his shoulders, no body to speak of, and then two patent-leather toes. He stood there hesitant; perhaps he did not know that his client had already arrived, perhaps he did not care. She thought it more probable that he did not care. He appeared to be in no hurry to find out. Lady Slane crept down a few steps, that she might get a better view of him. He wore a long linen coat like a house-painter's; he had a rosy and somewhat chubby face, and he held one finger pressed against his lips, as though archly and impishly preoccupied with some problem in his mind. What on earth is he going to do, she wondered, observing this strange little figure. Still pressing his finger, as though enjoining silence, he tiptoed across the hall to where a stain on the wall indicated that a barometer had once hung there; then rapidly tapped the wall like a wood-pecker tapping a tree; shook his head; muttered 'Falling! fall-ing!'; and, picking up the skirts of his coat, he executed two neat pirouettes which brought him back to the centre of the hall, his foot pointed nicely before him.

'Mr. Bucktrout?' said Lady Slane, descending.

Mr. Bucktrout gave a skip and changed the foot pointed before him. He paused to admire his instep. Then he looked up. 'Lady Slane?' he said, performing a bow full of elaborate courtesy.

'I came about the house,' said Lady Slane, quite at her ease and drawn by an instant sympathy to this eccentric person.

Mr. Bucktrout dropped his skirts and stood on two feet like anybody else. 'Ah yes, the house,' he said; 'I had forgotten. One must be business-like, although the glass is falling. So you want to see the house, Lady Slane. It is a nice house—so nice that I wouldn't care to let it to everybody. It is my own house, you understand; I am the owner, as well as the agent. If I had been merely the agent, acting on the owner's behalf, I should have felt it my duty to let when I could. That is why it has remained empty for so long. I have had many applicants, but I liked none of them. But you shall see it.' He put a slight emphasis on the 'you'.

'I have seen it,' siad Lady Slane; 'the caretaker showed me over.'

'Of course. A horrid woman. So harsh, so sordid. Did you give her a tip?'

'Yes,' said Lady Slane, amused. 'I gave her half-a-crown.'

'Ah, that's a pity. Too late now, though. Well, you have seen the house. Have you seen it all? Bedrooms, three; bath-room, one; lavatories, two, one upstairs and one down; reception rooms, three; lounge hall; usual offices. Company's water; electric light. Half an acre of garden; ancient fruit-trees, including a mulberry. Fine cellar; do you care for mushrooms? you could grow mushrooms in the cellar. Ladies, I find, seldom care much for wine, so the cellar might as well be used for mushrooms. I have never yet met with a lady who troubled to lay down a pipe of port. And so, Lady Slane, having seen the house, what do you think of it?'

Lady Slane hesitated, as the fanciful idea crossed her mind of telling Mr. Bucktrout the exact thoughts which had occurred to her while she awaited him; she felt confident that he would receive them with complete gravity and without surprise. But, instead, she confined herself to saying with the approved caution and reticence of a potential tenant, 'I think it would probably suit me very well.'

'Ah, but the question is,' said Mr. Bucktrout, again putting his finger to his lips, 'will you suit *it?* I have a feeling that you might. And, in any case, you would not want it after the end of the world.'

'I expect my own end will come before that,' said Lady Slane, smiling.

'Not unless you are very old indeed,' said Mr. Bucktrout seriously. 'The end of the world is due in two years' time—I could convince you by a few simple mathematical calculations. Perhaps you are no mathematician. Few ladies are. But if the subject interests you I could come to tea with you one day when you are established and give you my demonstration.'

'So I am going to be established here, am I?' said Lady Slane.

'I think so—yes—I think so,' said Mr. Bucktrout, putting his head on one side and looking obliquely at her. 'It seems likely. Otherwise, why should you have remembered the house for thirty years—you said so in your letter—and why should I have turned away so many tenants? The two things seem to come together, do they not, to converge at a point, after describing separate arcs? I am a great believer in the geometrical designs of destiny. That is another thing I should like to demonstrate to you one day if I may come to tea. Of course, if I were only the agent I should never suggest coming to tea. It would not be meet. But, being also the owner, I feel that once we have finished all our business we may meet upon an equal footing.'

'Indeed, I hope you will come whenever you feel inclined, Mr. Bucktrout,' said Lady Slane.

'You are most gracious, Lady Slane. I have few friends, and I find that as one grows older one relies more and more on the society of one's contemporaries and shrinks from the society of the young. They are so tiring. So unsettling. I can scarcely, nowadays, endure the company of anybody under seventy. Young people compel one to look forward on a life full of effort. Old people permit one to look backward on a life whose effort is over and done with. That is reposeful. Repose, Lady Slane, is one of the most important things in life, yet how few people achieve it? How few people, indeed, desire it? The old have it imposed upon them. Either they are infirm, or weary. But half of them still sigh for the energy which once was theirs. Such a mistake.'

'That, at any rate, is a mistake of which I am not guilty,' said Lady Slane, betraying herself with relief to Mr Bucktrout.

'No? Then we are agreed upon at least one of the major subjects. It is terrible to be twenty, Lady Slane. It is as bad as being faced with riding over the Grand National course. One knows one will almost certainly fall into the Brook of Competition, and break one's leg over the Hedge of Disappointment, and stumble over the Wire of Intrigue, and quite certainly come to grief over the Obstacle of Love. When one is old, one can throw oneself down as a rider on the evening after the race, and think, Well, I shall never have to ride that course again.'

'But you forget, Mr. Bucktrout,' said Lady Slane, delving into her own memories, 'when one was young, one enjoyed living dangerously—one desired it—one wasn't appalled.'

'Yes,' said Mr. Bucktrout, 'that is true. When I was a young man I was a Hussar. My greatest pleasure was pig-sticking. I assure you, Lady Slane, that I touched the highest moment of life whenever I saw a fine pair of tusks coming at me. I have several pairs, mounted, in my house to-day, which I should be pleased to show you. But I had no ambition—no military ambition. I never had the slightest wish to command my regiment. So of course I resigned my commission, since when I have learnt that the pleasures of contemplation are greater than the pleasures of activity.'

The image of Mr. Bucktrout as a Hussar, thus evoked by his queerly stilted phrases, moved Lady Slane to an amusement which she was careful to conceal. She found it easy to believe that he had never cherished any military ambition. She found him entirely to her liking. Still, it was necessary to recall him to practical matters, she supposed, though heaven knows that this rambling conversation was for her a new and luxurious indulgence. 'But now, about the house, Mr. Bucktrout,' she began, much as Carrie had resumed the topic with herself after that flow of passing jewels; it was a relapse into the old viceregal manner that brought Mr. Bucktrout back from pig-sticking in the scrub to the subject of rents in Hampstead. 'I like the house,' said Lady Slane, 'and apparently,' she added with a smile that undid the viceregal manner, 'you approve of me as a tenant. But what about business? What about the rent?'

He gave her a startled look; evidently, he had been busy pig-sticking by himself in the interval; had returned to life as a Hussar, forgetting himself as owner and agent. He put his finger to his nose this time, quizzing Lady Slane, giving himself time to think. The subject seemed distasteful to him, though relics of a business training tugged at him, jerking some string in his mind; he lived, naturally, in a world where rents were not of much importance. So did Lady Slane; and thus a pair more ill-assorted, and yet better assorted, to discuss rents could scarcely be imagined. 'The rent . . . the rent . . .' said Mr. Bucktrout, as one who endeavours to establish connection with some word in a foreign language he once has known.

Then he brightened. 'Of course: the rent,' he said briskly. 'You want to take the house on a yearly tenancy?' he said, recovering his vocabulary after his excursion of fifty years back into his pig-sticking days as a Hussar. 'It would scarcely be worth your while,' he added, 'to take it on more than a yearly tenancy. You might vacate it at any moment, and your heirs would not wish to have it on their hands. I think that on that basis we might come to a satisfactory agreement. I like the idea of a tenant who will give me recovery of the house within a short period. Apart from my personal predilection for you, Lady Slane, abruptly sprung though that predilection may be, I relish the idea that this particular house should return at short intervals again into my keeping. From that point of view alone, you would suit me admirably as a tenant. There are other points of view, of course—as in this life there invariably are—but in the interests of business I must for the present ignore them. Those other points of view are purely sentimental—*ee gee*, that I should fancy you as the occupier of this particular house (speaking as the owner, not the agent), and that I may look forward to agreeable afternoons at tea-time when I may set before you, as a lady of understanding, my several little demonstrations. Those considerations must stand aside for the moment. We are here to discuss the question of rent.' He pointed a foot; recollected himself; took it back; and cocked at Lady Slane an eye full of satisfaction and triumph.

He puts it delicately, admirably, thought Lady Slane; it would scarcely be worth my while to take the house on more than a yearly tenancy, since at any moment I might vacate it by being carried out of it in my coffin. But what if he should pre-decease me? for although I am certainly an old woman, he is equally certainly an old man. Any delicacy of speech between people so near to death, is surely absurd? But people do not willingly speak in plain English of death, however fixedly its imminence may weigh on their hearts; so Lady Slane refrained from pointing out the possible fallacies of Mr. Bucktrout's argument, and merely said, 'A yearly tenancy would suit me very well. Still, that doesn't reply to my inquiry about the rent?'

Mr. Bucktrout was manifestly embarrassed at being thus chased into a corner. Although both owner and agent, he was one of those who resent seeing their fantasies reduced to terms of pounds and pence. Moreover, he had set his heart upon Lady Slane as a tenant. He temporised. 'Well, Lady Slane, I counter your inquiry. What rent would you be willing to pay?'

Delicacy again, thought Lady Slane. He doesn't say: 'What rent could you afford to pay?' This fencing, this walking round one another like two courting pigeons, was becoming ludicrous. Henry would have struck down between them, cleaving the situation with an axe of cold sense. Yet she liked the odd little man, and was thankful, heartily thankful, that she had rejected Carrie's company. Carrie, like her father, would drastically have intervened, shattering thereby a relationship which had grown up, creating itself, as swiftly and exquisitely as a little rigged ship of blown glass, each strand hardening instantly as it left the tube and met the air, yet remaining so brittle that a false note, jarring on the ethereal ripples, could splinter it. Shrinking, Lady Slane named a sum, too large; which Mr. Bucktrout immediately halved, too small.

But between them they came to a settlement. Though it might not be everybody's method of conducting business, it suited them very well, and they parted very much pleased with each other.

Carrie found her mother curiously reticent about the house. Yes, she had seen it; yes, she had seen the agent; yes, she had arranged to take it. On a yearly tenancy. Carrie exclaimed. What if the agent got a better offer and turned her out? Lady Slane smiled wisely. The agent, she said, wouldn't turn her out. But, said Carrie, agents were such dreadfully grasping people— quite naturally—they had to be grasping—what guarantee had her mother that at the end of a year she might not be obliged to look for another house? Lady Slane said that she anticipated no such thing; Mr. Bucktrout was not that kind of person. Well, but, said Carrie, exasperated, Mr. Bucktrout had his living to make, hadn't he? Business wasn't based on philanthropy. And had her mother made any arrangements about repairs and decoration, she asked? whisking off on to another subject, since she gave up all hope of doing something about the lease; what about papering, and distempering, and leaks in the roof? Had her mother thought of that? Carrie, who had controlled all her mother's decision for years, really suffered a frenzy of mortification and anxiety, intensified by her inability to give free rein to her indignation, for she could not reasonably assume authority over an old lady of eighty-eight, if that old lady chose suddenly to imply that having reached the age of eighty-eight she was capable of managing her affairs for herself. Carrie was sure that she was capable of nothing of the sort; apart from her consternation at seeing herself deposed, she was genuinely concerned at seeing her mother heading straight and unrescuable into the most terrible muddle. Lady Slane meanwhile replied calmly that Mr. Bucktrout had promised to arrange with carpenters, painters, plumbers, and upholsterers on her behalf. It was kind of Carrie to worry, but quite unnecessary. She and Mr. Bucktrout would manage everything between them.

Carrie felt that it was useless even to mention the word Estimate. Her mother seemed to have gone right away from her, into a world ruled not by sense but by sentiment. A world in which one took other people's delicacy and nice feelings for granted. A world which, as Carrie knew very well, bore no relation to anything on this planet. It was all a part of the same thing as her mother's extraordinary indifference and obtuseness about the jewels. Who, in their senses, would have handed over five, perhaps seven, thousand pounds worth of jewels like that? Who, with any proper perception, would have failed to realise that Carrie and Lavinia ought to have at least a share? Not to mention Edith. They would not have grudged poor Edith a brooch. After all, Edith was Father's daughter. But her mother had given everything away, as though it were so much useless lumber, just as she had now delivered herself and her purse gaily into the hands of an old shark called Bucktrout.

Carrie, however, found great consolation in talking the matter over at immense and repetitive length with her relations. Their solidarity was thereby increased. They all thoroughly enjoyed their gatherings over the tea-table—tea was their favourite, perhaps because the cheapest, meal—and nobody minded how often somebody else said the same thing, even framed in the same words. They listened each time with renewed approval, nodding their heads as though some new and illuminating discovery had just been made. Carrie and her relations found great reassurance in assertion and re-assertion. Say a thing often enough, and it becomes true; by hammering in sufficient stakes of similar pattern they erected a stockade between themselves and the wild dangers of life. The phrase 'Mother is wonderful,' so prevalent between the death and the funeral, was rapidly replaced by the phrase 'Dear Mother—so hopeless over anything practical.' But having said that—and having said it with commendable perseverance, in Queen's Gate where William and Lavinia lived, in Lower Sloane Street where Carrie and Roland lived, in the Cromwell Road where Charles had his flat, in Cadogan Square where Herbert and Mabel lived—having said that, they were brought up short against their inability to cope with that softly hopeless Mother. So amenable, so malleable always, she had routed them completely—she, and her house at Hampstead, and her Mr. Bucktrout. They had none of them seen Mr. Bucktrout; they had none of them been allowed to see him; even Carrie had been rejected, and her offer of lifts in the motor; but his invisibility added only fuel to the fire of their mistrust. He became 'This man who has Got Hold of Mother.' If Lady Slane had not already given all the pearls, the jade, the rubies, and the emeralds in that haphazard fashion to Herbert and Mabel, they would have suspected her of handing them all over to Mr. Bucktrout at Mr. Bucktrout's suggestion. This Mr. Bucktrout, with his vagueness about the lease, with his helpfulness about carpenters, painters, plumbers, and upholsterers— what could he be but a shark? At the very best, his motive resolved itself for Carrie and her family into the ominous word Commission.

Meanwhile, Mr. Bucktrout had secured the services of Mr. Gosheron.

'You must understand,' he said to this estimable tradesman, 'that Lady Slane, despite her high position, is a lady of limited means. It is not always safe, Mr. Gosheron, to assume affluence in the aristocracy. Because a gentleman has been Viceroy of India and Prime Minister of England it does not mean that his relict is left well-off. Our public services, Mr. Gosheron, are conducted on very different principles. Therefore it becomes incumbent on you, Mr. Gosheron, to keep your estimate as low as is compatible with your own reasonable profit. As an agent, and also as an owner of property, I have some experience in such matters. And I assure you that I shall make it my business to check your estimates on Lady Slane's behalf as it were upon my own.'

Mr. Gosheron assured Mr. Bucktrout in return that he would never dream of taking advantage of her ladyship.

Genoux, from the first time that she saw him, took a fancy to Mr. Gosheron. 'Voilà un monsieur,' she said, 'qui connaît son travail. Il sait par exemple,' she added, 'quels weights il faut mettre dans les rideaux. Et il sait faire de la peinture pour que ça ne stick pas. J'aime,' she added, 'le bon travail—pas trop cher, mais pas de pacotille.' Genoux and Lady Slane, liberated from Carrie, spent very happy days with Mr. Bucktrout and Mr. Gosheron. Lady Slane liked everything about Mr. Gosheron, even to his appearance. He looked most respectable, and invariably wore an old bowler hat, green with age, which he never removed even in the house, but which, in order to show some respect to Lady Slane, he would tilt forward by the back brim, and would then resettle into place. His hair, which had once been brown, but now was grey and stringy, invariably became disarranged by this tilting of the hat, so that after the tilting a strand stuck out at the back, fascinating Lady Slane, but unnoticed by its owner. He carried a pencil always behind his ear, a pencil so broad and of so soft a lead that it could serve for nothing except making a mark across a plank of wood, but which Lady Slane never saw used for any other purpose than scratching his head. In him she quickly recognised one of those craftsmen who find fault with all work not carried out under their own auspices. 'That's a poor sort of contraption,' Mr. Gosheron would mutter, examining the damper of the kitchen range. He contrived to imply always that, had the job been left to him, he would have managed it a great deal better. Nevertheless, he implied at the same time, a man of his experience could put it right; could improve, though not quite satisfactorily, on a thoroughly bad job. Silent as a rule, and subdued in the presence of Mr. Bucktrout, he occasionally indulged in an outburst of his own. Lady Slane was especially delighted when he indulged in outbursts, such as his outbursts against asbestos-roofed sectional bungalows. These outbursts were the more valuable for their rarity. 'I can't understand, my lady,' he said, 'how people can live without beauty.' Mr. Gosheron could see beauty in a deal board, if it were well-fitted, though naturally he preferred an oak one. 'And to think,' he said, 'that some people cover up the grain with paint!' Mr. Gosheron was not a young man; he was seventy if a day, but his traditions went back a hundred years or more. 'These lorries,' he said, 'shaking down the walls!' Henry Slane, always progressive, had seen beauty in lorries even as Mr. Gosheron saw it in a well-carpentered board; but Lady Slane, who for years had striven loyally to keep up with the beauty of lorries, now found herself released back into a far more congenial set of values. She could dally for hours with Mr. Bucktrout and Mr. Gosheron, with Genoux following them about as a solid and stocky chorus. Planted squarely on her two feet, creaking within her brown paper linings, Genoux who had spent her life disapproving on principle of nearly everybody, regarded Mr. Bucktrout and Mr. Gosheron with an approval amounting almost to love. How different they were, how puzzlingly, pleasingly different, from the children of miladi!—for whom, nevertheless, Genoux nourished an awed respect. The two old gentlemen seemed so genuinely anxious that Lady Slane should have everything just as she liked it, yet should be spared all possible expense; when she made tentative suggestions, as to the inclusion of a glass shelf in the bathroom, or whatever it might be, they looked at each other with a glance of confederacy, almost a wink, and invariably said they thought that could be managed. That was the way Genoux liked to see miladi treated—as though she were something precious, and fragile, and unselfish, needing a protective insistence on the rights she would never claim for herself. No one had ever treated her quite like that before. Milord had loved her, of course, and had guarded her always from trouble (milord who always had such beautiful manners with everyone), but he himself was so dominating a personality that other people fell naturally into his shadow. Her children loved her too, or so Genoux supposed, for it was unthinkable to Genoux that a child should not love its mother, even after the age of sixty, but there had been times when Genoux could not at all approve of their manner towards their mother; Lady Charlotte, for instance, was really too tyrannical, arriving at Elm Park Gardens at all hours of the day, her very aspect enough to make a timid old lady tremble. Very often one could detect a veiled impatience behind her words. And they were all too energetic, in Genoux's opinion, except for Lady

Edith and Mr. Kay; they bustled their poor mother about, talking loudly and taking it for granted that her powers were equal with their own. Once, when Lady Slane was going out with Mr. William, she had proposed taking a taxi; but Mr. William had said no, they could quite well go in a bus, and Genoux, who was holding the front door open for them, had nearly produced her purse to offer Mr. William eighteen-pence. She wished now that she had indulged in that piece of irony. It was not reasonable to treat a lady of eighty-eight as though she were only sixty-five. Genoux, who herself was only two years younger than Lady Slane, waxed indignant whenever she put on Lady Slane's galoshes in the hall of Elm Park Gardens and handed her an umbrella to go out into the rain. It was not right, especially when one considered the state Lady Slane had been accustomed to, sitting up on an elephant with a mahout behind her holding a parasol over her head. Genoux had preferred Calcutta to Elm Park Gardens.

But at Hampstead, thanks to Mr. Bucktrout and Mr. Gosheron, the proper atmosphere had been at last achieved. It was modest; there were no aides-de-camp, no princes, but though modest it was warm, and affectionate, and respectful, and vigilant, and generous, just as it should be. Mr. Bucktrout expressed himself in a style which Genoux thought extremely distinguished. He was odd, certainly, but he was a gentleman— un vrai monsieur. He had strange and beautiful ideas; he was never in a hurry; he would break off in the middle of business to talk about Descartes or the satisfying quality of pattern. And when he said pattern, he did not mean the pattern on a wall-paper; he meant the pattern of life. Mr. Gosheron was never in a hurry either. Sometimes, by way of comment, he lifted his bowler hat at the back and scratched his head with his pencil. He spoke very little, and always in a low voice. He deplored the decay of craftsmanship in the modern world; refused to employ trades-union men, and had assembled a troop of workmen most of whom he had trained himself, and who were consequently so old that Genoux was sometimes afraid they would fall off their ladders. The workmen, too, had entered into the conspiracy to please Lady Slane; they greeted her arrival always with beaming smiles, took off their caps, and hastened to move the paint-pots out of her way. Yet for all this leisurely manner pervading the house, the work seemed to proceed quite fast, and there was always some little surprise prepared for Lady Slane every time she came up to Hampstead.

Mr. Bucktrout even gave her little presents, though his delicacy restrained them to a nature so modest and inexpensive that she could accept them without embarrassment. Sometimes it was a plant for her garden, sometimes a vase of flowers set with a curious effect of brilliance on a window-sill in an empty room. He was compelled to set them on a window-sill, he explained, since there were as yet no tables or other furniture, but Lady Slane suspected that he really preferred the window-sill, where he could so dispose his gift that the rays of the sun would fall upon it at the very hour when he expected his tenant. She teased him sometimes by arriving half-an-hour late, but he was undefeated; and once a ring of wet three inches away betrayed him: seeing that she was late, he had gone upstairs again to shift his flowers along into the sun. Old age, thought Lady Slane, must surely content itself with very small pleasures, judging by the pleasure she experienced at this confirmation of her suspicions. Weary, enfeebled, ready to go, she still could amuse herself by playing a tiny game in miniature with Mr. Bucktrout and Mr. Gosheron, a sort of minuet stepped out to a fading music, artificial perhaps, yet symbolic of some reality she had never achieved with her own children. The artificiality lay in the manner, the reality in the heart which invented it. Courtesy ceased to be blankly artificial, when prompted by real esteem; it became, simply, one of the decent, veiling graces; a formula by which a profounder feeling might be conveyed.

They were too old, all three of them, to feel keenly; to compete and circumvent and score. They must fall back upon the old measure of the minuet, in which the gentleman's bow expressed all his appreciative gallantry towards women, and the lady's fan raised a breeze insufficient to flutter her hair. That was old age, when people knew everything so well that they could no longer afford to express it save in symbols. Those days were gone when feeling burst its bounds and poured hot from the foundry, when the heart seemed likely to split with complex and contradictory desires; now there was nothing left but a landscape in monochrome, the features identical but all the colours gone from them, and nothing but a gesture left in the place of speech.

Meanwhile Mr. Bucktrout brought his little offerings, and Lady Slane liked them best when they took the form of flowers. Mr. Bucktrout, as she began to discover him, revealed many little talents, among which a gift for arranging a bunch was not the least. He would make daring and surprising combinations of colour and form, till the result was more like a still-life painting than like a bunch of living flowers, yet informed with a life that no paint could rival. Set upon their window-sill, luminous in the sun, more luminous for the bare boards and plaster surrounding them, their texture appeared lit from within rather than from without. Nor did his inventiveness ever falter, for this week he would produce a bunch as garish as a gipsy, all blue and purple and orange, but next week a bunch discreet as a pastel, all rose and grey with a dash of yellow, and some feathery spray lightly touched with cream. Lady Slane, who might have been a painter, could appreciate his effects. Mr. Bucktrout was an artist, said Lady Slane; and even Genoux, who did not care for flowers in the house because they dropped their petals over tables, and eventually had to be thrown away, making a damp mess in the waste-paper basket, even Genoux commented one day that 'Monsieur aurait dû se faire floriste.'

Little by little, seeing that his efforts were appreciated, his offerings became more personal. The vase of flowers was supplemented by a bunch for Lady Slane to pin against her shoulder. The first occasion having given rise to a difficulty, because, searching under her laces and ruffles, anxious not to disappoint the old gentleman, she could discover no pin, he thereafter always provided a large black safety pin pushed securely through the silver paper wrapped round the stalks, and Lady Slane dutifully used it, though she had been presciently careful to bring one with her. Of such small, tacit, and mutual courtesies was their relationship compact.

One day she asked him why he took so much trouble on her behalf. Why had he made it his business to find Mr. Gosheron for her, to supervise his estimates, to look into every detail of the work? That, surely, was not customary in an agent, even in an owner-agent? Mr. Bucktrout instantly became very serious. 'I have been wondering, Lady Slane,' he said, 'whether you would ask me that question. I am glad that you should have asked it, for I am always in favour of letting the daylight into the thickets of misunderstanding. You are right: it is not customary. Let us say that I do it because I have very little else to do, and that so long as you do not object, I am grateful to you for affording me the occupation.'

'No,' said Lady Slane, shy but determined; 'that is not the reason. Why do you take my interests in this way? You see, Mr. Bucktrout, not only do you control Mr. Gosheron—who, as a matter of fact, needs less controlling than any tradesman I ever met—but from the first you have been anxious to spare me as much as possible. I may not be very well versed in practical matters,' she said with her charming smile, 'but I have seen

enough of the world to realise that business is not usually conducted on your system. Besides, my daughter Charlotte . . .
well, never mind about my daughter Charlotte. The fact
remains that I am puzzled, and also rather curious.'

'I should not like you to think me a simpleton, Lady Slane,'
said Mr. Bucktrout very gravely. He hesitated, as though
wondering whether he should take her into his confidence, then
went off with a rush on another little speech. 'I am not a
simpleton,' he said, 'nor am I a childish old man. I dislike
childishness and all such rubbish. I feel nothing but impatience
with the people who pretend that the world is other than it is.
The world, Lady Slane, is pitiably horrible. It is horrible because
it is based upon competitive struggle—and really one does not
know whether to call the basis of that struggle a convention or a
necessity. Is it some extraordinary delusion, or is it a law of life?
Is it perhaps an animal law from which civilisation may eventually free us? At present it seems to me, Lady Slane, that man
has founded all his calculations upon a mathematical system
fundamentally false. His sums work out right for his own pur-
poses, because he has crammed and constrained his planet into
accepting his premises. Judged by other laws, though the
answers would remain correct, the premises would appear
merely crazy; ingenious enough, but crazy. Perhaps some day a
true civilisation may supervene and write a big W. against all
our answers. But we have a long road to travel yet—a long road
to travel.' He shook his head, pointed his foot, and became sunk
in his musings.

'Then you think,' said Lady Slane, seeing that she must recall
him from his abstractions, 'that anyone who goes against this
extraordinary delusion is helping civilisation on?'

'I do, Lady Slane; most certainly I do. But in a world as at
present constituted, it is a luxury that only poets can afford, or
people advanced in age. I assure you that when I first went into

business, after I had resigned my commission, I was fierce. It is really the only word. Fierce. No one could get the better of me. And the more severe my conduct, the more respect I earned. Nothing earns respect so quickly as letting your fellows see that you are a match for them. Other methods may earn you respect in the long run, but for a short-cut there is nothing like setting a high valuation on yourself and forcing others to accept it. Modesty, moderation, consideration, nicety—no good; they don't pay. If you were to meet one of my earlier colleagues, Lady Slane, he would tell you that in my day I had been a regular Juggernaut.'

'And when did you give up these principles of ruthlessness, Mr. Bucktrout?' asked Lady Slane.

'You do not suspect me of boasting, Lady Slane, do you?' asked Mr. Bucktrout, eyeing her. 'I am telling you all this so that you should realise that *naïveté* is not my weakness. As I said, you must not be allowed to think me a simpleton.— When did I give up these principles? Well, I set a term upon them; I determined that at sixty-five business properly speaking should know me no more. On my sixty-fifth birthday—or, to put it more correctly, on my sixty-sixth—I woke a free man. For my practice had always been a discipline rather than an inclination.'

'But what about this house?' asked Lady Slane. 'You told me that for thirty years you had refused tenants if you didn't like them. Surely that was inclination, wasn't it? It could hardly be described as business?'

'Ah,' said Mr. Bucktrout, putting his finger to his nose, 'you are too shrewd, Lady Slane; you have too good a memory. But don't be too hard on me: this house was always my one little patch of folly. Or, should I say, my one little patch of sanity? I like to be exact in my expressions. I see, Lady Slane, that you are something of a tease. I mean no impertinence. If ladies did not tease, we should be in danger of taking ourselves too seriously. I always had a fancy, you see, that I should like to end my days in this house, so naturally I did not wish its atmosphere contaminated by any unsympathetic influence. You may have noticed—of course you have noticed—that its atmosphere is curiously ripened and detached. I have preserved that atmosphere with the greatest care, for although one cannot create an atmosphere, one can at least safeguard it against disturbance.'

'But if you want to live here yourself—very well, die here yourself,' said Lady Slane, seeing that he had raised a hand and was about to correct her, 'why have you let it to me?'

'Oh,' said Mr. Bucktrout easily and consolingly, 'your tenancy, Lady Slane, is not likely to interfere with my intentions.'

For courteous though he was, Mr. Bucktrout in this respect remained firmly unsentimental, making no bones about the fact that Lady Slane would require the house for a short period only. Whenever he discouraged her from unnecessary expenditure, he did so on the grounds that it was scarcely worth her while. When she mentioned central heating, he reminded her that she would spend but few winters, if any, in this her last abode. 'Though to be sure,' he added sympathetically, 'there is no reason why one should not be comfortable while one may.' Genoux, overhearing this remark, summoned her religion to the support of her indignation. 'Monsieur pense donc qu'il n'y a pas de radiateurs au paradis? Il se fait une idée bien mièvre d'un Bon Dieu peu up-to-date.' Still, Mr. Bucktrout persisted in his idea that oil lamps would suffice to warm the rooms. He worked out the amount of gallons of paraffin they would consume in one winter, and balanced them against the cost of a furnace and pipes to pierce the walls. 'But, Mr. Bucktrout,' said Lady Slane, now without malice, 'as owner and agent you ought to encourage me to put in central heating. Think how strongly it would appeal to your next tenant.' 'Lady Slane,' replied Mr. Bucktrout, 'consideration of my text tenant remains in a separate compartment from consideration of my present tenant. That has always been my rule in life; and thanks to it I have always been able to keep my relationships distinct. I am a great believer in sharp outline. I dislike a fuzz. Most people fell into the error of making their whole life a fuzz, pleasing nobody, least of all themselves. Compromise is the very breath of negation. My principle has been, that it is better to please one person a great deal than to please a number of persons a little, no matter how much offence you give. I have given a great deal of offence in my life, but of not one offensive instance do I repent. I believe in taking the interest of the moment. Life is so transitory, Lady Slane, that one must grab it by the tail as it flies past. No good in thinking of yesterday or to-morrow. Yesterday is gone, and to-morrow problematical. Even to-day is precarious enough, God knows. Therefore I say unto you,' said Mr. Bucktrout, relapsing into Biblical language and pointing his foot as though to point his words, 'do not put in central heating, for you know not how long you may live to enjoy it. My next tenant is welcome to warm himself in hell. I am here to advise you; and my advice is, buy an oil-lamp—several oil-lamps. They will warm you and see you out, however often you may have to renew the wicks.' He changed his foot, and frisked his coat-tails in a little perorative flourish. Mr. Gosheron, rather embarrassed, tilted his hat.

This conviction of the transcience of her tenure arose, Lady Slane discovered, from two causes: Mr. Bucktrout's estimate of her own age, and his prophetic views as to the imminent end of the world. He discoursed gravely on this subject, undeterred by the presence of Genoux and Mr. Gosheron, who preferred to avoid such topics and wanted respectively to talk of linen-cupboards and distemper. Genoux's sheets must wait, and Mr. Gosheron's little discs of colour, miniature full-moons, called

Pompeian-red, Stone-grey, Olive-green, Shrimp-pink. Mr. Bucktrout's attention was too closely engaged with eternity for linen-cupboards and distemper to catch him in more than a perfunctory interest. He could bear with them for five minutes; not longer. After that he would stick his sarcasm into Mr. Gosheron, saying such things as that his yard-measure varied in length from room to room, according as it ran north and south, or east and west, and that Genoux's shelves could never be truly level, seeing that the whole universe was based upon a curve, all of which disconcerted Genoux and Mr. Gosheron, but made Genoux respect Mr. Bucktrout the more for his learning, and made Mr. Gosheron's hat tilt nearly on to the tip of his nose. Mr. Bucktrout, observing this confusion, enlarged with sadistic pleasure. He knew that he had an appreciative audience in Lady Slane, even while he kept his feet on the ground sufficiently for her protection. 'As you may know,' he said, standing in an unfinished room while painters suspended their brushes in order to listen, 'there are at least four theories presaging the end of the world. Flame, flood, frost, and collision. There are others, but they are so unscientific and so improbable as to be negligible. Then there are, of course, the prophetic numbers. In so far as I believe numbers to be a basic part of the eternal harmonies, I am a convinced Pythagorean. Numbers exist in the void; it is impossible to imagine the destruction of numbers, even though you imagine the destruction of the universe. I do not mean by this that I hold with such ingenuities as the great sacred number of the Babylonians, twelve million nine hundred and sixty thousand, as you remember, nor yet in such calculations as William Miller's, who, by a system of additions and deductions, decided that the world would end on March 21, 1843. No. I have worked out my own system, Lady Slane, and I can assure you that, though distressing, it is irrefutable. The great annihilation is close at hand.' Mr. Bucktrout was launched; he tiptoed across to the wall, and very carefully wrote up PΩMH with a bit of chalk. A painter came after him, and as carefully obliterated it with his brush.

'Mais en attendant, miladi,' said Genoux, 'mes draps?'

Lady Slane had never taken so much pleasure in anybody's company. She had never been so happy as with her two old gentleman. She had played her part among brilliant people, important people, she had accommodated herself to their conversation, and, during the years of her association with worldly affairs, she had learnt to put together the scattered bits of information which to her were so difficult to collate or even to remember; thus she was always reminded of the days of her girlhood, when vast gaps seemed to exist in her knowledge, and when she was at a loss to know what people meant when they referred to the Irish Question or the Woman's Movement, or to Free Trade and Protection, two especial stumbling blocks between which she could never distinguish instinctively, although she had had them explained to her a dozen times. She had always taken an enormous amount of trouble to disguise her ignorance from Henry. In the end she had learnt to succeed quite well, and he would disburden himself of his political perplexities without the slightest suspicion that his wife had long since lost the basis of his argument. She was secretly and bitterly ashamed of her insufficiency. But what was to be done about it? She could not, no, she simply could not, remember why Mr. Asquith disliked Mr. Lloyd George, or what exactly were the aims of Labour, that new and alarming Party. The most that she could do was to conceal her ignorance, while she scrambled round frenziedly in her brain for some recollected scrap of associated information which would enable her to make some adequate reply. During their years in Paris she had suffered especially, for the cleverness of French conversation (which she greatly admired) always made her feel outwitted; and though she could sit listening for hours in rapture to the spitting pyrotechnics of epigram and summary, marvelling at the ability of other people to compress into a phrase some aspect of life which, to her, from its very importance, demanded a lifetime of reflection, yet her quiescent pleasure was always spoilt by the dread that at a given moment some guest in mistaken politeness would turn to her, throwing her the ball she would be unable to catch, saying, 'Et Madame l'Ambassadrice, qu'en pense-t-elle?' And though she knew that inwardly she had understood what they were saying far better than they had understood it themselves—for the conversation of the French always seemed to turn upon the subjects which interested her most deeply, and about which she felt that she really knew something, could she but have expressed it—she remained stupidly inarticulate, saying something non-committal or something that she did not in the least mean, conscious meanwhile that Henry, sitting by, must be suffering wretchedly from the poor figure his wife cut. Yet, in private, he was apt to say, though rarely, that she was the most intelligent woman he knew because, although often inarticulate, she never made a foolish remark.

That these agonies should remain private to herself was her constant prayer; neither Henry nor the guests at her table must ever find her out. There were other allied weaknesses of which she was also ashamed, though in a slightly less degree: her inability, for instance, to write out a cheque correctly, putting the same amount in figures as in words, remembering to cross it, remembering to sign her name; her inability to understand what a debenture was, or the difference between ordinary and deferred stock; and as for that extraordinary menagerie of bulls, bears, stags, and contango, she might as well have found herself in a circus of wild animals. She supposed dutifully that these things were of major importance, since they were clearly the things which kept the world on the move; she supposed that party politics and war and industry, and a high birth-rate (which she had learned to call manpower), and competition and secret diplomacy and suspicion, were all part of a necessary game, necessary since the cleverest people she knew made it their business, though to her, as a game, unintelligible; she supposed it must be so, though the feeling more frequently seized her of watching figures moving in the delusion of a terrible and ridiculous dream. The whole tragic system seemed to be based upon an extraordinary convention, as incomprehensible as the theory of money, which (so she had been told) bore no relation to the actual supply of gold. It was chance which had made men turn gold into their symbol, rather than stones; it was chance which had made men turn strife into their principle, rather than amity. That the planet might have got on better with stones and amity —a simple solution—had apparently never occurred to its inhabitants.

Her own children, do what she might, had grown up in the same traditions. Naturally. There they were, trying and striving, not content merely to *be*. Herbert, so sententious always, so ambitious in his stupid way; Carrie with her committees and her harsh managing voice, interfering with people who did not want to be interfered with, all for the love of interference, her mother felt sure; Charles with his perpetual grievances; William and Lavinia, always scraping and saving and paring, an occupation in itself. There was no true kindliness, no grace, no privacy in any of them. For Edith and Kay alone their mother could feel some sympathy: Edith, always in a muddle, trying to get things straight and only getting them more tangled, trying to stand back and take a look at life, the whole of it, an impossibility accepted by most people, but which really bothered Edith and made her unhappy (still, the uneasiness did her credit); Kay— well, of all her children, perhaps Kay, messing about among his compasses and astrolabes, was the one who strove and struggled least; the one who had, without knowing it, the strongest sense of his own entity, when he shut his door behind him and took out his duster to potter with it along the alignment of his shelves. Yes, Kay and Edith were nearest to her; that would be one of the secrets, one of the jokes, she would take away with her into the grave.

For the rest, she had been a lonely woman, always at variance with the creeds to which she apparently conformed. Every now and then she had known some delicious encounter with a spirit attuned to her own. There had been the young man who accompanied them to Fatihpur Sikhri; a young man whose name she had forgotten, or had never known; but into whose eyes she had looked for one moment, and then, disturbed, had dismissed by her very gesture of strolling off to rejoin the Viceroy and his group of sun-helmeted officials. Such encounters had been rare, and, thanks to the circumstances of her life, brief. (She retained, however, a conviction that many spirits were fundamentally attuned, but so thickly overlaid by the formulas of the world that the clear requisite note could no longer be struck.) With Mr. Bucktrout and Mr. Gosheron she found herself entirely at ease. She could tell Mr. Bucktrout without embarrassment that she was unable to distinguish rates from taxes. She could tell Mr. Gosheron that she was unable to distinguish between a volt and an ampère. Neither of them tried to explain. They gave up at once, and simply said, leave it to me. She left it, and knew that her trust would not be misplaced.

Strange, the relief and release that this companionship brought her! Was it due to the weariness of old age, or to the long-awaited return to childhood, when all decisions and responsibilities might again be left in the hands of others, and one might be free to dream in a world of whose sunshine and benignity one was convinced? And she thought, if only I were young once more I would stand for all that was calm and contemplative, opposed to the active, the scheming, the striving, the false—yes! the false, she exclaimed, striking her fist into the palm of the other hand with unaccustomed energy; and then, trying to correct herself, she wondered whether this were not merely a negative creed, a negation of life; perhaps even a confession of insufficient vitality; and came to the conclusion that it was not so, for in contemplation (and also in the pursuit of the one chosen avocation which she had had to renounce) she could pierce to a happier life more truly than her children who reckoned things by their results and activities.

She remembered how, crossing the Persian desert with Henry, their cart had been escorted by flocks of butterflies, white and yellow, which danced on either side and overhead and all around them, now flying ahead in a concerted movement, now returning to accompany them, amused as it were to restrain their swift frivolity to a flitting round this lumbering conveyance, but still unable to suit their pace to such sobriety, so, to relieve their impatience, soaring up into the air or dipping between the very axles, coming out on the other side before the horses had had time to put down another hoof; making, all the while, little smuts of shadow on the sand, like little black anchors dropped, tethering them by invisible cables to earth, but dragged about with the same capricious swiftness, obliged to follow; and she remembered thinking, lulled by the monotonous progression that trailed after the sun from dawn to dusk, like a plough that should pursue the sun in one straight slow furrow round and round the world—she remembered thinking that this was something like her own life, following Henry Holland like the sun, but every now and then moving into a cloud of butterflies which were her own irreverent, irrelevant thoughts, darting and dancing, but altering the pace of the progression not by one tittle; never brushing the carriage with their wings; flickering always, and evading; sometimes rushing on ahead, but returning again to tease and to show off, darting between the axles; having an independent and a lovely life; a flock of ragamuffins skimming above the surface of the desert and around the trundling waggon; but Henry, who was travelling on a tour of investigation, could only say, 'Terrible, the ophthalmia among these people—I must really do something about it,' and, knowing that he was right and would speak to the missionaries, she had withdrawn her attention from the butterflies and had transferred it to her duty, determining that when they reached Yezd or Shiraz, or wherever it might be, she also would take the missionaries' wives to task about the ophthalmia in the villages and would make arrangements for a further supply of boracic to be sent out from England.

But, perversely, the flittering of the butterflies had always remained more important.

Part Two

Her heart sat silent through the noise
And concourse of the street;
There was no hurry in her hands,
No hurry in her feet.
                    CHRISTINA ROSSETTI

Sitting there in the sun at Hampstead, in the late summer, under the south wall and the ripened peaches, doing nothing with her hands, she remembered the day she had become engaged to Henry. She had plenty of leisure now, day in, day out, to survey her life as a tract of country traversed, and at last become a landscape instead of separate fields or separate years and days, so that it became a unity and she could see the whole view, and could even pick out a particular field and wander round it again in spirit, though seeing it all the while as it were from a height, fallen into its proper place, with the exact pattern drawn round it by the hedge, and the next field into which the gap in the hedge would lead. So, she thought, could she at last put circles round her life. Slowly she crossed that day, as one crosses a field by a little path through the grasses, with the sorrel and the buttercups waving on either side; she crossed it again slowly, from breakfast to bed-time, and each hour, as one hand of the

689

clock passed over the other, regained for her its separate character: this was the hour, she thought, when I first came downstairs that day, swinging my hat by its ribbons; and this was the
hour when he persuaded me into the garden, and sat with me on
the seat beside the lake, and told me it was not true that with one
blow of its wing a swan could break the leg of a man. She had
listened to him, paying dutiful attention to the swan which had
actually drifted up to them by the bank, dipping its beak and
then curving to probe irritably into the snowy tuft of feathers
on its breast; but she was thinking less of the swan than of
the young whiskers on Henry's cheek, only her thoughts had
merged, so that she wondered whether Henry's brown curls
were as soft as the feathers on the breast of the swan, and all but
reached out an idle hand to feel them. Then he passed from the
swan, as though that had been but a gambit to cover his hesitation, and the next thing she knew was that he was speaking
earnestly, bending forward and even fingering a flounce of her
dress, as though anxious, although unaware of his anxiety, to
establish some kind of contact between himself and her; but for
her all true contact had been severed from the moment he began
to speak so earnestly, and she felt no longer even the slight tug of
desire to put out her hand and touch the curly whiskers on his
cheek. Those words which he must utter so earnestly, in order
that his tone might carry their full weight; those words which
he seemed to produce from some serious and secret place,
hauling them up from the bottom of the well of his personality;
those words which belonged to the region of weighty and adult
things—those words removed him from her more rapidly than
an eagle catching him up in its talons to the sky. He had gone.
He had left her. Even while she conscientiously gazed at him and
listened, she knew that he was already miles and miles away. He
had passed into the sphere where people marry, beget and bear
children, bring them up, give orders to servants, pay income-

tax, understand about dividends, speak mysteriously in the presence of the young, take decisions for themselves, eat what they like, and go to bed at the hour which pleases them. Mr. Holland was asking her to accompany him into that sphere. He was asking her to be his wife.

It was clearly impossible, to her mind, that she should accept. The idea was preposterous. She could not possibly follow Mr. Holland into that sphere; could follow him, perhaps, less than any man, for she knew him to be very brilliant, and marked out for that most remote and impressive of mysteries, a Career. She had heard her father say that young Holland would be Viceroy of India before they had heard the last of him. That would mean that she must be Vicereine, and at the thought she had turned upon him the glance of a startled fawn. Instantly interpreting that glance according to his desires, Mr. Holland had clasped her in his arms and had kissed her with ardour but with restraint upon the lips.

What was a poor girl to do? Before she well knew what was happening, there was her mother smiling through tears, her father putting his hand on Mr. Holland's shoulder, her sisters asking if they might all be bridesmaids, and Mr. Holland himself standing very upright, very proud, very silent, smiling a little, bowing, and looking at her with an expression that even her inexperience could define only as proprietary. In a trice, like that, she had been changed from the person she was into somebody completely different. Or had she not? She could not detect any metamorphosis as having taken place within herself to match the sudden crop of smiles on all those faces. She certainly felt the same as before. A sense of terror possessed her over the novelty of her opinion being sought on any matter, and she hastily restored the decision into the hands of others. By this method she felt that she might delay the moment when she must definitely and irrevocably become that other person.

She could go on, for a little, secretly continuing to be herself.

And what, precisely, had been herself, she wondered—an old woman looking back on the girl she once had been? This wondering was the softest, most wistful, of occupations; yet it was not melancholy; it was, rather, the last, supreme luxury; a luxury she had waited all her life to indulge. There was just time, in this reprieve before death, to indulge herself to the full. She had, after all, nothing else to do. For the first time in her life—no, for the first time since her marriage—she had nothing else to do. She could lie back against death and examine life. Meanwhile, the air was full of the sound of bees.

She saw herself as a young girl walking beside the lake. She walked slowly, swinging her hat; she walked meditatively, her eyes cast down, and as she walked she prodded the tip of her parasol into the spongy earth. She wore the flounced and feminine muslins of 1860. Her hair was ringleted, and one ringlet escaped and fell softly against her neck. A curly spaniel accompanied her, snuffling into the bushes. They had all the appearance of a girl and a dog in an engraving from some sentimental keepsake. Yes, that was she, Deborah Lee, not Deborah Holland, not Deborah Slane; the old woman closed her eyes, the better to hold the vision. The girl walking beside the lake was unaware, but the old woman beheld the whole of adolescence, as who should catch a petal in the act of unfolding; dewy, wavering, virginal, eager, blown by generous yet shy impulses, as timid as a leveret and as swift, as confiding as a doe peeping between the tree trunks, as light-foot as a dancer waiting in the wings, as soft and scented as a damask rose, as full of laughter as a fountain—yes, that was youth, hesitant as one upon an unknown threshold, yet ready to run her breast against a spear. The old woman looked closer; she saw the tender flesh, the fragile curves, the deep and glistening eyes, the untried mouth, the ringless hands; and, loving the girl that she had been, she

tried to catch some tone of her voice, but the girl remained
silent, walking as though behind a wall of glass. She was alone.
That meditative solitude seemed a part of her very essence.
Whatever else might be in her head, it was certain that neither
love, nor romance, nor any of the emotions usually ascribed to
the young, were in it. If she dreamed, it was of no young Adam.
And there again, thought Lady Slane, one should not wrong the
young by circumscribing them with one sole set of notions, for
youth is richer than that; youth is full of hopes reaching out,
youth will burn the river and set all the belfries of the world
ringing; there is not only love to be considered, there are also
such things as fame and achievement and genius—which might
be in one's heart, knocking against one's ribs, who knows? let
us retire quickly to a turret, and see if the genius within one will
not declare itself. But, dear me, thought Lady Slane, it was a
poor lookout in eighteen-sixty for a girl to think of fame.

For Lady Slane was in the fortunate position of seeing into the
heart of the girl who had been herself. She could mark not only
the lingering step, the pause, the frowning brows, the prod of
the parasol into the earth, the broken reflection quivering down
into the waters of the lake; she could read also into the thoughts
which accompanied this solitary ramble. She could make herself
a party to their secrecy and their extravagance. For the thoughts
which ran behind this delicate and maidenly exterior were of an
extravagance to do credit even to a wild young man. They were
thoughts of nothing less than escape and disguise; a changed
name, a travestied sex, and freedom in some foreign city—
schemes on a par with the schemes of a boy about to run away to
sea. Those ringlets would drop beneath the scissors—and here a
hand stole upward, as though prophetically to caress a shorn
sleek head; that fichu would be replaced by a shirt—and here the
fingers felt for the knot of a tie; those skirts would be kicked
for ever aside—and here, very shyly this time, the hand dropped

towards the opening of a trouser pocket. The image of the girl faded, and in its place stood a slender boy. He was a boy, but essentially he was a sexless creature, a mere symbol and emanation of youth, one who had forsworn for ever the delights and rights of sex to serve what seemed to his rioting imagination a nobler aim. Deborah, in short, at the age of seventeen, had determined to become a painter.

The sun, which had been warming her old bones and the peaches on the wall, crept westering behind a house so that she shivered slightly, and rising, dragged her chair forward on to the still sunlit grass. She would follow that bygone ambition from its dubious birth, through the months when it steadied and increased and coursed like blood through her, to the days when it languished and lost heart, for all her efforts to keep it alive. She saw it now for what it was: the only thing of value that had entered her life. Reality she had had in plenty, or what with other women passed for reality—but she could not go into those realities now, she must attach herself to that transcending reality for as long as she could hold it, it was so firm, it made her so happy even to remember how it had once sustained her; for she was not merely telling herself about it now, but feeling it again, right down in some deep place; it had the pervading nature of love while love is strong, unlike the cold recital of love in reminiscence. She burned again with the same ecstasy, the same exaltation. How fine it had been, to live in that state of rapture! how fine, how difficult, how supremely worth while! A nun in her novitiate was not more vigilant than she. Drawn tight as a firm wire, she had trembled then to a touch; she had been poised as a young god in the integrity of creation. Images clustered in her mind, but every image must be of a nature extravagantly lyrical. Nothing else would fit. A crimson cloak, a silver sword, were neither sumptuous enough nor pure enough to express the ardours of that temper. By God, she exclaimed, the young blood running again generously through her, that is a life worth living! The life of the artist, the creator, looking closely, feeling widely; detail and horizon included in the same sweep of the glance. And she remembered how the shadow on the wall was a greater delight to her than the thing itself, and how she had looked at a stormy sky, or at a tulip in the sun, and, narrowing her eyes, had forced those things into relation with everything that made a pattern in her mind.

So for months she had lived intensely, secretly, building herself in preparation, though she never laid brush to canvas, and only dreamed herself away into the far future. She could gauge the idleness of ordinary life by the sagging of her spirits whenever the flame momentarily burnt lower. Those glimpses of futility alarmed her beyond all reason. The flame had gone out, she thought in terror, every time it drooped; it would never revive; she must be left cold and unillumined. She could never learn that it would return, as the great garland of rhythm swept once more upwards and the light poured over her, warm as the reappearing sun, incandescent as a star, and on wings she rose again, steadying in their flight. It was thus a life of extremes that she lived, at one moment rapt, at another moment sunk in despondency. But of all this not one flicker mounted to the surface.

Some instinct, perhaps, warned her to impart her unsuitable secret to none, knowing very well that her parents, indulgent indeed, but limited, as was natural, would receive her declaration with a smile and a pat on the head, and an interchanged glance passing between themselves, saying as plainly as possible, 'That's our pretty bird! and the first personable young man who comes along will soon put these notions to rout.' Or, perhaps, it was merely the treasured privacy of the artist which kept her silent. She was as docile as could be. She would run errands in the house for her mother, strip the lavender into a great cloth, make bags for it to lie between the sheets, write labels for the pots of jam, brush the pug, and fetch her cross-stitch after dinner without being bidden. Acquaintances envied her parents their eldest daughter. There were many who already had an eye on her as a wife for their son. But a thread of ambition was said to run through the modest and ordered household, a single thread, for Deborah's parents, arrived at middle age with their quiver-full of sons and daughters, preferred their easy rural domesticity to any worldly advantage, but for Deborah their aims were different: Deborah must be the wife of a good man, certainly, but if also the wife of a man to whose career she might be a help and an ornament—why, then, so much the better. Of this, naturally, nothing was said to Deborah. It would not do to turn the child's head.

Lady Slane rose again and drew her chair a little farther forward into the sun, for the shadow was beginning to creep, chilling her.

Her eldest brother had been away, she remembered; he was twenty-three; he had left home, as young men do; he had gone out into the world. She wondered sometimes what young men did, out in the world; she imagined them laughing and ruffling; going here and there, freely; striding home through the empty streets at dawn, or hailing a hansom and driving off to Richmond. They talked with strangers; they entered shops; they frequented the theatres. They had a club—several clubs. They were accosted by importunate women in the shadows, and could take their bodies for a night into their thoughtless embrace. Whatever they did, they did with a fine carelessness, a fine freedom, and when they came home they need give no account of their doings; moreover, there was an air of free-masonry among men, based upon their common liberty, very different from the freemasonry among women, which was always prying and personal and somehow a trifle obscene. But if the difference between her lot and her brother's occurred to Deborah, she said nothing of it. Beside the spaciousness of his opportunity and experience, she might justifiably feel a little cramped. If he, choosing to read for the Bar, were commended and applauded in his choice, why should she, choosing to be a painter, so shrink from announcing her decision that she was driven to secret and desperate plans for travesty and flight? There was surely a discrepancy somewhere. But everybody seemed agreed—so well agreed, that the matter was not even discussed: there was only one employment open to women.

The solidity of this agreement was brought home to Deborah from the moment that Mr. Holland led her to her mother from the lake. She had been a favourite child, but never had the rays of approval beaten down so warmly upon her. She was put in mind of those Italian pictures, showing heaven opened and the Eternal Father beaming down between golden rays like the sticks of a fan, so that one stretched out one's fingers to warm them at the glow of his benignity, as at the bars of a fire. So now with Deborah and her parents, not to mention the rest of her world, she was made to feel that in becoming engaged to Mr. Holland she had performed an act of exceeding though joyful virtue, had in fact done that which had always been expected of her; had fulfilled herself, besides giving enormous satisfaction to other people. She found herself suddenly surrounded by a host of assumptions. It was assumed that she trembled for joy in his presence, languished in his absence, existed solely (but humbly) for the furtherance of his ambitions, and thought him the most remarkable man alive, as she herself was the most favoured of women, a belief in which everybody was fondly prepared to indulge her. Such was the unanimity of these assumptions that she was almost persuaded into believing them true.

This was all very well, and for some days she allowed herself a little game of make-believe, imagining that she would be able to extricate herself without too much difficulty, for she was but eighteen, and it is pleasant to be praised, especially by those of whom one stands in affectionate awe; but presently she perceived that innumerable little strands like the thread of a spider were fastening themselves round her wrists and ankles, and that each one of them ran up to its other end in somebody's heart. There was her father's heart, and Mr. Holland's—whom she had learnt to call, but not very readily, Henry—and as for her mother's heart, that might have been a railway terminus, so many shining threads ran up into it out of sight—threads of pride and love and relief and maternal agitation and feminine welcome of fuss. Deborah stood there, bound and perplexed, and wondering what she should do next. Meanwhile, as she stood, feeling as silly as a May-queen with the streamers winding round her, she discerned upon the horizon people arriving with gifts, all converging upon her, as vassals bearing tribute: Henry with a ring—and the placing of it upon her finger was a real ceremony; her sisters with a dressing-bag they had clubbed together to buy; and then her mother with enough linen to rig a wind-jammer: table-cloths, dinner-napkins, towels (hand and bath), tea-cloths, kitchen rubbers, pantry cloths, dusters, and, of course, sheets, which when displayed proved to be double, and all embroidered with a monogram, not at first sight decipherable, but which on closer inspection Deborah disentangled into the letters D.H. After that, she was lost. She was lost into the foam and billows of silks, satins, poplins, and alpacas, while women knelt and crawled around her with their mouths full of pins, and she herself was made to stand, and turn, and bend her arm, and straighten it again, and was told to step out carefully, while the skirt made a ring on the floor, and was told that she must bear having her stays pulled a little tighter, for the lining had been cut a shade too small. It seemed to her then that she was always tired, and that people showed their love for her by making her more tired than she already was, by piling up her obligations and dancing round her until she knew not whether she stood still or spun round like a top; and time also seemed to have entered into the conspiracy, maliciously shortening the days, so that they rushed her along and were no more than a snowstorm of notes and tissue paper and of white roses that came every day from the florist by Henry's order. Yet all the time, as an undercurrent, the older women seemed to have a kind of secret among themselves, a reason for sage smiles and glances, a secret whereby something of Deborah's strength must be saved from this sweet turmoil and stored up for some greater demand that would be put upon her.

Indeed, these weeks before the wedding were dedicated wholly to the rites of a mysterious feminism. Never, Deborah thought, had she been surrounded by so many women. Matriarchy ruled. Men might have dwindled into insignificance on the planet. Even Henry himself did not count for much. (Yet he was there, terribly there, in the background; and thus, she thought, might a Theban mother have tired her daughter before sending her off to the Minotaur.) Women appeared from all quarters: aunts, cousins, friends, dressmakers, corsetières, milliners, and even a young French maid, whom Deborah was to have for her own, and who regarded her new mistress with wondering eyes, as one upon whom the gods had set their seal. In these rites Deborah—another assumption—was expected to play a most complicated part. She was expected to know what it was all about, and yet the core of the mystery was to remain hidden from her. She was to be the recipient of smiling congratulations, yet also she must be addressed as 'My little Deborah!' an exclamation from which she suspected that the adjective 'poor' was missing just by chance, and clipped in long embraces, almost valedictory in their benevolence. Oh, what a pother, she thought, women make about marriage! and yet who can blame them, she added, when one recollects that marriage—and its consequences—is the only thing that women have to make a pother about in the whole of their lives? Though the excitement be vicarious, it will do just as well. Is it not for this function that they had been formed, dressed, bedizened, educated—if so one-sided an affair may be called education—safeguarded, kept in the dark, hinted at, segregated, repressed, all that at a given moment they may be delivered, or may deliver their daughters over, to Minister to a Man?

But how on earth she was going to minister to him, Deborah did not know. She knew only that she remained completely alien to all this fuss about the wonderful opportunity which was to be hers. She supposed that she was not in love with Henry, but, even had she been in love with him, she could see therein no reason for foregoing the whole of her own separate existence. Henry was in love with her, but no one proposed that he should forego his. On the contrary, it appeared that in acquiring her he was merely adding something extra to it. He would continue to lunch with his friends, travel down to his constituency, and spend his evenings at the House of Commons; he would continue to enjoy his free, varied, and masculine life, with no ring upon his finger or difference in his name to indicate the change in his estate; but whenever he felt inclined to come home she must be there, ready to lay down her book, her paper, or her letters; she must be prepared to listen to whatever he had to say; she must entertain his political acquaintances; and even if he beckoned her across the world she must follow. Well, she thought, that recalled Ruth and Boaz and was very pleasant for Henry. No doubt he would do his part by her, as he understood it. Sitting down by her, as her needle plucked in and out of her embroidery, he would gaze fondly at her bent head, and would say he was lucky to have such a pretty little wife to come back to. For all his grandeur as a Cabinet Minister, he would say it

like any middle-class or working-man husband. And she ought
to look up, rewarded. For all his grandeur and desirability as
Governor or Viceroy, he would disregard the blandishments of
women ambitious for their husbands, beyond the necessary
gallantries of social intercourse, and would be faithful to her, so
that the green snake of jealousy would never slip across her path.
He would advance in honours, and with a genuine pride would
see a coronet appear on the head of the little black shadow which
had doubled him for so many years. But where, in such a programme, was there room for a studio?

It would not do if Henry were to return one evening and be
met by a locked door. It would not do if Henry, short of ink or
blotting-paper, were to emerge irritably only to be told that
Mrs. Holland was engaged with a model. It would not do if
Henry were appointed governor to some distant colony, to tell
him that the drawing-master unfortunately lived in London. It
would not do, if Henry wanted another son, to tell him that she
had just embarked on a special course of study. It would not do,
in such a world of assumptions, to assume that she had equal
rights with Henry. For such privileges marriage was not
ordained.

But for certain privileges marriage had been ordained, and
going to her bedroom Deborah took out her prayer-book and
turned up the Marriage Service. It was ordained for the pro-
creation of children—well, she knew that; one of her friends had
told her, before she had time to stop her ears. It was ordained so
that women might be loving and amiable, faithful and obedient
to their husbands, holy and godly matrons in all quietness,
sobriety, and peace. All this no doubt was, to a certain extent,
parliamentary language. But still it bore a certain relation to fact.
And still she asked, where, in this system, was there room for a
studio?

Henry, always charming and courteous, and now very much

in love, smiled most indulgently when she finally brought herself to ask him if he would object to her painting after they were married. Object! of course he would not object. He thought an elegant accomplishment most becoming in a woman. 'I confess,' he said, 'that of all feminine accomplishments the piano is my favourite, but since your talent lies in another direction, my dearest, why then we'll make the best of it.' And he went on to say how pleasant it would be for them both if she kept a record of their travels, and mentioned something about water-colour sketches in an album, which they could show their friends at home. But when Deborah said that that was not quite what she had in mind—she had thought of something more serious, she said, though her heart was in her mouth as she said it—he had smiled again, more fondly and indulgently than ever, and had said there would be plenty of time to see about that, but for his own part, he fancied that after marriage she would find plenty of other occupations to help her pass the days.

Then, indeed, she felt trapped and wild. She knew very well what he meant. She hated him for his Jovian detachment and superiority, for his fond but nevertheless smug assumptions, for his easy kindliness, and most of all for the impossibility of blaming him. He was not to blame. He had only taken for granted the things he was entitled to take for granted, thereby ranging himself with the women and entering into the general conspiracy to defraud her of her chosen life.

She was very childish, very tentative, very uncertain, very unaware. But at least she did recognise that the conversation had been momentous. She had her answer. She never referred to it again.

Yet she was no feminist. She was too wise a woman to indulge in such luxuries as an imagined martyrdom. The rift between herself and life was not the rift between man and woman, but the rift between the worker and the dreamer. That she was a woman, and Henry a man, was really a matter of chance. She would go no further than to acknowledge that the fact of her being a woman made the situation a degree more difficult.

Lady Slane dragged her chair this time half-way down the little garden. Genoux saw her from the windows and came out with a rug, 'pour m'assurer que miladi ne prendra pas froid. Que dirait ce pauvre milord, s'il pensait que miladi prenait froid? Lui, qui toujours avait tant de soin de miladi!'

Yes, she had married Henry, and Henry had always been extremely solicitous that she should not catch cold. He had taken the greatest possible care of her; she might say with truth that she had always led a sheltered life. (But was that what she had wanted?) Whether in England, or in Africa, or in Australia, or in India, Henry had always seen to it that she had the least possible amount of trouble. Perhaps that was his way of compensating her for the independence she had foregone for his sake. Perhaps Henry—an odd thought!—had realised more than his convenience would ever allow him to admit. Perhaps he had consciously or unconsciously tried to smother her longings under a pack of rugs and cushions, like putting a broken heart to sleep on a feather bed. She had always been surrounded by servants, secretaries, and aides-de-camp, fulfilling the function of those little fenders which prevent a ship from bumping too roughly against the quay. Usually, indeed, they had exceeded their duties, from sheer devotion to Lady Slane, from a sheer wish to protect and spare her, who was so gentle, so plucky, so self-effacing, and so feminine. Her fragility aroused the chivalry of men, her modesty precluded the antagonism of women, her spirit awoke the respect of both. And as for Henry himself, though he liked to dally with pretty and sycophantic women, bending over them in a way which often gave Lady Slane a pang, he had never thought another woman in the world worthy to compare.

Wrapped in the rug which in a sense had been put round her

knees by Henry, she wondered now how close had ever been the communion between them? The coldness with which she was now able to estimate their relationship frightened her a little, yet it took her back in some curious way to the days when she plotted to elude her parents and consecrate herself to an existence which, although conventionally reprehensible, should, essentially, be dedicated to the most severe and difficult integrity. *Then*, she had been face to face with life, and that had seemed a reason for a necessity for the clearest thinking; *now*, she was face to face with death, and that again seemed a reason for the truest possible estimate of values, without evasion. The middle period alone had been confused.

Confused. Other people would not think it confused. Other people would point to their marriage as a perfect marriage; to herself and Henry, severally, as the perfect wife and husband. They would say that neither had ever 'looked at' anybody else. They would envy them, as the partners in an honourable career and the founders of a satisfactory and promising dynasty. They would commiserate now with her in being left alone; but they would reflect that, after all, an old woman of eighty-eight who had had her life was not so much to be pitied, and might spend her remaining years in looking forward to the day when her husband—young once more, garlanded with flowers, and robed in some kind of night-gown—would stand waiting to greet her on the Other Side. They would say she had been happy.

But what was happiness? Had she been happy? That was a strange, clicking word to have coined—meaning something definite to the whole English-speaking race—a strange clicking word with its short vowel and its spitting double p's, and its pert tip-tilted y at the end, to express in two syllables a whole summary of life. Happy. But one was happy at one moment, unhappy two minutes later, and neither for any good reason; so what did it mean? It meant, if it meant anything at all, that some uneasy desire wanted black to be black, and white, white; it meant that in the jungle of the terrors of life, the tiny creeping creatures sought reassurance in a formula. Certainly, there had been moments of which one could say: *Then*, I was happy; and with greater certainty: *Then*, I was unhappy—when little Robert had lain in his coffin, for instance, strewn with rose-petals by his sobbing Syrian nurse—but whole regions had intervened, which were just existence. Absurd to ask of those, had she been happy or unhappy? It seemed merely as though someone were asking a question about someone that was not herself, clothing the question in a word that bore no relation to the shifting, elusive, iridescent play of life; trying to do something impossible, in fact, like compressing the waters of a lake into a tight, hard ball. Life was that lake, thought Lady Slane, sitting under the warm south wall amid the smell of the peaches; a lake offering its even surface to many reflections, gilded by the sun, silvered by the moon, darkened by a cloud, roughened by a ripple; but level always, a plane, keeping its bounds, not to be rolled up into a tight, hard ball, small enough to be held in the hand, which was what people were trying to do when they asked if one's life had been happy or unhappy.

No, that was not the question to ask her—not the question to ask anybody. Things were not so simple as all that. Had they asked her whether she had loved her husband, she could have answered without hesitation: yes, she had loved him. There had been no moments when she could differentiate and say: *Then*, at such a moment, I loved him; and again, *Then*, at such another, I loved him not. The stress had been constant. Her love for him had been a straight black line drawn right through her life. It had hurt her, it had damaged her, it had diminished her, but she had been unable to curve away from it. All the parts of her that were not Henry Holland's had pulled in opposition, yet by this single giant of love they had all been pulled over, as the weaker team in a tug-of-war. Her ambitions, her secret existence, all had given way. She had loved him so much, that even her resentment was subdued. She could not grudge him even the sacrifice he had imposed upon her. Yet she was not one of those women whose gladness in sacrifice is such that the sacrifice ceases to be a sacrifice. Her own youthful visions had been incompatible with such a love, and in giving them up she knew that she gave up something of incomparable value. That was what she had done for Henry Holland, and Henry Holland had never known it.

At last, she could see him and herself in retrospect; more precious than that, she could bear to examine him without disloyalty. She could bear to shed the frenzied loyalty of the past. Not that the anguish of her love had faded from her memory. She could still remember the days when she had prayed for the safety and happiness of Henry Holland, superstitiously, to a God in whom she had never wholly believed. Childish and ardent, the words of her prayer had grown, fitting themselves to her necessity. 'O Lord,' she had prayed nightly, 'take care of my beloved Henry, make him happy, keep him safe, O Lord, from all dangers, whether of illness or accident, preserve him for me who love him better than anything in heaven or earth.' Thus she had prayed; and as she prayed, every night, the words renewed their sharpness; whenever she whispered 'safe from all dangers, whether of illness or accident,' she had seen Henry knocked down by a dray, Henry breathing in pneumonia, as though either disaster were actually present; and when she whispered 'me who love him better than anything in heaven or earth,' she had undergone the nightly anxiety of wondering whether the inclusion of heaven were not blasphemous and might not offend a jealous God, for surely it was fringing on blasphemy to flaunt Henry as dearer to her than anything in earth or heaven—which involved God Himself, the very God she would propitiate—a blasphemy which might strike deeper than her intended appeal? Yet she persisted in her prayer, for it was strictly up against the truth. Henry was dearer, far dearer, to her than anything else in heaven or earth. He had decoyed her even into holding him dearer than her own ambition. She could not say otherwise, to a God who (if He existed at all) would certainly know her heart whether she whispered it out in prayer or not. Therefore, she might as well give herself the nightly luxury of whispering the truth, heard of God, she hoped; unheard, she hoped, of Henry Holland. It was a comfort to her. After her prayer, she could sleep, having ensured safety for Henry for at least twenty-four hours, the limit she set upon the efficacy of her prayer. And Henry Holland, she remembered, had been a difficult and dangerous treasure to preserve, even with the support of secret intercession. His career had been so active, so detached from the sheltered life of her petitions! She, who would have chosen for him the methodical existence of a Dutch bulb-grower, a mynheer concerned with nothing more disturbing than the fertilisation of a new tulip, while the doves in their wicker cage cooed and spread their wings in the sun, she had seen him always in a processional life, threatened by bombs, riding on an elephant through Indian cities, shut away from her by ceremony or business; and when physical danger was temporarily suspended in some safe capital, London, Paris, or Washington—when, great servant of the State, he found employment at home or travelled abroad on some peaceful mission—then other demands were made upon her watchfulness: she must be swift to detect his need for reassurance when a momentary discouragement overcame him; when, mooning, he strayed up to her and drooped over her chair, saying nothing, but waiting (as she knew) for some soft protection to come from her and fold itself around him like a cloak, yet it must all be done without a word directly spoken; she must restore his belief that the obstructiveness of his Government or the opposition of his rivals was due to their short-sightedness or envy, and to no deficiency within himself, yet must not allow him to know that she guessed at his mood of self-mistrust or the whole fabric of her comfort would be undone. And when she had accomplished this feat, this reconstruction of extreme delicacy and extreme solidity—when he left her, to go back strengthened to his business—then, with her hands lying limp, symbol of her exhaustion, and a sweet emptiness within her, as though her self had drained away to flow into the veins of another person— then, sinking, drowning, she wondered whether she had not secretly touched the heights of rapture.

Yet even this, the statement of her love and the recollection of its more subtle demands, failed to satisfy her in its broad simplification. The statement that she had loved, though indisputable, still admitted of infinite complexity. Who was the she, the 'I,' that had loved? And Henry, who and what was he? A physical presence, threatened by time and death, and therefore the dearer for that factual menace? Or was his physical presence merely the palpable projection, the symbol, of something which might justly be called himself? Hidden away under the symbol of their corporeality, both in him and in her, doubtless lurked something which was themselves. But that self was hard to get at; obscured by the too familiar trappings of voice, name, appearance, occupation, circumstance, even the fleeting perception of self became blunted or confused. And there were many selves. She could never be the same self with him as when she was alone; and even that solitary self which she pursued, shifted, changed, melted away as she approached it, she could never drive it into a dark corner, and there, like a robber in the night, hold it by the throat against the wall, the hard core of self chased into a blind alley or refuge. The very words which clothed her thoughts were but another falsification; no word could stand alone, like a column of stone or the trunk of a tree, but must riot instantly into a tropical tangle of associations; the fact, it seemed, was as elusive and as luxuriant as the self. Only in a wordless trance did any true apprehension become possible, a wordless trance of sheer feeling, an extra-physical state, in which nothing but the tingling of the finger-tips recalled the existence of the body, and a series of images floated across the mind, un-named, unrelated to language. That state, she supposed, was the state in which she approached most closely to the self concealed within her, but it was a state having nothing to do with Henry. Was this why she had welcomed, as the next best thing, the love which by its very pain gave her the illusion of contact?

She was, after all, a woman. Thwarted as an artist, was it perhaps possible to find fulfilment in other ways? Was there, after all, some foundation for the prevalent belief that woman should minister to man? Had the generations been right, the personal struggle wrong? Was there something beautiful, something active, something creative even, in her apparent submission to Henry? Could she not balance herself upon the tight-rope of her relationship with him, as dangerously and precariously as in the act of creating a picture? Was it not possible to see the tones and half-tones of her life with him as she might have seen the blue and violet shadows of a landscape; and so set them in relation and ordain their values, that she thereby forced them into beauty? Was not this also an achievement of the sort peculiarly suited to women? of the sort, indeed, which women alone could compass; a privilege, a prerogative, not to be despised? All the woman in her answered, yes! All the artist in her countered, no!

And then again, were not women in their new Protestant spirit defrauding the world of some poor remnant of enchantment, some illusion, foolish perhaps, but lovely? This time the woman and artist in her alike answered, yes.

She remembered a young couple she had known—the man a secretary at the Paris Embassy; very young they were—receiving her visits, as their ambassadress, with suitable reverence. She knew that they loved her, but at the same time she always felt her visits to be an intrusion. She divined them to be so much in love that they must grudge any half-hour filched from their allowance of years together. And she, for her part, counted her visits to them as an agony, yet she was drawn towards them partly from affection, partly from a desire to martyrise herself by the sight of their union. 'Male and female created he them,' she said to herself always, coming away. Sometimes, coming away, she felt herself to be so falsely placed in relation to Henry that the burden of life became too heavy, and she wished she might die. It was no phrase: she really wished it. She was too honest not to suffer under the burden of such falsity. She longed at times for a relationship as simple, as natural, and as right as the relationship between those two very uninteresting but engaging young people. She envied Alec as he stood before the fire jingling the coins in his pocket and looking down on his wife curled into a corner of the sofa. She envied Madge her unquestioning acceptance of everything that Alec said or did. Yet in the midst of her envy something offended her: this intolerably masculine lordliness, this abject feminine submission.

Where, then, lay the truth? Henry by the compulsion of love had cheated her of her chosen life, yet had given her another life, an ample life, a life in touch with the greater world, if that took her fancy; or a life, alternatively, pressed close up against her own nursery. For a life of her own, he had substituted his life with its interests, or the lives of her children with their potentialities. He assumed that she might sink herself in either, if not in both, with equal joy. It had never occurred to him that she might prefer simply to be herself.

A part of her had acquiesced. She remembered acquiescing in

the assumption that she should project herself into the lives of her children, especially her sons, as though their entities were of far greater importance than her own, and she herself but the vehicle of their creation and the shelter of their vulnerable years. She remembered the birth of Kay. She had wanted to call him Kay, because just before his birth she had been reading Malory. Up till then, her sons had succeeded automatically to the family names—Herbert, Charles, Robert, William—but over the fifth son, for some reason, her wishes were consulted, and when she suggested Kay as a name Henry did not protest. He had been in a good humour and had said, 'Have it your own way.' She remembered that even in her weakness she had thought Henry generous. Looking down into the crumpled red face of her new baby—though crumpled red faces had become quite usual to her by then, at the sixth repetition—she had realised the responsibility of launching the little creature labelled by a name not of its own choosing, like launching a battleship, only instead of turrets and decks and guns she had to do with the miraculous tissue of flesh and brain. Was it fair to call a child Kay? A name, a label, exerted an unseen though continuous pressure. People were said to grow up in accordance with their names. But Kay, at any rate, had not grown up unduly romantic, though certainly he could not be said to resemble his brothers or elder sister.

Yet of all her children, Kay and Edith had alone inherited something of their mother—Kay with his astrolabes, Edith with her muddles. Carrie, characteristically, had given her least trouble; Carrie had managed her own way into the world. Herbert, as the eldest son, had arrived in pomp and with difficulty. William had been a mean, silent baby, with small eyes; greedy, too, as though determined to squeeze all the provision of her breast even as, to-day, he and Lavinia, his fitting mate, were determined to squeeze all their advantage from the local dairy.

Charles had arrived protesting, even as he protested to-day, only
at that time he knew nothing of War Offices. Edith had had to
be beaten into drawing her first breath; she had been able to
manage life no better at its beginning than at its end. The fact
remained that in Kay and Edith alone she divined an unexpressed
sympathy. All the rest were Henry's children, with his energy
just gone wrong. Yet when her children were babies—small,
prone things, or things so young and feeble that one could sit
them up in safety only by supporting their insecure heads—she,
trying to compensate herself for her foregone independence, had
made an effort to look forward from the day when the skull over
the pulse which so terrifyingly and openly throbbed should have
closed up, when their hold on life would no longer be so
alarmingly precarious, when she would no longer be afraid of
their drawing their last breath even as she bent over their cradle
in the absence of the nurse. She had tried to look forward to the
day when they would develop characters of their own; when
they would hold opinions different from their parents', when
they would make plans and arrangements for themselves. Even
in this, she had been suppressed, thwarted. 'How amused we
shall be,' she had said to Henry as they stood together looking
down on Herbert netted in his cot, 'when he starts writing us
letters from school.' Henry had not liked that remark; she
divined his criticism instantly. Henry thought that all real
women ought to prefer their children helpless, and to deplore
the day when they would begin to grow up. Long-clothes
should be preferable to smocks; smocks to knickers; knickers to
trousers. Henry had definite, masculine ideas about women and
motherhood. Although secretly proud of his rising little sons, he
pretended even to himself that they were, so far, entirely their
mother's concern. So, naturally, she had endeavoured to adopt
those views. Herbert, at two years old, had been deposed in
favour of Carrie; Carrie, at a year, in favour of Charles. Because

it was expected of her, the baby had always been officially her darling. But none of these things had held any truth in them. She had always been aware that the self of her children was as far removed from her as the self of Henry, or, indeed, her own.

Shocking, unnatural thoughts had floated into her mind. 'If only I had never married . . . if only I had never had any children.' Yet she loved Henry—to the point of agony—and she loved her children—to the point of sentimentality. She wove theories about them, which she confided to Henry in moments of privacy and expansion. Herbert would be a statesman, she said, for had he not questioned her (at the age of twelve) about problems of native government? And Kay, aged four, had asked to be taken to see the Taj Mahal. Henry had indulged her in these fancies, not seeing that she was, in fact, indulging him.

But all this had been as nothing compared with Henry's ambitions which drove her down a path hedged with thorns. Everything in Henry's conceptions of the world had run counter to her own grain. Realist and idealist, they represented the extreme opposites of their points of view, with the difference that whereas Henry need make no bones about his creed, she must protect hers from shame and ridicule. Yet there, again, confusion swathed her. There were moments when she could enter into the excitement of the great game that Henry was always playing; moments when the private, specialised, intense, and lovely existence of the artist—whose practice had been denied her, but after whose ideal of life she still miserably and imaginatively hankered—seemed a poor and selfish and over-delicate thing compared with the masculine business of empire and politics and the strife of men. There were moments when she could understand not only with her brain but with her sensibility, that Henry should crave for a life of action even as she herself craved for a life of contemplation. They were indeed two halves of one dissevered world.

Part Three

This Life we live is dead for all its breath;
Death's self it is, set off on pilgrimage,
Travelling with tottering steps the first short stage.
                                    CHRISTINA ROSSETTI

Summer over, the October days were no longer warm enough for Lady Slane to sit in the garden. In order to get her airing she must go for a little walk, loaded with cloaks and furs by Genoux, who accompanied her to the front door to make sure that she did not discard any of her wrappings in the hall on the way. Lady Slane sometimes protested, as Genoux dragged one garment after another from the cupboard. 'But, Genoux, you are making me look like an old bundle.' Genoux, hanging the last cloak firmly round her shoulders, replied, 'Miladi est bien trop distinguée pour avoir jamais l'air d'un vieux bundle.' 'Do you remember, Genoux,' said Lady Slane, drawing on her gloves, 'how you always wanted me to wear woollen stockings for dinner?' It was indeed true. Genoux in cold weather had never been willing to put out silk stockings with her mistress's evening dress; or if she put them, after many remonstrances, she hopefully put also a woollen pair to wear underneath. 'Mais pourquoi pas, miladi?' said Genoux sensibly;

715

'dans ce temps-là les dames, même les jeunes dames, portaient les jupes convenablement longues, et un jupon par dessus le marché. Pourquoi s'enrhumer, pour des chevilles qui n'y paraissent pas? C'était la même histoire pour les combinaisons que miladi voulait à tout prix ôter pour le dîner, précisément au soir lorsqu'il fait plus froid.' She accompanied Lady Slane downstairs, talking in this strain, for all her volubility had been released since quitting Elm Park Gardens and the household of English servants with their cold discreet ways. She hovered and clucked over Lady Slane, half-scolding, half-cherishing. 'Miladi n'a jamais su se soigner. Elle ferait beaucoup mieux d'écouter sa vieille Genoux. Les premiers jours d'octobre, c'est tout ce qu'il y a de plus malin. Ça vous attrape sans crier gare. A l'âge de miladi on ne doit pas prendre de libertés.' 'Don't bury me till you need, Genoux,' said Lady Slane, escaping from her Anglicisms and pessimism alike.

She went down the steps carefully, for there had been a frost and they might be slippery. Genoux would watch her out of sight, she knew, so at the corner she must turn round to wave. Genoux would be hurt if she forgot to turn round. Yet by the gesture she would not be reassured; she would not be happy again until she had readmitted the muffled figure of the old lady to the safety of the house; drawn her in, taken off her boots, brought her slippers and perhaps a cup of hot soup, carried away her wraps, and left her to her book beside the sitting-room fire. Yet Genoux, for all her adages and croakings, was a gay and philosophical old soul, full of wisdom of the sturdy peasant kind. (She waved back to Lady Slane as Lady Slane after dutifully looking round turned the corner and pursued her way slowly towards the Heath.) Now she would go back to the kitchen and talk to the cat while she busied herself with her pots and pans. Lady Slane frequently heard her talking to the cat, 'Viens, mon bo-bo,' she would say; 'nice dinner, look, that's all for you,'—for she had an idea that English animals understood English only, and once, hearing the jackals bark round Gul-a-hek, had remarked to Lady Slane, 'C'est drôle tout de même, miladi, comme on entend tout de suite que ce ne sont pas des Anglais.' Well, it was a gentle life they led now, she and Genoux, thought Lady Slane making her way slowly up the hill towards the Heath; she and Genoux, living in such undisturbed intimacy, bound by the ties respectively of gratitude and devotion, bound also by the tie of their unspoken speculation as to which would be taken from the other first. Whenever the front door shut behind one of their rare visitors, each was conscious of a certain relief at the departure of intruders. The routine of their daily life was all they wanted—all, indeed, that they had strength for. Effort tired them both, though they had never admitted it to one another.

Fortunately, the intruders came but seldom. Lady Slane's children had come first, in rotation, as a duty, but most of them indicated to their mother so clearly the extreme inconvenience of coming as far as Hampstead that she felt justified in begging them to spare themselves the trouble, and except at intervals they took her at her word. Lady Slane was quite shrewd enough to imagine what they said to one another to appease their consciences: 'Well, we *asked* Mother to make her home with us. . . .' Edith alone had shown some disposition to come frequently and, as she called it, help. But Edith was now living in such a state of bliss in her own flat, that she had been easily able to decide that her mother didn't really want her. Kay she had not seen for some time. Last time he came, he had said after a great deal of shuffling and embarrassment that a friend of his, old FitzGeorge, wanted to be brought to call upon her. 'I think,' said Kay, poking the fire, 'that he said he had met you in India.' 'In India?' said Lady Slane vaguely. 'It's quite possible, dear, but

I don't remember the name. So many people came, you see. We were often twenty to luncheon. Could you put him off, do you think, Kay? I don't want to be rude, but somehow I seem to have lost my taste for strangers.'

Kay longed to ask his mother what Fitz had meant by saying he had seen him in his cradle. He had in fact come up to Hampstead determined to clear up this mystery. But, of course, he went away without asking.

No great-grandchildren. They were forbidden. The grand-children did not count; they were insignificant as the middle distance. But the great-grandchildren, who were not insignificant, but might be disturbing, were forbidden. Lady Slane had adhered to that, with the strange firmness sometimes and suddenly displayed by the most docile people. Mr. Bucktrout was the only regular visitor, coming once a week to tea, on Tuesdays. But she was not tired by Mr. Bucktrout; they would sit on either side of the fire, not lighting the lamps, while Mr. Bucktrout's conversation ran on like a purling brook, and Lady Slane listened or not, as she felt inclined.

Meanwhile, it was very beautiful, up on the Heath, with the brown trees and the blue distance. Lady Slane sat down on a bench and rested. Little boys were flying kites; they ran dragging the string across the turf, till like an ungainly bird the kite rose trailing its untidy tail across the sky. Lady Slane remembered other little boys flying kites in China. Her foreign memories and her English present played at *chassé-croisé* often now in her mind, mingling and superimposing, making her wonder sometimes whether her memory were not becoming a little confused, so immediate and simultaneous did both impressions appear. Was she on a hillside near Pekin with Henry, a groom walking their horses up and down at a respectful distance; or was she alone, old, and dressed in black, resting on a bench on Hampstead Heath? But there were the chimney-pots of London to steady her. No doubt about it, these little boys were Cockneys in rags, not celestial urchins in blue cotton; and her own limbs, as she shifted her position a little on the hard bench, gave her a rheumatic tweak bearing no relation to her young and physical well-being as she cantered up the scorched hillside with Henry. She tried, in a dim and groping way, to revive the sensation of that well-being. She found it impossible. A dutiful inner voice summoned from the past as some old melody might float unseizable into the outskirts of recollection, reproduced for her in words the facts of that sensation without awakening any response in her dulled old body. In vain she now told herself that once she had woken up on a summer morning longing to spring from her bed and to run out for sheer exuberance of spirit into the air. In vain she tried, and most deliberately, to renew the sharpness of waiting for the moment when—their official life suspended—she would turn in the darkness into Henry's arms. It was all words now, without reality. The only things which touched reality were the routine of her life with Genoux; the tiny interests of that life—the tradesmen's ring at the back door, the arrival of a parcel of books from Mudie's, the consultation as to Mr. Bucktrout's Tuesday tea, should they buy muffins or crumpets? the agitation over an announced visit from Carrie; and then the growth of her bodily ailments, for which she was beginning to feel quite an affection. Her body had, in fact, become her companion, a constant resource and preoccupation; all the small squalors of the body, known only to oneself, insignificant in youth, easily dismissed, in old age became dominant and entered into fulfilment of the tyranny they had always threatened. Yet it was, rather than otherwise, an agreeable and interesting tyranny. A hint of lumbago caused her to rise cautiously from her chair and reminded her of the day she had ricked her back at Nervi, since when her back had never been very reliable. The small intimacies of her teeth were known to her, so that she ate carefully, biting on one side rather than on the other. She instinctively crooked one finger—the third on the left hand—to save it from the pang of neuritis. An in-growing toe-nail obliged Genoux to use the shoe-horn with the greatest precaution. And all these parts of the body became intensely personal: my back, my tooth, my finger, my toe; and Genoux, again, was the only person who knew exactly what she meant by a sudden exclamation as she fell back into her chair, the bond between herself and Genoux thereby strengthening to the pitch of the bond between lovers, of an exclusive physical intimacy. Of such small things was her life now made: of communion with Genoux, of interest in her own disintegrating body, of Mr. Bucktrout's courtesy and weekly visits, of her pleasure in the frosty morning and the little boys flying kites on the Heath; even of her anxiety about slipping upon a frozen doorstep, for the bones of the aged, she knew, were brittle. All tiny things, contemptibly tiny things, ennobled only by their vast back-ground, the background of Death. Certain Italian paintings depicted trees—poplar, willow, alder—each leaf separate, and sharp, and veined, against a green translucent sky. Of such a quality were the tiny things, the shapely leaves, of her present life: redeemed from insignificance by their juxtaposition with a luminous eternity.

She felt exalted, she escaped from an obvious pettiness, from a finicking life, whenever she remembered that no adventure could now befall her except the supreme adventure for which all other adventures were but a preparation.

She miscalculated, however, forgetting that life's surprises were inexhaustible, even up to the end. On re-entering her house that afternoon she found a man's hat of peculiar square shape reposing upon the hall table, and Genoux in a state of excitement greeted her with a whisper: 'Miladi! il y a un monsieur . . . je lui ai dit que miladi était sortie, mais c'est un

monsieur qui n'écoute pas . . . il attend miladi au salon.
Faut-il servir le thé?—Miladi ôtera bien ses souliers,
de peur qu'ils ne soient humides?'

Lady Slane looked back upon her meeting with Mr. FitzGeorge.
So did Mr. FitzGeorge look back upon his meeting with Lady
Slane. Having waited long enough, and vainly, for Kay to bring
him, he had taken the law into his own hands and had come by
himself. Miserly in spite of his millions, he had travelled up to
Hampstead by Underground; had walked from the station; had
paused before Lady Slane's house, and with the eye of a connoisseur had appreciated its Georgian dignity. 'Ah,' he had said
with satisfaction, 'the house of a woman of taste.' He soon
discovered his error, for, having over-ridden Genoux's objec-
tions and pushed his way into the hall, he found that Lady Slane
had no taste at all. Perversely, this delighted him the more. The
room into which Genoux reluctantly showed him was simple
and comfortable. 'Arm-chairs and chintz, and the light in the
right place,' he muttered, wandering about. He was extraordinarily moved at the prospect of seeing Lady Slane again. But
when she came it was obvious that she did not remember him in
the least. She greeted him politely, with a return to the viceregal
manner; apologised for her absence, asked him to sit down; said
that Kay had mentioned his name; said that tea would come in a
minute; but was manifestly puzzled as to what errand had
brought him. Perhaps she wondered whether he wished to write
her husband's life? Mr. FitzGeorge, as this reflection struck
him, cackled suddenly, and, to his hostess, inexplicably. He
could scarcely explain at once that the Vicereine and not the
Viceroy had touched his imagination, more than half a century
ago, at Calcutta.
    As it was, he was compelled to explain that, as a young man,
he had come with letters of introduction to Government House

and had perfunctorily been asked to dinner. Mr. FitzGeorge, however, was not embarrassed; he was too genuinely detached from such social conventions. He accounted for himself quite simply and without evasions. 'You see,' he said, 'I was a name-less young man, to whom an unknown father had left a large fortune, with the wish that I should travel round the world. I was naturally delighted to avail myself of such an opportunity. It is always pleasant to gratify wishes which coincide with one's own. The solicitors, who were also my guardians,' he added dryly, 'commended my promptitude in complying with the wish expressed in the will. In their view, old dotards mould-ering in Lincoln's Inn, a young man who would desert London for the far East at his father's suggestion was a filial young man indeed. I suppose they thought the stage-doors of Shaftesbury Avenue a greater attraction than the bazaars of Canton. Well, they erred. Half the treasures of my collection to-day, Lady Slane, I owe to that journey round the world sixty years ago.'

It was clear that Lady Slane had never heard of his collection. She said as much. He was delighted, much as he had been delighted when he discovered that she had no taste.

'Capital, Lady Slane! My collection is, I suppose, at least twice as valuable as that of Eumorphopoulos, and twice as famous—though, I may add, I have paid a hundredth part of its present value for it. And, unlike most experts, I have never lost sight of beauty. Rarity, curiosity, antiquity are not enough for me. I must have beauty or, at any rate, craftmanship. And I have been justified. There is no piece in my collection to-day which any museum would not despoil its best show-case to possess.'

Lady Slane, knowing nothing of such things, was amused by such innocently childish boastfulness. She egged him on, this naïf old magpie, this collector of beautiful objects, who had suddenly made his way into her house, and now sat by her fire, bragging, forgetting that dinner-party at Calcutta and his friendship with Kay, which alone could have justified his intrusion. He had for her, from the first moment, the charm of a completely detached and isolated figure. The very fact that he had no known parents and no legitimate name, but was purely and simply himself, invested him with a certain legendary charm in her eyes. She had had enough, in her life, of people whose worldly status was their passport to admission. Mr. FitzGeorge had no such passport; even his wealth could scarcely be considered a passport, for his reputation as a miser instantly destroyed the hopes of the most sanguine seeker after benefit. Curiously enough, Lady Slane was not offended by his avarice as she was offended by it in her own son William. William and Lavinia were furtively avaricious; they couldn't help being stingy, since parsimony ran in their blood—she remembered thinking when they became engaged that that was the real link between them—but they were not frank about it, they tried to cover it up. Mr. FitzGeorge indulged his weakness on the grander scale, making no bones about it. Lady Slane liked people who, if they had vices, were not ashamed of them. She despised all hypocritical disguises. So when Mr. FitzGeorge told her that he hated parting with money, could only be induced to do so when irresistibly tempted by beauty, and could console himself only by the lure of a bargain, she frankly laughed and frankly gave him her respect. He looked at her across the fire. His coat, she observed, was shabby. 'I remember,' he said, 'that you laughed at me in Calcutta.'

He seemed to remember a great many things about Calcutta. 'Lady Slane,' he said, fencing, when she taxed him with his excellent memory, 'have you not yet noticed that youthful memories sharpen with advancing age?' That little 'yet' made her laugh again: he was playing the part of a man pretending to a woman that she still retained her youth. She was eighty-eight, but the man-to-woman mainspring still coiled like a cobra between them. Innumerable years had elapsed since she had felt that stimulus; it came as an unexpected revival, a flicker, a farewell, stirring her strangely and awaking some echo whose melody she could not quite recapture. Had she really seen FitzGeorge before, or did his slight and old-fashioned gallantry awaken only the general memory of years when all men had looked at her with admiration in their eyes? Whichever it was, his presence disquieted her, though she could not pretend that her faint agitation was anything but pleasant, and he had looked at her, too, in such a way as to suggest that he could provide her with the explanation if he would. All the evening, after he had gone, she sat gazing into the fire, her book neglected, wondering, trying to remember, trying to put her hand on something that remained tantalisingly just round the corner, just out of reach. Something had knocked against her as the clapper might knock against a cracked old bell in a disused steeple. No music travelled out over the valleys, but within the steeple itself a tingling vibration arose, disturbing the starlings in their nests and causing the cobwebs to quiver.

Next morning she, of course, derided her evening mood. What queer freak of sentimentality had caught her? For two hours she had been as dreamy as a girl! It was FitzGeorge's fault for entering her house in that way, for sitting down beside her fire as though he had some right to be there, for talking about the past, for teasing her gently about her dignity as the young Vicereine, for looking at her as though he were saying only half of what he would say later on, for being slightly mocking, slightly gallant, wholly admiring, and, secretly, moved. Although he had preserved a surface manner, she knew that his visit had not been without import to him. She wondered whether he would come again.

If the gentleman returned, said Genoux, was he to be admitted? Next time she would be prepared for him; he should not brush her aside as though she were yesterday's newspaper and walk straight into the hall, laying his funny little hat on the table. 'Ah, mon Dieu, miladi, quel drôle de chapeau!' She doubled herself up, rubbing her hands down her thighs as she laughed. Lady Slane loved Genoux's whole-hearted enjoyment of anything that struck her as funny. In response, she permitted herself a smile at Mr. FitzGeorge's hat. Where did he get such hats? asked Genoux; car jamais je n'ai vu un pareil chapeau en devanture. Did he have them made purposely for himself alone? And his muffler—had her ladyship seen it? All checks, like a stud-groom. 'C'est un original,' Genoux concluded sagely; but, unlike an English servant, she was not interested merely in making fun of Mr. FitzGeorge. She wanted to know more about him. It was pathetic, she said, to be like that—un vieux monsieur, and all alone. Had he never been married? He did not look as though he had been married. She followed Lady Slane about, eager for the information Lady Slane was unable to provide. He had made a good tea, said Genoux; she had noticed the shabbiness of his coat, assuming an excessive poverty: 'J'ai vite couru au coin de la rue, attraper l'homme aux muffins;' and was noticeably disappointed when Lady Slane told her rather dryly that Mr. FitzGeorge, to the best of her knowledge, was a millionaire. 'Un milliardaire! et s'affubler comme ça!' Genoux could not get over it. But what was the long and short of it to be? she asked. Was she to let him in next time, or was she not?

Lady Slane said she did not suppose Mr. FitzGeorge would come again, but even as she said it she detected herself in a lie, for as he took his leave, Mr. FitzGeorge had kept her hand and had asked for permission to return. Why should she lie to Genoux? 'Yes, let him in,' she said, moving away towards her sitting-room.

There were three of them now, three old gentlemen—Mr. Bucktrout, Mr. Gosheron, and Mr. FitzGeorge. A funny trio—

an agent, a builder, and a connoisseur! all old, all eccentric, and all unworldly. How oddly it had come about, that the whole of her life should have fallen away from her—her activities, her children, and Henry—and should have been so completely replaced in this little interlude before the end by a new existence so satisfyingly populated! She supposed that she herself was responsible for its creation, but could not imagine how she had done it. 'Perhaps,' she said aloud, 'one always gets what one wants in the end.' And taking down an old book, she opened it at random and read:

Cease of your oaths, cease of your great swearing,
Cease of your pomp, cease of your vainglory,
Cease of your hate, cease of your blaspheming,
Cease of your malice, cease of your envy,
Cease of your wrath, cease of your lechery,
Cease of your fraud, cease your deception,
Cease of your tongues making detraction.

It was surely remarkable that someone should have expressed her longing in—she looked at the date—1493?
She read the next verse:

Flee faint falsehood, fickle, foul, and fell,
Flee fatal flatterers, full of fairness,
Flee fair feigning, fables of favell,
Flee folks' fellowship, frequenting falseness,
Flee frantic facers fulfilled of frowardness,
Flee fools' fallacies, flee fond fantasies,
Flee from fresh babblers, feigning flatteries.

She had fled them all, except the fond fantasies; her three old gentlemen werc fond fantasies—fond fantasticks, she amended, smiling. As for pomp, vainglory, and tongues making detraction, they were things that never crossed her threshold now except when Carrie brought them in on a gust of chilly air. Then she caught herself up for so readily adopting Mr. Fitz-George and adding him to her intimates: what reason had she to suppose, beyond a phrase spoken in parting civility, that he would ever come again?

He came again, and she heard Genoux welcoming him as an old friend in the hall. Yes, her ladyship was in; yes, her ladyship had said she would be delighted to receive monsieur at any time. Lady Slane listened, wishing that Genoux would not be quite so hospitable on her behalf. She was not at all sure, now, that she liked her privacy being laid open to invasion by Mr. FitzGeorge. She must ask Kay to drop him a hint.

Meanwhile she received him, rising in her soft black draperies and giving him her hand with the smile he remembered. Why should she not? After all, they were two old people, very old people, so old that they were all the time age-conscious, and being so old it was agreeable to sit like two cats on either side of the fire warming their bones, stretching out hands so transparent as to let the pink light of the flames through them, while their conversation without effort rose or fell. Lady Slane, all her life long, had made people feel that they could talk if they liked, but need not talk if disinclined—one of the reasons why Henry Holland had first decided to marry her. Having a fund of quietness within herself, she could understand that other people also enjoyed being quiet. Few women, Henry Holland said, could be quiet without being dull, and fewer women could talk without being a bore; but then Henry Holland, although he enjoyed women, had a low opinion of them and was satisfied by none except his own wife. FitzGeorge with really remarkable shrewdness had diagnosed this in Calcutta where the Viceroy, heaven knows, had been sufficiently surrounded by pretty and animated women all flatteringly deluded by the apparently close and exclusive attention he accorded to each one in turn.

Thank goodness, thought Mr. FitzGeorge, she has no taste. He was sick to death of women who prided themselves on their taste, and thereby assumed an understanding with him as a connoisseur. There was no relation between the two things— between 'decoration' and real beauty. His works of art belonged to a different world from the skilful interiors of women of taste. He looked almost tenderly at Lady Slane's pink shaded lamps and Turkey rug. If one wanted beauty, one had only to rest one's eyes on her, so fine and old and lovely, like an ivory carving; flowing down like water into her chair, so slight and supple were her limbs, the firelight casting a flush of rose over her features and snowy hair. Youth had no beauty like the beauty of an old face; the face of youth was an unwritten page. Youth could never sit as still as that, in absolute repose, as though all haste, all movement, were over and done with, and nothing left but waiting and acquiescence. He was glad that he had never seen her in the middle years, so that he might keep untarnished his memory of her when she was young, lively, and full of fire, completing it with this present vision of her, having arrived at the other end of the story. The same woman, but he himself in ignorance of what had happened in between.

He became aware that he had not spoken for quite five minutes. Lady Slane appeared to have forgotten him. Yet she was not asleep, for she was looking quietly into the fire, her hands lying loose in their usual attitude, and her foot resting on the fender. He was surprised that she should accept him so naturally. 'But we are old,' he thought, 'and our perceptions are muted. She takes it for granted that I should sit here as though I had known her all my life. Lady Slane,' he said aloud, 'I don't believe you took much pleasure in your viceroyalty?'

His voice was always rather harsh and sardonic, and even in her company he made no attempt to soften it. He disregarded and despised mankind so much that he seldom spoke without a sneer. Kay was his only friend, but even Kay got the rough side of his tongue oftener than the smooth.

Lady Slane stiffened, out of a reviving loyalty to Henry. 'Even viceroyalty has its uses, Mr. FitzGeorge.'

'But not for such as you,' Mr. FitzGeorge said, unrepentant. 'Do you know,' he said, leaning forward, 'I was really upset by seeing you trapped among those mummers. You submitted and did your part—oh, admirably!—but all the time you were denying your nature. I remember waiting for you and Lord Slane to appear before dinner; we were assembled in some big drawing-room, thirty of us, I daresay, people wearing jewels and uniforms, all standing about feeling more or less foolish on an immense expanse of carpet. I remember there was a huge chandelier all lit up with candles; it tinkled whenever anybody walked overhead. I wondered whether it was your footstep that made it tinkle. And then a great folding-door was thrown open and you came in with the Viceroy, and all the women curtsied. After dinner you both came round the circle of your guests, saying something to each; you wore white, with diamonds in your hair, and you asked me if I hoped to get any big-game shooting. I suppose you thought that was the right thing to say to a rich young man; you couldn't know that I abominated the idea of killing animals. I said no, I was just a traveller; but although you smiled attentively I don't believe you listened to my answer. You were thinking what you should say to the next person, and no doubt you said something just as well composed and just as inappropriate. It was the Viceroy, not you, who suggested that I should accompany you on your trip.'

'On our trip?' said Lady Slane, amazed.

'You know that easy amiable way he had of throwing out suggestions? Half the time one knew that he didn't mean what he said, and that he never expected one to act upon it. One was expected to bow and say, Thank you so much, that would be delightful, and then never to refer to it again. He would say, China? yes, I am going to China next week; very interesting country, China; you ought to come with me. But he would have been very much surprised if one had taken him at his word, though I daresay that with his perfect manners he would have concealed his surprise. Now, Lady Slane, isn't it true?'

Without waiting to hear whether it were true, he went on. 'But on this one occasion somebody did take him at his word. I did. He said, You're an antiquarian, FitzGeorge—antiquarian for him was a vague term—you're an antiquarian, he said, and you're in no hurry. Why don't you come with us to Fatihpur Sikhri?'

The broken puzzle in Lady Slane's mind shook itself suddenly down into shape. The half-heard notes reassembled themselves into their tune. She stood again on the terrace of the deserted Indian city looking across the brown landscape where puffs of rising dust marked at intervals the road to Agra. She leant her arms upon the warm parapet and slowly twirled her parasol. She twirled it because she was slightly ill at ease. She and the young man beside her were isolated from the rest of the world. The Viceroy was away from them, inspecting the mother-of-pearl mosque, accompanied by a group of officials in white uniforms and sun-helmets; he was pointing with his stick, and saying that the ring-doves ought to be cleared away from under the eaves. The young man beside Lady Slane said softly that it was a pity the ring-doves should be condemned, for if a city were abandoned by man, why should the doves not inherit it? The doves, the monkeys, and the parrots, he went on, as a flight of jade-green parakeets swept past them, quarrelling in the air; look at their green plumage against these damask walls, he added, raising his head, as the flock swirled round again like a handful of emeralds blown across the Poet's House. There was something unusual, he said, in a city of mosques, palaces, and courts, inhabited solely by birds and animals; he would like to see a tiger going up Akbar's steps, and a cobra coiling its length neatly in the council chamber. They would be more becoming, he thought, to the red city than men in boots and solar topees. Lady Slane, keeping an ear pricked to observe the movements of the Viceroy and his group, had smiled at his fancies and had said that Mr. FitzGeorge was a romantic.

Mr. FitzGeorge. The name came back to her now. It was not surprising that, among so many thousands of names, she should have forgotten it. But she remembered it now, as she remembered the look he had given her when she twitted him. It was more than a look; it was a moment that he created, while he held her eyes and filled them with all the implications he dared not, or would not, speak. She had felt as though she stood naked before him.

'Yes,' he said, watching her across the fire at Hampstead; 'you were right: I *was* a romantic.'

She was startled to hear him thus audibly joining up with her recollections; the moment, then, had possessed equal significance, equal intensity, for him as for her? Its significance had indeed troubled her, and, for a while, made her more uneasy than she would acknowledge. Her loyalty to Henry was impeccable; but after the departure of FitzGeorge, that stray young traveller whose name her consciousness had scarcely registered, she had felt as though someone had exploded a charge of dynamite in her most secret cellar. Someone by a look had discovered the way into a chamber she kept hidden even from herself. He had committed the supreme audacity of looking into her soul.

'It was queer, wasn't it?' he said, still watching her.

'And after you left us at Agra,' said Lady Slane conversationally, unwilling to admit that he had shaken her, 'what did you do?'

'I went up into Cashmir,' said Mr. FitzGeorge, leaning back

in his chair and putting his fingertips together; 'I went up the river for a fortnight in a houseboat. I had plenty of time to think, and while I gazed over lakes of pink lotus I thought of a young woman in a white dress, so dutiful, so admirably trained, and so wild at heart. I used to flatter myself that for a minute I had come close to her, and then I remembered how after one glance she had turned away and had sauntered off towards her husband. But whether she did it because she was frightened, or because she intended to rebuke me, I could never decide. Perhaps both.'

'If she was frightened,' said Lady Slane, surprising both herself and FitzGeorge, 'it was of herself, not of you.'

'I didn't flatter myself it was of me,' said Mr. FitzGeorge; 'I knew even then that I had no charm for women, especially for lovely, eminent young women like yourself. I didn't desire it,' he said, looking at her as defiantly as his rather absurd old-maidish appearance would allow.

'Of course you didn't,' said Lady Slane, respecting this flicker of a thwarted pride.

'No,' said Mr. FitzGeorge, relapsing appeased; 'I didn't. And yet, you know,' he added, stung by some recollection to a fresh honesty, 'although I had never fallen in love with a woman before, and never have since, I fell in love with you at Fatihpur Sikhri. I suppose I really fell in love with you at that ridiculous dinner-party at Calcutta. Otherwise I should not have come to Fatihpur Sikhri. It took me out of my way, and I have never gone out of my way for man, woman, or child. I am the complete egoist, Lady Slane; you had better know it. Nothing but a work of art could tempt me out of my way. In China, where I went after Cashmir, I was so intoxicated by the works of art that I soon forgot you.'

This strange, incivil, and retarded love-making created a medley of feelings in Lady Slane. It offended her loyalty to Henry. It disturbed her old-age peacefulness. It revived the perplexities of her youth. It shocked her slightly, and pleased her more than it shocked. It was the very last thing she had ever expected—she whose days were now made up of retrospect and of only one anticipation. It was as though Mr. FitzGeorge had arrived with deliberate and malicious purpose to do violence to her settled mood.

'But even in China,' Mr. FitzGeorge went on, 'I still found leisure to think of you and Lord Slane. You seemed to me ill-assorted, as one might say of biscuits, only with biscuits one always assumes that it is the other way round. By saying that you were ill-assorted I don't mean to imply that you did not do your job admirably. You did. So admirably, that it awoke my suspicions. What would you have done with your life, Lady Slane, had you not married that very delightful and disconcerting charlatan?'

'Charlatan, Mr. FitzGeorge?'

'Oh no, of course he wasn't altogether a charlatan,' said Mr. FitzGeorge; 'on the contrary, he managed to be an undisastrous Prime Minister of England during five (I am told) difficult years. Nearly all years, incidentally, are difficult. Perhaps I misjudge him. But you will admit that he was handicapped. He had more charm than any man I ever knew; and though charm pays up to a certain point, there comes a point beyond which no reasonable man can be expected to go. He went beyond it—far beyond. He was too good to be true. You yourself, Lady Slane, must often have suffered from his charm?'

The question was proffered in such a way that Lady Slane nearly replied to it truthfully and inadvertently. Mr. FitzGeorge seemed really interested; and yet, she remembered, she had often watched Henry bending his brows in interest over some human question which could not really interest him at all, withdrawn as he was into a world where human interests shrank to insignificance, and nothing but a cold, sardonic ambition lay at the kernel of his mind, and if so Henry, then why not Mr. FitzGeorge? The one was a statesman, the other a connoisseur; she did not want to be examined as though she were a Tang figure which might possibly turn out to be a fake. Observation of Henry had taught her a lesson she would not easily forget. It had been terrible to live with, and to love, a being so charming, so deceptive, and so chill. Henry, she discovered suddenly, had been a very masculine man; masculinity, in spite of his charm and his culture, was the keynote of his character. He was of the world worldly, for all his scorn.

'I should have been a painter,' said Lady Slane, answering the question before last.

'Ah!' said Mr. FitzGeorge with the relief of a man who has at last secured what he wanted. 'Thank you. That gives me the key. So you were an artist, were you, potentially? But being a woman, that had to go by the board. I see. Now I understand why you sometimes looked so tragic when your face was in repose. I remember looking at you and thinking, That is a woman whose heart is broken.'

'My dear Mr. FitzGeorge!' cried Lady Slane. 'You really mustn't talk as though my life had been a tragedy. I had everything that most women would covet: position, comfort, children, and a husband I loved. I had nothing to complain of—nothing.'

'Except that you were defrauded of the one thing that mattered. Nothing matters to an artist except the fulfilment of his gift. You know that as well as I do. Frustrated, he grows crooked like a tree twisted into an unnatural shape. All meaning goes out of life, and life becomes existence—a makeshift. Face it, Lady Slane. Your children, your husband, your splendour, were nothing but obstacles that kept you from yourself. They were what you chose to substitute for your real vocation. You were too young, I suppose, to know any better, but when you chose that life you sinned against the light.'

Lady Slane put her hand over her eyes. She was no longer strong enough to bear this shock of denouncement. Mr. Fitz-George, suddenly inspired like a preacher, had overturned her placidity without any pity.

'Yes,' she said weakly, 'I know you are right.'

'Of course I am right. Old Fitz may be a comic figure, but he retains some sense of values, and I see that you have offended against one of the first canons of my creed. No wonder that I scold.'

'Don't scold me any more,' said Lady Slane, looking up and smiling; 'I assure you that if I did wrong, I paid for it. But you mustn't blame my husband.'

'I don't. According to his lights, he gave you all you could desire. He merely killed you, that's all. Men do kill women. Most women enjoy being killed; so I am told. Being a woman, I daresay that even you took a certain pleasure in the process. And now, are you angry with me?'

'No,' said Lady Slane; 'I think it is rather a relief to have been found out.'

'Of course you realise that I found you out at Fatihpur Sikhri? Not in detail, certainly, but in principle. This conversation is only a sequel to the conversation we didn't have then.'

Shaken though she was, Lady Slane laughed frankly. She felt immensely grateful to the outrageous Mr. FitzGeorge, who, now that he had ceased to scold her, sat looking at her with humour and affection.

'A conversation interrupted for fifty years,' she said.

'And now never to be resumed,' he said with surprising tact, knowing that she might dread a repeated probing of his lancet into her discovered wound; 'but there are some things which need to be said—this was one of them. Now we can be friends.'

*   *   *

Having thus arranged their friendship, Mr. FitzGeorge took it quite for granted that she should welcome his company. He arrived without warning, installed himself in what rapidly became his own chair, teased Genoux who adored him, carried on extravagant discussions with Mr. Bucktrout, imposed his habits on the house, but nevertheless fitted himself neatly in to Lady Slane's ways of life. He even accompanied her on her slow and shaky walks up to the Heath. Her capes, and his square hat, became familiar objects moving under the wintry trees. They wandered tremulously together, often sitting down on a bench, not admitting to one another that they were tired, but pretending that they desired to admire the view. When they had admired it long enough to feel rested, they agreed to get up and go a little farther. Thus they revived memories of Constable, and even visited Keats' house, that little white box of strain and tragedy marooned among the dark green laurels. Like ghosts themselves, they murmured of the ghost of Fanny Brawne and of the passion which had wrecked Keats; and all the while, just out of reach, round the corner, lurked the passion for Lady Slane which might have wrecked Mr. FitzGeorge, had he not been so wary an egoist (unlike poor Keats), just too wise to let himself float away on a hopeless love for the young Vicereine, just unwise enough to remain remotely faithful for fifty years.

Up on the Heath one day he recalled her to an incident she had forgotten.

'Do you remember,' he said—those three opening words having become so familiar to them that now they smiled whenever they used them—'that the day after that dinner-party I came back to luncheon?'

'Dinner-party?' said Lady Slane vaguely, for her mind no longer worked very quickly. 'What dinner-party?'

'At Calcutta,' he said gently, for he never grew impatient

when she had to be prompted. 'The Viceroy asked me back to luncheon when I had accepted to meet you at Fatihpur Sikhri. He said, we must arrange the details. I arrived rather early, and found you alone. Not quite alone, though. Kay was with you.'

'Kay?' said Lady Slane. 'Oh, but surely Kay wasn't born then.'

'He was two months old. You had him in the room with you, in his crib. Don't you remember? You were rather embarrassed at being found with your baby by a strange young man. But you got over your embarrassment at once—I remember admiring the simplicity of your manners—and asked me to look at him. You held back the curtain of his crib, and for your sake I did give one glance at the horrid little object, but what I really looked at was your hand holding back the curtain. It was as white as the muslin, and stained only with the colour of your rings.'

'These rings,' said Lady Slane, touching the bumps under her black gloves.

'If you say so. I once told Kay I had seen him in his cradle,' said Mr. FitzGeorge, chuckling. 'I had been saving up that joke against him for years. I startled him, I can tell you. But I gave him no explanation. To this day he doesn't know. Unless he asked you?'

'No,' said Lady Slane, 'he never asked me. And if he had asked me I shouldn't have been able to tell him.'

'No; one forgets, one forgets,' said Mr. FitzGeorge, staring out over the Heath. 'Yet there are some things one never forgets. I remember your hand on the curtain, and I remember your expression as you looked down on that nasty little new thing which has grown up into Kay. I remember the twisted feeling it gave me, to have stumbled into your intimacy. It didn't last long. You rang the bell, and a nurse came and removed Kay complete with his furniture.'

'Are you fond of Kay?' asked Lady Slane.

'Fond?' said Mr. FitzGeorge, astonished. 'Well—I'm used to him. Yes, I suppose you might say I was fond. We understand each other well enough to let each other alone. We're used to each other—put it like that. At our age, anything else would be a nuisance.'

Fondness, indeed, seemed a remote thing even to Lady Slane. She was fond of Mr. FitzGeorge, she supposed, and of Genoux, and of Mr. Bucktrout, and in a less degree of Mr. Gosheron, but it was a fondness out of which all the trouble and the agitation had departed. Even as the vitality had departed out of her old body. All emotion now was a twilight thing. She could say no more than that it was pleasant to stroll and sit on the Heath with Mr. FitzGeorge while he evoked memories of a day whose light, even through those veils, flared up too strongly for her faded eyes.

Even so, Mr. FitzGeorge had not told Lady Slane the whole of the truth. He had not reminded her that when he came that day and found her alone with Kay in his cradle in a corner of the room, he had also found her kneeling on the floor surrounded by a mass of flowers. To his idea, fresh from England, the season was winter; yet, cut from an Indian garden, roses, larkspurs, and sweet-peas lay sorted into heaps around her. Transparent glasses filled with water made points of light as they stood about all over the carpet. She had looked up at him, the unexpected visitor, catching her at an employment improbable in a Vicereine. Secretaries or gardeners should have fulfilled this function with which she preferred to deal herself. Her fingers dripping, she had looked up, pushing the hair out of her eyes. But she had pushed something else out of her eyes with the same gesture; she had pushed her whole private life out of them, and had replaced it by the perfunctory courtesy with which she rose, and, giving him her hand, wiping it first on a duster, said, 'Oh,

Mr. FitzGeorge,'—she had known his name then, temporarily
—'do forgive me, I had no idea it was so late.'

Down in St. James's Street, Mr. FitzGeorge's frequent absences
were noticed. Kay Holland himself observed that Fitz was now
less readily available for dinner than formerly, though the
explanation lay beyond the wildest range of his suspicion. Far
from coming near to the truth, he was full of an undeserved
solicitude for his old friend, wondering whether perhaps fatigue
or even ill-health compelled him to betake himself early to bed;
but on so ceremonious a basis had their relationship always been
placed that Kay could venture on no inquiries. He was acquainted with Mr. FitzGeorge's rooms and could form some idea
of how the old gentleman lived; could, in fact, imagine him
shuffling about in a dressing-gown and slippers among the disorder of his incomparable works of art, dissolving a soup-tablet for
his supper over the gas-ring, economising the electric light so
that one bulb alone illuminated the small Jaeger-clad figure and
touched the gilding on the stacked-up frames—or did he resort
to a candle-end stuck into a bottle? Kay was sure that Mr.
FitzGeorge did not allow himself enough to eat, nor could it be
very healthy to live among so much dust in the low, over-
crowded rooms where a daily charwoman was permitted only
the minimum of service. How Fitz himself contrived to emerge
presentably spruce and well-groomed from this sordid confusion
was a mystery to Kay, who spent a great deal of his time in
keeping his own surroundings as shiningly clean as possible. No
spinster, in fact, could be more house-proud than Kay Holland
supervising his annual spring-cleaning; washing, with his shirt-
sleeves rolled up, the more fragile of his treasures with his own
hands in a basin of water. But old Fitz! Kay supposed that those
two rooms had never been turned out since Fitz had moved into
them, untold years ago; a magpie's nest under the eaves of

Bernard Street, filled with the accumulation carried in, piece by piece; dumped on a chair or on the floor when the chairs gave out, stuffed into a drawer, crowded into a cupboard that would no longer shut; never touched, never dusted, except when Mr. FitzGeorge consenting to reveal his masterpieces to a visitor would blow the grimy coating away and hold picture, bronze, or carving up to the light.

And now Fitz was seldom to be seen. When he did walk into the Club, he seemed the same as usual and Kay's misgivings dwindled; if anything, he seemed a little more lively than before, abusing Kay with greater gusto, a twinkle in his eye as though he were enjoying a secret joke. Which indeed he was. Kay sat there, warmed and happy. No one had ever made fun of him as FitzGeorge made fun. But although Kay longed to revert to that conversation about having been seen in his cradle, shyness and habit forbade.

Fitz, however, had ceased asking to be introduced to Lady Slane, much to Kay's relief. He had been sure that his mother would not at all welcome the advent of a stranger in her retirement at Hampstead. He flattered himself, indeed, on his perception in this matter and on the skill he had shown in staving old Fitz off. Yet from time to time he felt a qualm: had he perhaps been rather unkindly firm in discouraging Fitz's one attempt at a new friendship? It must have cost Fitz a great effort to make the suggestion; an even greater effort to renew it. Still, his first duty was to his mother. Neither Carrie, nor Herbert, nor Charles could understand their mother's desire for retirement; but he, Kay, could understand it. It was, therefore, his duty to protect his mother in her desire. He had protected her—though he was usually overawed by Fitz—and thanks to his evasiveness Fitz had apparently forgotten all about his whim. Kay thought that he must go and see his mother one of these days and tell her how clever he had been.

He kept on putting off the expedition, however, for the January weather was bitterly cold, and Kay, who loved warmth and snugness as much as a cat, easily persuaded himself that draughty Underground stations were no place for a coddled person of his advancing years. Well wrapped up in overcoat and muffler, he could just undertake the walk from his rooms in the Temple across Fountain Court, through pigeons too fat to get out of his way, down the steps to the Embankment, up Northumberland Avenue and then through the Park to St. James's Street, his daily constitutional, but farther abroad than that he would not venture. He walked, not only for the sake of exercise, but because he had a lively sense of the presence of microbes in all public conveyances; a microbe to him was a horror even greater than a reptile; he seldom got through the day without imagining himself the victim of at least one deadly disease, and never drank a cup of tea without remembering thankfully that the water had been boiled into immunity. As it was, he welcomed a day of rain or sleet which gave him a pretext for remaining indoors. He quieted his conscience by writing little friendly notes to his mother, saying that he had had a cold, that he understood a great deal of influenza was about, and that he hoped Genoux was taking proper care of her. All the same, he thought, on the first fine day he must go to Hampstead and tell his mother about FitzGeorge. She would be amused. She would be grateful.

But Kay, like many a wiser man, deferred his plan just a little too long. He had forgotten Mr. FitzGeorge's twenty-five years of seniority. Eighty-one was not an age which permitted the playing of tricks with time. At twenty, thirty, forty, fifty, sixty, one might reasonably say, I will put that off until next summer—though, to be sure, even at twenty, the unexpected perils of life were always present—but at eighty-one such deferments became a mere taunt in the face of Fate. That which had been an unexpected and improbable peril in earlier years, swelled to a certainty after eighty. Kay's standards were perhaps distorted by the longevity of his own family. Certainly FitzGeorge's death came to him as a shock which he received with incredulity and resentment.

The first indication he had of it appeared on the posters: DEATH OF WEST-END CLUB-MAN. He registered this piece of news unconsciously as he walked down the Embankment and turned up Northumberland Avenue on his way to luncheon; it meant no more to him than the news of an omnibus mounting the pavement in Brixton. A little farther on he saw other posters, lunch edition: LONELY MILLIONAIRE DIES IN WEST-END. If the thought of FitzGeorge crossed his mind, he dismissed it; for Bernard Street, even by a journalist, could scarcely be described as West End. Kay had no experience of Fleet Street. Still, he bought a paper. He crossed the Park, noticing that the crocuses were beginning to show green noses above the ground. Thus had he walked a thousand times. Serene, he turned into Boodle's and ordered his bottle of Vichy water, unfolded his napkin, propped the *Evening Standard* before him, and started on his lunch—a cut from the joint, and pickles. He had no need to tell the waiter what he wanted, so regular and recurrent was daily life. There it was, in the second column on the front page: WEST-END CLUB-MAN FOUND DEAD: STRANGE LIFE-STORY OF WEALTHY RECLUSE REVEALED. (Even then, it occurred to Kay to wonder how one could be both a club-man and a recluse.) Then the name hit him: Mr. FitzGeorge. . . .

He put down his knife and fork with a clatter on his plate so that the other lunchers, who had wondered at Kay Holland's impassivity, raised their heads and whispered: 'Ah, he's heard!' Heard, when they meant read. But indeed with some justice they might say heard, since the printed name had screamed at Kay loud enough to deafen him. He felt as though someone had fetched him a box on the ear. 'Fitz dead?' he said to the man at the next table—a man he did not know, except by sight for the last twenty years, and to whom he had been accustomed to nod.

Then without knowing how he got there, except for some dim recollection of plunging into his pockets to pay the taxi, he found himself in Bernard Street, climbing the stairs to Fitz's rooms. The door into Fitz's rooms was broken in—smashed—splintered—and the police were there, two large young men, pompous and apologetic, very civil and accommodating to Kay when they learnt his name. Fitz was there too, lying on his bed in his Jaeger dressing-gown, curiously stiff. On the table were a sardine and a half, and a half-eaten piece of toast and the remains of a boiled egg, as unappetising as only the cold remains of a boiled egg can be. Fitz wore a night-cap, which was a surprise to Kay, a night-cap with a sideways tassel. He looked much the same as he had looked in life, except that he looked completely different. It was hard to say where the difference came in; the rigidity could scarcely account for it; perhaps it might be attributed to the guilty sense of eavesdropping on old Fitz, of catching him transfixed in a moment hitherto unseen by all eyes, the slippered moment, the night-cap moment, the moment when the three last sardines had been taken from the cupboard. 'We mustn't remove him, sir,' said one of the young policemen, on the watch lest Kay should go too near and touch his friend, 'before the doctors is entirely satisfied.'

Kay shrank towards the window, contrasting this death with that of his own father. They had indeed chosen very different paths in life. Fitz had scorned the world, he had lived secretly and privately, finding his pleasures within himself, betraying himself to none. Only once had Kay seen him roused, when some newspaper published an article on the eccentrics of London. 'God!' he had said, 'is it eccentric to keep oneself apart?' He had been enraged by the inclusion of his own name. He could see no reason for the curiosity commonly displayed by people over other people; it seemed to him vulgar, boring, and unnecessary. All he asked was to be let alone; he had no desire to interfere in the workings of the world; he simply wanted to live withdrawn into his chosen world, absorbed in his possessions and their beauty. That was his form of spirituality, his form of contemplation. Thus the loneliness of his death held no pathos, since it was in accordance with what he had chosen.

But it worried the agents of the law and the State. They invaded his room, while Kay stood wretchedly by the window fingering the grimy curtains. This gentleman, they said, looking at the stiff and silent figure, had been extremely wealthy; in fact, it was reported that his fortune had run into seven numbers. And although they were accustomed to deal with the lonely death of paupers, no precedent told them how to deal with the lonely death of a millionaire. He must have had *some* relatives, they said, looking at Kay as though Kay were to blame. But Kay said no; so far as he knew, Mr. FitzGeorge had no relatives at all; no link with anyone on earth. 'Stay,' he added, 'the South Kensington Museum might be able to tell you something about him.'

At that the Inspector guffawed, and then put his hand over his mouth, remembering that he was in a death-chamber. A museum! he said; well, that was a pretty dreary source of information to go to about a man after he was dead. The Inspector doubtless had a comfortable wife, rows of rowdy children, and pots of red geranium on the window-sill. As a matter of fact, he said, Mr. Holland wasn't so far off the mark when he mentioned the Museum. But for the Museum, he, the Inspector, and his subordinates wouldn't be there at all. The presence of the police was most irregular, where there was no suggestion of murder or suicide. Only, thanks to the Museum ringing up Scotland Yard in what the Inspector described as a 'state,' had Scotland Yard sent police to Bernard Street to keep watch over valuable objects which might turn out to be a legacy to the nation. Much as the Inspector manifestly despised the objects, he responded with instant appreciation to the word valuable. But couldn't Mr. Holland suggest anything a bit more human than a museum? Mr. Holland couldn't. He suggested feebly that they might look Mr. FitzGeorge up in *Who's Who*.

Well, said the Inspector, getting out a note-book and settling down to business, who was his father, anyway? Keep those reporters out, he added angrily to his two subordinates. He never had a father, said Kay, feeling like a netted rabbit and wishing that he had never come near Bernard Street to be bullied by the officials of the law. He had, moreover, a suspicion that the Inspector was exceeding his duties in the interest of his curiosity by thus inquiring into the antecedents of the dead millionaire.

The Inspector stared, and a joke dawned in his eyes, but because of his self-importance he suppressed it. 'His mother, then?' he said, implying that although a man might have dispensed with a father he could scarcely dispense with a mother. But Kay had passed beyond the region of such implications; he could see FitzGeorge only as an isolated figure, fighting to maintain its independence. 'He never had a mother either,' he replied.

'Then what *did* he have?' asked the Inspector, glancing at his subordinates with an expression that summed Kay up in the sole word, Balmy.

Kay was tempted to reply, A private life; for he felt a little light-headed, and the discrepancy between FitzGeorge and the Inspector, with all that the Inspector stood for, was almost too much for him; but he compromised, and pointing to the jumble of works of art cluttering the room, said, 'These.'

'That's not enough,' said the Inspector.

'It was enough for him,' said Kay.

'That junk?' said the Inspector. Kay was silent.

One of the policemen came forward and whispered, showing the Inspector a card. 'All right,' said the Inspector after looking at the card; 'let him in.'

'There's a lot of reporters on the landing, sir, as well.'

'Keep them out, I told you.'

'They say they only want a peep at the room, sir.'

'Well, they can't have it. Tell them there's nothing to see.'

'Very good, sir.'

'Only a lot of junk.'

'Very good, sir.'

'Show in the gentleman from the Museum. Nobody else. It seems,' said the Inspector, turning to Kay, 'that we were right about this here Museum. Here it is, turning up as it might be an uncle of the corpse. Prompt.' He passed the card over to Kay, who read: 'Mr. Christopher Foljambe, Victoria and Albert Museum.'

A young man in a bowler-hat, a blue overcoat, kid-gloves, and horn-rimmed spectacles came in. He cast one glance at Mr. FitzGeorge and then averted his eyes, which roamed instead over the litter in the room, appraising, while he talked to the Inspector. His attitude, however, differed from the Inspector's, for every now and then his eye would light up and his hand would start out in an involuntary predatory movement towards some dusty but invaluable pile on chair or table. He had, moreover, greeted Kay Holland with deference, thereby increasing Kay's prestige in the Inspector's estimation. A museum, after all, was a public institution, authorised in a very practical (although meagre) way by Government subsidy; and that was the kind of thing which commanded, one might almost say bought, the Inspector's respect. He treated Mr. Foljambe with more deference than he had shown to Kay Holland. For in Kay Holland he had not recognised an ex-Prime Minister's son, whereas Mr. Foljambe had sent in a card definitely stating: 'Victoria and Albert Museum.'

Mr. Foljambe, to do him justice, was ill-at-ease. He had been dispatched by his superiors in a hurry to see that old Fitz's things were duly safeguarded. The Museum, thanks to hints thrown out by old Fitz during the past forty years, considered that they might reasonably expect to have a claim on his possible legacies. Kay Holland, again retreating to the window and again fingering the grimy curtains, gave to both the Inspector and to Mr. Foljambe the credit due to them. The Inspector had a duty to fulfil; and Mr. Foljambe had been dispatched by his museum on an uncongenial job. Old Fitz's delight in a new discovery, old Fitz's grumpy and restrained rapture over some lovely object, belonged to a different world than this practical protection of a dead man, than this interest in the dead man's dispositions. Kay knew just enough of the world to realise that it must be so. Even on behalf of his friend, he could feel no real irony. The Inspector and Mr. Foljambe were both acting according to their lights. And Mr. Foljambe, especially, was being very decent about it.

'Of course, I know we have no right to interfere,' he was saying, 'but considering the immense value of the collection, and considering the fact that Mr. FitzGeorge always gave us to understand that he would bequeath the majority of his possessions to the nation, my museum felt that some adequate steps should be taken for the safeguarding of the property. I was instructed to say that if you would like one of our men to take charge, he would be at your disposal.'

'Did I understand you to say, sir, that the collection was of immense value?'

'It runs into millions, I should say,' replied Mr. Foljambe with relish.

'Well . . .' said the Inspector. 'I don't know anything about such things myself. The room looks to me like a pawnbroker's shop. But if you say so, sir, I must take your word for it. The gentleman,' he jerked his thumb at Mr. FitzGeorge, 'appears to have had no family?'

'None that I ever heard of.'

'Very unusual, sir. Very unusual for such a wealthy man.'

'Solicitors?' suggested Mr. Foljambe.

'No firm has come forward as yet, sir. Yet the news was in the lunch edition of the papers; true, there's no telephone here,' said the Inspector, looking round in disgust. 'They'd have to come in person.'

'Mr. FitzGeorge was a retiring sort of man.'

'So I understand, sir—a real solitary, you might say. Can't understand it myself; I like a bit of company. All right up here, sir?' asked the Inspector, tapping his forehead.

'A bit eccentric perhaps; nothing more.'

'You would expect a gentleman of his sort to be a J.P., or something, wouldn't you, sir? To have some public work, I mean—hospital committees, or something.'

'I don't think Mr. FitzGeorge was very publicly minded,' said Mr. Foljambe in such a tone that Kay could not decide whether he was being sympathetic or censorious. 'And yet,' he added, 'I oughtn't to say that about a man who can leave such a priceless collection to the nation.'

'You don't know for sure that he has,' said the Inspector.

Mr. Foljambe shrugged. 'His hints were pretty clear. And if he hasn't left it to the nation, who could he leave it to? Unless he's left it all to you, Mr. Holland,' he said, turning to Kay, pleased by his own joke.

But Mr. FitzGeorge had left his collection neither to the nation nor to Kay Holland. He had left it all, including the whole of his fortune, to Lady Slane. The will was written on a half-sheet of paper, but it was perfectly lucid, perfectly in order, duly witnessed, and left no loophole for other interpretation. It revoked a previous will, by which the fortune went to charity and the collection to be divided between various museums and the National and Tate Galleries. It stated expressly that Lady Slane's possession was to be absolute, and that no obligation was imposed on her as to the ultimate disposal.

This news was made public amid general consternation. The rage and dismay of the museums were equalled only by the astonishment and delight of Lady Slane's own family, which gathered at once and in force round Carrie's tea-table. Carrie was in the strong and enviable position of having seen her mother that very afternoon; she had, in fact, rushed straight up to Hampstead. 'Dear Mother,' she said, 'I couldn't leave her alone with that great responsibility thrust upon her. You know how little fitted she is to deal with that kind of thing.' 'But how on earth,' said Herbert, particularly explosive that day, 'how on earth did it all come about? How did she know this man FitzGeorge? And what had Kay to do with it? We know Kay and FitzGeorge were friends; we never knew that Mother knew him so much as by sight. I never heard her mention his name.' Herbert's explosiveness crackled like a heath fire.

'It was a plot, that's what it was; and Kay was at the bottom of it. Kay wanted the old man's things for himself. Well, Kay at any rate has been nicely sold.'

'But has he?' said Charles. 'How do we know that Kay hasn't got some private arrangement with Mother? Kay always kept himself apart from us; I always felt that Kay might be a little unscrupulous.'

'Oh, surely,' began Mabel.

'Be quiet, Mabel,' said Herbert. 'I agree with Charles; certainly Kay has always been a bit of a dark horse. And Mother has never said anything to any of us about her will.'

'Up to now,' said Edith, who had joined her relations,

though she despised herself for doing so, 'she has never had anything to leave.'

Edith's remark passed unnoticed as usual.

'I disagree with all of you,' said William, who was respected in his family for having the best grasp of practical considerations; 'if Kay and Mother had had an understanding between them, they would not have arranged for this FitzGeorge's fortune to go first to Mother. Think of the duties.'

'Death-duties?' said Edith, tactless as usual, uttering the unpleasant word.

'Half a million at least,' said William. 'No. Much better that it should all have gone straight to Kay.'

'But Mother is so unpractical,' said Carrie with a sigh.

'Tragically unpractical,' said William. 'Why didn't she consult one of us? But it's done now,' he resumed more philosophically, 'and what in Heaven's name will she do with it all?'

'She seemed to take no interest in it,' said Carrie. 'I found her reading a book while Genoux fed scraps to the cat in the corner. I don't believe she was really reading it, for when I asked her the title—just trying to make conversation, you know—she couldn't tell me. She said it was something Mudie had sent, but, as you know, Mother always makes up her lists most carefully, and never leaves it to Mudie. I had some difficulty in getting in, because, it appears, the house had been so besieged by newspaper men that Mother had forbidden Genoux to answer the doorbell. I had to go round into the garden and shout "Mother!" under the window.'

'Well,' said Herbert, as Carrie paused, 'and when you had got in, what explanation did she give you?'

'None. She had known this FitzGeorge in India, it appears, and he had been to call on her once or twice recently. So she told me. But I am sure she was keeping something back. When she said FitzGeorge had been to call on her, Genoux, who was hovering about, began to cry and went out of the room. She picked up her apron and began to sniff into it. As she went she said something about "Un si gentil monsieur." From which I assume that he had always given her a tip."

'And what about Mother? Did she seem upset?'

'She was quiet,' said Carrie after a pause, judicially. 'Yes, on the whole, I'm sure she was keeping something back. She kept trying to change the subject. As though one could change the subject! She hadn't seen the posters in London; that was evident. Dear Mother, I was only trying to help her. I did feel it was a little hard to be so misunderstood. She seemed to want to keep me out of it—to keep me at arm's length.'

'But,' said Lavinia, 'what could one want to keep back, at your mother's age? Not . . .?

'Well,' said Carrie, 'one never knows, does one?'

'No,' said Herbert, 'no! I can't believe *that*!' He spoke righteously, as the head of the family.

'Perhaps not,' said Carrie, deferring to him; 'I'm sure your judgment is best, Herbert. And yet, you know, a very strange idea struck me.'

They all edged forward to hear Carrie's very strange idea.

'No, I really can't say it,' said Carrie, delighted at having aroused so much interest; 'I really can't, not even here where I know it would go no further.'

'Carrie!' said Herbert, 'you know we always had a pact that we would never start a sentence unless we meant to finish it.'

'When we were children,' said Carrie, keeping up her reluctance.

'Of course, if you would rather not . . .' said Herbert.

'Well, if you insist,' said Carrie. 'This is what struck me. None of us ever knew of Mother's friendship with this old man—this old FitzGeorge. She never mentioned him to any of us. Now it turns out that she knew him in India—just about the time when Kay was born—perhaps before. And he always took an interest in Kay. Then he dies, leaving everything to Mother—not to Kay, it's true. But that's no reason why Mother shouldn't leave it all in turn to Kay. And perhaps he always meant Kay to have it. He merely short-circuited Kay. Who knows that that may not have been a kind of bluff? Eccentric old men like that, you know, are always terrified of scandal.'

'Because . . .' said Herbert.

'Exactly. Because.'

'Oh no, no!' said Edith, 'it's horrible, Carrie, it's monstrous. Mother loved Father, she never would have deceived him.'

'Dear Edith!' said Carrie. 'So naïve! seeing everything in terms of black or white!' But already she regretted having spoken in the presence of Edith, who might betray her to their mother. She had the best of reasons for wishing to remain on good terms with her mother at present.

Edith took her departure in indignation, leaving a united family behind her. They drew their chairs a little closer.

'And then,' said Carrie, going on with her story, 'a young man came—a most unpleasant young man. Foljambe, from some museum. Genoux behaved most unsuitably. I suppose that he had given her his card, instead of merely giving her his name; anyway, she announced him as Monsieur Follejambe. I suspect that she did it on purpose. But I soon saw that it served him right. It was quite clear that he and his museum had designs on poor Mother's inheritance. He pretended that he had come with an offer from his museum to house the collection if Mother hadn't room for it. Mother, for once, was quite sensible. She would make no promises. She said she hadn't decided what to do. She looked at Foljambe as though he weren't there. And then, of course, Genoux burst in as she always does, asking whether Mother would rather have cutlets or a chicken for dinner. A chicken, she said, was less economical, but it could be finished up next day. And Mother with at least eighty thousand a year!'

Lavinia groaned.

'But Mother was just as reticent with me as with the young man,' Carrie continued. 'I kept on assuring her that I only wanted to help—and you all know me well enough to believe that that was the simple truth—but she looked at me just as vaguely as she looked at Foljambe. She seemed to be thinking of something else all the time. Sentimental memories, perhaps,' said Carrie viciously. 'She didn't even ask me to stay to dinner, when Genoux came in again to say the chicken was nearly ready and would spoil. I had to leave with Foljambe finally, and, of course, I had to offer him a lift in the car. He tells me that the collection, apart from the fortune, is estimated at a couple of million.'

'Poor Father,' said Herbert; 'for the first time I feel glad that he is no longer alive.'

'Yes, that's a great comfort,' said Carrie. 'Poor Father. He never knew.'

They silently digested this comforting fact.

'But,' said William, ever practical, resuming the conversation, 'what will Mother do with all those things—all that money? Eighty thousand a year! And two million or so locked up in works of art! Why, if she sold them, she'd have a hundred and sixty thousand a year—more, if she invested it at five per cent. As she easily could.' His voice became shrill, as it always did over any question of money. 'One never knows, with Mother. Look at the casual way she behaved over the jewels. She seems to have no idea of value, no idea of responsibility. For all we know, she may hand over the whole collection to the nation.'

Terror descended upon Lady Slane's family.

'You don't really believe that, William? Surely she must have *some* feeling for her children?'

'I do believe it,' said William, working himself up. 'Mother is like a child who treats rubies as though they were pebbles. She has never learnt; she has merely wandered through life. You know we have always tacitly felt that Mother wasn't quite like other people. One doesn't like to say that sort of thing about one's mother, but at moments like this one can't afford to be over-delicate. At any moment she may do something erratic, something which makes one wring one's hands in despair. And we are powerless. Powerless!'

'Nonsense, William,' said Carrie, feeling that William was dramatising the situation; 'Mother has always been amenable to reason.'

'Even when she went to live at Hampstead?' said William gloomily. 'I can't agree that people who strike out a new line for themselves at Mother's age are amenable to reason. Even when she gave away the jewels in that ridiculous way?' He looked at Mabel, who nervously tried to cover up the pearls by some stringy lace. 'No, Carrie. Mother is a person who has never had her feet on the ground. Cloud-cuckoo-land—that's Mother's natural home. And, unfortunately, she has met with another inhabitant: Mr. FitzGeorge.'

'And what about Bucktrout?' said Carrie.

'What, indeed?' said William. 'Bucktrout may well induce her to make the whole fortune over to him. Poor Mother—so simple, so unwise. A prey. What is to be done?'

Meanwhile, Mr. Bucktrout had called on Lady Slane to condole with her over this sudden responsibility.

'You see, Mr. Bucktrout,' said Lady Slane, who was looking ill and troubled, 'Mr. FitzGeorge couldn't have known what he was doing. He wanted me to enjoy his beautiful things—I realise that. But what did he imagine I could do with so much money? I have quite enough for my wants. I knew a millionaire once, Mr. Bucktrout, and he was the most unhappy of men. He was so much afraid of assassination that he lived surrounded by detectives. They were like mice in the walls. He wouldn't allow himself to make a friend, because he couldn't get ulterior motives out of his mind. When one sat beside him at dinner, he was all the time fearing that one would end by asking him for a subscription to a favourite charity. Most people disliked him. I liked him very much. I have seen a great deal of men who mistrusted others because they scented ulterior motives, Mr. Bucktrout, and I don't want to be put into the same position. It seems absurd that Mr. FitzGeorge, of all men, should have put me into it. I don't think he can have known what he was doing.'

'In the eyes of the world, Lady Slane,' said Mr. Bucktrout, 'Mr. FitzGeorge has conferred an enormous benefit upon you.'

'I know, I know,' said Lady Slane, deeply worried and distressed, and not wishing to appear ungrateful.

All her life long, she was thinking, people had conferred benefits on her, benefits she did not covet. Henry by making her first into a Vicereine, and then into a political hostess, and now FitzGeorge by heaping her quiet life with gold and treasures.

'I never wanted anything, Mr. Bucktrout,' she said, 'but to stand aside. One of the things, it appears, that the world doesn't allow! Even at the age of eighty-eight.'

'Even the smallest planet,' said Mr. Bucktrout sententiously, 'is compelled to circle round the sun.'

'But does that mean,' asked Lady Slane, 'that we must all, willy-nilly, circle round wealth, position, possessions? I thought Mr. FitzGeorge knew better. Don't *you* understand?' she said, appealing to Mr. Bucktrout in desperation. 'I thought I had escaped at last from all those things, and now Mr. FitzGeorge, of all people, pushes me back into the thick of them. What am I to do, Mr. Bucktrout? What am I to do? I believe Mr. Fitz-George collected very beautiful things, but I know nothing of such things. I always preferred the works of God to the works of man. The works of God, I always felt, were given freely to anyone who could appreciate them, whether millionaire or pauper, whereas the works of man were reserved for the million-aires. Unless, indeed, the works of man were sufficient to the man who made them; then, it wouldn't matter what millionaire bought them in after years. Not that Mr. FitzGeorge,' she added, 'bought the works of man because of their value. He was an artist in appreciation. Besides, he was a miser. Far from paying the market value of a work of art, it amused him to discover a work of art for less that its market value. Then he felt he had got it on terms of a work of God rather than a work of man, if you follow me.'

'I follow you perfectly,' said Mr. Bucktrout.

'Few people would,' said Lady Slane. 'You encourage me to think that you sympathise with my position as few people would sympathise. I don't want all these valuable things, beau-tiful though they may be. It would worry me to think that I had upon my mantelpiece a terra-cotta Cellini, which Genoux would certainly break, dusting one morning before breakfast. No, Mr. Bucktrout. I would rather go up on to the Heath, if I want something to look at, and look at Constable's trees.'

'Rather than own a Constable?' asked Mr. Bucktrout shrewdly. 'I believe that Mr. FitzGeorge's collection includes a very fine Constable of Hampstead Heath.'

'Well,' said Lady Slane, relaxing, 'I might perhaps keep that.'

'But for the rest, Lady Slane,' said Mr. Bucktrout, 'excluding a few pieces that you might be willing to keep for personal reasons, what shall you decide to do?'

'Give them away,' said Lady Slane wearily, not energetically. 'Let the nation have them. Let the hospitals have the money. As Mr. FitzGeorge first intended. Let me be rid of it all. Only let me be rid of it! Besides,' she added, with the twist to which Mr. Bucktrout had become accustomed, 'think how much I shall annoy my children!'

He fully appreciated the subtlety of the practical joke that Lady Slane was playing on her children. Practical jokes, in principle, did not amuse Mr. Bucktrout; he dismissed them as childish and silly; but this particular joke tickled his sense of humour. He had formed a shrewd idea of Lady Slane's children, although he had never seen them.

'But when you die,' said Mr. Bucktrout, with his usual forthrightness, 'your obituary notices will point to you as a disinterested benefactor of the public.'

'I shan't be there to read them,' said Lady Slane, who had learnt enough from Lord Slane's obituary notices about the possibilities of false interpretation.

Mr. Bucktrout walked away genuinely concerned with the perplexity of his old friend. It never occurred to him that most people would regard Lady Slane's wistful regrets as very peculiar regrets indeed. He accepted quite simply the fact that Lady Slane disagreed with the world's customary values, and accordingly it seemed natural to him that she should resent having them so constantly forced upon her. Moreover, he now knew all about her early ambitions, and their complete variance with her actual life. Mr. Bucktrout, although simple in many ways—most people thought him a little mad—was also endowed with a direct and unprejudiced wisdom of his own: he knew that standards must be altered to fit the circumstances, and that it was absurd, although usual, to expect the circumstances to adjust themselves to ready-made standards. Lady Slane thus, in his opinion, deserved as much sympathy in the frustration of her life as an athlete stricken with paralysis. It was an unconventional view to take, no doubt, but Mr. Bucktrout never questioned its rightness.

Genoux, however, was struck with horror when she heard what Lady Slane proposed to do. Her French soul was appalled. For a couple of days she had walked on air, and in order to celebrate this sudden, this unbelievable, accretion of wealth had bought some extra pieces of fish for the cat. Her ideas of the fortune bequeathed to Lady Slane—she had read the amount in the papers, and had counted the zeros on her fingers, incredulously doing the sum several times over—were curiously mixed: she knew well enough what a million was, what two millions were, but in practical application she decided only that she might now venture to ask Lady Slane for the charwoman three times a week instead of twice. Hitherto, in the interests of economy, she had not spared herself even when her rheumatism made her stiffer than usual. She had simply doubled her coverings of brown paper, had put on an extra petticoat, and gone about her business hoping for relief. She knew miladi was not rich, and would rather suffer herself than add to miladi's expenses. But with Lady Slane's decision, casually communicated to her one evening as she came to remove the tray, all visions of future extravagance vanished. 'C'est pas possible, miladi!' she exclaimed. 'Et moi qui pensais voir revenir nos plus beaux jours!' Genoux was really in despair. Moreover, she had been delighted by the light of publicity turned once more on Lady Slane. Both the daily papers and the weekly illustrated papers had flaunted Lady Slane's photograph; the photographs had been very out-of-date, it was true, since nothing recent was available; they had shown Lady Slane as Vicereine, as Ambassadress, young, bejewelled, in evening dress, a tiara crowning her elaborate *coiffure*, seated under a palm; curiously old-fashioned; holding an open book in which

she was not reading; surrounded by her children, Herbert in his
sailor suit, Carrie in her party frock—how well Genoux remembered it!—leaning affectionately over their mother's shoulders,
looking down at the baby—was it Charles? was it William?—
she held upon her knee. One paper even, accepting the impossibility of getting a photograph of Lady Slane to-day, had
boldly made the best of a bad job and had reproduced a photograph taken in her wedding dress seventy years ago. The
companion picture was of Lord Slane in jodhpurs, rifle in hand,
one foot resting on a tiger. These things, which Lady Slane so
inexplicably did not like, satisfied Genoux' sense of fitness. It
was not for her to dictate to miladi, she said, but had miladi
considered her position and what was due to it? miladi, who had
been accustomed to all those aides-de-camp, all those servants—
'bien que ce n'était que des nègres'—all those orderlies,
ready to run at any moment with a note or a message? 'Dans
ce temps-là, miladi était au moins bien servie.' Then, in
the midst of her despair, a thought struck Genoux which caused
her to double up suddenly and rub her hands up and down her
thighs. 'Ah, mon Dieu, miladi, c'est Lady Charlotte qui va
être contente! Et Monsieur William, donc! Ah, la belle
plaisanterie!'

Lady Slane was lonely, now that Mr. FitzGeorge had gone. The
excitement aroused by her gift to the nation, and the frenzy
displayed by her own children, all passed over her without
making much impression. She forbade Genoux to bring a newspaper into the house until the headlines should have dwindled to
a mere paragraph, and she refused to see any of her children until
they would consent to treat the matter as though it had never
happened. Carrie wrote a carefully composed and dignified letter; a few weeks, possibly even a few months must elapse, she
said, before this terrible wound could heal sufficiently to allow

her to observe her mother's condition of silence. Until then she could not trust herself. When she had recovered a little she would write again. Meanwhile it was clear that Lady Slane must consider herself in the direst disgrace.

But although this left her unmoved, and although, thanks to Kay and to Mr. Bucktrout, she had had very little trouble with the authorities, beyond appending her signature to a few documents, she felt tired now and emptied in spirit. Her friendship with FitzGeorge had been strange and lovely—the last strange and lovely thing that was ever likely to happen to her. She desired nothing more. She desired only peace and the laying-down of vexation.

From time to time she came across allusions to her family in the papers. Carrie had opened a bazaar. Carrie's granddaughter was taking part in a charity matinée. Charles had succeeded in getting one of his letters into *The Times*. Richard—Herbert's eldest grandson—had won a point-to-point race. Deborah, his sister, had become most suitably engaged to the eldest son of a duke. Herbert himself had been delivered of a speech in the House of Lords. It was rumoured that the next vacant Governor-generalship would be awarded to Herbert. As it was, he had received the K.C.M.G. in the New Year Honours. . . . From the immense distance of her years Lady Slane contemplated these happenings, tiny and far-off, bringing with them some echo of the events mixed up with her own life. 'How weary, flat, stale, and unprofitable,' she said to herself, going carefully down-stairs with the help of a stick and the banisters, and wondering why, at the end of one's life, one should ever trouble to read anything but Shakespeare; or, for the matter of that, at the beginning of one's life either, since he seemed to have understood both exuberance and maturity. But it was only in maturity, perhaps, that one could fully appreciate his deeper understanding.

She looked upon this group of people, sprung from her own loins, and saw them in mid-career or else starting out upon their course. Young Deborah, she supposed, was happy in her engagement, and young Richard felt himself filled to the brim with life as he rode across country. She smiled quite tenderly as she thought of the two young creatures. But they would harden, she thought, they would harden when their warm youth grew chilled; they would become worldly-wise, self-seeking; the rash generosity of youth would be replaced by the prudence of middle-age. There would be no battle for them, no struggle in their souls; they would simply set hard into the moulds prepared for them. Lady Slane sighed to think that she was responsible, though indirectly, for their existence. The long, weary serpent of posterity streamed away from her. She felt sick at heart, and looked forward only to release.

Still, she did an inexplicable thing. After she had done it— after she had written the letter, stamped it, and given it to Genoux to post—she looked back upon her action and decided that she had acted in a trance. She could not say what impulse had moved her, what strange desire had tugged at her to recreate a link with the life she had abjured. Perhaps her loneliness was greater than any human courage could stand; perhaps she had overrated her own fortitude. Only a very strong soul could stand quite alone. Be that as it might, she had written to a press-cutting agency with the instruction that any references to her own family should be supplied to her. Privately, she knew that she wanted only the references to her great-grandchildren. She cared very little what happened to Carrie, Herbert, Charles, and William; the path that they followed and would continue to follow was clearly marked, offering no surprises, no delights. But even in her trance she shrank from betraying herself to the eyes of an agency in Holborn: she disguised her real desire under the extravagance of a general order. When the little green packets began to arrive, however, all references to her own children went straight into the waste-paper basket, and references to her great-grandchildren only were pasted very carefully by Lady Slane into an album bought from the stationer round the corner.

She derived an extraordinary pleasure from this occupation, carried on every evening under the shade of the pink lamp. Every evening, for, realising that a fresh supply would not arrive more than twice or thrice a week, she economised her little hoard, and would allow herself the luxury of pasting in only a proportion of the cuttings every day, so that one or two might always remain left over for the morrow. Fortunately, out of Lady Slane's great-grandchildren, two were grown-up, and their activities manifold. They were, in fact, among the prominent young people of the day, and in the gossip columns they had their news-value. Many pleasant hours were spent by Lady Slane in constructing their characters and personalities from these snip-pets, reinforced by her previous knowledge of them; a recreation for their great-grandmother of which the children themselves were entirely ignorant, an ignorance which added considerably to Lady Slane's half-mischievous, half-sentimental pleasure, for pleasure to her was entirely a private matter, a secret joke, intense, redolent, but as easily bruised as the petals of a gardenia. Genoux alone knew of her nightly occupation, but Genoux was no intrusion, being as much a part of Lady Slane as her boots or her hot-water bottle, or as the cat John, who sat bunched with incomparable neatness and dignity before the fire. Genoux indeed shared Lady Slane's interest in the young Hollands, though from a different point of view. She had been quick to guess and to welcome Lady Slane's reviving interest, and trotted in with a green packet as soon as it had fallen through the letter-box. 'Voilà, miladi! c'est arrivé!' and she would stand by expectantly while Lady Slane stripped off the wrapper and revealed the print. They were futile enough, heaven knows, these paragraphs. Treasure-hunting in Underground stations; a ball; a party; sometimes a photograph, of Richard in riding-breeches or of Deborah representing Mary Queen of Scots at a fancy-dress ball. Futile, but young and harmless. Lady Slane turned them over, and who should presume to analyse her feelings? But Genoux frankly clasped her hands in ecstasy. 'Ah, miladi, qu'il est donc beau, Monsieur Richard! Ah, miladi, qu'elle est donc jolie!' That was Deborah. Lady Slane would smile, pleased by Genoux' admiration. She was, after all, an old woman, and small things pleased her now. 'Yes,' she said, looking at a photograph of Richard, muddy, holding a silver cup under one arm and a riding whip under the other, 'he is a well-built young man—pas si mal.' 'Pas si mal!' cried Genoux in indignation, 'he is superb, a god; such elegance, such chic. All the young women must be mad about him. And he will follow in the footsteps of his great-grandfather,' added Genoux, who had a wholesome appreciation of worldly prestige; 'he will be Viceroy, Prime Minister, Dieu sait quoi encore; miladi verra.' For Genoux had never estimated Lady Slane's contempt for such things. 'No, Genoux,' said Lady Slane; 'I shan't be there to see.'

She would see only, and at so queer a remove, their lovely, silly youth. Thank God, she would not be there to see their hardening into an even sillier adult life, redeemed not even by this wild, foolish, but decorative quality. 'Nymphs and shepherds, come away,' she murmured, looking at the thick hair, the slim elastic limbs. 'Ah, Genoux,' she said, 'it was good to be young.'

That depends, said Genoux sagely, on what sort of a youth one had. It was not good to be the twelfth child of poor parents, and to be sent to live with farmers near Poitiers; to sleep on straw in a barn; never to see one's parents; to get up at five every morning, winter and summer; to be beaten if one didn't do one's work properly; to know that one's brothers and sisters were growing up as strangers. Genoux had been with Lady Slane for nearly seventy years, yet Lady Slane had never heard this revelation. She turned to Genoux with curiosity. 'And when you did see your brothers and sisters again, Genoux, did it feel very strange to you?'

Not a bit, said Genoux; blood counted. One's own family was one's own family. She had walked into the little flat in Paris, at the age of sixteen, as though she belonged there by right. The farm near Poitiers had vanished, and she never thought of it again, though she knew better than anybody where the straying hens laid their eggs. She had walked straight into the lives of her brothers and sisters and had taken up her place there as though she had never been away. She had had a little trouble with one of her sisters, who had given birth to twins just after her elder child had died of diphtheria. They had tried to conceal the death from her, Genoux said, but she had guessed it somehow, and leaping straight out of bed had rushed as she was, in her nightgown, to the cemetery, there to fling herself upon the grave. Genoux had been sent to fetch her back, nor had it apparently struck her as odd that a girl of her age should be employed on such a mission. Necessity ruled; and her mother had to stay at home to look after the twins. But her sojourn with her family had been but a brief interlude. Her father had already put down her name at a registry office, and the next thing she knew was that she was crossing the Channel to England, to take service with miladi.

Lady Slane listened with some emotion to this simple and philosophical recital. She blamed herself for never having questioned Genoux before. She had taken Genoux for granted, all these years; yet a wealth of experience was locked up in that sturdy breast. It must have been a curious transition, from the farm near Poitiers, where she slept on straw and was beaten, to the magnificence of Government House and Viceregal

Lodge. . . . The experiences of her great-grandchildren seemed
shallow indeed by comparison; her own experiences seemed thin
and over-civilised, lacking any contact with reality. She, who
had brooded in secret over an unfulfilled vocation, had never
been obliged to tear a distraught sister away from a newly-dug
grave. Watching Genoux, who stood there imperturbably relating these trials out of the past, she wondered which wounds
went the deeper: the jagged wounds of reality, or the profound
invisible bruises of the imagination?

Since those days Genoux had never had any personal life, she
supposed. Her life was in her service, with self submerged. Lady
Slane suddenly condemned herself as an egoistic old woman.
Yet, she reflected, she also had given her life away, to Henry.
She need not blame herself overmuch for the last indulgence of
her melancholy.

She returned to Genoux. The Holland family had replaced
Genoux' own family, absorbing everything that Genoux possessed of pride, ambition, snobbery. She remembered Genoux'
paeans of delight when Henry had been given a peerage. Over
every child she had watched as though it were her own, and
nothing but her fierce protectiveness of Lady Slane could have
drawn from her a word of criticism about the Holland children.
Now she transferred her interest to the great-grandchildren,
making no difference since the day they had ceased to come to
the house. Her loyal soul had momentarily been torn in half by
Lady Slane's refusal to receive Deborah and Richard. But when
Lady Slane explained that youthful vitality was too tiring for
an old lady, she had at once readjusted her notions. 'Bien
sûr, miladi; la jeunesse, c'est très fatigant.'

She welcomed, however, this suitable revival of family pride
typified in the green packets and the album. Deep down in her
peasant wisdom, she recognised the wholesome instinct for
perpetuation in posterity. Her own womanhood unfulfilled, she

clung pathetically to a vicarious satisfaction through the medium of her adored Lady Slane. 'Ça me fait du bien,' she said, tears in her eyes, 'de voir miladi s'occuper avec son petit pot of Stickphast.' And once she lifted up John, the cat, to look at a full-page photograph of Richard in the *Tatler*. 'Regarde, mon bobo, le beau gars.' John struggled and would not look. She set him down again, disappointed. 'C'est drôle, miladi; les animaux, c'est si intelligent, mais ça ne reconnaît jamais les images.'

Common sense rarely laid its fingers on Lady Slane, these days. It did occur to her to wonder, however, what the young people had thought of her renunciation of FitzGeorge's fortune. They had been indignant probably; they had cursed their great-grandmother soundly for defrauding them of a benefit which would eventually have been theirs. They would certainly have given her no credit for romantic motives. Perhaps she owed them an explanation, though not an apology? But how could she get into touch with them, now especially? Pride caught her wrist even as she stretched her pen out towards the ink. She had, after all, behaved towards them in what to any reasonable person must seem a most unnatural way; first she had refused to see them, and then she had eliminated from their future the possibility of great and easy wealth. She must appear to them as the incarnation of egoism and inconsideration. Lady Slane was distressed, yet she knew that she had acted according to her convictions. Had not FitzGeorge himself once taken her to task for sinning against the light? And suddenly, in a moment of illumination, she understood why FitzGeorge had tempted her with this fortune: he had tempted her only in order that she should find the strength to reject it. He had offered her not so much a fortune as a chance to be true to herself. Lady Slane bent down and stroked the cat, whom as a rule she did not much like. 'John,' she said, 'John—how fortunate that I did what he wanted, before I realised what he wanted.'

After that she was happy, though her qualms about her young

descendants continued to worry her. By a curious twist, her qualms of conscience about them increased now that she had satisfactorily explained her own action to herself, as though she blamed herself for some extravagant gesture of self-indulgence. Perhaps she had come too hastily to her decision? Perhaps she had treated the children unfairly? Perhaps one should not demand sacrifices of others, consequent upon one's own ideas? She had consulted her own ideas entirely, with the added spice of pleasure, she must admit, in annoying Carrie, Herbert, Charles, and William. It had seemed wrong to her that private people should own such possessions, such exaggerated wealth; therefore she had hastened to dispose of both, the treasures to the public and the money to the suffering poor; the logic was simple though trenchant. Stated in these terms, she could not believe in her own wrong-doing; but on the other hand, should she not have considered her great-grandchildren? It was a subtle problem to decide alone; and Mr. Bucktrout, to whom she confided it, gave her no help, for not only was he entirely in sympathy with her first instinct but, moreover, in view of the approaching end of the world, he could not see that it mattered very much one way or the other. 'My dear lady,' he said, 'when your Cellinis, your Poussins, your grandchildren, and your great-grandchildren are all mingled in planetary dust your problem of conscience will cease to be of much importance.' That was true rather than helpful. Astronomical truths, enlarging though they may be to the imagination, contain little assistance for immediate problems. She continued to gaze at him in distress, a distress which at that very moment had been augmented by a sudden thought of what Henry, raising his eyebrows, would have said.

'Miss Deborah Holland,' said Genoux, throwing open the door. She threw it open in such a way as to suggest that she was retrospectively aping the manner of the grand major-domo at the Paris Embassy.

Lady Slane rose in a fluster, with the usual soft rustle of her silks and laces; her knitting slipped to the floor; she stooped ineffectually to retrieve it; her mind swept wildly round, seeking to reconcile this improbable encounter between her great-grand-daughter, Mr. Bucktrout, and herself. The circumstances were too complicated for her to govern successfully in a moment's thought. She had never been good at dealing with a situation that demanded nimbleness of wit; and, considering the conver-sations she had had with Mr. Bucktrout about her great-grand-children, of whom Herbert's granddaughter thus suddenly presented herself as a specimen, the situation demanded a very nimble wit indeed. 'My *dear* Deborah,' said Lady Slane, scurry-ing affectionately, dropping her knitting, trying to retrieve it, abandoning the attempt midway, and finally managing to kiss Deborah on the cheek.

She was the more confused, for Deborah was the first young person to enter the house at Hampstead since Lady Slane had removed herself from Elm Park Gardens. The house at Hampstead had opened its doors to no one but Mr. FitzGeorge, Mr. Bucktrout, and Mr. Gosheron—and, of course, on occasion, to Lady Slane's own children, who, although they might be unwelcome, were at any rate advanced in years. Deborah came in the person of youth knocking at the doors. She was pretty, under her fur cap; pretty and elegant; the very girl Lady Slane would have expected from her photographs in the society papers. In the year since Lady Slane had seen her, she had changed from a schoolgirl into a young lady. Of her activities in the fashionable world since she became a young lady, Lady Slane had had ample evidence. This observation reminded Lady Slane of her press-cutting album, which was lying on the table under the lamp; releasing Deborah's hand, she hurriedly removed the album to a dark place, as though it were a dirtied cup of tea. She put the blotter over it. A narrow escape; narrow and unforeseen;

but now she felt safe. She came back and introduced Deborah formally to Mr. Bucktrout.

Mr. Bucktrout had the tact to take his leave almost immediately. Lady Slane, knowing him, had feared that he might plunge instantly into topics of the deepest import, with references to her own recent and eccentric conduct, thereby embarrassing both the girl and herself. Mr. Bucktrout, however, behaved most unexpectedly as a man of the world. He made a few remarks about the beginning of spring—about the reappearance of flowers on barrows in the London streets—about the longevity of anemones in water, especially if you cut their stems—about the bunches of snowdrops that came up from the country, and how soon they would be succeeded by bunches of primroses—about Covent Garden. But about cosmic catastrophes or the right judgment of Deborah Holland's great-grandmother he said nothing. Only once did he verge on an indiscretion, when he leant forward, putting his finger against his nose, and said, 'Miss Deborah, you bear a certain resemblance to Lady Slane whom I have the honour to call my friend.' Fortunately, he did not follow up the remark, but after the correct interval merely rose and took his leave. Lady Slane was grateful to him, yet it was with dismay that she saw him go, leaving her face to face with a young woman bearing what had once been her own name.

She expected an evasive and meaningless conversation as a start, dreading the chance phrase that would fire it into realities, growing swiftly like Jack's beanstalk into a tangle of reproaches; she expected anything in the world but that Deborah should sit at her knee and thank her with directness and simplicity for what she had done. Lady Slane made no answer at all, except to lay her hand on the girl's head pressed against her knee. She was too much moved to answer; she preferred to let the young voice go on, imagining that she herself was the speaker, reviving her

adolescent years and deluding herself with the fancy that she had
at last found a confidant to whom she could betray her thoughts.
She was old, she was tired, she lost herself willingly in the sweet
illusion. Was it an echo that she heard? or had some miracle
wiped out the years? were the years being played over again,
with a difference? She allowed her fingers to ruffle Deborah's
hair, and, finding it short instead of ringleted, supposed vaguely
that she had put her own early plans for escape into execution.
Had she then really run away from home? had she, indeed,
chosen her own career instead of Henry's? Was she now sitting
on the floor beside a trusted friend, pouring out her reasons, her
aspirations, and her convictions, with a firmness and a certainty
lit as by a flame from within? Fortunate Deborah! she thought,
to be so firm, so trustful, and by one person at least so well
understood; but to which Deborah she alluded, she scarcely
knew.

She had told herself after FitzGeorge's death that no strange
and lovely thing would ever enter her life again, a foolish proph-
ecy. This unexpected confusion of her own life with that of her
great-granddaughter was as strange and as lovely. FitzGeorge's
death had aged her; at her time of life people aged suddenly and
alarmingly; her mind was, perhaps, no longer very clear; but at
least it was clear enough for her to recognise its weakness, and
to say, 'Go on, my darling; you might be myself speaking.'
Deborah, in her young egoism, failed to pick up the significance
of that remark, which Lady Slane, indeed, had inadvertently let
slip. She had no intention of revealing herself to her great-grand-
daughter; her hand upon the latch of the door of death, she had
no intention of troubling the young with a recital of her own
past problems; enough for her, now to submerge herself into a
listener, a pair of ears, though she might still keep her secrets
running in and out of her mind according to her fancy—for it
must be remembered that Lady Slane had always relished the

privacy of her enjoyments. This enjoyment was especially private now, though not very sharp; it was hazy rather than sharp, her perceptions intensified and yet blurred, so that she could feel intensely without being able or obliged to reason. In the deepening twilight of her life, in the maturity of her years, she returned to the fluctuations of adolescence; she became once more the reed wavering in the river, the skiff reaching out towards the sea, yet blown back again and again into the safe waters of the estuary. Youth! youth! she thought; and she, so near to death, imagined that all the perils again awaited her, but this time she would face them more bravely, she would allow no concessions, she would be firm and certain. This child, this Deborah, this self, this other self, this projection of herself, was firm and certain. Her engagement, she said, was a mistake; she had drifted into it to please her grandfather; (Mother doesn't count, she said, nor does Granny—poor Mabel!) her grandfather had ambitions for her, she said; he liked the idea of her being, some day, a duchess; but what was that, she said, compared with what she herself wanted to be, a musician?

When she said 'a musician,' Lady Slane received a little shock, so confidently had she expected Deborah to say 'a painter.' But it came to much the same thing, and her disappointment was quickly healed. The girl was talking as she herself would have talked. She had no prejudice against marriage with someone who measured his values against the same rod as herself. Understanding was impossible between people who did not agree as to the yard and the inch. To her grandfather and her late fiancé, wealth and so great a title measured a yard—two yards—a hundred yards—a mile. To her, they measured an inch—half an inch. Music, on the other hand, and all that it implied, could be measured by no terrestrial scale. Therefore she was grateful to her great-grandmother for reducing her value in the worldly market. 'You see,' she said amused, 'for a week I was supposed to be an heiress, and when it was found that I wasn't an heiress at all it became much easier for me to break off my engagement.'

'When did you break it off?' asked Lady Slane, thinking of her newspaper cuttings which had not mentioned the fact.

'The day before yesterday.'

Genoux came in with the evening post, glad of a pretext to take another look at Deborah. Lady Slane slipped the green packet under her knitting. 'I didn't know,' she said, 'that you had broken it off.'

And such a relief it was, said Deborah, wriggling her shoulders. She would have no more to do, she said, with that crazy world. 'Is it crazy, great-grandmother,' she asked, 'or am I? Or am I merely one of the people who can't fit in? Am I just one of the people who think a different set of things important? Anyhow, why should I accept other people's ideas? My own are just as likely to be right—right for me. I know one or two people who agree with me, but they are always people who don't seem to get on with grandfather or great-aunt Carrie. And another thing'—she paused.

'Go on,' said Lady Slane, moved to the heart by this stumbling and perplexed analysis.

'Well,' said Deborah, 'there seems to be a kind of solidarity between grandfather and great-aunt Carrie and the people that grandfather and great-aunt Carrie approve of. As though cement had been poured over the whole lot. But the people I like always seem to be scattered, lonely people—only they recognise each other as soon as they come together. They seem to be aware of something more important than the things grandfather and great-aunt Carrie think important. I don't yet know exactly what that something is. If it were religion—if I wanted to become a nun instead of a musician—I think that even grandfather would understand dimly what I was talking about. But it isn't religion; and yet it seems to have something of the nature of religion. A chord of music, for instance, gives me more satisfaction than a prayer.'

'Go on,' said Lady Slane.

'Then,' said Deborah, 'among the people I like, I find something hard and concentrated in the middle of them, harsh, almost cruel. A sort of stone of honesty. As though they were determined at all costs to be true to the things that they think matter. Of course,' said Deborah dutifully, remembering the comments of her grandfather and her great-aunt Carrie, 'I know that they are, so to speak, very useless members of society.' She said it with a childish gravity.

'They have their uses,' said Lady Slane; 'they act as a leaven.'

'I never know how to pronounce that word,' said Deborah; 'whether to rhyme with even or seven. I suppose you are right about them, great-grandmother. But the leaven takes a long time to work, and even then it only works among people who are more or less of the same mind.'

'Yes,' said Lady Slane, 'but more people are really of the same mind than you would believe. They take a great deal of trouble to conceal it, and only a crisis calls it out. For instance, if you were to die,'—but what she really meant was, If I were to die—'I daresay you would find that your grandfather had understood you (me) better than you (I) think.'

'That's mere sentimentality,' said Deborah firmly; 'naturally, death startles everybody, even grandfather and great-aunt Carrie—it reminds them of the things they prefer to ignore. My point about the people I like, is not that they dwell morbidly on death, but that they keep continually a sense of what, to them, matters in life. Death, after all, is an incident. Life is an incident too. The thing I mean lies outside both. And it doesn't seem compatible with the sort of life grandfather and great-aunt Carrie think I ought to lead. Am I wrong, or are they?'

Lady Slane perceived one last opportunity for annoying Herbert and Carrie. Let them call her a wicked old woman! she knew that she was no such thing. The child was an artist, and must have her way. There were other people in plenty to carry on the work of the world, to earn and enjoy its rewards, to suffer its malice and return its wounds in kind; the small and rare fraternity to which Deborah belonged, indifferent to gilded lures, should be free to go obscurely but ardently about its business. In the long run, with the strange bedlam always in process of sorting itself out, as the present-day became history, the poets and the prophets counted for more than the conquerors. Christ himself was of their company.

She could form no estimate of Deborah's talents; that was beside the point. Achievement was good, but the spirit was better. To reckon by achievements was to make a concession to the prevailing system of the world; it was a departure from the austere, disinterested, exacting standards that Lady Slane and her kindred recognised. Yet what she said was not at all in accordance with her thoughts; she said, 'Oh dear, if I hadn't given away that fortune I could have made you independent.'

Deborah laughed. She wanted advice, she said, not money. Lady Slane knew very well that she did not really want advice either; she wanted only to be strengthened and supported in her resolution. Very well, if she wanted approval, she should have it. 'Of course you are right, my dear,' she said quietly.

They talked for a while longer, but Deborah, feeling herself folded into peace and sympathy, noticed that her great-grandmother's mind wandered a little into some maze of confusion to which Deborah held no guiding thread. It was natural at Lady Slane's age. At moments she appeared to be talking about herself, then recalled her wits, and with pathetic clumsiness tried to cover up the slip, rousing herself to speak eagerly of the girl's future, not of some event which had gone wrong in the distant past. Deborah was too profoundly lulled and happy to wonder much what that event could be. This hour of union with the old woman soothed her like music, like chords lightly touched in the evening, with the shadows closing and the moths bruising beyond an open window. She leaned against the old woman's knee as a support, a prop, drowned, enfolded, in warmth, dimness, and soft harmonious sounds. The hurly-burly receded; the clangour was stilled; her grandfather and her great-aunt Carrie lost their angular importance and shrivelled to little gesticulating puppets with parchment faces and silly wavering hands; other values rose up like great archangels in the room, and towered and spread their wings. Inexplicable associations floated into Deborah's mind; she remembered how once she had seen a young woman in a white dress leading a white borzoi across the darkness of a southern port. This physical and mental contact with her great-grandmother—so far removed in years, so closely attuned in spirit—stripped off the coverings from the small treasure of short experience that she had jealously stored away. She caught herself wondering whether she could afterwards recapture the incantation of this hour sufficiently to render it into terms of music. Her desire to render an experience in terms of music transcended even her interest in her great-grandmother as a human being; a form of egoism which she knew her great-grandmother would neither resent nor misunderstand. The impulse which had led her to her great-grandmother was a right impulse. The sense of enveloping music proved that. On some remote piano the chords were struck, and they were chords which had no meaning, no existence, in the world inhabited by her grandfather and her great-aunt Carrie; but in her great-grandmother's world they had their value and their significance. But she must not tire her great-grandmother, thought Deborah, suddenly realising that the old voice had ceased its maunderings and that the spell of an hour was broken. Her great-grandmother was asleep. Her chin had fallen forward on to the laces at her breast. Her lovely hands were limp in their repose. As Deborah rose silently, and silently let herself out into the street, being careful not to slam the door behind her, the chords of her imagination died away.

Genoux, bringing in the tray an hour later, announcing 'Miladi est servie,' altered her formula to a sudden, 'Mon Dieu, mais qu'est-ce que c'est ça—Miladi est morte.'

'It was to be expected,' said Carrie, mopping her eyes as she had not mopped them over the death of her father; 'it was to be expected, Mr. Bucktrout. Yet it comes as a shock. My poor mother was such a very exceptional woman, as you know— though I'm sure I don't see how you should have known it, for she was, of course, only your tenant. A correspondent in *The Times* described her this morning as a rare spirit. Just what I always said myself: a rare spirit.' Carrie had forgotten the many other things she had said. 'A little difficult to manage some-times,' she added, stung by a sudden thought of FitzGeorge's fortune; 'unpractical to a degree, but practical things are not the only things that count, are they, Mr. Bucktrout?' *The Times* had said that too. 'My poor mother had a beautiful nature. I don't say that I should always have acted myself as she some-times acted. Her motives were sometimes a little difficult to follow. Quixotic, you know, and—shall we say?—injudicious. Besides, she could be very stubborn. There were times when she wouldn't be guided, which was unfortunate, considering how unpractical she was. We should all be in a very different position now had she been willing to listen to us. However, it's no good crying over spilt milk, is it?' said Carrie, giving Mr. Bucktrout what was meant to be a brave smile.

Mr. Bucktrout made no answer. He disliked Carrie. He wondered how anyone so hard and so hypocritical could be the daughter of someone so sensitive and so honest as his old friend. He was determined to reveal to Carrie by no word or look how deeply he felt the loss of Lady Slane.

'There is a man downstairs who can take the measurements for the coffin, should you wish,' he said.

Carrie stared. So they had been right about this Mr. Bucktrout: a heartless old man, lacking the decency to find one suitable phrase about poor Mother; Carrie herself had been generous enough to repeat those words about the rare spirit; really, on the whole, she considered her little oration over her mother to be a very generous tribute, when one remembered the tricks her mother had played on them all. She had felt extremely righteous as she pronounced it, and according to her code Mr. Bucktrout ought to have said something graceful in reply. No doubt he had expected to pull some plums out of the pudding himself, and had been embittered by his failure. The thought of the old shark's discomfiture was Carrie's great consolation. Mr. Bucktrout was just the sort of man who tried to hook an unsuspecting old lady. And now, full of revengefulness, he fell back on bringing a man to make the coffin.

'My brother, Lord Slane, will be here shortly to make all the necessary arrangements,' she replied haughtily.

Mr. Gosheron, however, was already at the door. He came in tilting his bowler hat, but whether he tilted it towards the silent presence of Lady Slane in her bed, or towards Carrie standing at the foot, was questionable. Mr. Gosheron in his capacity as an undertaker was well accustomed to death; still, his feeling for Lady Slane had always been much warmer than for a mere client. He had already tried to give some private expression to his emotion by determining to sacrifice his most treasured piece of wood as the lid for her coffin.

'Her ladyship makes a lovely corpse,' he said to Mr. Bucktrout. They both ignored Carrie.

'Lovely in life, lovely in death, is what I always say,' said

Mr. Gosheron. 'It's astonishing, the beauty that death brings out. My old grandfather told me that, who was in the same line of business, and for fifty years I've watched to see if his words were true. "Beauty in life," he used to say, "may come from good dressing and what-not, but for beauty in death you have to fall back on character." Now look at her ladyship, Mr. Bucktrout. Is it true, or isn't it? To tell you the truth,' he added confidentially, 'if I want to size a person up, I look at them and picture them dead. That always gives it away, especially as they don't know you're doing it. The first time I ever set eyes on her ladyship, I said, yes, she'll do; and now that I see her as I pictured her then I still say it. She wasn't never but half in this world, anyhow.'

'No, she wasn't,' said Mr. Bucktrout, who, now that Mr. Gosheron had arrived, was willing to talk about Lady Slane, 'and she never came to terms with it either. She had the best that it could give her—all the things she didn't want. She considered the lilies of the field, Mr. Gosheron.'

'She did, Mr. Bucktrout; many a phrase out of the Bible have I applied to her ladyship. But people will stand things in the Bible that they won't stand in common life. They don't seem to see the sense of it when they meet it in their own homes, although they'll put on a reverent face when they hear it read out from a lectern.'

Oh goodness, thought Carrie, will these two old men never stop talking across Mother like a Greek chorus? She had arrived at Hampstead in a determined frame of mind: she would be generous, she would be forgiving—and some genuine emotion had come to her aid—but now her self-possession cracked and her ill-temper and grievances came boiling up. This agent and this undertaker, who talked so securely and so sagaciously, what could they know of her mother?

'Perhaps,' she snapped, 'you had better leave my mother's

funeral oration to be pronounced by one of her own family.'

Mr. Bucktrout and Mr. Gosheron both turned gravely towards her. She saw them suddenly as detached figures; figures of fun certainly, yet also figures of justice. Their eyes stripped away the protection of her decent hypocrisy. She felt that they judged her; that Mr. Gosheron, according to his use and principle, was imagining her as a corpse; was narrowing his eyes to help the effort of his imagination; was laying her out upon a bed, examining her without the defences she could no longer control. That phrase about the rare spirit shrivelled to a cinder. Mr. Bucktrout and Mr. Gosheron were in league with her mother, and no phrases could cover up the truth from such an alliance.

'In the presence of death,' she said to Mr. Gosheron, taking refuge in a last convention, 'you might at least take off your hat.'

THE END